KIPPS

&

THE RESEARCH
MAGNIFICENT

KIPPS

and

THE RESEARCH MAGNIFICENT

by

H. G. WELLS

ODHAMS PRESS LIMITED
LONDON, W.C. 2

KIPPS

THOSE individuals who have led secluded or isolated lives, or have hitherto moved in other spheres than those wherein well-bred people move, will gather all the information necessary from these pages to render them thoroughly conversant with the manners and amenities of society."

MANNERS AND RULES OF GOOD SOCIETY.
By a Member of the Aristocracy.

CONTENTS

Book One
The Making of Kipps

Book Two
Mr. Coote the Chaperon

CONTENTS

Book Three

Kippses

Book One
The Making of Kipps

CHAPTER ONE

§ 1

UNTIL he was nearly arrived at manhood, it did not become clear to Kipps how it was that he had come into the care of an aunt and uncle instead of having a father and mother like other little boys. He had vague memories of a somewhere else, a dim room, a window looking down on white buildings, and of a some one else who talked to forgotten people and who was his mother. He could not recall her features very distinctly, but he remembered with extreme definition a white dress she wore, with a pattern of little sprigs of flowers and little bows upon it, and a girdle of straight-ribbed white ribbon about the waist. Linked with this, he knew not how, were clouded half-obliterated recollections of scenes in which there was weeping, weeping in which he was inscrutably moved to join. Some terrible tall man with a loud voice played a part in these scenes, and, either before or after them, there were impressions of looking for interminable periods out of the window of railway trains in the company of these two people.

He knew, though he could not remember that he had ever been told, that a certain faded wistful face that looked at him from a plush and gilt framed daguerrotype above the mantel of the "sitting-room" was the face of his mother. But that knowledge did not touch his dim memories with any elucidation. In that photograph she was a girlish figure, lean-ing against a photographer's stile, and with all the self-conscious shrinking natural to that position. She had curly hair and a face far younger and prettier than any other mother in his experience. She swung a Dolly Varden hat by the string, and looked with obedient, respectful eyes on the photographer-gentleman who had commanded the pose. She was very slight and pretty. But the phantom mother that haunted his memory so elusively was not like that, though he could not remember how she differed. Perhaps she was older or a little less shrink-ing, or, it may be, only dressed in a different way. . . .

It is clear she handed him over to his aunt and uncle at New Romney with explicit directions and a certain endow-ment. One gathers she had something of that fine sense of social distinctions that subsequently played so large a part in Kipps' career. He was not to go to a "Common" school, she provided, but to a certain seminary in Hastings, that was not only a "middle-class academy" with mortar-boards and every evidence of a higher social tone, but also remarkably cheap. She seems to have been animated by the desire to do

her best for Kipps even at a certain sacrifice of herself, as
though Kipps were in some way a superior sort of person. She
sent pocket-money to him from time to time for a year or more
after Hastings had begun for him, but her face he never saw
in the days of his lucid memory.

His aunt and uncle were already high on the hill of life
when first he came to them. They had married for comfort
in the evening or, at any rate, in the late afternoon of their
days. They were at first no more than vague figures in the
background of proximate realities, such realities as familiar
chairs and tables, quiet to ride and drive, the newel of the
staircase, kitchen furniture, pieces of firewood, the boiler tap,
old newspapers, the cat, the High Street, the back-yard and
the flat fields that are always so near in that little town. He
knew all the stones in the yard individually, the creeper in the
corner, the dustbin and the mossy wall, better than many
men know the faces of their wives. There was a corner under
the ironing-board which, by means of a shawl, could be made,
under propitious gods, a very decent cubby-house, a corner
that served him for several years as the indisputable hub of
the world, and the stringy places in the carpet, the knots upon
the dresser, and the several corners of the rag hearthrug his
uncle had made, became essential parts of his mental foundations. The shop he did not know so thoroughly ; it was a
forbidden region to him, yet somehow he managed to know
it very well.

His aunt and uncle were, as it were, the immediate gods of
this world, and, like the gods of the world of old, occasionally
descended right into it, with arbitrary injunctions and dis-
proportionate punishments. And, unhappily, one rose to their
Olympian level at meals. Then one had to say one's " grace,"
hold one's spoon and fork in mad, unnatural ways called
" properly," and refrain from eating even nice, sweet things
" too fast." If he " gobbled " there was trouble, and at the
slightest *abandon* with knife, fork, and spoon his aunt rapped
his knuckles, albeit his uncle always finished up his gravy with
his knife. Sometimes, moreover, his uncle would come pipe
in hand out of a sedentary remoteness in the most disconcerting way when a little boy was doing the most natural and
attractive things, with " Drat and drabbit that young rascal !
What's he a-doing of now ? " and his aunt would appear at
door or window to interrupt interesting conversation with
children who were upon unknown grounds considered " low "
and undesirable, and call him in. The pleasantest little noises,
however softly you did them, drumming on tea-trays, trumpet-
ing your fists, whistling on keys, ringing chimes with a couple
of pails, or playing tunes on the window-panes, brought down
the gods in anger. Yet what noise is fainter than your finger
on the window—gently done ? Sometimes, however, these
gods gave him broken toys out of the shop, and then one loved

them better—for the shop they kept was, among other things, a toy-shop. (The other things included books to read and books to give away, and local photographs ; it had some pretensions to be a china-shop and the fascia spoke of glass ; it was also a stationer's shop with a touch of haberdashery about it, and in the windows and odd corners were mats and terra-cotta dishes and milking-stools for painting, and there was a hint of picture-frames, and fire-screens, and fishing-tackle, and air-guns, and bathing-suits, and tents—various things, indeed, but all cruelly attractive to a small boy's fingers.) Once his aunt gave him a trumpet if he would *promise* faithfully not to blow it, and afterwards took it away again. And his aunt made him say his catechism, and something she certainly called the "Colic for the Day," every Sunday in the year.

As the two grew old as he grew up, and as his impression of them modified insensibly from year to year, it seemed to him at last that they had always been as they were when in his adolescent days his impression of things grew fixed ; his aunt he thought of as always lean, rather worried looking, and prone to a certain obliquity of cap, and his uncle massive, many chinned, and careless about his buttons. They neither visited nor received visitors. They were always very suspicious about their neighbours and other people generally ; they feared the " low " and they hated and despised the " stuck up," and so they " kept themselves *to* themselves," according to the English ideal. Consequently little Kipps had no playmates, except through the sin of disobedience. By inherent nature he had a sociable disposition. When he was in the High Street he made a point of saying " Hallo ! " to passing cyclists, and he would put his tongue out at the Quodling children whenever their nursemaid was not looking. And he began a friendship with Sid Pornick, the son of the haberdasher next door, that, with wide intermissions, was destined to last his lifetime through.

Pornick, the haberdasher, I may say at once, was, according to old Kipps, a " blaring jackass ; " he was a teetotaller, a " nyar, nyar, 'im-singing Methodis'," and altogether distasteful and detrimental, he and his together, to true Kipps ideals so far as little Kipps could gather them. This Pornick certainly possessed an enormous voice, and he annoyed old Kipps greatly by calling " You—Arn " and " Siddee " up and down his house. He annoyed old Kipps by private choral services on Sunday, all his family " nyar, nyar "-ing ; and by mushroom culture, by behaving as though the pilaster between the two shops was common property, by making a noise of hammering in the afternoon when old Kipps wished to be quiet after his midday meal, by going up and down uncarpeted stairs in his boots, by having a black beard, by attempting to be friendly, and by—all that sort of thing. In fact, he annoyed old Kipps. He annoyed him especially with his shop-door mat.

Old Kipps never beat his mat, preferring to let sleeping dust lie, and seeking a motive for a foolish proceeding, he held that Pornick waited until there was a suitable wind in order that the dust disengaged in that operation might defile his neighbour's shop. These issues would frequently develop into loud and vehement quarrels, and on one occasion came so near to violence as to be subsequently described by Pornick (who read his newspaper) as a " Disgraceful Frackass." On that occasion he certainly went into his own shop with extreme celerity.

But it was through one of these quarrels that the friendship of little Kipps and Sid Pornick came about. The two small boys found themselves one day looking through the gate at the doctor's goats together ; they exchanged a few contradictions about which goat could fight which, and then young Kipps was moved to remark that Sid's father was a " blaring jackass." Sid said he wasn't, and Kipps repeated that he was, and quoted his authority. Then Sid, flying off at a tangent rather alarmingly, said he could fight young Kipps with one hand, an assertion young Kipps with a secret want of confidence denied. There were some vain repetitions and the incident might have ended there, but happily a sporting butcher boy chanced on the controversy at this stage, and insisted upon seeing fair play.

The two small boys, under his pressing encouragement, did at last button up their jackets, square, and fight an edifying drawn battle until it seemed good to the butcher boy to go on with Mrs. Holyer's mutton. Then, according to his directions and under his experienced stage management, they shook hands and made it up. Subsequently, a little tear-stained, perhaps, but flushed with the butcher boy's approval (" tough little kids "), and with cold stones down their necks as he advised, they sat side by side on the doctor's gate, projecting very much behind, stanching an honourable bloodshed, and expressing respect for one another. Each had a bloody nose and a black eye—three days later they matched to a shade—neither had given in, and, though this was tacit, neither wanted any more.

It was an excellent beginning. After his first encounter the attributes of their parents and their own relative value in battle never rose between them, and if anything was wanted to complete the warmth of their regard it was found in a joint dislike of the eldest Quodling. The eldest Quodling lisped, had a silly sort of straw hat and a large pink face (all covered over with self-satisfaction), and he went to the National school with a green-baize bag—a contemptible thing to do. They called him names and threw stones at him, and when he replied by threatenings (" Look 'ere, young Art Kipth, you better *thtoppit !* ") they were moved to attack, and put him to flight.

And after that they broke the head of Ann Pornick's doll, so that she went home weeping loudly—a wicked and endearing proceeding. Sid was whacked, but, as he explained, he wore a newspaper tactically adjusted during the transaction, and really it didn't hurt him at all. . . . And Mrs. Pornick put her head out of the shop door suddenly and threatened Kipps as he passed.

§ 2

" Cavendish Academy," the school that had won the limited choice of Kipps' vanished mother, was established in a battered private house in the part of Hastings remotest from the sea ; it was called an Academy for Young Gentlemen, and many of the young gentlemen had parents in " India " and other unverifiable places. Others were the sons of credulous widows, anxious, as Kipps' mother had been, to get something a little " superior " to a board school education as cheaply as possible, and others, again, were sent to demonstrate the dignity of their parents and guardians. And of course there were boys from France.

Its " principal " was a lean, long creature of indifferent digestion and temper, who proclaimed himself on a gilt-lettered board in his front area, George Garden Woodrow, F.S.Sc., letters indicating that he had paid certain guineas for a bogus diploma. A bleak, whitewashed outhouse constituted his schoolroom, and the scholastic quality of its carved and worn desks and forms was enhanced by a slippery blackboard and two large, yellow out-of-date maps—one of Africa and the other of Wiltshire—that he had picked up cheap at a sale. There were other maps and globes in his study, where he interviewed inquiring parents, but these his pupils never saw. And in a glass cupboard in the passage were several shillings-worth of test-tubes and chemicals, a tripod, a glass retort, and a damaged Bunsen burner, manifesting that the " Scientific laboratory " mentioned in the prospectus was no idle boast.

This prospectus, which was in dignified but incorrect English, laid particular stress on the sound preparation for a commercial career given in the Academy, but the army, navy, and civil service were glanced at in an ambiguous sentence. There was something vague in the prospectus about " examinational successes "—though Woodrow, of course, disapproved of " cram "—and a declaration that the curriculum included " art," " modern foreign languages," and " a sound technical and scientific training." Then came insistence upon the " moral well-being " of the pupils, and an emphatic boast of the excellence of the religious instruction, " so often neglected nowadays even in schools of wide repute." " That's bound to fetch 'em," Mr. Woodrow had remarked when he drew up the prospectus. And in conjunction with the mortar-boards it certainly did. Attention was directed to the " motherly " care of Mrs. Woodrow, in reality a small, partially effaced woman with a plaintive face and a mind above cookery, and the prospectus concluded with a phrase intentionally vague, " Fare unrestricted, and our own milk and produce."

The memories Kipps carried from that school into after-life were set in an atmosphere of stuffiness and mental muddle and included countless pictures of sitting on creaking forms, bored and idle ; of blot licking and the taste of ink ; of torn books with covers that set one's teeth on edge ; of the slimy surface of the laboured slates ; of furtive marble-playing, whispered story-telling, and of pinches, blows, and a thousand such petty annoyances being perpetually " passed on " according to the custom of the place ; of standing up in class and being hit suddenly and unreasonably for imaginary mis-behaviour ; of Mr. Woodrow's raving days, when a scarcely sane injustice prevailed ; of the cold vacuity of the hour of preparation before the bread-and-butter breakfast ; and of horrible headaches and queer, unprecedented internal feelings, resulting from Mrs. Woodrow's motherly rather than intelligent cookery. There were dreary walks when the boys marched two by two, all dressed in the mortar-board caps that so impressed the widowed mothers ; there were dismal half-holidays when the weather was wet, and the spirit of evil temper and evil imagination had the pent boys to work its will on ; there were unfair, dishonourable fights, and miserable defeats and victories ; there was bullying and being bullied. A coward boy Kipps particularly afflicted, until at last he was goaded to revolt by incessant persecution, and smote Kipps to toler-ance with whirling fists. There were memories of sleeping three in a bed ; of the dense, leathery smell of the schoolroom when one returned thither after ten minutes' play ; of a play-ground of mud and incidental sharp flints. And there was much furtive foul language.

" Our Sundays are our happiest days," was one of Wood-row's formulæ with the inquiring parent, but Kipps was not called in evidence. They were to him terrible gaps of inanity, no work, no play, a drear expanse of time with the mystery of church twice and plum-duff once in the middle. The afternoon was given up to furtive relaxations, among which " Torture Chamber " games with the less agreeable weaker boys figured. It was from the difference between this day and common days that Kipps derived his first definite conceptions of the nature of God and Heaven. His instinct was to evade any closer acquaintance as long as he could.

The solid work varied, according to the prevailing mood of Mr. Woodrow. Sometimes that was a despondent lethargy, copy-books were distributed or sums were " set," or the great mystery of book-keeping was declared in being, and beneath these superficial activities lengthy conversations and interminable guessing games with marbles went on, while

Mr. Woodrow sat inanimate at his desk, heedless of school affairs, staring in front of him at unseen things. At times his face was utterly inane ; at times it had an expression of stagnant amazement, as if he saw before his eyes with pitiless clearness the dishonour and mischief of his being. . . .

At other times the F.S.Sc. roused himself to action, and would stand up a wavering class and teach it, goading it with bitter mockery and blows through a chapter of Ahn's " First French Course ; or, France and the French," or a dialogue about a traveller's washing, or the parts of an opera house. His own knowledge of French had been obtained years ago in another English private school, and he had refreshed it by occasional weeks of loafing and mean adventure in Dieppe. He would sometimes in their lessons hit upon some reminiscence of these brighter days, and then he would laugh inexplicably and repeat French phrases of an unfamiliar type.

Among the commoner exercises he prescribed the learning of long passages of poetry from a " Potry Book," which he would delegate an elder boy to " hear " ; and there was reading aloud from the Holy Bible, verse by verse—it was none of your " godless " schools!—so that you counted the verses up to your turn and then gave yourself to conversation ; and sometimes one read from a cheap History of this land. They did, as Kipps reported, " loads of catechsim." Also there was much learning of geographical names and lists, and sometimes Woodrow, in an outbreak of energy, would see these names were actually found in a map. And once, just once, there was a chemistry lesson—a lesson of indescribable excitement —glass things of the strangest shape, a smell like bad eggs, something bubbling in something, a smash and stench, and Mr. Woodrow saying quite distinctly—they threshed it out in the dormitory afterwards—"Damn ! " Followed by the whole school being kept in, with extraordinary severities, for an hour. . . .

But interspersed with the memories of this gray routine were certain patches of brilliant colour, the Holidays, his holidays, which, in spite of the feud between their seniors, he spent as much as possible with Sid Pornick, the son of the irascible black-bearded haberdasher next door. They seemed to be memories of a different world. There were glorious days of " mucking about " along the beach, the siege of unresisting Martello towers, the incessant interest of the mystery and motion of windmills, the windy excursions with boarded feet over the yielding shingle to Dungeness lighthouse—Sid Pornick and he far adrift from reality, smugglers and armed men from the moment they left Great Stone behind them—wanderings in the hedgeless, reedy marsh, long excursions reaching even to Hythe where the machine-guns of the Empire are for ever whirling and tapping, and to Rye and Winchelsea perched like dream-cities on their little hills. The sky in these memories was the blazing hemisphere of the marsh heavens in summer, or its wintry tumult of sky and sea ; and there were wrecks, real wrecks, in it (near Dymchurch pitched high and blackened and rotting were the ribs of a fishing smack, flung aside like an empty basket when the sea had devoured its crew), and there was bathing all naked in the sea, bathing to one's arm-pits, and even trying to swim in the warm sea-water (spite of his aunt's prohibition) and (with her indulgence) the rare eating of dinner from a paper parcel miles away from home. Toke and cold ground-rice puddin' with plums it used to be—there is no better food at all. And for the background, in the place of Woodrow's mean and fretting rule, were his aunt's spare but frequently quite amiable figure—for though she in-sisted on his repeating the English Church catechism every Sunday, she had an easy way over dinners that one wanted to take abroad—and his uncle, corpulent and irascible, but sedentary and easily escaped. And freedom !

The holidays were, indeed, very different from school. They were free, they were spacious, and though he never knew it in these words—they had an element of beauty. In his memory of his boyhood they shone like strips of stained-glass window in a dreary waste of scholastic wall, they grew brighter and brighter as they grew remoter. There came a time at last and moods when he could look back to them with a feeling akin to tears.

The last of these windows was the brightest, and instead of the kaleidoscopic effect of its predecessors its glory was a single figure. For in the last of his holidays before the Moloch of Retail Trade got hold of him, Kipps made his first tentative essays at the mysterious shrine of Love. Very tentative they were, for he had become a boy of subdued passions, and potential rather than actual affectionateness.

And the object of these first stirrings of the great desire was no other than Ann Pornick, the head of whose doll he and Sid had broken long ago, and rejoiced over long ago, in the days when he had yet to learn the meaning of a heart.

§ 3

Negotiations were already on foot to make Kipps into a draper before he discovered the lights that lurked in Ann Pornick's eyes. School was over, absolutely over, and it was chiefly present to him that he was never to go to school again. It was high summer. The " breaking up " of school had been hilarious ; and the excellent maxim, " Last Day's Pay Day," had been observed by him with a scrupulous attention to his honour. He had punched the heads of all his enemies, wrung wrists and kicked shins ; he had distributed all his unfinished copy-books, all his school books, his collection of marbles, and his mortar-board cap among such as loved him ; and he had secretly written in obscure pages of their books " re-member Art Kipps." He had also split the anæmic Woodrow's cane, carved his own name deeply in several places about the premises, and broken the scullery window. He had told everybody so often that he was to learn to be a sea captain, that he had come almost to believe the thing himself. And now he was home, and school was at an end for him for ever-more.

He was up before six on the day of his return, and out in the hot sunlight of the yard. He set himself to whistle a peculiarly penetrating arrangement of three notes, supposed by the boys of the Hastings Academy and himself and Sid Pornick, for no earthly reason whatever, to be the original Huron war-cry. As he did this he feigned not to be doing it, because of the hatred between his uncle and the Pornicks, but to be examining with respect and admiration a new wing of the dustbin recently erected by his uncle—a pretence that would not have deceived a nestling tom-tit.

Presently there came a familiar echo from the Pornick hunting-ground. Then Kipps began to sing, " Ar pars eight tra-la, in the lane be'ind the church." To which an unseen person answered, " Ar pars eight it is, in the lane be'ind the church." The " tra-la " was considered to render the sentence incomprehensible to the uninitiated. In order to conceal their operations still more securely, both parties to this duet then gave vent to a vocalisation of the Huron war-cry again, and after a lingering repetition of the last and shrillest note, dis-persed severally, as became boys in the enjoyment of holidays, to light the house fires for the day.

Half-past eight found Kipps sitting on the sunlit gate at the top of the long lane that runs towards the sea, clashing his boots in a slow rhythm, and whistling with great violence all that he knew of an excruciatingly pathetic air. There appeared along by the churchyard wall a girl in a short frock, brown-haired, quick-coloured, and with dark blue eyes. She had grown so that she was a little taller than Kipps, and her colour had improved. He scarcely remembered her, so changed was she since last holidays—if, indeed, he had seen her during his last holidays, a thing he could not clearly recollect.

Some vague emotion arose at the sight of her. He stopped whistling and regarded her, oddly tongue-tied.

" He can't come," said Ann, advancing boldly. " Not yet."

" What—not Sid ? "

" No. Father's made him dust all his boxes again."

" What for ? "

" I dunno. Father's in a stew 's morning."

" Oh ! "

Pause. Kipps looked at her, and then was unable to look at her again. She regarded him with interest. " You left school ? " she remarked, after a pause.

" Yes."

" So's Sid."

The conversation languished. Ann put her hands on the top of the gate, and began a stationary hopping, a sort of ineffectual gymnastic experiment.

" Can you run ? " she said presently.

" Run you any day," said Kipps.

" Gimme a start ? "

" Where for ? " said Kipps.

Ann considered, and indicated a tree. She walked towards it and turned. " Gimme to here ? " she called. Kipps, standing now and touching the gate, smiled to express conscious superiority. " Farther ! " he said.

" Here ? "

" Bit more ! " said Kipps ; and then, repenting of his magnanimity, said " Orf ! " suddenly, and so recovered his lost concession.

They arrived abreast at the tree, flushed and out of breath. " Tie ! " said Ann, throwing her hair back from her face with her hand. " I won," panted Kipps. They disputed firmly, but quite politely. " Run it again, then," said Kipps. " *I* don't mind."

They returned towards the gate.

" You don't run bad," said Kipps, temperately, expressing sincere admiration. " I'm pretty good, you know."

Ann sent her hair back by an expert toss of the head. " You give me a start," she allowed.

They became aware of Sid approaching them. " You better look out, young Ann," said Sid, with that irreverent want of sympathy usual in brothers. " You have been out nearly 'arf-'our. Nothing ain't been done upstairs. Father said he didn't know where you was, but when he did he'd warm y'r young ear."

Ann prepared to go.

" How about that race ? " asked Kipps.

" Lor ! " cried Sid, quite shocked. " You ain't been racing *her* ! "

Ann swung herself round the end of the gate with her eyes on Kipps, and then turned away suddenly and ran off down the lane. Kipps' eyes tried to go after her, and came back to Sid's.

" I give her a lot of start," said Kipps apologetically. " It wasn't a proper race." And so the subject was dismissed. But Kipps was *distrait* for some seconds perhaps, and the mischief had begun in him.

§ 4

They proceeded to the question of how two accomplished Hurons might most satisfactorily spend the morning. Manifestly their line lay straight along the lane to the sea. " There's a new wreck," said Sid, " and my !—don't it stink just ! "

" Stink ? "

" Fair make you sick. It's rotten wheat."

They fell to talking of wrecks, and so came to ironclads and wars and such-like manly matters. Half-way to the wreck Kipps made a casual, irrelevant remark.

" Your sister ain't a bad sort," he said off-handedly.

" I clout her a lot," said Sidney modestly ; and, after a pause, the talk reverted to more suitable topics.

The new wreck was full of rotting grain, and stank abominably, even as Sid had said. This was excellent. They had it all to themselves. They took possession of it in force, at Sid's suggestion, and had speedily to defend it against enormous numbers of imaginary " natives," who were at last driven off by loud shouts of *bang, bang,* and vigorous thrusting and shoving of sticks. Then, also at Sid's direction, they sailed with it into the midst of a combined French, German, and Russian fleet, demolishing the combination unassisted, and having descended to the beach, clambered up the side and cut out their own vessel in brilliant style, they underwent a magnificent shipwreck (with vocalised thunder) and floated " water-logged "—so Sid insisted—upon an exhausted sea.

These things drove Ann out of mind for a time. But at last, as they drifted without food or water upon a stagnant ocean, haggard-eyed, chins between their hands, looking in vain for a sail, she came to mind again abruptly.

" It's rather nice 'aving sisters," remarked one perishing mariner.

Sid turned round and regarded him thoughtfully.

" Not it ! " he said.

" No ? "

" Not a bit of it."

He grinned confidentially. " Know too much," he said, and afterwards, " get out of things."

He resumed his gloomy scrutiny of the hopeless horizon. Presently he fell spitting jerkily between his teeth, as he had read was the way with such ripe manhood as chews its quid.

" Sisters," he said, " is rot. That's what sisters are. Girls, if you like, but sisters—*No !* "

" But ain't sisters girls ? "

" *N-eaow !* " said Sid, with unspeakable scorn ; and Kipps answered, " Of course. I didn't mean—— I wasn't thinking of that."

" You got a girl ? " asked Sid, spitting very cleverly again.

Kipps admitted his deficiency. He felt compunction.

" You don't know who *my* girl is, Art Kipps, I bet."

" Who *is*, then ? " asked Kipps, still chiefly occupied by his own poverty.

" Ah ! "

Kipps let a moment elapse before he did his duty. " Tell us ! "

Sid eyed him and hesitated.

" Secret ? " he said.

" Secret."

" Dying solemn ? "

" Dying solemn ! "   Kipps' self-concentration passed into curiosity.

Sid administered a terrible oath.

Sid adhered lovingly to his facts. " It begins with a Nem," he said, doling it out parsimoniously.

" M-A-U-D," he spelt, with a stern eye on Kipps. " C-H-A-R-T-E-R-I-S."

Now, Maud Charteris was a young person of eighteen and the daughter of the vicar of St. Bavon's—besides which, she had a bicycle—so that as her name unfolded, the face of Kipps lengthened with respect. " Get out," he gasped incredulously. " She ain't your girl, Sid Pornick."

" She is ! " answered Sid stoutly.

" What—truth ? "

" *Truth.*"

Kipps scrutinised his face. " Reely ? "

Sid touched wood, whistled, and repeated a binding doggerel with great solemnity.

Kipps still struggled with the amazing new light on the world about him. " D'you mean—she knows ? "

Sid flushed deeply, and his aspect became stern and gloomy. He resumed his wistful scrutiny of the sunlit sea. " I'd die for that girl, Art Kipps," he said presently ; and Kipps did not press a question he felt to be ill-timed. " I'd do anything she asked me to do," said Sid ; " just anything. If she was to ask me to chuck myself into the sea." He met Kipps' eye. " I *would*," he said.

They were pensive for a space, and then Sid began to discourse in fragments of Love, a theme upon which Kipps had already in a furtive way meditated a little, but which, apart from badinage, he had never yet heard talked about in the light of day. Of course, many and various aspects of life had come to light in the muffled exchange of knowledge that went on under the shadow of Woodrow, but this of Sentimental Love was not among them. Sid, who was a boy with an imagination, having once broached this topic, opened his heart, or, at any rate, a new chamber of his heart, to Kipps, and found no fault with Kipps for a lack of return. He produced a thumbed novelette that had played a part in his sentimental awakening; he proffered it to Kipps, and confessed there was a character in it, a baronet, singularly like himself. This baronet was a person of volcanic passions, which he concealed beneath a demeanour of " icy cynicism." The utmost expression he permitted himself was to grit his teeth, and, now his attention was called to it, Kipps remarked that Sid also had a habit of gritting his teeth, and, indeed, had had all the morning. They read for a time, and presently Sid talked again. The conception of love Sid made evident, was compact of devotion and much spirited fighting and a touch of mystery, but through all that cloud of talk there floated before Kipps a face that was flushed and hair that was tossed aside.

So they budded, sitting on the blackening old wreck in which men had lived and died, looking out to sea, talking of that other sea upon which they must presently embark. . . .

They ceased to talk, and Sid read ; but Kipps, falling behind with the reading, and not wishing to admit that he read slowlier than Sid, whose education was of the inferior Elementary School brand, lapsed into meditation.

" I *would* like to 'ave a girl," said Kipps.

" I mean just to talk to, and all that. . . ."

A floating sack distracted them at last from this obscure topic. They abandoned the wreck, and followed the new interest a mile along the beach, bombarding it with stones until it came to land. They had inclined to a view that it would contain romantic mysteries, but it was simply an ill-preserved kitten—too much even for them. And at last they were drawn dinner-ward, and went home hungry and pensive side by side.

§ 5

But Kipps' imagination had been warmed by that talk of love, and in the afternoon when he saw Ann Pornick in the High Street and said " Hallo ! " it was a different " hallo " from that of their previous intercourse. And when they had passed they both looked back and caught each other doing so. Yes, he *did* want a girl badly. . . .

Afterwards he was distracted by a traction engine going through the town, and his aunt had got some sprats for supper. When he was in bed, however, sentiment came upon him again in a torrent quite abruptly and abundantly, and he put his head under the pillow and whispered very softly, " I love Ann Pornick," as a sort of supplementary devotion.

In his subsequent dreams he ran races with Ann, and they lived in a wreck together, and always her face was flushed and her hair about her face. They just lived in a wreck and ran races, and were very, very fond of one another. And their favourite food was rock chocolate, dates, such as one buys off barrows, and sprats—fried sprats. . . .

In the morning he could hear Ann singing in the scullery next door. He listened to her for some time, and it was clear to him that he must put things before her.

Towards dusk that evening they chanced on one another out by the gate by the church, but though there was much in his mind, it stopped there with a resolute shyness until he and Ann were out of breath catching cockchafers and were sitting on that gate of theirs again. Ann sat up upon the gate, dark against vast masses of flaming crimson and darkling purple, and her eyes looked at Kipps from a shadowed face. There came a stillness between them, and quite abruptly he was moved to tell his love.

"Ann," he said, "I *do* like you. I wish you was my girl. . . . "I say, Ann. Will you *be* my girl?"

Ann made no pretence of astonishment. She weighed the proposal for a moment with her eyes on Kipps. "If you like, Artie," she said lightly. "*I* don't mind if I am."

"All right," said Kipps, breathless with excitement, "then you are."

"All right," said Ann.

Something seemed to fall between them, they no longer looked openly at one another. "Lor!" cried Ann, suddenly, "see that one!" and jumped down and darted after a cockchafer that had boomed within a yard of her face. And with that they were girl and boy again. . . .

They avoided their new relationship painfully.

They did not recur to it for several days, though they met twice. Both felt that there remained something before this great experience was to be regarded as complete; but there was an infinite diffidence about the next step. Kipps talked in fragments of all sorts of matters, telling particularly of the great things that were being done to make a man and a draper of him; how he had two new pairs of trousers and a black coat and four new shirts. And all the while his imagination was urging him to that unknown next step, and when he was alone and in the dark he became even an enterprising wooer. It became evident to him that it would be nice to take Ann by the hand; even the decorous novelettes Sid affected egged him on to that greater nearness of intimacy.

Then a great idea came to him, in a paragraph called "Lover's Tokens" that he read in a torn fragment of *Tit Bits*. It fell in to the measure of his courage—a divided sixpence! He secured his aunt's best scissors, fished a sixpence out of his jejune tin money-box, and jabbed his finger in a varied series of attempts to get it in half. When they met again the sixpence was still undivided. He had not intended to mention the matter to her at that stage, but it came up spontaneously. He endeavoured to explain the theory of broken sixpences and his unexpected failure to break one.

"But what you break it for?" said Ann. "It's no good if it's broke."

"It's a Token," said Kipps.

"Like——?"

"Oh, you keep half and I keep half, and when we're sep'rated, you look at your half and I look at mine—see? Then we think of each other."

"Oh!" said Ann, and appeared to assimilate this information.

"Only, *I* can't get it in 'arf nohow," said Kipps.

They discussed this difficulty for some time without illumination. Then Ann had a happy thought.

" Tell you what," she said, starting away from him abruptly and laying a hand on his arm, " you let *me* 'ave it, Artie. I know where father keeps his file."

Kipps handed her the sixpence, and they came upon a pause. " I'll easy do it," said Ann.

In considering the sixpence side by side, his head had come near her cheek. Quite abruptly he was moved to take his next step into the unknown mysteries of love.

" Ann," he said, and gulped at his temerity, " I *do* love you. Straight. I'd do anything for you, Ann. Reely—I would."

He paused for breath. She answered nothing, but she was no doubt enjoying herself. He came yet closer to her, his shoulder touched hers. " Ann, I wish you'd——"

He stopped.

" What ? " said Ann.

" Ann—lemme kiss you."

Things seemed to hang for a space; his tone, the drop of his courage made the thing incredible as he spoke. Kipps was not of that bold order of wooers who impose conditions.

Ann perceived that she was not prepared for kissing after all. Kissing, she said, was silly, and when Kipps would have displayed a belated enterprise she flung away from him. He essayed argument. He stood afar off as it were—the better part of a yard—and said she *might* let him kiss her, and then that he didn't see what good it was for her to be his girl if he couldn't kiss her. . . .

She repeated that kissing was silly. A certain estrangement took them homeward. They arrived in the dusky High Street not exactly together, and not exactly apart, but straggling. They had not kissed, but all the guilt of kissing was between them. When Kipps saw the portly contours of his uncle standing dimly in the shop doorway his footsteps faltered, and the space between our young couple increased. Above, the window over Pornick's shop was open, and Mrs. Pornick was visible, taking the air. Kipps assumed an expression of extreme innocence. He found himself face to face with his uncle's advanced outposts of waistcoat buttons.

" Where ye bin, my boy ? "

' Bin for a walk, uncle."

" Not along of that brat of Pornick's ? "

" Along of who ? "

" That gell "—indicating Ann with his pipe.

" Oh, no, uncle ! "—very faintly.

" Run in, my boy." Old Kipps stood aside, with an oblique glance upward, and his nephew brushed clumsily by him and vanished out of sight of the street into the vague obscurity of the little shop. The door closed behind old Kipps with a nervous jangle of its bell, and he set himself to light the single oil-lamp that illuminated his shop at nights. It was an operation requiring care and watching, or else it flared and "smelt." Often it smelt after all. Kipps, for some reason, found the dusky living-room with his aunt in it too populous for his feelings, and went upstairs.

"That brat of Pornick's!" It seemed to him that a horrible catastrophe had occurred. He felt he had identified himself inextricably with his uncle and cut himself off from her for ever by saying "Oh, no!" At supper he was so visibly depressed that his aunt asked him if he wasn't feeling well. Under this imminent threat of medicine he assumed an unnatural cheerfulness. . . .

He lay awake for nearly half an hour that night, groaning because things had all gone wrong, because Ann wouldn't let him kiss her, and because his uncle had called her a brat. It seemed to Kipps almost as though he himself had called her a brat. . . .

There came an interval during which Ann was altogether inaccessible. One, two, three days passed and he did not see her. Sid he met several times ; they went fishing, and twice they bathed, but though Sid lent and received back two further love stories, they talked no more of love. They kept themselves in accord, however, agreeing that the most flagrantly senti-mental story was "proper." Kipps was always wanting to speak of Ann, and never daring to do so. He saw her on Sunday evening going off to chapel. She was more beautiful than ever in her Sunday clothes, but she pretended not to see him because her mother was with her. But he thought she pretended not to see him because she had given him up for ever. Brat!—who could be expected ever to forgive that ? He abandoned himself to despair, he ceased even to haunt the places where she might be found. . . .

With paralysing unexpectedness came the end.

Mr. Shalford, the draper at Folkestone to whom he was to be bound apprentice, had expressed a wish to "shape the lad a bit" before the autumn sale. Kipps became aware that his box was being packed, and gathered the full truth of things on the evening before his departure. He became feverishly eager to see Ann just once more. He made silly and needless excuses to go out into the yard, he walked three times across the street without any excuse at all to look up at the Pornick windows. Still she was hidden. He grew desperate. It was within half an hour of his departure that he came on Sid.

"Hallo !" he said, " I'm orf ! "

"Business ? "

"Yes."

Pause.

"I say Sid. You going 'ome ? "

"Straight now."

" D'you mind——. Ask Ann about that."

" About what ? "

" She'll know."

And Sid said he would. But even that, it seemed, failed to evoke Ann.

At last the Folkestone bus rumbled up, and he ascended. His aunt stood in the doorway to see him off. His uncle assisted with the box and portmanteau. Only furtively could he glance up at the Pornick windows, and still it seemed Ann hardened her heart against him. " Get up ! " said the driver, and the hoofs began to clatter. No—she would not come out even to see him off. The bus was in motion, and old Kipps was going back into his shop. Kipps stared in front of him, assuring himself that he did not care.

He heard a door slam, and instantly craned out his neck to look back. He knew that slam so well. Behold ! out of the haberdasher's door a small, untidy figure in homely pink print had shot resolutely into the road and was sprinting in pursuit. In a dozen seconds she was abreast of the bus. At the sight of her Kipps' heart began to beat very quickly, but he made no immediate motion of recognition.

" Artie ! " she cried breathlessly. " Artie ! Artie ! You know ! I got *that* ! "

The bus was already quickening its pace and leaving her behind again, when Kipps realised what " that " meant. He became animated, he gasped, and gathered his courage together and mumbled an incoherent request to the driver to " stop jest a jiff for sunthin'." The driver grunted, as the disparity of their years demanded, and then the bus had pulled up and Ann was below.

She leapt up upon the wheel. Kipps looked down into Ann's face, and it was foreshortened and resolute. He met her eyes just for one second as their hands touched. He was not a reader of eyes. Something passed quickly from hand to hand, something that the driver, alert at the corner of his eye, was not allowed to see. Kipps hadn't a word to say, and all she said was, " I done it, smorning." It was like a blank space in which something pregnant should have been written and wasn't. Then she dropped down, and the bus moved forward.

After the lapse of about ten seconds, it occurred to him to stand and wave his new bowler hat at her over the corner of the bus top, and to shout hoarsely, " Goo'-bye, Ann ! Don' forget me—while I'm away ! "

She stood in the road looking after him, and presently she waved her hand.

He remained standing unstably, his bright, flushed face looking back at her and his hair fluffing in the wind, and he waved his hat until at last the bend of the road hid her from his eyes. Then he turned about and sat down, and presently he began to put the half-sixpence he held clenched in his hand into his trouser pocket. He looked sideways at the driver to judge how much he had seen.

Then he fell a-thinking. He resolved that, come what might, when he came back to New Romney at Christmas, he would, by hook or by crook, kiss Ann.

Then everything would be perfect and right, and he would be perfectly happy.

CHAPTER TWO

THE EMPORIUM

§ 1

WHEN Kipps left New Romney, with a small yellow tin box, a still smaller portmanteau, a new umbrella, and a keepsake half-sixpence, to become a draper, he was a youngster of fourteen, thin, with whimsical drakes'-tails at the pole of his head, smallish features, and eyes that were sometimes very light and sometimes very dark, gifts those of his birth ; and by the nature of his training he was indistinct in his speech, confused in his mind, and retreating in his manners. Inexorable fate had appointed him to serve his country in commerce, and the same national bias towards private enterprise and leaving bad alone, which had left his general education to Mr. Woodrow, now indentured him firmly into the hands of Mr. Shalford of the Folkestone Drapery Bazaar. Apprenticeship is still the recognised English way to the distributing branch of the social service. If Mr. Kipps had been so unfortunate as to have been born a German he might have been educated in an elaborate and costly special school (" over-educated—crammed up "—old Kipps) to fit him for his end—such being their pedagogic way. He might—— But why make unpatriotic reflections in a novel ? There was nothing pedagogic about Mr. Shalford.

He was an irascible, energetic little man with hairy hands, for the most part under his coat-tails, a long, shiny, bald head, a pointed aquiline nose a little askew, and a neatly trimmed beard. He walked lightly and with a confident jerk, and he was given to humming. He had added to exceptional business " push," bankruptcy under the old dispensation, and judicious matrimony. His establishment was now one of the most considerable in Folkestone, and he insisted on every inch of frontage by alternate stripes of green and yellow down the houses over the shops. His shops were numbered 3, 5, and 7 on the street, and on his bill-heads 3 to 7. He encountered the abashed and awe-stricken Kipps with the praises of his System and himself. He spread himself out behind his desk with a grip on the lapel of his coat, and made Kipps a sort of speech. " We expect y'r to work, y'r know, and we expect y'r to study our interests," explained Mr. Shalford, in the regal and commercial plural. " Our System here is the best system y'r could have. I made it, and I ought to know. I began at the very bottom of the ladder when I was fourteen, and there isn't a step in it I don't know. Not a step. Mr. Booch in the desk will give y'r the card of rules and fines. Jest wait a minute." He pretended to be busy with some dusty memoranda under a paper-weight, while Kipps stood in a sort of paralysis of awe regarding his new master's oval baldness. " Two thous'n three forty-seven pounds," whispered Mr. Shalford audibly, feigning forgetfulness of Kipps. Clearly a place of great transactions !

Mr. Shalford rose, and, handing Kipps a blotting-pad and an inkpot to carry, mere symbols of servitude, for he made no use of them, emerged into a counting-house where three clerks had been feverishly busy ever since his door-handle had turned. " Booch," said Mr. Shalford, " 'ave y'r copy of the Rules ? " and a down-trodden, shabby little old man, with a ruler in one hand and a quill pen in his mouth, silently held out a small book with green and yellow covers, mainly devoted, as Kipps presently discovered, to a voracious system of Fines. He became acutely aware that his hands were full and that everybody was staring at him. He hesitated a moment before putting the inkpot down to free a hand.

" Mustn't fumble like *that*," said Mr. Shalford as Kipps pocketed the Rules. " Won't do here. Come along, come along," cocked his coat-tails high, as a lady might hold up her dress, and led the way into the shop.

A vast, interminable place it seemed to Kipps, with unending shining counters and innumerable faultlessly dressed young men and, presently, Houri-like young women staring at him. Here there was a long vista of gloves dangling from overhead rods, there ribbons and baby linen. A short young lady in black mittens was making out the account of a customer, and was clearly confused in her addition by Shalford's eagle eye.

A thick-set young man with a bald head and a round, very wise face, who was profoundly absorbed in adjusting all the empty chairs down the counter to absolutely equal distances, awoke out of his preoccupation and answered respectfully to a few Napoleonic and quite unnecessary remarks from his employer. Kipps was told that this young man's name was Mr. Buggins, and that he was to do whatever Mr. Buggins told him to do.

They came round a corner into a new smell, which was destined to be the smell of Kipps' life for many years, the vague, distinctive smell of Manchester goods. A fat man with a large nose jumped—actually jumped—at their appearance, and began to fold a pattern of damask in front of him exactly like an automaton that is suddenly set going. " Carshot, see to this boy to-morrow," said the master. " See he don't fumble. Smart'n 'im up."

" Yussir," said Carshot fatly, glanced at Kipps, and resumed his pattern-folding with extreme zeal.

" Whatever Mr. Carshot says y'r to do, ye *do*," said Mr. Shalford, trotting onward ; and Carshot blew out his face with an appearance of relief.

They crossed a large room full of the strangest things Kipps had ever seen. Lady-like figures, surmounted by black, wooden knobs in the place of the refined heads one might have reasonably expected stood about with a lifelike air of conscious fashion. " Costume Room," said Shalford. Two voices engaged in some sort of argument—" I can assure you, Miss Mergle, you are entirely mistaken—entirely, in supposing I should do anything so unwomanly,"—sank abruptly, and they discovered two young ladies, taller and fairer than any of the other young ladies, and with black trains to their dresses, who were engaged in writing at a little table. Whatever they told him to do Kipps gathered he was to do. He was also, he understood, to do whatever Carshot and Booch told him to do. And there were also Buggins and Mr. Shalford. And not to forget or fumble !

They descended into a cellar called " The Warehouse," and Kipps had an optical illusion of errand-boys fighting. Some aerial voice said " Teddy ! " and the illusion passed. He looked again, and saw quite clearly that they were packing parcels, and always would be, and that the last thing in the world that they would or could possibly do was to fight. Yet he gathered from the remarks Mr. Shalford addressed to their busy backs that they had been fighting—no doubt at some past period of their lives.

Emerging in the shop again among a litter of toys and what are called " fancy articles," Shalford withdrew a hand from beneath his coat-tails to indicate an overhead change carrier. He entered into elaborate calculations to show how many minutes in one year were saved thereby, and lost himself among the figures. " Seven tums eight seven nine—was it ? Or seven eight nine ? Now, *now* ! Why, when I was a boy your age I c'd do a sum like that as soon as hear it. We'll soon get y'r into better shape than that. Make you Fishent. Well, y'r must take my word it comes to pounds and pounds saved in the year—pounds and pounds. System ! System everywhere. Fishency." He went on murmuring " Fishency " and " System " at intervals for some time. They passed into a yard, and Mr. Shalford waved his hand to his three delivery vans, all striped green and yellow—" uniform—green, yell'r —System." All over the premises were pinned absurd little cards, " This door locked after 7.30. By order, Edwin Shalford," and the like.

Mr. Shalford always wrote " By Order," though it conveyed no earthly meaning to him. He was one of those people who collect technicalities upon them as the Reduvius bug collects dirt. He was the sort of man who is not only ignorant but absolutely incapable of English. When he wanted to say he had a sixpenny-ha'penny longcloth to sell, he put it thus to

startled customers : "Can DO you one six half, if y'like."
He always omitted pronouns and articles and so forth ; it
seemed to him the very essence of the efficiently business-like.
His only preposition was " as " or the compound " as per."
He abbreviated every word he could ; he would have considered
himself the laughing-stock of Wood Street if he had chanced
to spell *socks* in any way but " sox." But, on the other hand,
if he saved words here he wasted them there ; he never acknow-
ledged an order that was not an esteemed favour, nor sent a
pattern without begging to submit it. He never stipulated for
so many months' credit, but bought in November " as Jan."
It was not only words he abbreviated in his London communications. In paying his wholesalers his " System " admitted
of a constant error in the discount of a penny or twopence, and
it " facilitated business," he alleged, to ignore odd pence in
the cheques he wrote. His ledger clerk was so struck with the
beauty of this part of the System that he started a private one
on his own account with the stamp-box that never came to
Shalford's knowledge.

This admirable British merchant would glow with a particular
pride of intellect when writing his London orders.

" Ah ! do y'r think *you'll* ever be able to write London
orders ? " he would say with honest pride to Kipps, waiting
impatiently long after closing-time to take these triumphs
of commercial efficiency to post, and so end the interminable
day.

Kipps shook his head, anxious for Mr. Shalford to get on.

" Now, here, f'example, I've written—see ? ' 1 piece 1 in.
cott blk elas 1/or ' ; what do I mean by that *or*—eh ? d'ye
know ? "

Kipps promptly hadn't the faintest idea.

" And then, ' 2 ea silk net as per patts herewith ' ; *ea*—eh ? "

" Dunno, sir."

It was not Mr. Shalford's way to explain things. " Dear,
dear ! Pity you couldn't get some c'mercial education at your
school. 'Stid of all this lit'ry stuff. Well, my boy, if y'r not
a bit sharper, y'll never write London orders, *that's* pretty plain.
Jest stick stamps on all those letters and mind y'r stick 'em
right way up, and try and profit a little more by the opportunities your aunt and uncle have provided ye. Can't say *what'll*
happen t'ye if ye don't." And Kipps, tired, hungry, and belated,
set about stamping with vigour and despatch.

" Lick the *envelope*," said Mr. Shalford, " lick the *envelope*,
as though he grudged the youngster the postage-stamp gum.
" It's the little things mount up," he would say and, indeed,
that was his philosophy of life—to hustle and save, always to
hustle and save. His political creed linked Reform, which
meant nothing, with Peace and Economy, which meant a
sweated expenditure, and his conception of a satisfactory
municipal life was to " keep down the rates." Even his

religion was to save his soul and to preach a similar cheeseparing to the world.

§ 2

The indentures that bound Kipps to Mr. Shalford were antique and complex ; they insisted on the latter gentleman's parental privileges, they forbade Kipps to dice and game, they made him over, body and soul, to Mr. Shalford for seven long years, the crucial years of his life. In return there were vague stipulations about teaching the whole art and mystery of the trade to him, but as there was no penalty attached to negligence, Mr. Shalford, being a sound, practical, business man, considered this a mere rhetorical flourish, and set himself assiduously to get as much out of Kipps and to put as little into him as he could in the seven years of their intercourse.

What he put into Kipps was chiefly bread and margarine, infusions of chicory and tea-dust, colonial meat by contract at threepence a pound, potatoes by the sack, and watered beer. If, however, Kipps chose to buy any supplementary material for growth, Mr. Shalford had the generosity to place his kitchen resources at his disposal free—if the fire chanced to be going. He was also allowed to share a bedroom with eight other young men, and to sleep in a bed which, except in very severe weather, could be made, with the help of his overcoat and private under-linen, not to mention newspapers, quite sufficiently warm for any reasonable soul. In addition, Kipps was taught the list of fines, and how to tie up parcels, to know where goods were kept in Mr. Shalford's systematised shop, to hold his hands extended upon the counter, and to repeat such phrases as " What can I have the pleasure—— ? " " No trouble, I 'ssure you," and the like ; to block, fold, and measure materials of all sorts, to lift his hat from his head when he passed Mr. Shalford abroad, and to practise a servile obedience to a large number of people. But he was not, of course, taught the " cost " mark of the goods he sold, nor anything of the method of buying such goods. Nor was his attention directed to the unfamiliar social habits and fashions to which his trade ministered. The use of half the goods he saw sold and was presently to assist in selling he did not understand ; materials for hangings, cretonnes, chintzes, and the like ; serviettes, and all the bright, hard whitewear of a well-ordered house ; pleasant dress materials, linings, stiffenings ; they were to him from first to last no more than things, heavy and difficult to handle in bulk, that one folded up, unfolded, cut into lengths, and saw dwindle and pass away out into that mysterious, happy world in which the Customer dwells. Kipps hurried from piling linen table-cloths, that were, collectively, as heavy as lead, to eat off oilcloth in a gas-lit dining-room underground, and he dreamt of combing endless blankets beneath his over-coat, spare undershirt, and three newspapers. So he had at

least the chance of learning the beginnings of philosophy.
In return for these benefits he worked so that he commonly
went to bed exhausted and footsore. His round began at
half-past six in the morning, when he would descend, unwashed
and shirtless, in old clothes and a scarf, and dust boxes and
yawn, and take down wrappers and clean the windows until
eight. Then in half an hour he would complete his toilet, and
take an austere breakfast of bread and margarine and what only
an Imperial Englishman would admit to be coffee, after which
refreshment he ascended to the shop for the labours of the day.

Commonly these began with a mighty running to and fro
with planks and boxes and goods for Carshot, the window-
dresser, who, whether he worked well or ill, nagged persistently,
by reason of a chronic indigestion, until the window was done.
Sometimes the costume window had to be dressed, and then
Kipps staggered down the whole length of the shop from the
costume-room with one after another of those ladylike shapes
grasped firmly but shamefully each about her single ankle of
wood. Such days as there was no window-dressing there was a
mighty carrying and lifting of blocks and bales of goods into
piles and stacks. After this there were terrible exercises, at
first almost despairfully difficult ; certain sorts of goods that
came in folded had to be rolled upon rollers, and for the most
part refused absolutely to be rolled, at any rate by Kipps ;
certain other sorts of goods that came from the wholesalers
rolled had to be measured and folded, and folding makes
young apprentices wish they were dead. All of it, too, quite
avoidable trouble, you know, that is not avoided because of
the cheapness of the genteeler sorts of labour and the dearness
of forethought in the world. And then consignments of new
goods had to be marked off and packed into paper parcels,
and Carshot packed like conjuring tricks, and Kipps packed
like a boy with tastes in some other direction—not ascertained.
And always Carshot nagged——.

He had a curious formula of appeal to his visceral economy
that the refinement of our times and the earnest entreaties of
my friends oblige me to render by an etiolated paraphrase.

" My Heart and Liver ! I never see such a boy," so I will
present Carshot's refrain ; and even when he was within a
foot or so of the customer's face, the disciplined ear of Kipps
would still at times develop a featureless intercalary murmur
into—well, " My Heart and Liver ! "

There came a blessed interval when Kipps was sent abroad
" matching." This consisted chiefly in supplying unexpected
defects in buttons, ribbon, lining, and so forth in the dress-
making department. He was given a written paper of orders
with patterns pinned thereto and discharged into the sunshine
and interest of the street. Then until he thought it wise to
return and stand the racket of his delay, he was a free man,
clear of all reproach.

He made remarkable discoveries in topography, as, for example, that the most convenient way from the establishment of Mr. Adolphus Davis to the establishment of Messrs. Plummer, Roddis, and Tyrrell, two of his principal places of call, is not, as is generally supposed, down the Sandgate road, but up the Sandgate road, round by West Terrace and along the Leas to the lift, watch the lift up and down *twice*, but not longer, because that wouldn't do, back along the Leas, watch the Harbour for a short time, and then round by the churchyard, and so (hurrying) into Church Street and Rendezvous Street. But on some exceptionally fine days the route lay through Radnor Park to the pond where little boys sail ships and there are interesting swans.

He would return to find the shop settling down to the business of serving customers. And now he had to stand by to furnish any help that was necessary to the seniors who served, to carry parcels and bills about the shop, to clear away " stuff " after each engagement, to hold up curtains until his arms ached, and, what was more difficult than all, to do nothing and not stare disconcertingly at customers when there was nothing for him to do. He plumbed an abyss of boredom, or stood a mere carcass with his mind far away, fighting the enemies of the empire, or steering a dream-ship perilously into unknown seas. To be recalled sharply to our higher civilisation by some bustling senior's " Nar then, Kipps. *Look* alive ! Ketch 'old. (My Heart and Liver !) "

At half-past seven o'clock—except on late nights—a feverish activity of " straightening up " began, and when the last shutter was up outside, Kipps, with the speed of an arrow leaving a bow, would start hanging wrappers over the fixtures and over the piles of wares upon the counters, preparatory to a vigorous scattering of wet sawdust and the sweeping out of the shop.

Sometimes people would stay long after the shop was closed. " They don't mind a bit at Shalford's," these ladies used to say, and while they loitered it was forbidden to touch a wrapper or take any measures to conclude the day until the doors closed behind them.

Mr. Kipps would watch these later customers from the shadow of a stack of goods, and death and disfigurement was the least he wished for them. Rarely much later than nine, a supper of bread and cheese and watered beer awaited him downstairs, and, that consumed, the rest of the day was entirely at his disposal for reading, recreation, and the improvement of his mind. . . .

The front door was locked at half-past ten, and the gas in the dormitory extinguished at eleven.

§ 3

On Sundays he was obliged to go to church once, and commonly he went twice, for there was nothing else to do. He sat in the free seats at the back ; he was too shy to sing, and not always clever enough to keep his place in the Prayer Book, and he rarely listened to the sermon. But he had developed a sort of idea that going to church had a tendency to alleviate life. His aunt wanted to have him confirmed, but he evaded this ceremony for some years.

In the intervals between services he walked about Folkestone with an air of looking for something. Folkestone was not so interesting on Sundays as on week-days because the shops were shut ; but, on the other hand, there was a sort of confusing brilliance along the front of the Leas in the afternoon. Sometimes the apprentice next above him would condescend to go with him ; but when the apprentice next but one above him condescended to go with the apprentice next above him, then Kipps, being habited as yet in ready-made clothes without tails, and unsuitable, therefore, to appear in such company, went alone.

Sometimes he would strike out into the country—still as if looking for something he missed—but the rope of meal-times haled him home again, and sometimes he would invest the major portion of the weekly allowance of a shilling that old Booch handed out to him, in a sacred concert on the pier. He would sometimes walk up and down the Leas between twenty and thirty times after supper, desiring much the courage to speak to some other person in the multitude similarly employed. Almost invariably he ended his Sunday footsore.

He never read a book, there were none for him to read, and, besides, in spite of Mr. Woodrow's guidance through a cheap and cheaply annotated edition of the *Tempest* (English Literature), he had no taste that way ; he never read any newspapers except, occasionally, *Tit-Bits* or a ha'penny " comic." His chief intellectual stimulus was an occasional argey-bargey that sprang up between Carshot and Buggins at dinner. Kipps listened as if to unparalleled wisdom and wit, and treasured all the gems of repartee in his heart against the time when he, too, should be a Buggins and have the chance and courage for speech.

At times there came breaks in this routine—sale-times, darkened by extra toil and work past midnight, but brightened by a sprat supper and some shillings in the way of " premiums." And every year—not now and then, but every year—Mr. Shalford, with paranthetic admiration of his own generosity and glancing comparisons with the austerer days when *he* was apprenticed, conceded Kipps no less than ten days holiday— ten whole days every year ! Many a poor soul at Portland might well envy the fortunate Kipps. Insatiable heart of man ! but how those days were grudged and counted as they snatched themselves away from him one after another !

Once a year came stocktaking, and at intervals gusts of " marking off " goods newly arrived. Then the splendours of Mr. Shalford's being shone with oppressive brilliancy. " System ! " he would say, " system ! Come ! *'ussel* ! " and issue sharp, confusing, contradictory orders very quickly. Carshot trotted about, confused, perspiring, his big nose up in the air, his little eye on Mr. Shalford, his forehead crinkled, his lips always going to the formula, " Oh, my Heart and Liver ! " The smart junior and the second apprentice vied with one another in obsequious alacrity. The smart junior aspired to Carshot's position, and that made him almost violently subservient to Shalford. They all snapped at Kipps. Kipps held the blotting-pad and the safety inkpot and a box of tickets, and ran and fetched things. If he put the ink down before he went to fetch things, Mr. Shalford usually knocked it over, and if he took it away Mr. Shalford wanted it before he returned. " You make my tooth ache, Kipps," Mr. Shalford would say. " You gimme n'ralgia. You got no more System in you than a bad potato." And at the times when Kipps carried off the inkpot Mr. Shalford would become purple in the face, and jab round with his dry pen at imaginary inkpots and swear, and Carshot would stand and vociferate, and the smart junior would run to the corner of the department and vociferate, and the second apprentice would pursue Kipps, vociferating, " Look Alive, Kipps ! Look Alive ! Ink, Man ! Ink ! "

A vague self-disgust that shaped itself as an intense hate of Shalford and all his fellow-creatures filled the soul of Kipps during these periods of storm and stress. He felt that the whole business was unjust and idiotic, but the why and the wherefore was too much for his unfortunate brain. His mind was a welter. One desire, the desire to dodge some, at least, of a pelting storm of disagreeable comment, guided him through a fumbling performance of his duties. His disgust was infinite ! It was not decreased by the inflamed ankles and sore feet that form a normal incident in the business of making an English draper, and the senior apprentice, Minton, a gaunt, sullen-faced youngster with close-cropped, wiry, black hair, a loose, ugly mouth, and a moustache like a smudge of ink, directed his attention to deeper aspects of the question and sealed his misery.

" When you get too old to work they chuck you away." said Minton. " Lor ! you find old drapers everywhere— tramps, beggars, dock labourers, bus conductors—Quod. Anywhere but in a crib."

" Don't they get shops of their own ? "

" Lord ! *'Ow* are they to get shops of their own ? They

'aven't any Capital! How's a draper's shopman to save up five hundred pounds even? I tell you it can't be done. You got to stick to Cribs until it's over. I tell you we're in a blessed drain-pipe, and we've got to crawl along it till we die."

The idea that fermented perpetually in the mind of Minton was to " hit the little beggar slap in the eye "—the little beggar being Mr. Shalford—" and see how his blessed System met that."

This threat filled Kipps with splendid anticipations whenever Shalford went marking off in Minton's department. He would look at Minton and look at Shalford and decide where he would best like Shalford hit. . . . But for reasons known to himself Shalford never pished and tushed with Minton as he did at the harmless Carshot, and this interesting experiment upon the System was never attempted.

§ 4

There were times when Kipps would lie awake, all others in the dormitory asleep and snoring, and think dismally of the outlook Minton pictured. Dimly he perceived the thing that had happened to him, how the great stupid machine of retail trade had caught his life into its wheels, a vast, irresistible force which he had neither strength of will nor knowledge to escape. This was to be his life until his days should end. No adventures, no glory, no change, no freedom. Neither —though the force of that came home to him later—might he dream of effectual love and marriage. And there was a terrible something called the " swap," or " the key of the street," and " crib hunting," of which the talk was scanty but sufficient. Night after night he would resolve to enlist, to run away to sea, to set fire to the warehouse, or drown himself, and morning after morning he rose up and hurried downstairs in fear of a sixpenny fine. He would compare his dismal round of servile drudgery with those windy, sunlit days at Littlestone, those windows of happiness shining ever brighter as they receded. The little figure of Ann seemed in all these windows now.

She, too, had happened on evil things. When Kipps went home for the first Christmas after he was bound, that great suspended resolve of his to kiss her flared up to hot determination, and he hurried out and whistled in the yard. There was a silence, and then old Kipps appeared behind him.

" It's no good your whistling there, my boy," said old Kipps in a loud, clear tone, designed to be audible over the wall. " They've cleared out all you 'ad any truck with. *She's* gone as help to Ashford, my boy. *Help!* Slavey is what we used to call 'em, but times are changed. Wonder they didn't say lady-'elp while they was about it. It 'ud be like 'em."

And Sid—— ? Sid had gone too. " Arrand boy or somethink," said old Kipps. " To one of these here brasted cicycle shops."

" *Has* 'e ? " said Kipps, with a feeling that he had been gripped about the chest ; and he turned quickly and went indoors.

Old Kipps, still supposing him present, went on to further observations of an anti-Pornick tendency. . . .

When Kipps got upstairs, safe in his own bedroom, he sat down on the bed and stared at nothing. They were caught —they were all caught. All life took on the hue of one perpetual dismal Monday morning. The Hurons were scattered, the wrecks and the beach had passed away from him, the sun of those warm evenings at Littlestone had set for evermore. . . .

The only pleasure left for the brief remainder of his holiday after that was to think he was not in the shop. Even that was transient. Two more days, one more day, half a day. When he went back there were one or two very dismal nights indeed. He went so far as to write home some vague intimation of his feelings about business and his prospects, quoting Minton, but Mrs. Kipps answered him, " Did he want the Pornicks to say he wasn't good enough to be a draper ? " This dreadful possibility was, of course, conclusive in the matter. " No ; " he resolved they should not say he failed at that.

He derived much help from a " manly " sermon delivered in an enormous voice by a large, fat, sun-red clergyman, just home from a colonial bishopric he had resigned on the plea of ill-health, exhorting him that whatever his hand found to do, he was to do with all his might, and the revision of his catechism preparatory to his confirmation reminded him that it behoved him to do his duty in that state of life into which it had pleased God to call him.

After a time the sorrows of Kipps grew less acute, and, save for a miracle, the brief tragedy of his life was over. He subdued himself to his position even as his church required of him, seeing, moreover, no way out of it.

The earliest mitigation of his lot was that his soles and ankles became indurated to the perpetual standing. The next was an unexpected weekly whiff of freedom that came every Thursday. Mr. Shalford, after a brave stand for what he called " Innyvishal lib'ty " and the " Idea of my System," a stand which, he explained, he made chiefly on patriotic grounds, was at last, under pressure of certain of his customers, compelled to fall in line with the rest of the local Early Closing Association, and Mr. Kipps could emerge in daylight and go where he listed for long, long hours. Moreover, Minton, the pessimist, reached the end of his appointed time and left— to enlist in a cavalry regiment, and go about this planet leading an insubordinate but interesting life that ended at last in an intimate, vivid, and really, you know, by no means painful or tragic night grapple in the Terah Valley. In a little while

Kipps cleaned windows no longer ; he was serving customers (of the less important sort) and taking goods out on approval, and presently he was third apprentice, and his moustache was visible, and there were three apprentices whom he might legally snub and cuff. But one was (most dishonestly) too big to cuff, in spite of his greener years.

§ 5

There came still other distractions, the natural distractions of adolescence, to take his mind off the inevitable. His costume, for example, began to interest him more ; he began to realise himself as a visible object, to find an interest in the costume-room mirrors and the eyes of the girl-apprentices.

In this he was helped by counsel and example. Pearce, his immediate senior, was by way of being what was called a Masher, and preached his cult. During slack times grave discussions about collars, ties, the cut of trouser-legs, and the proper shape of a boot-toe, were held in the Manchester department. In due course Kipps went to a tailor, and his short jacket was replaced by a morning coat with tails. Stirred by this, he purchased at his own expense three stand-up collars to replace his former turn-down ones. They were nearly three inches high, higher than those Pearce wore, and they made his neck quite sore, and left a red mark under his ears. . . . So equipped, he found himself fit company even for this fashionable apprentice, who had now succeeded Minton in his seniority.

Most potent help of all in the business of forgetting his cosmic disaster was this, that so soon as he was in tail coats, the young ladies of the establishment began to discover that he was no longer a " horrid little boy." Hitherto they had tossed heads at him and kept him in his place. Now they discovered that he was a " nice boy," which is next door at least to being a " feller," and in some ways even preferable. It is painful to record that his fidelity to Ann failed at their first onset. I am fully sensible how entirely better this story would be, from a sentimental point of view, if he had remained true to that early love. Only then it would have been a different story altogether. And at least Kipps was thus far true, that with none of these later loves was there any of that particular quality that linked Ann's flushed face and warmth and the inner things of life so inseparably together. Though they were not without emotions of various sorts.

It was one of the young ladies in the costume-room who first showed by her manner that he was a visible object and capable of exciting interest. She talked to him, she encouraged him to talk to her, she lent him a book she possessed, and darned a sock for him and said she would be his elder sister. She allowed him to escort her to church with a great air of having induced him to go. Then she investigated his eternal welfare, overcame a certain affectation of virile indifference to religion, and extorted a promise that he would undergo "confirmation." This excited the other young lady in the costumes, her natural rival, and she set herself with great charm and subtlety to the capture of the ripening heart of Kipps. She took a more worldly line. She went for a walk with him to the pier on Sunday afternoon, and explained to him how a gentleman must always walk "outside" a lady on a pavement, and how all gentlemen wore, or, at least, carried gloves, and generally the broad beginnings of the British social ideal. Afterwards the ladies exchanged "words" upon Sabbatical grounds. In this way was the *toga virilis* bestowed on Kipps, and he became recognised as a suitable object for that Platonic Eros whose blunted darts devastate even the very highest class establishments. In this way, too, did that pervading ambition of the British young man to be, if not a "gentleman," at least mistakably like one, take root in his heart.

He took to these new interests with a quite natural and personal zest. He became initiated into the mysteries of "flirting" and—at a slightly later stage and with some leading hints from Pearce, who was of a communicative disposition in these matters—of the milder forms of "spooning." Very soon he was engaged. Before two years were out he had been engaged six times, and was beginning to be rather a desperate fellow, so far as he could make out. Desperate, but quite gentlemanly, be it understood, and without let or hindrance to the fact that he was in four brief lessons "prepared" by a distant-mannered and gloomy young curate, and "confirmed" a member of the Established Church.

The engagements in drapery establishments do not necessarily involve a subsequent marriage. They are essentially more refined, less coarsely practical, and altogether less binding than the engagements of the vulgar rich. These young ladies do not like not to be engaged, it is so unnatural, and Mr. Kipps was as easy to get engaged to as one could wish. There are, from the young lady's point of view, many conveniences in being engaged. You get an escort for church and walks, and so forth. It is not quite the thing to walk abroad with a "feller," much more to "spoon" with him, when he is neither one's fiancé nor an adopted brother; it is considered either a little fast or else as savouring of the "walking-out" habits of the servant girls. Now, such is the sweetness of human charity, that the shop young lady in England has just the same horror of doing anything that savours of the servant girl as the lady journalist, let us say, has of anything savouring of the shop-girl, or the really quite nice young lady has of anything savouring of any sort of girl who has gone down into the economic battlefield to earn herself a living. . . .

But the very deepest of these affairs was still among the shallow places of love, at best it was paddling where it is decreed that men must sink or swim. Of the deep and dangerous places, and of the huge, buoyant lift of its waves, he tasted nothing. Affairs of clothes and vanities they were, jealousies about a thing said, flatteries and mutual boastings, climaxes in the answering grasp of hands, the temerarious use of Christian names, culminations in a walk, or a near confidence, or a little pressure more or less. Close sitting on a seat after twilight with some little fondling was, indeed, the boldest of lover's adventures, the utmost limit of his enterprises in the service of that stark Great Lady who is daughter of Uranus and the sea. The " young ladies " who reigned in his heart came and went like people in an omnibus ; there was the vehicle, so to speak, upon the road, and they entered and left it without any cataclysm of emotion. For all that, this development of the sex interest was continuously very interesting to Kipps, and kept him going as much as anything through all these servile years. . . .

§ 6

For a tailpiece to this chapter one may vignette a specimen minute.

It is a bright Sunday afternoon ; the scene is a secluded little seat half-way down the front of the Leas, and Kipps is four years older than when he parted from Ann. There is a quite perceptible down upon his upper lip, and his costume is just as tremendous a " mash " as lies within his means. His collar is so high that it scars his inaggressive jaw-bone, and his hat has a curly brim, his tie shows taste, his trousers are modestly brilliant, and his boots have light cloth uppers and button at the side. He jabs at the gravel before him with a cheap cane and glances sideways at Flo Bates, the young lady from the cash desk. She is wearing a brilliant blouse and a gaily trimmed hat. There is an air of fashion about her that might disappear under the analysis of a woman of the world, but which is quite sufficient to make Kipps very proud to be distinguished as her particular " feller," and to be allowed at temperate intervals to use her Christian name.

The conversation is light and gay in the modern style, nd Flo keeps on smiling, good temper being her special charm.

" Ye see, you don't mean what *I* mean," he is saying.

" Well, what do *you* mean ? "

" Not what you mean ! "

" Well, tell me."

" *Ah!* That's another story."

Pause. They look meaningly at one another.

" You *are* a one for being roundabout," says the lady.

" Well, you're not so plain, you know."

" Not plain ? "

" No."

" You don't mean to say I'm roundabout ? "

" No. I mean to say—— Though——Pause.

" Well ? "

" You're not a bit plain—you're " (his voice jumps up to a squeak) " pretty. See ? "

" Oh, get *out* ! "—her voice lifts also—with pleasure.

She strikes him with her glove, then glances suddenly at a ring upon her finger. Her smile disappears momentarily. Another pause. Eyes meet and the smile returns.

" I wish I knew—— " says Kipps.

" Knew——? "

" Where you got that ring."

She lifts the hand with the ring until her eyes just show (very prettily) over it. " You'd just *like* to know," she says slowly, and smiles still more brightly with the sense of successful effect.

" I dessay I could guess."

" I dessay you couldn't."

" Couldn't I ? "

" No ! "

" Guess it in three."

" Not the name."

" Ah ! "

" *Ah !* "

" Well, anyhow, lemme look at it."

He looks at it. Pause. Giggles, slight struggle, and a slap on Kipps' coat-sleeve. A passer-by appears down the path and she hastily withdraws her hand.

She glances at the face of the approaching man. They maintain a bashful silence until he has passed. . . .

CHAPTER THREE

THE WOODCARVING CLASS

§ 1

THOUGH these services to Venus Epipontia and these studies in the art of dress, did much to distract his thoughts and mitigate his earlier miseries, it would be mere optimism to present Kipps as altogether happy. A vague dissatisfaction with life drifted about him, and every now and again enveloped him like a sea-fog. During these periods it was grayly evident that there was something, something vital in life, lacking. For no earthly reason that Kipps could discover, he was haunted by a suspicion that life was going wrong, or had already gone wrong in some irrevocable way. The ripening self-consciousness of adolescence developed this into a clearly felt insufficiency. It was all very well to carry gloves, open doors, never say " Miss " to a girl, and walk " outside," but were there not other things, conceivably even deeper things, before the complete thing was attained ? For example, certain matters of knowledge. He perceived great bogs of ignorance about him, fumbling traps, where other people, it was alleged, *real* gentlemen and ladies, for example, and the clergy, had knowledge and assurance, bogs which it was sometimes difficult to elude. A girl arrived in the millinery department who could, she said, *speak* French and German. She snubbed certain advances, and a realisation of inferiority blistered Kipps. But he tried to pass the thing off as a joke by saying " Parlez-vous Francey " whenever he met her, and inducing the junior apprentice to say the same.

He even made some dim, half-secret experiments towards remedying the deficiencies he suspected. He spent five shillings on five serial numbers of a Home Educator, and bought (and even thought of reading) a Shakespeare and a Bacon's " Advancement of Learning," and the poems of Herrick from a chap who was hard up. He battled with Shakespeare all one Sunday afternoon, and found the " English Literature," with which Mr. Woodrow had equipped him, had vanished down some crack in his mind. He had no doubt it was very splendid stuff, but he couldn't quite make out what it was all about. There was an occult meaning, he knew, in literature, and he had forgotten it. Moreover, he discovered one day, while taunting the junior apprentice with ignorance, that his " rivers of England " had also slipped his memory, and he laboriously restored that fabric of rote learning : " Ty Wear Tees 'Umber——"

I suppose some such phase of discontent is a normal thing in every adolescence. The ripening mind seeks something upon which its will may crystallise, upon which its discursive emotions, growing more abundant with each year of life, may concentrate. For many, though not for all, it takes a religious direction ; but in those particular years the mental atmosphere of Folkestone was exceptionally free from any revivalistic disturbance that might have reached Kipps' mental being. Sometimes they fall in love. I have known this uneasiness end in different cases in a vow to read one book (not a novel) every week, to read the Bible through in a year, to pass in the Honours division of the London Matriculation examination, to become an accomplished chemist, and never more to tell a lie. It led Kipps finally into Technical Education, as we understand it in the south of England.

It was in the last year of his apprenticeship that he had pursued his researches after that missing qualification into the Folkestone Young Men's Association, where Mr. Chester Coote prevailed. Mr. Chester Coote was a young man of semi-independent means, who inherited a share in a house agency, read Mrs. Humphry Ward, and took an interest in social work. He was a whitish-faced young man, with a

prominent nose, pale blue eyes, and a quivering quality in his
voice. He was very active upon committees ; he was very
prominent and useful on all social occasions, in evidence
upon platforms, and upon all those semi-public occasions
when the Great descend. He lived with an only sister. To
Kipps and his kind in the Young Men's Association he read a
stimulating paper on " Self-Help." He said it was the noblest
of all our distinctive English characteristics, and he was very
much down upon the " over-educated " Germans. At the
close a young German hairdresser made a few commendatory
remarks which developed somehow into an oration on Hano-
verian politics. As he became excited he became guttural
and obscure ; the meeting sniggered cheerfully at such ridiculous English, and Kipps was so much amused that he forgot
a private project to ask this Chester Coote how he might set
about a little Self-Help on his own private account in such
narrow margins of time as the System of Mr. Shalford spared
him. But afterwards in the night-time it came to him again.

It was a few months later, and after his apprenticeship
was over, and Mr. Shalford had with depreciatory observations taken him on as an Improver at twenty pounds a year,
that this question was revived by a casual article on Technical
Education in a morning paper that a commercial traveller left
behind him. It played the rôle of the word in season. Something in the nature of conversion, a faint sort of concentration
of purpose, really occurred in him then. The article was written
with penetrating vehemence, and it stimulated him to the
pitch of inquiring about the local Science and Art Classes ;
and after he had told everybody in the shop about it, and
taken the advice of all who supported his desperate resolution,
he joined. At first he attended the class in Freehand, that
being the subject taught on early closing night, and he had
already made some progress in that extraordinary routine of
reproducing freehand " copies," which for two generations
has passed with English people for instruction in art, when
the dates of the classes were changed. Thereby, just as the
March winds were blowing, he was precipitated into the Woodcarving class, and his mind diverted first to this useful and
broadening pursuit, and then to its teacher.

§ 2

The class in woodcarving was an extremely select class,
conducted at that time by a young lady named Walshingham ;
and as this young lady was destined by fortune to teach
Kipps a great deal more than woodcarving, it will be well
if the reader gets the picture of her correctly in mind. She
was only a year or so older than he was, she had a pale, intellectual face, dark gray eyes and black hair, which she
wore over her forehead in an original and striking way that
she had adapted from a picture by Rossetti in the South

Kensington Museum. She was slender, so that without un-
gainliness she had an effect of being tall, and her hands were
shapely and white when they came into contrast with hands
much exercised in rolling and blocking. She dressed in those
loose and pleasant forms and those soft and tempered shades
that arose in England in the socialistic-æsthetic epoch, and
remain to this day among us as the badge of those who read
Turgenev's novels, scorn current fiction, and think on higher
planes. I think she was as beautiful as most beautiful people,
and to Kipps she was altogether beautiful. She had, Kipps
learnt, matriculated at London University, an astounding feat
to his imagination, and the masterly way in which she de-
monstrated how to prod and worry honest pieces of wood
into useless and unedifying patterns in relief, extorted his
utmost admiration.

At first when Kipps had learnt he was to be taught by a
" girl " he was inclined to resent it, the more so as Buggins
had recently been very strong on the gross injustice of feminine
employment. " We have to keep wives," said Buggins (though,
as a matter of fact, he did not keep even one), " and how
are we to do it with a lot of girls coming in to take the work
out of our mouths ? " Afterwards, Kipps, in conjunction
with Pearce, looked at it from another point of view, and
thought it would be rather a " lark." Finally, when he saw
her, and saw her teaching and coming nearer to him with an
impressive deliberation, he was breathless with awe and the
quality of her dark, slender femininity.

The class consisted of two girls and a maiden lady of riper
years, friends of Miss Walshingham's, and anxious rather to
support her in an interesting experiment than to become
really expert woodcarvers ; an elderly, oldish young man
with spectacles and a black beard, who never spoke to any
one, and who was evidently too shortsighted to see his work
as a whole ; a small boy, who was understood to have a " gift "
for woodcarving ; and a lodging-house keeper, who " took
classes " every winter, she told Mr. Kipps, as though they
were a tonic, and " found they did her good." And occasionally
Mr. Chester Coote—refined and gentlemanly—would come into
the class, with or without papers, ostensibly on committee
business, but in reality to talk to the less attractive of the
two girl-students, and sometimes a brother of Miss Walshingham's, a slender, dark young man with a pale face and fluc-
tuating resemblances to the young Napoleon, would arrive
just at the end of the class-time to see his sister home.

All these personages impressed Kipps with a sense of inferiority that in the case of Miss Walshingham became positively
abysmal. The ideas and knowledge they appeared to have,
their personal capacity and freedom, opened a new world to
his imagination. These people came and went with a sense
of absolute assurance, against an overwhelming background

of plaster casts, diagrams and tables, benches and a blackboard, a background that seemed to him to be saturated with recondite knowledge and the occult and jealously guarded tips and secrets that constitute Art and the Higher Life. They went home, he imagined, to homes where the piano was played with distinction and freedom, and books littered the tables and foreign languages were habitually used. They had complicated meals, no doubt. They " knew etiquette," and how to avoid all the errors for which Kipps bought penny manuals —" What to Avoid," " Common Errors in Speaking," and the like. He knew nothing about it all, nothing whatever ; he was a creature of the outer darkness blinking in an unsuspected light.

He heard them speak easily and freely to one another of examinations, of books and paintings, of " last year's Academy" —a little contemptuously—and once, just at the end of the class-time, Mr. Chester Coote and young Walshingham and the two girls argued about something or other called, he fancied, " Vagner," or " Vargner "—they seemed to say it both ways—and which presently shaped itself more definitely as the name of a man who made up music. (Carshot and Buggins weren't in it with them.) Young Walshingham, it appeared, said something or other that was an " epigram," and they all applauded him. Kipps, I say, felt himself a creature of outer darkness, an inexcusable intruder in an altitudinous world. When the epigram happened he first of all smiled to pretend he understood, and instantly suppressed the smile to show he did not listen. Then he became extremely hot and uncomfortable, though nobody had noticed either phase.

It was clear his only chance of concealing his bottomless baseness was to hold his tongue, and meanwhile he chipped with earnest care and abased his soul before the very shadow of Miss Walshingham. She used to come and direct and advise him, with, he felt, an effort to conceal the scorn she had for him, and, indeed, it is true that at first she thought of him chiefly as the clumsy young man with the red ears.

And as soon as he emerged from the first effect of pure and awe-stricken humility—he was greatly helped to emerge from that condition to a perception of human equality by the need the lodging-house keeper was under to talk while she worked, and as she didn't like Miss Walshingham and her friends very much, and the young man with spectacles was deaf, she naturally talked to Kipps—he perceived that he was in a state of adoration for Miss Walshingham that it seemed almost a blasphemous familiarity to speak of as being in love.

This state, you must understand, had nothing to do with " flirting " or " spooning " and that superficial passion that flashes from eye to eye upon the Leas and Pier—absolutely nothing. That he knew from the first. Her rather pallid, intellectual young face beneath those sombre clouds of hair put her in a class apart ; towards her the thought of " attentions " paled and vanished. To approach such a being, to perform sacrifices and to perish obviously for her, seemed the limit he might aspire to, he or any man. For if his love was abasement, at any rate it had this much of manliness that it covered all his sex. It had not yet come to Kipps to acknowledge any man as his better in his heart of hearts. When one does that the game is played, and one grows old indeed.

The rest of his sentimental interests vanished altogether in this great illumination. He meditated about her when he was blocking cretonne, her image was before his eyes at teatime, and blotted out the more immediate faces and made him silent and preoccupied and so careless in his bearing that the junior apprentice, sitting beside him, mocked at and parodied his enormous bites of bread and butter unreproved. He became conspicuously less popular on the " fancy " side, the " costumes " was chilly with him and the " millinery " cutting. But he did not care. An intermittent correspondence with Flo Bates, that had gone on since she left Mr. Shalford's desk for a position at Tunbridge, " nearer home ", and which had roused Kipps in its earlier stages to unparalleled heights of epistolary effort, died out altogether by reason of his neglect. He heard with scarcely a pang that, as a consequence, perhaps, of his neglect, Flo was " carrying on with a chap who managed a farm."

Every Thursday he jabbed and gouged at his wood, jabbing and gouging intersecting circles and diamond traceries, and that laboured inane which our mad world calls ornament, and he watched Miss Walshingham furtively whenever she turned away. The circles, in consequence, were jabbed crooked, and his panels, losing their symmetry, became comparatively pleasing to the untrained eye—and once he jabbed his finger. He would cheerfully have jabbed all his fingers if he could have found some means of using the opening to express himself of the vague emotions that possessed him. But he shirked conversation just as earnestly as he desired it ; he feared that profound general ignorance of his might appear.

§ 3

There came a time when she could not open one of the class-room windows. The man with the black beard pored over his chippings heedlessly. . . .

It did not take Kipps a moment to grasp his opportunity. He dropped his gouge and stepped forward. " Lem *me*," he said. . . .

He could not open the window either !

" Oh, please don't trouble," she said.

" 'Sno trouble," he gasped.

Still the sash stuck. He felt his manhood was at stake.
He gathered himself together for a tremendous effort, and
the pane broke with a snap, and he thrust his hand into the
void beyond.

" *There !* " said Miss Walshingham, and the glass fell
ringing into the courtyard below.

Then Kipps made to bring his hand back and felt the
keen touch of the edge of the broken glass at his wrist. He
turned dolefully. " I'm tremendously sorry," he said, in
answer to the accusation in Miss Walshingham's eyes. " I
didn't think it would break like that "—as if he had expected
it to break in some quite different and entirely more satisfactory
manner. The boy with the gift for woodcarving, having
stared at Kipps' face for a moment, became involved in a
Laocoon struggle with a giggle.

" You've cut your wrist," said one of the girl friends,
standing up and pointing. She was a pleasant-faced, greatly
freckled girl, with a helpful disposition, and she said, " You've
cut your wrist " as brightly as if she had been a trained nurse.

Kipps looked down and saw a swift line of scarlet rush
down his hand. He perceived the other man-student regarding
this with magnified eyes. " You *have* cut your wrist," said
Miss Walshingham ; and Kipps regarded his damage with
greater interest.

" He's cut his wrist," said the maiden lady to the lodging-
house keeper, and seemed in doubt what a lady should do.
" It's——" she hesitated at the word " bleeding," and nodded
to the lodging-house keeper instead.

" Dreadfully," said the maiden lady, and tried to look and
tried not to look at the same time.

" Of *course* he's cut his wrist," said the lodging-house
keeper, momentarily quite annoyed at Kipps ; and the other
young lady, who thought Kipps rather common, went on
quietly with her wood-cutting with an air of its being the
proper thing to do—though nobody else seemed to know it.

" You must tie it up," said Miss Walshingham.

" We must tie it up," said the freckled girl.

" I 'adn't the slightest idea that window was going to
break like that," said Kipps, with candour. " Nort the
slightest."

He glanced again at the blood on his wrist, and it seemed
to him that it was on the very point of dropping on the floor
of that cultured class-room. So he very neatly licked it off,
feeling at the same time for his handkerchief. " Oh, *don't* ! "
said Miss Walshingham as he did so, and the girl with the
freckles made a movement of horror. The giggle got the
better of the boy with the gift, and celebrated its triumph
by unseemly noises, in spite of which it seemed to Kipps at
the moment that the act that had made Miss Walshingham

say, " Oh, *don't* ! " was rather a desperate and manly treatment of what was, after all, a creditable injury.

" It ought to be tied up," said the lodging-house keeper,
holding her chisel upright in her hand. " It's a bad cut to
bleed like that."

" We must tie it up," said the freckled girl, and hesitated
in front of Kipps. " Have you got a handkerchief ? " she
said.

" I dunno 'ow I managed *not* to bring one," said Kipps.
" I—— Not 'aving a cold, I suppose some 'ow I didn't
think—— ! "

He checked a further flow of blood.

The girl with the freckles caught Miss Walshingham's eye
and held it for a moment. Both glanced at Kipps' injury.
The boy with the gift, who had reappeared with a chastened
expression from some noisy pursuit beneath his desk, made
the neglected motions of one who proffers shyly. Miss Walshingham, under the spell of the freckled girl's eye, produced
a handkerchief. The voice of the maiden lady could be heard
in the background : " I've been through all the technical
education Ambulance classes twice, and I know you go *so*
if it's a vein, and *so* if it's an artery—at least you go *so* for
one, and *so* for the other, which-ever it may be—but . . ."

" If you will give me your hand," said the freckled girl ;
and proceeded, with Miss Walshingham's assistance, to bandage Kipps in a most businesslike way. Yes, they actually
bandaged Kipps. They pulled up his cuffs—happily they
were not a very frayed pair—and held his wrist and wrapped
the soft handkerchief round it, and tightened the knot together. And Miss Walshingham's face, the face of that almost
divine Over-human, came close to the face of Kipps.

" We're not hurting you, are we ? " she said.

" Not a bit," said Kipps, as he would have said if they
had been sawing his arm off.

" We're not experts, you know," said the freckled girl.

" I'm sure it's a dreadful cut," said Miss Walshingham.

" It ain't much, reely," said Kipps ; " and you're taking a
lot of trouble. I'm sorry I broke that window. I can't think
what I could have been doing."

" It isn't so much the cut at the time, it's the poisoning
afterwards," came the voice of the maiden lady.

" Of course, I'm quite willing to pay for the window,"
panted Kipps opulently.

" We must make it just as tight as possible to stop the
bleeding," said the freckled girl.

" I don't think it's much, reely," said Kipps. " I'm awful
sorry I broke that window, though."

" Put your finger on the knot, dear," said the freckled girl.

" Eh ? " said Kipps. " I mean—— "

Both the young ladies became very intent on the knot,

and Mr. Kipps was very red and very intent upon the two young ladies.

"Mortified, and had to be sawn off," said the maiden lady.

"Sawn off," said the lodging-house keeper.

"Sawn *right* off," said the maiden lady, and jabbed at her mangled design.

"*There*," said the freckled girl, "I think that ought to do. You're sure it's not too tight?"

"Not a bit," said Kipps.

He met Miss Walshingham's eyes and smiled to show how little he cared for wounds and pain. "It's only a little cut," he added.

The maiden lady appeared as an addition to their group. "You should have washed the wound, dear," she said. "I was just telling Miss Collis——" She peered through her glasses at the bandage. "That doesn't look *quite* right," she remarked critically. "You should have taken the ambulance classes. But I suppose it will have to do. Are you hurting?"

"Not a bit," said Kipps; and smiled at them all with the air of a brave soldier in hospital.

"I'm sure it *must* hurt," said Miss Walshingham.

"Anyhow, you're a very good patient," said the girl with the freckles.

Mr. Kipps became bright pink. "I'm only sorry I broke the window—that's all," he said. "But who would have thought it was going to break like that?"

Pause.

"I'm afraid you won't be able to go on carving to-night," said Miss Walshingham.

"I'll try," said Kipps. "It reely doesn't hurt—not anything to matter."

Presently Miss Walshingham came to him as he carved heroically with his hand bandaged in her handkerchief. There was a touch of novel interest in her eyes. "I'm afraid you're not getting on very fast," she said.

The freckled girl looked up and regarded Miss Walshingham.

"I'm doing a little, anyhow," said Kipps. "I don't want to waste any time. A feller like me hasn't much time to spare."

It struck the girls that there was a quality of modest disavowal about that "feller like me." It gave them a light into this obscure person, and Miss Walshingham ventured to commend his work as "promising" and to ask whether he meant to follow it up. Kipps didn't "altogether know"—"things depended on so much," but if he was in Folkestone next winter he certainly should. It did not occur to Miss Walshingham at the time to ask why his progress in art depended upon his presence in Folkestone. There were some more questions and answers—they continued to talk to him for a little time even when Mr. Chester Coote had come into the room—and when at last the conversation had died out it dawned upon Kipps just how much his cut wrist had done for him. . . .

He went to sleep that night revising that conversation for the twentieth time, treasuring this and expanding that, and inserting things he might have said to Miss Walshingham —things he might still say about himself—in relation, more or less explicit, to her. He wasn't quite sure if he wouldn't like his arm to mortify a bit, which would make him interesting, or to heal up absolutely, which would show the exceptional purity of his blood. . . .

§ 4

The affair of the broken window happened late in April, and the class came to an end in May. In that interval there were several small incidents and great developments of emotion. I have done Kipps no justice if I have made it seem that his face was unsightly. It was, as the freckled girl pointed out to Helen Walshingham, an " interesting " face, and that aspect of him which presented chiefly erratic hair and glowing ears ceased to prevail.

They talked him over, and the freckled girl discovered there was something " wistful " in his manner. They detected a " natural delicacy," and the freckled girl set herself to draw him out from that time forth. The freckled girl was nineteen, and very wise and motherly and benevolent, and really she greatly preferred drawing out Kipps to woodcarving. It was quite evident to her that Kipps was in love with Helen Walshingham, and it struck her as a queer and romantic and pathetic and extremely interesting phenomenon. And as at that time she regarded Helen as " simply lovely," it seemed only right and proper that she should assist Kipps in his modest efforts to place himself in a state of absolute abandon upon her altar.

Under her sympathetic management the position of Kipps was presently defined quite clearly. He was unhappy in his position—misunderstood. He told her he " didn't seem to get on like " with customers, and she translated this for him as " too sensitive." The discontent with his fate in life, the dreadful feeling that Education was slipping by him, troubles that time and usage were glazing over a little, revived to their old acuteness but not to their old hopelessness. As a basis for sympathy, indeed, they were even a source of pleasure.

And one day at dinner it happened that Carshot and Buggins fell talking of " these here writers," and how Dickens had been a labeller of blacking, and Thackeray " an artis' who couldn't sell a drawing," and how Samuel Johnson had walked to London without any boots, having thrown away his only pair " out of pride." " It's Luck," said Buggins, " to a very large extent. They just happen to hit on something that catches on, and there you are ! "

"Nice easy life they have of it, too," said Miss Mergle. "Write just an hour or so, and done for the day! Almost like gentlefolks."

"There's more work in it than you'd think," said Carshot, stooping to a mouthful.

"I wouldn't mind changing for all that," said Buggins. "I'd like to see one of these here authors marking off with Jimmy."

"I think they copy from each other a good deal," said Miss Mergle.

"Even then (chup, chup, chup)," said Carshot, "there's writing it out in their own hands."

They proceeded to enlarge upon the literary life, on its ease and dignity, on the social recognition accorded to those who led it, and on the ample gratifications their vanity achieved. "Pictures everywhere—never get a new suit without being photographed—almost like Royalty," said Miss Mergle. And all this talk impressed the imagination of Kipps very greatly. Here was a class that seemed to bridge the gulf. On the one hand essentially Low, but by fictitious circumstances capable of entering upon these levels of social superiority to which all true Englishmen aspire, these levels from which one may tip a butler, scorn a tailor, and even commune with those who lead "men" into battle. "Almost like gentlefolks"—that was it! He brooded over these things in the afternoon, until they blossomed into daydreams. Suppose, for example, he had chanced to write a book, a well-known book, under an assumed name, and yet kept on being a draper all the time. . . . Impossible, of course; but *suppose——* It made quite a long dream.

And at the next woodcarving class he let it be drawn from him that his real choice in life was to be a Nawther—"only one doesn't get a chance."

After this there were times when Kipps had the pleasant sense that comes of attracting interest. He was a mute, inglorious Dickens, or at any rate something of that sort, and they were all taking him at that. The discovery of this indefinable "something in" him, the development of which was now painfully restricted and impossible, did much to bridge the gulf between himself and Miss Walshingham. He was unfortunate, he was futile, but he was not "common." Even now with help—— ? The two girls, and the freckled girl in particular, tried to "stir him up" to some effort to do his imputed potentialities justice. They were still young enough to believe that to nice and niceish members of the male sex—more especially when under the stimulus of feminine encouragement—nothing is finally impossible.

The freckled girl was, I say, the stage manager of this affair, but Miss Walshingham was the presiding divinity. A touch of proprietorship came in her eyes at times when she

looked at him. He was hers—unconditionally—and she knew
it.

To her directly, Kipps scarcely ever made a speech. The
enterprising things that he was continually devising to say
to her, he usually did not say, or said, with a suitable modi-
fication, to the girl with the freckles. And one day the girl
with the freckles smote him to the heart. She said to him,
looking across the class-room to where her friend reached a
cast from the shelf, " I do think Helen Walshingham is sometimes the most lovely person in the world. Look at her now ! "

Kipps gasped for a moment. The moment lengthened,
and she regarded him as an intelligent young surgeon might
regard an operation without anæsthetics. " You're right,"
he said, and then looked at her with an entire abandonment
of visage.

She coloured under his glare of silent avowal, and he blushed
brightly. " I think so, too," he said hoarsely, cleared his
throat, and, after a meditative moment, proceeded sacra-
mentally with his woodcarving.

" You *are* wonderful," said the freckled girl to Miss Walshingham, apropos of nothing as they went on their way
home together. " He simply adores you."

" But, my dear, what have I done ? " said Helen.

" That's just it," said the freckled girl. " What *have* you
done ? "

And then with a terrible swiftness came the last class of
the course to terminate this relationship altogether. Kipps
was careless of dates, and the thing came upon him with an
effect of abrupt surprise. Just as his petals were expanding
so hopefully, " Finis," and the thing was at an end. But
Kipps did not fully appreciate that the end was indeed and
really and truly the end until he was back in the Emporium
after the end was over.

The end began practically in the middle of the last class,
when the freckled girl broached the topic of terminations.
She developed the question of just how he was going on
after the class ended. She hoped he would stick to certain
resolutions of self-improvement he had breathed. She said
quite honestly that he owed it to himself to develop his
possibilities. He expressed firm resolve, but dwelt on difficulties.
He had no books. She instructed him how to get books from
the public library. He was to get a form of application for a
ticket signed by a ratepayer, and he said " of course " when
she said Mr. Shalford would do that, though all the time
he knew perfectly well it would " never do " to ask Mr. Shalford
for anything of the sort. She explained that she was going to
North Wales for the summer, information he received without
immediate regret. At intervals he expressed his intention of
going on with woodcarving when the summer was over, and
once he added, " if——"

She considered herself extremely delicate not to press for the completion of that " if——"

After that talk there was an interval of languid woodcarving and watching Miss Walshingham.

Then presently there came a bustle of packing, a great ceremony of handshaking all round by Miss Collis and the maiden lady of ripe years, and then Kipps found himself outside the class-room, on the landing with his two friends. It seemed to him he had only just learnt that this was the last class of all. There came a little pause, and the freckled girl suddenly went back into the class-room, and left Kipps and Miss Walshingham alone together for the first time. Kipps was instantly breathless. She looked at his face with a glance that mingled sympathy and curiosity, and held out her white hand.

" Well, good-bye, Mr. Kipps," she said.

He took her hand and held it.

" I'd do anything," said Kipps, and had not the temerity to add " for you." He stopped awkwardly.

He shook her hand and said " Good-bye."

There was a little pause. " I hope you will have a pleasant holiday," she said.

" I shall come back to the class next year, anyhow," said Kipps, valiantly, and turned abruptly to the stairs.

" I hope you will," said Miss Walshingham.

He turned back towards her.

" Really ? " he said.

" I hope everybody will come back."

" I will—anyhow," said Kipps. " You may count on that ; " and he tried to make his tones significant.

They looked at one another through a little pause.

" Good-bye," she said.

Kipps lifted his hat.

She turned towards the class-room.

" Well ? " said the freckled girl, coming back towards her.

" Nothing," said Helen. " At least—presently."

And she became very energetic about some scattered tools on a desk. The freckled girl went out and stood for a moment at the head of the stairs. When she came back she looked very hard at her friend. The incident struck her as important —wonderfully important. It was unassimilable, of course, and absurd, but there it was, the thing that is so cardinal to a girl, the emotion, the subservience, the crowning triumph of her sex. She could not help feeling that Helen took it on the whole a little too hardly.

CHAPTER FOUR

CHITTERLOW

§ I

THE hour of the class on the following Thursday found Kipps in a state of nearly incredible despondency. He was sitting with his eyes on the reading-room clock, his chin resting on his fists, and his elbows on the accumulated comic papers, that were comic, alas! in vain. He paid no heed to the little man in spectacles glaring opposite to him, famishing for *Fun*. In this place it was he had sat night after night, each night more blissful than the last, waiting until it should be time to go to Her! And then—bliss! And now the hour had come and there was no class! There would be no class now until next October. It might be there would never be a class, so far as he was concerned, again.

It might be there would never be a class again, for Shalford, taking exception at a certain absent-mindedness that led to mistakes, and more particularly to the ticketing of several articles in Kipps' Manchester window upside down, had been " on to " him for the past few days in an exceedingly onerous manner. . . .

He sighed profoundly, pushed the comic papers back—they were rent away from him instantly by the little man in spectacles—and tried the old engravings of Folkestone in the past that hung about the room. But these, too, failed to minister to his bruised heart. He wandered about the corridors for a time and watched the Library Indicator for a while. Wonderful thing that! But it did not hold him for long. People came and laughed near him, and that jarred with him dreadfully. He went out of the building, and a beastly cheerful barrel-organ mocked him in the street. He was moved to a desperate resolve to go down to the beach. There, it might be, he would be alone. The sea might be rough—and attuned to him. It would certainly be dark.

" If I 'ad a penny I'm blest if I wouldn't go and chuck myself off the end of the pier. . . . *She'd* never miss me. . . ."

He followed a deepening vein of thought.

" Penny, though! It's tuppence," he said, after a space.

He went down Dover Street in a state of profound melancholia—at the pace and mood, as it were, of his own funeral procession—and he crossed at the corner of Tontine Street, heedless of all mundane things. And there it was that Fortune came upon him, in disguise and with a loud shout, the shout of a person endowed with an unusually rich, full voice, followed immediately by a violent blow in the back.

His hat was over his eyes, and an enormous weight rested

on his shoulders, and something kicked him in the back of his calf.

Then he was on all fours in some mud that Fortune, in conjunction with the Folkestone corporation and in the pursuit of equally mysterious ends, had heaped together even lavishly for his reception.

He remained in that position for some seconds, awaiting further developments, and believing almost anything broken before his heart. Gathering at last that this temporary violence of things in general was over, and being perhaps assisted by a clutching hand, he arose, and found himself confronting a figure holding a bicycle and thrusting forward a dark face in anxious scrutiny.

" You aren't hurt, Matey ? " gasped the figure.

" Was that *you* 'it me ? " said Kipps.

" It's these handles, you know," said the figure, with an air of being a fellow-sufferer. "They're too *low*. And when I go to turn, if I don't remember, Bif !—and I'm *in* to something."

" Well—you give me a oner in the back—anyhow," said Kipps, taking stock of his damages.

" I was coming downhill, you know," explained the bicyclist. " These little Folkestone hills are a Fair Treat. It isn't as though I'd been on the level. I came rather a whop."

" You did *that*," said Kipps.

" I was back-pedalling for all I was worth, anyhow," said the bicyclist. " Not that I *am* worth much back-pedalling."

He glanced round and made a sudden movement almost as if to mount his machine. Then he turned as rapidly to Kipps again, who was now stooping down, pursuing the tale of his injuries.

" Here's the back of my trouser-leg all tore down," said Kipps, " and I believe I'm bleeding. You reely ought to be more careful——"

The stranger investigated the damage with a rapid movement. " Holy Smoke, so you are ! " He laid a friendly hand on Kipps' arm. " I say—look here ! Come up to my diggings and sew it up. I'm—— Of course I'm to blame, and I say——" His voice sank to a confidential friendliness. " Here's a slop. Don't let on I ran you down. Haven't a lamp, you know. Might be a bit awkward, for *me*."

Kipps looked up towards the advancing policeman. The appeal to his generosity was not misplaced. He immediately took sides with his assailant. He stood as the representative of the law drew nearer. He assumed an air which he considered highly suggestive of an accident not having happened.

" All right," he said, " go on ! "

" Right you are," said the cyclist, promptly, and led the way ; and then, apparently with some idea of deception, called over his shoulder, " I'm tremendous glad to have met you, old chap."

" It really isn't a hundred yards," he said, after they had passed the policeman ; " it's just round the corner."

" Of course," said Kipps, limping slightly. " I don't want to get a chap into trouble. Accidents *will* happen. Still——"

" Oh, *rather* ! I believe you. Accidents *will* happen. Especially when you get *me* on a bicycle." He laughed. " You aren't the first I've run down, not by any manner of means ! I don't think you can be hurt much, either. It isn't as though I was scorching. You didn't see me coming. I was back-pedalling like anything. Only naturally it seems to you I must have been coming fast. And I did all I could to ease off the bump as I hit you. It was just the treadle, I think, came against your calf. But it was All Right of you about that policeman, you know. That was a Fair Bit of All Right. Under the Circs., if you'd told him I was riding, it might have been forty bob ! Forty bob ! I'd have had to tell 'em Time is Money just now for Mr. H. C.

" I shouldn't have blamed you either, you know. Most men, after a bump like that, might have been spiteful. The least I can do is to stand you a needle and thread. And a clothes' brush. It isn't every one who'd have taken it like you.

" Scorching ! Why, if I'd been scorching you'd have—coming as we did—you'd have been knocked silly.

" But, I tell you, the way you caught on about that slop was something worth seeing. When I asked you—I didn't half expect it. Bif ! Right off. Cool as a cucumber. Had your line at once. I tell you that there isn't many men would have acted as you have done, I *will* say that. You acted like a gentleman over that slop."

Kipps' first sense of injury disappeared. He limped along a pace or so behind, making depreciatory noises in response to these flattering remarks, and taking stock of the very appreciative person who uttered them.

As they passed the lamps he was visible as a figure with a slight anterior plumpness, progressing buoyantly on knicker-bockered legs, with quite enormous calves, legs that, contrasting with Kipps' own narrow practice, were even exuberantly turned out at the knees and toes. A cycling cap was worn very much on one side, and from beneath it protruded carelessly straight wisps of dark-red hair, and ever and again an ample nose came into momentary view round the corner. The muscular cheeks of this person and a certain generosity of chin he possessed were blue shaven, and he had no moustache. His carriage was spacious and confident, his gestures up and down the narrow, deserted back street they traversed were irresistibly suggestive of ownership ; a succession of broadly gesticulating shadows were born squatting on his feet, and grew and took possession of the road and reunited at last with the shadows of the infinite, as lamp after lamp was

passed. Kipps saw by the flickering light of one of them that
they were in Little Fenchurch Street, and then they came round
a corner sharply into a dark court and stopped at the door
of a particularly ramshackle-looking little house, held up
between two larger ones, like a drunken man between policemen.

The cyclist propped his machine carefully against the
window, produced a key and blew down it sharply. " The
lock's a bit tricky," he said, and devoted himself for some
moments to the task of opening the door. Some mechanical
catastrophe ensued, and the door was open.

" You'd better wait here a bit while I get the lamp," he
remarked to Kipps ; " very likely it isn't filled," and vanished
into the blackness of the passage. " Thank God for matches ! "
he said ; and Kipps had an impression of a passage in the
transitory pink flare and the bicyclist disappearing into a
farther room. Kipps was so much interested by these things
that for the time he forgot his injuries altogether.

An interval, and Kipps was dazzled by a pink-shaded
kerosene lamp. " You go in," said the red-haired man, " and
I'll bring in the bike," and for a moment Kipps was alone
in the lamp-lit room. He took in rather vaguely the shabby
ensemble of the little apartment, the round table covered
with a torn, red, glass-stained cover on which the lamp stood,
a mottled looking-glass over the fireplace reflecting this, a
disused gas-bracket, an extinct fire, a number of dusty post-
cards and memoranda stuck round the glass, a dusty, crowded
paper-rack on the mantel with a number of cabinet photographs,
a table littered with papers and cigarette ash, and a siphon of
soda-water. Then the cyclist reappeared, and Kipps saw
his blue-shaved, rather animated face, and bright, reddish-
brown eyes for the first time. He was a man, perhaps, ten
years older than Kipps, but his beardless face made them in a
way contemporary.

" You behaved all right about that policeman, anyhow,"
he repeated as he came forward.

" I don't see 'ow else I could 'ave done," said Kipps, quite
modestly. The cyclist scanned his guest for the first time,
and decided upon hospitable details.

" We'd better let that mud dry a bit before we brush it.
Whisky there is, good old Methusaleh, Canadian Rye ; and
there's some brandy that's all right. Which'll you have ? "

" I dunno," said Kipps, taken by surprise ; and then seeing
no other course but acceptance, " Well, whisky, then."

" Right you are, old boy ; and if you'll take my advice
you'll take it neat. I may not be a particular judge of this
sort of thing, but I do know old Methusaleh pretty well.
Old Methusaleh—four stars. That's me ! Good old Harry
Chitterlow, and good old Methusaleh. Leave 'em together.
Bif ! He's gone ! "

He laughed loudly, looked about him, hesitated, and retired, leaving Kipps in possession of the room, and free to
make a more precise examination of its contents.

§ 2

He particularly remarked the photographs that adorned
the apartment. They were chiefly photographs of ladies, in
one case in tights, which Kipps thought a " bit 'ot ; " but
one represented the bicyclist in the costume of some remote
epoch. It did not take Kipps long to infer that the others
were probably actresses, and that his host was an actor, and
the presence of the half of a large coloured playbill seemed
to confirm this. A note in an Oxford frame that was a little
too large for it he presently demeaned himself to read. " Dear
Mr. Chitterlow," it ran its brief course, " if, after all, you
will send the play you spoke of, I will endeavour to read it,"
followed by a stylish but absolutely illegible signature, and
across this was written in pencil, " What price Harry now ? "
And in the shadow by the window was a rough and rather
able sketch of the bicyclist in chalk on brown paper, calling
particular attention to the curvature of the forward lines of
his hull and calves and the jaunty carriage of his nose, and
labelled unmistakably " Chitterlow." Kipps thought it
" rather a take-off." The papers on the table by the siphon
were in manuscript, Kipps observed, manuscript of a particularly convulsive and blottesque sort, and running obliquely
across the page.

Presently he heard the metallic clamour as if of a series of
irreparable breakages with which the lock of the front door
discharged its function, and then Chitterlow reappeared, a
little out of breath, and with a starry-labelled bottle in his
large, freckled hand.

" Sit down, old chap," he said, " sit down. I had to go
out for it, after all. Wasn't a solitary bottle left. However,
it's all right now we're here. No, don't sit on that chair,
there's sheets of my play on that. That's the one—with the
broken arm. I think this glass is clean, but, anyhow, wash
it out with a squizz of siphon and shy it in the fireplace. Here,
I'll do it ! Lend it here ! "

As he spoke Mr. Chitterlow produced a corkscrew from a
table drawer, attacked and overcame good old Methusaleh's
cork in a style a bar-tender might envy, washed out two
tumblers in his simple, effectual manner, and poured a couple
of inches of the ancient fluid into each. Kipps took his tumbler,
said " Thenks " in an off-hand way, and, after a momentary
hesitation whether he should say " Here's to you ! " or not,
put it to his lips without that ceremony. For a space fire in
his throat occupied his attention to the exclusion of other
matters, and then he discovered Mr. Chitterlow with an intensely bulldog pipe alight, seated on the opposite side of the

empty fireplace, and pouring himself out a second dose of whisky.

"After all," said Mr. Chitterlow, with his eye on the bottle and a little smile wandering to hide amidst his larger features, "this accident might have been worse. I wanted some one to talk to a bit, and I didn't want to go to a pub, leastways not a Folkestone pub, because, as a matter of fact, I'd promised Mrs. Chitterlow, who's away, not to, for various reasons, though, of course, if I'd wanted to, I'm just that sort, I should have all the same—and here we are ! It's curious how one runs up against people out bicycling ! "

"Isn't it ! " said Kipps, feeling that the time had come for him to say something.

"Here we are, sitting and talking like old friends, and half an hour ago we didn't know we existed. Leastways we didn't know each other existed. I might have passed you in the street, perhaps, and you might have passed me, and how was I to tell that, put to the test, you would have behaved as decently as you have behaved. Only it happened otherwise, that's all. You're not smoking ! " he said. " Have a cigarette ? "

Kipps made a confused reply that took the form of not minding if he did, and drank another sip of old Methusaleh in his confusion. He was able to follow the subsequent course of that sip for quite a long way. It was as though the old gentleman was brandishing a burning torch through his vitals, lighting him here and lighting him there, until at last his whole being was in a glow. Chitterlow produced a tobacco-pouch and cigarette-papers, and, with an interesting parenthesis that was a little difficult to follow about some lady, named Kitty something or other, who had taught him the art when he was as yet only what you might call a nice boy, made Kipps a cigarette, and, with a consideration that won Kipps' gratitude, suggested that, after all, he might find a little soda-water an improvement on the whisky. " Some people like it that way," said Chitterlow ; and then with voluminous emphasis, " *I* don't."

Emboldened by the weakened state of his enemy, Kipps promptly swallowed the rest of him, and had his glass at once hospitably replenished. He began to feel he was of a firmer consistency than he commonly believed, and turned his mind to what Chitterlow was saying with the resolve to play a larger part in the conversation than he had hitherto done. Also he smoked through his nose quite successfully, an art he had only very recently acquired.

Meanwhile, Chitterlow explained that he was a playwright, and the tongue of Kipps was unloosened to respond that he knew a chap, or rather one of their fellows knew a chap, or at least, to be perfectly correct, this fellow's brother did, who had written a play. In response to Chitterlow's inquiries, he could not recall the title of the play, nor where it had appeared, nor the name of the manager who produced it, though he thought the title was something about " Love's Ransom," or something like that.

" He made five 'undred pounds by it, though," said Kipps. " I know that."

" That's nothing," said Chitterlow, with an air of experience that was extremely convincing. " Noth-ing. May seem a big sum to *you*, but *I* can assure you it's just what one gets any day. There's any amount of money, an-ny amount, in a good play."

" I dessay," said Kipps, drinking.

" Any amount of money ! "

Chitterlow began a series of illustrative instances. He was clearly a person of quite unequalled gift for monologue. It was as though some conversational dam had burst upon Kipps, and in a little while he was drifting along upon a copious rapid of talk about all sorts of theatrical things by one who knew all about them, and quite incapable of anticipating whither that rapid meant to carry him. Presently, somehow, they had got to anecdotes about well-known theatrical managers—little Teddy Bletherskite, artful old Chumps, and the magnificent Behemoth, " petted to death, you know, fair sickened, by all these society women." Chitterlow described various personal encounters with these personages, always with modest self-depreciation, and gave Kipps a very amusing imitation of old Chumps in a state of intoxication. Then he took two more stiff doses of old Methusaleh in rapid succession.

Kipps reduced the hither end of his cigarette to a pulp as he sat " dessaying " and " quite believing " Chitterlow in the sagest manner, and admiring the easy way in which he was getting on with this very novel and entertaining personage. He had another cigarette made for him, and then Chitterlow, assuming by insensible degrees more and more of the manner of a rich and successful playwright being interviewed by a young admirer, set himself to answer questions which sometimes Kipps asked, and sometimes Chitterlow, about the particulars and methods of his career. He undertook this self-imposed task with great earnestness and vigour, treating the matter, indeed, with such fullness that at times it seemed lost altogether under a thicket of parentheses, footnotes, and episodes that branched and budded from its stem. But it always emerged again, usually by way of illustration, to its own digressions. Practically it was a mass of material for the biography of a man who had been everywhere and done everything (including the Hon. Thomas Norgate, which was a record), and in particular had acted with great distinction and profit (he dated various anecdotes, " when I was getting thirty, or forty, or fifty dollars a week ") throughout America and the entire civilised world.

And as he talked on and on in that full, rich, satisfying voice he had, and as old Methusaleh, indisputably a most drunken old reprobate of a whisky, busied himself throughout Kipps, lighting lamp after lamp until the entire framework of the little draper was illuminated and glowing like some public building on a festival, behold Chitterlow, and Kipps with him, and the room in which they sat were transfigured ! Chitterlow became in very truth that ripe, full man of infinite experience and humour and genius, fellow of Shakespeare and Ibsen and Mæterlinck (three names he placed together quite modestly far above his own), and no longer ambiguously dressed in a sort of yachting costume with cycling knickerbockers, but elegantly if unconventionally attired, and the room ceased to be a small and shabby room in a Folkestone slum, and grew larger and more richly furnished, and the flyblown photographs were curious old pictures, and the rubbish on the walls the most rare and costly bric-à-brac, and the indisputable paraffin lamp a soft and splendid light. A certain youthful heat that to many minds might have weakened old Methusaleh's starry claim to a ripe antiquity vanished in that glamour ; two burnt holes and a clamant darn in the table-cloth, moreover, became no more than the pleasing contradictions natural in the house of genius ; and as for Kipps—Kipps was a bright young man of promise, distinguished by recent quick, courageous proceedings not too definitely insisted upon, and he had been rewarded by admission to a sanctum and confidences for which the common prosperous, for which " society women " even, were notoriously sighing in vain. " Don't *want* them, my boy ; they'd simply play old Harry with the Work, you know ! Chaps outside, bank clerks and university fellows, think the life's all *that* sort of thing. Don't you believe 'em ! Don't you believe 'em."

And then——!

" Boom . . . Boom . . . Boom . . . Boom . . ." right in the middle of a most entertaining digression on flats who join touring companies under the impression that they are actors, Kipps much amused at their flatness as exposed by Chitterlow.

" Lor ! " said Kipps, like one who awakens, " that's not eleven ! "

" Must be," said Chitterlow. " It was nearly ten when I got that whisky. It's early yet——"

" All the same, I must be going," said Kipps, and stood up. " Even now—maybe. Fact is—I 'ad *no* idea. The 'ouse door shuts at 'arf-past ten, you know. I ought to 'ave thought before."

" Well, if you *must* go— ! I tell you what. I'll come too. . . . Why ! There's your leg, old man ! Clean forgot it ! You can't go through the streets like that. I'll sew up the tear. And meanwhile have another whisky."

" I ought to be getting on *now*," protested Kipps, feebly ; and then Chitterlow was showing him how to kneel on a chair in order that the rent trouser leg should be attainable, and old Methusaleh on his third round was busy repairing the temporary

eclipse of Kipps' arterial glow. Then suddenly Chitterlow was
seized with laughter, and had to leave off sewing to tell Kipps
that the scene wouldn't make a bad bit of business in a farcical
comedy, and then he began to sketch out the farcical comedy,
and that led him to a digression about another farcical comedy
of which he had written a ripping opening scene which wouldn't
take ten minutes to read. It had something in it that had never
been done on the stage before, and was yet perfectly legitimate,
namely, a man with a live beetle down the back of his neck
trying to seem at his ease in a roomful of people. . . .

" *They* won't lock you out," he said, in a singularly reassuring
tone, and began to read and act what he explained to be (not
because he had written it, but simply because he knew it was
so on account of his exceptional experience of the stage), and
what Kipps also quite clearly saw to be, one of the best opening
scenes that had ever been written.

When it was over, Kipps, who rarely swore, was inspired
to say the scene was " damned fine " about six times over,
whereupon, as if by way of recognition, Chitterlow took a
simply enormous portion of the inspired antediluvian, declaring
at the same time that he had rarely met a " *finer* " intelligence
than Kipps' (stronger there might be, *that* he couldn't say with
certainty as yet, seeing how little, after all, they had seen of
each other, but a finer *never*), that it was a shame such a gallant
and discriminating intelligence should be nightly either locked
up or locked out at ten—well, ten-thirty, then—and that he
had half a mind to recommend old somebody or other (apparently the editor of a London daily paper) to put on Kipps
forthwith as a dramatic critic in the place of the current
incapable.

" I don't think I've ever made up anything for print," said
Kipps, " ever. I'd have a thundering good try, though, if ever
I got a chance. I would that ! I've written window tickets orfen
enough. Made 'em up and everything. But that's different."

" You'd come to it all the fresher for not having done it
before. And the way you picked up every point in that scene,
my boy, was a Fair Treat ! I tell you, you'd knock William
Archer into fits. Not so literary, of course, you'd be, but I
don't believe in literary critics any more than in literary playwrights. Plays *aren't* literature—that's just the point they
miss. Plays are plays. No ! That won't hamper you, anyhow.
You're wasted down here, I tell you. Just as I was, before I
took to acting. I'm hanged if I wouldn't like your opinion on
these first two acts of that tragedy I'm on to. I haven't told
you about that. It wouldn't take me more than an hour to
read." . . .

§ 3

Then, so far as he could subsequently remember, Kipps had
" another," and then it would seem that, suddenly regardless

of the tragedy, he insisted that he " really *must* be getting on," and from that point his memory became irregular. Certain things remained quite clearly, and as it is a matter of common knowledge that intoxicated people forget what happens to them, it follows that he was not intoxicated. Chitterlow came with him, partly to see him home and partly for a freshener before turning in. Kipps recalled afterwards very distinctly how in Little Fenchurch Street he discovered that he could not walk straight, and also that Chitterlow's needle and thread in his still unmended trouser leg was making an annoying little noise on the pavement behind him. He tried to pick up the needle suddenly by surprise, and somehow tripped and fell, and then Chitterlow, laughing uproariously, helped him up. " It wasn't a bicycle this time, old boy," said Chitterlow, and that appeared to them both at the time as being a quite extraordinarily good joke indeed. They punched each other about on the strength of it.

For a time after that Kipps certainly pretended to be quite desperately drunk and unable to walk, and Chitterlow entered into the pretence and supported him. After that Kipps remembered being struck with the extremely laughable absurdity of going downhill to Tontine Street in order to go uphill again to the Emporium, and trying to get that idea into Chitterlow's head and being unable to do so on account of his own merriment and Chitterlow's evident intoxication ; and his next memory after that was of the exterior of the Emporium, shut and darkened, and, as it were, frowning at him with all its stripes of yellow and green. The chilly way in which " SHALFORD " glittered in the moonlight printed itself with particular vividness on his mind. It appeared to Kipps that that establishment was closed to him for evermore. Those gilded letters, in spite of appearances, spelt FINIS for him and exile from Folkestone. He would never do wood-carving, never see Miss Walshingham again. Not that he had ever hoped to see her again. But this was the knife, this was final. He had stayed out, he had got drunk, there had been that row about the Manchester window dressing only three days ago. . . . In the retrospect he was quite sure that he was perfectly sober then and at bottom extremely unhappy, but he kept a brave face on the matter nevertheless, and declared stoutly he didn't care if he *was* locked out.

Whereupon Chitterlow slapped him on the back very hard and told him that was a " Bit of All-Right," and assured him that when he himself had been a clerk in Sheffield, before he took to acting, he had been locked out sometimes for six nights running.

" What's the result ? " said Chitterlow. " I could go back to that place now, and they'd be glad to have me. . . . Glad to have me," he repeated, and then added, " That is to say, if they remember me—which isn't very likely."

Kipps asked a little weakly, " What am I to do ? "

" Keep out," said Chitterlow. " You can't knock 'em up now—that would give you Right away. You'd better try and sneak in in the morning with the Cat. That'll do you. You'll probably get in all right in the morning if nobody gives you away."

Then for a time—perhaps as the result of that slap on the back—Kipps felt decidedly queer, and, acting on Chitterlow's advice, went for a bit of a freshener upon the Leas. After a time he threw off the temporary queerness, and found Chitterlow patting him on the shoulder and telling him that he'd be all right now in a minute and all the better for it—which he was. And the wind having dropped and the night being now a really very beautiful moonlight night indeed, and all before Kipps to spend as he liked, and with only a very little tendency to spin round now and again to mar its splendour, they set out to walk the whole length of the Leas to the Sandgate lift and back, and as they walked Chitterlow spoke first of moonlight transfiguring the sea and then of moonlight transfiguring faces, and so at last he came to the topic of Love, and upon that he dwelt a great while, and with a wealth of experience and illustrative anecdote that seemed remarkably pungent and material to Kipps. He forgot his lost Miss Walshingham and his outraged employer again. He became, as it were, a desperado by reflection.

Chitterlow had had adventures, a quite astonishing variety of adventures, in this direction ; he was a man with a past, a really opulent past, and he certainly seemed to like to look back and see himself amidst its opulence.

He made no consecutive history, but he gave Kipps vivid momentary pictures of relations and entanglements. One moment he was in flight—only too worthily in flight—before the husband of a Malay woman in Cape Town. At the next he was having passionate complications with the daughter of a clergyman in York. Then he passed to a remarkable grouping at Seaford.

" They say you can't love two women at once," said Chitterlow. " But I tell you——" He gesticulated and raised his ample voice. " It's *Rot ! Rot !* "

" *I* know that," said Kipps.

" Why, when I was in the smalls with Bessie Hopper's company there were Three." He laughed, and decided to add, " not counting Bessie, that is."

He set out to reveal Life as it is lived in touring companies, a quite amazing jungle of interwoven " affairs " it appeared to be, a mere amorous winepress for the crushing of hearts.

"People say this sort of thing's a nuisance and interferes with Work. I tell you it isn't. The Work couldn't go on without it. They *must* do it. They haven't the Temperament if

they don't. If they hadn't the Temperament they wouldn't
want to act ; if they have— Bif ! "

"You're right," said Kipps. "I see that."

Chitterlow proceeded to a close criticism of certain historical
indiscretions of Mr. Clement Scott respecting the morals of the
stage. Speaking in confidence, and not as one who addresses
the public, he admitted regretfully the general truth of these
comments. He proceeded to examine various typical instances
that had almost forced themselves upon him personally, and
with especial regard to the contrast between his own character
towards women and that of the Hon. Thomas Norgate, with
whom it appeared he had once been on terms of great
intimacy. . . .

Kipps listened with emotion to these extraordinary recollections. They were wonderful to him, they were incredibly
credible. This tumultuous, passionate, irregular course was
the way life ran—except in high-class establishments ! Such
things happened in novels, in plays—only he had been fool
enough not to understand they happened. His share in the conversation was now, indeed, no more than faint writing in the
margin ; Chitterlow was talking quite continuously. He
expanded his magnificent voice into huge guffaws, he drew it
together into a confidential intensity, it became drawlingly
reminiscent, he was frank, frank with the effect of a revelation,
reticent also with the effect of a revelation, a stupendously
gesticulating moonlit black figure, wallowing in itself, preach-
ing Adventure and the Flesh to Kipps. Yet withal shot with
something of sentiment, with a sort of sentimental refinement
very coarsely and egotistically done. The Times he had had !
—even before he was as old as Kipps he had had innumerable
Times.

Well, he said with a sudden transition, he had sown his
wild oats—one had to somewhen—and now, he fancied he had
mentioned it earlier in the evening, he was happily married.
She was, he indicated, a "born lady." Her father was a
prominent lawyer, a solicitor in Kentish Town, "done a lot
of public-house business ; " her mother was second cousin
to the wife of Abel Jones, the fashionable portrait painter—
"almost Society people in a way." That didn't count with
Chitterlow. He was no snob. What *did* count was that she
possessed what he ventured to assert, without much fear of
contradiction, was the very finest completely untrained
contralto voice in all the world. ("But to hear it properly,"
said Chitterlow, "you want a Big Hall.") He became rather
vague, and jerked his head about to indicate when and how
he had entered matrimony. She was, it seemed, "away with
her people." It was clear that Chitterlow did not get on with
these people very well. It would seem they failed to appreciate
his playwriting, regarding it as an unremunerative pursuit,
whereas, as he and Kipps knew, wealth beyond the dreams of

avarice would presently accrue. Only patience and persistence were needful.

He went off at a tangent to hospitality. Kipps must come down home with him. They couldn't wander about all night, with a bottle of the right sort pining at home for them. " You can sleep on the sofa. You won't be worried by broken springs, anyhow, for I took 'em all out myself two or three weeks ago. I don't see what they ever put 'em in for. It's a point I know about. I took particular notice of it when I was with Bessie Hopper. Three months we were, and all over England, North Wales, and the Isle of Man, and I never struck a sofa in diggings anywhere that hadn't a broken spring. Not once—all the time."

He added, almost absently, " It happens like that at times."

They descended the slant road towards Harbour Street and went on past the Pavilion Hotel.

§ 4

They came into the presence of old Methusaleh again, and that worthy, under Chitterlow's direction, at once resumed the illumination of Kipps' interior with the conscientious thoroughness that distinguished him. Chitterlow took a tall portion to himself with an air of asbestos, lit the bulldog pipe again, and lapsed for a space into meditation, from which Kipps roused him by remarking that he expected " a nacter 'as a lot of ups and downs like, now and then."

At which Chitterlow seemed to bestir himself. " Ra-ther," he said. " And sometimes it's his own fault and sometimes it isn't. Usually it is. If it isn't one thing it's another. If it isn't the manager's wife it's bar-bragging. I tell you things happen at times. I'm a fatalist. The fact is, Character has you. You can't get away from it. You may think you do, but you don't."

He reflected for a moment. " It's that what makes tragedy. Psychology really. It's the Greek irony—Ibsen and—all that. Up to date."

He emitted this exhaustive summary of high-toned modern criticism as if he was repeating a lesson while thinking of something else ; but it seemed to rouse him as it passed his lips, by including the name of Ibsen.

He became interested in telling Kipps, who was, indeed, open to any information whatever about this quite novel name, exactly where he thought Ibsen fell short, points where it happened that Ibsen was defective just where it chanced that he, Chitterlow, was strong. Of course, he had no desire to place himself in any way on an equality with Ibsen ; still, the fact remained that his own experience in England and America and the colonies was altogether more extensive than Ibsen could have had. Ibsen had probably never seen " one decent bar scrap " in his life. That, of course, was not Ibsen's fault, or his own merit, but there the thing was. Genius, he knew, was supposed to be able to do anything or to do without anything ; still, he was now inclined to doubt that. He had a play in hand that might perhaps not please William Archer—whose opinion, after all, he did not value, as he valued Kipps' opinion—but which, he thought, was, at any rate, as well constructed as anything Ibsen ever did.

So with infinite deviousness Chitterlow came at last to his play. He decided he would not read it to Kipps, but tell him about it. This was the simpler, because much of it was still unwritten. He began to explain his plot. It was a complicated plot, and all about a nobleman who had seen everything and done everything and knew practically all that Chitterlow knew about women, that is to say, " all about women " and such-like matters. It warmed and excited Chitterlow. Presently he stood up to act a situation, which could not be explained. It was an extremely vivid situation.

Kipps applauded the situation vehemently. " Tha's dam fine," said the new dramatic critic, quite familiar with his part now, striking the table with his fist and almost upsetting his third portion (in the second series) of old Methusaleh. " Tha's *dam* fine, Chit'low ! "

" You see it ? " said Chitterlow, with the last vestiges of that incidental gloom disappearing. " Good old boy ! I thought you'd see it. But it's just the sort of thing the literary critic can't see. However, it's only a beginning——"

He replenished Kipps and proceeded with his exposition.

In a little while it was no longer necessary to give that over-advertised Ibsen the purely conventional precedence he had hitherto had. Kipps and Chitterlow were friends, and they could speak frankly and openly of things not usually admitted. " Any'ow," said Kipps, a little irrelevantly, and speaking over the brim of the replenishment, " what you read jus' now was dam fine. Nothing can't alter that."

He perceived a sort of faint buzzing vibration about things that was very nice and pleasant, and with a little care he had no difficulty whatever in putting his glass back on the table. Then he perceived Chitterlow was going on with the scenario, and then that old Methusaleh had almost entirely left his bottle. He was glad there was so little more Methusaleh to drink, because that would prevent his getting drunk. He knew that he was not now drunk, but he knew that he had had enough. He was one of those who always know when they have had enough. He tried to interrupt Chitterlow to tell him this, but he could not get a suitable opening. He doubted whether Chitterlow might not be one of those people who did not know when they had had enough. He discovered that he disapproved of Chitterlow. Highly. It seemed to him that Chitterlow went on and on like a river. For a time he was inexplicably and quite unjustly cross with Chitterlow, and wanted to say to him " you got the gift of the gab," but he only got so far as to say " the gift," and then Chitterlow thanked him and said he was better than Archer any day. So he eyed Chitterlow with a baleful eye until it dawned upon him that a most extraordinary thing was taking place. Chitterlow kept mentioning some one named Kipps. This presently began to perplex Kipps very greatly. Dimly but decidedly he perceived this was wrong.

"Look 'ere," he said suddenly, " *what* Kipps ? "

"This chap Kipps I'm telling you about."

"What chap Kipps you're telling which about ? "

"I told you."

Kipps struggled with a difficulty in silence for a space. Then he reiterated firmly, " *What* chap Kipps ? "

"This chap in my play—man who kisses the girl."

"Never kissed a girl," said Kipps, "leastways——" and subsided for a space. He could not remember whether he had kissed Ann or not—he knew he had meant to. Then, suddenly, in a tone of great sadness, and addressing the hearth, he said, " *My* name's Kipps."

"Eh ? " said Chitterlow.

"Kipps," said Kipps, smiling a little cynically.

"What about him ? "

"He's me." He tapped his breastbone with his middle finger to indicate his essential self.

He leant forward very gravely towards Chitterlow. "Look 'ere, Chit'low," he said. "You haven't no business putting my name into play. You mustn't do things like that. You'd lose me my crib, right away." And they had a little argument— so far as Kipps could remember. Chitterlow entered upon a general explanation of how he got his names. These he had, for the most part, got out of a newspaper that was still, he believed, "lying about." He even made to look for it, and while he was doing so Kipps went on with the argument, addressing himself more particularly to the photograph of the girl in tights. He said that at first her costume had not commended her to him, but now he perceived she had an extremely sensible face. He told her she would like Buggins if she met him, he could see she was just that sort. She would admit—all sensible people would admit—that using names in plays was wrong. You could, for example, have the law of him.

He became confidential. He explained that he was already in sufficient trouble for stopping out all night, without having his name put in plays. He was certain to be in the deuce of a row, the deuce of a row. Why had he done it ? Why hadn't he gone at ten ? Because one thing leads to another. One thing, he generalised, always does lead to another. . . .

He was trying to tell her that he was utterly unworthy of Miss Walshingham, when Chitterlow gave up the search, and suddenly accused him of being drunk and talking " Rot——"

CHAPTER FIVE

" SWAPPED "

§ I

HE awoke on the thoroughly comfortable sofa that had
had all its springs removed, and although he had certainly not been intoxicated, he awoke with what
Chitterlow pronounced to be, quite indisputably, a Head and
a Mouth. He had slept in his clothes, and he felt stiff and uncomfortable all over, but the head and mouth insisted that he
must not bother over little things like that. In the head was
one large, angular idea that it was physically painful to have
there. If he moved his head, the angular idea shifted about in
the most agonising way. This idea was that he had lost his
situation and was utterly ruined, and that it really mattered
very little. Shalford was certain to hear of his escapade, and
that, coupled with that row about the Manchester window—— !

He raised himself into a sitting position under Chitterlow's
urgent encouragement.

He submitted apathetically to his host's attentions. Chitterlow, who admitted being a " bit off it " himself and in need of
an egg-cupful of brandy, just an egg-cupful neat, dealt with
that Head and Mouth as a mother might deal with the fall
of an only child. He compared it with other Heads and Mouths
that he had met, and in particular to certain experienced by
the Hon. Thomas Norgate. " Right up to the last," said
Chitterlow, " he couldn't stand his liquor. It happens like that
at times." And after Chitterlow had pumped on the young
beginner's head and given him some anchovy paste piping hot
on buttered toast, which he preferred to all the other remedies
he had encountered, Kipps resumed his crumpled collar,
brushed his clothes, tacked up his knee, and prepared to face
Mr. Shalford and the reckoning for this wild, unprecedented
night—the first " night out " that ever he had taken.

Acting on Chitterlow's advice to have a bit of a freshener
before returning to the Emporium, Kipps walked some way
along the Leas and back, and then went down to a shop near
the Harbour to get a cup of coffee. He found that extremely
reinvigorating, and he went on up the High Street to face the
inevitable terrors of the office, a faint touch of pride in his
depravity tempering his extreme self-abasement. After all,
it was not an unmanly headache ; he had been out all night,
and he had been drinking, and his physical disorder was there
to witness the fact. If it wasn't for the thought of Shalford,
he would have been even a proud man to discover himself at
last in such a condition. But the thought of Shalford was
very dreadful. He met two of the apprentices snatching a

walk before shop began. At the sight of them he pulled his spirits together, put his hat back from his pallid brow, thrust his hands into his trousers pockets, and adopted an altogether more dissipated carriage ; he met their innocent faces with a wan smile. Just for a moment he was glad that his patch at the knee was, after all, visible, and that some, at least, of the mud on his clothes had refused to move at Chitterlow's brushing. What wouldn't they think he had been up to ? He passed them without speaking. He could imagine how they regarded his back. Then he recollected Mr. Shalford. . . .

The deuce of a row certainly, and perhaps―― ! He tried to think of plausible versions of the affair. He could explain he had been run down by rather a wild sort of fellow who was riding a bicycle, almost stunned for the moment (even now he felt the effects of the concussion in his head), and had been given whisky to restore him, and " the fact is, Sir,"―with an upward inflection of the voice, an upward inflection of the eyebrows, and an air of its being the last thing one would have expected whisky to do, the manifestation, indeed, of a practically unique physiological weakness―" it got into my '*ed* ! ". . .

Put like that it didn't look so bad.

He got to the Emporium a little before eight, and the housekeeper, with whom he was something of a favourite (" There's no harm in Mr. Kipps," she used to say), seemed to like him, if anything, better for having broken the rules, and gave him a piece of dry toast and a good hot cup of tea.

" I suppose the G. V.―― " began Kipps.

" He knows," said the housekeeper.

He went down to shop a little before time, and presently Booch summoned him to the presence.

He emerged from the private office after an interval of ten minutes.

The junior clerk scrutinised his visage. Buggins put the frank question.

Kipps answered with one word.

" Swapped ! " said Kipps.

§ 2

Kipps leant against the fixtures with his hands in his pockets and talked to the two apprentices under him.

" I don't care if I *am* swapped," said Kipps. " I been sick of Teddy and his System some time.

" I was a good mind to chuck it when my time was up," said Kipps. " Wish I 'ad now."

Afterwards Pearce came round, and Kipps repeated this.

" What's it for ? " said Pearce. " That row about the window tickets ? "

" No fear ! " said Kipps, and sought to convey a perspective of splendid depravity. " I wasn't in las' night," he said, and made even Pearce, " man about town " Pearce, open his eyes.

" Why, where did you get to ? " asked Pearce.

He conveyed that he had been " fair round the town."
" With a Nactor chap I know."

" One can't *always* be living like a curit," he said.

" No fear," said Pearce, trying to play up to him.

But Kipps had the top place in that conversation.

" My lor ! " said Kipps, when Pearce had gone, " but wasn't
my mouth and 'ed bad this morning before I 'ad a pick-me-
up ! "

" Whad jer 'ave ? "

" Anchovy on 'ot buttered toast. It's the very best pick-
me-up there is. You trust me, Rogers. I never take no
other, and I don't advise you to. See ? "

And when pressed for further particulars, he said again he
had been " fair all *round* the town, with a Nactor chap " he
knew. They asked curiously all he had done, and he said,
" Well, what do *you* think ? " And when they pressed for
still further details, he said there were things little boys ought
not to know, and laughed darkly, and found them some hucka-
back to roll.

And in this manner for a space did Kipps fend off the contemplation of the " key of the street " that Shalford had
presented him.

§ 3

This sort of thing was all very well when junior apprentices were about, but when Kipps was alone with himself it
served him not at all. He was uncomfortable inside, and his
skin was uncomfortable, and the Head and Mouth, palliated
perhaps, but certainly not cured, were still with him. He felt,
to tell the truth, nasty and dirty, and extremely disgusted
with himself. To work was dreadful, and to stand still and
think still more dreadful. His patched knee reproached him.
These were the second best of his three pairs of trousers, and
they had cost him thirteen and sixpence. Practically ruined
they were. His dusting pair was unfit for shop, and he would
have to degrade his best. When he was under inspection he
affected the slouch of a desperado, but directly he found himself alone, this passed insensibly into the droop.

The financial aspect of things grew large before him. His
whole capital in the world was the sum of five pounds in the
Post Office Savings Bank, and four and sixpence cash. Besides,
there would be two months' " screw." His little tin box upstairs was no longer big enough for his belongings, he would
have to buy another, let alone that it was not calculated to
make a good impression in a new " crib." Then there would
be paper and stamps needed in some abundance for answering
advertisements and railway fares when he went " crib hunting." He would have to write letters, and he never wrote
letters. There was spelling, for example, to consider. Probably

if nothing turned up before his month was up, he would have
to go home to his Uncle and Aunt.

How would they take it ? . . .

For the present, at any rate, he resolved not to write to
them.

Such disagreeable things as this it was that lurked below
the fair surface of Kipps' assertion, " I been wanting a change.
If 'e 'adn't swapped me, I should very likely 'ave swapped
'*im*."

In the perplexed privacies of his own mind he could not
understand how everything had happened. He had been the
Victim of Fate, or at least of one as inexorable—Chitterlow.
He tried to recall the successive steps that had culminated so
disastrously. They were difficult to recall. . . .

Buggins that night abounded in counsel and reminiscence.

" Curious thing," said Buggins, " but every time I've had
the swap I've never believed I should get another Crib—never.
But I have," said Buggins. " Always. So don't lose heart,
whatever you do.

" Whatever you do," said Buggins, " keep hold of your
collars and cuffs—shirts, if you can, but collars anyhow.
Spout them last. And, anyhow, it's summer ! you won't
want your coat. . . . You got a good umbrella. . . .

" You'll no more get a shop from New Romney than—
anything. Go straight up to London, get the cheapest room
you can find—and hang out. Don't eat too much. Many a
chap's put his prospects in his stomach. Get a cup o' coffee
and a slice—egg, if you like—but remember you got to turn
up at the Warehouse tidy. The best places *now*, I believe,
are the old cabmen's eating houses. Keep your watch and
chain as long as you can. . . .

" There's lots of shops going," said Buggins. " Lots ! "

And added reflectively, " But not this time of year, perhaps."

He began to recall his own researches. " 'Stonishing lot of
chaps you see," he said. " All sorts. Look like Dukes, some
of 'em. High hat. Patent boots. Frock-coat. All there. All
right for a West End crib. Others—Lord ! It's a caution,
Kipps. Boots been inked in some reading-rooms—*I* used to
write in a Reading Room in Fleet Street, regular penny club
—hat been wetted, collar frayed, tail-coat buttoned up, black
chest-plaster tie—spread out. Shirt, you know, gone——"
Buggins pointed upwards with a pious expression.

" No shirt, I expect ? "

" Eat it," said Buggins.

Kipps meditated. " I wonder where old Minton is," he said
at last. " I often wondered about 'im."

§ 4

It was the morning following Kipps' notice of dismissal
that Miss Walshingham came into the shop. She came in with

a dark, slender lady, rather faded, rather tightly dressed, whom Kipps was to know some day as her mother. He discovered them in the main shop, at the counter of the ribbon department. He had come to the opposite glove counter with some goods enclosed in a parcel that he had unpacked in his own department. The two ladies were both bent over a box of black ribbon.

He had a moment of tumultuous hesitations. The etiquette of the situation was incomprehensible. He put down his goods very quietly and stood, hands on counter, staring at these two ladies. Then, as Miss Walshingham sat back, the instinct of flight seized him. . . .

He returned to his Manchester shop wildly agitated. Directly he was out of sight of her he wanted to see her. He fretted up and down the counter, and addressed some snappish remarks to the apprentice in the window. He fumbled for a moment with a parcel, untied it needlessly, began to tie it up again, and then bolted back again into the main shop. He could hear his own heart beating.

The two ladies were standing in the manner of those who have completed their purchases and are waiting for their change. Mrs. Walshingham regarded some remnants with impersonal interest ; Helen's eyes searched the shop. They distinctly lit up when they discovered Kipps.

He dropped his hands to the counter by habit, and stood for a moment regarding her awkwardly. What would she do ? Would she cut him ? She came across the shop to him.

" How are *you*, Mr. Kipps ? " she said, in her clear, distinct tones, and she held out her hand.

" Very well, thank you," said Kipps ; " how are you ? "

She said she had been buying some ribbon.

He became aware of Mrs. Walshingham very much surprised. This checked something allusive about the class, and he said instead that he supposed she was glad to be having her holidays now. She said she was, it gave her more time for reading and that sort of thing. He supposed that she would be going abroad, and she thought that perhaps they *would* go to Knocke or Bruges for a time.

Then came a pause, and Kipps' soul surged within him. He wanted to tell her he was leaving and would never see her again. He could find neither words nor voice to say it. The swift seconds passed. The girl in the ribbons was handing Mrs. Walshingham her change. " Well," said Miss Walshingham, " good-bye," and gave him her hand again.

Kipps bowed over her hand. His manners, his counter manners were the easiest she had ever seen upon him. She turned to her mother. It was no good now, no good. Her mother ! You couldn't say a thing like that before her mother ! All was lost but politeness. Kipps rushed for the door. He stood at the door bowing with infinite gravity, and she smiled and nodded as she went out. She saw nothing of the struggle within him, nothing but a gratifying emotion. She smiled like a satisfied goddess as the incense ascends.

Mrs. Walshingham bowed stiffly and a little awkwardly.

He remained holding the door open for some seconds after they had passed out, then rushed suddenly to the back of the " costume " window to watch them go down the street. His hands tightened on the window-rack as he stared. Her mother appeared to be asking discreet questions. Helen's bearing suggested the off-hand replies of a person who found the world a satisfactory place to live in. " Really, Mumsie, you cannot expect me to cut my own students dead," she was, in fact, saying. . . .

They vanished round Henderson's corner.

Gone ! And he would never see her again—never !

It was as though some one had struck his heart with a whip. Never ! Never ! Never ! And she didn't know ! He turned back from the window, and the department, with its two apprentices, was impossible. The whole glaring world was insupportable.

He hesitated, and made a rush, head down, for the cellar that was his Manchester warehouse. Rogers asked him a question that he pretended not to hear.

The Manchester warehouse was a small cellar apart from the general basement of the building, and dimly lit by a small gas flare. He did not turn that up, but rushed for the darkest corner, where, on the lowest shelf, the Sale window-tickets were stored. He drew out the box of these with trembling hands and upset them on the floor, and so, having made himself a justifiable excuse for being on the ground with his head well in the dark, he could let his poor bursting little heart have its way with him for a space.

And there he remained until the cry of " Kipps ! Forward ! " summoned him once more to face the world.

CHAPTER SIX

THE UNEXPECTED

§ 1

Now in the slack of that same day, after the midday dinner and before the coming of the afternoon customers, this disastrous Chitterlow descended upon Kipps with the most amazing coincidence in the world. He did not call formally, entering and demanding Kipps, but privately, in a confidential and mysterious manner.

Kipps was first aware of him as a dark object bobbing about excitedly outside the hosiery window. He was stooping and craning and peering in the endeavour to see into the interior between and over the socks and stockings. Then he transferred his attention to the door, and after a hovering scrutiny, tried the baby-linen display. His movements and gestures suggested a suppressed excitement.

Seen by daylight, Chitterlow was not nearly such a magnificent figure as he had been by the subdued nocturnal lightings and beneath the glamour of his own interpretation. The lines were the same, indeed, but the texture was different. There was a quality about the yachting cap, an indefinable finality of dustiness, a shiny finish on all the salient surfaces of the reefer coat. The red hair and the profile, though still forcible and fine, were less in the quality of Michelangelo and more in that of the merely picturesque. But it was a bright, brown eye still that sought amidst the interstices of the baby-linen.

Kipps was by no means anxious to interview Chitterlow again. If he had felt sure that Chitterlow would not enter the shop, he would have hid in the warehouse until the danger was past, but he had no idea of Chitterlow's limitations. He decided to keep up the shop in the shadows until Chitterlow reached the side window of the Manchester department, and then to go outside as if to inspect the condition of the window and explain to him that things were unfavourable to immediate intercourse. He might tell him he had already lost his situation. . . .

" 'Ullo, Chit'low," he said, emerging.

" Very man I want to see," said Chitterlow, shaking with vigour. " Very man I want to see." He laid a hand on Kipps' arm. " How *old* are you, Kipps ? "

" One-and-twenty," said Kipps. " Why ? "

" Talk about coincidences ! And your name, now ? Wait a minute." He held out a finger. " *Is* it Arthur ? "

" Yes," said Kipps.

" You're the man," said Chitterlow.

" What man ? "

" It's about the thickest coincidence I ever struck," said Chitterlow, plunging his extensive hand into his breast-coat pocket. " Half a jiff and I'll tell you your mother's Christian name." He laughed and struggled with his coat for a space, produced a washing-book and two pencils, which he deposited in his side pocket, then in one capacious handful, a bent but by no means finally disabled cigar, the rubber proboscis of a bicycle pump, some twine and a lady's purse, and finally a small pocket-book, and from this, after dropping and recovering several visiting-cards, he extracted a carelessly torn piece of newspaper. " Euphemia," he read, and brought his face close to Kipps'. " Eh ? " He laughed noisily. " It's about as fair a Bit of All Right as any one *could* have—outside a coincidence play. Don't say her name wasn't Euphemia, Kipps, and spoil the whole blessed show."

" Whose name—Euphemia ? " asked Kipps.

" Your mother's."

" Lemme see what it says on the paper."

Chitterlow handed him the fragment and turned away. " You may say what you like," he said, addressing a vast, deep laugh to the street generally.

Kipps attempted to read. " WADDY or KIPPS. If Arthur Waddy or Arthur Kipps, the son of Margaret Euphemia Kipps, who——"

Chitterlow's finger swept over the print. " I went down the column, and every blessed name that seemed to fit my play I took. I don't believe in made-up names. As I told you. I'm all with Zola in that. Documents whenever you can. I like 'em hot and real. See ? Who was Waddy ? "

" Never heard his name."

" Not Waddy ? "

" No ! "

Kipps tried to read again, and abandoned the attempt. " What does it mean ? " he said. " I don't understand."

" It means," said Chitterlow, with a momentary note of lucid exposition, " so far as I can make out, that you're going to strike it Rich. Never mind about the Waddy—that's a detail. What does it usually mean ? You'll hear of something to your advantage—very well. I took that newspaper up to get my names by the merest chance. Directly I saw it again and read that—I knew it was you. I believe in coincidences. People say they don't happen. *I* say they do. Everything's a coincidence. Seen properly. Here you are. Here's one ! Incredible ? Not a bit of it ! See ? It's you ! Kipps ! Waddy be damned ! It's a Mascot. There's luck in my play. Bif ! You're there. *I'm* there. Fair *in* it ! Snap ! " And he discharged his fingers like a pistol. " Never you mind about the ' Waddy.' "

" Eh ? " said Kipps, with a nervous eye on Chitterlow's fingers.

" You're all right," said Chitterlow, " you may bet the seat of your only breeches on that ! Don't you worry about the Waddy—that's as clear as day. You're about as right side up as a billiard ball . . . whatever you do. Don't stand there gaping, man ! Read the paper if you don't believe me. Read it ! "

He shook it under Kipps' nose.

Kipps became aware of the second apprentice watching them from the shop. His air of perplexity gave place to a more confident bearing.

" —— ' who was born at East Grinstead.' I certainly was born there. I've 'eard my Aunt say—— "

" I knew it," said Chitterlow, taking hold of one edge of the paper and bringing his face close alongside Kipps'.

" —— ' on September the first, eighteen hundred and seventy-eight—— '

" *That's* all right," said Chitterlow. " It's all, all right, and all you have to do is to write to Watson and Bean and get it——"

" Get what ? "

" Whatever it is."

Kipps sought his moustache. " You'd write ? " he asked.

" Ra-ther."

" But what do you think it is ? "

" That's the fun of it ! " said Chitterlow, taking three steps in some as yet uninvented dance. " That's where the joke comes in. It may be anything—it may be a million. If so ! Where does little Harry come in ? Eh ?"

Kipps was trembling slightly. " But——" he said, and thought. " If you was me——" he began. " About that Waddy——? "

He glanced up and saw the second apprentice disappear with amazing swiftness from behind the goods in the window.

" *What ?* " asked Chitterlow, but he never had an answer.

" Lor ! There's the guv'nor ! " said Kipps, and made a prompt dive for the door.

He dashed in, only to discover that Shalford, with the junior apprentice in attendance, had come to mark off remnants of Kipps' cotton dresses, and was demanding him. " Hallo, Kipps," he said, " outside——? "

" Seein' if the window was straight, Sir," said Kipps.

" Umph ! " said Shalford.

For a space Kipps was too busily employed to think at all of Chitterlow or the crumpled bit of paper in his trouser pocket. He was, however, painfully aware of a suddenly disconnected excitement at large in the street. There came one awful moment when Chitterlow's nose loomed interrogatively over the ground glass of the department door, and his bright little red-brown eye sought for the reason of Kipps' disappearance, and then it became evident that he saw the high light of Shalford's baldness, and grasped the situation and went away. And then Kipps (with that advertisement in his pocket) was able to come back to the business in hand.

He became aware that Shalford had asked a question. " Yessir, nosir, rightsir. I'm sorting up zephyrs to-morrow, Sir," said Kipps.

Presently he had a moment to himself again, and, taking up a safe position behind a newly unpacked pile of summer lace curtains, he straightened out the piece of paper and re-perused it. It was a little perplexing. That " Arthur Waddy or Arthur Kipps "—did that imply two persons or one ? He would ask Pearce or Buggins. Only——

It had always been impressed upon him that there was something demanding secrecy about his mother.

" Don't you answer no questions about your mother," his aunt had been wont to say. " Tell them you don't know, whatever it is they ask you."

" Now, this——? "

Kipps' face became portentously careful, and he tugged at his moustache, such as it was, hard.

He had always represented his father as being a " gentleman farmer." " It didn't pay," he used to say, with a picture in his own mind of a penny magazine aristocrat prematurely worn out by worry. " I'm a Norfan, both sides," he would explain, with the air of one who had seen trouble. He said he lived with his uncle and aunt, but he did not say that they kept a toy-shop, and to tell any one that his uncle had been a butler—*a servant!*—would have seemed the maddest of indiscretions. Almost all the assistants in the Emporium were equally reticent and vague, so great is their horror of " Lowness " of any sort. To ask about this " Waddy or Kipps " would upset all these little fictions. He was not, as a matter of fact, perfectly clear about his real status in the world (he was not, as a matter of fact, perfectly clear about anything), but he knew that there was a quality about his status that was—detrimental.

Under the circumstances——?

It occurred to him that it would save a lot of trouble to destroy the advertisement there and then.

In which case he would have to explain to Chitterlow !

" Eng ! " said Mr Kipps.

" Kipps! " cried Carshot, who was shop-walking. " Kipps Forward ! "

He thrust back the crumpled paper into his pocket, and sallied forth to the customer.

" I want," said the customer, looking vaguely about her through glasses, " a little bit of something to cover a little stool I have. Anything would do—a remnant or anything."

The matter of the advertisement remained in abeyance for half an hour, and at the end the little stool was still a candidate for covering, and Kipps had a thoroughly representative collection of the textile fabrics in his department to clear away. He was so angry about the little stool that the crumpled advertisement lay for a space in his pocket, absolutely forgotten.

§ 2

Kipps sat on his tin box under the gas-bracket that evening, and looked up the name Euphemia, and learnt what it meant in the " Inquire Within About Everything " that constituted Buggins' reference library. He hoped Buggins, according to his habit, would ask him what he was looking for, but Buggins was busy turning out his week's washing. " Two collars," said Buggins, " half pair socks, two dickeys. Shirt ? . . . M'm. There ought to be another collar somewhere."

" Euphemia," said Kipps at last, unable altogether to keep to himself this suspicion of a high origin that floated so delight-

fully about him. "Eu-phemia; it isn't a name *common*
people would give to a girl, is it ?"

"It isn't the name any decent people would give to a girl,"
said Buggins, " common or not."

"Lor!" said Kipps. "Why ?"

"It's giving girls names like that," said Buggins, "that
nine times out of ten makes 'em go wrong. It unsettles 'em.
If ever I was to have a girl, if ever I was to have a dozen
girls, I'd call 'em all Jane. Every one of 'em. You couldn't
have a better name than that. Euphemia, indeed! What
next ? . . . . Good Lord ! . . . That isn't one of my collars
there, is it, under your bed ?"

Kipps got him the collar.

"I don't see no great 'arm in Euphemia," he said as he did so.

After that he became restless. "I'm a good mind to write
that letter," he said ; and then, finding Buggins preoccupied
wrapping his washing up in the " ½ sox," added to himself,
"a thundering good mind."

So he got his penny bottle of ink, borrowed the pen from
Buggins, and with no very serious difficulty in spelling or
composition, did as he had resolved.

He came back into the bedroom about an hour afterwards,
a little out of breath and pale. "Where you been ?" said
Buggins, who was now reading the *Daily World Manager*,
which came to him in rotation from Carshot.

"Out to post some letters," said Kipps, hanging up his hat.

"Crib hunting ?"

"Mostly," said Kipps.

"Rather," he added, with a nervous laugh ; "what else ?"

Buggins went on reading. Kipps sat on his bed and regarded
the back of the *Daily World Manager* thoughtfully.

"Buggins," he said at last.

Buggins lowered his paper and looked.

"I say, Buggins, what do these here advertisements mean
that say so-and-so will hear of something greatly to his advantage ?"

"Missin' people," said Buggins, making to resume reading.

"How d'yer mean ?" asked Kipps. "Money left, and that
sort of thing ?"

Buggins shook his head. "Debts," he said, "more often
than not."

"But that ain't to his advantage."

"They put that to get 'old of 'em,' said Buggins. "Often
it's wives."

"What you mean ?"

"Deserted wives try and get their husbands back that
way."

"I suppose it *is* legacies sometimes, eh ? Perhaps if some
one was left a hundred pounds by some one——"

"Hardly ever," said Buggins.

" Well, 'ow——? " began Kipps, and hesitated.

Buggins resumed reading. He was very much excited by a leader on Indian affairs. " By Jove ! " he said, " it won't do to give these here Blacks votes."

" No fear," said Kipps.

" They're different altogether," said Buggins. " They 'aven't the sound sense of Englishmen, and they 'aven't the character. There's a sort of tricky dishonesty about 'em— false witness and all that—of which an Englishman has no idea. Outside their courts of law—it's a pos'tive fact, Kipps —there's witnesses waitin' to be 'ired. Reg'lar trade. Touch their 'ats as you go in. Englishmen 'ave no idea, I tell you— not ord'nary Englishmen. It's in their blood. They're too timid to be honest. Too slavish. They aren't used to being free like we are, and if you gave 'em freedom they wouldn't make a proper use of it. Now, *we*—— Oh, *Damn* ! "

For the gas had suddenly gone out, and Buggins had the whole column of Society Club Chat still to read.

Buggins could talk of nothing after that but Shalford's meanness in turning off the gas, and after being extremely satirical about their employer, undressed in the dark, hit his bare toe against a box, and subsided, after unseemly ejaculations, into silent ill-temper.

Though Kipps tried to get to sleep before the affair of the letter he had just posted resumed possession of his mind, he could not do so. He went over the whole thing again, quite exhaustively.

Now that his first terror was abating, he couldn't quite determine whether he was glad or sorry that he had posted that letter. If it *should* happen to be a hundred pounds !

It *must* be a hundred pounds !

If it was he could hold out for a year, for a couple of years even, before he got a Crib.

Even if it was fifty pounds—— !

Buggins was already breathing regularly when Kipps spoke again. " *Bug*-gins," he said.

Buggins pretended to be asleep, and thickened his regular breathing (a little too hastily) to a snore.

" I say, Buggins," said Kipps, after an interval.

" *What's* up now ? " said Buggins, unamiably.

" S'pose *you* saw an advertisement in a paper, with your name in it, see, asking you to come and see some one, like, so as to hear of something very much to your—— "

" Hide," said Buggins, shortly.

" But—— "

" I'd hide."

" Er ? "

" Goo'-night, o' man," said Buggins, with convincing earnestness. Kipps lay still for a long time, then blew profoundly, turned over and stared at the other side of the dark.

He had been a fool to post that letter !
Lord ! *Hadn't* he been a fool !

It was just five days and a half after the light had been
turned out while Buggins was reading, that a young man
with a white face, and eyes bright and wide open, emerged
from a side road upon the Leas front. He was dressed in his
best clothes, and, although the weather was fine, he carried
his umbrella, just as if he had been to church. He hesitated,
and turned to the right. He scanned each house narrowly as he
passed it, and presently came to an abrupt stop. " Hughenden," said the gateposts in firm, black letters, and the fanlight
in gold repeated " Hughenden." It was a stucco house, fit to
take your breath away, and its balcony was painted a beautiful
sea green, enlivened with gilding. He stood looking up at it.
" Gollys ! " he said at last, in an awe-stricken whisper.

It had rich-looking crimson curtains to all the lower windows,
and brass-railed blinds above. There was a splendid tropical
plant in a large artistic pot in the drawing-room window.
There was a splendid bronzed knocker (ring also) and two
bells—one marked " servants."

" Gollys ! *Servants*, eh ? "

He walked past away from it with his eyes regarding it,
and then turned and came back. He passed through a further
indecision, and finally drifted away to the sea front, and sat
down on a seat a little way along the Leas and put his arm
over the back and regarded " Hughenden." He whistled an
air very softly to himself, put his head first on one side and
then on the other. Then for a space he scowled fixedly at it.

A very stout old gentleman with a very red face and very
protuberant eyes sat down beside Kipps, removed a Panama
hat of the most abandoned desperado cut, and mopped his
brow and blew. Then he began mopping the inside of his hat.
Kipps watched him for a space, wondering how much he might
have a year, and where he bought his hat. Then "Hughenden"
reasserted itself.

An impulse overwhelmed him. " I say," he said, leaning
forward to the old gentleman.

The old gentleman started and stared.

" *What* did you say ? " he asked fiercely.

" You wouldn't think," said Kipps, indicating with his
forefinger, " that that 'ous there belongs to me."

The old gentleman twisted his neck round to look at " Hughenden." Then he came back to Kipps, looked at his mean
little garments with apoplectic intensity, and blew at him by
way of reply.

" It does," said Kipps, a little less confidently.

" Don't be a Fool," said the old gentleman, and put his
hat on and wiped out the corners of his eyes. " It's hot enough,"

panted the old gentleman indignantly, " without Fools." Kipps looked from the old gentleman to the house, and back to the old gentleman. The old gentleman looked at Kipps, and snorted and looked out to sea, and again, snorting very contemptuously, at Kipps.

" Mean to say it doesn't belong to me ? " said Kipps.

The old gentleman just glanced over his shoulder at the house in dispute, and then fell to pretending Kipps didn't exist. " It's been lef' me this very morning," said Kipps. " It ain't the only one that's been lef' me, neither."

" Aw ! " said the old gentleman, like one who is sorely tried. He seemed to expect the passers-by presently to remove Kipps.

" It '*as*," said Kipps. He made no further remark to the old gentleman for a space, but looked with a little less certitude at the house. . . .

" I got—— " he said, and stopped.

" It's no good telling you if you don't believe," he said.

The old gentleman, after a struggle with himself, decided not to have a fit. " Try that game on with me," he panted. " Give you in charge."

" What game ? "

" Wasn't born yesterday," said the old gentleman, and blew. " Besides," he added, " *Look* at you !

" I know you," said the old gentleman, and coughed shortly and nodded to the horizon, and coughed again.

Kipps looked dubiously from the house to the old gentleman, and back to the house. Their conversation, he gathered, was over.

Presently he got up and went slowly across the grass to its stucco portal again. He stood, and his mouth shaped the precious word, " Hughenden." It was all *right* ! He looked over his shoulder as if in appeal to the old gentleman, then turned and went his way. The old gentleman was so evidently past all reason !

He hung for a moment some distance along the parade, as though some invisible string was pulling him back. When he could no longer see the house from the pavement he went out into the road. Then with an effort he snapped the string.

He went on down a quiet side street, unbuttoned his coat furtively, took out three bank-notes in an envelope, looked at them, and replaced them. Then he fished up five new sovereigns from his trouser pocket and examined them. To such a confidence had his exact resemblance to his dead mother's portrait carried Messrs. Watson and Bean.

It was right enough.

It really was *all* right.

He replaced the coins with grave precaution, and went his way with a sudden briskness. It was all right—he had it now —he was a rich man at large. He went up a street and round a corner and along another street, and started towards the Pavilion, and changed his mind and came round back, resolved to go straight to the Emporium and tell them all.

He was aware of some one crossing a road far off ahead of him, some one curiously relevant to his present extraordinary state of mind. It was Chitterlow. Of course, it was Chitterlow who had told him first of the whole thing ! The playwright was marching buoyantly along a cross street. His nose was in the air, the yachting cap was on the back of his head, and the large freckled hand grasped two novels from the library, a morning newspaper, a new hat done up in paper, and a lady's net bag full of onions and tomatoes. . . .

He passed out of sight behind the wine-merchant's at the corner, as Kipps decided to hurry forward and tell him of the amazing change in the Order of the Universe that had just occurred.

Kipps uttered a feeble shout, arrested as it began, and waved his umbrella. Then he set off at a smart pace in pursuit. He came round the corner, and Chitterlow had gone ; he hurried to the next, and there was no Chitterlow ; he turned back unavailingly, and his eyes sought some other possible corner. His hand fluttered to his mouth, and he stood for a space on the pavement edge, staring about him. No good !

But the sight of Chitterlow was a wholesome thing, it connected events together, joined him on again to the past at a new point, and that was what he so badly needed. . . .

It was all right—all right.

He became suddenly very anxious to tell everybody at the Emporium, absolutely everybody, all about it. That was what wanted doing. He felt that telling was the thing to make this business real. He gripped his umbrella about the middle, and walked very eagerly.

He entered the Emporium through the Manchester department. He flung open the door (over whose ground glass he had so recently, in infinite apprehension, watched the nose of Chitterlow), and discovered the second apprentice and Pearce in conversation. Pearce was prodding his hollow tooth with a pin and talking in fragments about the distinctive characteristics of Good Style.

Kipps came up in front of the counter.

" I say," he said. " What d'yer think ? "

" What ? " said Pearce over the pin.

" Guess."

" You've slipped out because Teddy's in London."

" Something more."

" What ? "

" Been left a fortune."

" Garn ! "

" I 'ave."

" Get out ! "

"Straight. I been lef' twelve 'undred pounds—twelve 'undred pounds a year!"

He moved towards the little door out of the department into the house, moving, as heralds say, *regardant passant*. Pearce stood with mouth wide open and pin poised in air. "No!" he said at last.

"It's right," said Kipps, "and I'm going."

And he fell over the doormat into the house.

§ 4

It happened that Mr Shalford was in London buying summer sale goods, and, no doubt, also interviewing aspirants to succeed Kipps.

So that there was positively nothing to hinder a wild rush of rumour from end to end of the Emporium. All the masculine members began their report with the same formula. "Heard about Kipps?"

The new girl in the cash desk had had it from Pearce, and had dashed out into the fancy shop to be the first with the news on the fancy side. Kipps had been left a thousand pounds a year—twelve thousand pounds a year. Kipps had been left twelve hundred thousand pounds. The figures were uncertain, but the essential facts they had correct. Kipps had gone upstairs. Kipps was packing his box. He said he wouldn't stop another day in the old Emporium not for a thousand pounds! It was said that he was singing ribaldry about old Shalford.

He had come down! He was in the counting-house. There was a general movement thither. (Poor old Buggins had a customer, and couldn't make out what the deuce it was all about! Completely out of it, was Buggins.)

There was a sound of running to and fro, and voices saying this, that, and the other thing about Kipps. Ring-a-dinger, ring-a-dinger went the dinner-bell, all unheeded. The whole of the Emporium was suddenly bright-eyed, excited, hungry to tell somebody, to find at any cost some body who didn't know, and be first to tell them, "Kipps has been left thirty—forty—fifty thousand pounds!"

"*What!*" cried the senior porter, "Him!" and ran up to the counting-house as eagerly as though Kipps had broken his neck.

"One of our chaps just been left sixty thousand pounds," said the first apprentice, returning after a great absence, to his customer.

"Unexpectedly?" said the customer.

"Quite," said the first apprentice. . . .

"I'm sure if Any One deserves it, it's Mr. Kipps," said Miss Mergle; and her train rustled as she hurried to the counting-house.

There stood Kipps amidst a pelting shower of congratula-

tions. His face was flushed, and his hair disordered. He still
clutched his hat and best umbrella in his left hand. His right
hand was any one's to shake rather than his own. (Ring-a-
dinger, ring-a-dinger ding, ding, ding, dang you ! " went the
neglected dinner-bell.)

"Good old Kipps ! " said Pearce, shaking. "Good old
Kipps ! "

Booch rubbed one anæmic hand upon the other. "You're
sure it's all right, Mr. Kipps ? " he said in the background.

"I'm sure we all congratulate him," said Miss Mergle.

"Great Scott ! " said the new young lady in the glove
department. "Twelve hundred a year ! Great Scott ! You
aren't thinking of marrying any one, are you, Mr Kipps ? "

"Three pounds five and ninepence a day," said Mr. Booch,
working in his head almost miraculously. . . .

Every one, it seemed, was saying how glad they were it was
Kipps, except the junior apprentice, upon whom—he being
the only son of a widow, and used to having the best of everything as a right—an intolerable envy, a sense of unbearable
wrong, had cast its gloomy shade. All the rest were quite
honestly and simply glad—gladder, perhaps, at that time than
Kipps, because they were not so overpowered. . . .

Kipps went downstairs to dinner, emitting fragmentary
disconnected statements. "Never expected anything of the
sort. . . . When this here old Bean told me, you could have
knocked me down with a feather. . . . He says, ' You ben
lef' money.' Even then I didn't expect it'd be mor'n a
hundred pounds, perhaps. Something like that."

With the sitting down to dinner and the handing of plates,
the excitement assumed a more orderly quality. The housekeeper emitted congratulations as she carved, and the maidservant became dangerous to clothes with the plates—she
held them anyhow ; one expected to see one upside down,
even—she found Kipps so fascinating to look at. Every one
was the brisker and hungrier for the news (except the junior
apprentice), and the housekeeper carved with unusual
liberality. It was High Old Times there under the gaslight,
High Old Times. "I'm sure if Any One deserves it," said
Miss Mergle—"pass the salt, please—it's Mr Kipps."

The babble died away a little as Carshot began barking
across the table at Kipps. "You'll be a bit of a Swell, Kipps,"
he said. "You won't hardly know yourself."

"Quite the gentleman," said Miss Mergle.

"Many real gentlemen's families," said the housekeeper,
"have to do with less."

"See you on the Leas," said Carshot. "My—— ! " He
met the housekeeper's eye. She had spoken about that expression before. "My eye ! " he said, tamely, lest words
should mar the day.

"You'll go to London, I reckon," said Pearce. "You'll be

a man about town. We shall see you mashing 'em, with violets in your button 'ole, down the Burlington Arcade."

" One of these West End Flats. That'd be *my* style," said Pearce. " And a first-class club."

" Aren't these Clubs a bit 'ard to get into ? " asked Kipps, open-eyed over a mouthful of potato.

" No fear. Not for Money," said Pearce. And the girl in the laces, who had acquired a cynical view of Modern Society from the fearless exposures of Miss Marie Corelli, said, " Money goes everywhere nowadays, Mr. Kipps."

But Carshot showed the true British strain.

" If I was Kipps," he said, pausing momentarily for a knifeful of gravy, " I should go to the Rockies and shoot bears."

" I'd certainly 'ave a run over to Boulogne," said Pearce, " and look about a bit. I'm going to do that next Easter myself, anyhow—see if I don't."

" Go to Oireland, Mr. Kipps," came the soft insistence of Biddy Murphy, who managed the big workroom, flushed and shining in the Irish way as she spoke. " Go to Oireland. Ut's the loveliest country in the world. Outside currs. Fishin', shootin', huntin'. An' pretty gals ! Eh ! You should see the Lakes of Killarney, Mr. Kipps ! " And she expressed ecstasy by a facial pantomime, and smacked her lips.

And presently they crowned the event.

It was Pearce who said, " Kipps, you ought to stand Sham ! "

And it was Carshot who found the more poetical word " Champagne."

" Rather ! " said Kipps hilariously ; and the rest was a question of detail and willing emissaries. " Here it comes ! " they said, as the apprentice came down the staircase. " How about the shop ? " said some one. " Oh, *hang* the shop ! " said Carshot ; and made gruntulous demands for a corkscrew with a thing to cut the wire. Pearce, the dog ! had a wire-cutter in his pocket-knife. How Shalford would have stared at the gold-tipped bottles if he had chanced to take an early train ! Bang went the corks, and bang ! Gluck, gluck, gluck, and sizzle!

When Kipps found them all standing about him under the gas flare, saying almost solemnly " Kipps ! " with tumblers upheld, " Have it in tumblers," Carshot had said, " have it in tumblers. It isn't a wine like you have in glasses. Not like port and sherry. It cheers you up, but you don't get drunk. It isn't hardly stronger than lemonade. They drink it at dinner, some of 'em, every day."

" What ! At three and six a bottle ! " said the house-keeper, incredulously.

" *They* don't stick at *that*," said Carshot. " Not the champagne sort."

The housekeeper pursed her lips and shook her head. . . .

When Kipps, I say, found them all standing up to toast him in that manner, there came such a feeling in his throat and face that for the life of him he scarcely knew for a moment whether he was not going to cry. "Kipps!" they all said, with kindly eyes. It was very good of them, and hard there wasn't a stroke of luck for them all!

But the sight of upturned chins and glasses pulled him together again. . . .

They did him honour. Unenviously and freely they did him honour.

For example, Carshot, being subsequently engaged in serving cretonne, and desiring to push a number of rejected blocks up the counter in order to have space for measuring, swept them by a powerful and ill-calculated movement of the arm, with a noise like thunder, partly on to the floor, and partly on to the foot of the still gloomily preoccupied junior apprentice. And Buggins, whose place it was to shopwalk while Carshot served, shopwalked with quite unparalleled dignity, dangling a new season's sunshade with a crooked handle on one finger. He arrested each customer who came down the shop with a grave and penetrating look. "Showing very tractive line new sheason's shunshade," he would remark ; and after a suitable pause, "'Markable thing, one our 'sistant leg'sy twelve 'undred a year. Very tractive. Nothing more to-day, mum ? No!" And he would then go and hold the door open for them with perfect decorum, and with the sunshade dangling elegantly from his left hand. . . .

And the second apprentice, serving a customer with cheap ticking, and being asked suddenly if it was strong, answered remarkably,—

"Oo, *no*, mum! Strong! Why, it ain't 'ardly stronger than lemonade." . . .

The head porter, moreover, was filled with a virtuous resolve to break the record as a lightning packer, and make up for lost time. Mr. Swaffenham of the Sandgate Riviera, for example, who was going out to dinner that night at seven, received at half-past six, instead of the urgently needed dress shirt he expected, a corset specially adapted to the needs of persons inclined to embonpoint. A parcel of summer underclothing selected by the elder Miss Waldershawe was somehow distributed in the form of gratis additions throughout a number of parcels of a less intimate nature, and a box of millinery on approval to Lady Pamshort (at Wampachs) was enriched by the addition of the junior porter's cap. . . .

These little things, slight in themselves, witness, perhaps, none the less eloquently to the unselfish exhilaration felt throughout the Emporium at the extraordinary and unexpected enrichment of Mr. Kipps.

§ 5

The bus that plies between New Romney and Folkestone is painted a British red, and inscribed on either side with the word " Tip-top " in gold amidst voluptuous scrolls. It is a slow and portly bus ; even as a young bus it must have been slow and portly. Below it swings a sort of hold, hung by chains between the wheels, and in the summer time the top has garden seats. The front over those two dauntless, un-hurrying horses rises in tiers like a theatre ; there is first a seat for the driver and his company, and above that a seat, and above that, unless my memory plays me false, a seat. You sit in a sort of composition by some Italian painter—a celestial group of you. There are days when this bus goes, and days when it doesn't go—you have to find out. And so you get to New Romney. So you will continue to get to New Romney for many years, for the light railway concession along the coast is happily in the South Eastern Railway Company's keeping, and the peace of the marsh is kept inviolate save for the bicycle bells of such as Kipps and I. This bus it was, this ruddy, venerable and, under God's mercy, immortal bus, that came down the Folkestone hill with unflinching delibera-tion, and trundled through Sandgate and Hythe, and out into the windy spaces of the Marsh, with Kipps and all his fortunes on its brow.

You figure him there. He sat on the highest seat diametri-cally above the driver, and his head was spinning and spinning with champagne and this stupendous Tomfoolery of Luck ; and his heart was swelling, swelling indeed at times as though it would burst him, and his face towards the sunlight was transfigured. He said never a word, but ever and again, as he thought of this or that, he laughed. He seemed full of chuckles for a time, detached and independent chuckles, chuckles that rose and burst on him like bubbles in a wine. . . . He held a banjo sceptre-fashion and resting on his knee. He had always wanted a banjo, now he had got one at Melchior's, while he was waiting for the bus.

There sat beside him a young servant, who was sucking peppermint, and a little boy with a sniff whose flitting eyes showed him curious to know why ever and again Kipps laughed, and beside the driver were two young men in gaiters talking about " tegs." And there sat Kipps, all unsuspected, twelve hundred a year, as it were, except for the protrusion of the banjo, disguised as a common young man. And the young man in gaiters to the left of the driver eyed Kipps and his banjo, and especially his banjo, ever and again, as if he found it and him, with his rapt face, an insoluble enigma. And many a King has ridden into a conquered city with a lesser sense of splendour than Kipps.

Their shadows grew long behind them, and their faces

were transfigured in gold as they rumbled on towards the splendid west. The sun set before they had passed Dymchurch, and as they came lumbering into New Romney past the wind-mill the dusk had come.

The driver handed down the banjo and the portmanteau, and Kipps having paid him, " That's aw right," he said to the change as a gentleman should, turned about, and ran the portmanteau smartly into Old Kipps, whom the sound of the stopping of the bus had brought to the door of the shop in an aggressive mood and with his mouth full of supper.

" 'Ullo, uncle ; didn't see you," said Kipps.

" Blunderin' ninny," said Old Kipps. " What's brought *you* here? Ain't early closing, is it? Not Toosday ? "

" Got some news for you, uncle," said Kipps, dropping the portmanteau.

" Ain't lost your situation, 'ave you ? What's that you got there ? I'm blowed if it ain't a banjo, Goolord ! Spendin' your money on banjoes ! Don't put down your portmanty there—anyhow. Right in the way of everybody. I'm blowed if ever I saw such a boy as you've got lately. Here ! Molly ! And look here ! What you got a portmanty for ? Why ! Goolord ! You ain't *really* lost your place, 'ave you ? "

" Somethin's happened," said Kipps, slightly dashed. " It's all right, Uncle. I'll tell you in a minute."

Old Kipps took the banjo as his nephew picked up the portmanteau again.

The living-room door opened quickly, showing a table equipped with elaborate simplicity for supper, and Mrs. Kipps appeared.

" If it ain't young Artie ! " she said. " Why, whatever's brought *you* 'ome ? "

" 'Ullo, Aunt," said Artie. " I'm coming in. I got somethin' to tell you. I've 'ad a bit of luck."

He wouldn't tell them all at once. He staggered with the portmanteau round the corner of the counter, set a bundle of children's tin pails into clattering oscillation, and entered the little room. He deposited his luggage in the corner beside the tall clock, and turned to his Aunt and Uncle again. His aunt regarded him doubtfully ; the yellow light from the little lamp on the table escaped above the shade, and lit her forehead and the tip of her nose. It would be all right in a minute. He wouldn't tell them all at once. Old Kipps stood in the shop door with the banjo in his hand, breathing noisily.

" The fact is, Aunt, I've 'ad a bit of Luck."

" You ain't been backin' gordless 'orses, Artie ? " she asked. " No fear."

" It's a draw he's been in," said Old Kipps, still panting from the impact of the portmanteau, " it's a dratted draw. Jest look here, Molly. He's won this 'ere trashy banjer and throwd up his situation on the strength of it—that's what

he's done. Goin' about singing. Dash and plunge. Jest the
very fault poor Pheamy always 'ad. Blunder right in, and
no one mustn't stop 'er ! "

"You ain't thrown up your place, Artie, 'ave you ? " said
Mrs. Kipps.

Kipps perceived his opportunity. "I 'ave," he said ; "I've
throwed it up."

"What for ? " said Old Kipps.

"So's to learn the banjo ! "

"Goo *Lord* !" said Old Kipps, in horror to find himself verified.

"I'm going about playing," said Kipps, with a giggle.
"Goin' to black my face, Aunt, and sing on the beach. I'm
going to 'ave a most tremenjous lark and earn any amount
of money—you see. Twenty-six fousand pounds I'm going
to earn just as easy as nothing ! "

"Kipps," said Mrs. Kipps, "he's been drinking ! "

They regarded their nephew across the supper table with
long faces. Kipps exploded with laughter, and broke out
again when his aunt shook her head very sadly at him. Then
suddenly he fell grave. He felt he could keep it up no longer.
"It's all right, Aunt. Reely. I ain't mad, and I ain't been
drinking. I been lef' money. I been left twenty-six fousand
pounds."

Pause.

"And you thrown up your place ? " said Old Kipps.

"Yes," said Kipps, "Rather ! "

"And bort this banjer, put on your best noo trousers, and
come right on 'ere ? "

"Well," said Mrs. Kipps, "I—never—did ! "

"These ain't my noo trousers, Aunt," said Kipps, regretfully. "My noo trousers wasn't done."

"I shouldn't ha' thought that *even you* could ha' been such
a fool as that," said Old Kipps.

Pause.

"It's *all* right," said Kipps, a little disconcerted by their
distrustful solemnity. "It's all right—reely ! Twenny-six
thousan' pounds. And a 'ouse."

Old Kipps pursed his lips and shook his head.

"A 'ouse on the Leas. I could have gone there. Only I
didn't. I didn't care to. I didn't know what to say. I wanted
to come and tell you."

"How d'yer know the 'ouse—— ?"

"They told me."

"Well," said Old Kipps, and nodded his head portentously
towards his nephew, with the corners of his mouth pulled
down in a strikingly discouraging way. "Well, you *are* a
young Gaby."

"I didn't *think* it of you, Artie ! " said Mrs. Kipps.

"Wadjer mean ? " asked Kipps, faintly, looking from one
to the other with a withered face.

Old Kipps closed the shop door. " They been 'avin a lark with you," said Old Kipps, in a mournful undertone. " That's what I mean, my boy. They jest been seein' what a Gaby like you 'ud do."

" I dessay that young Quodling was in it," said Mrs. Kipps. " 'E's jest that sort."

(For Quodling of the green-baize bag had grown up to be a fearful dog, the terror of New Romney.)

" It's somebody after your place, very likely," said Old Kipps.

Kipps looked from one sceptical reproving face to the other, and round him at the familiar shabby little room, with his familiar cheap portmanteau on the mended chair, and that banjo amidst the supper-things like some irrevocable deed. Could he be rich indeed ? Could it be that these things had really happened ? Or had some insane fancy whirled him hither ?

Still—perhaps a hundred pounds——

" But," he said. " It's all right, reely, Uncle. You don't think—— ? I 'ad a letter."

" Got up," said Old Kipps.

" But I answered it and went to a norfis."

Old Kipps felt staggered for a moment, but he shook his head and chins sagely from side to side. As the memory of old Bean and Shalford's revived, the confidence of Kipps came back to him.

" I saw a nold gent, Uncle—perfect gentleman. And 'e told me all about it. Mos' respectable 'e was. Said 'is name was Watson and Bean—leastways 'e was Bean. Said it was lef' me "—Kipps suddenly dived into his breast pocket—" by my Grandfather—— "

The old people started.

Old Kipps uttered an exclamation and wheeled round towards the mantelshelf, above which the daguerrotype of his lost younger sister smiled its fading smile upon the world.

" Waddy, 'is name was," said Kipps, with his hand still deep in his pocket. " It was 'is son was my father—— "

" Waddy ! " said Old Kipps.

" Waddy ! " said Mrs. Kipps.

" She'd never say," said Old Kipps.

There was a long silence.

Kipps fumbled with a letter, a crumpled advertisement and three banknotes. He hesitated between these items.

" Why ! That young chap what was arsting questions—— " said Old Kipps, and regarded his wife with an eye of amazement.

" Must 'ave been," said Mrs. Kipps.

" Must 'ave been," said Old Kipps.

" James," said Mrs. Kipps, in an awe-struck voice. " After all—perhaps—— It's true ! "

" '*Ow* much did you say ?" asked Old Kipps. " 'Ow much did you say 'e'd lef' you, me b'y ? "

It was thrilling, though not quite in the way Kipps had expected. He answered almost meekly across the meagre supper-things, with his documentary evidence in his hand,—

" Twelve 'undred pounds. Proximately," he said. "Twelve 'undred pounds a year. 'E made 'is will jest before 'e died—not more'n a month ago. When 'e was dying, 'e seemed to change like, Mr. Bean said. 'E'd never forgiven 'is son, never —not till then. 'Is son 'ad died in Australia, years and years ago, and *then* 'e 'adn't forgiven 'im. You know—'is son what was my father. But jest when 'e was ill and dying 'e seemed to get worried like, and longing for some one of 'is own. And 'e told Mr. Bean it was 'im that had prevented them marrying. So 'e thought. That's 'ow it all come about. . . ."

§ 6

At last Kipps' flaring candle went up the narrow, uncarpeted staircase to the little attic that had been his shelter and refuge during all the days of his childhood and youth. His head was whirling. He had been advised, he had been warned, he had been flattered and congratulated, he had been given whisky and hot water and lemon and sugar, and his health had been drunk in the same. He had also eaten two Welsh rarebits—an unusual supper. His Uncle was chiefly for his going into Parliament, his Aunt was consumed with a great anxiety. " I'm afraid he'll go and marry beneath 'im."

" Y'ought to 'ave a bit o' shootin' somewheer," said Old Kipps.

" It's your *duty* to marry into a county family, Artie—remember that.

" There's lots of young noblemen'll be glad to 'eng on to you," said Old Kipps. " You mark my words. And borrow your money. And then good-day to ye."

" I got to be precious careful," said Kipps. " Mr. Bean said that."

" And you got to be precious careful of this old Bean," said Old Kipps. " We may be out of the world in Noo Romney, but I've 'eard a bit about solicitors for all that. You keep your eye on old Bean, me b'y.

" 'Ow do we know what 'e's up to, with your money, even now ? " said Old Kipps, pursuing his uncomfortable topic.

" 'E *looked* very respectable," said Kipps.

Kipps undressed with great deliberation and with vast gasps of pensive margin. Twenty-six thousand pounds !

His aunt's solicitude had brought back certain matters into the foreground that his " Twelve 'undred a year ! " had for a time driven away altogether. His thoughts went back to the woodcarving class. Twelve Hundred a Year. He sat on the edge of the bed in profound meditation, and his boots fell " whop " and " whop " upon the floor, with a long interval between each " whop." Twenty-six thousand pounds. " By Gum !" He dropped the remainder of his costume about him on the floor, got into bed, pulled the patchwork quilt over him, and put his head on the pillow that had been first to hear of Ann Pornick's accession to his heart. But he did not think of Ann Pornick now.

It was about everything in the world except Ann Pornick that he seemed to be trying to think of—simultaneously. All the vivid happenings of the day came and went in his over-taxed brain—" that old Bean " explaining and explaining, the fat man who wouldn't believe, an overpowering smell of peppermint, the banjo, Miss Mergle saying he deserved it, Chitterlow vanishing round a corner, the wisdom and advice and warnings of his Aunt and Uncle. She was afraid he would marry beneath him, *was* she ? She didn't know. . . .

His brain made an excursion into the woodcarving class and presented Kipps with the picture of himself amazing that class by a modest yet clearly audible remark, " I been left twenty-six thousand pounds." Then he told them all quietly but firmly that he had always loved Miss Walshingham—always, and so he had brought all his twenty-six thousand pounds with him to give to her there and then. He wanted nothing in return. . . . Yes, he wanted nothing in return. He would give it to her all in an envelope and go. Of course he would keep the banjo—and a little present for his Aunt and Uncle—and a new suit perhaps—and one or two other things she would not miss. He went off at a tangent. He might buy a motor-car, he might buy one of these here things that will play you a piano—that would make old Buggins sit up ! He could pretend he had learnt to play—he might buy a bicycle and a cyclist suit. . . .

A terrific multitude of plans of what he might do, and in particular of what he might buy, came crowding into his brain, and he did not so much fall asleep as pass into a disorder of dreams in which he was driving a four-horse Tip-Top coach down Sandgate Hill (" I shall have to be precious careful "), wearing innumerable suits of clothes, and through some terrible accident wearing them all wrong. Consequently, he was being laughed at. The coach vanished in the interest of the costume. He was wearing golfing suits and a silk hat. This passed into a nightmare that he was promenading on the Leas in a Highland costume, with a kilt that kept shrinking, and Shalford was following him with three policemen. " He's my assistant," Shalford kept repeating ; " he's escaped. He's an escaped Improver. Keep by him, and in a minute you'll have to run him in. I know 'em. We say they wash, but they won't." . . . He could feel the kilt creeping up his legs. He would have tugged at it to pull it down, only his arms were paralysed. He had an impression of giddy crises. He uttered a shriek of despair. " *Now* ! " said Shalford. He woke in horror, his quilt had slipped off the bed.

He had a fancy he had just been called, that he had somehow overslept himself and missed going down for dusting. Then he perceived it was still night, and light by reason of the moonlight, and that he was no longer in the Emporium. He wondered where he could be. He had a curious fancy that the world had been swept and rolled up like a carpet, and that he was nowhere. It occurred to him that perhaps he was mad. " Buggins ! " he said. There was no answer, not even the defensive snore. No room, no Buggins, nothing !

Then he remembered better. He sat on the edge of his bed for some time. Could any one have seen his face, they would have seen it white, and drawn, with staring eyes. Then he groaned weakly. " Twenty-six thousand pounds ! " he whispered.

Just then it presented itself in an almost horribly overwhelming mass.

He remade his bed and returned to it. He was still dreadfully wakeful. It was suddenly clear to him that he need never trouble to get up punctually at seven again. That fact shone out upon him like a star through clouds. He was free to lie in bed as long as he liked, get up when he liked, go where he liked ; have eggs every morning for breakfast, or rashers, or bloater-paste, or . . . Also he was going to astonish Miss Walshingham. . . .

Astonish her and astonish her. . . .

.   .   .   .

He was awakened by a thrush singing in the fresh dawn. The whole room was flooded with warm, golden sunshine. " I say ! " said the thrush. " I say ! I say ! Twelve 'Undred a Year ! Twelve 'UNDRED a Year ! I say ! I say ! I say ! "

He sat up in bed and rubbed the sleep from his eyes with his knuckles. Then he jumped out of bed and began dressing very eagerly. He did not want to lose any time in beginning the new life.

Book Two

Mr. Coote the Chaperon

CHAPTER ONE

THE NEW CONDITIONS

§ I

THERE comes a gentlemanly figure into these events, and for a space takes a leading part therein, a Good Influence, a refined and amiable figure, Mr. Chester Coote. You must figure him as about to enter our story, walking with a curious rectitude of bearing through the evening dusk towards the Public Library, erect, large-headed—he had a great big head, full of the suggestion of a powerful mind well under control—with a large, official-looking envelope in his white and knuckly hand. In the other he carries a gold-handled cane. He wears a silken gray jacket suit, buttoned up, and anon he coughs behind the official envelope. He has a prominent nose, slaty gray eyes, and a certain heaviness about the mouth. His mouth hangs breathing open, with a slight protrusion of the lower jaw. His straw hat is pulled down a little in front, and he looks each person he passes in the eye, and, directly his look is answered, looks away.

Thus Mr. Chester Coote, as he was on the evening when he came upon Kipps. He was a local house-agent, and a most active and gentlemanly person, a conscious gentleman, equally aware of society and the serious side of life. From amateur theatricals of a nice refined sort to science classes, few things were able to get along without him. He supplied a fine full bass, a little flat and quavery perhaps, but very abundant, to the St. Stylites' choir. . . .

He goes on towards the Public Library, lifts the envelope in salutation to a passing curate, smiles, and enters. . . .

It was in the Public Library that he came upon Kipps.

By that time Kipps had been rich a week or more, and the change in his circumstances was visible upon his person. He was wearing a new suit of drab flannels, a Panama hat, and a red tie for the first time, and he carried a silver-mounted stick with a tortoiseshell handle. He felt extraordinarily different, perhaps more different than he really was, from the meek Improver of a week ago. He felt as he felt Dukes must feel, yet at bottom he was still modest. He was leaning on his stick and regarding the indicator with a respect that never palled. He faced round to meet Mr. Coote's overflowing smile.

" What are you doang hea ? " asked Mr. Chester Coote.

Kipps was momentarily abashed. " Oh," he said slowly, and then, " Mooching round a bit."

That Coote should address him with this easy familiarity was a fresh reminder of his enhanced social position. " Jest mooching round," he said. " I been back in Folkestone free days now. At my 'ouse, you know."

" Ah ! " said Mr. Coote. " I haven't yet had an opportunity of congratulating you on your good fortune."

Kipps held out his hand. " It was the cleanest surprise that ever was," he said. " When Mr. Bean told me of it—you could have knocked me down with a feather."

" It must mean a tremendous change for you."

" O-o. Rather. Change ? Why, I'm like the chap in the song they sing, I don't 'ardly know where I are. *You* know."

" An extraordinary change," said Mr. Coote. " I can quite believe it. Are you stopping in Folkestone ? "

" For a bit. I got a 'ouse, you know. What my gran'father 'ad. I'm stopping there. His housekeeper was kep' on. Fancy —being in the same town and everything ! "

" Precisely," said Mr. Coote. " That's it," and coughed like a sheep behind four straight fingers.

" Mr. Bean got me to come back to see to things. Else I was out in New Romney, where my uncle and aunt live. But it's a lark coming back. In a way . . ."

The conversation hung for a moment.

" Are you getting a book ? " asked Coote.

" Well, I 'aven't got a ticket yet. But I shall get one all right, and have a go in at reading. I've often wanted to. Rather. I was just 'aving a look at this Indicator. First-class idea. Tells you all you want to know."

" It's simple," said Coote, and coughed again, keeping his eyes fixed on Kipps. For a moment they hung, evidently disinclined to part. Then Kipps jumped at an idea he had cherished for a day or more—not particularly in relation to Coote, but in relation to any one.

" You doing anything ? " he asked.

" Just called with a papah about the classes."

" Because——— Would you care to come up and look at my 'ouse and 'ave a smoke and a chat—eh ? " He made indicative back jerks of the head, and was smitten with a horrible doubt whether possibly this invitation might not be some hideous breach of etiquette. Was it, for example, the correct hour ? " I'd be awfully glad if you would," he added.

Mr. Coote begged for a moment while he handed the official-looking envelope to the librarian, and then declared himself quite at Kipps' service. They muddled a moment over precedence at each door they went through, and so emerged to the street.

" It feels awful rum to me at first, all this," said Kipps. " 'Aving a 'ouse of my own—and all that. It's strange, you know. 'Aving all day. Reely I don't 'ardly know what to do with my time.

" D'ju smoke ? " he said suddenly, proffering a magnificent gold-decorated, pigskin cigarette-case, which he produced from nothing, almost as though it was some sort of trick, Coote hesitated and declined, and then with great liberality. " Don't let me hinder you . . ."

They walked a little way in silence, Kipps being chiefly concerned to affect ease in his new clothes and keeping a wary eye on Coote. " It's rather a big windfall," said Coote presently. " It yields you an income——? "

" Twelve 'undred a year," said Kipps.   " Bit over—if anything."

" Do you think of living in Folkestone ? "

" Don't know 'ardly yet. I *may*. Then again, I may not. I got a furnished 'ouse, but I may let it."

" Your plans are undecided ? "

" That's jest it," said Kipps.

" Very beautiful sunset it was to-night," said Coote, and Kipps said, " Wasn't it ? " and they began to talk of the merits of sunsets. Did Kipps paint ? Not since he was a boy. He didn't believe he could now. Coote said his sister was a painter, and Kipps received this intimation with respect. Coote sometimes wished he could find time to paint himself, but one couldn't do everything, and Kipps said that was " jest it."

They came out presently upon the end of the Leas, and looked down to where the squat, dark masses of the harbour and harbour station, gemmed with pin-point lights, crouched against the twilit gray of the sea. " If one could do *that*," said Coote ; and Kipps was inspired to throw his head back, cock it on one side, regard the harbour with one eye shut, and say that it would take some doing. Then Coote said something about "Abend," which Kipps judged to be in a foreign language, and got over by lighting another cigarette from his by no means completed first one. " You're right—*puff, puff*."

He felt that so far he had held up his end of the conversation in a very creditable manner, but that extreme discretion was advisable.

They turned away, and Coote remarked that the sea was good for crossing, and asked Kipps if he had been over the water very much. Kipps said he hadn't been—" much," but he thought very likely he'd have a run over to Boulogne soon ; and Coote proceeded to talk of the charms of foreign travel, mentioning quite a number of unheard-of places by name. He had been to them ! Kipps remained on the defensive, but behind his defences his heart sank. It was all very well to pretend, but presently it was bound to come out. *He* didn't know anything of all this. . . .

So they drew near the house. At his own gate Kipps became extremely nervous. It was a fine impressive door. He knocked neither a single knock nor a double, but about one and a half —an apologetic half. They were admitted by an irreproachable housemaid with a steady eye, before which Kipps cringed dreadfully. He hung up his hat and fell about over hall chairs and things. " There's a fire in the study, Mary ? " he had the audacity to ask, though evidently he knew, and led the way upstairs panting. He tried to shut the door and discovered the housemaid behind him coming to light his lamp. This enfeebled him further. He said nothing until the door closed behind her. Meanwhile, to show his *sang-froid*, he hummed and flitted towards the window and here and there.

Coote went to the big hearthrug and turned and surveyed his host. His hand went to the back of his head and patted his occiput—a gesture frequent with him.

" 'Ere we are," said Kipps, hands in his pockets, and glancing round him.

It was a gaunt, Victorian room, with a heavy, dirty cornice, and the ceiling enriched by the radiant plaster ornament of an obliterated gas chandelier. It held two large glass-fronted bookcases, one of which was surmounted by a stuffed terrier encased in glass. There was a mirror over the mantel, and hangings and curtains of magnificent crimson patternings. On the mantel were a huge black clock of classical design, vases in the Burslem Etruscan style, spills, and toothpicks in large receptacles of carved rock, large lava ash-trays, and an exceptionally big box of matches. The fender was very great and brassy. In a favourable position under the window was a spacious rosewood writing-desk, and all the chairs and other furniture were of rosewood and well stuffed.

" This," said Kipps, in something near an undertone, " was the o' gentleman's study—my grandfather that was. 'E used to sit at that desk and write."

" Books ? "

" No. Letters to the *Times* and things like that. 'E's got 'em all cut out—stuck in a book. . . . Leastways he *'ad*. It's in that bookcase. . . . Won't you sit down ? "

Coote did, blowing very slightly, and Kipps secured his vacated position on the extensive black-skin rug. He spread out his legs compass fashion, and tried to appear at his ease. The rug, the fender, the mantel, and mirror, conspired with great success to make him look a trivial and intrusive little creature amidst their commonplace hauteur, and his own shadow on the opposite wall seemed to think everything a great lark, and mocked and made tremendous fun of him. . . .

§ 2

For a space Kipps played a defensive game, and Coote drew the lines of the conversation. They kept away from the theme of Kipps' change of fortune, and Coote made remarks upon local and social affairs. " You must take an interest in these things now," was as much as he said in the way of personalities. But it speedily became evident that he was a person of wide and commanding social relationships. He spoke of " society " being mixed in the neighbourhood, and of the difficulty of getting people to work together and "do" things; they were cliquish. Incidentally he alluded quite familiarly to men with military titles, and once even to some one with a title, a Lady Punnet. Not snobbishly, you understand, nor deliberately, but quite in passing. He had, it appeared, talked to Lady Punnet about private theatricals! In connection with the hospitals. She had been unreasonable, and he had put her right—gently, of course, but firmly. "If you stand up to these people," said Coote, "they like you all the better." It was also very evident he was at his ease with the clergy; "my friend Mr. Densemore—a curate, you know, and rather curious, the Reverend *and* Honourable." Coote grew visibly in Kipps' eyes as he said these things; he became, not only the exponent of "Vagner or Vargner," the man whose sister had painted a picture to be exhibited at the Royal Academy, the type of the hidden thing called culture, but a delegate, as it were, or at least an intermediary from that great world "up there", where there were men-servants, where there were titles, where people dressed for dinner, drank wine at meals, wine costing very often as much as three and sixpence the bottle, and followed through a maze of etiquette, the most stupendous practices. . . .

Coote sat back in the arm-chair smoking luxuriously and expanding pleasantly with the delightful sense of *savoir faire*; Kipps sat forward, his elbows on his chair arm, alert, and his head a little on one side. You figure him as looking little and cheap, and feeling smaller and cheaper amidst his new surroundings. But it was a most stimulating and interesting conversation. And soon it became less general, and more serious and intimate. Coote spoke of people who had got on, and of people who hadn't; of people who seemed to be in everything, and people who seemed to be out of everything; and then he came round to Kipps.

"You'll have a good time," he said abruptly, with a smile that would have interested a dentist.

"I dunno," said Kipps.

"There's mistakes, of course."

"That's jest it."

Coote lit a new cigarette. "One can't help being interested in what you will do," he remarked. "Of course—for a young man of spirit, come suddenly into wealth—there's temptations."

"I got to go careful," said Kipps. "O' Bean told me that at the very first."

Coote went on to speak of pitfalls, of Betting, of Bad Companions. "I know," said Kipps, "I know." "There's Doubt again," said Coote. "I know a young fellow—a solicitor—handsome, gifted. And yet, you know—utterly sceptical. Practically altogether a Sceptic."

"Lor!" said Kipps, "not a Natheist?"

" I fear so," said Coote. " Really, you know, an awfully
fine young fellow—Gifted! But full of this dreadful Modern
Spirit—Cynical! All this Overman stuff. Nietzsche and all
that. . . . I wish I could do something for him."

" Ah! " said Kipps, and knocked the ash off his cigarette.
" I know a chap—one of our apprentices he was—once.
Always scoffing. . . . He lef'."

He paused. " Never wrote for his refs," he said, in the deep
tone proper to a moral tragedy ; and then, after a pause,
" Enlisted ! "

" Ah ! " said Coote.

" And often," he said, after a pause, " it's just the most
spirited chaps, just the chaps one likes best, who Go Wrong."

" It's temptation," Kipps remarked.

He glanced at Coote, leant forward, knocked the ash from
his cigarette into the mighty fender. " That's jest it," he said,
" you get tempted. Before you know where you are."

" Modern life," said Coote, " is so—complex. It isn't every
one is Strong. Half the young fellows who go wrong aren't
really bad."

" That's jest it," said Kipps.

" One gets a tone from one's surroundings——"

" That's exactly it," said Kipps.

He meditated. " *I* picked up with a chap," he said. " A
Nacter. Leastways, he writes plays. Clever feller. But——"

He implied extensive moral obloquy by a movement of his
head. " Of course it's seeing life," he added.

Coote pretended to understand the full implications of
Kipps' remark. " Is it *worth* it ? " he asked.

" That's jest it," said Kipps.

He decided to give some more. " One gets talking," he
said. " Then it's " 'ave a drink ! " Old Methusaleh three stars
—and where *are* you ? *I* been drunk," he said, in a tone of
profound humility, and added, " lots of times."

" Tt—tt " said Coote.

" Dozens of times," said Kipps, smiling sadly ; and added,
" Lately."

His imagination became active and seductive. " One thing
leads to another. Cards, p'raps. Girls——"

" I know," said Coote, " I know."

Kipps regarded the fire, and flushed slightly. He borrowed
a sentence that Chitterlow had recently used. " One can't
tell tales out of school," he said.

" I can imagine it," said Coote.

Kipps looked with a confidential expression into Coote's
face. " It was bad enough when money was limited," he
remarked. " But now "—he spoke with raised eyebrows—
" I got to steady down."

" You *must*," said Coote, protruding his lips into a sort of
whistling concern for a moment.

" I must," said Kipps, nodding his head slowly, with raised eyebrows. He looked at his cigarette end and threw it into the fender. He was beginning to think he was holding his own in this conversation rather well after all.

Kipps was never a good liar. He was the first to break silence. " I don't mean to say I been reely bad or reely bad drunk. " A 'eadache, perhaps—three or four times, say. But there it is ! "

" I have never tasted alcohol in my life," said Coote, with an immense frankness, " never ! "

" No ? "

" Never. I don't feel *I* should be likely to get drunk at all —it isn't that. And I don't go so far as to say even that in small quantities—at meals—it does one harm. But if I take it, some one else who doesn't know where to stop—you see ? "

" That's jest it," said Kipps. with admiring eyes.

" I smoke," admitted Coote. " One doesn't want to be a Pharisee."

It struck Kipps what a tremendously Good chap this Coote was, not only tremendously clever and educated and a gentleman, and one knowing Lady Punnet, but Good. He seemed to be giving all his time and thought to doing good things to other people. A great desire to confide certain things to him arose. At first Kipps hesitated whether he should confide an equal desire for Benevolent activities or for further Depravity—either was in his mind. He rather affected the pose of the Good Intentioned Dog. Then suddenly his impulses took quite a different turn—fell, indeed, into what was a far more serious rut in his mind. It seemed to him Coote might be able to do for him something he very much wanted done.

" Companionship accounts for so much," said Coote.

" That's jest it." said Kipps. " Of course, you know, in my new position—— That's just the difficulty."

He plunged boldly at his most secret trouble. He knew that he wanted refinement—culture. It was all very well—but he knew. But how was one to get it ? He knew no one, knew no people—— He rested on the broken sentence. The shop chaps were all very well, very good chaps and all that, but not what one wanted. " I feel be'ind," said Kipps. " I feel out of it. And consequently I feel it's no good. And then if temptation comes along——"

" Exactly," said Coote.

Kipps spoke of his respect for Miss Walshingham and her freckled friend. He contrived not to look too self-conscious. " You know, I'd like to talk to people like that, but I can't. A chap's afraid of giving himself away."

" Of course," said Coote, " of course."

" I went to a middle-class school, you know. You mustn't fancy I'm one of these here board-school chaps, but you know it reely wasn't a first-class affair. Leastways he didn't

take pains with us. If you didn't want to learn you needn't—
I don't believe it was *much* better than one of these here national
schools. We wore mortar-boards, o' course. But what's
that ?

" I'm a regular fish out of water with this money. When
I got it—it's a week ago—reely I thought I'd got everything
I wanted. But I dunno what to *do*."

His voice went up into a squeak. " Practically," he said,
" it's no good shuttin' my eyes to things—I'm a gentleman."

Coote indicated a serious assent.

" And there's the responsibilities of a gentleman," he remarked.

" That's jest it," said Kipps.

" There's calling on people," said Kipps. " If you want
to go on knowing Some one you knew before, like. People
that's refined." He laughed nervously. " I'm a regular fish
out of water," he said, with expectant eyes on Coote.

But Coote only nodded for him to go on.

" This actor chap," he meditated, " is a good sort of chap.
But 'e isn't what *I* call a gentleman. I got to 'old myself in
with 'im. 'E'd make me go it wild in no time. 'E's pretty
near the on'y chap I know. Except the shop chaps. They've
come round to 'ave supper once already and a bit of a sing-
song afterwards. I sang. I got a banjo, you know, and I
vamp a bit. Vamping—you know. Haven't got far in the
book—'Ow to Vamp—but still I'm getting on. Jolly, of course,
in a way, but what does it *lead* to ? . . . Besides that, there's
my Aunt and Uncle. *They're* very good old people—very—jest
a bit interfering p'r'aps, and thinking one isn't grown up,
but Right enough. Only— It isn't what I *want*. I feel I've
got be'ind with everything. I want to make it up again. I
want to get with educated people who know 'ow to do things
—in the regular proper way."

His beautiful modesty awakened nothing but benevolence
in the mind of Chester Coote.

" If I had some one like you," said Kipps, " that I knew
regular like—— "

From that point their course ran swift and easy. " If I
could be of any use to you," said Coote. . . .

" But you're so busy, and all that."

" Not *too* busy. You know, your case is a very interesting
one. It was partly that made me speak to you and draw you
out. Here you are with all this money and no experience, a
spirited young chap—— "

" That's jest it," said Kipps.

" I thought I'd see what you were made of, and I must
confess I've rarely talked to any one that I've found quite
so interesting as you have been—— "

" I seem able to say things to you, like, somehow," said
Kipps.

"I'm glad. I'm tremendously glad."

"I want a Friend. That's it—straight."

"My dear chap, if I—— "

"Yes ; but—— "

"*I* want a Friend too."

"Reely ? "

"Yes. You know, my dear Kipps — if I may call you that."

"Go on," said Kipps.

"I'm rather a lonely dog myself. *This* to-night——I've not had any one I've spoken to so freely of my Work for months."

"No ? "

"Yes. And, my dear chap, if I can do anything to guide or help you—— "

Coote displayed all his teeth in a kindly tremulous smile, and his eyes were shiny. "Shake 'ands," said Kipps, deeply moved ; and he and Coote rose and clasped with mutual emotion.

"It's reely too good of you," said Kipps.

"Whatever I can do I will," said Coote.

And so their compact was made. From that moment they were Friends—intimate, confidential, high-thinking, *sotto-voce* friends. All the rest of their talk (and it inclined to be interminable) was an expansion of that. For that night Kipps wallowed in self-abandonment, and Coote behaved as one who had received a great trust. That sinister passion for pedagogy to which the Good-Intentioned are so fatally liable, that passion of infinite presumption that permits one weak human being to arrogate the direction of another weak human being's affairs, had Coote in its grip. He was to be a sort of lay confessor and director of Kipps ; he was to help Kipps in a thousand ways ; he was, in fact, to chaperon Kipps into the higher and better sort of English life. He was to tell him his faults, advise him about the right thing to do—— "

"It's all these things I don't know," said Kipps. "I don't know, for instance, what's the right sort of dress to wear—I don't even know if I'm dressed right now—— "

"All these things "—Coote stuck out his lips and nodded rapidly to show he understood—"trust me for that," he said ; "trust me."

As the evening wore on Coote's manner changed, became more and more the manner of a proprietor. He began to take up his rôle, to survey Kipps with a new, with a critical affection. It was evident the thing fell in with his ideas. "It will be awfully interesting," he said. "You know, Kipps, you're really good stuff." (Every sentence now he said "Kipps," or "my dear Kipps," with a curiously authoritative intonation.)

"I know," said Kipps, "only there's such a lot of things

I don't seem to be up to some'ow. That's where the trouble comes in."

They talked and talked, and now Kipps was talking freely. They rambled over all sorts of things. Among others Kipps' character was dealt with at length. Kipps gave valuable lights on it. "When I'm reely excited," he said, "I don't seem to care *what* I do. I'm like that." And again, "I don't like to do anything under'and. I *must* speak out. . . ."

He picked a piece of cotton from his knee, the fire grimaced behind his back, and his shadow on the wall and ceiling was disrespectfully convulsed.

§ 3

Kipps went to bed at last with an impression of important things settled, and he lay awake for quite a long time. He felt he was lucky. He had known—in fact Buggins and Carshot and Pearce had made it very clear indeed—that his status in life had changed, and that stupendous adaptations had to be achieved ; but how they were to be effected had driven that adaptation into the incredible. Here, in the simplest, easiest way, was the adapter. The thing had become possible. Not, of course, easy, but possible.

There was much to learn, sheer intellectual toil, methods of address, bowing, an enormous complexity of laws. One broken, you are an outcast. How, for example, would one encounter Lady Punnet ? It was quite possible some day he might really have to do that. Coote might introduce him. "Lord !" he said aloud to the darkness between grinning and dismay. He figured himself going into the Emporium, to buy a tie, for example, and there in the face of Buggins, Carshot, Pearce, and the rest of them, meeting "my friend, Lady Punnet !" It might not end with Lady Punnet ! His imagination plunged and bolted with him, galloped, took wings, and soared to romantic, to poetical altitudes. . . .

Suppose some day one met Royalty. By accident, say ! He soared to that ! After all—twelve hundred a year is a lift, a tremendous lift. How did one address Royalty ? "Your Majesty's Goodness' it would be, no doubt—something like that—and on the knees. He became impersonal. Over a thousand a year made him an Esquire, didn't it ? He thought that was it. In which case, wouldn't he have to be presented at court ? Velvet breeches, like you wear cycling, and a sword ! What a curious place a court must be ! Kneeling and bowing ; and what was it Miss Mergle used to talk about ? Of course ! —ladies with long trains walking about backward. Everybody walked about backward at court, he knew, when not actually on their knees. Perhaps, though, some people regular stood up to the King ! Talked to him, just as one might talk to Buggins, say. Cheek, of course ! Dukes, it might be, did that—by permission ? Millionaires ? . . .

From such thoughts this free citizen of our Crowned Republic passed insensibly into dreams—turgid dreams of that vast ascent which constitutes the true-born Briton's social scheme, which terminates with retrogressive progression and a bending back.

§ 4

The next morning he came down to breakfast looking grave —a man with much before him in the world.

Kipps made a very special thing of his breakfast. Daily once hopeless dreams came true then. It had been customary in the Emporium to supplement Shalford's generous, indeed unlimited, supply of bread and butter-substitute by private purchases, and this had given Kipps very broad artistic conceptions of what the meal might be. Now there would be a cutlet or so or a mutton chop—this splendour Buggins had reported from the great London clubs—haddock, kipper, whiting, or fish-balls, eggs, boiled or scrambled, or eggs and bacon, kidney also frequently, and sometimes liver. Amidst a garland of such themes, sausages, black and white puddings, bubble-and-squeak, fried cabbage and scallops, came and went. Always as camp followers came potted meat in all varieties, cold bacon, German sausage, brawn, marmalade, and two sorts of jam ; and when he had finished these he would sit among his plates and smoke a cigarette, and look at all these dishes crowded round him with beatific approval. It was his principal meal. He was sitting with his cigarette regarding his apartment with the complacency begotten of a generous plan of feeding successfully realised, when newspapers and post arrived.

There were several things by the post, tradesmen's circulars and cards, and two pathetic begging letters—his luck had got into the papers—and there was a letter from a literary man and a book to enforce his request for 10s. to put down Socialism. The book made it very clear that prompt action on the part of property owners was becoming urgent, if property was to last out the year. Kipps dipped in it, and was seriously perturbed. And there was a letter from Old Kipps, saying it was difficult to leave the shop and come over and see him again just yet, but that he had been to a sale at Lydd the previous day, and bought a few good old books and things it would be difficult to find the equal of in Folkestone. "They don't know the value of these things out here," wrote Old Kipps, " but you may depend upon it they are valuable," and a brief financial statement followed. "There is an engraving some one might come along and offer you a lot of money for one of these days. Depend upon it, these old things are about the best investment you could make. . . ."

Old Kipps had long been addicted to sales, and his nephew's good fortune had converted what had once been but a looking and a craving—he had rarely even bid for anything in the old days, except the garden tools or the kitchen gallipots or things like that, things one gets for sixpence and finds a use for— into a very active pleasure. Sage and penetrating inspection, a certain mystery of bearing, tactical bids and Purchase— Purchase!—the old man had had a good time.

While Kipps was re-reading the begging letters, and wishing he had the sound, clear common sense of Buggins to help him a little, the Parcels Post brought along the box from his uncle. It was a large, insecure-looking case, held together by a few still loyal nails, and by what the British War Office would have recognised at once as an Army Corps of string— rags, and odds and ends tied together. Kipps unpacked it with a table knife, assisted at a critical point by the poker, and found a number of books and other objects of an antique type.

There were three bound volumes of early issues of *Chambers's Journal*, a copy of Punch's Pocket Book for 1875, Sturm's *Reflections*, an early version of Gill's *Geography* (slightly torn), an illustrated work on Spinal Curvature, an early edition of Kirke's *Human Physiology*, *The Scottish Chiefs*, and a little volume on the Language of Flowers. There was a fine steel engraving, oak-framed, and with some rusty spots, done in the Colossal style and representing the Handwriting on the Wall. There were also a copper kettle, a pair of candle-snuffers, a brass shoe-horn, a tea-caddy to lock, two decanters (one stoppered), and what was probably a portion of an eigh-teenth-century child's rattle. Kipps examined these objects one by one, and wished he knew more about them. Turning over the pages of the *Physiology* again, he came upon a striking plate, in which a youth of agreeable profile displayed his interior in an unstinted manner to the startled eye. It was a new view of humanity altogether for Kipps, and it arrested his mind. "Chubes," he whispered. "Chubes!"

This anatomised figure made him forget for a space that he was "practically a gentleman" altogether, and he was still surveying its extraordinary complications when another reminder of a world quite outside those spheres of ordered gentility into which his dreams had carried him overnight arrived (following the servant) in the person of Chitterlow.

§ 5

"Ul-*lo*!" said Kipps, rising.

"Not busy?" said Chitterlow, enveloping Kipps' hand for a moment in one of his own, and tossing the yachting cap upon the monumental carved oak sideboard.

"Only a bit of reading," said Kipps.

"Reading, eh?" Chitterlow cocked the red eye at the books and other properties for a moment, and then. "I've been expecting you round again one night."

" I been coming round," said Kipps ; " on'y there's a chap 'ere—— I was coming round last night, on'y I met 'im."

He walked to the hearthrug. Chitterlow drifted round the room for a time, glancing at the things as he talked. " I've altered that play tremendously since I saw you," he said.

" Pulled it all to pieces."

" What play's that, Chit'low ? "

" The one we were talking about. You know. You said something—I don't know if you meant it—about buying half of it. Not the tragedy. I wouldn't sell my own twin brother a share in that. That's my investment. That's my Serious Work. No ! I mean that new farce I've been on to. Thing with the business about a beetle."

" Oo yes," said Kipps. " *I* remember."

" I thought you would. Said you'd take a fourth share for a hundred pounds. *You* know."

" I seem to remember something—— "

" Well, it's all different. Every bit of it. I'll tell you. You remember what you said about a butterfly. You got confused, you know—Old Meth. Kept calling the beetle a butterfly, and that set me off. I've made it quite different. Quite different. Instead of Popplewaddle—thundering good farce-name that, you know, for all that it came from a Visitors' List—instead of Popplewaddle getting a beetle down his neck and rushing about, I've made him a collector—collects butterflies, and this one you know's a rare one. Comes in at window, centre ! " Chitterlow began to illustrate with appropriate gestures. " Pop rushes about after it. Forget he mustn't let on he's in the house. After that—— Tells 'em. Rare butterfly, worth lots of money. Some are, you know. Every one's on to it after that. Butterfly can't get out of room ; every time it comes out to have a try, rush, and scurry. Well, I've worked on that. Only—— "

He came very close to Kipps. He held up one hand horizontally and tapped it in a striking and confidential manner with the fingers of the other. " Something else," he said. " That's given me a Real Ibsenish Touch—like the Wild Duck. You know that woman—I've made her lighter—and she sees it. When they're chasing the butterfly the third time, she's on ! She looks. ' That's me !' she says. Bif ! Pestered Butterfly. *She's* the Pestered Butterfly. It's legitimate. Much more legitimate than the Wild Duck—where there isn't a duck !

" Knock 'em ! The very title ought to knock 'em. I've been working like a horse at it. . . . You'll have a goldmine in that quarter share, Kipps. . . . *I* don't mind. It's suited me to sell it, and suited you to buy. Bif !"

Chitterlow interrupted his discourse to ask, " You haven't any brandy in the house, have you ? Not to drink, you know. But I want just an eggcupful to pull me steady. My liver's

a bit queer. . . . It doesn't matter if you haven't. Not a bit.
I'm like that. Yes, whisky'll do. Better ! "

Kipps hesitated for a moment, then turned and fumbled
in the cupboard of his sideboard. Presently he disinterred
a bottle of whisky and placed it on the table. Then he put out
first one bottle of soda-water, and, after the hesitation of a
moment, another. Chitterlow picked up the bottle and read
the label. "Good old Methusaleh," he said. Kipps handed
him the corkscrew, and then his hand fluttered up to his
mouth. "I'll have to ring now," he said, "to get glasses."
He hesitated for a moment before doing so, leaning doubtfully, as it were, towards a bell.

When the housemaid appeared, he was standing on the
hearthrug with his legs wide apart, with the bearing of a
desperate fellow. And after they had both had whiskies, " You
know a decent whisky," Chitterlow remarked, and took
another, " just to drink." Kipps produced cigarettes, and the
conversation flowed again.

Chitterlow paced the room. He was, he explained, taking
a day off ; that was why he had come round to see Kipps.
Whenever he thought of any extensive change in a play he
was writing, he always took a day off. In the end it saved
time to do so. It prevented his starting rashly upon work that
might have to be re-written. There was no good in doing
work when you might have to do it over again, none whatever.

Presently they were descending the steps by the Parade
en route for the Warren, with Chitterlow doing the talking
and going with a dancing drop from step to step. . . .

They had a great walk, not a long one, but a great one.
They went up by the Sanatorium, and over the East Cliff
and into that queer little wilderness of slippery and tumbling
clay and rock under the chalk cliffs—a wilderness of thorn
and bramble, wild rose and wayfaring tree, that adds so
greatly to Folkestone's charm. They traversed its intricacies
and clambered up to the crest of the cliffs at last by a precipitous path that Chitterlow endowed in some mysterious
way with suggestions of Alpine adventure. Every now and
then he would glance aside at sea and cliffs with a fresh boyishness of imagination that brought back New Romney and the
stranded wrecks to Kipps' memory ; but mostly he talked of
his great obsession of plays and playwriting, and that empty
absurdity that is so serious to his kind, his Art. That was
a thing that needed a monstrous lot of explaining. Along they
went, sometimes abreast, sometimes in single file, up the
little paths and down the little paths, and in among the
bushes and out along the edge above the beach ; and Kipps
went along trying ever and again to get an insignificant word
in edgeways, and the gestures of Chitterlow flew wide and
far, and his great voice rose and fell, and he said this and he said
that, and he biffed and banged into the circumambient Inane.

It was assumed that they were embarked upon no more trivial enterprise than the Reform of the British Stage, and Kipps found himself classed with many opulent and even royal and noble amateurs—the Honourable Thomas Norgate came in here—who had interested themselves in the practical realisation of high ideals about the Drama. Only he had a finer understanding of these things, and instead of being preyed upon by the common professional—" and they *are* a lot," said Chitterlow ; " I haven't toured for nothing "—he would have Chitterlow. Kipps gathered few details. It was clear he had bought the quarter of a farcical comedy—practically a gold-mine—and it would appear it would be a good thing to buy the half. A suggestion, or the suggestion of a suggestion, floated out that he should buy the whole play and produce it forthwith. It seemed he was to produce the play upon a royalty system of a new sort, whatever a royalty system of any sort might be. Then there was some doubt, after all, whether that farcical comedy was in itself sufficient to revolutionise the present lamentable state of the British Drama. Better, perhaps, for such a purpose was that tragedy —as yet unfinished—which was to display all that Chitterlow knew about women, and which was to centre about a Russian nobleman embodying the fundamental Chitterlow personality. Then it became clearer that Kipps was to produce several plays. Kipps was to produce a great number of plays. Kipps was to found a National Theatre. . . .

It is probable that Kipps would have expressed some sort of disavowal, if he had known how to express it. Occasionally his face assumed an expression of whistling meditation, but that was as far as he got towards protest.

In the clutch of Chitterlow and the Incalculable, Kipps came round to the house in Fenchurch Street, and was there made to participate in the midday meal. He came to the house forgetting certain confidences, and was reminded of the existence of a Mrs. Chitterlow (with the finest completely untrained contralto voice in England) by her appearance. She had an air of being older than Chitterlow, although probably she wasn't, and her hair was a reddish brown, streaked with gold. She was dressed in one of those complaisant garments that are dressing-gowns, or tea-gowns, or bathing wraps, or rather original evening robes, according to the exigencies of the moment—from the first Kipps was aware that she possessed a warm and rounded neck, and her well-moulded arms came and vanished from the sleeves—and she had large, expressive brown eyes, that he discovered ever and again fixed in an enigmatical manner upon his own.

A simple but sufficient meal had been distributed with careless spontaneity over the little round table in the room with the photographs and looking-glass, and when a plate had, by Chitterlow's direction, been taken from under the marmalade in the cupboard, and the kitchen fork and a knife that was not loose in its handle had been found for Kipps, they began and made a tumultuous repast. Chitterlow ate with quiet enormity, but it did not interfere with the flow of his talk. He introduced Kipps to his wife very briefly ; she had obviously heard of Kipps before, and he made it vaguely evident that the production of the comedy was the thing chiefly settled. His reach extended over the table, and he troubled nobody. When Mrs. Chitterlow, who for a little while seemed socially self-conscious, reproved him for taking a potato with a jab of his fork, he answered, " Well, you shouldn't have married a man of Genius," and from a subsequent remark it was perfectly clear that Chitterlow's standing in this respect was made no secret of in his household.

They drank old Methusaleh and syphon soda, and there was no clearing away ; they just sat among the plates and things, and Mrs. Chitterlow took her husband's tobacco-pouch and made a cigarette and smoked, and blew smoke, and looked at Kipps with her large brown eyes. Kipps had seen cigarettes smoked by ladies before, " for fun," but this was real smoking. It frightened him rather. He felt he must not encourage this lady—at any rate, in Chitterlow's presence.

They became very cheerful after the repast, and as there was now no waste to deplore, such as one experiences in the windy open air, Chitterlow gave his voice full vent. He fell to praising Kipps very highly and loudly. He said he had known Kipps was the right sort, he had seen it from the first, almost before he got up out of the mud on that memorable night. " You can," he said, " sometimes. That was why——" He stopped, but he seemed on the verge of explaining that it was his certainty of Kipps being the right sort had led him to confer this great Fortune upon him. He left that impression. He threw out a number of long sentences and material for sentences of a highly philosophical and incoherent character about Coincidences. It became evident he considered dramatic criticism in a perilously low condition. . . .

About four Kipps found himself stranded, as it were, by a receding Chitterlow on a seat upon the Leas.

He was chiefly aware that Chitterlow was an overwhelming personality. He puffed his cheeks and blew.

No doubt this was seeing life, but had he particularly wanted to see life that day ? In a way Chitterlow had interrupted him. The day he had designed for himself was altogether different from this. He had been going to read through a precious little volume called *Don't* that Coote had sent round for him—a book of invaluable hints, a summary of British deportment, that had only the one defect of being at points a little out of date.

That reminded him he had intended to perform a difficult exercise called an Afternoon Call upon the Cootes, as a preliminary to doing it in deadly earnest upon the Walshinghams. It was no good to-day, anyhow, now.

He came back to Chitterlow. He would have to explain to Chitterlow he was taking too much for granted—he would have to do that. It was so difficult to do in Chitterlow's presence, though ; in his absence it was easy enough. This half-share, and taking a theatre and all of it, was going too far.

The quarter share was right enough, he supposed, but even that——! A hundred pounds ! What wealth is there left in the world after one has paid out a hundred pounds from it ?

He had to recall that, in a sense, Chitterlow had indeed brought him his fortune before he could face even that.

You must not think too hardly of him. To Kipps, you see, there was as yet no such thing as proportion in these matters. A hundred pounds went to his horizon. A hundred pounds seemed to him just exactly as big as any other large sum of money.

CHAPTER TWO

THE WALSHINGHAMS

§ 1

THE Cootes lived in a little house in Bouverie Square, with a tangle of Virginia creeper up the veranda.

Kipps had been troubled in his mind about knocking double or single—it is these things show what a man is made of—but happily there was a bell.

A queer little maid with a big cap admitted Kipps, and took him through a bead curtain and a door into a little drawing-room, with a black and gold piano, a glazed bookcase, a Moorish cosy corner, and a draped looking-glass overmantel, bright with Regent Street ornaments and photographs of various intellectual lights. A number of cards of invitation to meetings and the match list of a Band of Hope cricket club were stuck into the looking-glass frame, with Coote's name as a Vice-President. There was a bust of Beethoven over the book case, and the walls were thick with conscientiously executed but carelessly selected " views " in oil and water colours and gilt frames. At the end of the room, facing the light, was a portrait that struck Kipps at first as being Coote in spectacles and feminine costume, and that he afterwards decided must be Coote's mother. Then the original appeared, and he discovered that it was Coote's elder and only sister, who kept house for him. She wore her hair in a knob behind, and the sight of the knob suggested to Kipps an explanation for a frequent gesture of Coote's, a patting exploratory movement to the back of his head. And then it occurred to him that this was quite an absurd idea altogether.

She said, " Mr. Kipps, I believe," and Kipps laughed

pleasantly, and said, " That's it ! " and then she told him
that " Chester " had gone down to the art school to see about
sending off some drawings or other, and that he would be
back soon. Then she asked Kipps if he painted, and showed
him the pictures on the wall. Kipps asked her where each one
was " of," and when she showed him some of the Leas slopes,
he said he never would have recognized them. He said it was
funny how things looked in a picture very often. " But they're
awfully *good*," he said. " Did you do them ? " He would look
at them with his neck arched like a swan's, his head back and
on one side, and then suddenly peer closely into them. " They
are good. I wish I could paint.' " That's what Chester says,"
she answered. " I tell him he has better things to do." Kipps
seemed to get on very well with her.

Then Coote came in, and they left her and went upstairs
together, and had a good talk about reading and the Rules
of Life. Or rather Coote talked, and the praises of thought
and reading were in his mouth. . . .

You must figure Coote's study, a little bedroom put to
studious uses, and over the mantel an array of things he had
been led to believe indicative of culture and refinement—an
autotype of Rossetti's " Annunciation," an autotype of
Watts's " Minotaur," a Swiss carved pipe with many joints
and a photograph of Amiens Cathedral (these two the spoils
of travel), a phrenological bust, and some broken fossils from
the Warren. A rotating bookshelf carried the *Encyclopædia
Britannica* (tenth edition), and on the top of it a large official-
looking, age-grubby envelope, bearing the mystic words, " On
His Majesty's Service," a number or so of the *Bookman*, and
a box of cigarettes were lying. A table under the window bore
a little microscope, some dust in a saucer, some grimy glass
slips, and broken cover glasses, for Coote had " gone in for "
biology a little. The longer side of the room was given over
to bookshelves, neatly edged with pinked American cloth, and
with an array of books—no worse an array of books than you
find in any public library ; an almost haphazard accumulation of obsolete classics, contemporary successes, the Hundred Best Books (including Samuel Warren's *Ten Thousand
a Year*), old school-books, directories, the *Times* Atlas, Ruskin
in bulk, Tennyson complete in one volume, Longfellow, Charles
Kingsley, Smiles, a guide-book or so, several medical pamphlets,
odd magazine numbers, and much indescribable rubbish—in
fact, a compendium of the contemporary British mind. And
in front of this array stood Kipps, ill-taught and untrained,
respectful, awe-stricken, and, for the moment at any rate,
willing to learn, while Coote, the exemplary Coote, talked to
him of reading and the virtue in books.

" Nothing enlarges the mind," said Coote, " like Travel
and Books. . . . And they're both so easy nowadays, and
so cheap ! "

" I've often wanted to 'ave a good go in at reading," Kipps replied.

" You'd hardly believe," Coote said, " how much you can get out of books. Provided you avoid trashy reading, that is. You ought to make a rule, Kipps, and read one Serious Book a week. Of course we can Learn even from Novels, Nace Novels, that is, but it isn't the same thing as serious reading. I made a rule, One Serious Book and One Novel —no more. There's some of the Serious Books I've been reading lately—on that table ; *Sartor Resartus*, Mrs. Twaddle-tome's *Pond Life, The Scottish Chiefs, Life and Letters of Dean Farrar.* . . ."

§ 2

There came at last the sound of a gong, and Kipps descended to tea in that state of nervous apprehension at the difficulties of eating and drinking that his Aunt's knuckle rappings had implanted in him for ever. Over Coote's shoulder he became aware of a fourth person in the Moorish cosy corner, and he turned, leaving incomplete something incoherent he was saying to Miss Coote about his modest respect and desire for literature, to discover this fourth person was Miss Helen Walshingham, hatless, and looking very much at home.

She rose at once with an extended hand to meet his hesitation.

" You're stopping in Folkestone, Mr. Kipps ? "

" 'Ere on a bit of business," said Kipps. " I thought you was away in Bruges."

" That's later," said Miss Walshingham. " We're stopping until my brother's holiday begins, and we're trying to let our house. Where are you staying in Folkestone ? "

" I got a 'ouse of mine—on the Leas."

" I've heard all about your good fortune—this afternoon."

" Isn't it a Go ! " said Kipps. " I 'aven't nearly got to believe it's reely 'appened yet. When that—Mr. Bean told me of it, you could 'ave knocked me down with a feather. . . It's a tremenjous change for me."

He discovered Miss Coote was asking him whether he took milk and sugar. " *I* don't mind," said Kipps. " Jest as you like."

Coote became active, handing tea and bread-and-butter. It was thinly cut, and the bread was rather new, and the half of the slice that Kipps took fell upon the floor. He had been holding it by the edge, for he was not used to this migratory method of taking tea without plates or table. This little incident ruled him out of the conversation for a time, and when he came to attend to it again, they were talking about something or other prodigious — a performer of some sort — that was coming, called, it seemed, " Padrooski ! " So Kipps, who had dropped quietly into a chair, ate his bread-and-butter, said " no, thank you " to any more, and by this discreet restraint got more freedom with his cup and saucer.

Apart from the confusion natural to tea, he was in a state of tremulous excitement on account of the presence of Miss Walshingham. He glanced from Miss Coote to her brother, and then at Helen. He regarded her over the top of his cup as he drank. Here she was, solid and real. It was wonderful. He remarked, as he had done at times before, the easy flow of the dark hair back from her brow over her ears, the shapeliness of the white hands that came out from her simple white cuffs, the delicate pencilling of her brow.

Presently she turned her face to him almost suddenly, and smiled with the easiest assurance of friendship.

" You will go, I suppose ? " she said, and added, " to the Recital."

" If I'm in Folkestone I shall," said Kipps, clearing away a little hoarseness. " I don't *know* much about music, but what I do know I like."

" I'm sure you'll like Paderewski," she said.

" If you do," he said, " I dessay I shall."

He found Coote very kindly taking his cup.

" Do you think of living in Folkestone ? " asked Miss Coote, in a tone of proprietorship from the hearthrug.

" No," said Kipps, " that's jest it—I hardly know." He also said that he wanted to look round a bit before doing anything. " There's so much to consider," said Coote, smoothing the back of his head.

" I may go back to New Romney for a bit," said Kipps. " I got an Uncle and Aunt there. I reely don't know."

Helen regarded him thoughtfully for a moment.

" You must come and see us," she said, " before we go to Bruges."

" Oo, rather ! " said Kipps. " If I may."

" Yes, do," she said, and suddenly stood up before Kipps could formulate an inquiry when he should call.

" You're sure you can spare that drawing-board ? " she said to Miss Coote ; and the conversation passed out of range.

And when he had said " Good-bye " to Miss Walshingham, and she had repeated her invitation to call, he went upstairs again with Coote to look out certain initiatory books they had had under discussion. And then Kipps, blowing very resolutely, went back to his own place, bearing in his arm (1) *Sesame and Lilies* ; (2) *Sir George Tressady* ; (3) an anonymous book on *Vitality* that Coote particularly esteemed. And having got to his own sitting-room, he opened *Sesame and Lilies* and read with ruthless determination for some time.

§ 3

Presently he leant back and gave himself up to the business of trying to imagine just exactly what Miss Walshingham could have thought of him when she saw him. Doubts about the precise effect of the gray flannel suit began to trouble him. He turned to the mirror over the mantel, and then got into a chair to study the hang of the trousers. It looked all right. Luckily she had not seen the Panama hat. He knew he had the brim turned up wrong, but he could not find out which way the brim was right. However, that she had not seen. He might, perhaps, ask at the shop where he bought it.

He meditated for a while on his reflected face—doubtful whether he liked it or not—and then got down again and flitted across to the sideboard where there lay two little books, one in a cheap magnificent cover of red and gold, and the other in green canvas. The former was called, as its cover witnessed, *Manners and Rules of Good Society*, by a Member of the Aristocracy, and after the cover had indulged in a band of gilded decoration, light-hearted, but natural under the circumstances, it added, " TWENTY-FIRST EDITION." The second was that admirable classic, *The Art of Conversing*. Kipps returned with these to his seat, placed the two before him, opened the latter with a sigh, and flattened it under his hand.

Then with knitted brows he began to read onward from a mark, his lips moving.

" Having thus acquired possession of an idea, the little ship should not be abruptly launched into deep waters, but should be first permitted to glide gently and smoothly into the shallows ; that is to say, the conversation should not be commenced by broadly and roundly stating a fact, or didactically expressing an opinion, as the subject would be thus virtually or summarily disposed of, or perhaps be met with a ' Really ' or ' Indeed,' or some equally brief monosyllabic reply. If an opposite opinion were held by the person to whom the remark were addressed, he might not, if a stranger, care to express it in the form of a direct contradiction or actual dissent. To glide imperceptibly into conversation is the object to be attained——"

At this point Mr. Kipps rubbed his fingers through his hair with an expression of some perplexity, and went back to the beginning.

§ 4

When Kipps made his call on the Walshinghams, it all happened so differently from the *Manners and Rules* prescription (" Paying Calls ") that he was quite lost from the very outset. Instead of the footman or maidservant proper in these cases, Miss Walshingham opened the door to him herself. " I'm so glad you've come," she said, with one of her rare smiles.

She stood aside for him to enter the rather narrow passage.

" I thought I'd call," he said, retaining his hat and stick.

She closed the door and led the way to a little drawing-room, which impressed Kipps as being smaller and less emphatically coloured than that of the Cootes, and in which, at first, only a copper bowl of white poppies upon the brown tablecloth caught his particular attention.

" You won't think it unconventional to come in, Mr. Kipps, will you ? " she remarked. " Mother is out."

" I don't mind," he said, smiling amiably, " if you don't."

She walked round the table and stood regarding him across it, with that same look between speculative curiosity and appreciation that he remembered from the last of the art-class meetings.

" I wondered whether you would call or whether you wouldn't before you left Folkestone."

" I'm not leaving Folkestone for a bit, and any'ow I should have called on you."

" Mother will be sorry she was out. I've told her about you, and she wants, I know, to meet you."

" I saw 'er—if that was 'er—in the shop," said Kipps.

" Yes—you did, didn't you ? . . . She has gone out to make some duty calls, and I didn't go. I had something to write. I write a little, you know."

" Reely," said Kipps.

" It's nothing much," she said, " and it comes to nothing." She glanced at a little desk near the window, on which there lay some paper. " One must do something." She broke off abruptly. " Have you seen our outlook ? " she asked, and walked to the window, and Kipps came and stood beside her. " We look on the Square. It might be worse, you know. That out-porter's truck there is horrid—and the railings, but it's better than staring one's social replica in the face, isn't it ? It's pleasant in early spring—bright green laid on with a dry brush—and it's pleasant in autumn."

" I like it," said Kipps. " That laylock there is pretty, isn't it ?"

" Children come and pick it at times," she remarked.

" I dessay they do," said Kipps.

He rested on his hat and stick and looked appreciatively out of the window, and she glanced at him for one swift moment. A suggestion that might have come from the *Art of Conversing* came into his head. " Have you a garden ? " he said.

She shrugged her shoulders. " Only a little one," she said, and then, " Perhaps you would like to see it."

" I like gardening," said Kipps, with memories of a pennyworth of nasturtiums he had once trained over his uncle's dustbin.

She led the way with a certain relief.

They emerged through a four-seasons' coloured glass door to a little iron veranda, that led by iron steps to a minute walled garden. There was just room for a patch of turf and a flower-bed ; one sturdy variegated Euonymus grew in the corner. But the early June flowers, the big narcissus, snow upon the mountains, and a fine show of yellow wallflowers, shone gay.

" That's our garden," said Helen. " It's not a very big one, is it ? "

" I like it," said Kipps.

" It's small," she said, " but this is the day of small things."

Kipps didn't follow that.

" If you were writing when I came," he remarked, " I'm interrupting you."

She turned round with her back to the railing and rested, leaning on her hands. " I had finished," she said. " I couldn't get on."

" Were you making up something ? " asked Kipps.

There was a little interval before she smiled. " I try—quite vainly—to write stories," she said. " One must do something. I don't know whether I shall ever do any good—at that—anyhow. It seems so hopeless. And, of course—one must study the popular taste. But now my brother has gone to London—I get a lot of leisure."

" I seen your brother, 'aven't I ? "

" He came to the class once or twice. Very probably you have. He's gone to London to pass his examinations and become a solicitor. And then I suppose he'll have a chance. Not much, perhaps, even then. But he's luckier than I am."

" You got your classes and things."

" They ought to satisfy me. But they don't. I suppose I'm ambitious. We both are. And we hadn't much of a spring board." She glanced over her shoulder at the cramped little garden with an air of reference in her gesture.

" I should think you could do anything if you wanted to ? " said Kipps.

" As a matter of fact, I can't do anything I want to."

" You done a good deal."

" What ? "

" Well, didn't you pass one of these here University things ? "

" Oh, I matriculated ! "

" I should think I was no end of a swell if *I* did—I know that."

" Mr. Kipps, do you know how many people matriculate into London University every year ? "

" How many, then ? "

" Between two and three thousand."

" Well, just think how many don't ! "

Her smile came again and broke into a laugh. " Oh, *they* don't count," she said ; and then realizing that might penetrate Kipps if he was left with it, she hurried on to, " The fact is, I'm a discontented person, Mr. Kipps. Folkestone, you know, is a Sea Front, and it values people by sheer vulgar prosperity. We're not prosperous, and we live in a back street. We have to live here because this is our house. It's a mercy we haven't to ' let.' One feels one hasn't opportunities. If one had, I suppose one wouldn't use them. Still——"

Kipps felt he was being taken tremendously into her confidence. " That's jest it," he said.

He leant forward on his stick and said very earnestly, " I believe you could do anything you wanted to, if you tried."

She threw out her hands in disavowal.

" I *know*," said he, very sagely, and nodding his head. " I watched you once or twice when you were teaching that woodcarving class."

For some reason this made her laugh—a rather pleasant laugh, and that made Kipps feel a very witty and successful person. " It's very evident," she said, " that you're one of those rare people who believe in me, Mr. Kipps," to which he answered, " Oo, I *do* ! " and then suddenly they became aware of Mrs. Walshingham coming along the passage. In another moment she appeared through the four-seasons' door, bonneted and ladylike, and a little faded, exactly as Kipps had seen her in the shop. Kipps felt a certain apprehension at her appearance, in spite of the reassurances he had had from Coote.

" Mr. Kipps has called on us," said Helen ; and Mrs. Walshingham said it was very, very kind of him, and added that new people didn't call on them very much nowadays. There was nothing of the scandalised surprise Kipps had seen in the shop ; she had heard, perhaps, he was a gentleman now. In the shop he had thought her rather jaded and haughty, but he had scarcely taken her hand, which responded to his touch with a friendly pressure, before he knew how mistaken he had been. She then told her daughter that some one called Mrs. Wace had been out, and turned to Kipps again to ask him if he had had tea. Kipps said he had not, and Helen moved towards some mysterious interior. " But, *I* say," said Kipps, " don't you on my account——"

Helen vanished, and he found himself alone with Mrs. Walshingham. Which, of course, made him breathless and Boreas-looking for a moment.

" You were one of Helen's pupils in the woodcarving class ? " asked Mrs. Walshingham, regarding him with the quiet watchfulness proper to her position.

" Yes," said Kipps ; " that's 'ow I 'ad the pleasure——"

" She took a great interest in her woodcarving class. She is so energetic, you know, and it gives her an Outlet."

" I thought she taught something splendid."

" Every one says she did very well. Helen, I think, would do anything well that she undertook to do. She's so very clever. And she throws herself into things so."

She untied her bonnet-strings with a pleasant informality.

" She has told me all about her class. She used to be full of it. And about your cut hand."

" Lor ! " said Kipps ; " fancy telling that ! "

" Oh, yes. And how brave you were ! "

(Though, indeed, Helen's chief detail had been his remark-able expedient for checking bloodshed.)

Kipps became bright pink. " She said you didn't seem to feel it a bit."

Kipps felt he would have to spend weeks over *The Art of Conversing*.

While he still hung fire, Helen returned with the apparatus for afternoon tea upon a tray.

" Do you mind pulling out the table ? " asked Mrs. Walsh-ingham.

That again was very homelike. Kipps put down his hat and stick in the corner, and amidst an iron thunder pulled out a little rusty, green-painted, iron table, and then in the easiest manner followed Helen in to get chairs.

So soon as he had got rid of his teacup—he refused all food, of course, and they were merciful—he became wonderfully at his ease. Presently he was talking. He talked quite modestly and simply about his changed condition, and his difficulties and plans. He spread what indeed had an air of being all his simple little soul before their eyes. In a little while his clipped, defective accent had become less perceptible to their ears, and they began to realise, as the girl with the freckles had long since realised, that there were passable aspects of Kipps. He confided, he submitted, and for both of them he had the realest, the most seductively flattering undertone of awe and reverence.

He remained about two hours, having forgotten how terribly incorrect it is to stay at such a length. They did not mind at all.

CHAPTER THREE

ENGAGED

§ 1

WITHIN two months, within a matter of three-and-fifty days, Kipps had clambered to the battlements of Heart's Desire.

It all became possible by the Walshinghams—it would seem at Coote's instigation—deciding, after all, not to spend the holidays at Bruges. Instead they remained in Folkestone, and this happy chance gave Kipps just all those opportunities of which he stood in need.

His crowning day was at Lympne, and long before the summer warmth began to break, while, indeed, August still flamed on high. They had organised—no one seemed to know who suggested it first—a water party on the still reaches of the old military canal at Hythe, and they were to picnic by the brick bridge, and afterwards to clamber to Lympne Castle. The host of the gathering, it was understood very clearly, was Kipps.

They went a merry party. The canal was weedy, with only a few inches of water at the shallows, and so they went in three canoes. Kipps had learnt to paddle—it had been his first athletic accomplishment; and his second—with the last three or four of ten private lessons still to come—was to be cycling. But Kipps did not paddle at all badly; muscles hardened by lifting pieces of cretonne could cut a respectable figure by the side of Coote's exertions, and the girl with the freckles, the girl who understood him, came in his canoe. They raced the Walshinghams, brother and sister; and Coote, in a liquefying state and blowing mightily, but still persistent, and always quite polite and considerate, toiled behind with Mrs. Walshingham. She could not be expected to paddle (though, of course, she " offered "), and she reclined upon specially adjusted cushions under a black-and-white sunshade, and watched Kipps and her daughter, and feared at intervals that Coote was getting hot.

They were all more or less in holiday costume; the eyes of the girls looked out under the shade of wide-brimmed hats; even the freckled girl was unexpectedly pretty, and Helen, swinging sunlit to her paddle, gave Kipps, almost for the first time, the suggestion of a graceful body. Kipps was arrayed in the completest boating costume, and when his fashionable Panama was discarded and his hair blown into disorder, he became, in his white flannels, as sightly as most young men. His complexion was a notable asset.

Things favoured him, the day favoured him, every one favoured him. Young Walshingham, the girl with the freckles, Coote, and Mrs. Walshingham, were playing up to him in the most benevolent way, and between the landing-place and Lympne, Fortune, to crown their efforts, had placed a small convenient field entirely at the disposal of an adolescent bull. Not a big, real, resolute bull, but, on the other hand, no calf; a young bull, at the same stage of emotional development as Kipps, " where the brook and river meet." Detachedly our party drifted towards him.

When they landed, young Walshingham, with the simple directness of a brother, abandoned his sister to Kipps and secured the freckled girl, leaving Coote to carry Mrs. Walshingham's light wool wrap. He started at once in order to put an effectual distance between himself and his companion on the one hand, and a certain pervasive chaperonage that went with Coote, on the other. Young Walshingham I think I have said, was dark, with a Napoleonic profile, and it was natural for him therefore to be a bold thinker and an epigrammatic speaker, and he had long ago discovered great possibilities of appreciation in the freckled girl. He was in a very happy frame that day because he had just been entrusted with the management of Kipps' affairs (old Bean inexplicably dismissed), and that was not a bad beginning for a solicitor of only a few months' standing ; and, moreover, he had been reading Nietzsche, and he thought that in all probability he was the Non-Moral Overman referred to by that writer. He wore fairly large-sized hats. He wanted to expand the theme of the Non-Moral Overman in the ear of the freckled girl, to say it over, so to speak, and in order to seclude his exposition they went aside from the direct path and trespassed through a coppice, avoiding the youthful bull. They escaped to these higher themes but narrowly, for Coote and Mrs. Walshingham, subtle chaperones both, and each indisposed, for excellent reasons, to encumber Kipps and Helen, were hot upon their heels. These two kept the direct route to the stile of the bull's field, and the sight of the animal at once awakened Coote's innate aversion to brutality in any shape or form. He said the stiles were too high, and that they could do better by going round by the hedge, and Mrs. Walshingham, nothing loath, agreed.

This left the way clear for Kipps and Helen, and they encountered the bull. Helen did not observe the bull ; Kipps did ; but that afternoon, at any rate, he was equal to facing a lion. And the bull really came at them. It was not an affair of the bull-ring exactly, no desperate rushes and gorings, but he came ; he regarded them with a large, wicked, bluish eye, opened a mouth below his moistly glistening nose, and booed, at any rate, if he did not exactly bellow, and he shook his head wickedly, and showed that tossing was in his mind. Helen was frightened, without any loss of dignity, and Kipps went extremely white. But he was perfectly calm, and he seemed to her to have lost the last vestiges of his accent and his social shakiness. He directed her to walk quietly towards the stile and made an oblique advance towards the bull.

" You be orf ! " he said. . . .

When Helen was well over the stile, Kipps withdrew in good order. He got over the stile under cover of a feint, and the thing was done—a small thing, no doubt, but just enough to remove from Helen's mind an incorrect deduction that a man who was so terribly afraid of a teacup as Kipps must necessarily be abjectly afraid of everything else in the world. In her moment of reaction she went, perhaps, too far in the opposite direction. Hitherto Kipps had always had a certain flimsiness of effect for her. Now, suddenly, he was discovered solid. He was discovered possible in many new ways. Here, after all, was the sort of back a woman can get behind ! . . .

As they went past the turf-crowned mass of Portus Lemanus, up the steep slopes towards the castle on the crest, the thing was almost manifest in her eyes.

Every one who stays in Folkstone goes sooner or later to Lympne. The castle became a farm-house, and the farm-house, itself now ripe and venerable, wears the walls of the castle as a little man wears a big man's coat. The kindliest of farm ladies entertains a perpetual stream of visitors, and shows you her vast mangle and her big kitchen, and takes you out upon the sunniest little terrace-garden in all the world, and you look down the sheep-dotted slopes, to where, beside the canal and under the trees, the crumbled memories of Rome sleep for ever. One climbs the Keep, up a tortuous spiral of stone, worn now to the pitch of perforation, and there one is lifted to the centre of far more than a hemisphere of view. Away below one's feet, almost at the bottom of the hill, the Marsh begins and spreads and spreads in a mighty crescent that sweeps about the sea, the Marsh dotted with the church towers of forgotten mediæval towns, and breaking at last into the low blue hills by Winchelsea and Hastings ; east hangs France between the sea and sky ; and round the north, bounding the wide perspectives of farms and houses and woods, the Downs, with their hangers and chalk-pits, sustain the passing shadows of the sailing clouds.

And here it was, high out of the world of every day, and in the presence of spacious beauty, that Kipps and Helen found themselves agreeably alone. All six, it had seemed, had been coming for the Keep ; but Mrs. Walshingham had hesitated at the horrid little stairs, and then suddenly felt faint, and so she and the freckled girl had remained below, walking up and down in the shadow of the house ; and Coote had re-membered they were all out of cigarettes, and had taken off young Walshingham into the village. There had been shouting to explain between ground and parapet, and then Helen and Kipps turned again to the view and commended it, and fell silent.

Helen sat fearlessly in an embrasure, and Kipps stood beside her.

" I've always been fond of scenery," Kipps repeated, after an interval.

Then he went off at a tangent. " D'you reely think that was right what Coote was saying ? "

She looked interrogation.

" About my name."

" Being really C-U-Y-P-S ? I have my doubts. I thought at first—— What makes Mr. Coote add an ' S ' to Cuyp ? "

" _I_ dunno," said Kipps, foiled. " I was jest thinking." . . .

She shot one wary glance at him, and then turned her eyes to the sea.

Kipps was out for a space. He had intended to lead from

this question to the general question of surnames and change
of names ; it had seemed a light and witty way of saying
something he had in mind, and suddenly he perceived that
this was an unutterably vulgar and silly project. The hitch
about that " S " had saved him. He regarded her profile for
a moment, framed in weather-beaten stone, and backed by
the blue elements.

He dropped the question of his name out of existence, and
spoke again of the view. " When I see scenery—and things
that—that are beautiful, it makes me feel—— "

She looked at him suddenly, and saw him fumbling for his
words.

" Silly like," he said.

She took him in with her glance, the old look of proprietorship it was, touched with a certain warmth. She spoke in a
voice as unambiguous as her eyes. " You needn't," she said.
" You know, Mr. Kipps, you hold yourself too cheap."

Her eyes and words smote him with amazement. He stared
at her like a man who awakens. She looked down.

" You mean—— " he said ; and then, " Don't you hold
me cheap ? "

She glanced up again and shook her head.

" But—for instance—you don't think of me—as an equal
like."

" Why not ? "

" Oo ! But, reely—— "

His heart beat very fast.

" If I thought—— " he said ; and then, " You know so
much."

" That's nothing," she said.

Then for a long time, as it seemed to them, both kept silence
—a silence that said and accomplished many things.

" I know what I am," he said at length. . . . " If I thought
it was possible. . . . If I thought you. . . . I believe I could
do anything—— "

He stopped, and she sat downcast and strikingly still.

" Miss Walshingham," he said, " is it possible that you
. . . could care for me enough to—to 'elp me ? Miss Walshingham, do you care for me at all ? "

It seemed she was never going to answer. She looked up
at him. " I think," she said, " you are the most generous—
look at what you have done for my brother !—the most generous and the most modest of—men. And this afternoon—I
thought you were the bravest."

She turned her head, glanced down, waved her hand to
some one on the terrace below, and stood up.

" Mother is signalling," she said. " We must go down."

Kipps became polite and deferential by habit, but his
mind was a tumult that had nothing to do with that.

He moved before her towards the little door that opened

on the winding stairs—" always precede a lady down or up
stairs "—and then, on the second step, he turned resolutely.
" But—— " he said, looking up out of the shadow, flannel
clad and singularly like a man.

She looked down on him, with her hand upon the stone
lintel.

He held out his hand as if to help her. " Can you tell me ? "
he said. " You must know—— "

" What ? "

" If you care for me ? "

She did not answer for a long time. It was as if everything
in the world was drawn to the breaking-point, and in a minute
must certainly break.

" Yes," she said at last, " I know."

Abruptly, by some impalpable sign, he knew what the
answer would be, and he remained still.

She bent down over him and softened to her wonderful
smile.

" Promise me," she insisted.

He promised with his still face.

" If *I* do not hold you cheap, you will never hold yourself
cheap."

" If you do not hold me cheap ! You mean—— ? "

She bent down quite close to him. " I hold you," she said,
and then whispered, " *dear*."

" Me ? "

She laughed aloud.

He was astonished beyond measure. He stipulated lest
there might yet be some misconception. " You will marry
me ? "

She was laughing, inundated by the sense of bountiful
power, of possession and success. He looked quite a nice
little man to have. " Yes," she laughed. " What else could
I mean ? " and, " Yes."

He felt as a praying hermit might have felt, snatched from
the midst of his quiet devotions, his modest sack-cloth and
ashes, and hurled neck and crop over the glittering gates of
Paradise, smack among the iridescent wings, the bright-eyed
Cherubim. He felt like some lowly and righteous man dyna-
mited into Bliss. . . .

His hand tightened on the rope that steadies one upon
the stairs of stone. He was for kissing her hand and did not.

He said not a word more. He turned about, and, with
something very like a scared expression on his face, led the
way into the obscurity of their descent. . . .

§ 3

Every one seemed to understand. Nothing was said, nothing
was explained ; the merest touch of the eyes sufficed. As
they clustered in the castle gateway, Coote, Kipps remembered

afterwards, laid hold of his arm as if by chance, and pressed it. It was quite evident he knew. His eyes, his nose, shone with benevolent congratulation ; shone, too, with the sense of a good thing conducted to its climax. Mrs. Walshingham, who had seemed a little fatigued by the hill, recovered, and was even obviously stirred by affection for her daughter. There was in passing a motherly caress. She asked Kipps to give her his arm in walking down the steep. Kipps in a sort of dream obeyed. He found himself trying to attend to her, and soon he was attending.

She and Kipps talked like sober, responsible people and went slowly, while the others drifted down the hill together, a loose little group of four. He wondered momentarily what they would talk about, and then sank into his conversation with Mrs. Walshingham. He conversed, as it were, out of his superficial personality, and his inner self lay stunned in un-suspected depths within. It had an air of being an interesting and friendly talk, almost their first long talk together. Hitherto he had had a sort of fear of Mrs. Walshingham as of a person possibly satirical, but she proved a soul of sense and sentiment, and Kipps, for all his abstraction, got on with her unexpectedly well. They talked a little upon scenery and the inevitable melancholy attaching to old ruins and the thought of vanished generations.

" Perhaps they jousted here," said Mrs. Walshingham.

" They was up to all sorts of things," said Kipps ; and then the two came round to Helen. She spoke of her daughter's literary ambitions. " She will do something, I feel sure. You know, Mr. Kipps, it's a great responsibility to a mother to feel her daughter is—exceptionally clever."

" I dessay it is," said Kipps. " There's no mistake about that."

She spoke, too, of her son—almost like Helen's twin— alike yet different. She made Kipps feel quite fatherly. " They are so quick, so artistic," she said, " so full of ideas. Almost they frighten me. One feels they need opportunities—as other people need air."

She spoke of Helen's writing. " Even when she was quite a little dot she wrote verse."

(Kipps, sensation.)

" Her father had just the same tastes—— " Mrs. Walshing-ham turned a little beam of half-pathetic reminiscence on the part. " He was more artist than business man. That was the trouble. . . . He was misled by his partner, and when the crash came every one blamed him. . . . Well, it doesn't do to dwell on horrid things . . . especially to-day. There are bright days, Mr. Kipps, and dark days. And mine have not always been bright."

Kipps presented a face of Coote-like sympathy.

She diverged to talk of flowers, and Kipps' mind was filled with the picture of Helen bending down towards him in the Keep. . . .

They spread the tea under the trees before the little inn,
and at a certain moment Kipps became aware that every
one in the party was simultaneously and furtively glancing
at him. There might have been a certain tension had it not
been first of all for Coote and his tact, and afterwards for a
number of wasps. Coote was resolved to make this memorable
day pass off well, and displayed an almost boisterous sense of
fun. Then young Walshingham began talking of the Roman
remains below Lympne, intending to lead up to the Overman.
" These old Roman chaps—— " he said ; and then the wasps
arrived. They killed three in the jam alone.

Kipps killed wasps, as it were in a dream, and handed
things to the wrong people, and maintained a thin surface
of ordinary intelligence with the utmost difficulty. At times
he became aware—aware with an extraordinary vividness—of
Helen. Helen was carefully not looking at him, and behaving
with amazing coolness and ease. But just for that one time
there was the faintest suggestion of pink beneath the ivory of
her cheeks. . . .

Tacitly the others conceded to Kipps the right to paddle
back with Helen ; he helped her into the canoe and took
his paddle, and, paddling slowly, dropped behind the others.
And now his inner self stirred again. He said nothing to her.
How could he ever say anything to her again ? She spoke to
him at rare intervals about reflections and flowers and the
trees, and he nodded in reply. But his mind moved very
slowly forward now from the point at which it had fallen
stunned in the Lympne Keep, moving forward to the beginnings
of realisation. As yet he did not say even in the recesses of
his heart that she was his ! But he perceived that the goddess
had come from her altar, amazingly, and had taken him by
the hand !

The sky was a vast splendour, and then close to them were
the dark protecting trees, and the shining, smooth still water.
He was an erect black outline to her ; he plied his paddle
with no unskilful gesture ; the water broke to snaky silver
and glittered far behind his strokes. Indeed, he did not seem
so bad to her. Youth calls to youth the wide world through,
and her soul rose in triumph over his subjection. And behind
him was money and opportunity, freedom, and London, a
great background of seductively indistinct hopes. To him her
face was a warm dimness. In truth he could not see her eyes,
but it seemed to his love-witched brain he did, and that they
shone out at him like dusky stars.

All the world that evening was no more than a shadowy
frame of darkling sky and water and dipping boughs about
Helen. He seemed to see through things with an extraordinary
clearness ; she was revealed to him certainly, as the cause
and essence of it all.

He was, indeed, at his Heart's Desire. It was one of those times when there seems to be no future, when Time has stopped and we are at the end. Kipps that evening could not have imagined a to-morrow ; all that his imagination had pointed towards was attained. His mind stood still, and took the moments as they came.

§ 4

About nine that night Coote came round to Kipps' new apartment in the Upper Sandgate Road—the house on the Leas had been let furnished and Kipps made an effort towards realisation. He was discovered sitting at the open window and without a lamp—quite still. Coote was deeply moved, and he pressed Kipps' palm and laid a knobby white hand on his shoulder, and displayed the sort of tenderness becoming in a crisis. Kipps, too, was moved that night, and treated Coote like a very dear brother.

" She's splendid," said Coote, coming to it abruptly.

" Isn't she ? " said Kipps.

" I couldn't help noticing her face," said Coote. . . . " You know, my dear Kipps, this is better than a legacy."

" I don't deserve it," said Kipps.

" You can't say that."

" I don't. I can't 'ardly believe it. I can't believe it at all. No ! "

There followed an expressive stillness.

" It's wonderful," said Kipps. " It takes me like that."

Coote made a faint blowing noise, and so again they came for a time on silence.

" And it began—before your money ? "

" When I was in 'er class," said Kipps solemnly.

Coote, speaking out of a darkness which he was illuminating strangely with efforts to strike a match, said it was beautiful. He could not have *wished* Kipps a better fortune. . . .

He lit a cigarette, and Kipps was moved to do the same, with a sacramental expression.

Presently speech flowed more freely.

Coote began to praise Helen, and her mother and brother ; he talked of when " it " might be ; he presented the thing as concrete and credible. " It's a county family, you know," he said. " She is connected, you know, with the Beauprés family—you know Lord Beauprés."

" No ! " said Kipps, " reely ! "

" Distantly, of course," said Coote. " Still——"

He smiled a smile that glimmered in the twilight.

" It's too much," said Kipps, overcome. " It's so all like that."

Coote exhaled. For a time Kipps listened to Helen's praises and matured a point of view.

" I say, Coote," he said. " What ought I to do now ? "

" What do you mean ? " said Coote.

" I mean about calling on 'er and all that."

He reflected. " Naturally I want to do it all right."

" Of course," said Coote.

" It would be awful to go and do something now—all wrong."

Coote's cigarette glowed as he meditated. " You must call, of course," he decided. " You'll have to speak to Mrs. Walshingham."

" 'Ow ? " said Kipps.

" Tell her you mean to marry her daughter."

" I dessay she knows," said Kipps, with defensive penetration.

Coote's head was visible, shaking itself judicially.

" Then there's the ring," said Kipps. " What 'ave I to do about that ? "

" What ring do you mean ? "

" 'Ngagement Ring. There isn't anything at all about that in *Manners and Rules of Good Society*—not a word."

" Of course you must get something—tasteful. Yes."

" What sort of ring ? "

" Something nace. They'll show you in the shop."

" O' course. I s'pose I got to take it to 'er, eh ? Put it on 'er finger."

" Oh, no ! Send it. Much better."

" Ah ! " said Kipps for the first time with a note of relief.

" Then 'ow about this call ?—on Mrs. Walshingham I mean. 'Ow ought one to go ? "

" Rather a ceremonial occasion," reflected Coote.

" Wadyer mean ? Frock coat ? "

" I *think* so," said Coote, with discrimination.

" Light trousers, and all that ? "

" Yes."

" Rose ? "

" I think it might run to a buttonhole."

The curtain that hung over the future became less opaque to the eyes of Kipps. To-morrow, and then other days, became perceptible at least as existing. Frock-coat, silk hat, and a rose ! With a certain solemnity he contemplated himself in the process of slow " transformation into an English gentleman, Arthur Cuyps, frock-coated on occasions of ceremony, the familiar acquaintance of Lady Punnet, the recognised wooer of a distant connection of the Earl of Beauprés.

Something like awe at the magnitude of his own fortunes came upon him. He felt the world was opening out like a magic flower in a transformation scene at the touch of this wand of gold. And Helen, nestling beautiful in the red heart of the flower. Only ten weeks ago he had been no more than the shabbiest of improvers and shamefully dismissed for dissipation, the mere soil-buried seed, as it were, of these glories. He resolved the engagement ring should be of expressively excessive quality and appearance, in fact the very best they had.

" Ought I to send 'er flowers ? " he speculated.

" Not necessarily," said Coote. " Though, of course, it's an attention." . . .

Kipps meditated on flowers.

" When you see her," said Coote, " you'll have to ask her to name the day."

Kipps started. " That won't be just yet a bit, will it ? "

" Don't know any reason for delay."

" Oo, but—a year say."

" Rather a long taime," said Coote.

" Is it ? " said Kipps, turning his head sharply. " But——"
There was quite a long pause.

" I say ! " he said at last, and in an altered voice, " you'll 'ave to 'elp me about the wedding."

" Only too happy ! " said Coote.

" O' course," said Kipps, " I didn't think——" He changed his line of thought. " Coote," he asked, " wot's a ' tate-eh-tate ' ? "

" A ' tate-ah-tay,' " said Coote improvingly, " is a conversation alone together."

" Lor ! " said Kipps, " but I thought—— It says *strictly* we oughtn't to enjoy a tater-tay, not sit together, walk together, ride together, or meet during any part of the day. That don't leave much time for meeting, does it ? "

" The book says that ? " asked Coote.

" I jest learnt it by 'eart before you came. I thought that was a bit rum, but I s'pose it's all right."

" You won't find Mrs. Walshingham so strict as all that," said Coote. " I think that's a bit extreme. They'd only do that now in very strict old aristocratic families. Besides, the Walshinghams are so modern—advanced you might say. I expect you'll get plenty of chances of talking together."

" There's a tremendous lot to think about," said Kipps, blowing a profound sigh. " D'you mean—p'raps we might be married in a few months or so ? "

" You'll *have* to be," said Coote. " Why not ? " . . .

Midnight found Kipps alone, looking a little tired, and turning over the leaves of the red-covered text-book with a studious expression. He paused for a moment at page 233, his eye caught by the words :—

" FOR AN UNCLE OR AUNT BY MARRIAGE the period is six weeks black with jet trimmings."

" No," said Kipps, after a vigorous mental effort. " That's not it." The pages rustled again. He stopped and flattened out the little book decisively at the beginning of the chapter on " Weddings."

He became pensive. He stared at the lamp-wick. " I suppose I ought to go over and tell them," he said at last.

§ 5

Kipps called on Mrs. Walshingham attired in the proper costume for Ceremonial Occasions in the Day. He carried a silk hat, and he wore a deep-skirted frock-coat ; his boots were patent leather, and his trousers a dark gray. He had generous white cuffs with gold links, and his gray gloves, one thumb of which had burst when he put them on, he held loosely in his hand. He carried a small umbrella, rolled to an exquisite tightness. A sense of singular correctness pervaded his being and warred with the enormity of the occasion for possession of his soul. Anon he touched his silk cravat. The world smelt of his rosebud.

He seated himself on a newly re-covered chintz arm-chair, and stuck out the elbow of the arm that held his hat.

" I know," said Mrs. Walshingham, " I know everything," and helped him out most amazingly. She deepened the impression he had already received of her sense and refinement. She displayed an amount of tenderness that touched him.

" This is a great thing," she said, " to a mother," and her hand rested for a moment on his impeccable coat-sleeve.

" A daughter, Arthur," she explained, " is so much more than a son."

Marriage, she said, was a lottery, and without love and toleration—there was much unhappiness. Her life had not always been bright—there had been dark days and bright days. She smiled rather sweetly. " This is a bright one," she said.

She said very kind and flattering things to Kipps, and she thanked him for his goodness to her son. (" That wasn't anything," said Kipps.) And then she expanded upon the theme of her two children. " Both so accomplished," she said, " so clever. I call them my Twin Jewels."

She was repeating a remark she had made at Lympne, that she always said her children needed opportunities as other people needed air, when she was abruptly arrested by the entry of Helen. They hung on a pause, Helen perhaps surprised by Kipps' week-day magnificence. Then she advanced with outstretched hand.

Both the young people were shy. " I jest called round," began Kipps, and became uncertain how to end.

" Won't you have some tea ? " asked Helen.

She walked to the window, looked at the familiar outporter's barrow, turned, surveyed Kipps for a moment ambiguously, said, " I will get some tea," and so departed again.

Mrs. Walshingham and Kipps looked at one another, and the lady smiled indulgently. " You two young people mustn't be shy of each other," said Mrs. Walshingham, which damaged Kipps considerably.

She was explaining how sensitive Helen always had been, even about quite little things, when the servant appeared with the tea-things ; and then Helen followed, and, taking up a secure position behind the little bamboo tea-table, broke the ice with officious teacup clattering. Then she introduced the topic of a forthcoming open-air performance of *As You Like It*, and steered past the worst of the awkwardness. They discussed stage illusion. " I mus' say," said Kipps, " I don't quite like a play in a theayter. It seems sort of unreal some'ow."

" But most plays are written for the stage," said Helen, looking at the sugar.

" I know," admitted Kipps.

They got through tea. " Well," said Kipps, and rose.

" You mustn't go yet," said Mrs. Walshingham, rising and taking his hand. " I'm sure you two must have heaps to say to each other ; " and so she escaped towards the door.

§ 6

Among other projects that seemed almost equally correct to Kipps at that exalted moment was one of embracing Helen with ardour so soon as the door closed behind her mother, and one of headlong flight through the open window. Then he remembered he ought to hold the door open for Mrs. Walshingham, and turned from that duty to find Helen still standing, beautifully inaccessible, behind the tea-things. He closed the door and advanced towards her with his arms akimbo and his hands upon his coat skirts. Then feeling angular, he moved his right hand to his moustache. Anyhow, he was dressed all right. Somewhere at the back of his mind, dim and mingled with doubt and surprise, appeared the perception that he felt now quite differently towards her, that something between them had been blown from Lympne Keep to the four winds of heaven. . . .

She regarded him with an eye of critical proprietorship.

" Mother has been making up to you," she said, smiling slightly.

She added, " It was nice of you to come round to see her."

They stood through a brief pause, as though each had expected something different in the other, and was a little perplexed at its not being there. Kipps found he was at the corner of the brown-covered table, and he picked up a little flexible book that lay upon it to occupy his mind.

" I bought you a ring to-day," he said, bending the book and speaking for the sake of saying something, and then he moved to genuine speech. " You know," he said, " I can't 'ardly believe it."

Her face relaxed slightly again. " No ? " she said, and may have breathed, " Nor I."

" No," he went on. " It's as though everything 'ad changed.

More even than when I got that money. 'Ere we are going to marry. It's like being some one else. What I feel is——"

He turned a flushed and earnest face to her. He seemed to come alive to her with one natural gesture. " I don't *know* things. I'm not good enough. I'm not refined. The more you see of me, the more you'll find me out."

" But I'm going to help you."

" You'll 'ave to 'elp me a fearful lot."

She walked to the window, glanced out of it, made up her mind, turned and came towards him, with her hands clasped behind her back.

" All these things that trouble you are very little things. If you don't mind—if you will let me tell you things——"

" I wish you would."

" Then I will."

" They're little things to you, but they aren't to me."

" It all depends, if you don't mind being told."

" By you ? "

" I don't expect you to be told by strangers."

" Oo ! " said Kipps, expressing much.

" You know, there are just a few little things—— For instance, you know, you are careless with your pronunciation. . . . You don't mind my telling you ? "

" I like it," said Kipps.

" There's aitches."

" I know," said Kipps, and then endorsingly, " I been told. Fact is, I know a chap, a Nacter, *he's* told me. He's told me, and he's going to give me a lesson or so."

" I'm glad of that. It only requires a little care."

" Of course, on the stage they got to look out. They take regular lessons."

" Of course," said Helen, a little absently.

" I dessay I shall soon get into it," said Kipps.

" And then there's dress," said Helen, taking up her thread again.

Kipps became pink, but he remained respectfully attentive.

" You don't mind ? " she said.

" Oo no."

" You mustn't be too—too dressy. It's possible to be over conventional, over elaborate. It makes you look like a shop . . . like a common well-off person. There's a sort of easiness that is better. A real gentleman looks right, without looking as though he had tried to be right."

" Jest as though 'e'd put on what came first ? " said the pupil in a faded voice.

" Not exactly that, but a sort of ease."

Kipps nodded his head intelligently. In his heart he was kicking his silk hat about the room in an ecstasy of disappointment.

" And you must accustom yourself to bè more at your

ease when you are with people," said Helen. " You've only got to forget yourself a little and not be anxious——"

" I'll try," said Kipps, looking rather hard at the teapot. " I'll do my best to try."

" I know you will," she said ; and laid a hand for an instant upon his shoulder and withdrew it.

He did not perceive her caress. " One has to learn," he said. His attention was distracted by the strenuous efforts that were going on in the back of his head to translate, " I say, didn't you ought to name the day ? " into easy as well as elegant English, a struggle that was still undecided when the time came for them to part. . . .

He sat for a long time at the open window of his sitting-room with an intent face, recapitulating that interview. His eyes rested at last almost reproachfully on the silk hat beside him. " 'Ow *is* one to know ? " he asked. His attention was caught by a rubbed place in the nap, and, still thoughtful, he rolled up his handkerchief skilfully into a soft ball and began to smooth this down.

His expression changed slowly.

" 'Ow the Juice is one to know ? " he said, putting down the hat with some emphasis.

He rose up, went across the room to the sideboard, and, standing there, opened and began to read in *Manners and Rules*."

CHAPTER FOUR

THE BICYCLE MANUFACTURER

§ 1

So Kipps embarked upon his engagement, steeled himself to the high enterprise of marrying above his breeding. The next morning found him dressing with a certain quiet severity of movement, and it seemed to his landlady's housemaid that he was unusually dignified at breakfast. He meditated profoundly over his kipper and his kidney and bacon. He was going to New Romney to tell the old people what had happened and where he stood. And the love of Helen had also given him courage to do what Buggins had once suggested to him as a thing he would do were he in Kipps' place, and that was to hire a motor-car for the afternoon. He had an early cold lunch, and then, with an air of quiet resolution, assumed a cap and coat he had purchased to this end, and, thus equipped, strolled round, blowing slightly, to the motor shop. The transaction was unexpectedly easy, and within the hour, Kipps, spectacled and wrapped about, was tootling through Dymchurch.

They came to a stop smartly and neatly outside the little toy-shop. " Make that thing 'oot a bit, will you ? " said

Kipps. Yes. That's it." " Whup," said the motor-car. " Whur-rup." Both his Aunt and Uncle came out on the pavement. " Why, it's Artie ! " cried his Aunt ; and Kipps had a moment of triumph.

He descended to hand-claspings, removed wraps and spectacles, and the motor-driver retired to take " an hour off." Old Kipps surveyed the machinery and disconcerted Kipps for a moment by asking him, in a knowing tone, what they asked him for a thing like that. The two men stood inspecting the machine and impressing the neighbours for a time, and then they strolled through the shop into the little parlour for a drink.

" They ain't settled," old Kipps had said at the neighbours. " They ain't got no further than experiments. There's a bit of take-in about each. You take my advice and wait, me boy, even if it's a year or two before you buy one for your own use."

(Though Kipps had said nothing of doing anything of the sort.)

" 'Ow d'you like that whisky I sent ? " asked Kipps, dodging the old familiar bunch of children's pails.

Old Kipps became tactful. " It's very good whisky, my boy," said old Kipps. " I 'aven't the slightest doubt it's a very good whisky, and cost you a tidy price. But—dashed if it soots me ! They put this here Foozle Ile in it, my boy, and it ketches me jest 'ere." He indicated his centre of figure. " Gives me the heartburn," he said, and shook his head rather sadly.

" It's a very good whisky," said Kipps. " It's what the actor-manager chaps drink in London, I 'appen to know."

" I dessay they do, my boy," said old Kipps, " but then they've 'ad their livers burnt out—and I 'aven't. They ain't dellicat like me. My stummik always 'as been extry-dellicat. Sometimes it's almost been as though nothing would lay on it. But that's in passing. I liked those segars. You can send me some more of them segars. . . ."

You cannot lead a conversation straight from the gastric consequences of Foozle Ile to Love, and so Kipps, after a friendly inspection of a rare old engraving after Morland (perfect except for a hole kicked through the centre) that his Uncle had recently purchased by private haggle, came to the topic of the old people's removal.

At the outset of Kipps' great fortunes there had been much talk of some permanent provision for them. It had been conceded they were to be provided for comfortably, and the phrase, " retire from business," had been very much in the air. Kipps had pictured an ideal cottage with a creeper always in exuberant flower about the door, where the sun shone for ever, and the wind never blew, and a perpetual welcome hovered in the doorway. It was an agreeable dream, but when it came to the point of deciding upon this particular cottage or that, and on this particular house or that, Kipps was surprised by an unexpected clinging to the little home, which he had always understood to be the worst of all possible houses.

" We don't want to move in a 'urry," said Mrs. Kipps.

" When we want to move, we want to move for life. I've had enough moving about in my time," said old Kipps.

" We can do here a bit more now we done here so long," said Mrs. Kipps.

" You lemme look about a bit *fust*," said old Kipps.

And in looking about old Kipps found perhaps a finer joy than any mere possession could have given. He would shut his shop more or less effectually against the intrusion of customers, and toddle abroad seeking new matter for his dream ; no house was too small and none too large for his knowing inquiries. Occupied houses took his fancy more than vacant ones, and he would remark, " You won't be a-livin' 'ere for ever, even if you think you will," when irate householders protested against the unsolicited examination of their more intimate premises. . . .

Remarkable difficulties arose, of a totally unexpected sort.

" If we 'ave a larger 'ouse," said Mrs. Kipps, with sudden bitterness, " we shall want a servant, and I don't want no gells in the place larfin' at me, sniggerin' and larfin' and prancin' and trapesin', lardy da !

" If we 'ave a smaller 'ouse," said Mrs. Kipps, " there won't be room to swing a cat."

Room to swing a cat, it seemed, was absolutely essential. It was an infrequent but indispensable operation.

" When we *do* move," said old Kipps, " if we could get a bit of shootin'——

" I don't want to sell off all this here stock for nothin'," said old Kipps. " It's took years to 'cumulate. I put a ticket in the winder sayin', ' sellin' orf,' but it 'asn't brought nothing like a roosh. One of these 'ere dratted visitors, pretendin' to want an air-gun, was all we 'ad in yesterday. Jest an excuse for spyin' round, and then go away and larf at you. No thanky to everything, it didn't matter what. . . . That's 'ow *I* look at it, Artie."

They pursued meandering fancies about the topic of their future settlement for a space, and Kipps became more and more hopeless of any proper conversational opening that would lead to his great announcement, and more and more uncertain how such an opening should be taken. Once, indeed, old Kipps, anxious to get away from this dangerous subject of removals, began, " And what are you a-doin' of in Folkestone ? I shall have to come over and see you one of these days," but before Kipps could get in upon that, his Uncle had passed into a general exposition of the proper treatment of landladies and their humbugging, cheating ways, and so the opportunity banished. It seemed to Kipps the only thing to do was to go out into the town for a stroll, compose an effectual opening at leisure, and then come back and discharge it at them in its consecutive completeness. And even out-of-doors and alone, he found his mind distracted by irrelevant thoughts.

§ 2

His steps led him out of the High Street towards the church, and he leant for a time over the gate that had once been the winning-post of his race with Ann Pornick, and presently found himself in a sitting position on the top rail. He had to get things smooth again, he knew ; his mind was like a mirror of water after a breeze. The image of Helen and his great future was broken and mingled into fragmentary reflections of remoter things, of the good name of Old Methusaleh Three Stars, of long-dormant memories the High Street saw fit, by some trick of light and atmosphere, to arouse that afternoon. . . .

Abruptly a fine full voice from under his elbow shouted, " What-o, Art ! " and behold Sid Pornick was back in his world, leaning over the gate beside him, and holding out a friendly hand.

He was oddly changed, and yet oddly like the Sid that Kipps had known. He had the old broad face and mouth, abundantly freckled, the same short nose, and the same blunt chin, the same odd suggestion of his sister Ann without a touch of her beauty ; but he had quite a new voice, loud, and a little hard, and his upper lip carried a stiff and very fair moustache.

Kipps shook hands. " I was just thinking of *you*, Sid," he said, " jest this very moment, and wondering if ever I should see you again—ever. And 'ere you are ! "

" One likes a look round at times," said Sid. " How are *you*, old chap ? "

" All right," said Kipps. " I just been lef'——"

" You aren't changed much," interrupted Sid.

" Ent I ? " said Kipps, foiled.

" I knew your back directly I came round the corner. Spite of that 'at you got on. Hang it, I said, that's Art Kipps or the devil. And so it was."

Kipps made a movement of his neck as if he would look at his back and judge. Then he looked Sid in the face. " You got a moustache, Sid," he said.

" I s'pose you're having your holidays ? " said Sid.

" Well, partly. But I just been lef'——"

" *I'm* taking a bit of a holiday," Sid went on. " But the fact is, I have to give *myself* holidays nowadays. I've set up for myself."

" Not down here ? "

" No fear ! I'm not a turnip. I've started in Hammersmith,

manufacturing." Sid spoke off-hand, as though there was no such thing as pride.

" Not drapery ? "

" No fear ! Engineer. Manufacture bicycles." He clapped his hand to his breast pocket and produced a number of pink handbills. He handed one to Kipps, and prevented him reading it by explanations and explanatory dabs of a pointing finger. " That's our make—my make, to be exact—the Red Flag— see ? I got a transfer with my name—Pantocrat tyres, eight pounds—yes, *there*—Clinchers ten, Dunlops eleven, Ladies' one pound more—that's the lady's. Best machine at a democratic price in London. No guineas and no discounts—honest trade. I build 'em—to order. I've built," he reflected, looking away seaward, " seventeen. Counting orders in 'and. . . .

" Come down to look at the old place a bit," said Sid. " Mother likes it at times."

" Thought you'd all gone away——"

" What ! after my father's death ? No ! My mother's come back, and she's living at Muggett's cottages. The sea-air suits 'er. She likes the old place better than Hammersmith . . . and I can afford it. Got an old crony or so here. . . . Gossip . . . have tea. . . . S'pose *you* ain't married, Kipps ? "

Kipps shook his head. " I——" he began.

" *I* am," said Sid. " Married these two years, and got a nipper. Proper little chap."

Kipps got his word in at last. " I got engaged day before yesterday," he said.

" Ah ! " said Sid airily. " That's all right. Who's the fortunate lady ? "

Kipps tried to speak in an off-hand way. He stuck his hands in his pockets as he spoke. " She's a solicitor's daughter," he said, " in Folkestone. Rather'r nice set. County family. Related to the Earl of Beauprés——"

" Steady on ! " cried Sid.

" You see, I've 'ad a bit of luck, Sid. Been lef' money."

Sid's eye travelled instinctively to mark Kipps' garments. " How much ? " he asked.

" 'Bout twelve 'undred a year," said Kipps, more off-handedly than ever.

" Lord ! " said Sid, with a note of positive dismay, and stepped back a pace or two.

" My granfaver it was," said Kipps, trying hard to be calm and simple. " 'Ardly knew I 'ad a granfaver. And then— bang ! When o' Bean, the solicitor, told me of it, you could 'ave knocked me down——"

" '*Ow* much ? " demanded Sid, with a sharp note in his voice.

" Twelve 'undred pound a year—proximately, that is. . . ."

Sid's attempt at genial unenvious congratulation did not last a minute. He shook hands with an unreal heartiness, and said he was jolly glad. " It's a blooming stroke of Luck," he said.

" It's a bloomin' stroke of Luck," he repeated, " that's what it is," with the smile fading from his face. " Of course, better you 'ave it than me, o' chap. So I don't envy you, anyhow. *I* couldn't keep it if I did 'ave it."

" 'Ow's that ? " said Kipps, a little hipped by Sid's patent chagrin.

" I'm a Socialist, you see," said Sid. " I don't 'old with Wealth. What *is* Wealth ? Labour robbed out of the poor. At most it's only yours in trust. Leastways, that's 'ow *I* should take it."

He reflected. " The Present distribution of Wealth," he said, and stopped.

Then he let himself go, with unmasked bitterness. " It's no sense at all. It's jest damn foolishness. Who's going to work and care in a muddle like this ? Here first you do—something anyhow—of the world's work and it pays you hardly anything, and then it invites you to do nothing, nothing whatever, and pays you twelve hundred pounds a year. Who's going to respect laws and customs when they come to damn silliness like that ? "

He repeated, " Twelve hundred pounds a year ! "

At the sight of Kipps' face he relented slightly.

" It's not you I'm thinking of, o' man ; it's the system. Better you than most people. Still——"

He laid both hands on the gate and repeated to himself, " Twelve 'undred a year. . . . Gee-whiz, Kipps ! You'll be a swell ! "

" I shan't," said Kipps, with imperfect conviction. " No fear."

" You can't 'ave money like that and not swell out. You'll soon be too big to speak to—'ow do they put it ?—a mere mechanic like me."

" No fear, Siddee," said Kipps, with conviction. " I ain't that sort."

" Ah ! " said Sid, with a sort of unwilling scepticism, " money'll be too much for you. Besides—you're caught by a swell already."

" 'Ow d'yer mean ? "

" That girl you're going to marry. Masterman says——"

" Oo's Masterman ? "

" Rare good chap I know—takes my first-floor front room. Masterman says it's always the wife pitches the key. Always. There's no social differences—till women come in."

" Ah ! " said Kipps profoundly. " You don't know."

Sid shook his head. " Fancy ! " he reflected, " Art Kipps ! . . . Twelve 'Undred a Year ! "

Kipps tried to bridge that opening gulf. " Remember the Hurons, Sid ? "

"Rather," said Sid.

"Remember that wreck?"

"I can smell it now—sort of sour smell."

Kipps was silent for a moment, with reminiscent eyes on Sid's still troubled face.

"I say, Sid, 'ow's Ann?"

"*She's* all right," said Sid.

"Where is she now?"

"In a place . . . Ashford."

"Oh!"

Sid's face had become a shade sulkier than before.

"The fact is," he said, "we don't get on very well together. *I* don't hold with service. We're common people, I suppose, but I don't like it. I don't see why a sister of mine should wait at other people's tables. No. Not even if they got Twelve 'Undred a Year."

Kipps tried to change the point of application. "Remember 'ow you came out once when we were racing here? . . . She didn't run bad for a girl."

And his own words raised an image brighter than he could have supposed, so bright it seemed to breathe before him, and did not fade altogether, even when he was back in Folkestone an hour or so later.

But Sid was not to be deflected from that other rankling theme by any reminiscences of Ann.

"I wonder what you will do with all that money," he speculated. "I wonder if you will do any good at all. I wonder what you *could* do. You should hear Masterman. He'd tell you things. Suppose it came to me; what should I do? It's no good giving it back to the State as things are. Start an Owenite profit-sharing factory perhaps. Or a new Socialist paper. We want a new Socialist paper."

He tried to drown his personal chagrin in elaborate exemplary suggestions. . . .

§ 3

"I must be gettin' on to my motor," said Kipps at last, having to a large extent heard him out.

"What! Got a motor?"

"No!" said Kipps apologetically. "Only jobbed for the day."

"'Ow much?"

"Five pounds."

"Keep five families for a week! Good Lord!" That seemed to crown Sid's disgust.

Yet drawn by a sort of fascination, he came with Kipps and assisted at the mounting of the motor. He was pleased to note it was not the most modern of motors, but that was the only grain of comfort. Kipps mounted at once, after one violent agitation of the little shop-door to set the bell ajangle and warn his Uncle and Aunt. Sid assisted with the great fur-lined overcoat and examined the spectacles.

" Good-bye, o' chap ! " said Kipps.

" Good-bye, o' chap ! " said Sid.

The old people came out to say good-bye.

Old Kipps was radiant with triumph. " 'Pon my sammy, Artie ! I'm a goo' mind to come with you," he shouted ; and then, " I got something you might take with you ! "

He dodged back into the shop and returned with the per-forated engraving after Morland.

" You stick to this, my boy," he said. " You get it repaired by some one who knows. It's the most vallyble thing I got you so far—you take my word."

" Warrup ! " said the motor, and tuff, tuff, tuff, and backed and snorted, while old Kipps danced about on the pavement as if foreseeing complex catastrophes, and told the driver, " That's all right."

He waved his stout stick to his receding nephew. Then he turned to Sid. " Now, if you could make something like that, young Pornick, you *might* blow a bit ! "

" I'll make a doocid sight better than *that* before I done," said Sid, hands deep in his pockets.

" Not *you*," said old Kipps.

The motor set up a prolonged sobbing moan and vanished round the corner. Sid stood motionless for a space, unheeding some further remark from old Kipps. The young mechanic had just discovered that to have manufactured seventeen bicycles, including orders in hand, is not so big a thing as he had supposed, and such discoveries trying one's manhood. . . .

" Oh, well ! " said Sid at last, and turned his face towards his mother's cottage.

She had got a hot teacake for him, and she was a little hurt that he was dark and preoccupied as he consumed it. He had always been such a boy for teacake, and then when one went out specially and got him one——!

He did not tell her—he did not tell any one—he had seen young Kipps. He did not want to talk about Kipps for a bit to any one at all.

CHAPTER FIVE

THE PUPIL LOVER

§ 1

WHEN Kipps came to reflect upon his afternoon's work, he had his first inkling of certain comprehensive in-compatibilities lying about the course of true love in his particular case. He had felt without understanding the incongruity between the announcement he had failed to make and the circle of ideas of his Aunt and Uncle. It was this rather than the want of a specific intention that had silenced him, the perception that when he travelled from Folkestone to New Romney he travelled from an atmosphere where his engagement to Helen was sane and excellent to an atmosphere where it was only to be regarded with incredulous suspicion. Coupled and associated with this jar was his sense of the altered behaviour of Sid Pornick, the evident shock to that ancient alliance caused by the fact of his enrichment, the touch of hostility in his " You'll soon be swelled too big to speak to a poor mechanic like me." Kipps was unprepared for the unpleasant truth—that the path of social advancement is, and must be, strewn with broken friendships. This first protrusion of that fact caused a painful confusion in his mind. It was speedily to protrude in a far more serious fashion in relation to the " hands " from the Emporium, and Chitterlow.

From the day at Lympne Castle his relations with Helen had entered upon a new footing. He had prayed for Helen as good souls pray for Heaven, with as little understanding of what it was he prayed for. And now that period of standing humbly in the shadows before the shrine was over, and the goddess, her veil of mystery flung aside, had come down to him and taken hold of him, a good strong firm hold, and walked by his side. She liked him. What was singular was, that very soon she had kissed him thrice, whimsically upon the brow, and he had never kissed her at all. He could not analyse his feelings, only he knew the world was wonderfully changed about them ; but the truth was that, though he still wor-shipped and feared her, though his pride in his engagement was ridiculously vast, he loved her now no more. That subtle something, woven of the most delicate strands of self-love and tenderness and desire, had vanished imperceptibly, and was gone now for ever. But that she did not suspect in him, nor, as a matter of fact, did he.

She took him in hand in perfect good faith. She told him things about his accent ; she told him things about his bearing, about his costume and his way of looking at things. She thrust the blade of her intelligence into the tenderest corners of Kipps' secret vanity ; she slashed his most intimate pride to bleeding tatters. He sought very diligently to anticipate some at least of these informing thrusts by making great use of Coote. But the unanticipated made a brave number. . . .

She found his simple willingness a very lovable thing.

Indeed, she liked him more and more. There was a touch of motherliness in her feelings towards him. But his upbringing and his associations had been, she diagnosed, " awful." At New Romney she glanced but little—that was remote. But in her inventory—she went over him as one might go over a newly taken house, with impartial thoroughness—she dis-covered more proximate influences, surprising intimations of nocturnal " sing-songs "—she pictured it as almost shocking

that Kipps should sing to the banjo—much low-grade wisdom
treasured from a person called Buggins—" Who *is* Buggins ? "
said Helen—vague figures of indisputable vulgarity—Pearce
and Carshot—and more particularly a very terrible social
phenomenon—Chitterlow.

Chitterlow blazed upon them with unheralded oppressive
brilliance the first time they were abroad together.

They were going along the front of the Leas to see a school-
play in Sandgate—at the last moment Mrs. Walshingham had
been unable to come with them—when Chitterlow loomed up
into the new world. He was wearing the suit of striped flannel
and the straw hat that had followed Kipps' payment in advance
for his course in elocution, his hands were deep in his side-
pockets and animated the corners of his jacket, and his attentive
gaze at the passing loungers, the faint smile under his boldly
drawn nose, showed him engaged in studying character—no
doubt for some forthcoming play.

" What HO ! " said he, at the sight of Kipps, and swept
off the straw hat with so ample a clutch of his great flat hand
that it suggested to Helen's startled mind a conjurer about to
palm a halfpenny.

" 'Ello, Chitt'low," said Kipps, a little awkwardly, and not
saluting.

Chitterlow hesitated. " Half a mo', my boy," he said, and
arrested Kipps by extending a large hand over his chest.
" Excuse me, my dear," he said, bowing like his Russian count
by way of apology to Helen, and with a smile that would have
killed at a hundred yards. He effected a semi-confidential
grouping of himself and Kipps, while Helen stood in white
amazement.

" About that play," he said.

" 'Ow about it ? " asked Kipps, acutely aware of Helen.

" It's all right," said Chitterlow. " There's a strong smell of
syndicate in the air, I may tell you. Strong."

" That's aw right," said Kipps.

" You needn't tell everybody," said Chitterlow, with a
transitory confidential hand to his mouth, which pointed the
application of the " everybody " just a trifle too strongly.
" But I think it's coming off. However—— I mustn't detain
you now. So long. You'll come round, eh ? "

" Right you are," said Kipps.

" To-night ? "

" At eight."

And then, and more in the manner of a Russian prince than
any common count, Chitterlow bowed and withdrew. Just
for a moment he allowed a conquering eye to challenge Helen's,
and noted her for a girl of quality. . . .

There was a silence between our lovers for a space.

" That," said Kipps, with an allusive movement of the head,
" was Chitt'low."

" Is he—a friend of yours ? "

" In a way. . . . You see, I met 'im. Leastways 'e met me. Run into me with a bicycle, 'e did, and so we got talking together."

He tried to appear at his ease. The young lady scrutinised his profile.

" What is he ? "

" E's a Nacter chap," said Kipps. " Leastways 'e writes plays."

" And sells them ? "

" Partly."

" Whom to ? "

" Different people. Shares he sells. . . . It's all right, reely— I meant to tell you about him before."

Helen looked over her shoulder to catch a view of Chitterlow's retreating aspect. It did not compel her complete confidence.

She turned to her lover, and said in a tone of quiet authority, " You must tell me all about Chitterlow. Now."

The explanation began. . . .

The School Play came almost as a relief to Kipps. In the flusterment of going in he could almost forget, for a time, his Laocoon struggle to explain, and in the intervals he did his best to keep forgetting. But Helen, with a gentle insistence, resumed the explanation of Chitterlow as they returned towards Folkestone.

Chitterlow was confoundedly difficult to explain. You could hardly imagine !

There was an almost motherly anxiety in Helen's manner, blended with the resolution of a schoolmistress to get to the bottom of the affair. Kipps' ears were soon quite brightly red.

" Have you seen one of his plays ? "

" 'E's tole me about one."

" But on the stage."

" No. He 'asn't 'ad any on the stage yet. That's all coming. . . ."

" Promise me," she said in conclusion, " you won't do anything without consulting me."

And, of course, Kipps promised. " Oo no ! "

They went on their way in silence.

" One can't know everybody," said Helen, in general.

" Of course," said Kipps, " in a sort of way it was him that helped me to my money." And he indicated in a confused manner the story of the advertisement. " I don't like to drop 'im all at once," he added.

Helen was silent for a space, and when she spoke she went off at a tangent. " We shall live in London—soon," she remarked. " It's only while we are here."

It was the first intimation she gave him of their post-nuptial prospects.

"We shall have a nice little flat somewhere, not too far west, and there we shall build up a circle of our own."

§ 2

All that declining summer Kipps was the pupil lover. He made an extraordinarily open secret of his desire for self-improvement ; indeed Helen had to hint once or twice that his modest frankness was excessive, and all this new circle of friends did, each after his or her manner, everything that was possible to supplement Helen's efforts and help him to ease and skill in the more cultivated circles to which he had come. Coote was still the chief teacher, the tutor—there are so many little difficulties that a man may take to another man that he would not care to propound to the woman he loves—but they were all, so to speak, upon the staff. Even the freckled girl said to him once in a pleasant way, "You mustn't say ' contre temps,' you must say ' contraytom,' " when he borrowed that expression from *Manners and Rules*, and she tried, at his own suggestion, to give him clear ideas upon the subject of "as" and "has." A certain confusion between these words was becoming evident, the first fruits of a lesson from Chitterlow on the aspirate. Hitherto he had discarded that dangerous letter almost altogether, but now he would pull up at words beginning with "h" and draw a sawing breath—rather like a startled kitten—and then aspirate with vigour.

Said Kipps one day, "*As* 'e ?—I should say, ah—Has 'e ? Ye know I got a lot of difficulty over them two words, which is which ? "

"Well, ' as ' is a conjunction, and ' has ' is a verb."

"I know," said Kipps, "but when is ' has ' a conjunction and when is ' as ' a verb ? "

"Well," said the freckled girl, preparing to be very lucid. "It's *has* when it means one has, meaning having, but if it isn't it's *as*. As, for instance, one says 'e—I mean *he*—He has. But one says—' as he has.' "

"I see," said Kipps. "So I ought to say ' as 'e ? ' "

"No, if you are asking a question you say *has* 'e—I mean he—'as he ? " She blushed quite brightly, but still clung to her air of lucidity.

"I see," said Kipps. He was about to say something further, but he desisted. "I got it much clearer now. *Has* 'e ? *Has* 'e as. Yes."

"If you remember about having."

"Oo, I will," said Kipps. . . .

Miss Coote specialised in Kipps' artistic development. She had early formed an opinion that he had considerable artistic sensibility ; his remarks on her work had struck her as decidedly intelligent, and whenever he called round to see them she would show him some work of art—now an illustrated book, now perhaps a colour print of a Botticelli, now the Hundred Best Paintings, now " Academy Pictures," now a German art handbook, and now some magazine of furniture and design. " I know you like these things," she used to say, and Kipps said, " Oo, I *do*." He soon acquired a little armoury of appreciative sayings. When presently the Walshinghams took him up to the Arts and Crafts, his deportment was intelligent in the extreme. For a time he kept a wary silence and suddenly pitched upon a colour print. " That's rather nace," he said to Mrs. Walshingham. " That lill' thing. There." He always said things like that by preference to the mother rather than the daughter unless he was perfectly sure.

He quite took to Mrs. Walshingham. He was impressed by her conspicuous tact and refinement ; it seemed to him that the ladylike could go no farther. She was always dressed with a delicate fussiness that was never disarranged, and even a sort of faded quality about her hair, and face, and bearing, and emotions, contributed to her effect. Kipps was not a big man, and commonly he did not feel a big man, but with Mrs. Walshingham he always felt enormous and distended, as though he was a navvy who had taken some disagreeable poison which puffed him up inside his skin as a preliminary to bursting. He felt, too, as though he had been rolled in clay and his hair dressed with gum. And he felt that his voice was strident and his accent like somebody swinging a crowded pig's-tail in a free and careless manner. All this increased and enforced his respect for her. Her hand, which flitted often and again to his hand and arm, was singularly well shaped and cool. " Arthur," she called him from the very beginning.

She did not so much positively teach and tell him as tactfully guide and infect him. Her conversation was not so much didactic as exemplary. She would say, " I *do* like people to do " so and so. She would tell him anecdotes of nice things done, of gentlemanly feats of graceful consideration ; she would record her neat observations of people in trains and omnibuses, how, for example, a man had passed her change to the conductor, " quite a common man he looked," but he had lifted his hat. She stamped Kipps so deeply with the hat-raising habit that he would uncover if he found himself in the same railway ticket-office with a lady, and so stand ceremoniously until the difficulties of change drove him to an apologetic provisional oblique resumption of his headgear. . . . And robbing these things of any air of personal application, she threw about them an abundant talk about her two children—she called them her Twin Jewels quite frequently—about their gifts, their temperaments, their ambition, their need of opportunity. They needed opportunity, she would say, as other people needed air. . . .

In his conversations with her Kipps always assumed—and she seemed to assume—that she was to join that home in London Helen foreshadowed ; but he was surprised one day to gather that this was not to be the case. " It wouldn't do," said Helen, with decision. " We want to make a circle of our own." " But won't she be a bit lonely down here ? " asked Kipps.

" There's the Waces, and Mrs. Prebble, and Mrs. Bindon Botting, and—lots of people she knows." And Helen dismissed this possibility. . . .

Young Walshingham's share in the educational syndicate was smaller. But he shone out when they went to London on that Arts and Crafts expedition. Then this rising man of affairs showed Kipps how to buy the more theatrical weeklies for consumption in the train, how to buy and what to buy in the way of cigarettes with gold tips and shilling cigars, and how to order hock for lunch and sparkling Moselle for dinner, how to calculate the fare of a hansom cab—penny a minute while he goes—how to look intelligently at an hotel tape, and how to sit still in a train like a thoughtful man instead of talking like a fool and giving yourself away. And he, too, would glance at the good time coming when they were to be in London for good and all.

That prospect expanded and developed particulars. It presently took up a large part of Helen's conversation. Her conversations with Kipps were never of a grossly sentimental sort ; there was a shyness of speech in that matter with both of them ; but these new adumbrations were at least as interesting, and not so directly disagreeable, as the clear-cut intimations of personal defect that for a time had so greatly chastened Kipps' delight in her presence. The future presented itself with an almost perfect frankness as a joint campaign of Mrs. Walshingham's Twin Jewels upon the Great World, with Kipps in the capacity of baggage and supply. They would still be dreadfully poor, of course—this amazed Kipps, but he said nothing—until " Brudderkins " began to succeed ; but if they were clever and lucky they might do a great deal.

When Helen spoke of London, a brooding look as of one who contemplates a distant country, came into her eyes. Already it seemed they had the nucleus of a set. Brudderkins was a member of the Theatrical Judges, an excellent and influential little club of journalists and literary people, and he knew Shimer and Stargate and Whiffle of the " Red Dragon," and besides these were the Revels. They knew the Revels quite well. Sidney Revel, before his rapid rise to prominence as a writer of epigrammatic essays that were quite above the ordinary public, had been an assistant master at one of the best Folkestone schools. Brudderkins had brought him home to tea several times, and it was he had first suggested Helen should try and write. " It's perfectly easy," Sidney had said. He had been writing occasional things for the evening papers and for the weekly reviews even at that time. Then he had gone up to London, and had almost unavoidably become a dramatic critic. Those brilliant essays had followed, and then *Red Hearts a-Beating*, the romance that had made him. It was a tale of spirited adventure, full of youth and beauty and naïve passion and generous devotion, bold, as the *Bookman* said, and frank in places, but never in the slightest degree morbid. He had met and married an American widow with quite a lot of money, and they had made a very distinct place for themselves, Kipps learnt, in the literary and artistic society of London. Helen seemed to dwell on the Revels a great deal ; it was her exemplary story, and when she spoke of Sidney—she often called him Sidney—she would become thoughtful. She spoke most of him, naturally, because she had still to meet Mrs. Revel. . . . . Certainly they would be in the world in no time, even if the distant connection with the Beauprés family came to nothing.

Kipps gathered that with his marriage and the movement to London they were to undergo that subtle change of name Coote had first adumbrated. They were to become " Cuyps," Mr. and Mrs. Cuyps. Or was it Cuyp ?

" It'll be rum at first," said Kipps.

" I dessay I shall soon get into it," he said. . . .

So in their several ways they all contributed to enlarge and refine and exercise the intelligence of Kipps. And behind all these other influences, and as it were presiding over and correcting these influences, was Kipps' nearest friend, Coote, a sort of master of the ceremonies. You figure his face, blowing slightly with solicitude, his slate-coloured, projecting, but not unkindly eye intent upon our hero. The thing, he thought, was going off admirably. He studied Kipps' character immensely. He would discuss him with his sister, with Mrs. Walshingham, with the freckled girl, with any one who would stand it. " He is an interesting character," he would say, " likeable—a sort of gentleman by instinct. He takes to all these things. He improves every day. He'll soon get *Sang-Froid*. We took him up just in time. He wants now—— Well —— next year, perhaps, if there is a good Extension Literature course he might go in for it. He wants to go in for something like that."

" He's going in for his bicycle now," said Mrs. Walshingham.

" That's all right for summer," said Coote, " but he wants to go in for some serious intellectual interest, something to take him out of himself a little more. *Savoir Faire* and self-forgetfulness is more than half the secret of *Sang-Froid*. . . ."

§ 3

The world, as Coote presented it, was in part an endorsement, in part an amplification, and in part a rectification of the world of Kipps—the world that derived from the old couple in New Romney and had been developed in the Emporium ; the world, in fact, of common British life. There was the same subtle sense of social gradation that had moved Mrs. Kipps to prohibit intercourse with labourers' children, and the same dread of anything " common " that had kept the personal quality of Mr. Shalford's establishment so high. But now a certain disagreeable doubt about Kipps' own position was removed, and he stood with Coote inside the sphere of gentlemen assured. Within the sphere of gentlemen there are distinctions of rank indeed, but none of class; there are the Big People, and the modest, refined, gentlemanly little people, like Coote, who may even dabble in the professions and counterless trades ; there are lords and magnificences, and there are gentle-folk who have to manage—but they can all call on one another, they preserve a general equality of deportment throughout, they constitute that great state within the state—Society.

" But reely," said the Pupil, " not what you call being in Society ? "

" Yes," said Coote. " Of course, down here, one doesn't see much of it, but there's local society. It has the same rules."

" Calling and all that ? "

" Precisely," said Coote.

Kipps thought, whistled a bar, and suddenly broached a question of conscience. " I often wonder," he said, " whether I oughtn't to dress for dinner—when I'm alone 'ere."

Coote protruded his lips and reflected. " Not full dress," he adjudicated ; " that would be a little excessive. But you should *change*, you know. Put on a mess jacket, and that sort of thing—easy dress. That is what *I* should do, certainly, if I wasn't in harness—and poor."

He coughed modestly, and patted his hair behind.

And after that the washing-bill of Kipps quadrupled, and he was to be seen at times by the bandstand with his light summer overcoat unbuttoned, to give a glimpse of his nice white tie. He and Coote would be smoking the gold-tipped cigarettes young Walshingham had prescribed as " chic," and appreciating the music highly. " That's—puff—a very nice bit," Kipps would say ; or better, " That's nace." And at the first grunts of the loyal anthem they stood with religiously uplifted hats. Whatever else you might call them, you could never call them disloyal.

The boundary of Society was admittedly very close to Coote and Kipps, and a leading solicitude of the true gentleman was to detect clearly those " beneath " him, and to behave towards them in a proper spirit. " It's jest there it's so 'ard for me," said Kipps. He had to cultivate a certain " distance " to acquire altogether the art of checking the presumption of bounders and old friends. It was difficult, Coote admitted.

" I got mixed up with this lot 'ere," said Kipps. " That's what's so harkward—I mean awkward."

" You could give them a hint," said Coote.

" 'Ow ? "

" Oh—the occasion will suggest something."

The occasion came one early-closing night, when Kipps was sitting in a canopy chair near the bandstand with his summer overcoat fully open, and a new Gibus pulled slightly forward over his brow, waiting for Coote. They were to hear the band for an hour, and then go down to assist Miss Coote and the freckled girl in trying over some Beethoven duets, if they remembered them, that is, sufficiently well. And as Kipps lounged back in his chair and occupied his mind with his favourite amusement on such evenings, which consisted chiefly in supposing that every one about him was wondering who he was, came a rude rap at the canvas back and the voice of Pearce.

" It's nice to be a gentleman," said Pearce, and swung a penny chair into position, while Buggins appeared smiling agreeably on the other side, and leant upon his stick. *He was smoking a common briar pipe !*

Two real ladies, very fashionably dressed, and sitting close at hand, glanced quickly at Pearce, and then away again, and it was evident *their* wonder was at an end.

" *He's* all right," said Buggins, removing his pipe and surveying Kipps.

" 'Ello, Buggins ! " said Kipps, not too cordially.   " 'Ow goes it ? "

" All right.   Holidays next week.   If you don't look out, Kipps, I shall be on the Continong before you.   Eh ? "

" You going t' Boologne ? "

" Ra-ther.   Parley vous Francey.   You bet."

" *I* shall 'ave a bit of a run over there one of these days," said Kipps.

There came a pause.   Pearce applied the top of his stick to his mouth for a space, and regarded Kipps.   Then he glanced at the people about them.

" I say, Kipps," he said in a distinct loud voice, " see 'er Ladyship lately ? "

Kipps perceived the audience was to be impressed, but he responded half-heartedly.   " No, I 'aven't," he said.

" She was along of Sir William the other night," said Pearce, still loud and clear, " and she asked to be remembered to you."

It seemed to Kipps that one of the two ladies smiled faintly, and said something to the other, and then certainly they glanced at Pearce.   Kipps flushed scarlet.   " *Did* she ? " he answered.

Buggins laughed good-humouredly over his pipe.

" Sir William suffers a lot from his gout," Pearce continued unabashed.

(Buggins much amused with his pipe between his teeth.)

Kipps became aware of Coote at hand.

Coote nodded rather distantly to Pearce.   " Hope I haven't kept you waiting, Kipps," he said.

" I kep' a chair for you," said Kipps, and removed a guardian foot.

" But you've got your friends," said Coote.

" Oh, *we* don't mind," said Pearce cordially, " the more the merrier ; " and, " Why don't you get a chair, Buggins ? " Buggins shook his head in a sort of aside to Pearce, and Coote coughed behind his hand.

" Been kep' late at business ? " asked Pearce.

Coote turned quite pale, and pretended not to hear. His eyes sought in space for a time, and with a convulsive movement he recognised a distant acquaintance and raised his hat.

Pearce had also become a little pale. He addressed himself to Kipps in an undertone.

" Mr. Coote, isn't he ? " he asked.

Coote addressed himself to Kipps directly and exclusively. His manner had the calm of extreme tension.

" I'm rather late," he said. " I think we ought almost to be going on *now*."

Kipps stood up. " That's all right," he said.

" Which way are you going ? " said Pearce, standing also, and brushing some crumbs of cigarette ash from his sleeve.

For a moment Coote was breathless. " Thank you," he said, and gasped. Then he delivered the necessary blow, " I don't think we're in need of your society, you know," and turned away.

Kipps found himself falling over chairs and things in the wake of Coote, and then they were clear of the crowd.

For a space Coote said nothing ; then he remarked abruptly, and quite angrily for him, " I think that was *awful* Cheek ! "

Kipps made no reply. . . .

The whole thing was an interesting little object-lesson in " distance," and it stuck in the front of Kipps' mind for a long time. He had particularly vivid the face of Pearce with an expression between astonishment and anger. He felt as though he had struck Pearce in the face under circumstances that gave Pearce no power to reply. He did not attend very much to the duets, and even forgot at the end of one of them to say how perfectly lovely it was.

§ 4

But you must not imagine that the national ideal of a gentleman, as Coote developed it, was all a matter of deportment and selectness, a mere isolation from debasing associations. There is a Serious Side, a deeper aspect of the true True Gentleman. But it is not vocal. The True Gentleman does not wear his heart on his sleeve. For example, he is deeply religious, as Coote was, as Mrs. Walshingham was ; but outside the walls of a church it never appears, except perhaps now and then in a pause, in a profound look, in a sudden avoidance. In quite a little while Kipps also had learnt the pause, the profound look, the sudden avoidance, that final refinement of spirituality, impressionistic piety

And the True Gentleman is patriotic also. When one saw Coote lifting his hat to the National Anthem, then perhaps one got a glimpse of what patriotic emotions, what worship, the polish of a gentleman may hide. Or singing out his deep notes against the Hosts of Midian, in the St. Stylites' choir ; then indeed you plumbed his spiritual side.

> " Christian dost thou heed them
>   On the holy ground,
>   How the hosts of Mid-i-an
>   Prowl and prowl around ?
>   Christian, up and smai-it them . . ."

But these were but gleams. For the rest, Religion, Nationality, Passion, Finance, Politics, much more so those cardinal issues Birth and Death, the True Gentleman skirted about, and became facially rigid towards, and ceased to speak, and panted and blew.

" One doesn't talk of that sort of thing," Coote would say, with a gesture of the knuckly hand.

" O' course," Kipps would reply, with an equal significance. Profundities. Deep, as it were, blowing to deep.

One does not talk, but on the other hand one is punctilious to do. Action speaks. Kipps—in spite of the fact that the Walshinghams were more than a little lax—Kipps, who had formerly flitted Sunday after Sunday from one Folkestone church to another, had now a sitting of his own, paid for duly, at Saint Stylites. There he was to be seen, always at the surplice evening service, and sometimes of a morning, dressed with a sober precision, and with an eye on Coote in the chancel. No difficulties now about finding the place in his book. He became a communicant again—he had lapsed soon after his confirmation when the young lady in the costume-room who was his adopted sister left the Emporium—and he would sometimes go round to the Vestry for Coote, after the service. One evening he was introduced to the Hon. and Rev. Densmore. He was much too confused to say anything, and the noble cleric had nothing to say, but they were introduced. . . .

No ! You must not imagine that the national ideal of a gentleman is without its " serious side," without even its stern and uncompromising side. The imagination, no doubt, refuses to see Coote displaying extraordinary refinements of courage upon the striken field, but in the walks of peace there is sometimes sore need of sternness. Charitable as one may be, one must admit there are people who *do* things—impossible things ; people who place themselves " out of it " in countless ways ; people, moreover, who are by a sort of predestination out of it from the beginning ; and against these Society has invented a terrible protection for its Cootery—the Cut. The cut is no joke for any one. It is excommunication. You may be cut by an individual, you may be cut by a set, or you may be—and this is so tragic that beautiful romances have been written about it—" Cut by the County." One figures Coote discharging this last duty and cutting somebody—Coote, erect and pale, never speaking, going past with eyes of pitiless slate, lower jaw protruding a little, face pursed up and cold and stiff. . . .

It never dawned upon Kipps that he would one day have to face this terrible front, to be to Coote not only as one dead, but as one gone more than a stage or so in decay, cut and passed, banned and outcast for ever. It never dawned upon either of them.

Yet so it was to be !

One cannot hide any longer that all this fine progress of Kipps is doomed to end in collapse. So far, indeed, you have seen him ascend. You have seen him becoming more refined and careful day by day, more carefully dressed, less clumsy in the uses of social life. You have seen the gulf widening between himself and his former low associates. I have brought you at last to the vision of him, faultlessly dressed and posed, in an atmosphere of candlelight and chanting, in his own sitting, his own sitting ! in one of the most fashionable churches in Folkestone. . . . I have refrained from the lightest touch upon the tragic note that must now creep into my tale. Yet the net of his low connections has been about his feet, and, moreover, there was something interwoven in his being. . . .

CHAPTER SIX

DISCORDS

§ 1

ONE day Kipps set out upon his newly mastered bicycle to New Romney, to break the news of his engagement to his Uncle and Aunt—positively. He was now a finished cyclist, but as yet an unseasoned one ; the south-west wind, even in its summer guise, as one meets it in the Marsh, is the equivalent of a reasonable hill, and ever and again he got off and refreshed himself by a spell of walking. He was walking just outside New Romney preparatory to his triumphal entry (one hand off), when abruptly he came upon Ann Pornick.

It chanced he was thinking about her at the time. He had been thinking curious things ; whether, after all, the atmosphere of New Romney and the Marsh had not some difference, some faint impalpable quality that was missing in the great and fashionable world of Folkestone behind there on the hill. Here there was a homeliness, a familiarity. He had noted as he passed that old Mr. Cliffordown's gate had been mended with a fresh piece of string. In Folkestone he didn't take notice, and he didn't care if they built three hundred houses. Come to think of it, that was odd. It was fine and grand to have twelve hundred a year ; it was fine to go about on trams and omnibuses and think not a person aboard was as rich as oneself ; it was fine to buy and order this and that and never have any work to do, and to be engaged to a girl distantly related to the Earl of Beauprés ; but yet there had been a zest in the old time out here, a rare zest in the holidays, in sunlight, on the sea beach, and in the High Street, that failed from these new things. He thought of those bright windows of holiday that had seemed so glorious to him in the retrospect from his apprentice days. It was strange that now, amidst his present splendours, they were glorious still !

All those things were over now—perhaps that was it ! Something had happened to the world, and the old light had been turned out. He himself was changed, and Sid was changed, terribly changed, and Ann, no doubt, was changed.

He thought of her with the hair blown about her flushed cheeks as they stood together after their race. . . .

Certainly she must be changed, and all the magic she had been fraught with to the very hem of her short petticoats gone, no doubt, for ever. And as he thought that, or before and while he thought it—for he came to all these things in his own vague and stumbling way—he looked up, and there was Ann !

She was seven years older, and greatly altered ; yet for the moment it seemed to him that she had not changed at all. " Ann ! " he said ; and she, with a lifting note, " It's Art Kipps ! "

Then he became aware of changes—improvements. She was as pretty as she had promised to be, her blue eyes as dark as his memory of them, and with a quick, high colour ; but now Kipps by several inches was the taller again. She was dressed in a simple gray dress, that showed her very clearly as a straight and healthy little woman, and her hat was Sunday-fied, with pink flowers. She looked soft and warm and welcoming. Her face was alight to Kipps with her artless gladness at their encounter.

" It's Art Kipps ! " she said.

" Rather," said Kipps.

" You got your holidays ? "

It flashed upon Kipps that Sid had not told her of his great fortune. Much regretful meditation upon Sid's behaviour had convinced him that he himself was to blame for exasperating boastfulness in that affair, and this time he took care not to err in that direction. So he erred in the other.

" I'm taking a bit of a 'oliday," he said.

" So'm I," said Ann.

" You been for a walk ? " asked Kipps.

Ann showed him a bunch of wayside flowers.

" It's a long time since I seen you, Ann. Why, 'ow long must it be ? Seven—eight years nearly."

" It don't do to count," said Ann.

" It don't look like it," said Kipps, with the slightest emphasis.

" You got a moustache," said Ann, smelling her flowers and looking at him over them, not without admiration.

Kipps blushed. . . .

Presently they came to the bifurcation of the roads.

" I'm going down this way to mother's cottage," said Ann.

" I'll come a bit your way, if I may."

In New Romney social distinctions that are primary realities in Folkestone are absolutely non-existent, and it seemed quite permissible for him to walk with Ann, for all that she was no more than a servant. They talked with remarkable ease to one another, they slipped into a vein of intimate reminiscence in the easiest manner. In a little while Kipps was amazed to find Ann and himself at this—

" You r'member that half-sixpence ? What we cut to-gevver ? "

" Yes ? "

" I got it still."

She hesitated. " Funny, wasn't it ? " she said, and then, " You got yours, Artie ? "

" Rather," said Kipps. " What do *you* think ? " and wondered in his heart of hearts why he had never looked at that sixpence for so long.

Ann smiled at him frankly.

" I didn't expect you'd keep it," she said. " I thought often —it was silly to keep mine.

" Besides," she reflected, " it didn't mean anything really."

She glanced at him as she spoke and met his eye.

" Oh, didn't it ! " said Kipps, a little late with his response, and realising his infidelity to Helen even as he spoke.

" It didn't mean much anyhow," said Ann. " You still in the drapery ? "

" I'm living at Folkestone," began Kipps, and decided that that sufficed. " Didn't Sid tell you he met me ? "

" No ! Here ? "

" Yes. The other day. 'Bout a week or more ago."

" That was before I came."

" Ah, that was it," said Kipps.

" E's got on," said Ann. " Got 'is own shop now, Artie."

" 'E tole me."

They found themselves outside Muggett's cottages. " You're going in ? " said Kipps.

" I s'pose so," said Ann.

They both hung upon the pause. Ann took a plunge.

" D'you often come to New Romney ? " she asked.

" I ride over a bit at times," said Kipps.

K-RM 6

Another pause. Ann held out her hand.

" I'm glad I seen you," she said.

Extraordinary impulses arose in neglected parts of Kipps' being. " Ann," he said, and stopped.

" Yes," said she, and was bright to him.

They looked at one another.

All, and more than all, of those first emotions of his adolescence had come back to him. Her presence banished a multitude of countervailing considerations. It was Ann more than ever. She stood breathing close to him with her soft-looking lips a little apart and gladness in her eyes.

" I'm awful glad to see you again," he said ; " it brings back old times."

" Doesn't it ? "

Another pause. He would have liked to have had a long talk to her, to have gone for a walk with her or something, to have drawn nearer to her in any conceivable way, and above all to have had some more of the appreciation that shone in her eyes, but a vestige of Folkestone, still clinging to him, told him it " wouldn't do." " Well," he said, " I must be getting on," and turned away reluctantly, with a will under compulsion. . . .

When he looked back from the corner she was still at the gate. She was perhaps a little disconcerted by his retreat. He felt that. He hesitated for a moment, half turned, stood, and suddenly did great things with his hat. That hat ! The wonderful hat of our civilisation ! . . .

In another minute he was engaged in a singularly absent-minded conversation with his Uncle about the usual topics.

His Uncle was very anxious to buy him a few upright clocks as an investment for subsequent sale. And there were also some very nice globes, one terrestrial and the other celestial, in a shop at Lydd that would look well in a drawing-room, and inevitably increase in value. . . . Kipps either did or did not agree to this purchase, he was unable to recollect.

The south-west wind perhaps helped him back ; at any rate he found himself through Dymchurch without having noticed the place. There came an odd effect as he drew near Hythe. The hills on the left and the trees on the right seemed to draw together and close in upon him until his way was straight and narrow. He could not turn round on that treacherous half-tamed machine, but he knew that behind him, he knew so well, spread the wide vast flatness of the Marsh shining under the afternoon sky. In some way this was material to his thoughts. And as he rode through Hythe he came upon the idea that there was a considerable amount of incompatability between the existence of one who was practically a gentleman and of Ann.

In the neighbourhood of Seabrook he began to think he had, in some subtle way, lowered himself by walking along

by the side of Ann. . . . After all, she was only a servant.
Ann !

She called out all the least gentlemanly instincts of his
nature. There had been a moment in their conversation when
he had quite distinctly thought it would really be an extremely
nice thing for some one to kiss her lips. . . . There was something warming about Ann—at least for Kipps. She impressed
him as having, somewhen during their vast interval of
separation, contrived to make herself in some distinctive way
his.

Fancy keeping that half-sixpence all this time !

It was the most flattering thing that ever happened to Kipps.

§ 2

He found himself presently sitting over *The Art of Conversing*,
lost in the strangest musings. He got up, walked about, became
stagnant at the window for a space, roused himself, and by
way of something lighter tried *Sesame and Lilies*. From that,
too, his attention wandered. He sat back. Anon he smiled,
anon sighed. He arose, pulled his keys from his pocket, looked
at them, decided, and went upstairs. He opened the little
yellow box that had been the nucleus of all his possessions in
the world, and took out a small *Escritoire*, the very humblest
sort of present, and opened it—kneeling. And there in the
corner was a little packet of paper, sealed as a last defence
against any prying invader with red sealing-wax. It had gone
untouched for years. He held this little packet between finger
and thumb for a moment, regarding it, and then put down the
escritoire and broke the seal. . . .

As he was getting into bed that night he remembered something for the first time !

" Dash it ! " he said. " Deshed if I told 'em *this* time. . .
Well !

" I shall 'ave to go over to New Romney again ! "

He got into bed, and remained sitting pensively on the
pillow for a space.

" Rum world," he reflected, after a vast interval.

Then he recalled that she had noticed his moustache. He
embarked upon a sea of egotistical musing.

He imagined himself telling Ann how rich he was. What
a surprise that would be for her !

Finally he sighed profoundly, blew out his candle, and
snuggled down, and in a little while he was asleep. . . .

But the next morning, and at intervals afterwards, he found
himself thinking of Ann—Ann the bright, the desirable, the
welcoming, and with an extraordinary streakiness he wanted
quite badly to go, and then as badly not to go, over to New
Romney again.

Sitting on the Leas in the afternoon, he had an idea. " I
ought to 'ave told 'er, I suppose, about my being engaged.

" Ann ! "

All sorts of dreams and impressions that had gone clean
out of his mental existence came back to him, changed and
brought up to date to fit her altered presence. He thought of
how he had gone back to New Romney for his Christmas
holidays, determined to kiss her, and of the awful blankness
of the discovery that she had gone away.

It seemed incredible now, and yet not wholly incredible,
that he had cried real tears for her—how many years was it
ago ?

§ 3

Daily I should thank my Maker that He did not delegate
to me the Censorship of the world of men. I should temper a
fierce injustice with a spasmodic indecision, that would prolong
rather than mitigate the bitterness of the Day. For human
dignity, for all conscious human superiority I should lack the
beginnings of charity ; for bishops, prosperous schoolmasters,
judges, and all large respect-pampered souls. And more
especially bishops, towards whom I bear an atavistic Viking
grudge, dreaming not infrequently and with invariable zest
of galleys and landings, and well-known living ornaments of the
episcopal bench sprinting inland on twinkling gaiters before
my thirsty blade—all these people, I say, I should treat below
their deserts ; but, on the other hand, for such as Kipps——
There the exasperating indecisions would come in. The Judgment would be arrested at Kipps. Every one and everything
would wait. The balance would sway and sway, and whenever
it heeled towards an adverse decision, my finger would set it
swaying again. Kings, warriors, statesmen, brilliant women,
" personalities," panting with indignation, headline humanity
in general, would stand undamned, unheeded, or be damned in
the most casual manner for their importunity, while my eye
went about for anything possible that could be said on behalf of
Kipps. . . . Albeit I fear nothing can save him from con-
demnation upon this present score, that within two days he
was talking to Ann again.

One seeks excuses. Overnight there had been an encounter
of Chitterlow and young Walshingham in his presence that had
certainly warped his standards. They had called within a
few minutes of each other, and the two, swayed by virile
attentions to Old Methusaleh Three Stars, had talked against
each other, over and at the hospitable presence of Kipps.
Walshingham had seemed to win at the beginning, but finally
Chitterlow had made a magnificent display of vociferation
and swept him out of existence. At the beginning Chitterlow
had opened upon the great profits of playwrights, and young
Walshingham had capped him at once with a cynical but
impressive display of knowledge of the High Finance. If
Chitterlow boasted his thousands, young Walshingham boasted

his hundreds of thousands, and was for a space left in sole possession of the stage, juggling with the wealth of nations. He was going on by way of Financial Politics to the Overman, before Chitterlow recovered from his first check, and came back to victory. " Talking of women," said Chitterlow, coming in abruptly upon some things not generally known, beyond Walshingham's more immediate circle, about a recently departed Empire-builder ; " Talking of Women and the way they Get at a man——"

(Though, as a matter of fact, they had been talking of the Corruption of Society by Speculation.)

Upon this new topic Chitterlow was soon manifestly invincible. He knew so much, he had known so many. Young Walshingham did his best with epigrams and reservations, but even to Kipps it was evident that his was a book-learned depravity. One felt Walshingham had never known the inner realities of passion. But Chitterlow convinced and amazed. He had run away with girls, he had been run away with by girls, he had been in love with several at a time—" not counting Bessie "—he had loved and lost, he had loved and refrained, and he had loved and failed. He threw remarkable lights upon the moral state of America—in which country he had toured with great success. He set his talk to the tune of one of Mr. Kipling's best-known songs. He told an incident of simple romantic passion, a delirious dream of love and beauty in a Saturday to Monday steamboat trip up the Hudson, and tagged his end with " I learnt about women from 'er ! " After that he adopted the refrain, and then lapsed into the praises of Kipling. " Little Kipling," said Chitterlow, with the familiarity of affection, " *he* knows," and broke into quotation :—

> " I've taken my fun where I've found it ;
>   I've rogued and I've ranged in my time ;
>   I've 'ad my picking of sweet'earts,
>   An' four of the lot was Prime."

(These things, I say, affect the moral standards of the best of us.)

" *I'd* have liked to have written that," said Chitterlow. " That's Life, that is ! But go and put it on the Stage, put even a bit of the Realities of Life on the Stage and see what they'll do to you ! Only Kipling could venture on a job like that. That Poem KNOCKED me ! I won't say Kipling hasn't knocked me before and since, but that was a Fair Knock Out. And yet—you know—there's one thing in it . . . this,—

> " I've taken my fun where I've found it,
>   And now I must pay for my fun,
>   For the more you 'ave known o' the others
>   The less will you settle to one."

Well. In my case anyhow—I don't know how much that
proves, seeing I'm exceptional in so many things and there's
no good denying it—but so far as I'm concerned—I tell you
two, but, of course, you needn't let it go any farther—I've
been perfectly faithful to Muriel ever since I married her—
ever since. . . . Not once. Not even by accident have I ever
said or done anything in the slightest——" His little brown
eye became pensive after this flattering intimacy, and the
gorgeous draperies of his abundant voice fell into graver folds.
" *I learnt about women from 'er*," he said impressively.

" Yes," said Walshingham, getting into the hinder spaces
of that splendid pause, " a man must know about women.
And the only sound way of learning is the experimental method."

" If you want to know about the experimental method, my
boy," said Chitterlow, resuming. . . .

So they talked. *Ex pede Herculem*, as Coote, that cultivated
polyglot, would have put it. And in the small hours Kipps
went to bed, with his brain whirling with words and whisky,
and sat for an unconscionable time upon his bed edge, musing
sadly upon the unmanly monogamy that had cast its shadow
upon his career, musing with his thoughts pointing round more
and more certainly to the possibility of at least duplicity with
Ann.

§ 4

For some days he had been refraining with some insistence
from going off to New Romney again. . . .

I do not know if this may count in palliation of his mis-
conduct. Men, real Strong-Souled, Healthy Men, should be,
I suppose, impervious to conversational atmospheres, but I
have never claimed for Kipps a place at these high levels.
The fact remains, that next day he spent the afternoon with
Ann, and found no scruple in displaying himself a budding
lover.

He had met her in the High Street, had stopped her, and
almost on the spur of the moment had boldly proposed a
walk, " for the sake of old times."

" *I* don't mind," said Ann.

Her consent almost frightened Kipps. His imagination
had not carried him to that. " It would be a lark," said Kipps,
and looked up the street and down. " Now ? " he said.

" I don't mind a bit, Artie. I was just going for a walk
along towards St Mary's."

" Let's go that way be'ind the church," said Kipps ; and
presently they found themselves drifting seaward in a mood
of pleasant commonplace. For a while they talked of Sid.
It went clean out of Kipps' head, at that early stage even,
that Ann was a " girl " according to the exposition of Chitterlow, and for a time he remembered only that she was Ann.
But afterwards, with the reek of that talk in his head, he

lapsed a little from that personal relation. They came out upon the beach and sat down in a tumbled pebbly place where a meagre grass and patches of sea poppy were growing, and Kipps reclined on his elbow and tossed pebbles in his hand, and Ann sat up, sunlit, regarding him. They talked in fragments. They exhausted Sid, they exhausted Ann, and Kipps was chary of his riches.

He declined to a faint lovemaking. " I got that 'arf-sixpence still," he said.

" Reely ? "

That changed the key. " I always kept mine, some'ow," said Ann ; and there was a pause.

They spoke of how often they had thought of each other during those intervening years. Kipps may have been untruthful, but Ann, perhaps, was not. " I met people here and there," said Ann ; " but I never met any one quite like you, Artie."

" It's jolly our meeting again, anyhow," said Kipps. " Look at that ship out there. She's pretty close in. . . ."

He had a dull period, became, indeed, almost pensive, and then he was enterprising for a while. He tossed up his pebbles so that, as if by accident, they fell on Ann's hand. Then, very penitently, he stroked the place. That would have led to all sorts of coquetries on the part of Flo Bates, for example, but it disconcerted and checked Kipps to find Ann made no objection, smiled pleasantly down on him, with eyes half shut because of the sun. She was taking things very much for granted.

He began to talk, and Chitterlow standards resuming possession of him, he said he had never forgotten her.

" I never forgotten you either, Artie," she said. " Funny, 'sn't it ? "

It impressed Kipps also as funny.

He became reminiscent, and suddenly a warm summer's evening came back to him. " Remember them cockchafers, Ann ? " he said. But the reality of the evening he recalled was not the chase of cockchafers. The great reality that had suddenly arisen between them was that he had never kissed Ann in his life. He looked up, and there were her lips.

He had wanted to very badly, and his memory leaped and annihilated an interval. That old resolution came back to him, and all sorts of new resolutions passed out of mind. And he had learnt something since those boyish days. This time he did not ask. He went on talking, his nerves began very faintly to quiver, and his mind grew bright.

Presently, having satisfied himself that there was no one to see, he sat up beside her, and remarked upon the clearness of the air, and how close Dungeness seemed to them. Then they came upon a pause again.

" Ann," he whispered, and put an arm that quivered about her.

She was mute and unresisting, and, as he was to remember, solemn.

He turned her face towards him and kissed her lips, and she kissed him back again—kisses frank and tender as a child's.

§ 5

It was curious that in the retrospect he did not find nearly the satisfaction in this infidelity he had imagined was there. It was no doubt desperately doggish, doggish to an almost Chitterlowesque degree, to recline on the beach at Littlestone with a " girl," to make love to her and to achieve the triumph of her, kissing when he was engaged to another " girl " at Folkestone ; but somehow these two people were not " girls," they were Ann and Helen. Particularly Helen declined to be considered as a " girl." And there was something in Ann's quietly friendly eyes, in her frank smile, in the naïve pressure of her hand, there was something undefended and welcoming that imparted a flavour to the business upon which he had not counted. He had learnt about women from her. That refrain ran through his mind and deflected his thoughts, but, as a matter of fact, he had learnt about nothing but himself.

He wanted very much to see Ann some more and explain—— He did not clearly know what it was he wanted to explain.

He did not clearly know anything. It is the last achievement of the intelligence to get all of one's life into one coherent scheme, and Kipps was only in a measure more aware of himself as a whole than is a tree. His existence was an affair of dissolving and recurring moods. When he thought of Helen or Ann, or any of his friends, he thought sometimes of this aspect and sometimes of that—and often one aspect was finally incongruous with another. He loved Helen, he revered Helen. He was also beginning to hate her with some intensity. When he thought of that expedition to Lympne, profound, vague, beautiful emotions flooded his being ; when he thought of paying calls with her perforce, or of her latest comment on his bearing, he found himself rebelliously composing fierce and pungent insults, couched in the vernacular. But Ann, whom he had seen so much less of, was a simpler memory. She was pretty, she was almost softly feminine, and she was possible to his imagination just exactly where Helen was impossible. More than anything else, she carried the charm of respect for him, the slightest glance of her eyes was balm for his perpetually wounded self-conceit.

Chance suggestions it was set the tune of his thoughts, and his state of health and repletion gave the colour. Yet somehow he had this at least almost clear in his mind, that to have gone to see Ann a second time, to have implied that she had been in possession of his thoughts through all this interval, and, above all, to have kissed her, was shabby and wrong. Only, unhappily, this much of lucidity had come now just a few hours after it was needed.

§ 6

Four days after this it was that Kipps got up so late. He got up late, cut his chin while shaving, kicked a slipper into his sponge bath, and said " Dash ! "

Perhaps you know those intolerable mornings, dear Reader, when you seem to have neither the heart nor the strength to rise, and your nervous adjustments are all wrong and your fingers thumbs, and you hate the very birds for singing. You feel inadequate to any demand whatever. Often such awakenings follow a poor night's rest, and commonly they mean indiscriminate eating, or those subtle mental influences old Kipps ascribed to " Foozle Ile " in the system, or worry. And with Kipps—albeit Chitterlow had again been his guest overnight—assuredly worry had played a leading rôle. Troubles had been gathering upon him for days, there had been a sort of concentration of these hosts of Midian overnight, and in the gray small hours Kipps had held his review.

The predominating trouble marched under this banner—a

MR. KIPPS.

MRS. BINDON BOTTING

At Home,

Thursday, September 16th.

Anagrams, 4 to 6.30.   R.S.V.P.

banner that was the facsimile of a card upon his looking-glass in the room below. And in relation to this terribly significant document, things had come to a pass with Helen, that he would only describe in his own expressive idiom as " words."

It had long been a smouldering issue between them that Kipps was not availing himself with any energy or freedom of the opportunities he had of social exercises, much less was he seeking additional opportunities. He had, it was evident, a peculiar dread of that universal afternoon enjoyment, the Call, and Helen made it unambiguously evident that this dread was " silly " and had to be overcome. His first display of this unmanly weakness occurred at the Cootes on the day before he kissed Ann. They were all there, chatting very pleasantly, when the little servant with the big cap announced the younger Miss Wace.

Whereupon Kipps manifested a lively horror and rose partially from his chair. "O Gum!" he protested. "Carn't I go upstairs?"

Then he sank back, for it was too late. Very probably the younger Miss Wace had heard him as she came in.

Helen said nothing of that, though her manner may have shown her surprise, but afterwards she told Kipps he must get used to seeing people, and suggested that he should pay a series of calls with Mrs. Walshingham and herself. Kipps gave a reluctant assent at the time, and afterwards displayed a talent for evasion that she had not expected in him. At last she did succeed in securing him for a call upon Miss Punchafer of Radnor Park—a particularly easy call, because, Miss Punchafer being so deaf, one could say practically what one liked—and then outside the gate he shirked again. "I can't go in," he said, in a faded voice.

"You must," said Helen, beautiful as ever, but even more than a little hard and forbidding.

"I can't."

He produced his handkerchief hastily, thrust it to his face, and regarded her over it with rounded hostile eyes.

"Possible," he said in a hoarse, strange voice out of the handkerchief. "Nozzez bleedin'." . . .

But that was the end of his power of resistance, and when the rally for the Anagram Tea occurred, she bore down his feeble protests altogether. She insisted. She said frankly, "I am going to give you a good talking to about this"; and she did. . . .

From Coote he gathered something of the nature of Anagrams and Anagram parties. An anagram, Coote explained, was a word spelt the same way as another, only differently arranged; as, for instance, T.O.C.O.E. would be an anagram for his own name Coote.

"T.O.C.O.E.," repeated Kipps, very carefully.

"Or T.O.E.C.O.," said Coote.

"Or T.O.E.C.O.," said Kipps, assisting his poor head by nodding it at each letter.

"Toe Company, like," he said, in his efforts to comprehend.

When Kipps was clear what an anagram meant, Coote came to the second heading, the Tea. Kipps gathered there might be from thirty to sixty people present, and that each one would have an anagram pinned on. "They gave you a card to put your guesses on, rather like a dence programme, and then, you know, you go round and guess," said Coote. "It's rather good fun."

'Oo, rather!" said Kipps, with simulated gusto.

" It shakes everybody up together," said Coote.

Kipps smiled and nodded. . . .

In the small hours all his painful meditations were threaded by the vision of that Anagram Tea ; it kept marching to and fro and in and out of his other troubles, from thirty to sixty people, mostly ladies and callers, and a great number of the letters of the alphabet, and more particularly P.I.K.P.S. and T.O.E.C.O., and he was trying to make one word out of the whole interminable procession. . . .

This word, as he finally gave it with some emphasis to the silence of the night, was, " *Demn !* "

Then wreathed as it were in this lettered procession was the figure of Helen as she had appeared at the moment of " words " ; her face a little hard, a little irritated, a little disappointed. He imagined himself going round and guessing under her eye. . . .

He tried to think of other things, without lapsing upon a still deeper uneasiness that was decorated with yellow sea-poppies, and the figures of Buggins, Pearce, and Carshot, three murdered friendships, rose reproachfully in the stillness and changed horrible apprehensions into unspeakable remorse. Last night had been their customary night for the banjo, and Kipps, with a certain tremulous uncertainty, had put Old Methusaleh amidst a retinue of glasses on the table and opened a box of choice cigars. In vain. They were in no need, it seemed, of *his* society. But instead Chitterlow had come, anxious to know if it was all right about that syndicate plan. He had declined anything but a very weak whisky-and-soda, " just to drink," at least until business was settled, and had then opened the whole affair with an effect of great orderliness to Kipps. Soon he was taking another whisky by sheer inadvertency, and the complex fabric of his conversation was running more easily from the broad loom of his mind. Into that pattern had interwoven a narrative of extensive alterations in the Pestered Butterfly—the neck-and-beetle business was to be restored—the story of a grave difference of opinion with Mrs. Chitterlow, where and how to live after the play had succeeded, the reasons why the Hon. Thomas Norgate had never financed a syndicate, and much matter also about the syndicate now under discussion. But if the current of their conversation had been vortical and crowded, the outcome was perfectly clear. Kipps was to be the chief participator in the syndicate, and his contribution was to be two thousand pounds. Kipps groaned and rolled over, and found Helen again, as it were, on the other side. " Promise me," she had said, " you won't do anything without consulting me."

Kipps at once rolled back to his former position, and for a space lay quite still. He felt like a very young rabbit in a trap.

Then suddenly, with extraordinary distinctness, his heart

cried out for Ann, and he saw her as he had seen her at New Romney, sitting amidst the yellow sea-poppies with the sunlight on her face. His heart called out for her in the darkness as one calls for rescue. He knew, as though he had known it always, that he loved Helen no more. He wanted Ann, he wanted to hold her and be held by her, to kiss her again and again, to turn his back for ever on all these other things. . . .

He rose late, but this terrible discovery was still there, undispelled by cockcrow or the day. He rose in a shattered condition, and he cut himself while shaving, but at last he got into his dining-room, and could pull the bell for the hot constituents of his multifarious breakfast. And then he turned to his letters. There were two real letters in addition to the customary electric-belt advertisement, continental lottery circular, and betting tout's card. One was in a slight mourning envelope, and addressed in an unfamiliar hand. This he opened first, and discovered a note,—

MRS. RAYMOND WACE

requests the pleasure of

MR. KIPPS'

Company at Dinner

on Tuesday, Sept. 21st, at 8 o'clock.

R.S.V.P.

With a hasty movement Kipps turned his mind to the second letter. It was an unusually long one from his Uncle, and ran as follows :—

" MY DEAR NEPHEW,—We are considerably startled by your letter, though expecting something of the sort and disposed to hope for the best. If the young lady is a relation to the Earl of Beauprés well and good but take care you are not being imposed upon for there are many who will be glad enough to snap you up now your circumstances are altered. I waited on the old Earl once while in service and he was remarkably close with his tips and suffered from corns. A hasty old gent and hard to please—I dare say he has forgotten me altogether—and anyhow there is no need to rake up bygones. To-morrow is bus day and as you say the young lady is living near by we shall shut up shop for there is really nothing doing now what with all the visitors bringing everything with them down to their very children's pails and say how de do to her and give her a bit of a kiss and encouragement if we think her suitable—she will be pleased to see your old uncle. We wish we could have had a look at her first but still there is not much mischief done and hoping that all will turn out well yet I am

" Your affectionate Uncle

" EDWARD GEORGE KIPPS.

" My heartburn still very bad. I shall bring over a few bits of rhubarb I picked up, a sort you won't get in Folkestone and if possible a good bunch of flowers for the young lady."

" Comin' over to-day," said Kipps, standing helplessly with the letter in his hand.

" 'Ow the Juice—— ? "

" I carn't."

" Kiss 'er ! "

A terrible anticipation of that gathering framed itself in his mind, a hideous, impossible disaster.

" I carn't even face 'er—— ! "

His voice went up to a note of despair. " And it's too late to telegraf and stop 'em ! "

§ 7

About twenty minutes after this, an out-porter in Castle Hill Avenue was accosted by a young man with a pale, desperate face, an exquisitely rolled umbrella, and a heavy Gladstone bag.

" Carry this to the station, will you ? " said the young man. " I want to ketch the nex' train to London. . . . You'll 'ave to look sharp ; I 'even't very much time."

CHAPTER SEVEN

LONDON

§ 1

LONDON was Kipps' third world. There were, no doubt, other worlds, but Kipps knew only these three : firstly, New Romney and the Emporium, constituting his primary world, his world of origin, which also contained Ann ; secondly, the world of culture and refinement, the world of which Coote was chaperon, and into which Kipps was presently to marry, a world, it was fast becoming evident, absolutely incompatible with the first ; and thirdly, a world still to a large extent unexplored, London. London presented itself as a place of great gray spaces and incredible multitudes of people, centring about Charing Cross station and the Royal Grand Hotel, and containing at unexpected arbitrary points shops of the most amazing sort, statuary, squares, restaurants—where it was possible for clever people like Walshingham to order a lunch item by item to the waiters' evident respect and sympathy—exhibitions of incredible things—the Walshinghams had taken him to the Arts and Crafts and to a Picture Gallery —and theatres. London, moreover, is rendered habitable by hansom cabs. Young Walshingham was a natural cab-taker ; he was an all-round, large-minded young man, and he had

in the course of their two days' stay taken Kipps into no
less than nine, so that Kipps was singularly not afraid of these
vehicles. He knew that wherever you were, so soon as you
were thoroughly lost, you said " Hi ! " to a cab, and then
" Royal Grend Hotel." Day and night these trusty con-
veyances are returning the strayed Londoner back to his
point of departure, and were it not for their activity, in a
little while the whole population, so vast and incomprehensible
is the intricate complexity of this great city, would be hopelessly lost for ever. At any rate, that is how the thing
presented itself to Kipps, and I have heard much the same
from visitors from America.

His train was composed of corridor carriages, and he forgot
his troubles for a time in the wonders of this modern substitute
for railway compartments. He went from the non-smoking
to the smoking carriage, and smoked a cigarette, and strayed
from his second-class carriage to a first and back. But
presently Black Care got aboard the train and came and
sat beside him. The exhilaration of escape had evaporated
now, and he was presented with a terrible picture of his Aunt
and Uncle arriving at his lodgings and finding him fled. He
had left a hasty message that he was called away suddenly
on business, " ver' important business," and they were to
be sumptuously entertained. His immediate motive had been
his passionate dread of an encounter between these excellent
but unrefined old people and the Walshinghams, but now
that end was secured, he could see how thwarted and ex-
asperated they would be.

How to explain to them ?

He ought never to have written to tell them !

He ought to have got married, and told them afterwards.

He ought to have consulted Helen.

" Promise me," she had said.

" Oh, *desh* ! " said Kipps, and got up and walked back
into the smoking car and began to consume cigarettes.

Suppose, after all, they found out the Walshinghams'
address and went there !

At Charing Cross, however, were distractions again. He
took a cab in an entirely Walshingham manner, and was
pleased to note the enhanced respect of the cabman when
he mentioned the Royal Grand. He followed Walshingham's
routine on their previous visit with perfect success. They were
very nice in the office, and gave him an excellent room at
fourteen shillings the night. He went up and spent a considerable time examining the
furniture of his room, scrutinising himself in its various mirrors,
and sitting on the edge of the bed whistling. It was a vast
and splendid apartment, and cheap at fourteen shillings.
But finding the figure of Ann inclined to resume possession
of his mind, he roused himself and descended by the staircase,

after a momentary hesitation before the lift. He had thought of lunch, but he drifted into the great drawing-room, and read a guide to the Hotels of Europe for a space, until a doubt whether he was entitled to use this palatial apartment without extra charge arose in his mind. He would have liked something to eat very much now, but his inbred terror of the table was strong. He did at last get by a porter in uniform towards the dining-room, but at the sight of a number of waiters and tables with remarkable complications of knives and glasses, terror seized him, and he backed out again with a mumbled remark to the waiter in the doorway about this not being the way.

He hovered in the hall and lounge until he thought the presiding porter regarded him with suspicion, and then went up to his room again by the staircase, got his hat and umbrella, and struck out boldy across the courtyard. He would go to a restaurant instead.

He had a moment of elation in the gateway. He felt all the Strand must notice him as he emerged through the great gate of the hotel. " One of these here rich swells," they would say. " Don't they go it just ! " A cabman touched his hat. " No fear," said Kipps pleasantly. . . .

Then he remembered he was hungry again.

Yet he decided he was in no great hurry for lunch, in spite of an internal protest, and turned eastward along the Strand in a leisurely manner. He would find a place to suit him soon enough. He tried to remember the sort of things Walshingham had ordered. Before all things he didn't want to go into a place and look like a fool. Some of these places rook you dreadful, besides making fun of you. There was a place near Essex Street where there was a window brightly full of chops, tomatoes, and lettuce. He stopped at this and reflected for a time, and then it occurred to him that you were expected to buy these things raw and cook them at home. Anyhow, there was sufficient doubt in the matter to stop him. He drifted on to a neat window with champagne bottles, a dish of asparagus, and a framed menu of a two-shilling lunch. He was about to enter, when fortunately he perceived two waiters looking at him over the back screen of the window with a most ironical expression, and he sheered off at once. There was a wonderful smell of hot food half-way down Fleet Street, and a nice-looking tavern with several doors, but he could not decide which door. His nerve was going under the strain.

He hesitated at Farringdon Street, and drifted up to St. Paul's and round the churchyard, full chiefly of dead bargains in the shop windows, to Cheapside. But now Kipps was getting demoralised, and each house of refreshment seemed to promise still more complicated obstacles to food. He didn't know how you went in, and what was the correct thing to do with your hat ; he didn't know what you said to the waiter, or what you called the different things ; he was convinced absolutely he would " fumble," as Shalford would have said, and look like a fool. Somebody might laugh at him ! The hungrier he got, the more unendurable was the thought that any one should laugh at him. For a time he considered an extraordinary expedient to account for his ignorance. He would go in and pretend to be a foreigner, and not know English. Then they might understand. . . . Presently he had drifted into a part of London where there did not seem to be any refreshment places at all.

" Oh, *desh* ! " said Kipps, in a sort of agony of indecisiveness. " The very nex' place I see, in I go."

The next place was a fried-fish shop in a little side street, where there were also sausages on a gas-lit grill.

He would have gone in, but suddenly a new scruple came to him, that he was too well dressed for the company he could see dimly through the steam sitting at the counter and eating with a sort of nonchalant speed.

§ 2

He was half minded to resort to a hansom and brave the terrors of the dining-room of the Royal Grand—they wouldn't know why he had gone out really—when the only person he knew in London appeared (as the only person one does know will do in London) and slapped him on the shoulder. Kipps was hovering at a window at a few yards from the fish shop pretending to examine some really strikingly cheap pink baby-linen, and trying to settle finally about those sausages. " Hullo, Kipps ! " cried Sid, " spending the millions ? "

Kipps turned and was glad to perceive no lingering vestige of the chagrin that had been so painful at New Romney. Sid looked grave and important, and he wore a quite new silk hat that gave a commercial touch to a generally socialistic costume. For the moment the sight of Sid uplifted Kipps wonderfully. He saw him as a friend and helper, and only presently did it come clearly into his mind that this was the brother of Ann.

He made amiable noises.

" I've just been up this way," Sid explained, " buying a second-hand 'namelling stove. . . . I'm going to 'namel myself."

" Lor ! " said Kipps.

" Yes. Do me a lot of good. Let the customer choose his colour. See ? What brings *you* up ? "

Kipps had a momentary vision of his foiled Uncle and Aunt. " Jest a bit of a change," he said.

Sid came to a swift decision. " Come down to my little show. I got some one I'd like to see talking to you."

Even then Kipps did not think of Ann in this connection.

"Well," he said, trying to invent an excuse on the spur of the moment. "Fact is," he explained, "I was jest looking round to get a bit of lunch."

"Dinner we call it," said Sid. "But that's all right. You can't get anything to eat hereabout. If you're not too haughty to do a bit of slumming, there's some mutton spoiling for me now——"

The word mutton affected Kipps greatly.

"It won't take us 'arf an hour," said Sid, and Kipps was carried.

He discovered another means of London locomotion in the Underground Railway, and recovered his self-possession in that interest. "You don't mind going third?" asked Sid; and Kipps said, "Nort a *bit* of it." They were silent in the train for a time, on account of strangers in the carriage, and then Sid began to explain who it was he wanted Kipps to meet. "It's a chap named Masterman do you no end of good.

"He occupies our first-floor front room, you know. It isn't so much for gain I let as company. We don't *want* the whole 'ouse, that's one thing, and another is I knew the man before. Met him at our Sociological, and after a bit he said he wasn't comfortable where he was. That's how it came about. He's a first-class chap—first class. Science! You should see his books!

"Properly he's a sort of journalist. He's written a lot of things, but he's been too ill lately to do very much. Poetry he's written, all sorts. He writes for the *Commonweal* sometimes, and sometimes he reviews books. 'E's got 'eaps of books —'eaps. Besides selling a lot.

"He knows a regular lot of people, and all sorts of things. He's been a dentist, and he's a qualified chemist, and I seen 'im often reading German and French. Taught 'imself. He was here——"

Sid indicated South Kensington, which had come opportunely outside the carriage windows, with a nod of his head, "—— three years. Studying science. But you'll see 'im. When he really gets to talking—he *pours* it out."

"Ah!" said Kipps, nodding sympathetically, with his two hands on his umbrella knob.

"He'll do big things some day," said Sid. "He's written a book on science already. *Physiography*, it's called. *Elementary Physiography*! Some day he'll write an Advanced—when he gets time."

He let this soak into Kipps.

"I can't introduce you to lords and swells," he went on, "but I *can* show you a Famous Man, that's going to be. I *can* do that. Leastways—— Unless——"

Sid hesitated.

"He's got a frightful cough," he said.

"He won't care to talk to me," weighed Kipps.

"That's all right ; *he* won't mind. He's fond of talking. He'd talk to any one," said Sid reassuringly, and added a perplexing bit of Londonised Latin. "He doesn't *pute* anything, *non alienum*. You know."

"*I* know," said Kipps intelligently, over his umbrella knob, though of course that was altogether untrue.

§ 3

Kipps found Sid's shop a practical-looking establishment, stocked with the most remarkable collection of bicycles and pieces of bicycle that he had ever beheld. "My hiring stock," said Sid, with a wave to this ironmongery ; "and there's the best machine at a democratic price in London, The Red Flag, built by *me*. See ? "

He indicated a graceful gray brown framework in the window. "And there's my stock of accessories—store prices."

"Go in for motors a bit," added Sid.

"Mutton ? " said Kipps, not hearing him distinctly.

"Motors, I *said*. . . . 'Owever, Mutton Department here " ; and he opened a door that had a curtain-guarded window in its upper panel, to reveal a little room with ,ed walls and green furniture, with a white-clothed table and the generous promise of a meal. "Fanny ! " he shouted. "Here's Art Kipps."

A bright-eyed young woman of five or six-and-twenty in a pink print appeared, a little flushed from cooking, and wiped a hand on an apron and shook hands and smiled and said it would all be ready in a minute. She went on to say she had heard of Kipps and his luck, and meanwhile Sid vanished to draw the beer, and returned with two glasses for himself and Kipps.

"Drink that," said Sid ; and Kipps felt all the better for it.

"I give Mr. Masterman '*is* upstairs a hour ago," said Mrs. Sid. "I didn't think 'e ought to wait."

A rapid succession of brisk movements on the part of every one and they were all four at dinner—the fourth person being Master Walt Whitman Pornick, a cheerful young gentleman of one and a half, who was given a spoon to hammer on the table with, to keep him quiet, and who got "Kipps" right at the first effort and kept it all through the meal, combining it first with this previous acquisition and then that. "Peacock Kipps," said Master Walt, at which there was great laughter, and also "More Mutton Kipps."

"He's a regular oner," said Mrs. Sid, "for catching up words. You can't say a word but what 'e's on to it."

There were no serviettes and less ceremony, and Kipps thought he had never enjoyed a meal so much. Every one was a little excited by the meeting and chatting and disposed

to laugh, and things went easily from the very beginning.
If there was a pause, Master Walt filled it in. Mrs. Sid, who
tempered her enormous admiration for Sid's intellect and his
Socialism and his severe business methods by a motherly
sense of her sex and seniority, spoke of them both as " you
boys," and dilated—when she was not urging Kipps to have
some more of this or that—on the disparity between herself
and her husband.

" Shouldn't ha' thought there was a year between you,"
said Kipps ; " you seem jest a match."

" *I'm his* match anyhow," said Mrs. Sid, and no epigram
of young Walshingham's was ever better received.

" Match," said young Walt, coming in on the tail of the
joke and getting a round for himself.

Any sense of superior fortune had long vanished from
Kipps' mind, and he found himself looking at host and
hostess with enormous respect. Really old Sid was a wonderful
chap, here in his own house at two-and-twenty, carving his
own mutton and lording it over wife and child. No legacies
needed by him ! And Mrs. Sid, so kind and bright and hearty !
And the child, old Sid's child ! Old Sid had jumped round a
bit. It needed the sense of his fortune at the back of his
mind to keep Kipps from feeling abject. He resolved he'd buy
young Walt something tremendous in toys at the very first
opportunity.

" Drop more beer, Art ? "

" Right you are, old man."

" Cut Mr. Kipps a bit more bread, Sid."

" Can't I pass *you* a bit ? " . . .

Sid was all right, Sid was ; there was no mistake about
that.

It was growing up in his mind that Sid was the brother
of Ann, but he said nothing about her, for excellent reasons.
After all, Sid's irritation at her name when they had met
in New Romney seemed to show a certain separation. They
didn't tell each other much. . . . He didn't know how things
might be between Ann and Mrs. Sid either.

Still, for all that, Sid was Ann's brother.

The furniture of the room did not assert itself very much
above the cheerful business of the table, but Kipps was impressed with the idea that it was pretty. There was a dresser
at the end with a number of gay plates and a mug or so, a
Labour Day poster by Walter Crane on the wall, and through
the glass and over the blind of the shop door one had a glimpse
of the bright-colour advertisement cards of bicycle dealers,
and a shelfful of boxes labelled The Paragon Bell, The Scarum
Bell, and The Patent Omi ! Horn. . . .

It seemed incredible that he had been in Folkestone that
morning, that even now his Aunt and Uncle—— !

B-r-r-r. It didn't do to think of his Aunt and Uncle.

§ 4

When Sid repeated his invitation to come and see Masterman, Kipps, now flushed with beer and Irish stew, said he
didn't mind if he did, and after a preliminary shout from
Sid that was answered by a voice and a cough, the two went
upstairs.

"Masterman's a rare one," said Sid over his arm and in
an undertone. "You should hear him speak at a meeting.
. . . If he's in form, that is."

He rapped, and went into a large, untidy room.

"This is Kipps," he said. "You know. The chap I told
you of. With twelve 'undred a year."

Masterman sat gnawing an empty pipe, and as close to
the fire as though it was alight and the season mid-winter.
Kipps concentrated upon him for a space, and only later
took in something of the frowsy furniture, the little bed
half behind, and evidently supposed to be wholly behind
a careless screen, the spittoon by the fender, the remains of
a dinner on the chest of drawers, and the scattered books
and papers. Masterman's face showed him a man of forty
or more, with curious hollows at the side of his forehead and
about his eyes. His eyes were very bright, there was a spot
of red in his cheeks, and the wiry black moustache under his
short red nose had been trimmed with scissors into a sort
of brush along his upper lip. His teeth were darkened ruins.
His jacket collar was turned up about a knitted white neck-
wrap, and his sleeves betrayed no cuffs. He did not rise to
greet Kipps, but he held out a thin-wristed hand and pointed
with the other to a bedroom arm-chair.

"Glad to see you," he said. "Sit down and make yourself
at home. Will you smoke?"

Kipps said he would, and produced his store. He was
about to take one, and then with a civil afterthought handed
the packet first to Masterman and Sid. Masterman pretended
surprise to find his pipe out before he took one. There was
an interlude of matches. Sid pushed the end of the screen
out of his way, sat down on the bed thus frankly admitted,
and prepared, with a certain quiet satisfaction of manner,
to witness Masterman's treatment of Kipps.

"And how does it feel to have twelve hundred a year?"
asked Masterman, holding his cigarette to his nose tip in a
curious manner.

"It's rum," confided Kipps, after a reflective interval.
"It feels juiced rum."

"I've never felt it," said Masterman.

"It takes a bit of getting into," said Kipps. "I can tell
you that."

Masterman smoked and regarded Kipps with curious eyes.

" I expect it does," he said presently.

" And has it made you perfectly happy ? " he asked abruptly.

" I couldn't 'ardly say *that*," said Kipps.

Masterman smiled. " No," he said. " Has it made you much happier ? "

" It did at first."

" Yes. But you got used to it. How long, for example, did the real delirious excitement last ? "

" Oo, *that* ! Perhaps a week," said Kipps.

Masterman nodded his head. " That's what discourages *me* from amassing wealth," he said to Sid. " You adjust yourself. It doesn't last. I've always had an inkling of that, and it's interesting to get it confirmed. I shall go on sponging for a bit longer on *you*, I think."

" You don't," said Sid. " No fear."

" Twenty-four thousand pounds," said Masterman, and blew a cloud of smoke. " Lord ! Doesn't it worry you ? "

" It is a bit worrying at times. . . . Things 'appen."

" Going to marry ? "

" Yes."

" H'm. Lady, I guess, of a superior social position ? "

" Rather," said Kipps. " Cousin to the Earl of Beauprés."

Masterman readjusted his long body with an air of having accumulated all the facts he needed. He snuggled his shoulder-blades down into the chair and raised his angular knees. " I doubt," he said, flicking cigarette ash into the atmosphere, " if any great gain or loss of money does—as things are at present—make more than the slightest difference in one's happiness. It ought to—if money was what it ought to be, the token given for service, one ought to get an increase in power and happiness for every pound one got. But the plain fact is, the times are out of joint, and money—money, like everything else—is a deception and a disappointment."

He turned his face to Kipps and enforced his next words with the index finger of his lean lank hand. " If I thought otherwise," he said, " I should exert myself to get some. But—if one sees things clearly one is so discouraged. So confoundedly discouraged. . . . When you first got your money you thought that it meant you might buy just anything you fancied ? "

" It was a bit that way," said Kipps.

" And you found you couldn't. You found that for all sorts of things it was a question of where to buy and how to buy, and what you didn't know how to buy with your money, straight away this world planted something else upon you."

" I got rather done over a banjo first day," said Kipps. " Leastways, my uncle says so."

" Exactly," said Masterman.

Sid began to speak from the bed. " That's all very well,

Masterman," he said, " but after all, money *is* Power, you
know. You can do all sorts of things——"

" I'm talking of happiness," said Masterman. " You can
do all sorts of things with a loaded gun in the Hammersmith
Broadway, but nothing—practically—that will make you or
any one else very happy. Nothing. Power's a different matter
altogether. As for happiness, you want a world in order
before money or property, or any of those things have any
real value, and this world, I tell you, is hopelessly out of
joint. Man is a social animal with a mind nowadays that
goes round the globe, and a community cannot be happy in
one part and unhappy in another. It's all or nothing, no
patching any more for ever. It is the standing mistake of the
world not to understand that. Consequently people think
there is a class or order somewhere just above them or just
below them, or a country or place somewhere that is really
safe and happy. . . . The fact is, Society is one body, and it
is either well or ill. That's the law. This society we live in
is ill. It's a fractious, feverish invalid, gouty, greedy, ill-
nourished. You can't have a happy left leg with neuralgia,
or a happy throat with a broken leg. That's my position,
and that's the knowledge you'll come to. I'm so satisfied of
it that I sit here and wait for my end quite calmly, sure that
I can't better things by bothering—in my time and so far
as I am concerned that is. I'm not even greedy any more—
my egotism's at the bottom of a pond with a philosophical
brick round its neck. The world is ill, my time is short, and
my strength is small. I'm as happy here as anywhere."

He coughed, was silent for a moment, then brought the
index finger round to Kipps again. " You've had the opportunity of sampling two grades of society, and you don't find
the new people you're among much better or any happier
than the old ? "

" No," said Kipps reflectively. " No. I 'aven't seen it
quite like that before, but—— No. They're not."

" And you might go all up the scale and down the scale
and find the same thing. Man's a gregarious beast, a gregarious beast, and no money will buy you out of your own
time—any more than out of your own skin. All the way up
and all the way down the scale there's the same discontent.
No one is quite sure where they stand, and every one's fretting.
The herd's uneasy and feverish. All the old tradition goes
or has gone, and there's no one to make a new tradition.
Where are your nobles now ? Where are your gentlemen ?
They vanished directly the peasant found out he wasn't
happy and ceased to be a peasant. There's big men and
little men mixed up together, and that's all. None of us
know where we are. Your cads in a bank-holiday train, and
your cads on a two-thousand-pound motor, except for a
difference in scale, there's not a pin to choose between them.

Your smart society is as low and vulgar and uncomfortable
for a balanced soul as a gin palace, no more and no less ;
there's no place or level of honour or fine living left in the
world, so what's the good of climbing ? "

" 'Ear, 'ear," said Sid.

" It's true," said Kipps.

" *I* don't climb," said Masterman, and accepted Kipps'
silent offer of another cigarette.

" No," he said. " This world is out of joint. It's broken
up, and I doubt if it'll heal. I doubt very much if it'll heal.
We're in the beginning of the Sickness of the World."

He rolled his cigarette in his lean fingers and repeated with
satisfaction, " The Sickness of the World."

" It's we've got to make it better," said Sid, and looked
at Kipps.

" Ah, Sid's an optimist," said Masterman.

" So you are, most times," said Sid.

Kipps lit another cigarette with an air of intelligent participation.

" Frankly," said Masterman, recrossing his legs and ex-
pelling a jet of smoke luxuriously, " frankly, I think this
civilisation of ours is on the topple."

" There's Socialism," said Sid.

" There's no imagination to make use of it."

" We've got to *make* one," said Sid.

" In a couple of centuries, perhaps," said Masterman.
" But meanwhile we're going to have a pretty acute attack
of universal confusion. Universal confusion. Like one of
those crushes when men are killed and maimed for no reason
at all, going into a meeting or crowding for a train. Commercial and Industrial Stresses. Political Exploitation. Tariff
Wars. Revolutions. All the bloodshed that will come of
some fools calling half the white world yellow. These things
alter the attitude of everybody to everybody. Everybody's
going to feel 'em. Every fool in the world panting and shoving.
We're all going to be as happy and comfortable as a household
during a removal. What else can we expect ? "

Kipps was moved to speak, but not in answer to Masterman's inquiry. " I've never rightly got the 'eng of this
Socialism," he said. " What's it going to do, like ? "

They had been imagining that he had some elementary idea
in the matter, but as soon as he had made it clear that he
hadn't, Sid plunged at exposition, and in a little while Masterman, abandoning his pose of the detached man ready to die,
joined in. At first he joined in only to correct Sid's version,
but afterwards he took control. His manner changed. He
sat up and rested his elbow on his knees, and his cheek flushed
a little. He expanded his case against property and the
property class with such vigour that Kipps was completely
carried away, and never thought of asking for a clear vision

of the thing that would fill the void this abolition might create. For a time he quite forgot his own private opulence. And it was as if something had been lit in Masterman. His languor passed. He enforced his words by gestures of his long thin hands. And as he passed swiftly from point to point of his argument, it was evident he grew angry.

"To-day," he said, "the world is ruled by rich men : they may do almost anything they like with the world. And what are they doing ? Laying it waste ! "

"Hear, hear ! " said Sid, very sternly.

Masterman stood up, gaunt and long, thrust his hands in his pockets, and turned his back to the fireplace.

"Collectively, the rich to-day have neither heart nor imagination. No ! They own machinery, they have knowledge and instruments and powers beyond all previous dreaming, and what are they doing with them ? Think what they are doing with them, Kipps, and think what they might do. God gives them a power like the motor-car, and all they can do with it is to go careering about the roads in goggled masks, killing children and making machinery hateful to the soul of man ! (" True," said Sid, " true.") God gives them means of communication, power unparalleled of every sort, time, and absolute liberty ! They waste it all in folly ! Here under their feet (and Kipps' eyes followed the direction of a lean index finger to the hearthrug), under their accursed wheels, the great mass of men festers and breeds in darkness, darkness those others make by standing in the light. The darkness breeds and breeds. It knows no better. . . . Unless you can crawl or pander or rob you must stay in the stew you are born in. And those rich beasts above claw and clutch as though they had nothing ! They grudge us our schools, they grudge us a gleam of light and air, they cheat us, and then seek to forget us. . . . There is no rule, no guidance, only accidents and happy flukes. . . . Our multitudes of poverty increase, and this crew of rulers makes no provision, foresees nothing, anticipates nothing ! "

He paused, and made a step, and stood over Kipps in a white heat of anger. Kipps nodded in a non-committal manner, and looked hard and rather gloomily at his host's slipper as he talked.

"It isn't as though they had something to show for the waste they make of us, Kipps. They haven't. They are ugly and cowardly and mean. Look at their women ! Painted, dyed, and drugged, hiding their ugly shapes under a load of dress ! There isn't a woman in the swim of society at the present time who wouldn't sell herself body and soul, who wouldn't lick the boots of a Jew or marry a nigger, rather than live decently on a hundred a year ! On what would be wealth for you or me ! They know it. They know we know it. . . . No one believes in them. No one believes in nobility any more. Nobody believes in kingship any more. Nobody believes there is justice in the law. . . . But people have habits, people go on in the old grooves, as long as there's work, as long as there's weekly money. . . . It won't last, Kipps."

He coughed and paused. "Wait for the lean years," he cried. "Wait for the lean years." And suddenly he fell into a struggle with his cough, and spat a gout of blood. "It's nothing," he said to Kipps' note of startled horror.

He went on talking, and the protests of his cough interlaced with his words, and Sid beamed in an ecstasy of painful admiration.

"Look at the fraud they have let life become, the miserable mockery of the hope of one's youth. What have *I* had ? I found myself at thirteen being forced into a factory like a rabbit into a chloroformed box. Thirteen !—when *their* children are babies. But even a child of that age could see what it meant, that Hell of a factory ! Monotony and toil and contempt and dishonour ! And then death. So I fought—at thirteen !"

Minton's "crawling up a drainpipe till you die" echoed in Kipps' mind, but Masterman, instead of Minton's growl, spoke in a high indignant tenor.

"I got out at last—somehow," he said quietly, suddenly plumping back in his chair. He went on after a pause. "For a bit, some of us get out by luck, some by cunning, and crawl on to the grass, exhausted and crippled, to die. That's a poor man's success, Kipps. Most of us don't get out at all. I worked all day, and studied half the night, and here I am with the common consequences. Beaten ! And never once have I had a fair chance, never once ! " His lean, clenched fist flew out in a gust of tremulous anger. "These Skunks shut up all the university scholarships at nineteen for fear of men like me. And then—do *nothing*. . . . We're wasted for nothing. By the time I'd learnt something the doors were locked. I thought knowledge would do it—I did think that ! I've fought for knowledge as other men fight for bread. I've starved for knowledge. I've turned my back on women ; I've done even that. I've burst my accursed lung. . . ." His voice rose with impotent anger. "I'm a better man than any ten princes alive. And I'm beaten and wasted. I've been crushed, trampled, and defiled by a drove of hogs. I'm no use to myself or the world. I've thrown my life away to make myself too good for use in this huckster's scramble. If I had gone in for business, if I had gone in for plotting to cheat my fellow-men. . . . Ah, well ! It's too late. It's too late for that, anyhow. It's too late for anything now ! And I couldn't have done it. . . . And over in New York now there's a pet of society making a corner in wheat !

"By God ! " he cried hoarsely, with a clutch of the lean

hand. " By God ! if I had his throat ! Even now ! I might do something for the world."

He glared at Kipps, his face flushed deep, his sunken eyes glowing with passion, and then suddenly he changed altogether.

There was a sound of tea-things rattling upon a tray outside the door, and Sid rose to open it.

" All of which amounts to this," said Masterman, suddenly quiet again and talking against time. " The world is out of joint, and there isn't a soul alive who isn't half waste or more. You'll find it the same with you in the end, wherever your luck may take you. . . . I suppose you won't mind my having another cigarette ? "

He took Kipps' cigarette with a hand that trembled so violently it almost missed its object, and stood up, with something of guilt in his manner, as Mrs. Sid came into the room.

Her eye met his, and marked the flush upon his face.

" Been talking Socialism ? " said Mrs. Sid, a little severely.

§ 5

Six o'clock that day found Kipps drifting eastward along the southward margin of Rotten Row. You figure him a small, respectably attired person going slowly through a sometimes immensely difficult and always immense world. At times he becomes pensive, and whistles softly ; at times he looks about him. There are a few riders in the Row ; a carriage flashes by every now and then along the roadway, and among the great rhododendrons and laurels and upon the green sward there are a few groups and isolated people dressed—in the style Kipps adopted to call upon the Walshinghams when first he was engaged. Amid the complicated confusion of Kipps' mind was a regret that he had not worn his other things. . . .

Presently he perceived that he would like to sit down ; a green chair tempted him. He hesitated at it, took possession of it, and leant back and crossed one leg over the other.

He rubbed his under lip with his umbrella handle, and reflected upon Masterman and his denunciation of the world.

" Bit orf 'is 'ead, poor chap," said Kipps ; and added, " I wonder——"

He thought intently for a space.

" I wonder what 'e meant by the lean years. . . ."

The world seemed a very solid and prosperous concern just here, and well out of reach of Masterman's dying clutch. And yet——

It was curious he should have been reminded of Minton.

His mind turned to a far more important matter. Just at the end Sid had said to him, " Seen Ann ? " and as he was about to answer, " You'll see a bit more of her now. She's got a place in Folkestone."

It had brought him back from any concern about the world being out of joint or anything of that sort.

Ann !

One might run against her any day.

He tugged at his little moustache.

He would like to run against Ann very much. . . .

And it would be juiced awkward if he did !

In Folkestone ! It was a jolly sight too close. . . .

Then at the thought that he might run against Ann in his beautiful evening dress on the way to the band, he fluttered into a momentary dream, that jumped abruptly into a nightmare.

Suppose he met her when he was out with Helen ! " Oh, Lor ! " said Kipps. Life had developed a new complication that would go on and go on. For some time he wished with the utmost fervour that he had not kissed Ann, that he had not gone to New Romney the second time. He marvelled at his amazing forgetfulness of Helen on that occasion. Helen took possession of his mind. He would have to write to Helen, an easy, off-hand letter to say he had come to London for a day or so. He tried to imagine her reading it. He would write just such another letter to the old people, and say he had had to come up on business. That might do for *them* all right, but Helen was different. She would insist on explanations.

He wished he could never go back to Folkestone again. That would about settle the whole affair.

A passing group attracted his attention, two faultlessly dressed gentlemen and a radiantly expensive lady. They were talking, no doubt, very brilliantly. His eyes followed them. The lady tapped the arm of the left-hand gentleman with a daintily tinted glove. Swells ! No end. . . .

His soul looked out upon life in general as a very small nestling might peep out of its nest. What an extraordinary thing life was to be sure, and what a remarkable variety of people there were in it !

He lit a cigarette, and speculated upon that receding group of three, and blew smoke and watched them. They seemed to do it all right. Probably they all had incomes of very much over twelve hundred a year. Perhaps not. Probably they none of them suspected as they went past that he, too, was a gentleman of independent means, dressed as he was without distinction. Of course things were easier for them. They were brought up always to dress well and do the right thing from their very earliest years ; they started clear of all his perplexities ; they had never got mixed up with all sorts of different people who didn't go together. If, for example, that lady there got engaged to that gentleman, she would be quite safe from any encounter with a corpulent, osculatory Uncle, or Chitterlow, or the dangerously significant eye of Pearce.

His thoughts came round to Helen.

When they were married and Cuyps, or Cuyp—Coote had failed to justify his " s "—and in that West end flat, and shaken free of all these low-class associations, would he and she parade here of an afternoon dressed like that ? It would be rather fine to do so. If one's dress was all right.

Helen !

She was difficult to understand at times.

He blew extensive clouds of cigarette smoke.

There would be teas, there would be dinners, there would be calls—— Of course he would get into the way of it.

But Anagrams were a bit stiff to begin with !

It was beastly confusing at first to know when to use your fork at dinner, and all that. Still——

He felt an extraordinary doubt whether he would get into the way of it. He was interested for a space by a girl and groom on horseback, and then he came back to his personal preoccupations.

He would have to write to Helen. What could he say to explain his absence from the Anagram Tea ? She had been pretty clear she wanted him to come. He recalled her resolute face without any great tenderness. He *knew* he would look like a silly ass at that confounded tea ! Suppose he shirked it and went back in time for the dinner ! Dinners were beastly difficult too, but not so bad as anagrams. The very first thing that might happen when he got back to Folkestone would be to run against Ann. Suppose, after all, he did meet Ann when he was with Helen !

What queer encounters were possible in the world !

Thank goodness they were going to live in London !

But that brought him round to Chitterlow. The Chitterlows would be coming to London too. If they didn't get money they'd come after it ; they weren't the sort of people to be choked off easily, and if they did, they'd come to London to produce their play. He tried to imagine some seemly social occasion invaded by Chitterlow and his rhetoric, by his torrential thunder of self-assertion, the whole company flattened thereunder like wheat under a hurricane.

Confound and hang Chitterlow ! Yet somehow, somewhen, one would have to settle accounts with him ! And there was Sid ! Sid was Ann's brother. He realised with sudden horror the social indiscretion of accepting Sid's invitation to dinner.

Sid wasn't the sort of chap one could snub or cut, and besides—Ann's brother ! He didn't want to cut him ; it would be worse than cutting Buggins and Pearce—a sight worse. And after that lunch ! It would be next thing to cutting Ann herself. And even as to Ann !

Suppose he was with Helen or Coote ! . . .

" Oh, Blow ! " he said at last, and then viciously, " *Blow !* " and so rose and flung away his cigarette end and pursued

his reluctant dubitating way towards the really quite uncongenial splendours of the Royal Grand. . . .

And it is vulgarly imagined that to have money is to have
no troubles at all !

§ 6

Kipps endured splendour at the Royal Grand Hotel for
three nights and days, and then he retreated in disorder.
The Royal Grand defeated and overcame and routed Kipps
not of intention, but by sheer royal grandeur, grandeur combined with an organisation for his comfort carried to excess.
On his return he came upon a difficulty, he had lost his
circular piece of cardboard with the number of his room,
and he drifted about the hall and passages in a state of perplexity for some time, until he thought all the porters and
officials in gold lace caps must be watching him, and jesting
to one another about him. Finally, in a quiet corner down
below near the hairdresser's shop, he found a kindly-looking
personage in bottle green, to whom he broached his difficulty.
" I say," he said, with a pleasant smile, " I can't find my
room nohow." The personage in bottle green, instead of
laughing in a nasty way, as he might well have done, became
extremely helpful, showed Kipps what to do, got his key,
and conducted him by lift and passage to his chamber. Kipps
tipped him half a crown.

Safe in his room, Kipps pulled himself together for dinner.
He had learnt enough from young Walshingham to bring
his dress clothes, and now he began to assume them. Unfortunately, in the excitement of his flight from his Aunt and
Uncle, he had forgotten to put in his other boots, and he
was some time deciding between his purple cloth slippers
with a golden marigold and the prospect of cleaning the boots
he was wearing with the towel, but finally, being a little
footsore, he took the slippers.

Afterwards, when he saw the porters and waiters and the
other guests catch sight of the slippers, he was sorry he had
not chosen the boots. However, to make up for any want
of style at that end, he had his crush hat under his arm.

He found the dining-room without excessive trouble. It
was a vast and splendidly decorated place, and a number
of people, evidently quite *au fait*, were dining there at little
tables lit with electric red-shaded candles, gentlemen in
evening dress, and ladies with dazzling, astonishing necks.
Kipps had never seen evening dress in full vigour before,
and he doubted his eyes. And there were also people not
in evening dress, who no doubt wondered what noble family
Kipps represented. There was a band in a decorated recess,
and the band looked collectively at the purple slippers, and
so lost any chance they may have had of a donation so far
as Kipps was concerned. The chief drawback to this mag-

nificent place was the excessive space of floor that had to be crossed before you got your purple slippers hidden under a table.

He selected a little table—not the one where a rather impudent-looking waiter held a chair, but another—sat down, and, finding his gibus in his hand, decided after a moment of thought to rise slightly and sit on it. (It was discovered in his abandoned chair at a late hour by a supper-party and restored to him next day.)

He put the napkin carefully on one side, selected his soup without difficulty, " Clear, please," but he was rather floored by the presentation of a quite splendidly bound wine-card. He turned it over, discovered a section devoted to whisky and had a bright idea.

" 'Ere," he said to the waiter, with an encouraging movement of the head ; and then in a confidential manner, " You 'aven't any Old Methusaleh Three Stars, 'ave you ? "

The waiter went away to inquire, and Kipps went on with his soup with an enhanced self-respect. Finally, Old Methusaleh being unattainable, he ordered a claret from about the middle of the list. " Let's 'ave some of this," he said. He knew claret was a good sort of wine.

" A half bottle ? " said the waiter.

" Right you are," said Kipps.

He felt he was getting on. He leant back after his soup, a man of the world, and then slowly brought his eyes round to the ladies in evening dress on his right. . . .

He couldn't have thought it !

They were scorchers. Jest a bit of black velvet over the shoulders !

He looked again. One of them was laughing, with a glass of wine half raised—wicked-looking woman she was ; the other, the black velvet one, was eating bits of bread with nervous quickness and talking fast.

He wished old Buggins could see them.

He found a waiter regarding him and blushed deeply. He did not look again for some time, and became confused about his knife and fork over the fish. Presently he remarked a lady in pink to the left of him eating the fish with an entirely different implement.

It was over the *vol au vent* that he began to go to pieces. He took a knife to it ; then saw the lady in pink was using a fork only, and hastily put down his knife, with a considerable amount of rich creaminess on the blade, upon the cloth. Then he found that a fork in his inexperienced hand was an instrument of chase rather than capture. His ears became violently red, and then he looked up to discover the lady in pink glancing at him, and then smiling, as she spoke to the man beside her.

He hated the lady in pink very much.

He stabbed a large piece of the *vol au vent* at last, and was too glad of his luck not to make a mouthful of it. But it was an extensive fragment, and pieces escaped him. Shirt-front! " Desh it ! " he said, and had resort to his spoon. His waiter went and spoke to two other waiters, no doubt jeering at him. He became very fierce suddenly. " 'Ere ! " he said, gesticulating ; and then, " Clear this away ! "

The entire dinner-party on his right, the party of the ladies in advanced evening dress, looked at him. . . . He felt that every one was watching him and making fun of him, and the injustice of this angered him. After all, they had had every advantage he hadn't. And then, when they got him there doing his best, what must they do but glance and sneer and nudge one another. He tried to catch them at it, and then took refuge in a second glass of wine.

Suddenly and extraordinarily he found himself a Socialist. He did not care how close it was to the lean years when all these things would end.

Mutton came with peas. He arrested the hand of the waiter. " No peas," he said. He knew something of the danger and difficulty of eating peas. Then, when the peas went away, he was embittered again. . . . Echoes of Masterman's burning rhetoric began to reverberate in his mind. Nice lot of people these were to laugh at any one ! Women half undressed—— It was that made him so beastly uncomfortable. How could one eat one's dinner with people about him like that ? Nice lot they were. He was glad he wasn't one of them anyhow. Yes, they might look. He resolved, if they looked at him again, he would ask one of the men who he was staring at. His perturbed and angry face would have concerned any one. The band, by an unfortunate accident, was playing truculent military music. The mental change Kipps underwent was, in its way, what psychologists call a conversion. In a few moments all Kipps' ideals were changed. He who had been " practically a gentleman," the sedulous pupil of Coote, the punctilious raiser of hats, was instantly a rebel, an outcast, the hater of everything " stuck-up," the foe of Society and the social order of to-day. Here they were among the profits of their robbery, these people who might do anything with the world. . . .

" No, thanks," he said to a dish.

He addressed a scornful eye at the shoulders of the lady to his left.

Presently he was refusing another dish. He didn't like it —fussed-up food ! Probably cooked by some foreigner. He finished up his wine and his bread. . . .

" No, thenks."

" No, thenks. . . ."

He discovered the eye of a diner fixed curiously upon his flushed face. He responded with a glare. Couldn't he go without things if he liked ?

"What's this?" said Kipps, to a great green cone.

"Ice," said the waiter.

"I'll 'ave some," said Kipps.

He seized fork and spoon and assailed the bombe. It cut rather stiffly. "Come up!" said Kipps, with concentrated bitterness, and the truncated summit of the bombe flew off suddenly, travelling eastward with remarkable velocity. Flop, it went upon the floor a yard away, and for a while time seemed empty.

At the adjacent table they were laughing altogether.

Shy the rest of the bombe at them?

Flight?

At any rate, a dignified withdrawal.

"No!" said Kipps, "no more," arresting the polite attempt of the waiter to serve him with another piece. He had a vague idea he might carry off the affair as though he meant the ice to go on the floor—not liking ice, for example, and being annoyed at the badness of his dinner. He put both hands on the table, thrust back his chair, disengaged a purple slipper from his napkin, and rose. He stepped carefully over the prostrate ice, kicked the napkin under the table, thrust his hands deep into his pockets, and marched out—shaking the dust of the place, as it were, from his feet. He left behind him a melting fragment of ice upon the floor, his gibus hat, warm and compressed in his chair, and, in addition, every social ambition he had ever entertained in the world.

§ 7

Kipps went back to Folkestone in time for the Anagram Tea. But you must not imagine that the change of heart that came to him in the dining-room of the Royal Grand Hotel involved any change of attitude towards this promised social and intellectual treat. He went back because the Royal Grand was too much for him.

Outwardly calm, or at most a little flushed and ruffled, inwardly Kipps was a horrible, tormented battleground of scruples, doubts, shames, and self-assertions during that three days of silent, desperate grappling with the big hotel. He did not intend the monstrosity should beat him without a struggle; but at last he had sullenly to admit himself overcome. The odds were terrific. On the one hand himself—with, among other things, only one pair of boots; on the other a vast wilderness of rooms, covering several acres, and with over a thousand people, staff and visitors, all chiefly occupied in looking queerly at Kipps, in laughing at him behind his back, in watching for difficult corners at which to confront and perplex him and inflict humiliations upon him. For example, the hotel scored over its electric light. After the dinner the chambermaid, a hard, unsympathetic young woman with a superior manner, was summoned by a bell Kipps had rung under the impression the button was the electric-light switch. " Look 'ere," said Kipps, rubbing a shin that had suffered during his search in the dark, " why aren't there any candles or matches ? " The hotel explained and scored heavily.

" It isn't every one is up to these things," said Kipps.

" No, it isn't," said the chambermaid, with ill-concealed scorn, and slammed the door at him.

" S'pose I ought to have tipped her," said Kipps.

After that Kipps cleaned his boots with a pocket-handker-chief and went for a long walk, and got home in a hansom ; but the hotel scored again by his not putting out his boots, and so having to clean them again in the morning. The hotel also snubbed him by bringing him hot water when he was fully dressed and looking surprised at his collar, but he got a breakfast, I must admit, with scarcely any difficulty.

After that the hotel scored heavily by the fact that there are twenty-four hours in the day and Kipps had nothing to do in any of them. He was a little footsore from his previous day's pedestrianism, and he could make up his mind for no long excursions. He flitted in and out of the hotel several times, and it was the polite porter who touched his hat every time that first set Kipps tipping.

" What 'e wants is a tip," said Kipps.

So at the next opportunity he gave the man an unexpected shilling, and, having once put his hand in his pocket, there was no reason why he should not go on. He bought a news-paper at the bookstall and tipped the boy the rest of the shilling, and then went up by the lift and tipped the man sixpence, leaving his newspaper inadvertently in the lift. He met his chambermaid in the passage and gave her half a crown. He resolved to demonstrate his position to the entire establishment in this way. He didn't like the place ; he disapproved of it politically, socially, morally; but he re-solved no taint of meanness should disfigure his sojourn in its luxurious halls. He went down by the lift (tipping again), and, being accosted by a waiter with his gibus, tipped the finder half a crown. He had a vague sense that he was making a flank movement upon the hotel and buying over its staff. They would regard him as a " character " ; they would get to like him. He found his stock of small silver diminishing and replenished it at a desk in the hall. He tipped a man in bottle green, who looked like the man who had shown him his room the day before ; and then he saw a visitor eyeing him, and doubted whether he was in this instance doing right. Finally he went out and took chance buses to their destinations, and wandered a little in remote wonderful suburbs, and returned. He lunched at a chop-house in Isling-ton, and found himself back in the Royal Grand, now un-mistakably footsore and London-weary, about three. He was

attracted to the drawing-room by a neat placard about afternoon tea.

It occurred to him that the campaign of tipping upon
which he had embarked was, perhaps, after all, a mistake.
He was confirmed in this by observing that the hotel officials
were watching him, not respectfully, but with a sort of
amused wonder, as if to see whom he would tip next. However, if he backed out now, they would think him an awful
fool. Every one wasn't so rich as he was. It was his way
to tip. Still——

He grew more certain the hotel had scored again.

He pretended to be lost in thought, and so drifted by,
and, having put hat and umbrella in the cloakroom, went
into the drawing-room for afternoon tea.

There he did get what for a time he held to be a point
in his favour. The room was large and quiet at first, and
he sat back restfully until it occurred to him that his attitude
brought his extremely dusty boots too prominently into the
light, so instead he sat up, and then people of the upper and
upper middle classes began to come and group themselves about
him and have tea likewise, and so revive the class animosities
of the previous day.

Presently a fluffy fair-haired lady came into prominent
existence a few yards away. She was talking to a respectful
low-voiced clergyman, whom she was possibly entertaining at
tea. " No," she said ; " dear Lady Jane wouldn't do that ! "

" Mumble, mumble, mumble," from the clergyman.

" Poor dear Lady Jane was always so sensitive," the voice
of the lady sang out clear and emphatic.

A fat, hairless, important-looking man joined this group,
took a chair, and planted it firmly with its back in the face
of Kipps, a thing that offended Kipps mightily. " Are you
telling him," gurgled the fat, hairless man, " about dear
Lady Jane's affliction ? " A young couple, lady brilliantly
attired, and the man in a magnificently cut frock-coat, arranged
themselves to the right, also with an air of exclusion towards
Kipps. " I've told him," said the gentleman in a flat, abundant
voice. " My ! " said the young lady with an American smile.
No doubt they all thought Kipps was out of it. A great desire
to assert himself in some way surged up in his heart. He felt
he would like to cut in on the conversation in some dramatic
way. A monologue, something in the manner of Masterman ?
At any rate, abandoning that as impossible, he would like
to appear self-centred and at ease. His eye, wandering over
the black surfaces of a noble architectural mass close by,
discovered a slot and an enamelled plaque of directions.

It was some sort of musical box !

It occurred to Kipps that he would like some music, that
to inaugurate some would show him a man of taste and at
his ease at the same time. He rose, read over a list of tunes,

selected one haphazard, pressed his sixpence—it was sixpence !
—home, and prepared for a confidential refined little melody.

Considering the high social tone of the Royal Grand, it
was really a very loud instrument indeed. It gave vent to
three deafening brays, and so burst the dam of silence that
had long pent it in. It seemed to be chiefly full of the great-
uncles of trumpets, megalo-trombones, and railway-brakes.
It made sounds like shunting trains. It did not so much begin
as blow up your counterscarp and rush forward to storm
under cover of melodious shrapnel. It had not so much an
air as a ricochet. The music had, in short, the inimitable
quality of Sousa. It swept down upon the friend of Lady Jane
and carried away something socially striking into the eternal
night of the unheard ; the American girl to the left of it was
borne off shrieking. " HIGH cockalorum Tootletootle tootle
loo. HIGH cockalorum tootle lootle loo. BUMP, bump,
bump—BUMP,"—Native American music, full of native
American notes, full of the spirit of western college yells and
election howls, joyous, exorbitant music from the gigantic
nursery of the Future, bearing the hearer along upon its
torrential succession of sounds, as if he was in a cask on Niagara.
Whiroo ! Yah ! Have at you ! The Strenuous Life ! Yaha !
Stop ! A Reprieve ! A Reprieve ! No ! Bang ! Bump !

Everybody looked round, conversation ceased and gave
place to gestures.

The friend of Lady Jane became terribly agitated.

" Can't it be stopped ? " she vociferated, pointing a gloved
finger and saying something to the waiter about " that dreadful young man."

" Ought not to be working," said the clerical friend of Lady
Jane.

The waiter shook his head at the fat, hairless gentleman.

People began to move away. Kipps leant back luxurious,
and then tapped with a half-crown to pay.

He paid, tipped liked a gentleman, rose with an easy gesture,
and strolled towards the door. His retreat evidently completed
the indignation of the friend of Lady Jane, and from the door
he could still discern her gestures as asking, " Can't it be
stopped ? " The music followed him into the passage and
pursued him to the lift, and only died away completely in the
quiet of his own room, and afterwards from his window he
saw the friend of Lady Jane and her party having their tea
carried out to a little table in the court.

Certainly that was a point to him. But it was his only
score ; all the rest of the game lay in the hands of the upper
classes and the big hotel. And presently he was doubting
whether even this was really a point. It seemed a trifle vulgar,
come to think it over, to interrupt people when they were
talking.

He saw a clerk peering at him from the office, and suddenly

it occurred to him that the place might get back at him tremendously over the bill.

They would probably take it out of him by charging pounds
and pounds.

Suppose they charged more than he had !

The clerk had a particularly nasty face, just the face to
take advantage of a vacillating Kipps.

He became aware of a man in a cap touching it, and produced his shilling automatically, but the strain was beginning
to tell. It was a deuce and all of an expense—this tipping.

If the hotel chose to stick it on to the bill something tremendous, what was Kipps to do ? Refuse to pay ? Make a
row ?

If he did he couldn't fight all these men in bottle green. . . .

He went out about seven and walked for a long time, and
dined at last upon a chop in the Euston Road ; then he walked
along to the Edgeware Road and sat and rested in the Metro-
politan Music Hall for a time, until a trapeze performance
unnerved him, and finally he came back to bed. He tipped
the lift-man sixpence and wished him good-night.   In the
silent watches of the night he reviewed the tale of the day's
tipping, went over the horrors of the previous night's dinner,
and heard again the triumphant bray of the harmonicon devil
released from its long imprisonment. Every one would be
told about him to-morrow. He couldn't go on ! He admitted
his defeat. Never in their whole lives had any of these people
seen such a Fool as he ! Ugh ! . . .

His method of announcing his withdrawal to the clerk was
touched with bitterness.

" I'm going to get out of this," said Kipps, blowing windily.
" Let's see what you got on my bill."

" One breakfast ? " asked the clerk.

" Do I *look* as if I'd ate two ? " . . .

At his departure, Kipps, with a hot face, convulsive gestures,
and an embittered heart, tipped every one who did not promptly
and actively resist, including an absent-minded South African
diamond merchant who was waiting in the hall for his wife.
He paid his cabman a four-shilling piece at Charing Cross,
having no smaller change, and wished he could burn him alive.
Then in a sudden reaction of economy he refused the proffered
help of a porter, and carried his bag quite violently to the
train.

CHAPTER EIGHT

KIPPS ENTERS SOCIETY

§ 1

SUBMISSION to Inexorable Fate took Kipps to the Anagram Tea.

At any rate he would meet Helen there in the presence of other people, and be able to carry off the worst of the difficulty of explaining his little jaunt to London. He had not seen her since his last portentous visit to New Romney. He was engaged to her, he would have to marry her, and the sooner he faced her again the better. Before wild plans of turning Socialist, defying the world and repudiating all calling for ever, his heart, on second thoughts, sank. He felt Helen would never permit anything of the sort. As for the Anagrams, he could do no more than his best, and that he was resolved to do. What had happened at the Royal Grand, what had happened at New Romney, he must bury in his memory and begin again at the reconstruction of his social position. Ann, Buggins, Chitterlow—all these, seen in the matter-of-fact light of the Folkestone corridor train, stood just as they stood before—people of an inferior social position, who had to be eliminated from his world. It was a bother about Ann, a bother and a pity. His mind rested so for a space on Ann until the memory of those Anagrams drew him away. If he could see Coote that evening he might, he thought, be able to arrange some sort of connivance about the anagrams, and his mind was chiefly busy sketching proposals for such an arrangement. It would not, of course, be ungentlemanly cheating, but only a little mystification. Coote, very probably, might drop him a hint of the solution of one or two of the things—not enough to win a prize, but enough to cover his shame. Or failing that, he might take a humorous, quizzical line, and pretend he was pretending to be very stupid. There were plenty of ways out of it if one kept a sharp lookout. . . .

The costume Kipps wore to the Anagram Tea was designed as a compromise between the strict letter of high fashion and seaside laxity—a sort of easy semi-state for afternoon. Helen's first reproof had always lingered in his mind. He wore a frock-coat, but mitigated it by a Panama hat of romantic shape with a black band, gray gloves, but, for relaxation, brown button boots. The only other man besides the clergy present —a new doctor with an attractive wife—was in full afternoon dress. Coote was not there.

Kipps was a little pale, but quite self-possessed, as he approached Mrs. Bindon Botting's door. He took a turn while some people went in, and then faced it manfully. The door opened and revealed—Ann !

In the background, through a draped doorway, behind a big fern in a great art pot, the elder Miss Botting was visible talking to two guests ; the auditory background was a froth of feminine voices. . . .

Our two young people were much too amazed to give one another any formula of greeting, though they had parted warmly enough. Each was already in a state of extreme tension to meet the demands of this great and unprecedented occasion—an Anagram Tea. " Lor ! " said Ann, her sole remark ; and then the sense of Miss Botting's eye ruled her straight again. She became very pale, but she took his hat mechanically, and he was already removing his gloves. " Ann," he said in a low tone, and then " Fency ! "

The eldest Miss Botting knew Kipps was the sort of guest who requires nursing, and she came forward vocalising charm. She said it was " awfully jolly of him to come—awfully jolly. It was awfully difficult to get any good men ! "

She handed Kipps forward, mumbling, and in a dazed condition, to the drawing-room, and there he encountered Helen, looking unfamiliar in an unfamiliar hat. It was as if he had not met her for years.

She astonished him. She didn't seem to mind in the least his going to London. She held out a shapely hand, and smiled encouragingly. " You've faced the anagrams ? " she said.

The second Miss Botting accosted them, a number of oblong pieces of paper in her hand, mysteriously inscribed. " Take an anagram," she said ; " take an anagram," and boldly pinned one of these brief documents to Kipps' lapel. The letters were " Cypshi," and Kipps from the very beginning suspected this was an anagram for Cuyps. She also left a thing like a long dance programme, from which dangled a little pencil, in his hand. He found himself being introduced to people, and then he was in a corner with the short lady in a big bonnet, who was pelting him with gritty little bits of small talk, that were gone before you could take hold of them and reply.

" Very hot," said this lady. " Very hot indeed—hot all the summer—remarkable year—all the years remarkable now—don't know what we're coming to. Don't you think so, Mr. Kipps ? "

" Oo, rather," said Kipps, and wondered if Ann was still in the hall. Ann !

He ought not to have stared at her like a stuck fish, and pretended not to know her. That couldn't be right. But what *was* right ?

The lady in the big bonnet proceeded to a second discharge. " Hope you're fond of anagrams, Mr. Kipps—difficult exercise —still, one must do something to bring people together—

better than Ludo, anyhow. Don't you think so, Mr. Kipps? "

Ann fluttered past the open door. Her eyes met his in amazed inquiry. Something had got dislocated in the world for both of them. . . .

He ought to have told her he was engaged. He ought to have explained things to her. Perhaps, even now, he might be able to drop her a hint.

" Don't you think so, Mr. Kipps? "

" Oo, rather," said Kipps for the third time.

A lady with a tired smile, who was labelled conspicuously, " Wogdelenk," drifted towards Kipps' interlocutor, and the two fell into conversation. Kipps found himself socially aground. He looked about him. Helen was talking to a curate and laughing. Kipps was overcome by a vague desire to speak to Ann. He was for sidling doorward.

" What are *you*, please ? " said an extraordinarily bold, tall girl, and arrested him while she took down " Cypshi."

" I'm sure I don't know what it means," she explained. " I'm Sir Bubh. Don't you think anagrams are something chronic ? "

Kipps made stockish noises, and the young lady suddenly became the nucleus of a party of excited friends who were forming a syndicate to guess, and barred his escape. She took no further notice of him. He found himself jammed against an occasional table and listening to the conversation of Mrs. " Wogdelenk " and his lady with the big bonnet.

" She packed her two beauties off together," said the lady in the big bonnet. " Time enough, too. Don't think much of this girl she's got as housemaid now. Pretty, of course, but there's no occasion for a housemaid to be pretty—none whatever. And she doesn't look particularly up to her work either. Kind of 'mazed expression."

" You never can tell," said the lady labelled " Wogdelenk " ; " you never can tell. My wretches are big enough, Heaven knows, and do they work ? Not a bit of it ! . . ."

Kipps felt dreadfully out of it with regard to all these people, and dreadfully in it with Ann.

He scanned the back of the big bonnet, and concluded it was an extremely ugly bonnet indeed. It got jerking forward as each short, dry sentence was snapped off at the end, and a plume of osprey on it jerked excessively. " She hasn't guessed even one ! " followed by a shriek of girlish merriment, came from the group about the tall, bold girl. They'd shriek at him presently, perhaps ! Beyond thinking his own anagram might be Cuyps, he hadn't a notion. What a chatter they were all making ! It was just like a summer sale ! Just the sort of people who'd give a lot of trouble and swap you ! And suddenly the smouldering fires of rebellion leapt to flame again. These were a rotten lot of people, and the anagrams were rotten nonsense, and he (Kipps) had been a rotten fool to come.

There was Helen away there still laughing with her curate. Pity she couldn't marry a curate, and leave him (Kipps) alone ! Then he'd know what to do. He disliked the whole gathering, collectively and in detail. Why were they all trying to make him one of themselves ? He perceived unexpected ugliness everywhere about him. There were two great pins jabbed through the tall girl's hat, and the swirls of her hair below the brim, with the minutest piece of tape tie-up showing, did not repay close examination. Mrs. "Wogdelenk" wore a sort of mumps bandage of lace, and there was another lady perfectly dazzling with beads and jewels and bits of trimming. They were all flaps and angles and flounces, these women. Not one of them looked as neat and decent a shape as Ann's clean, trim little figure. Echoes of Masterman woke up in him again. Ladies indeed ! Here were all these chattering people, with money, with leisure, with every chance in the world, and all they could do was to crowd like this into a couple of rooms and jabber nonsense about anagrams.

" Could Cypshi really mean Cuyps ? " floated like a dissolving wreath of mist across his mind.

Abruptly resolution stood armed in his heart. He was going to get out of this !

" 'Scuse me," he said, and began to wade neck-deep through the bubbling tea-party.

He was going to get out of it all !

He found himself close by Helen. " I'm orf," he said, but she gave him the briefest glance. She did not appear to hear him. " Still, Mr. Spratlingdown, you *must* admit there's a limit even to conformity," she was saying. . . .

He was in a curtained archway, and Ann was before him carrying a tray supporting several small sugar-bowls.

He was moved to speech. " *What* a Lot !" he said, and then mysteriously, " I'm engaged to *her*." He indicated Helen's new hat, and became aware of a skirt he had stepped upon.

Ann stared at him helplessly, borne past in the grip of incomprehensible imperatives.

Why shouldn't they talk together ?

He was in a small room, and then at the foot of the staircase in the hall. He heard the rustle of a dress, and what was conceivably his hostess was upon him.

" But you're not going, Mr. Kipps ? " she said.

" I must," he said. " I got to."

" But, Mr. Kipps ! "

" I must," he said. " I'm not well."

" But before the guessing ! Without any tea ! "

Ann appeared and hovered behind him.

" I got to go," said Kipps.

If he parleyed with her Helen might awake to his desperate attempt.

" Of course, if you *must* go."

" It's something I've forgotten," said Kipps, beginning to feel regrets. " Reely, I must."

Mrs. Botting turned with a certain offended dignity, and Ann, in a state of flushed calm that evidently concealed much, came forward to open the door.

" I'm very sorry," he said. " I'm very sorry," half to his hostess and half to her, and was swept past her by superior social forces—like a drowning man in a mill-race—and into the Upper Sandgate Road. He half turned upon the step, and then slam went the door. . . .

He retreated along the Leas, a thing of shame and perplexity, Mrs. Botting's aggrieved astonishment uppermost in his mind. . . .

Something—reinforced by the glances of the people he was passing—pressed its way to his attention through the tumultuous disorder of his mind.

He became aware that he was still wearing his little placard with the letters " Cypshi."

" Desh it ! " he said, clutching off this abomination. In another moment its several letters, their task accomplished, were scattering gleefully before the breeze down the front of the Leas.

§ 2

Kipps was dressed for Mrs. Wace's dinner half an hour before it was time to start, and he sat waiting until Coote should come to take him round. *Manners and Rules of Good Society* lay beside him neglected. He had read the polished prose of the Member of the Aristocracy on page 96 as far as,—

> " the acceptance of an invitation is, in the eyes of diners out, a binding obligation which only ill-health, family bereavement, or some all-important reason justifies its being set on one side or otherwise evaded "—

and then he had lapsed into gloomy thoughts.

That afternoon he had had a serious talk with Helen.

He had tried to express something of the change of heart that had happened to him. But to broach the real state of the matter had been altogether too terrible for him. He had sought a minor issue. " I don't like all this Seciety," he had said.

" But you must *see* people," said Helen.

" Yes, but—— It's the sort of people you see." He nerved himself. " I didn't think much of that lot at the Enegram Tea."

" You have to see all sorts of people if you want to see the world," said Helen.

Kipps was silent for a space, and a little short of breath.

" My dear Arthur," she began almost kindly, " I shouldn't ask you to go to these affairs if I didn't think it good for you, should I ? "

Kipps acquiesced in silence.

" You will find the benefit of it all when we get to London. You learn to swim in a tank before you go out into the sea. These people here are good enough to learn upon. They're stiff and rather silly, and dreadfully narrow, and not an idea in a dozen of them, but it really doesn't matter at all. You'll soon get *Savoir Faire*."

He made to speak again, and found his powers of verbal expression lacking. Instead he blew a sigh.

" You'll get used to it all very soon," said Helen helpfully. . . .

As he sat meditating over that interview, and over the vistas of London that opened before him, on the little flat and teas and occasions, and the constant presence of Brudderkins and all the bright prospect of his new and better life, and how he would never see Ann any more, the housemaid entered with a little package, a small, square envelope for " Arthur Kipps, Esquire."

" A young woman left this, Sir," said the housemaid, a little severely.

" Eh ? " said Kipps. " What young woman ? " and then suddenly began to understand.

" She looked an ordinary young woman," said the housemaid coldly.

" Ah ! " said Kipps. " *That's* orlright."

He waited till the door had closed behind the girl, staring at the envelope in his hand, and then, with a curious feeling of increasing tension, tore it open. As he did so, some quicker sense than sight or touch told him its contents. It was Ann's half-sixpence. And besides, not a word !

Then she must have heard him——!

He was standing with the envelope in his hand when Coote became audible without.

Coote appeared in evening dress, a clean and radiant Coote, with large greenish-white gloves, and a particularly large white tie edged with black. " For a third cousin," he presently explained. " Nace, isn't it ? " He could see Kipps was pale and disturbed, and put this down to the approaching social trial. " You keep your nerve up, Kipps, my dear chap, and you'll be all right," said Coote, with a big brotherly glove on Kipps' sleeve.

§ 3

The dinner came to a crisis so far as Kipps' emotions were concerned with Mrs. Bindon Botting's talk about servants, but before that there had been several things of greater or smaller magnitude to perturb and disarrange his social front.

One little matter that was mildly insurgent throughout the entire meal was, if I may be permitted to mention so intimate a matter, the behaviour of his left brace. The webbing—which was of a cheerful scarlet silk—had slipped away from its buckle, fastened, no doubt, in agitation, and had developed a strong tendency to place itself obliquely, in the manner rather of an official decoration, athwart his spotless front. It first asserted itself before they went in to dinner. He replaced this ornament by a dexterous thrust when no one was looking, and thereafter the suppression of this novel innovation upon the stereotyped sombreness of evening dress became a standing preoccupation. On the whole, he was inclined to think his first horror excessive ; at any rate, no one remarked upon it. However, you imagine him constantly throughout the evening with one eye and one hand, whatever the rest of him might be doing, predominantly concerned with the weak corner.

But this, I say, was a little matter. What exercised him much more was to discover Helen, quite terribly in evening dress.

The young lady had let her imagination rove London-ward, and this costume was perhaps an anticipation of that clever little flat, not too far west, which was to become the centre of so delightful a literary and artistic set. It was, of all the feminine costumes present, most distinctly an evening dress. One was advised Miss Walshingham had arms and shoulders of a type by no means despicable ; one was advised Miss Walshingham was capable not only of dignity but charm, even a certain glow of charm. It was, you know, her first evening dress, a tribute paid by Walshingham finance to her brightening future. Had she wanted keeping in countenance, she would have had to have fallen back upon her hostess, who was resplendent in black and steel. The other ladies had to a certain extent compromised. Mrs. Walshingham had dressed with just a refined little V, and Mrs. Bindon Botting, except for her dear mottled arms, confided scarcely more of her plump charm to the world. The elder Miss Botting stopped short of shoulders, and so did Miss Waoe. But Helen didn't. She was—had Kipps had eyes to see it—a quite beautiful human figure ; she knew it, and she met him with a radiant smile that had forgotten all the little difference of the afternoon. But to Kipps her appearance was the last release. With that she had become as remote, as foreign, as incredible as a wife and mate, as though the Cnidian Venus herself, in all her simple elegance, was, before witnesses, declared to be his. If, indeed, she had ever been credible as a wife and mate !

She ascribed his confusion to modest reverence, and, having blazed smiling upon him for a moment, turned a shapely shoulder towards him and exchanged a remark with Mrs. Bindon Botting. Ann's poor little half-sixpence came against Kipps' fingers in his pocket, and he clutched at it suddenly

as though it was a talisman. Then he abandoned it to suppress
his cough. He was affected by a cough. "Miss
Wace tells me Mr. Revel is coming," Mrs. Botting was saying.

"Isn't it delightful?" said Helen. "We saw him last
night. He's stopped on his way to Paris. He's going to meet
his wife there."

Kipps' eyes rested for a moment on Helen's dazzling deltoid,
and then went inquiringly, accusingly, almost, to Coote's
face. Where in the presence of this terrible emergence was
the gospel of suppression now? that Furtive treatment of
Religion and Politics, and Birth and Death, and Bathing and
Babies and "all those things," which constitute your True
Gentleman? He had been too modest even to discuss this
question with his Mentor, but surely, surely this quintessence
of all that is good and nice could regard these unsolicited
confidences only in one way. With something between relief
and the confirmation of his worst fears he perceived, by a
sort of twitching of the exceptionally abundant muscles about
Coote's lower jaw, in a certain deliberate avoidance of one
particular direction by those pale but resolute gray eyes, by
the almost convulsive grip of the ample, greenish-white gloves
behind him, a grip broken at times for controlling pats at the
black-bordered tie and the back of that spacious head, and by
a slight but increasing disposition to cough, that *Coote did not
approve!*

To Kipps Helen had once supplied a delicately beautiful
dream, a thing of romance and unsubstantial mystery. But
this was her final materialisation, and the last thin wreath of
glamour about her was dispelled. In some way (he had forgotten how, and it was perfectly incomprehensible) he was
bound to this dark, solid and determined young person, whose
shadow and suggestion he had once loved. He had to go
through with the thing as a gentleman should. Still——

And when he was sacrificing Ann!

He wouldn't stand this sort of thing, whatever else he
stood. . . . Should he say something about her dress to her
—to-morrow?

He could put his foot down firmly. He could say, " Look
'ere. I don't care. I ain't going to stand it. See?"

She'd say something unexpected, of course. She always
did say something unexpected.

Suppose, for once, he overrode what she said, and simply
repeated his point.

He found these thoughts battling with certain conversational aggressions from Mrs. Wace, and then Revel arrived
and took the centre of the stage.

The author of that brilliant romance, *Red Hearts a-Beating*,
was a less imposing man than Kipps had anticipated, but he
speedily effaced that disappointment by his predominating
manners. Although he lived habitually in the vivid world of

London, his collar and tie were in no way remarkable, and
he was neither brilliantly handsome, nor curly, nor long-
haired. His personal appearance suggested arm-chairs rather
than the equestrian exercises and amorous toyings and passionate intensities of his masterpiece ; he was inclined to be
fat, with whitish flesh, muddy-coloured straight hair ; he had
a rather shapeless and truncated nose, and his chin was
asymmetrical. One eye was more inclined to stare than the
other. He might have been esteemed a little undistinguished-
looking were it not for his beeswaxed moustache, which came
amidst his features with a pleasing note of incongruity, and
the whimsical wrinkles above and about his greater eye. His
regard sought and found Helen's as he entered the room, and
they shook hands presently with an air of intimacy Kipps,
for no clear reason, found objectionable. He saw them clasp
their hands, heard Coote's characteristic cough—a sound
rather more like a very, very old sheep a quarter of a mile
away being blown to pieces by a small charge of gunpowder
than anything else in the world—did some confused beginnings
of a thought, and then they were all going in to dinner, and
Helen's shining bare arm lay along his sleeve. Kipps was in
no state for conversation. She glanced at him, and, though he
did not know it, very slightly pressed his elbow. He struggled
with strange respiratory dislocations.   Before them went
Coote, discoursing in amiable reverberations to Mrs. Walshingham, and at the head of the procession was Mrs. Bindon
Botting, talking fast and brightly beside the erect military
figure of little Mr. Wace. (He was not a soldier really, but he
had caught a martinet bearing by living so close to Shorncliffe.) Revel came at last, in charge of Mrs. Wace's queenly
black and steel, politely admiring in a flute-like cultivated
voice the mellow wall-paper of the staircase. Kipps marvelled
at everybody's self-possession.

From the earliest spoonful of soup it became evident that
Revel considered himself responsible for the table-talk. And
before the soup was over it was almost as manifest that Mrs.
Bindon Botting inclined to consider his sense of responsibility
excessive. In her circle Mrs. Bindon Botting was esteemed
an agreeable rattle, her manner and appearance were conspicuously vivacious for one so plump, and she had an almost
Irish facility for humorous description. She would keep people
amused all through an afternoon call with the story of how
her jobbing gardener had got himself married and what his
home was like, or how her favourite butt, Mr. Stigson Warder,
had all his unfortunate children taught almost every conceivable instrument because they had the phrenological bump
of music abnormally large. The family itself was also abnormally large. " They got to trombones, my dear ! " she would
say, with her voice coming to a climax. Usually her friends
conspired to draw her out, but on this occasion they neglected

to do so, a thing that militated against her keen desire to shine in Revel's eyes. After a time she perceived that the only thing for her to do was to cut in on the talk, on her own account, and this she began to do. She made several ineffectual snatches at the general attention, and then Revel drifted towards a topic she regarded as particularly her own—the ordering of households.

They came to the thing through talk about localities. " We are leaving our house in The Boltons," said Revel, " and taking a little place at Wimbledon, and I think of having rooms in Dane's Inn. It will be more convenient in many ways. My wife is furiously addicted to golf and exercise of all sorts, and I like to sit about in clubs—I haven't the strength necessary for these hygienic proceedings—and the old arrangement suited neither of us. And besides, no one could imagine the demoralisation the domestics of West London have undergone during the last three years."

" It's the same everywhere," said Mrs. Bindon Botting.

" Very possibly it is. A friend of mine calls it the servile tradition in decay, and regards it all as a most hopeful phenomenon—— "

" He ought to have had my last two criminals," said Mrs. Bindon Botting.

She turned to Mrs. Wace, while Revel came again a little too late with a " Possibly—— "

" And I haven't told you, my dear," she said, speaking with voluble rapidity, " I'm in trouble again."

" That last girl ? "

" The last girl. Before I can get a cook, my hard-won housemaid "—she paused—" chucks it."

" Panic ? " asked young Walshingham.

" Mysterious grief ! Everything merry as a marriage-bell until my Anagram Tea ! Then in the evening a portentous rigour of bearing, a word or so from my Aunt, and immediately—Floods of Tears and Notice ! " For a moment her eye rested thoughtfully on Kipps as she said, " Is there anything heartrending about Anagrams ? "

" I find them so," said Revel. " I—— "

But Mrs. Bindon Botting got away again. " For a time it made me quite uneasy—— "

Kipps jabbed his lip with his fork rather painfully, and was recalled from a fascinated glare at Mrs. Botting to the immediate facts of dinner.

" ——whether anagrams might not have offended the good domestic's Moral Code—you never can tell. We made inquiries. No. No. No. She *must* go, and that's all ! "

" One perceives," said Revel, " in these disorders, dimly and distantly, the last dying glow of the age of Romance. Let us suppose, Mrs. Botting, let us at least try to suppose —it is Love."

Kipps clattered with his knife and fork.

" It's love," said Mrs. Botting ; " what else can it be? Beneath the orderly humdrum of our lives these romances are going on, until at last they bust up and give Notice and upset our humdrum altogether. Some fatal, wonderful soldier—— "

" The passions of the common or house-domestic—— " began Revel, and recovered possession of the table.

Upon the troubled disorder of Kipps' table manners there had supervened a quietness, an unusual calm. For once in his life he had distinctly made up his mind on his own account. He listened no more to Revel. He put down his knife and fork and refused everything that followed. Coote regarded him with tactful concern, and Helen flushed a little.

§ 4

About half-past nine that night there came a violent pull at the bell of Mrs. Bindon Botting, and a young man in a dress-suit and a gibus and other marks of exalted social position stood without. Athwart his white expanse of breast lay a ruddy bar of patterned silk that gave him a singular distinction and minimised the glow of a few small stains of Burgundy. His gibus was thrust back, and exposed a disorder of hair that suggested a reckless desperation. He had, in fact, burnt his boats and refused to join the ladies. Coote, in the subsequent conversation, had protested quietly, " You're going on all right, you know," to which Kipps had answered he didn't care a " Eng " about that, and so, after a brief tussle with Walshingham's detaining arm, had got away. " I got something to do," he said. " 'Ome." And here he was— panting an extraordinary resolve. The door opened, revealing the pleasantly furnished hall of Mrs. Bindon Botting, lit by rose-tinted lights, and in the centre of the picture, neat and pretty in black and white, stood Ann. At the sight of Kipps her colour vanished.

" Ann," said Kipps, " I want to speak to you. I got something to say to you right away. See ? I'm—— "

" This ain't the door to speak to me at," said Ann.

" But, Ann ! It's something special."

" You spoke enough," said Ann.

" Ann ! "

" Besides, that's my door, down there. Basement. If I was caught talking at *this* door—— ! "

" But, Ann, *I'm*—— "

" Basement after nine. Them's my hours. I'm a servant, and likely to keep one. If you're calling here, what name, please? But you got your friends and I got mine, and you mustn't go talking to *me*."

" But, Ann, I want to ask you—— "

Some one appeared in the hall behind Ann. " Not here,"

said Ann. "Don't know any one of that name," and incontinently slammed the door in his face.

"What was that, Ann?" said Mrs. Bindon Botting's invalid Aunt.

"Ge'm a little intoxicated, Ma'am—asking for the wrong name, Ma'am."

"What name did he want?" asked the lady doubtfully.

"No name that *we* know, Ma'am," said Ann, hustling along the hall towards the kitchen stairs.

"I hope you weren't too short with him, Ann."

"No shorter than he deserved, considering 'ow he be'aved," said Ann, with her bosom heaving.

And Mrs. Bindon Botting's invalid Aunt, perceiving suddenly that this call had some relation to Ann's private and sentimental trouble, turned, after one moment of hesitating scrutiny, away.

She was an extremely sympathetic lady was Mrs. Bindon Botting's invalid Aunt ; she took an interest in the servants, imposed piety, extorted confessions and followed human nature, blushing and lying defensively to its reluctantly revealed recesses ; but Ann's sense of privacy was strong, and her manner, under drawing-out and encouragement, sometimes even alarming. . . .

So the poor old lady went upstairs again.

§ 5

The basement door opened, and Kipps came into the kitchen. He was flushed and panting.

He struggled for speech.

"'Ere," he said, and held out two half-sixpences.

Ann stood behind the kitchen table—face pale and eyes round, and now—and it simplified Kipps very much—he could see she had indeed been crying.

"Well?" she said.

"Don't you see?"

Ann moved her head slightly.

"I kep' it all these years."

"You kep' it too long."

His mouth closed and his flush died away. He looked at her. The amulet, it seemed, had failed to work.

"Ann!" he said.

"Well?"

"Ann."

The conversation still hung fire.

"Ann," he said ; made a movement with his hands that suggested appeal and advanced a step.

Ann shook her head more definitely, and became defensive.

"Look here, Ann," said Kipps. "I been a fool."

They stared into each other's miserable eyes.

"Ann," he said. "I want to marry you."

Ann clutched the table edge. " You can't," she said faintly.

He made as if to approach her round the table, and she took a step that restored their distance.

" I must," he said.

" You can't."

" I must. You *got* to marry me, Ann."

" You can't go marrying everybody. You got to marry *'er*."

" I shan't."

Ann shook her head. " You're engaged to that girl. Lady, rather. You can't be engaged to me."

" I don't want to be engaged to you. I *been* engaged. I want to be married to you. See ? Right away."

Ann turned a shade paler. " But what d'you mean ? " she asked.

" Come right off to London and marry me. Now."

" What d'you mean ? "

Kipps became extremely lucid and earnest.

" I mean, come right off and marry me now before any one else can. See ? "

" In London ? "

" In London."

They stared at one another again. They took things for granted in the most amazing way.

" I couldn't," said Ann. " For one thing, my month's not up for mor'n free weeks yet."

They hung before that for a moment as though it was insurmountable.

" Look 'ere, Ann ! Arst to go. Arst to go ! "

" *She* wouldn't," said Ann.

" Then come without arsting," said Kipps.

" She'd keep my box—— "

" She won't."

" She will."

" She won't."

" You don't know 'er."

" Well, desh 'er—let 'er ! LET 'ER ! Who cares ? I'll buy you a 'undred boxes if you'll come."

" It wouldn't be right towards Her."

" It isn't Her you got to think about, Ann. It's me."

" And you 'aven't treated me properly," she said. " You 'aven't treated me properly, Artie. You didn't ought to 'ave—— "

" I didn't say I 'ad," he interrupted, " did I ? Ann," he appealed, " I didn't come to arguefy. I'm all wrong. I never said I wasn't. It's yes or no. Me or not. . . . I been a fool. There ! See ? I been a fool. Ain't that enough ? I got myself all tied up with every one and made a fool of myself all round. . . ."

He pleaded, " It isn't as if we didn't care for one another, Ann."

She seemed impassive, and he resumed his discourse.

"I thought I wasn't likely ever to see you again, Ann. I reely did. It isn't as though I was seein' you all the time. I didn't know what I wanted, and I went and be'aved like a fool—jest as any one might. I know what I want, and I know what I don't want now.

"Ann!"

"Well?"

"Will you come? . . . Will you come? . . ."

Silence.

"If you don't answer me, Ann—I'm desprit—if you don't answer me now, if you don't say you'll come, I'll go right out now——"

He turned doorward passionately as he spoke, with his threat incomplete.

"I'll go," he said. "I 'aven't a friend in the world! I been and throwed everything away. I don't know why I done things and why I 'aven't. All I know is I can't stand nothing in the world any more." He choked. "The pier," he said.

He fumbled with the door-latch, grumbling some inarticulate self-pity, as if he sought a handle, and then he had it open.

Clearly he was going.

"Artie!" said Ann sharply.

He turned about, and the two hung white and tense.

"I'll do it," said Ann.

His face began to work, he shut the door and came a step back to her, staring; his face became pitiful, and then suddenly they moved together. "Artie!" she cried, "don't go!" and held out her arms, weeping.

They clung close to one another. . . .

"Oh, I *been* so mis'bel!" cried Kipps, clinging to this lifebuoy; and suddenly his emotion, having no further serious work in hand, burst its way to a loud *boohoo!* His fashionable and expensive gibus flopped off, and fell and rolled and lay neglected on the floor.

"I been so mis'bel," said Kipps, giving himself vent. "Oh, I *been* so mis'bel, Ann!"

"Be quiet," said Ann, holding his poor blubbering head tightly to her heaving shoulder, herself all a-quiver; "be quiet. She's there! Listenin'. She'll 'ear you, Artie, on the stairs. . . ."

§ 6

Ann's last words when, an hour later, they parted—Mrs. and Miss Bindon Botting having returned very audibly upstairs—deserve a section to themselves.

"I wouldn't do this for every one, mind you," whispered Ann.

CHAPTER NINE

THE LABYRINTHODON

§ 1

YOU imagine them fleeing through our complex and difficult
social system as it were for life, first on foot and severally
to the Folkestone Central Station, then in a first-class
carriage, with Kipps' bag as sole chaperon to Charing Cross,
and then in a four-wheeler, a long, rumbling, palpitating, slow
flight through the multitudinous swarming London streets
to Sid. Kipps kept peeping out of the window. " It's the
next corner after this, I believe," he would say. For he had
a sort of feeling that at Sid's he would be immune from the
hottest pursuit. He paid the cabman in a manner adequate
to the occasion, and turned to his prospective brother-in-law.
" Me and Ann," he said, " we're going to marry."

" But I thought——" began Sid.

Kipps motioned him towards explanations in the shop. . . .

" It's no good my arguing with you," said Sid, smiling
delightedly as the case unfolded. " You done it now." And
Masterman, being apprised of the nature of the affair, descended
slowly in a state of flushed congratulation.

" I thought you might find the Higher Life a bit difficult,"
said Masterman, projecting a bony hand. " But I never thought
you'd have the originality to clear out. . . . Won't the young
lady of the superior classes swear ! Never mind—it doesn't
matter anyhow."

" You were starting a climb," he said at dinner, " that
doesn't lead anywhere. You would have clambered from
one refinement of vulgarity to another, and never got to any
satisfactory top. There isn't a top. It's a squirrel's cage.
Things are out of joint, and the only top there is is a lot of
blazing card-playing women and betting men, seasoned with
archbishops and officials and all that sort of glossy pandering
Tosh. . . . You'd have hung on, a disconsolate, dismal little
figure, somewhere up the ladder, far below even the motor-
car class, while your wife larked about, or fretted because
she wasn't a bit higher than she was. . . . I found it all out
long ago. I've seen women of that sort. And I don't climb
any more."

" I often thought about what you said last time I saw
you," said Kipps.

" I wonder what I said," said Masterman, in parenthesis.
" Anyhow, you're doing the right and sane thing, and that's
a rare spectacle. You're going to marry your equal, and
you're going to take your own line, quite independently of
what people up there, or people down there, think you ought

or ought not to do. That's about the only course one can take
nowadays, with everything getting more muddled and upside
down every day. Make your own little world and your own
house first of all ; keep that right side up whatever you do,
and marry your mate. . . . That, I suppose, is what *I* should
do—if *I* had a mate. . . . But people of my sort, luckily for
the world, don't get made in pairs. No !

" Besides—— However—— " And abruptly, taking
advantage of an interruption by Master Walt, he lapsed
into thought.

Presently he came out of his musings.

" After all," he said, " there's Hope."

" What about ? " said Sid.

" Everything," said Masterman.

" Where there's life there's hope," said Mrs. Sid. " But
none of you aren't eating anything like you ought to."

Masterman lifted his glass.

" Here's to Hope ! " he said, " the Light of the World ! "

Sid beamed at Kipps, as who should say, " You don't meet
a character like *this* every dinner-time."

" Here's to Hope ! " repeated Masterman. " The best thing
one can have. Hope of life—— Yes."

He imposed his moment of magnificent self-pity on them
all. Even young Walt was impressed.

§ 2

They spent the days before their marriage in a number
of agreeable excursions together. One day they went to Kew
by steamboat, and admired the house full of paintings of
flowers extremely ; and one day they went early to have
a good long day at the Crystal Palace, and enjoyed themselves very much indeed. They got there so early that nothing
was open inside ; all the stalls were wrappered up, and all
the minor exhibitions locked and barred. They seemed the
minutest creatures even to themselves in that enormous
empty aisle, and their echoing footsteps indecently loud.
They contemplated realistic groups of plaster savages, and
Ann thought they'd be queer people to have about. She was
glad there were none in this country. They meditated upon
replicas of classical statuary without excessive comment.
Kipps said, at large, it must have been a queer world then ;
but Ann very properly doubted if they really went about like
that. But the place at that early hour was really lonely. One
began to fancy things. So they went out into the October
sunshine of the mighty terraces, and wandered amidst miles
of stucco tanks, and about those quiet Gargantuan grounds.
A great gray emptiness it was, and it seemed marvellous to
them, but not nearly so marvellous as it might have seemed.
" I never see a finer place, never," said Kipps, turning to

survey the entirety of the enormous glass front with Paxton's vast image in the centre.

"What it must 'ave cost to build!" said Ann, and left her sentence eloquently incomplete.

Presently they came to a region of caves and waterways, and amidst these waterways strange reminders of the possibilities of the Creator. They passed under an arch made of a whale's jaws, and discovered amidst herbage, browsing or standing unoccupied and staring as if amazed at themselves, huge effigies of iguanodons, and deinotheria, and mastodons and such-like cattle gloriously done in green and gold.

"They got everything," said Kipps. "Earl's Court isn't a patch on it."

His mind was very greatly exercised by these monsters, and he hovered about them and returned to them. "You'd wonder 'ow they ever got enough to eat," he said several times.

§ 3

It was later in the day, and upon a seat in the presence of the green and gold Labyrinthodon that looms so splendidly above the lake, that the Kippses fell into talk about their future. They had made a sufficient lunch in the palace, they had seen pictures and no end of remarkable things, and that and the amber sunlight made a mood for them, quiet and philosophical—a haven mood. Kipps broke a contemplative silence with an abrupt allusion to one principal preoccupation. "I shall offer an 'pology, and I shall offer 'er brother damages. If she likes to bring an action for Breach after that, well—I done all I can. . . . They can't get much out of reading my letters in court, because I didn't write none. I dessay a thousan' or two'll settle all that, anyhow. I ain't much worried about that. That don't worry me very much, Ann—No."

And then, "It's a lark our marrying.

"It's curious 'ow things come about. If I 'adn't run against you, where should I 'ave been now—eh? . . . Even after we met I didn't seem to see it like—not marrying you, I mean —until that night I came. I didn't—reely."

"I didn't neither," said Ann, with thoughtful eyes on the water.

For a time Kipps' mind was occupied by the prettiness of her thinking face. A faint tremulous network of lights, reflected from the ripples of a passing duck, played subtly over her cheek and faded away.

Ann reflected. "I s'pose things 'ad to be," she said.

Kipps mused. "It's curious 'ow ever I got on to be engaged to 'er."

"She wasn't suited to you," said Ann.

"Suited? No fear! That's jest it. 'Ow did it come about?"

" I expect she led you on," said Ann.

Kipps was half minded to assent. Then he had a twinge of conscience. " It wasn't that, Ann," he said. " It's curious. I don't know what it was, but it wasn't that. I don't re-collect. . . . No. . . . Life's jolly rum ; that's one thing, any'ow. And I suppose I'm a rum sort of feller. I get excited sometimes, and then I don't seem to care *what* I do. That's about what it was, reely. Still——"

They meditated, Kipps with his arms folded and pulling at his scanty moustache. Presently a faint smile came over his face.

" We'll get a nice little 'ouse out 'Ithe way."

" It's 'omelier than Folkstone," said Ann.

" Jest a nice *little* 'ouse," said Kipps. " There's Hughenden, of course. But that's let. Besides being miles too big. And I wouldn't live in Folkestone again some'ow—not for anything."

" I'd like to 'ave a 'ouse of my own," said Ann. " I've often thought, being in service, 'ow much I'd like to manage a 'ouse of my own."

" You'd know all about what the servants was up to, any-how," said Kipps, amused.

" Servants ! We don't want no servants," said Ann, startled.

" You'll 'ave to 'ave a servant," said Kipps. " If it's only to do the 'eavy work of the 'ouse."

" What ! and not be able 'ardly to go into my own kitchen ?" said Ann.

" You ought to 'ave a servant," said Kipps.

" One could easy 'ave a woman in for anything that's 'eavy," said Ann. " Besides—— If I 'ad one of the girls one sees about nowadays, I should want to be taking the broom out of 'er 'and and do it all over myself. I'd manage better without 'er."

" We ought to 'ave one servant, anyhow," said Kipps, " else 'ow should we manage if we wanted to go out together or anything like that ? "

" I might get a *young* girl," said Ann, " and bring 'er up in my own way."

Kipps left the matter at that and came back to the house.

" There's little 'ouses going into Hythe just the sort we want, not too big and not too small. We'll 'ave a kitching and a dining-room and a little room to sit in of a night."

" It mustn't be a 'ouse with a basement," said Ann.

" What's a basement ? "

" It's a downstairs, where there's not 'arf enough light and everything got to be carried—up and down, up and down, all day—coals and everything. And it's got to 'ave a water-tap and sink and things upstairs. You'd 'ardly believe, Artie, if you 'adn't been in service, 'ow cruel and silly some 'ouses are built—you'd think they 'ad a spite against servants the way the stairs are made."

" We won't 'ave one of that sort," said Kipps. . . . " We'll 'ave a quiet little life. Now go out a bit—now come 'ome again. Read a book, perhaps, if we got nothing else to do. 'Ave old Buggins in for an evening at times. 'Ave Sid down. There's bicycles—— "

" I don't fancy myself on a bicycle," said Ann.

" 'Ave a trailer," said Kipps, " and sit like a lady. I'd take you out to New Romney easy as anything, jest to see the old people."

" I wouldn't mind that," said Ann.

" We'll jest 'ave a sensible little 'ouse, and sensible things. No art or anything of that sort, nothing stuck-up or anything, but jest sensible. We'll be as right as anything, Ann."

" No Socialism," said Ann, starting a lurking doubt.

" No Socialism," said Kipps, " just sensible—that's all."

" I dessay it's all right for them that understand it, Artie, but I don't agree with this Socialism."

" I don't neither, reely," said Kipps. " I can't argue about it, but it don't seem real like to me. All the same, Masterman's a clever fellow, Ann."

" I didn't like 'im at first, Artie, but I do now—in a way. You don't understand 'im all at once."

" 'E's so clever," said Kipps. " 'Arf the time I can't make out what 'e's up to. 'E's the cleverest chap I ever met. I never 'eard such talking. 'E ought to write a book. . . . It's a rum world, Ann, when a chap like that isn't 'ardly able to earn a living."

" It's 'is 'ealth," said Ann.

" I expect it is," said Kipps, and ceased to talk for a little while.

" We shall be 'appy in that little 'ouse, Ann, don't y' think ?" She met his eyes and nodded.

" I seem to see it," said Kipps, " sort of cosy like. 'Bout tea-time and muffins, kettle on the 'ob, cat on the 'earthrug —we must get a cat, Ann—and *you* there. Eh ? "

They regarded each other with appreciative eyes, and Kipps became irrelevant.

" I don't believe, Ann," he said, " I 'aven't kissed you not for 'arf an hour. Leastways, not since we was in those caves."

For kissing had already ceased to be a matter of thrilling adventure for them.

Ann shook her head. " You be sensible and go on talking about Mr. Masterman," she said. . . .

But Kipps had wandered to something else. " I like the way your 'air turns back jest there," he said, with an indicative finger. " It was like that, I remember, when you was a girl. Sort of wavy. I've often thought of it. . . . 'Member when we raced that time—out be'ind the church ? "

Then for a time they sat idly, each following out agreeable meditations.

" It's rum," said Kipps.

" What's rum ? "

" 'Ow everything's 'appened," said Kipps. " Who'd 'ave thought of our being 'ere like this six weeks ago ? . . . Who'd 'ave thought of my ever 'aving any money ? "

His eyes went to the big Labyrinthodon. He looked first carelessly and then suddenly with a growing interest in its vast face. " I'm deshed," he murmured. Ann became interested. He laid a hand on her arm and pointed. Ann scrutinised the Labyrinthodon, and then came round to Kipps' face in mute interrogation.

" Don't you see it ? " said Kipps.

" See what ? "

" 'E's *jest* like old Coote."

" It's extinct," said Ann, not clearly apprehending.

" I dessay 'e is. But 'e's jest like old Coote, all the same for that."

Kipps meditated on the monstrous shapes in sight. " I wonder 'ow all these old antediluvium animals *got* extinct," he asked. " No one couldn't possibly 'ave killed 'em."

" Why, *I* know that ! " said Ann. " They was overtook by the Flood. . . . "

Kipps meditated for a while. " But I thought they had to take two of everything there was—— "

" Within reason they 'ad," said Ann. . . .

The Kippses left it at that.

The great green and gold Labyrinthodon took no notice of their conversation. It gazed with its wonderful eyes over their heads into the infinite—inflexibly calm. It might, indeed, have been Coote himself there, Coote the unassuming, cutting them dead.

There was something about its serenity that suggested patience, suggested the indifference of a power that waits. In the end this quality, dimly apprehended, made the Kippses uneasy, and after a while they got up, and, glancing backward, went their way.

§ 4

And in due course these two simple souls married, and Venus Urania, the Goddess of Wedded Love, who is indeed a very great and noble and kindly goddess, bent down and blessed their union.

Book Three

Kippses

CHAPTER ONE

THE HOUSING PROBLEM

§ I

HONEYMOONS and all things come to an end, and you see at last Mr. and Mrs. Arthur Kipps descending upon the Hythe platform—coming to Hythe to find that nice *little* house, to realise that bright dream of a home they had first talked about in the grounds of the Crystal Palace. They are a valiant couple, you perceive, but small, and the world is a large, incongruous system of complex and difficult things. Kipps wears a gray suit, with a wing poke collar and a neat, smart tie. Mrs. Kipps is the same bright and healthy little girl-woman you saw in the marsh, not an inch has been added to her stature in all my voluminous narrative. Only now she wears a hat.

It is a hat very unlike the hats she used to wear on her Sundays out—a flourishing hat, with feathers and a buckle and bows and things. The price of that hat would take many people's breath away—it cost two guineas ! Kipps chose it. Kipps paid for it. They left the shop with flushed cheeks and smarting eyes, glad to be out of range of the condescending saleswoman.

" Artie," said Ann, " you didn't ought to 'ave—— "

That was all. And, you know, the hat didn't suit Ann a bit. Her clothes did not suit her at all. The simple cheap, clean brightness of her former style had given place not only to this hat, but to several other things in the same key. And out from among these things looked her pretty face, the face of a wise little child—an artless wonder struggling through a preposterous dignity.

They had bought that hat one day when they had gone to see the shops in Bond Street. Kipps had looked at the passers-by, and it had suddenly occurred to him that Ann was dowdy. He had noted the hat of a very proud-looking lady passing in an electric brougham, and had resolved to get Ann the nearest thing to that.

The railway porters perceived some subtle incongruity in Ann, so did the knot of cabmen in the station doorway, the two golfers, and the lady with daughters, who had also got out of the train. And Kipps, a little pale, blowing a little, not in complete possession of himself, knew that they noticed her and him. And Ann—— It is hard to say just what Ann observed of these things.

" 'Ere ! " said Kipps to a cabman, and regretted too late a vanished " H."

" I got a trunk up there," he said to a ticket-inspector, " marked A. K."

" Ask a porter," said the inspector, turning his back.

" Demn ! " said Kipps, not altogether inaudibly.

§ 2

It is all very well to sit in the sunshine and talk of the house you will have, and another altogether to achieve it. We English—all the world, indeed, to-day—live in a strange atmosphere of neglected great issues, of insistent, triumphant petty things ; we are given up to the fine littlenesses of intercourse ; table manners and small correctitudes are the substance of our lives. You do not escape these things for long, even by so catastrophic a proceeding as flying to London with a young lady of no wealth and inferior social position. The mists of noble emotion swirl and pass, and there you are, divorced from all your deities, and grazing in the meadows under the Argus eyes of the social system, the innumerable mean judgments you feel raining upon you, upon your clothes and bearing, upon your pretensions and movements.

Our world to-day is a meanly conceived one—it is only an added meanness to conceal that fact. For one consequence, it has very few nice little houses. Such things do not come for the asking ; they are not to be bought with money during ignoble times. Its houses are built on the ground of monstrously rich, shabbily extortionate landowners, by poor, parsimonious, greedy people in a mood of elbowing competition. What can you expect from such ridiculous conditions ? To go house-hunting is to spy out the nakedness of this pretentious world, to see what our civilisation amounts to when you take away curtains and flounces and carpets, and all the fluster and distraction of people and fittings. It is to see mean plans meanly executed for mean ends, the conventions torn aside, the secrets stripped, the substance underlying all such Chester Cootery, soiled and worn and left.

So you see our poor dear Kippses going to and fro, in Hythe, in Sandgate, in Ashford, and Canterbury and Deal and Dover —at last even in Folkestone—with " orders to view," pink and green and white and yellow orders to view, and labelled keys in Kipps' hand, and frowns and perplexity upon their faces. . . .

They did not clearly know what they wanted, but whatever it was they saw, they knew they did not want that. Always they found a confusing multitude of houses they could not take, and none they could. Their dreams began to turn mainly on empty, abandoned-looking rooms, with unfaded patches of paper to mark the place of vanished pictures, and doors that had lost their keys. They saw rooms floored with boards that yawned apart and were splintered, skirtings eloquent of the industrious mouse, kitchens with a dead black-beetle in the empty cupboard, and a hideous variety of coal-holes and dark cupboards under the stairs. They stuck their little heads through roof trap-doors, and gazed at disorganised ball-taps, at the black filthiness of unstopped roofs. There were occasions when it seemed to them that they must be the victims of an elaborate conspiracy of house agents, so bleak and cheerless is a second-hand empty house in comparison with the humblest of inhabited dwellings.

Commonly the houses were too big. They had huge windows that demanded vast curtains in mitigation, countless bed-rooms, acreage of stone steps to be cleaned, kitchens that made Ann protest. She had come so far towards a proper conception of Kipps' social position as to admit the prospect of one servant. " But lor ! " she would say, " you'd want a man-servant in this 'ouse." When the houses were not too big, then they were almost always the product of speculative building, of that multitudinous, hasty building for the extra-vagant swarm of new births that was the essential disaster of the nineteenth century. The new houses Ann refused as damp, and even the youngest of those that had been in use showed remarkable signs of a sickly constitution—the plaster flaked away, the floors gaped, the paper moulded and peeled, the doors dropped, the bricks were scaled, and the railings rusted ; Nature, in the form of spiders, earwigs, cockroaches, mice, rats, fungi, and remarkable smells, was already fighting her way back. . . .

And the plan was invariably inconvenient, invariably. All the houses they saw had a common quality for which she could find no word, but for which the proper word is " in-civility." " They build these 'ouses," she said, " as though girls wasn't 'uman beings." Sid's social democracy had got into her blood, perhaps, and, anyhow, they went about dis-covering the most remarkable inconsiderateness in the con-temporary house. " There's kitching stairs to go up, Artie ! " Ann would say. " Some poor girl's got to go up and down, up and down, and be tired out, jest because they haven't the sense to leave enough space to give their steps a proper rise—and no water upstairs anywhere—every drop got to be carried ! It's 'ouses like this wear girls out.

" It's 'aving 'ouses built by men, I believe, makes all the work and trouble," said Ann. . . .

The Kippses, you see, thought they were looking for a reasonably simple little contemporary house, but indeed they were looking either for dreamland or A.D. 1975, or thereabouts, and it hadn't come.

§ 3

But it was a foolish thing of Kipps to begin building a house.

He did that out of an extraordinary animosity for house-agents he had conceived.

Everybody hates house-agents, just as everybody loves sailors. It is, no doubt, a very wicked and unjust hatred, but

the business of a novelist is not ethical principle, but facts.
Everybody hates house-agents because they have everybody
at a disadvantage. All other callings have a certain amount
of give and take, the house-agent simply takes. All other
callings want you ; your solicitor is afraid you may change
him, your doctor cannot go too far, your novelist—if only
you knew it—is mutely abject towards your unspoken wishes ;
and as for your tradespeople, milkmen will fight outside your
front door for you, and greengrocers call in tears if you discard
them suddenly ; but who ever heard of a house-agent struggling to serve any one ? You want a house ; you go to him ;
you, dishevelled and angry from travel, anxious, inquiring ;
he calm, clean, inactive, reticent, quietly doing nothing. You
beg him to reduce rents, whitewash ceilings, produce other
houses, combine the summer-house of No. 6 with the conservatory of No. 4—much he cares ! You want to dispose of a
house ; then he is just the same—serene, indifferent. On one
occasion I remember he was picking his teeth all the time he
answered me. Competition is a mockery among house-agents ;
they are all alike ; you cannot wound them by going to the
opposite office, you cannot dismiss them, you can at most
dismiss yourself. They are invulnerably placed behind maho-
gany and brass, too far usually even for a sudden swift lunge
with an umbrella ; to throw away the keys they lend you
instead of returning them is larceny, and punishable as such. . . .

It was a house-agent in Dover who finally decided Kipps
to build. Kipps, with a certain faltering in his voice, had
delivered his ultimatum—no basement, not more than eight
rooms, hot and cold water upstairs, coal-cellar in the house,
but with intervening doors to keep dust from the scullery and
so forth. He stood blowing. " You'll have to build a house,"
said the house-agent, sighing wearily, " if you want all that."
It was rather for the sake of effective answer than with any
intention at the time that Kipps mumbled, " That's about
what I shall do—this goes on."

Whereupon the house-agent smiled. He smiled !

When Kipps came to turn the thing over in his mind, he
was surprised to find quite a considerable intention had ger-
minated and was growing up in him. After all, lots of people
have built houses. How could there be so many if they hadn't ?
Suppose he " reely " did ! Then he would go to the house-
agent and say, " 'Ere, while you been getting me a sootable
'ouse, blowed if I 'aven't built one ! " Go round to all of them
—all the house-agents in Folkestone, in Dover, Ashford,
Canterbury, Margate, Ramsgate, saying that——! Perhaps
then they might be sorry. It was in the small hours that he
awoke to a realisation that he had made up his mind in the
matter.

" Ann," he said, " Ann," and also used the sharp of his
elbow.

Ann was at last awakened to the pitch of an indistinct inquiry what was the matter.

" I'm going to build a house, Ann."

" Eh ? " said Ann, suddenly, as if awake.

" Build a house."

Ann said something incoherent about he'd better wait until the morning before he did anything of the sort, and immediately, with a fine trustfulness, went fast asleep again.

But Kipps lay awake for a long while building his house, and in the morning at breakfast he made his meaning clear. He had smarted under the indignities of house-agents long enough, and this seemed to promise revenge—a fine revenge. " And, you know, we might reely make rather a nice little 'ouse out of it—like we want."

So resolved, it became possible for them to take a house for a year, with a basement, no service life, blackleading to do everywhere, no water upstairs, no bathroom, vast sash windows to be cleaned from the sill, stone steps with a twist and open to the rain, into the coal-cellar, insufficient cupboards, unpaved path to the dustbin, no fireplace to the servants' bedroom, no end of splintery wood to scrub—in fact, a very typical English middle-class house. And having added to this house some furniture, and a languid young person with unauthentic golden hair named Gwendolen, who was engaged to a sergeant-major and had formerly been in an hotel, having " moved in " and spent some sleepless nights, varied by nocturnal explorations in search of burglars, because of the strangeness of being in a house for which they were personally responsible, Kipps settled down for a time and turned himself with considerable resolution to the project of building a home.

§ 4

At first Kipps gathered advice, finding an initial difficulty in how to begin. He went into a builder's shop at Seabrook one day and told the lady in charge that he wanted a house built. He was breathless, but quite determined, and he was prepared to give his order there and then ; but she temporised with him, and said her husband was out, and he left without giving his name. Also he went and talked to a man in a cart, who was pointed out to him by a workman as the builder of a new house near Saltwood, but he found him first sceptical and then overpoweringly sarcastic. " I suppose you build a 'ouse every 'oliday," he said, and turned from Kipps with every symptom of contempt.

Afterwards Carshot told alarming stories about builders, and shook Kipps' expressed resolution a good deal, and then Pearce raised the question whether one ought to go in the first instance to a builder at all, and not rather to an architect. Pearce knew a man at Ashford whose brother was an architect, and as it is always better in these matters to get some one you know, the Kippses decided, before Pearce had gone, and Carshot's warnings had resumed their sway, to apply to him. They did so—rather dubiously.

The architect, who was brother of Pearce's friend, appeared as a small, alert individual with a black bag and a cylindrical silk hat, and he sat at the dining-room table, with his hat and his bag exactly equidistant right and left of him, and maintained a demeanour of impressive woodenness, while Kipps, on the hearthrug, with a quaking sense of gigantic enterprise, vacillated answers to his inquiries. Ann held a watching brief for herself, in a position she had chosen as suitable to the occasion, beside the corner of the carved oak sideboard. They felt, in a sense, at bay.

The architect began by asking for the site, and seemed a little discomposed to discover this had still to be found. " I thought of building just anywhere," said Kipps. " I 'aven't made up my mind about that yet." The architect remarked that he would have preferred to see the site in order to know where to put what he called his " ugly side," but it was quite possible, of course, to plan a house " in the air," on the level, " simply with back and front assumed "—if they would like to do that. Kipps flushed slightly, and secretly hoping it would make no great difference in the fees, said a little doubtfully that he thought that would be all right.

The architect then marked off, as it were, the first section of his subject, with a single dry cough, opened his bag, took out a spring tape measure, some hard biscuits, a metal flask, a new pair of dogskin gloves, a clockwork motor-car partially wrapped in paper, a bunch of violets, a paper of small brass screws, and, finally, a large distended notebook ; he replaced the other objects carefully, opened his notebook, put a pencil to his lips and said, " And what accommodation will you require ? " To which Ann, who had followed his every movement with the closest attention and a deepening dread, replied with the violent suddenness of one who has lain in wait, " Cubbuds ! "

" Anyhow," she added, catching her husband's eye.

The architect wrote it down.

" And how many rooms ? " he said, coming to secondary matters.

The young people regarded one another. It was dreadfully like giving an order.

" How many bedrooms, for example ? " asked the architect.

" One ? " suggested Kipps, inclined now to minimise at any cost.

" There's Gwendolen ! " said Ann.

" Visitors, perhaps," said the architect ; and temperately, " You never know."

" Two, p'r'aps ? " said Kipps. " We don't want no more than a *little* 'ouse, you know."

" But the merest shooting-box——" said the architect. . . .

They got to six, he beat them steadily from bedroom to bedroom, the word " nursery " played across their imaginative skies—he mentioned it as the remotest possibility—and then six being reluctantly conceded, Ann came forward to the table, sat down, and delivered herself of one of her prepared conditions. " 'Ot and cold water," she said, " laid on to each room—any'ow."

It was an idea long since acquired from Sid.

" Yes," said Kipps, on the hearthrug, " 'ot and cold water laid on to each bedroom—we've settled on that."

It was the first intimation to the architect that he had to deal with a couple of exceptional originality, and as he had spent the previous afternoon in finding three large houses in *The Builder*, which he intended to combine into an original and copyright design of his own, he naturally struggled against these novel requirements. He enlarged on the extreme expensiveness of plumbing, on the extreme expensiveness of everything not already arranged for in his scheme, and only when Ann declared she'd as soon not have the house as not have her requirements, and Kipps, blenching the while, had said he didn't mind what a thing cost him so long as he got what he wanted, did he allow a kindred originality of his own to appear beneath the acquired professionalism of his methods. He dismissed their previous talk with his paragraphic cough. " Of course," he said, " if you don't mind being unconventional——"

He explained that he had been thinking of a Queen Anne style of architecture (Ann, directly she heard her name, shook her head at Kipps in an aside) so far as the exterior went. For his own part, he said, he liked to have the exterior of a house in a style, not priggishly in a style, but mixed, with one style uppermost, and the gables and dormers and casements of the Queen Anne style, with a little roughcast and sham timbering here and there, and perhaps a bit of an overhang, diversified a house and made it interesting. The advantages of what he called a Queen Anne style was that it had such a variety of features. . . . Still, if they were prepared to be unconventional it could be done. A number of houses were now built in the unconventional style, and were often very pretty. In the unconventional style one frequently had what perhaps he might call Internal Features—for example, an old English oak staircase and gallery. White roughcast and green paint were a good deal favoured in houses of this type.

He indicated that his excursus on style was finished by a momentary use of his cough, and reopened his notebook, which he had closed to wave about in a moment of descriptive enthusiasm while expatiating on the unbridled wealth of External Features associated with Queen Anne. " Six bedrooms," he said, moistening his pencil. " One with barred windows, suitable for a nursery if required."

Kipps endorsed this huskily and reluctantly.

There followed a most interesting discussion upon house-building, in which Kipps played a minor part. They passed from bedrooms to the kitchen and scullery, and there Ann displayed an intelligent exactingness that won the expressed admiration of the architect. They were particularly novel upon the position of the coal-cellar, which Ann held to be altogether too low in the ordinary house, necessitating much heavy carrying. They dismissed as impracticable the idea of having coal-cellar and kitchen at the top of the house, because that would involve carrying all the coal through the house, and therewith much subsequent cleaning, and for a time they dealt with a conception of a coal-cellar on the ground floor with a light staircase running up outside to an exterior shoot. " It might be made a Feature," said the architect a little doubtfully, jotting down a note of it. " It would be apt to get black, you know."

Thence they passed to the alternative of service lifts, and then, by an inspiration of the architect's, to the possibilities of gas-heating. Kipps did a complicated verbal fugue on the theme, " gas-heating heats the air," with variable aspirates ; he became very red, and was lost to the discussion altogether for a time, though his lips kept silently moving.

Subsequently the architect wrote to say that he found in his notebook very full and explicit directions for bow windows to all rooms, for bedrooms, for water supply, lift, height of stairs and absence of twists therein, for a well-ventilated kitchen twenty feet square, with two dressers and a large box window-seat, for scullery and outhouses and offices, but nothing whatever about drawing-room, dining-room, library, or study, or approximate cost, and he awaited further instruc-tions. He presumed there would be a breakfast-room, dining-room, drawing-room, and study for Mr. Kipps—at least that was his conception—and the young couple discussed this matter long and ardently.

Ann was distinctly restrictive in this direction. " I don't see what you want a drawin'-room and a dinin' *and* a kitchin for. If we was going to let in summer—well and good. But we're not going to let. Consequently we don't want so many rooms. Then there's a 'all. What use is a 'all ? It only makes work. And a study ! "

Kipps had been humming and stroking his moustache since he had read the architect's letter. " I think I'd like a little bit of a study—not a big one, of course, but one with a desk and bookshelves, like there was in Hughenden. I'd like that."

It was only after they had talked to the architect again and seen how scandalised he was at the idea of not having a draw-ing-room, that they consented to that Internal Feature. They consented to please him. " But we shan't never use it," said Ann.

Kipps had his way about a study. "When I get that study," said Kipps, "I shall do a bit of reading I've long wanted to do. I shall make a nabit of going in there and reading something an hour every day. There's Shakespeare and a lot of things a man like me ought to read. Besides, we got to 'ave *somewhere* to put the Encyclopædia. I've always thought a study was about what I've wanted all along. You can't 'elp reading if you got a study. If you 'aven't, there's nothing for it, so far's *I* can see, but treshy novels."

He looked down at Ann, and was surprised to see a joyless thoughtfulness upon her face.

"Fency, Ann!" he said, not too buoyantly, "'aving a little 'ouse of our own!"

"It won't be a little 'ouse," said Ann, "not with all them rooms."

§ 5

Any lingering doubt in that matter was dispelled when it came to plans.

The architect drew three sets of plans on a transparent bluish sort of paper that smelt abominably. He painted them very nicely; brick-red and ginger, and arsenic green and a leaden sort of blue, and brought them over to show our young people. The first set were very simple, with practically no External Features—"a plain style," he said it was—but it looked a big sort of house, nevertheless; the second had such extras as a conservatory, bow windows of various sorts, one roughcast gable and one half-timbered ditto in plaster, and a sort of overhung veranda, and was much more imposing; and the third was quite fungoid with External Features, and honeycombed with Internal ones; it was, he said, "practically a mansion," and altogether a very noble fruit of the creative mind of man. It was, he admitted, perhaps almost too good for Hythe; his art had run away with him and produced a modern mansion in the "best Folkestone style"; it had a central hall with a staircase, a Moorish gallery, and a Tudor stained-glass window, crenelated battlements to the leading over the portico, an octagonal bulge with octagonal bay windows, surmounted by an Oriental dome of metal, lines of yellow bricks to break up the red and many other richnesses and attractions. It was the sort of house, ornate and in its dignified way voluptuous, that a city magnate might build, but it seemed excessive to the Kippses. The first plan had seven bedrooms, the second eight, the third eleven; they had, the architect explained, "worked in," as if they were pebbles in a mountaineer's boot.

"They're big 'ouses," said Ann, directly the elevations were unrolled.

Kipps listened to the architect, with round eyes and an exuberant caution in his manner, anxious not to commit him-

self further than he had done to the enterprise, and the architect
pointed out the Features and other objects of interest with
the scalpel belonging to a pocket manicure set that he carried.
Ann watched Kipps' face, and communicated with him furtively over the architect's head. " *Not so big*," said Ann's lips.

" It's a bit big for what I meant," said Kipps, with a reassuring eye on Ann.

" You won't think it big when you see it up," said the
architect ; " you take my word for that."

" We don't want no more than six bedrooms," said Kipps.

" Make this one a box-room, then," said the architect.

A feeling of impotence silenced Kipps for a time.

" Now which," said the architect, spreading them out,
" is it to be ? "

He flattened down the plans of the most ornate mansion
to show it to better effect.

Kipps wanted to know how much each would cost " at the
outside," which led to much alarmed signalling from Ann.
But the architect could estimate only in the most general
way.

They were not really committed to anything when the
architect went away ; Kipps had promised to think it over
—that was all.

" We can't 'ave that 'ouse," said Ann.

" They're miles too big—all of them," agreed Kipps.

" You'd want—— Four servants wouldn't be 'ardly
enough," said Ann.

Kipps went to the hearthrug and spread himself. His tone
was almost off-hand. " Nex' time 'e comes," said Kipps, " I'll
'splain to him. It isn't at all the sort of thing we want. It's
—it's a misunderstanding. You got no occasion to be anxious
'bout it, Ann."

" I don't see much good reely in building an 'ouse at all,"
said Ann.

" Oo, we *got* to build a 'ouse now we begun," said Kipps.
" But now supposin' we 'ad—— "

He spread out the most modest of the three plans and
scratched his cheek.

§ 6

It was unfortunate that old Kipps came over the next day.

Old Kipps always produced peculiar states of mind in his
nephew—a rash assertiveness, a disposition towards display
unlike his usual self. There had been great difficulty in re-
conciling both these old people to the Pornick *mésalliance*,
and at times the controversy echoed in old Kipps' expressed
thoughts. This, perhaps, it was, and no ignoble vanity, that
set the note of florid successfulness going in Kipps' conversation whenever his uncle appeared. Mrs. Kipps was, as a
matter of fact, not reconciled at all ; she had declined all

invitations to come over on the bus, and was a taciturn hostess on the one occasion when the young people called at the toy-shop *en route* for Mrs. Pornick. She displayed a tendency to sniff that was clearly due to pride rather than catarrh, and, except for telling Ann she hoped she would not feel too " stuck up " about her marriage, confined her conversation to her nephew or the infinite. The call was a brief one, and made up chiefly of pauses, no refreshment was offered or asked for, and Ann departed with a singularly high colour. For some reason she would not call at the toy-shop a second time when they found themselves again in New Romney.

But old Kipps, having adventured over and tried the table of the new *ménage* and found it to his taste, showed many signs of softening towards Ann. He came again, and then again. He would come over by the bus, and, except when his mouth was absolutely full, he would give his nephew one solid and continuous mass of advice of the most subtle and disturbing description until it was time to toddle back to the High Street for the afternoon bus. He would walk with him to the sea front, and commence *pourparlers* with boatmen for the purchase of one of their boats—" You ought to keep a boat of your own," he said—though Kipps was a singularly poor sailor—or he would pursue a plan that was forming in his mind in which he should own and manage what he called " weekly " property in the less conspicuous streets of Hythe. The cream of that was to be a weekly collection of rents in person, the nearest approach to feudal splendour left in this democratised country. He gave no hint of the source of the capital he designed for this investment, and at times it would appear he intended it as an occupation for his nephew rather than himself.

But there remained something in his manner towards Ann —in the glances of scrutiny he gave her unawares, that kept Kipps alertly expansive whenever he was about ; and in all sorts of ways. It was on account of old Kipps, for example, that our Kipps plunged one day—a golden plunge—and brought home a box of cummerbundy ninepenny cigars, and substituted blue label old Methusaleh Four Stars for the common and generally satisfactory white brand.

" Some of this is whisky, my boy," said old Kipps, when he tasted it, smacking critical lips. . . .

" Saw a lot of young officery fellers coming along," said old Kipps. " You ought to join the volunteers, my boy, and get to know a few."

" I dessay I shall," said Kipps. " Later."

" They'd make you an officer, you know, 'n no time. They want officers," said old Kipps. " It isn't every one can afford it. They'd be regular glad to 'ave you. . . . Ain't bort a dog yet ? "

" Not yet, Uncle. 'Ave a segar ? "

" Nor a moty car ? "

" Not yet, Uncle."

" There's no 'urry about that. And don't get one of these 'ere trashy cheap ones when you do get it, my boy. Get one as'll last a lifetime. . . . I'm surprised you don't 'ire a bit more."

" Ann don't seem to fency a moty car," said Kipps.

" Ah," said old Kipps, " I expect not," and glanced a comment at the door. " She ain't used to going out," he said. " More at 'ome indoors."

" Fact is," said Kipps hastily, " we're thinking of building a 'ouse."

" I wouldn't do that, my boy," began old Kipps ; but his nephew was routing in the chiffonier drawer amidst the plans. He got them in time to check some further comment on Ann. " Um," said the old gentleman, a little impressed by the extraordinary odour and the unusual transparency of the tracing-paper Kipps put into his hands. " Thinking of building a 'ouse, are you ? "

Kipps began with the most modest of the three projects.

Old Kipps read slowly through his silver-rimmed spectacles, " Plan of a 'ouse for Arthur Kipps, Esquire. Um."

He didn't warm to the project all at once, and Ann drifted into the room to find him still scrutinising the architect's proposals a little doubtfully.

" We couldn't find a decent 'ouse anywhere," said Kipps, leaning against the table and assuming an off-hand note. " I didn't see why we shouldn't run up one for ourselves."

Old Kipps could not help liking the tone of that.

" We thought we might see—— " said Ann.

" It's a spekerlation, of course," said old Kipps, and held the plan at a distance of two feet or more from his glasses and frowned. " This isn't exactly the 'ouse I should expect you to 'ave thought of though," he said. " Practically, it's a villa. It's the sort of 'ouse a bank clerk might 'ave. 'Tisn't what I should call a gentleman's 'ouse, Artie."

" It's plain, of course," said Kipps, standing beside his Uncle and looking down at this plan, which certainly did seem a little less magnificent now than it had at the first encounter.

" You mustn't 'ave it too plain," said old Kipps.

" If it's comfortable—— " Ann hazarded.

Old Kipps glanced at her over his spectacles. " You ain't comfortable, my gel, in this world, not if you don't live up to your position "—so putting compactly into contemporary English that fine old phrase *noblesse oblige.* " A 'ouse of this sort is what a retired tradesman might 'ave, or some little whipper-snapper of a s'licitor. But *you*—— "

" Course that isn't the o'ny plan," said Kipps, and tried the middle one.

But it was the third one won over old Kipps. " Now, that's a *'ouse*, my boy," he said at the sight of it.

Ann came and stood just behind her husband's shoulder, while old Kipps expanded upon the desirability of the larger scheme. " You ought to 'ave a billiard-room," he said ; " I don't see that, but all the rest's about right ! A lot of these 'ere officers 'ere 'ud be glad of a game of billiards. . . .

" What's all these dots ? " said old Kipps.

" S'rubbery," said Kipps. " Flow'ing s'rubs."

" There's eleven bedrooms in that 'ouse," said Ann. " It's a bit of a lot, ain't it, Uncle ? "

" You'll want 'em, my girl. As you get on you'll be 'aving visitors. Friends of your 'usband's, p'r'aps, from the School of Musketry—what you want 'im to get on with. You can't never tell."

" If we 'ave a great s'rubbery," Ann ventured, " we shall 'ave to keep a gardener."

" If you don't 'ave a s'rubbery," said old Kipps, with a note of patient reasoning, " 'ow are you to prevent every jackanapes that goes by starin' into your drorin'-room winder —p'r'aps when you get some one a bit special to entertain ? "

" We ain't *used* to a s'rubbery," said Ann, mulishly ; " we get on very well 'ere."

" It isn't what you're used to," said old Kipps, " it's what you ought to 'ave *now*." And with that Ann dropped out of the discussion.

" Study and lib'ry," old Kipps read. " That's right. I see a Tantalus the other day over Brookland, the very thing for a gentleman's study. I'll try and get over and bid for it. . . ."

By bus time old Kipps was quite enthusiastic about the house-building, and it seemed to be definitely settled that the largest plan was the one decided upon.

But Ann had said nothing further in the matter.

§ 7

When Kipps returned from seeing his Uncle into the bus—there always seemed a certain doubt whether that portly figure would go into the little red " Tip-top " box—he found Ann still standing by the table, looking with an expression of comprehensive disapproval at the three plans.

" There don't seem much the matter with Uncle," said Kipps, assuming the hearthrug, " spite of 'is 'eartburn. 'E 'opped up them steps like a bird."

Ann remained staring at the plans.

" You don't like them plans ? " hazarded Kipps.

" No ; I don't, Artie."

" We got to build somethin' now."

" But—— It's a gentleman's 'ouse, Artie ! "

" It's—it's a decent size, o' course."

Kipps took a flirting look at the drawing and went to the window.

"Look at the cleanin'. Free servants 'll be lost in that 'ouse, Artie."

"We must '*ave* servants," said Kipps.

Ann looked despondently at her future residence.

"We got to keep up our position any'ow," said Kipps, turning towards her. "It stands to reason, Ann, we got a position. Very well! I can't 'ave you scrubbin' floors. You got to 'ave a servant, and you got to manage a 'ouse. You wouldn't 'ave me ashamed——"

Ann opened her lips and did not speak.

"What?" asked Kipps.

"Nothing," said Ann, "only I did want it to be a *little* 'ouse, Artie. I wanted it to be a 'andy little 'ouse, jest for us."

Kipps' face was suddenly flushed and obstinate. He took up the curiously smelling tracings again. "I'm not a-going to be looked down upon," he said. "It's not only Uncle I'm thinking of!"

Ann stared at him.

Kipps went on. "I won't 'ave that young Walshingham f'r instance, sneering and sniffing at me. Making out as if we was all wrong. I see 'im yesterday. . . . Nor Coote neether. I'm as good—we're as good—whatever's 'appened."

Silence, and the rustle of plans.

He looked up and saw Ann's eyes bright with tears. For a moment the two stared at one another.

"We'll 'ave the big 'ouse," said Ann, with a gulp. "I didn't think of that, Artie."

Her aspect was fierce and resolute, and she struggled with emotion. "We'll 'ave the big 'ouse," she repeated. "They shan't say I dragged you down wiv me—none of them shan't say that. I've thought—— I've always been afraid of that."

Kipps looked again at the plan, and suddenly the grand house had become very grand indeed. He blew.

"No, Artie. None of them shan't say that," and, with something blind in her motions, Ann tried to turn the plan round to her. . . .

After all, Kipps thought, there might be something to say for the milder project. . . . But he had gone so far that now he did not know how to say it.

And so the plans went out to the builders, and in a little while Kipps was committed to two thousand five hundred pounds' worth of building. But then, you know, he had an income of twelve hundred a year.

§ 8

It is extraordinary what minor difficulties cluster about house-building.

"I say, Ann," remarked Kipps one day. "We shall 'ave

to call this little 'ouse by a name. I was thinking of 'Ome Cottage. But I dunno whether 'Ome Cottage is quite the thing like. All these little fisherman's places are called Cottages."

" I like ' Cottage,' " said Ann.

" It's got eleven bedrooms, y'see," said Kipps. " I don't see 'ow you call it a cottage with more bedrooms than four. Prop'ly speaking, it's a Large Villa. Prop'ly it's almost a Big 'Ouse. Leastways a 'Ouse."

" Well," said Ann, " if you must call it Villa—Home Villa. . . . I wish it wasn't."

Kipps meditated.

" 'Ow about Eureka Villa ? " he said, raising his voice.

" What's Eureka ? "

" It's a name," he said. " There used to be Eureka Dress Fasteners. There's lots of names, come to think of it, to be got out of a shop. There's Pyjama Villa. I remember that in the hosiery. No, come to think, that wouldn't do. But Maraposa—sort of oatmeal cloth, that was. . . . No ! Eureka's better."

Ann meditated. " It seems silly like to 'ave a name that don't mean much."

" Perhaps it does," said Kipps. " Though it's what people 'ave to do."

He became meditative. " I got it ! " he cried.

" Not Oreeka ! " said Ann.

" No ! There used to be a 'ouse at Hastings opposite our school—quite a big 'ouse it was—St. Ann's. Now *that*—— "

" No," said Mrs. Kipps, with decision. " Thanking you kindly, but I don't have no butcher boys making game of me. . . ."

They consulted Carshot, who suggested, after some days of reflection, Waddycombe, as a graceful reminder of Kipps' grandfather ; old Kipps, who was for " Upton Manor House," where he had once been second footman ; Buggins, who favoured either a stern, simple number, " Number One "— if there were no other houses there, or something patriotic, as " Empire Villa "; and Pearce, who inclined to " Sandringham " ; but in spite of all this help they were still undecided, when amidst violent perturbations of the soul, and after the most complex and difficult hagglings, wranglings, fears, muddles, and goings to and fro, Kipps became the joyous owner of a freehold plot of three-eighths of an acre, and saw the turf being wheeled away from the site that should one day be his home.

CHAPTER TWO

THE CALLERS

§ 1

THE Kippses sat at their midday dinner-table amidst the vestiges of rhubarb pie, and discussed two post cards the one o'clock post had brought. It was a rare, bright moment of sunshine in a wet and windy day in the March that followed their marriage. Kipps was attired in a suit of brown, with a tie of fashionable green, while Ann wore one of those picturesque loose robes that are usually associated with sandals and advanced ideas. But there weren't any sandals on Ann or any advanced ideas, and the robe had come quite recently through the counsels of Mrs. Sid. Pornick. "It's Art-like," said Kipps, but giving way. "It's more comfortable," said Ann. The room looked out by French windows upon a little patch of green and the Hythe parade. The parade was all shiny wet with rain, and the green-gray sea tumbled and tumbled between parade and sky.

The Kipps furniture, except for certain chromo-lithographs of Kipps' incidental choice that struck a quiet note amidst the wall-paper, had been tactfully forced by an expert sales-man, and it was in a style of mediocre elegance. There was a sideboard of carved oak that had only one fault—it reminded Kipps at times of wood-carving, and its panel of bevelled glass now reflected the back of his head. On its shelf were two books from Parsons' Library, each with a "place" marked by a slip of paper; neither of the Kippses could have told you the title of either book they read, much less the author's name. There was an ebonised overmantel set with phials and pots of brilliant colour, each duplicated by looking-glass, and bearing also a pair of Japanese jars made in Birmingham, a wedding-present from Mr. and Mrs. Sidney Pornick, and several sumptuous Chinese fans. And there was a Turkey carpet of great richness. In addition to these modern exploits of Messrs. Bunt and Bubble, there were two inactive tall clocks, whose extreme dilapidation appealed to the connoisseur; a terrestrial and a celestial globe, the latter deeply indented; a number of good old iron-moulded and dusty books; and a stuffed owl, wanting one (easily replaceable) glass eye, obtained by the exertions of Uncle Kipps. The table equipage was as much as possible like Mrs. Bindon Botting's, only more costly, and in addition there were green and crimson wine-glasses—though the Kippses never drank wine. . . .

Kipps turned to the more legible of his two post cards again.

" ' Unavoidably prevented from seein' me to-day,' 'e says. I like 'is cheek. After I gave 'im 'is start and everything.' "

He blew.

" 'E certainly treats you a bit orf 'and," said Ann.

Kipps gave vent to his dislike of young Walshingham.

"He's getting too big for 'is britches," he said. "I'm beginning to wish she *'ad* brought an action for breach. Ever since *'e* said she wouldn't, 'e's seemed to think I've got no right to spend my own money."

" 'E's never liked your building the 'ouse," said Ann.

Kipps displayed wrath. "What the goodness 'as it got to do wiv 'im ?

"Overman, indeed ! " he added ; "Overmantel ! . . . 'E trys that on with me—I'll tell 'im something 'e won't like."

He took up the second card. "Dashed if I can read a word of it. I can jest make out Chit'low at the end, and that's all."

He scrutinised it. "It's like some one in a fit writing. This here might be W-H-A-T—*what*. P-R-I-C-E—*I* got it ! What price Harry now ? It was a sort of saying of 'is. I expect 'e's either done something or not done something towards starting that play, Ann."

"I expect that's about it," said Ann.

Kipps grunted with effort. "I can't read the rest," he said at last, "nohow."

A thoroughly annoying post. He pitched the card on the table, stood up and went to the window, where Ann, after a momentary reconnaissance at Chitterlow's hieroglyphics, came to join him.

"Wonder what I shall do this afternoon," said Kipps, with his hands deep in his pockets.

He produced and lit a cigarette.

"Go for a walk, I s'pose," said Ann.

"I *been* for a walk this morning.

"S'pose I must go for another," he added, after an interval.

They regarded the windy waste of sea for a space.

"Wonder why it is 'e won't see me," said Kipps, returning to the problem of young Walshingham. "It's all lies about 'is being too busy."

Ann offered no solution.

"Rain again ! " said Kipps—as the lash of the little drops stung the window.

"Oo, bother ! " said Kipps, "you got to do something. Look 'ere, Ann ! I'll go orf for a reg'lar tramp through the rain, up by Saltwood, round by Newington, over the camp, and so round and back, and see 'ow they're getting on about the 'ouse. See ? And look 'ere !—you get Gwendolen to go out a bit before I come back. If it's still rainy, she can easy go round and see 'er sister. Then we'll 'ave a bit of tea, with eacake—all buttery—see ? Toce it ourselves, p'r'aps. Eh ? "

" I dessay I can find something to do in the 'ouse," said Ann, considering. " You'll take your mackintosh and leggings, I s'pose ? You'll get wet without your mackintosh over those roads."

" Right-o," said Kipps ; and went to ask Gwendolen for his brown leggings and his other pair of boots.

§ 2

Things conspired to demoralise Kipps that afternoon.

When he got outside the house everything looked so wet under the drive of the south-wester that he abandoned the prospect of the clay lanes towards Newington altogether, and turned east to Folkestone along the Seabrook digue. His mackintosh flapped about him, the rain stung his cheek ; for a time he felt a hardy man. And then as abruptly the rain ceased and the wind fell, and before he was through Sandgate High Street it was a bright spring day. And there was Kipps in his mackintosh and squeaky leggings, looking like a fool !

Inertia carried him another mile to the Leas, and there the whole world was pretending there had never been such a thing as rain—ever. There wasn't a cloud in the sky ; except for an occasional puddle, the asphalte paths looked as dry as a bone. A smartly dressed man, in one of those overcoats that look like ordinary cloth, and are really most deceitfully and unfairly waterproof, passed him and glanced at the stiff folds of his mackintosh. " Demn ! " said Kipps. His mackintosh swished against his leggings, his leggings piped and whistled over his boot-tops.

" Why do I never get anything right ? " Kipps asked of a bright, implacable universe.

Nice old ladies passed him, refined people with tidy umbrellas, bright, beautiful supercilious-looking children. Of course, the right thing for such a day as this was a light overcoat and an umbrella. A child might have known that. He had them at home, but how could one explain that ? He decided to turn down by the Harvey monument and escape through Clifton Gardens towards the hills. And thereby he came upon Coote.

He already felt the most abject and propitiatory of social outcasts when he came upon Coote, and Coote finished him. He passed within a yard of Coote. Coote was coming along towards the Leas, and when Kipps saw him his legs hesitated about their office, and he seemed to himself to stagger about all over the footpath. At the sight of him Coote started visibly. Then a sort of *rigor vitæ* passed through his frame, his jaw protruded and errant bubbles of air seemed to escape and run about beneath his loose skin. (Seemed, I say,—I am perfectly well aware that there is really connective tissue in Coote, as in all of us, to prevent anything of the sort.) His eyes fixed themselves on the horizon and glazed. As he went by Kipps

could hear his even, resolute breathing. He went by, and
Kipps staggered on into a universe of dead cats and dust-
heaps, rind and ashes—*cut* !

It was part of the inexorable decrees of Providence that
almost immediately afterwards the residuum of Kipps had
to pass a very, very long and observant-looking girls' school.

Kipps recovered consciousness again on the road between
Shorncliffe station and Cheriton, though he cannot remember,
indeed, to this day he has never attempted to remember how
he got there. And he was back at certain thoughts suggested
by his last night's novel-reading, that linked up directly with
the pariah-like emotions of these last encounters. The novel
lay at home upon the chiffonier ; it was one about society
and politics—there is no need whatever to give the title or
name the author—written with a heavy-handed thoroughness
that overrode any possibility of resistance on the part of the
Kipps' mind. It had crushed all his poor edifice of ideals,
his dreams of a sensible, unassuming existence, of snugness,
of not caring what people said, and all the rest of it, to dust ;
it had reinstated, squarely and strongly again, the only proper
conception of English social life. There was a character in
the book who trifled with Art, who was addicted to reading
French novels, who dressed in a loose, careless way, who was
a sorrow to his dignified, silvery haired, politico-religious
mother, and met the admonitions of bishops with a front of
brass. He treated a " nice girl " to whom they had got him
engaged, badly ; he married beneath him—some low thing
or other. And sank. . . .

Kipps could not escape the application of the case. He was
enabled to see how this sort of thing looked to decent people ;
he was enabled to gauge the measure of the penalties due. His
mind went from that to the frozen marble of Coote's visage.

He deserved it !

That day of remorse ! Later it found him upon the site
of his building operations and surveying the disorder of preparation in a mood near to despair, his mackintosh over his arm.

Hardly any one was at work that day—no doubt the builders
were having him in some obscure manner—and the whole place
seemed a dismal and depressing litter. The builder's shed,
black-lettered WILKINS, BUILDER, HYTHE, looked like
a stranded thing amidst a cast-up disorder of wheelbarrows
and wheeling planks, and earth, and sand, and bricks. The
foundations of the walls were trenches full of damp concrete,
drying in patches ; the rooms—it was incredible they could
ever be rooms—were shaped out as squares and oblongs of
coarse wet grass and sorrel. They looked absurdly small—
dishonestly small. What could you expect ? Of course the
builders were having him, building too small, building all
wrong, using bad materials ! Old Kipps had told him a wrinkle
or two. The builders were having him, young Walshingham

was having him, everybody was having him! They were
having him and laughing at him because they didn't respect
him. They didn't respect him because he couldn't do things
right. Who could respect him ? . . .

He was an outcast, he had no place in the society of mankind. He had had his chance in the world and turned his
back on it. He had " behaved badly "—that was the phrase. . .

Here a great house was presently to arise—a house to be
paid for, a house neither he nor Ann could manage—with
eleven bedrooms, and four disrespectful servants having them
all the time !

How had it all happened exactly ?

This was the end of his great fortune ! What a chance he
had had ! If he had really carried out his first intentions and
stuck to things, how much better everything might have
been ! If he had got a tutor — that had been in his mind
originally — a special sort of tutor, to show him everything
right. A tutor for gentlemen of neglected education. If he
had read more and attended better to what Coote had said. . . .

Coote, who had just cut him ! . . .

Eleven bedrooms ! What had possessed him ?   No one
would ever come to see them ; no one would ever have
anything to do with them. Even his Aunt cut him ! His
Uncle treated him with a half-contemptuous sufferance. He
had not a friend worth counting in the world ! Buggins,
Carshot, Pearce—shop assistants ! The Pornicks—a low,
Socialist lot ! He stood among his foundations like a lonely
figure among ruins ; he stood among the ruins of his future,
and owned himself a foolish and mistaken man. He saw
himself and Ann living out their shameful lives in this great,
crazy place—as it would be—with everybody laughing secretly
at them, and the eleven bedrooms and nobody approaching
them—nobody nice and right, that is—for ever. And Ann !

What was the matter with Ann ? She'd given up going
for walks lately, got touchy and tearful, been fitful with her
food. Just when she didn't ought to. It was all a part of the
judgment upon wrong-doing ; it was all part of the social
penalties that Juggernaut of a novel had brought home to his
mind.

§ 3

He let himself in with his latch-key. He went moodily
into the dining-room and got out the plans to look at them.
He had a vague hope that there would prove to be only ten
bedrooms. But he found there were still eleven. He became
aware of Ann standing over him. " Look 'ere, Artie ! " said
Ann.

He looked up and found her holding a number of white
oblongs.

His eyebrows rose.

" It's Callers," said Ann.

He put his plans aside slowly, and took and read the cards in silence, with a sort of solemnity. Callers ! Then perhaps he wasn't to be left out of the world after all. Mrs. G. Porrett Smith ; Miss Porrett Smith ; Miss Mabel Porrett Smith ; and two smaller cards of the Rev. G. Porrett Smith. " Lor ! " he said. " *Clergy !* "

" There was a lady," said Ann, " and two growed-up gels —all dressed up ! "

" And *'im* ? "

" There wasn't no 'im."

" Not—— ? " He held out the little card.

" No.   There was a lady and two young ladies."

" But—these cards ! Whad they go and leave these two little cards with the Rev. G. Smith on for ? Not if 'e wasn't with 'em."

" 'E wasn't with 'em."

" Not a little chap—dodgin' about be'ind the others ? And didn't come in ? "

" I didn't see no gentleman with them at all," said Ann.

" Rum ! " said Kipps.   A half-forgotten experience came back to him. " I know," he said, waving the reverend gentleman's card, " 'e give 'em the slip ; that's what he'd done. Gone off while they was rapping before you let 'em in. It's a fair call any'ow." He felt a momentary base satisfaction at his absence. " What did they talk about, Ann ? "

There was a pause.   " I didn't let 'em in," said Ann.

He looked up suddenly and perceived that something unusual was the matter with Ann. Her face was flushed, her eyes were red and hard.

" Didn't let 'em in ? "

" No ! They didn't come in at all."

He was too astonished for words.

" I answered the door," said Ann.   " I'd been upstairs, 'namelling the floor. 'Ow was I to think about Callers, Artie ? We ain't never 'ad Callers, all the time we been 'ere. I'd sent Gwendolen out for a bref of fresh air, and there I was upstairs, 'namelling that floor she done so bad, so's to get it done before she came back. I thought I'd 'namel that floor and then get tea, and 'ave it quiet with you, toce and all, before she came back. 'Ow was I to think about Callers ? "

She paused.   " Well," said Kipps, " what then ? "

" They came and rapped.   'Ow was I to know ? I thought it was a tradesman or something. Never took my apron off, never wiped the 'namel off my 'ands—nothing. There they was ! "

She paused again.   She was getting to the disagreeable part.

" Wad they say ? " said Kipps.

" She says, ' Is Mrs. Kipps at home ? ' See ? To me."

" Yes."

" And me all painty and no cap on and nothing, neither missis not servant like. There, Artie, I could 'a sunk through the floor with shame, I really could. I could 'ardly get my voice. I couldn't think of nothing to say but just ' Not at 'Ome,' and out of 'abit like I 'eld the tray. And they give me the cards and went, and 'ow I shall ever look that lady in the face again I don't know. . . . And that's all about it, Artie ! They looked me up and down they did, and then I shut the door on 'em."

" Goo ! " said Kipps.

Ann went and poked the fire needlessly with a passion-quivering hand.

" I wouldn't 'ave 'ad that 'appen for five pounds," said Kipps. " Clergyman and all ! "

Ann dropped the poker into the fender with some éclat, and stood up and looked at her hot face in the glass. Kipps' disappointment grew. " You did ought to 'ave known better than that, Ann ! You reely did."

He sat forward, cards in hand, with a deepening sense of social disaster. The plates were laid upon the table, toast sheltered under a cover at mid-fender, the teapot warmed beside it, and the kettle, just lifted from the hob, sang amidst the coals. Ann glanced at him for a moment, then stooped with the kettle-holder to wet the tea.

" Tcha ! " said Kipps, with his mental state developing.

" I don't see it's any use getting in a state about it now," said Ann.

" Don't you ! I do. See ? 'Ere's these people, good people, want to 'ssociate with us, and 'ere you go and slap 'em in the face ! "

" I didn't slap 'em in the face."

" You do—practically. You slams the door in their face, and that's all we see of 'em ever ! I wouldn't 'ave 'ad this 'appen not for a ten-pound note."

He rounded his regrets with a grunt. For a while there was silence, save for the little stir of Ann's few movements preparing tea.

" Tea, Artie," said Ann, handing him a cup.

Kipps took it.

" I put sugar *once*," said Ann.

" Oo, dash it ! Oo cares ? " said Kipps, taking an extraordinarily large additional lump with fury-quivering fingers, and putting his cup, with a slight excess of force, on the recess cupboard. " Oo cares ? "

" I wouldn't 'ave 'ad that 'appen," he said, bidding steadily against accomplished things, " for twenty pounds."

He gloomed in silence through a long minute or so.

Then Ann said the fatal thing that exploded him. " Artie ! " she said.

" What ? "

" There's But-tud Toce down there ! By your foot ! "

There was a pause, husband and wife regarded one another.

" Buttud Toce, indeed ! " he said.   " You go and mess up them callers, and then you try and stuff me up with Buttud Toce ! Buttud Toce, indeed ! 'Ere's our first chance of knowing any one that's at all fit to 'sociate with—— Look 'ere, Ann ! Tell you what it is—you got to return that call."

" Return that call ! "

" Yes—you got to return that call. That's what you got to do ! I know—— " He waved his arm vaguely towards the miscellany of books in the recess. " It's in *Manners and Rools of Good S'ity*. You got to find jest 'ow many cards to leave, and you got to go and leave 'em. See ? "

Ann's face expressed terror. " But, Artie ! 'Ow *can* I ? "

" '*Ow can* you ? 'Ow *could* you ? You got to do it, any'ow. They won't know you—not in your Bond Street 'At ! If they do, they won't say nothing."

His voice assumed a note of entreaty. " You mus', Ann."

" I can't."

" You mus'."

" I can't, and I won't. Anything in reason I'll do, but face those people again I can't—after what 'as 'appened."

" You won't ? "

" *No!*" . . .

" So there they go—orf ! And we never see them again ! And so it goes on ! So it goes on ! We don't know nobody, and we *shan't* know anybody ! And you won't put yourself out not a little bit, or take the trouble to find out anything 'ow it ought to be done."

Terrible pause.

" I never ought to 'ave married you, Artie, that's the troof."

" Oh, *don't* go into that ! "

" I never ought to have married you, Artie. I'm not equal to the position. If you 'adn't said you'd drown yourself—— " She choked.

" I don' see why you shouldn't *try*, Ann—— *I've* improved. Why don't you ? 'Stead of which you go sending out the servant and 'namelling floors, and then when visitors come——"

" 'Ow was *I* to know about y'r old visitors ? " cried Ann in a wail, and suddenly got up and fled from amidst their ruined tea, the tea of which " toce, all buttery," was to be the crown and glory.

Kipps watched her with a momentary consternation. Then he hardended his heart. " Ought to 'ave known better," he said, " goin' on like that ! " He remained for a space rubbing his knees and muttering. He emitted scornfully, " I carn't, an' I won't." He saw her as the source of all his shames.

Presently, quite mechanically, he stooped down and lifted the flowery china cover. " Ter dash 'er Buttud Toce ! " he

shouted at the sight of it, and clapped the cover down again
hard. . . .

When Gwendolen came back she perceived things were in
a slightly unusual poise. Kipps sat by the fire in a rigid attitude, reading a casually selected volume of the *Encyclopædia
Britannica*, and Ann was upstairs and inaccessible—to reappear at a later stage with reddened eyes. Before the fire,
and still in a perfectly assimilable condition, was what was
evidently an untouched supply of richly buttered toast under
a cracked cover.

" They've 'ad a bit of a tiff," said Gwendolen, attending
to her duties in the kitchen with her outdoor hat still on, and
her mouth full. " They're rummuns—if ever ! My eye ! "

And she took another piece of Ann's generously buttered
toast.

§ 4

The Kippses spoke no more that day to one another.

The squabble about cards and buttered toast was as serious
to them as the most rational of differences. It was all rational
to them. Their sense of wrong burnt within them ; their sense
of what was owing to themselves, the duty of implacability,
the obstinacy of pride. In the small hours Kipps lay awake
at the nadir of unhappiness, and came near groaning. He
saw life as an extraordinarily desolating muddle ; his futile
house, his social discredit, his bad behaviour to Helen, his low
marriage with Ann. . . .

He became aware of something irregular in Ann's breathing. . . .

He listened. She was awake, and quietly and privately
sobbing ! . . .

He hardened his heart, resolutely he hardened his heart.
And presently Ann lay still.

§ 5

The stupid little tragedies of these clipped and limited lives !

As I think of them lying unhappily there in the darkness,
my vision pierces the night. See what I can see ! Above them,
brooding over them, I tell you there is a monster, a lumpish
monster, like some great, clumsy griffin thing, like the Crystal
Palace labyrinthodon, like Coote, like the leaden goddess of
the Dunciad, like some fat, proud flunkey, like pride, like
indolence, like all that is darkening and heavy and obstructive
in life. It is matter and darkness, it is the anti-soul, it is the
ruling power of this land, Stupidity. My Kippses live in its
shadow. Shalford and his apprenticeship system, the Hastings
Academy, the ideas of Coote, the ideas of the old Kippses,
all the ideas that have made Kipps what he is—all these are
a part of its shadow. But for that monster they might not be
groping among false ideas to hurt one another so sorely ; but

for that, the glowing promise of childhood and youth might have had a happier fruition ; thought might have awakened in them to meet the thought of the world, the quickening sunshine of literature pierced to the substance of their souls ; their lives might not have been divorced, as now they are divorced, from the apprehension of beauty that we favoured ones are given—the vision of the Grail that makes life fine for ever. I have laughed, and I laugh at these two people ; I have sought to make you laugh. . . .

But I see through the darkness the souls of my Kippses as they are, as little pink strips of quivering, living stuff, as things like the bodies of little, ill-nourished, ailing, ignorant children—children who feel pain, who are naughty and muddled and suffer, and do not understand why. And the claw of this Beast rests upon them !

CHAPTER THREE

TERMINATIONS

§ 1

NEXT morning came a remarkable telegram from Folkestone. " Please come at once—urgent—Walshingham," said the telegram, and Kipps, after an agitated but still ample breakfast, departed. . . .

When he returned his face was very white, and his countenance disordered. He let himself in with his latch-key and came into the dining-room, where Ann sat, affecting to work at a little thing she called a bib. She heard his hat fall in the hall before he entered, as though he had missed the peg. " I got something to tell you, Ann," he said, disregarding their overnight quarrel, and went to the hearthrug and took hold of the mantel and stared at Ann as though the sight of her was novel.

" Well ? " said Ann, not looking up, and working a little faster.

" 'E's gone ! "

Ann looked up sharply, and her hands stopped. " *Who's* gone ? " For the first time she perceived Kipps' pallor.

" Young Walshingham—I saw 'er, and she tole me."

" Gone ! What d'you mean ? "

" Cleared out ! Gone off for good ! "

" What for ? "

" For 'is 'ealth," said Kipps, with sudden bitterness. " 'E's been speckylating. He's speckylated our money, and 'e's speckylated their money, and now 'e's took 'is 'ook. That's all about it, Ann."

" You mean—— ? "

" I mean 'e's orf, and our twenty-four fousand's orf too !

And 'ere we are ! Smashed up ! That's all about it, Ann."
He panted.

Ann had no vocabulary for such an occasion. " Oh, Lor ! "
she said, and sat still.

Kipps came about and stuck his hands deeply in his trouser
pockets. " Speckylated every penny—lorst it all—and
gorn." . . .

Even his lips were white.

" You mean we ain't got nothin' left, Artie ? "

" Not a penny ! Not a bloomin' penny, Ann. No ! "

A gust of passion whirled across the soul of Kipps. He
flung out a knuckly fist. " If I 'ad 'im 'ere," he said, " I'd—
I'd—I'd wring 'is neck for 'im. I'd—I'd—— " His voice rose
to a shout. He thought of Gwendolen in the kitchen, and fell
to, " Ugh ! "

" But, Artie," said Ann, trying to grasp it, " d'you mean
to say he's took our money ? "

" Speckylated it ! " said Kipps, with an illustrative flourish
of the arm that failed to illustrate. " Bort things dear and
sold 'em cheap, and played the 'ankey-pankey jackass with
everything we got. That's what I mean 'e's done, Ann." He
repeated this last sentence with the addition of violent adverbs.

" D'you mean to say our money's *gone*, Artie ? "

" Ter-dash it, *Yes*, Ann ! " swore Kipps, exploding in a
shout. " Ain't I tellin' you ? "

He was immediately sorry. " I didn't mean to 'oller at
you, Ann," he said, " but I'm all shook up. I don't 'ardly
know what I'm sayin'. Ev'ry penny. . . ."

" But, Artie—— "

Kipps grunted. He went to the window and stared for
a moment at a sunlit sea. " Gord ! " he swore.

" I mean," he said, coming back to Ann, and with an air
of exasperation, " that he's 'bezzled and 'ooked it. That's
what I mean, Ann."

Ann put down the bib. " But wot are we going to *do*,
Artie ? "

Kipps indicated ignorance, wrath, and despair with one
comprehensive gesture of his hands. He caught an ornament
from the mantel and replaced it. " I'm going to bang about,"
he said, " if I ain't precious careful."

" You saw '*er*, you say ? "

" Yes."

" What did she say 'xactly ? " said Ann.

" Told me to see a s'licitor—tole me to get some one to 'elp
me at once. She was there in black—like she used to be, and
speaking cool and careful like. 'Elen ! . . . She's precious
'ard, is 'Elen. She looked at me straight. ' It's my fault,' she
said, ' I ought to 'ave warned you. . . . Only under the
circumstances it was a little difficult.' Straight as anything.
I didn't 'ardly say anything to 'er. I didn't seem to begin to

take it in until she was showing me out. I 'adn't anything to
say. Jest as well, perhaps. She talked—like a Call a'most.
She said—what *was* it she said about her mother ?—' My
mother's overcome with grief,' she said, ' so naturally everything comes on me.' "

" And she told you to get some one to 'elp you ? "

" Yes. I been to old Bean."

" O' Bean ? "

" Yes. What I took my business away from ! "

" What did he say ? "

" He was a bit off 'and at first, but then 'e come round.
He couldn't tell me anything till 'e knew the facts. What
I know of young Walshingham, there won't be much 'elp in
the facts. No ! "

He reflected for a space. " It's a Smash-up, Ann. More
likely than not, Ann—'e's left us over'ead in debt. We got to
get out of it just 'ow we can. . . .

" We got to begin again," he went on. " *Ow*, I don't know.
All the way 'ome—my 'ead's been going. We got to get a
living some'ow or other. 'Aving time to ourselves, and a bit
of money to spend, and no hurry and worry ; it's all over for
ever, Ann. We was fools, Ann. We didn't know our benefits.
We been caught. Gord ! . . . Gord ! "

He was on the verge of " banging about " again.

They heard a jingle in the passage, the large, soft impact
of a servant's indoor boots. As if she were a part, a mitigatory
part of Fate, came Gwendolen to lay the midday meal. Kipps
displayed self-control forthwith. Ann picked up the bib
again and bent over it, and the Kippses bore themselves
gloomily, perhaps, but not despairfully, while their dependant
was in the room. She spread the cloth and put out the cutlery
with a slow inaccuracy, and Kipps, after a whisper to himself,
went again to the window. Ann got up and put away her
work methodically in the chiffonier.

" When I think," said Kipps, as soon as the door closed
again behind Gwendolen—" when I think of the 'ole people,
and 'aving to tell 'em of it all, I want to smesh my 'ead against
the nearest wall. Smesh my silly brains out ! And Buggins
—Buggins, what I'd arf promised to start in a lill' outfitting
shop in Rendezvous Street. . . ."

Gwendolen returned and restored dignity.

The midday meal spread itself slowly before them. Gwendolen, after her custom, left the door open, and Kipps closed
it carefully before sitting down.

He stood for a moment, regarding the meal doubtfully.

" I don't feel as if I could swaller a moufful," he said.

" You got to eat," said Ann. . . .

For a time they said little, and once swallowing was achieved,
ate on with a sort of melancholy appetite. Each was now
busy thinking.

"After all," said Kipps, presently, "whatever 'appens, they can' turn us out or sell us up before nex' quarter day. I'm pretty sure about that."

"Sell us up!" said Ann.

"I dessay we're bankrup'," said Kipps, trying to say it easily, and helping himself with a trembling hand to unnecessary potatoes.

Then a long silence. Ann ceased to eat, and there were silent tears.

"More potatoes, Artie?" choked Ann.

"I couldn't," said Kipps. "No."

He pushed back his plate, which was indeed replete with potatoes, got up and walked about the room. Even the dinner-table looked distraught and unusual.

"What to do, I *don't* know," he said.

"Oh, *Lord*!" he ejaculated, and picked up and slapped down a book.

Then his eye fell upon another post card that had come from Chitterlow by the morning's post, and which now lay by him on the mantelshelf. He took it up, glanced at its imperfectly legible message, and put it down.

"Delayed!" he said scornfully. "Not prodooced in the smalls. Or is it smells 'e says? 'Ow can one understand that? Any'ow, 'e's 'umbugging again. Somefing about the Strand. No! . . . Well, 'e's 'ad all the money 'e'll ever get out of me! . . . I'm done."

He seemed to find a momentary relief in the dramatic effect of his announcement. He came near to a swagger of despair upon the hearthrug, and then suddenly came and sat down next to Ann, and rested his chin on the knuckles of his two clenched hands.

"I been a fool, Ann," he said in a gloomy monotone. "I been a brasted fool. But it's 'ard on us, all the same. It's 'ard."

"'Ow was you to know?" said Ann.

"I ought to 'ave known. I did in a sort of way know. And 'ere we are! I wouldn't care so much if it was myself, but it's *you*, Ann! 'Ere we are! Regular smashed up! And you——"

He checked at an unspeakable aggravation of their disaster. "I knew 'e wasn't to be depended upon, and there I left it! And you got to pay. . . . What's to 'appen to us all, I don't know."

He thrust out his chin and glared at fate.

"'Ow do you know 'e's speckylated everything?" said Ann, after a silent survey of him.

"'E 'as," said Kipps, irritably, holding firm to disaster.

"She say so?"

"She don't know, of course; but you depend upon it, that's it. She told me she knew something was on, and when she found 'im gone and a note lef' for her, she knew it was

up with 'im. 'E went by the night boat. She wrote that tele-
grarf off to me straight away."

Ann surveyed his features with tender, perplexed eyes ;
she had never seen him so white and drawn before, and her
hand rested an inch or so away from his arm. The actual loss
was still, as it were, afar from her. The immediate thing was
his enormous distress.

" 'Ow do you know—— ?" she said, and stopped. It would
irritate him too much.

Kipps' imagination was going headlong.

" Sold up ! " he emitted presently, and Ann flinched.

" Going back to work, day after day. I can't stand it,
Ann, I can't. And you—— "

" It don't do to think of it," said Ann.

Presently he came upon a resolve. " I keep on thinking
of it, and thinking of it, and what's to be done, and what's
to be done. I shan't be any good 'ome s'arfernoon. It keeps
on going round and round in my 'ead, and round and round.
I better go for a walk or something. I'd be no comfort to you,
Ann. I should want to 'owl and 'ammer things if I 'ung about
'ome. My fingers 'r all atwitch. I shall keep on thinking 'ow
I might 'ave stopped it, and callin' myself a fool. . . ."

He looked at her between pleading and shame. It seemed
like deserting her.

Ann regarded him with tear-dimmed eyes.

" You'd better do what's good for you, Artie," she said. . . .
" I'll be best cleaning. It's no use sending off Gwendolen
before her month, and the top room wants turning out." She
added with a sort of grim humour, " May as well turn it out
now while I got it."

" I better go for a walk," said Kipps.

And presently our poor, exploded Kipps was marching out
to bear his sudden misery. Habit turned him up the road
towards his growing house, and then suddenly he perceived
his direction—" Oh, Lor !"—and turned aside and went up
the steep way to the hill-crest and the Sandling Road, and
over the line by that tree-embowered Junction, and athwart
the wide fields towards Postling—a little, black, marching
figure—and so up the Downs and over the hills, whither he
had never gone before. . . .

§ 2

He came back long after dark, and Ann met him in the
passage.

" Where you been, Artie ? " she asked, with a strained
note in her voice.

" I been walking and walking—trying to tire myself out.
All the time I been thinking, what shall I do ? Trying to fix
something up, all out of nothing."

" I didn't know you meant to be out all this time."

Kipps was gripped by compunction. . . .

" I can't think what we ought to do," he said presently.

" You can't do anything much, Artie, not till you hear from Mr. Bean."

" No. I can't do anything much. That's jest it. And all this time I keep feelin' if I don't do something the top of my 'ead'll bust. . . . Been trying to make up advertisements 'arf the time I been out—'bout finding a place; good sales- man and stockkeeper, good Manchester dresses, window- dressing—Lor ! Fancy that all beginning again ! . . . If you went to stay with Sid a bit—— If I sent every penny I got to you—— I dunno ! I dunno ! "

When they had gone to bed there was an elaborate attempt to get to sleep. . . . In one of their great waking pauses Kipps remarked in a muffled tone, " I didn't mean to frighten you, Ann, being out so late. I kep' on walking and walking, and some'ow it seemed to do me good. I went out to the 'ill-top ever so far beyond Stanford, and sat there ever so long, and it seemed to make me better. Jest looking over the marsh like, and seeing the sun set. . . ."

" Very likely," said Ann, after a long interval, " it isn't so bad as you think it is, Artie."

" It's bad," said Kipps.

" Very likely, after all, it isn't quite so bad. If there's only a little—— "

There came another long silence.

" Ann," said Kipps, in the quiet darkness.

" Yes," said Ann.

" Ann," said Kipps, and stopped as though he had hastily shut a door upon speech.

" I kep' thinking," he said, trying again—" I kep' thinking, after all, I been cross to you and a fool about things—about them cards, Ann—but "—his voice shook to pieces—" we 'ave been 'appy, Ann . . . some'ow . . . togever."

And with that he and then she fell into a passion of weeping.

They clung very tightly together—closer than they had been since ever the first brightness of their married days turned to the gray of common life again. . . .

All the disaster in the world could not prevent their going to sleep at last, with their poor little troubled heads close together on one pillow. There was nothing more to be done ; there was nothing more to be thought. Time might go on with his mischiefs, but for a little while at least they still had one another.

§ 3

Kipps returned from his second interview with Mr. Bean in a state of strange excitement. He let himself in with his latch-key and slammed the door. " Ann ! " he shouted, in an unusual note ; " Ann ! "

Ann replied distantly.

" Something to tell you," said Kipps ; " something noo ! "

Ann appeared apprehensive from the kitchen.

" Ann," he said, going before her into the little dining-room, for his news was too dignified for the passage, " very likely, Ann, o' Bean says, we shall 'ave—— " He decided to prolong the suspense. " Guess ! "

" I can't, Artie."

" Think of a lot of money ! "

" A 'undred pounds p'r'aps ? "

He spoke with immense deliberation. " Over a fousand pounds! "

Ann stared and said nothing, only went a shade whiter.

" Over," he said. " A'most certainly over."

He shut the dining-room door and came forward hastily, for Ann, it was clear, meant to take this mitigation of their disaster with a complete abandonment of her self-control. She came near flopping ; she fell into his arms.

" Artie," she got to at last, and began to weep, clinging tightly to him.

" Pretty near certain," said Kipps, holding her. " A fousand pounds ! "

" I *said*, Artie," she wailed on his shoulder with the note of accumulated wrongs, " very likely it wasn't so bad. . . ."

" There's things," he said, when presently he came to particulars, " 'e couldn't touch. The noo place ! It's freehold and paid for, and with the bit of building on it, there's five or six 'undred pounds p'r'aps—say worf free 'undred for safety. We can't be sold up to finish it, like we thought. O' Bean says we can very likely sell it and get money. 'E says you often get a chance to sell a 'ouse lessen 'arf done, specially free'old. *Very* likely 'e says. Then there's Hughenden. Hughenden 'asn't been mortgaged not for more than 'arf its value. There's a 'undred or so to be got on that, and the furniture, and the rent for the summer still coming in. 'E says there's very likely other things. A fousand pounds ; that's what '*e* said. 'E said it might even be more. . . ."

They were sitting now at the table.

" It alters everything," said Ann.

" I been thinking that, Ann, all the way 'ome. I came in the motor-car. First ride I've had since the Smash. We needn't send off Gwendolen ; leastways, not till *after*. You know. We needn't turn out of 'ere—not for a long time. What we been doing for the o' people we can go on doing a'most as much. And your mother ! . . . I wanted to 'oller, coming along. I pretty near run coming down the road by the Hotel."

" Oh, I *am* glad we can stop 'ere and be comfortable a bit," said Ann. " I *am* glad for that."

" I pretty near told the driver on the motor—only 'e was the sort won't talk. . . . You see, Ann, we'll be able to start a shop, we'll be able to get *into* something like. All about our 'aving to go back to places and that—all that doesn't matter any more."

For a while they abandoned themselves to ejaculating transports. Then they fell talking to shape an idea to themselves of the new prospect that opened before them.

" We must start a sort of shop," said Kipps, whose imagination had been working. " It'll 'ave to be a shop."

" Drapery ? " said Ann.

" You want such a lot of capital for the drapery ; mor'n a thousand pounds you want by a long way—to start it anything like proper."

" Well, outfitting. Like Buggins was going to do."

Kipps glanced at that for a moment, because the idea had not occurred to him. Then he came back to his prepossession.

" Well, I thought of something else, Ann," he said. " You see, I've always thought a little bookshop—— It isn't like the drapery—'aving to be learnt. I thought, even before this Smash Up, 'ow I'd like to 'ave something to do, instead of always 'aving 'olidays always like we 'ave been 'aving."

She reflected.

" You don't know *much* about books, do you, Artie ? "

" You don't want to." He illustrated. " I noticed when we used to go to that Lib'ry at Folkestone, ladies weren't anything like what they was in a draper's—if you 'aven't got *just* what they want, it's ' Oh, no ! ' and out they go. But in a bookshop it's different. One book's very like another— after all, what is it ? Something to read and done with. It's not a thing that matters like print dresses or serviettes— where you either like 'em or don't, and people judge you by. They take what you give 'em in books and lib'ries, and glad to be told *what* to. See 'ow we was—up at that lib'ry. . . . "

He paused. " You see, Ann——

" Well, I read 'n 'dvertisement the other day—— I been asking Mr. Bean. It said—five 'undred pounds."

" What did ? "

" Branches," said Kipps.

Ann failed to understand. " It's a sort of thing that gets up bookshops all over the country," said Kipps. " I didn't tell you, but I arst about it a bit. On'y I dropped it again. Before this Smash, I mean. I'd thought I'd like to keep a shop for a lark, on'y then I thought it silly. Besides, it 'ud 'ave been beneath me."

He blushed vividly. " It was a sort of projek of mine, Ann.

" On'y it wouldn't 'ave done," he added.

It was a tortuous journey when the Kippses set out to explain anything to each other. But through a maze of fragmentary elucidations and questions, their minds did presently begin to approximate to a picture of a compact, bright little shop, as a framework for themselves.

" I thought of it one day when I was in Folkestone. I thought of it one day when I was looking in at a window. I see a chap dressin' a window, and he was whistlin', reg'lar light-hearted. . . . I thought—I'd like to keep a bookshop any'ow, jest for something to do. And when people weren't about, then you could sit and read the books. See ? It wouldn't be arf bad. . . ."

They mused, each with elbows on table and knuckles to lips, looking with speculative eyes at each other.

" Very likely we'll be 'appier than we should 'ave been with more money," said Kipps, presently.

" We wasn't 'ardly suited—— " reflected Ann, and left her sentence incomplete.

" Fish out of water like," said Kipps. . . .

" You won't 'ave to return that call now," said Kipps, opening a new branch of the question. " That's one good thing."

" Lor ! " said Ann, " no more I shan't ! "

" I don't s'pose they'd want you to even if you did—with things as they are."

A certain added brightness came into Ann's face. " Nobody won't be able to come leaving cards on us, Artie, now, any more. We are out of *that* ! "

" There isn't no necessity for us to be Stuck Up," said Kipps, " any more for ever ! 'Ere we are, Ann, common people, with jest no position at all, as you might say, to keep up. No se'v'nts not if you don't like. No dressin' better than other people. If it wasn't we been robbed—dashed if I'd care a rap about losing that money. I b'lieve "—his face shone with the rare pleasure of paradox—" I reely b'lieve, Ann, it'll prove a savin' in the end."

§ 4

The remarkable advertisement which had fired Kipps' imagination with this dream of a bookshop opened out in the most alluring way. It was one little facet in a comprehensive scheme of transatlantic origin, which was to make our old-world methods of bookselling " sit up," and it displayed an imaginative briskness, a lucidity and promise that aroused the profoundest scepticism in the mind of Mr. Bean. To Kipps' renewed investigations it presented itself in an expository illustrated pamphlet (far too well printed, Mr. Bean thought, for a reputable undertaking) of the most convincing sort. Mr. Bean would not let him sink his capital in shares in its projected company that was to make all things new in the world of books, but he could not prevent Kipps becoming one of their associated booksellers. And so, when presently it became apparent that an Epoch was not to be made, and the " Associated Booksellers' Trading Union (Limited) " receded and dissolved and liquidated (a few drops) and vanished and went away to talk about something else, Kipps remained floating undamaged in this interestingly uncertain universe as an independent bookseller.

Except that it failed, the Associated Booksellers' Trading Union had all the stigmata of success. Its fault, perhaps, was that it had them all instead of only one or two. It was to buy wholesale for all its members and associates and exchange stock, having a common books-in-stock list and a common lending library, and it was to provide a uniform registered shop-front to signify all these things to the intelligent passer-by. Except that it was controlled by buoyant young Overmen, with a touch of genius in their arithmetic, it was, I say, a most plausible and hopeful project. Kipps went several times to London, and an agent came to Hythe, Mr. Bean made some timely interventions, and then behind a veil of planks and an announcement in the High Street, the uniform registered shop-front came rapidly into being. " Associated Book-sellers' Trading Union," said this shop-front, in a refined artistic lettering that bookbuyers were going to value, as wise men over forty value the proper label for Berncasteler Doctor, and then, "Arthur Kipps."

Next to starting a haberdasher's shop, I doubt if Kipps could have been more truly happy than during those weeks of preparation.

There is, of course, nothing on earth, and I doubt at times if there is a joy in heaven, like starting a small haberdasher's shop. Imagine, for example, having a drawerful of tapes (one whole piece most exquisitely blocked) of every possible width of tape, or again, an army of neat, large packages, each displaying one sample of hooks and eyes. Think of your cottons, your drawer of coloured silks, the little, less, least of the compartments and thin packets of your needle-drawer ! Poor princes and wretched gentlefolk, mysteriously above retail trade, may taste only the faint unsatisfactory shadow of these delights with trays of stamps or butterflies. I write, of course, for those to whom these things appeal ; there are clods alive who see nothing, or next to nothing, in spools of mercerised cotton and endless bands of paper-set pins. I write for the wise, and as I write I wonder that Kipps resisted haberdashery. He did. Yet even starting a bookshop is at least twenty times as interesting as building your own house to your own design in unlimited space and time, or any possible thing people with indisputable social position and sound securities can possibly find to do. Upon that I rest.

You figure Kipps "going to have a look to see how the little shop is getting on," the shop that is not to be a loss and a spending of money, but a gain. He does not walk too fast towards it ; as he comes into view of it his paces slacken and his head goes to one side. He crosses to the pavement opposite in order to inspect the fascia better, already his name is adumbrated in faint white lines ; stops in the middle of the road and scrutinises imaginary details, for the benefit of his future next-door neighbour, the curiosity-shop man, and so at last, in. . . A smell of paint and of the shavings of imperfectly seasoned pinewood ! The shop is already glazed, and a carpenter is busy over the fittings for adjustable shelves in the side windows. A painter is busy on the fixtures round about (shelving above and drawers below), which are to accommodate most of the stock, and the counter—the counter and desk are done. Kipps goes inside the desk, the desk which is to be the strategic centre of the shop, brushes away some sawdust, and draws out the marvellous till : here gold is to be, here silver, here copper—notes locked up in a cash-box in the well below. Then he leans his elbows on the desk, rests his chin on his fist and fills the shelves with imaginary stock ; books beyond reading. Every day a man who cares to wash his hands and read uncut pages artfully may have his cake and eat it, among that stock. Under the counter to the right paper and string are to lurk, ready to leap up and embrace goods sold ; on the table to the left, art publications —whatever they may prove to be. He maps it out, serves an imaginary customer, receives a dream seven-and-sixpence, packs, bows out. He wonders how it was he ever came to fancy a shop a disagreeable place.

" It's different," he says at last, after musing on that difficulty, " being your own."

It *is* different. . . .

Or, again, you figure Kipps with something of the air of a young sacristan, handling his brightly virginal account books, and looking and looking again, and then still looking, at an unparalleled specimen of copperplate engraving, ruled money below, and above bearing the words, " In Account with ARTHUR KIPPS (loud flourishes), The Booksellers' Trading Union " (temperate decoration). You figure Ann sitting and stitching at one point of the circumference of the light of the lamp, stitching queer little garments for some unknown stranger, and over against her sits Kipps. Before him is one of those engraved memorandum forms, a moist pad, wet with some thick and greasy, greenish-purple ink, that is also spreading quietly but steadily over his fingers, a cross-nibbed pen for first-aid surgical assistance to the patient in his hand, a dating rubber stamp. At intervals he brings down this latter with great care and emphasis upon the paper, and when he lifts it there appears a beautiful oval design, of which " Paid, Arthur Kipps, The Associated Booksellers' Trading Union," and a date, are the essential ingredients, stamped in purple ink.

Anon he turns his attention to a box of small, round, yellow labels, declaring " This book was bought from the Associated Booksellers' Trading Union." He licks one with deliberate care, sticks it on the paper before him and defaces it with-great solemnity. "I can do it, Ann," he says, looking up brightly. For the Associated Booksellers' Trading Union, among other brilliant notions and inspirations, devised an ingenious system of taking back its books again in part payment for new ones within a specified period. When it failed, all sorts of people were left with these unredeemed pledges in hand

§ 5

Amidst all this bustle and interest, all this going to and fro before they " moved in " to the High Street, came the great crisis that hung over the Kippses, and one morning in the small hours Ann's child was born. . . .

Kipps was coming to manhood swiftly now. The once rabbit-like soul that had been so amazed by the discovery of " chubes " in the human interior and so shocked by the sight of a woman's shoulder-blades, that had found shame and anguish in a mislaid Gibus and terror in an Anagram Tea, was at last facing the greater realities. He came suddenly upon the master thing in life—birth. He passed through hours of listening, hours of impotent fear in the night and in the dawn, and then there was put into his arms something most wonderful, a weak and wailing creature, incredibly, heart-stirringly soft and pitiful, with minute appealing hands that it wrung his heart to see. He held it in his arms and touched its tender cheek as if he feared his lips might injure it. And this marvel was his Son !

And there was Ann, with a greater strangeness and a greater familiarity in her quality than he had ever found before. There were little beads of perspiration on her temples and her lips, and her face was flushed, not pale, as he had feared to see it. She had the look of one who emerges from some strenuous and invigorating act. He bent down and kissed her, and he had no words to say. She wasn't to speak much yet, but she stroked his arm with her hand and had to tell him one thing.

"He's over nine pounds, Artie," she whispered. " Bessie's —— Bessie's wasn't no more than eight."

To have given Kipps a pound of triumph over Sid seemed to her almost to justify Nunc Dimittis. She watched his face for a moment, then closed her eyes in a kind of blissful exhaustion as the nurse, with something motherly in her manner, pushed Kipps out of the room.

§ 6

Kipps was far too much preoccupied with his own life to worry about the further exploits of Chitterlow. The man had got his two thousand ; on the whole, Kipps was glad he had had it rather than young Walshingham, and there was an end to the matter. As for the complicated transactions he

achieved and proclaimed by mainly illegible and always incomprehensible post-cards, they were like passing voices heard
in the street as one goes about one's urgent concerns. Kipps
put them aside, and they got in between the pages of the stock
and were lost for ever, and sold in with the goods to customers,
who puzzled over them mightily.

Then one morning as our bookseller was dusting round
before breakfast, Chitterlow returned, appeared suddenly in
the shop doorway.

It was the most unexpected thing in the world. The man
was in evening dress, evening dress in that singularly crumpled
state it assumes after the hour of dawn, and above his dishevelled red hair a smallish Gibus hat tilted remarkably
forward. He opened the door and stood tall and spread, with
one vast white glove flung out, as if to display how burst a
glove might be, his eyes bright, such wrinkling of brow and
mouth as only an experienced actor can produce, and a singular
radiance of emotion upon his whole being—an altogether
astonishing spectacle.

The bell jangled for a bit, and then gave it up and
was silent. For a long, long second everything was quietly
attentive. Kipps was amazed to his uttermost ; had he
had ten times the capacity, he would still have been fully
amazed. " It's Chit'low ! " he said at last, standing duster in
hand.

But he doubted whether it was not a dream.

" Tzit ! " gasped that most extraordinary person, still in an
incredibly expanded attitude, and then with a slight forward
jerk of the starry split glove, " Bif ! "

He could say no more. The tremendous speech he had had
ready vanished from his mind. Kipps stared at his facial
changes, vaguely conscious of the truth of the teachings of
Nisbet and Lombroso concerning men of genius.

Then suddenly Chitterlow's features were convulsed, the
histrionic fell from him like a garment, and he was weeping.
He said something indistinct about " Old Kipps ! *Good* old
Kipps ! Oh, old Kipps ! " and somehow he managed to mix
a chuckle and a sob in the most remarkable way. He emerged
from somewhere near the middle of his original attitude, a
merely life-size creature. " My play, boohoo ! " he sobbed,
clutching at his friend's arm. " My play, Kipps! (sob). You
know ? "

" Well ? " cried Kipps, with his heart sinking in sympathy.
" It ain't—— ? "

" No," howled Chitterlow. " No. It's a Success ! My dear
chap ! my dear boy ! Oh ! It's a—Bu—boohoo !—a Big
Success ! " He turned away and wiped streaming tears with
the back of his hand. He walked a pace or so and turned.
He sat down on one of the specially designed artistic chairs
of the Associated Booksellers' Trading Union and produced

an exiguous lady's handkerchief, extraordinarily belaced. He
choked. " *My* play," and covered his face here and there.

He made an unsuccessful effort to control himself, and shrank
for a space to the dimensions of a small and pathetic creature.
His great nose suddenly came through a careless place in the
handkerchief.

" I'm knocked," he said in a muffled voice, and so remained
for a space—wonderful—veiled.

He made a gallant effort to wipe his tears away. " I had
to tell you," he said, gulping.

" Be all right in a minute," he added, " Calm ! " and sat
still. . . .

Kipps stared in commiseration of such success. Then he
heard footsteps, and went quickly to the house doorway.
" Jest a minute," he said. " Don't go in the shop, Ann, for a
minute. It's Chitterlow. He's a bit essited. But he'll be
better in a minute. It's knocked him over a bit. You see "—
his voice sank to a hushed note as one who announces death—
" 'e's made a success with his play."

He pushed her back, lest she should see the scandal of
another male's tears. . . .

Soon Chitterlow felt better, but for a little while his manner
was even alarmingly subdued. " I *had* to come and tell you,"
he said. " I *had* to astonish some one. Muriel—she'll be first-
rate, of course. But she's over at Dymchurch." He blew his
nose with enormous noise, and emerged instantly, a merely
garrulous optimist.

" I expect she'll be precious glad."

" She doesn't know yet, my dear boy. She's at Dymchurch
—with a friend. She's seen some of my first nights before. . . .
Better out of it. . . . I'm going to her now. I've been up all
night—talking to the Boys and all that. I'm a bit off it just
for a bit. But—it Knocked 'em. It Knocked everybody."

He stared at the floor and went on in a monotone. " They
laughed a bit at the beginning—but nothing like a settled
laugh—not until the second act—you know—the chap with
the beetle down his neck. Little Chisholme did that bit to
rights. Then they began—*to* rights." His voice warmed and
increased. " Laughing ! It made *me* laugh ! We jumped 'em
into the third act before they had time to cool. Everybody
was on it. I never saw a first night go so fast. Laugh, laugh,
laugh, LAUGH, LAUGH, LAUGH " (he howled the last
repetition with stupendous violence). " Everything they
laughed at. They laughed at things that we hadn't meant to
be funny—not for one moment. Bif ! Bizz ! Curtain. A Fair
Knock Out ! . . . I went on—but I didn't say a word. Chisholme did the patter. Shouting ! It was like walking under
Niagara—going across that stage. It was like never having
seen an audience before. . . .

" Then afterwards—the Boys ! "

His emotion held him for a space. " Dear old Boys ! " he murmured.

His word multiplied, his importance increased. In a little while he was restored to something of his old self. He was enormously excited. He seemed unable to sit down anywhere. He came into the breakfast-room so soon as Kipps was sure of him, shook hands with Mrs. Kipps parenthetically, sat down and immediately got up again. He went to the bassinet in the corner and looked absent-mindedly at Kipps junior, and said he was glad if only for the youngster's sake. He immediately resumed the thread of his discourse. . . . He drank a cup of coffee noisily and walked up and down the room talking, while they attempted breakfast amidst the gale of his excitement. The infant slept marvellously through it all.

" You won't mind my not sitting down, Mrs. Kipps—I couldn't sit down for any one, or I'd do it for you. It's you I'm thinking of more than any one, you and Muriel, and all Old Pals and Good Friends. It means wealth, it means money —hundreds and thousands. . . . If you'd heard 'em, *you'd know.*"

He was silent through a portentous moment, while topics battled for him, and finally he burst and talked of them all together. It was like the rush of water when a dam bursts and washes out a fair-sized provincial town ; all sorts of things floated along on the swirl. For example, he was discussing his future behaviour. " I'm glad it's come now. Not before. I've had my lesson. I shall be very discreet now, trust me. We've learnt the value of money." He discussed the possibility of a country house, of taking a Martello tower as a swimming-box (as one might say a shooting-box), of living in Venice because of its artistic associations and scenic possibilities, of a flat in Westminster or a house in the West End. He also raised the question of giving up smoking and drinking, and what classes of drink were especially noxious to a man of his constitution. But discourses on all this did not prevent a parenthetical computation of the probable profits on the supposition of a thousand nights here and in America, nor did it ignore the share Kipps was to have, nor the gladness with which Chitterlow would pay that share, nor the surprise and regret with which he had learnt, through an indirect source which awakened many associations, of the turpitude of young Walshingham, nor the distaste Chitterlow had always felt for young Walshingham, and men of his type. An excursus upon Napoleon had got into the torrent somehow, and kept bobbing up and down. The whole thing was thrown into the form of a single complex sentence, with parenthetical and subordinate clauses fitting one into the other like Chinese boxes, and from first to last it never even had an air of approaching anything in the remotest degree partaking of the nature of a full stop.

Into this deluge came the *Daily News*, like the gleam of

light in Watts' picture, the waters were assuaged while its
sheet was opened, and it had a column, a whole column of
praise. Chitterlow held the paper, and Kipps read over his
left hand, and Ann under his right. It made the affair more
real to Kipps ; it seemed even to confirm Chitterlow against
lurking doubts he had been concealing. But it took him away.
He departed in a whirl, to secure a copy of every morning
paper, every blessed rag there is, and take them all to Dymchurch and Muriel forthwith. It had been the send-off the
Boys had given him that had prevented his doing as much
at Charing Cross—let alone that he only caught it by the skin
of his teeth. . . . Besides which, the bookstall wasn't open.
His white face, lit by a vast excitement, bid them a tremendous
farewell, and he departed through the sunlight, with his
buoyant walk, buoyant almost to the tottering pitch. His
hair, as one got it sunlit in the street, seemed to have grown in
the night.

They saw him stop a newsboy.

" Every blessed rag," floated to them on the notes of that
gorgeous voice.

The newsboy, too, had happened on luck. Something like
a faint cheer from the newsboy came down the air to terminate
that transaction.

Chitterlow went on his way swinging a great budget of
papers, a figure of merited success. The newsboy recovered
from his emotion with a jerk, examined something in his
hand again, transferred it to his pocket, watched Chitterlow
for a space, and then in a sort of hushed silence resumed his
daily routine. . . .

Ann and Kipps regarded that receding happiness in silence,
until it vanished round the bend of the road.

" I *am* glad," said Ann at last, speaking with a little sigh.

" So'm I," said Kipps, with emphasis. " For if ever a feller
'as worked and waited—it's 'im. . . . "

They went back through the shop rather thoughtfuly, and,
after a peep at the sleeping baby, resumed their interrupted
breakfast. " If ever a feller 'as worked and waited, it's
'im," said Kipps, cutting bread.

" Very likely it's true," said Ann, a little wistfully.

" What's true ? "

" About all that money coming."

Kipps meditated. " I don't see why it shouldn't be," he
decided, and handed Ann a piece of bread on the tip of his
knife.

" But we'll keep on the shop," he said, after an interval
for further reflection, " all the same. . . . I 'aven't much trust
in money after the things we've seen."

§ 7

That was two years ago, and, as the whole world knows, the *Pestered Butterfly* is running still. It *was* true. It has made the fortune of a once declining little theatre in the Strand ; night after night the great beetle scene draws happy tears from a house packed to repletion, and Kipps—for all that Chitterlow is not what one might call a business man—is almost as rich as he was in the beginning. People in Australia, people in Lancashire, Scotland, Ireland, in New Orleans, in Jamaica, in New York, and Montreal, have crowded through doorways to Kipps' enrichment, lured by the hitherto unsuspected humours of the entomological drama. Wealth rises like an exhalation all over our little planet, and condenses, or at least some of it does, in the pockets of Kipps.

" It's rum," said Kipps.

He sat in the little kitchen out behind the bookshop and philosophised and smiled while Ann gave Arthur Waddy Kipps his evening tub before the fire. Kipps was always present at this ceremony, unless customers prevented ; there was something in the mixture of the odours of tobacco, soap, and domesticity that charmed him unspeakably.

" Chuckerdee, o' man," he said affably, wagging his pipe at his son, and thought incidentally, after the manner of all parents, that very few children could have so straight and clean a body.

" Dadda's got a cheque," said Arthur Waddy Kipps, emerging for a moment from the towel.

" 'E gets 'old of everything," said Ann. " You can't say a word—— "

" Dadda got a cheque," this marvellous child repeated.

" Yes, o' man, I got a cheque. And it's got to go into a bank for you, against when you got to go to school. See ? So's you'll grow up knowing your way about a bit."

" Dadda's got a cheque," said the wonder son, and then gave his mind to making mighty splashes with his foot. Every time he splashed, laughter overcame him, and he had to be held up for fear he should tumble out of the tub in his merriment. Finally he was towelled to his toe-tips, wrapped up in warm flannel, and kissed and carried off to bed by Ann's cousin and lady help, Emma. And then after Ann had carried away the bath into the scullery, she returned to find her husband with his pipe extinct and the cheque still in his hand.

" Two fousand pounds," he said. " It's dashed rum. Wot 'ave *I* done to get two fousand pounds, Ann ? "

" What 'aven't you—not to ? " said Ann.

He reflected upon this view of the case.

" I shan't never give up this shop," he said at last.

" We're very 'appy 'ere," said Ann.

" Not if I 'ad *fifty* fousand pounds."

" No fear," said Ann.

" You got a shop," said Kipps, " and you come along in a year's time and there it is. But money—look 'ow it comes and goes ! There's no sense in money. You may kill yourself trying to get it, and then it comes when you aren't looking. There's my 'riginal money ! Where is it now ? Gone ! And it's took young Walshingham with it, and 'e's gone, too. It's like playing skittles. 'Long comes the ball, right and left you fly, and there it is rolling away and not changed a bit. No sense in it. 'E's gone, and she's gone—gone off with that chap Revel, that sat with me at dinner. Married man ! And Chit'low rich ! Lor !—what a fine place that Gerrik Club is to be sure, where I 'ad lunch wiv' 'im ! Better'n *any* 'otel. Footmen in powder they got—not waiters, Ann—footmen ! 'E's rich and me rich—in a sort of way. . . . Don't seem much sense in it, Ann—'owever you look at it." He shook his head.

" I know one thing," said Kipps.

" What ? "

" I'm going to put it in jest as many different banks as I can. See ? Fifty 'ere, fifty there. 'Posit. I'm not going to 'nvest it—no fear."

" It's only frowing money away," said Ann.

" I'm arf a mind to bury some of it under the shop. Only I expect one 'ud always be coming down at nights to make sure it was there. . . . I don't seem to trust any one—not with money." He put the cheque on the table corner and smiled and tapped his pipe on the grate, with his eyes on that wonderful document. " S'pose old Bean started orf," he reflected. . . . " One thing—'e *is* a bit lame."

" 'E wouldn't," said Ann ; " not 'im."

" I was only joking like." He stood up, put his pipe among the candlesticks on the mantel, took up the cheque and began folding it carefully to put it back in his pocket-book.

A little bell jangled.

" Shop ! " said Kipps. " That's right. Keep a shop and the shop'll keep you. That's 'ow I look at it, Ann."

He drove his pocket-book securely into his breast-pocket before he opened the living-room door. . . .

But whether, indeed, it is the bookshop that keeps Kipps, or whether it is Kipps who keeps the bookshop, is just one of those commercial mysteries people of my unarithmetical temperament are never able to solve. They do very well, the dears, anyhow, thank Heaven !

The bookshop of Kipps is on the left-hand side of the Hythe High Street coming from Folkestone, between the yard of the livery stable and the shop window full of old silver and such-like things—it is quite easy to find—and there you may see him for yourself and speak to him and buy this book of him if you like. He has it in stock, I know. Very delicately I've seen to that. His name is not Kipps, of course, you must understand that ; but everything else is exactly as I have told you. You can talk to him about books, about politics, about going to Boulogne, about life, and the ups and downs of life. Perhaps he will quote you Buggins—from whom, by the bye, one can now buy everything a gentleman's wardrobe should contain at the little shop in Rendezvous Street, Folkestone. If you are fortunate to find Kipps in a good mood, he may even let you know how he inherited a fortune " once." " Run froo it," he'll say with a not unhappy smile. " Got another afterwards—speckylating in plays. Needn't keep this shop if I didn't like. But it's something to do. . . . "

Or he may be even more intimate. " I seen some things," he said to me once. " Raver ! Life ! Why, once I—I *loped* ! I did—reely ! "

(Of course, you will not tell Kipps that he *is* " Kipps," or that I have put him in this book. He hasn't the remotest suspicion of that. And, you know, you never can tell how people are going to take that sort of thing. I am an old and trusted customer now, and for many amiable reasons I should prefer that things remained exactly on their present footing.)

§ 8

One early-closing evening in July they left the baby to the servant cousin, and Kipps took Ann for a row on the Hythe canal. The sun set in a mighty blaze, and left a world warm, and very still. The twilight came. And there was the water, shining bright, and the sky a deepening blue, and the great trees that dipped their boughs towards the water, exactly as it had been when he paddled home with Helen, when her eyes had seemed to him like dusky stars. He had ceased from rowing and rested on his oars, and suddenly he was touched by the wonder of life—the strangeness that is a presence stood again by his side.

Out of the darkness beneath the shallow, weedy stream of his being rose a question, a question that looked up dimly and never reached the surface. It was the question of the wonder of the beauty, the purposeless, inconsecutive beauty, that falls so strangely among the happenings and memories of life. It never reached the surface of his mind, it never took to itself substance or form ; it looked up merely as the phantom of a face might look, out of deep waters, and sank again into nothingness.

" Artie," said Ann.

He woke up and pulled a stroke. " What ? " he said.

" Penny for your thoughts, Artie."

He considered.

" I reely don't think I was thinking of anything," he said at last, with a smile. " No."

He still rested on his oars.

"I expect," he said, "I was thinking jest what a Rum Go everything is. I expect it was something like that."

"Queer old Artie!"

"Ain't I? I don't suppose there ever was a chap quite like me before."

He reflected for just another minute.

"Oo!—I dunno," he said at last, and roused himself to pull.

THE RESEARCH
MAGNIFICENT

CONTENTS

The Prelude

The Story

CONTENTS

THE PRELUDE

ON FEAR AND ARISTOCRACY

§ 1

THE story of William Porphyry Benham is the story of a man who was led into adventure by an idea. It was an idea that took possession of his imagination quite early in life, it grew with him and changed with him, it interwove at last completely with his being. His story is its story. It was traceably germinating in the schoolboy ; it was manifestly present in his mind at the very last moment of his adventurous life. He belonged to that fortunate minority who are independent of daily necessities, so that he was free to go about the world under its direction. It led him far. It led him into situations that bordered upon the fantastic, it made him ridiculous, it came near to making him sublime. And this idea of his was of such a nature that in several aspects he could document it. Its logic forced him to introspection and to the making of a record.

An idea that can play so large a part in a life must necessarily have something of the complication and protean quality of life itself. It is not to be stated justly in any formula, it is not to be rendered by an epigram. As well one might show a man's skeleton for his portrait. Yet, essentially, Benham's idea was simple. He had an incurable, an almost innate persuasion that he had to live life nobly and thoroughly. His commoner expression for that thorough living is " the aristocratic life." But by " aristocratic " he meant something very different from the quality of a Russian prince, let us say, or an English peer. He meant an intensity, a clearness. . . . Nobility for him was to get something out of his individual existence, a flame, a jewel, a splendour—it is a thing easier to understand than to say.

One might hesitate to call this idea " innate," and yet it comes soon into a life when it comes at all. In Benham's case we might trace it back to the Day Nursery at Seagate, we might detect it stirring already at the petticoat stage, in various private struttings and valiant dreamings with a helmet of pasteboard and a white-metal sword. We have most of us been at least as far as that with Benham. And we have died like Horatius, slaying our thousands for our country, or we have perished at the stake or faced the levelled muskets of the firing party—" No, do not bandage my eyes "—because we would not betray the secret path that meant destruction to our city. But with Benham the vein was stronger, and it increased instead of fading out as he grew to manhood. It was less obscured by those earthy acquiescences, those discretions, that saving sense of proportion, which have made most of us so satisfactorily what we are. " Porphyry," his mother had discovered before he was seventeen, " is an excellent boy, a brilliant boy, but, I begin to see, just a little unbalanced."

The interest of him, the absurdity of him, the story of him, is that.

Most of us are—balanced ; in spite of occasional reveries we do come to terms with the limitations of life, with those desires and dreams and discretions that, to say the least of it, qualify our nobility ; we take refuge in our sense of humour and congratulate ourselves on a certain amiable freedom from priggishness or presumption ; but for Benham that easy declension to a humorous acceptance of life as it is did not occur. He found his limitations soon enough ; he was perpetually rediscovering them, but out of these interments of the spirit he rose again—remarkably. When we others have decided that, to be plain about it, we are not going to lead the noble life at all, that the thing is too ambitious and expensive even to attempt, we have done so because there were other conceptions of existence that were good enough for us ; we decided that instead of that glorious impossible being of ourselves, we would figure in our own eyes as jolly fellows, or sly dogs, or sane, sound, capable men, or brilliant successes, and so forth—practicable things. For Benham, exceptionally, there were not these practicable things. He blundered, he fell short of himself, he had—as you will be told—some astonishing rebuffs, but they never turned him aside for long. He went by nature for this preposterous idea of nobility as a linnet hatched in a cage will try to fly.

And when he discovered—and in this he was assisted not a little by his friend at his elbow—when he discovered that Nobility was not the simple thing he had at first supposed it to be, he set himself in a mood only slightly disconcerted to the discovery of Nobility. When it dawned upon him, as it did, that one cannot be noble, so to speak, *in vacuo*, he set himself to discover a Noble Society. He began with simple beliefs and fine attitudes and ended in a conscious research. If he could not get through by a stride, then it followed that he must get through by a climb. He spent the greater part of his life studying and experimenting in the noble possibilities of man. He never lost his absurd faith in that conceivable splendour. At first it was always just round the corner or just through the wood ; to the last it seemed still but a little way beyond the distant mountains.

For this reason this story has been called *The Research Magnificent.* It was a real research, it was documented. In the rooms in Westhaven Street that at last were as much as one could call his home, he had accumulated material for— one hesitates to call it a book—let us say it was an analysis of, a guide to the noble life. There after his tragic death came his old friend White, the journalist and novelist, under a promise, and found these papers, he found them to the extent of a crammed bureau, half a score of patent files quite distended, and a writing-table drawer-full ; and he was greatly exercised to find them. They were, White declares, they are still after much experienced handling, an indigestible aggregation. On this point White is very assured. When Benham thought he was gathering together a book he was dreaming, White says. There is no book in it. . . .

Perhaps too, one might hazard, Benham was dreaming when he thought the noble life a human possibility. Perhaps man, like the ape and the hyæna and the tapeworm and many other of God's necessary but less attractive creatures, is not for such exalted ends. That doubt never seems to have got a lodgment in Benham's skull ; though at times one might suppose it the basis of White's thought. You will find in all Benham's story, if only it can be properly told, now subdued, now loud and amazed and distressed, but always traceable, this startled, protesting question, " *But why the devil aren't we?* " As though necessarily we ought to be. He never faltered in his persuasion that behind the dingy face of this world, the earthy stubbornness, the baseness and dullness of himself and all of us, lurked the living jewels of heaven, the light of glory, things unspeakable. At first it seemed to him that one had only just to hammer and will ; and at the end, after a life of willing and hammering, he was still convinced there was something, something in the nature of an Open Sesame, perhaps a little more intricate than one had supposed at first, a little more difficult to secure, but still in that nature, which would suddenly roll open for mankind the magic cave of the universe, that precious cave at the heart of all things in which one must believe.

And then life—life would be the wonder it so perplexingly just isn't. . . .

§ 2

Benham did not go about the world telling people of this consuming research. He was not the prophet or preacher of his idea. It was too living and intricate and uncertain a part of him to speak freely about. It was his secret self ; to expose it casually would have shamed him. He drew all sorts of reserves about him, he wore his manifest imperfections turned up about him like an overcoat in bitter wind. He was content to be inexplicable. His thoughts led him to the conviction that this magnificent research could not be, any more than any other research can be, a solitary enterprise, but he delayed expression ; in a mighty writing and stowing away of these papers he found a relief from the unpleasant urgency to confess and explain himself prematurely. So that White, though he knew Benham with the intimacy of an old schoolfellow who had renewed his friendship and had shared his last days and been a witness of his death, read the sheets of manuscript often with surprise and with a sense of added acidation.

And, being also a trained maker of books, White as he read was more and more distressed that an accumulation so interesting should be so entirely unshaped for publication. "But this will never make a book," said White with a note of personal grievance. His hasty promise in their last moments together had bound him, it seemed, to a task he now found impossible. He would have to work upon it tremendously ; and even then he did not see how it could be done.

This collection of papers was not a story, not an essay, not a confession, not a diary. It was—nothing definable. It went into no conceivable covers. It was just, White decided, a proliferation. A vast proliferation. It wanted even a title. There were signs that Benham had intended to call it *The Aristocratic Life*, and that he had tried at some other time the title of *An Essay on Aristocracy*. Moreover, it would seem that towards the end he had been disposed to drop the word "aristocratic" altogether, and adopt some such phrase as *The Larger Life*. Once it was *Life Set Free*. He had fallen away more and more from nearly everything that one associates with aristocracy—at the end only its ideals of fearlessness and generosity remained.

Of all these titles *The Aristocratic Life* seemed at first most like a clue to White. Benham's erratic movements, his sudden impulses, his angers, his unaccountable patiences, his journeys to strange places, and his lapses into what had seemed to be pure adventurousness, could all be put into system with that. Before White had turned over three pages of the great fascicle of manuscript that was called Book Two, he had found the word "Bushido" written with a particularly flourishing capital letter and twice repeated. "That was inevitable," said White with the comforting regret one feels at a friend's banalities. "And it dates . . . Yes—this was early. . . ."

"Modern aristocracy, the new aristocracy," he read presently, "has still to be discovered and understood. This is the necessary next step for mankind. As far as possible I will discover and understand it, and as far as I know it I will be it. This is the essential disposition of my mind. God knows I have appetites and sloths and habits and blindnesses, but so far as it is in my power to release myself I will escape to this. . . ."

§ 3

White sat far into the night and for several nights turning over papers and rummaging in untidy drawers. Memories came back to him of his dead friend and pieced themselves together with other memories and joined on to scraps in this writing. Bold yet convincing guesses began to leap across the gaps. A story shaped itself. . . .

The story began with the schoolfellow he had known at Minchinghampton School.

Benham had come up from his father's preparatory school at Seagate. He had been a boy reserved rather than florid in his acts and manners, a boy with a pale face, incorrigible hair, and brown eyes that went dark and deep with excitement. Several times White had seen him excited, and when he was excited Benham was capable of tensely daring things. On one occasion he had insisted upon walking across a field in which was an aggressive bull. It had been put there to prevent the boys taking a short cut to the swimming place. It had bellowed tremendously and finally charged him. He had dodged it and got away ; at the time it had seemed an immense feat to White and the others who were safely up the field. He had walked to the fence, risking a second charge by his deliberation. Then he had sat on the fence and declared his intention of always crossing the field so long as the bull remained there. He had said this with white intensity, he had stopped abruptly in mid-sentence, and then suddenly he had dropped to the ground, clutched the fence, struggled with heaving shoulders, and been sick.

The combination of apparently stout heart and manifestly weak stomach had exercised the Minchinghampton intelligence profoundly.

On one or two other occasions Benham had shown courage of the same rather screwed-up sort. He showed it not only in physical but in mental things. A boy named Prothero set a fashion of religious discussion in the school, and Benham, after some self-examination, professed an atheistical republicanism rather in the manner of Shelley. This brought him into open conflict with Roddles, the History Master. Roddles had discovered these theological controversies in some mysterious way, and he took upon himself to talk at Benham and Prothero. He treated them to the common misapplication of that fool who " hath said in his heart there is no God." He did not perceive there was any difference between the fool who says a thing in his heart and one who says it in the dormitory. He revived that delectable anecdote of the Eton boy who professed disbelief and was at once " soundly flogged " by his head master. " Years afterwards that boy came back to thank——"

" Gurr," said Prothero softly. " *Stew*—ard ! "

" Your turn next, Benham," whispered an orthodox controversialist.

" Good Lord ! I'd like to see him," said Benham with a forced loudness that could scarcely be ignored.

The subsequent controversy led to an interview with the head. From it Benham emerged more whitely strung up than ever. " He said he would certainly swish me if I deserved it, and I said I would certainly kill him if he did."

" And then ? "

" He told me to go away and think it over. Said he would preach about it next Sunday. . . . Well, a swishing isn't a likely thing anyhow. But I would. . . . There isn't a master here I'd stand a thrashing from—not one. . . . And because I choose to say what I think ! . . . I'd run amuck."

For a week or so the school was exhilarated by a vain and ill-concealed hope that the head might try it just to see if Benham would. It was tantalisingly within the bounds of possibility. . . .

These incidents came back to White's mind as he turned over the newspapers in the upper drawer of the bureau. The drawer was labelled " Fear—the First Limitation," and the material in it was evidently designed for the opening volume of the great unfinished book. Indeed, a portion of it was already arranged and written up.

As White read through this manuscript he was reminded of a score of schoolboy discussions Benham and he and Prothero had had together. Here was the same old toughness of mind, a kind of intellectual hardihood, that had sometimes shocked his schoolfellows. Benham had been one of those boys who do not originate ideas very freely, but who go out to them with a fierce sincerity. He believed and disbelieved with emphasis. Prothero had first set him doubting, but it was Benham's own temperament took him on to denial. His youthful atheism had been a matter for secret consternation in White. White did not believe very much in God even then, but this positive disbelieving frightened him. It was going too far. There had been a terrible moment in the dormitory, during a thunderstorm, a thunderstorm so vehement that it had awakened them all, when Latham, the humorist and a quietly devout boy, had suddenly challenged Benham to deny his Maker.

" *Now* say you don't believe in God ? "

Benham sat up in bed and repeated his negative faith, while little Hopkins, the Bishop's son, being less certain about the accuracy of Providence than His aim, edged as far as he could away from Benham's cubicle and rolled his head in his bed-clothes.

" And anyhow," said Benham, when it was clear that he was not to be struck dead forthwith, " you show a poor idea of your God to think he'd kill a schoolboy for honest doubt. Even old Roddles——"

"I can't listen to you," cried Latham, the humorist, "I can't listen to you. It's—*horrible.*"

"Well, who began it ? " asked Benham.

A flash of lightning lit the dormitory and showed him to White white-faced and ablaze with excitement, sitting up with the bed-clothes about him. "Oh *wow* ! " wailed the muffled voice of little Hopkins as the thunder burst like a giant pistol overhead, and he buried his head still deeper in the bed-clothes and gave way to unappeasable grief.

Latham's voice came out of the darkness. "This *Atheism* that you and Billy Prothero have brought into the school——"

He started violently at another vivid flash, and every one remained silent, waiting for the thunder. . . .

But White remembered no more of the controversy because he had made a frightful discovery that filled and blocked his mind. Every time the lightning flashed, there was a red light in Benham's eyes. . . .

It was only three days after when Prothero discovered exactly the same phenomenon in the School House boothole and talked of cats and cattle, that White's confidence in their friend was partially restored. . . .

§ 4

"Fear, the First Limitation "—his title indicated the spirit of Benham's opening book very clearly. His struggle with fear was the very beginning of his soul's history. It continued to the end. He had hardly decided to lead the noble life before he came bump against the fact that he was a physical coward. He felt fear acutely. "Fear," he wrote, "is the foremost and most persistent of the shepherding powers that keep us in the safe fold, that drive us back to the beaten track and comfort and—futility. The beginning of all aristocracy is the subjugation of fear."

At first the struggle was so great that he hated fear without any qualification ; he wanted to abolish it altogether.

"When I was a boy," he writes, "I thought I would conquer fear for good and all, and never more be troubled by it. But it is not to be done in that way. One might as well dream of having dinner for the rest of one's life. Each time and always I have found that it has to be conquered afresh. To this day I fear, little things as well as big things. I have to grapple with some little dread every day—urge myself. . . . Just as I have to wash and shave myself every day. . . . I believe it is so with every one, but it is difficult to be sure ; few men who go into dangers care very much to talk about fear. . . ."

Later Benham found some excuses for fear, came even to dealings with fear. He never, however, admits that this universal instinct is any better than a kindly but unintelligent nurse from whose fostering restraints it is man's duty to escape. Discretion, he declared, must remain ; a sense of proportion, an " adequacy of enterprise," but the discretion of an aristocrat is in his head, a tactical detail, it has nothing to do with this visceral sinking, this ebb in the nerves. " From top to bottom, the whole spectrum of fear is bad, from panic fear at one extremity down to that mere disinclination for enterprise, that reluctance and indolence which is its lowest phase. These are things of the beast, these are for creatures that have a settled environment, a life history, that spin in a cage of instincts. But man is a beast of that kind no longer, he has left his habitat, he goes out to limitless living. . . ."

This idea of man going out into new things, leaving securities, habits, customs, leaving his normal life altogether behind him, underlay all Benham's aristocratic conceptions. And it was natural that he should consider fear as entirely inconvenient, treat it indeed with ingratitude, and dwell upon the immense liberations that lie beyond for those who will force themselves through its remonstrances. . . .

Benham confessed his liability to fear quite freely in these notes. His fear of animals was ineradicable. He had had an overwhelming dread of bears until he was twelve or thirteen, the child's irrational dread of impossible bears, bears lurking under the bed and in the evening shadows. He confesses that even up to manhood he could not cross a field containing cattle without keeping a wary eye upon them—his bull adventure rather increased than diminished that disposition—he hated a strange dog at his heels and would manœuvre himself as soon as possible out of reach of the teeth or heels of a horse. But the peculiar dread of his childhood was tigers. Some gaping nursemaid confronted him suddenly with a tiger in a cage in the menagerie annexe of a circus. " My small mind was overwhelmed."

" I had never thought," White read, " that a tiger was much larger than a St. Bernard dog. . . . This great creature ! . . . I could not believe any hunter would attack such a monster except by stealth and with weapons of enormous power. . . .

" He jerked himself to and fro across his cramped, rickety cage and looked over my head with yellow eyes—at some phantom far away. Every now and then he snarled. The contempt of his detestable indifference sank deeper and deeper into my soul. I knew that were the cage to vanish I should stand there motionless, his helpless prey. I knew that were he at large in the same building with me I should be too terror-stricken to escape him. At the foot of a ladder leading clear to escape I should have awaited him paralysed. At last I gripped my nurse's hand. ' Take me away,' I whispered.

" In my dreams that night he stalked me. I made my

frozen flight from him, I slammed a door on him, and he thrust his paw through a panel as though it had been paper and clawed for me. The paw got longer and longer. . . .

"I screamed so loudly that my father came up from his study.

"I remember that he took me in his arms.

"'It's only a big sort of pussy, Poff,' he said. '*Felis tigris. Felis*, you know, means cat.'

"But I knew better. I was in no mood then for my father's insatiable pedagoguery.

"'And my little son mustn't be a coward. . . .'

"After that I understood I must keep silence and bear my tigers alone.

"For years the thought of that tiger's immensity haunted my mind. In my dreams I cowered before it a thousand times; in the dusk it rarely failed me. On the landing on my way to bed there was a patch of darkness beyond a chest that became a lurking horror for me, and sometimes the door of my father's bedroom would stand open and there was a long buff and crimson-striped shape, by day indeed an ottoman, but by night—— Could an ottoman crouch and stir in the flicker of a passing candle? Could an ottoman come after you noiselessly, and so close that you could not even turn round upon it? No!"

§ 5

When Benham was already seventeen and, as he supposed hardened against his fear of beasts, his friend Prothero gave him an account of the killing of an old labouring man by a stallion which had escaped out of its stable. The beast had careered across a field, leapt a hedge and come upon its victim suddenly. He had run a few paces and stopped, trying to defend his head with the horse rearing over him. It beat him down with two swift blows of its fore hoofs, one, two, lifted him up in its long yellow teeth and worried him as a terrier does a rat—the poor old wretch was still able to make a bleating sound at that—dropped him, trampled and kicked him as he tried to crawl away, and went on trampling and battering him until he was no more than a bloody inhuman bundle of clothes and mire. For more than half an hour this continued, and then its animal rage was exhausted and it desisted, and went and grazed at a little distance from this misshapen, hoof-marked, torn, and muddy remnant of a man. No one it seems but a horror-stricken child knew what was happening. . . .

This picture of human indignity tortured Benham's imagination much more than it tortured the teller of the tale. It filled him with shame and horror. For three or four years every detail of that circumstantial narrative seemed unforgettable. A little lapse from perfect health and the obsession returned. He could not endure the neighing of horses; when he saw horses galloping in a field with him his heart stood still. And all his life thereafter he hated horses.

§ 6

A different sort of fear that also greatly afflicted Benham was due to a certain clumsiness and insecurity he felt in giddy and unstable places. There he was more definitely balanced between the hopelessly rash and the pitifully discreet.

He had written an account of a private struggle between himself and a certain path of planks and rock edges called the Bisse of Leysin. This happened in his adolescence. He had had a bad attack of influenza and his doctor had sent him to a little hotel—the only hotel it was in those days —at Montana in Valais. There, later, when he had picked up his strength, his father was to join him and take him mountaineering, that second-rate mountaineering which is so dear to dons and schoolmasters. When the time came he was ready for that, but he had had his experiences. He had gone through a phase of real cowardice. He was afraid, he confessed, before even he reached Montana he was afraid of the steepness of the mountains. He had to drive ten or twelve miles up and up the mountain-side, a road of innumerable hairpin bends and precipitous banks, and the horse was gaunt and ugly with a disposition to shy, and he confesses he clutched the side of the vehicle and speculated how he should jump if presently the whole turnout went tumbling over. . . .

"And afterwards I dreamt dreams of precipices. I made strides over precipices, I fell and fell with a floating swiftness towards remote valleys, I was assailed by eagles upon a perilous ledge that crumbled away and left me clinging by my nails to nothing."

The Bisse of Leysin is one of those artificial watercourses which bring water from some distant source to pastures that have an insufficient or uncertain supply. It is a little better now than most because of a certain exceptional boldness in its construction; for a distance of a few score yards it runs supported by iron staples across the front of a sheer precipice, and for perhaps half a mile it hangs like an eyebrow over nearly or quite vertical walls of pine-set rock. Beside it, on the outer side of it, runs a path, which becomes an offhand gangway of planking at the overhanging places. At one corner, which gives the favourite picture-postcard from Montana, the rocks project so sharply above the water that the passenger on the gangway must crouch down upon the bending plank as he walks. There is no hand-hold at all.

A path from Montana takes one over a pine-clad spur and down a precipitous zig-zag upon the middle of the Bisse, and thither Benham came, fascinated by the very fact that

here was something of which the mere report frightened him.
He had to walk across the cold clear rush of the Bisse upon
a pine log, and then he found himself upon one of the gentler
interludes of the Bisse track. It was a scrambling path nearly
two feet wide, and below it were slopes, but not so steep as
to terrify. At a vast distance below he saw through tree-stems
and blue haze a twisted strand of bright whiteness, the river
that joins the Rhone at Sion. It looped about and passed
out of sight remotely beneath his feet. He turned to the
right, and came to a corner that overhung a precipice. He
craned his head round this corner and saw the evil place of
the picture-postcards.

He remained for a long time trying to screw himself up
to walk along the jagged six-inch edge of rock between cliff
and torrent into which the path has shrunken, to the sagging
plank under the overhanging rock beyond.

He could not bring himself to do that.

" It happened that close to the corner a large lump of rock
and earth was breaking away, a cleft was opening, so that
presently, it seemed possible at any moment, the mass would
fall headlong into the blue deeps below. This impending
avalanche was not in my path along the Bisse, it was no sort
of danger to me, but in some way its insecurity gave a final
touch to my cowardice. I could not get myself round that
corner."

He turned away. He went and examined the planks in
the other direction, and these he found less forbidding. He
crossed one precipitous place, with a fall of two score feet
or less beneath him, and found worse ahead. There also
he managed. A third place was still more disagreeable. The
plank was worn and thin, and sagged under him. He went
along it supporting himself against the rock above the Bisse
with an extended hand. Halfway the rock fell back, so that
there was nothing whatever to hold. He stopped, hesitating
whether he should go back—but on this plank there was no
going back because no turning round seemed practicable.
While he was still hesitating there came a helpful intervention. Behind him he saw a peasant appearing and disappearing
behind trees and projecting rock masses, and coming across
the previous plank at a vigorous trot. . . .

Under the stimulus of a spectator Benham got to the end
of this third place without much trouble. Then very politely
he stood aside for the expert to go ahead so that he could
follow at his own pace.

There were, however, more difficulties yet to come, and a
disagreeable humiliation. That confounded peasant developed
a parental solicitude. After each crossing he waited, and
presently began to offer advice and encouragement. At last
came a place where everything was overhanging, where the
Bisse was leaking, and the plank wet and slippery. The wate

ran out of the leak near the brim of the wooden channel and fell in a long shivering thread of silver. *There was no sound of its fall.* It just fell—into a void. Benham wished he had not noted that. He groaned, but faced the plank ; he knew this would be the slowest affair of all.

The peasant surveyed him from the farther side.

" Don't be afraid ! " cried the peasant in his clumsy Valaisian French, and returned, returning along the plank that seemed quite sufficiently loaded without him, extending a charitable hand.

" Damn ! " whispered Benham, but he took the hand.

Afterwards, rather ignobly, he tried to explain in his public-school French. " *Pas de peur*," he said. " *Pas de peur. Mais la tête, n'a pas l'habitude.*"

The peasant, failing to understand, assured him again that there was no danger.

(" Damn ! ")

Benham was led over all the other planks, he was led as if he was an old lady crossing a glacier. He was led into absolute safety, and shamefacedly he rewarded his guide. Then he went a little way and sat down, swore softly, and watched the honest man go striding and plunging down towards Lens until he was out of sight.

" Now," said Benham to himself, " if I do not go back along the planks my secret honour is gone for ever."

He told himself that he had not a good head, that he was not well, that the sun was setting and the light no longer good, that he had a very good chance indeed of getting killed. Then it came to him suddenly as a clear and simple truth, as something luminously plain, that it is better to get killed than go away defeated by such fears and unsteadiness as his. The change came into his mind as if a white light were suddenly turned on—where there had been nothing but shadows and darkness. He rose to his feet and went swiftly and intently the whole way back, going with a kind of temperate reckless-ness, and, because he was no longer careful, easily. He went on beyond his starting place toward the corner, and did that supreme bit, to and fro, that bit where the lump was falling away, and he had to crouch, as gaily as the rest. Then he recrossed the Bisse upon the pine log, clambered up through the pines to the crest, and returned through the meadows to his own hotel.

After that he should have slept the sleep of contentment, but instead he had quite dreadful nightmares, of hanging in frozen fear above incredible declivities, of ill-aimed leaps across chasms to slippery footholds, of planks that swayed and broke suddenly in the middle and headed him down and down. . . .

The next day in the sunshine he walked the Bisse again with those dreams like trailing mists in his mind, and by comparison the path of the Bisse was nothing, it was like walking along a kerbstone, it was an exercise for young ladies. . . .

§ 7

In his younger days Benham had regarded Fear as a shameful secret and as a thing to be got rid of altogether. It seemed to him that to feel fear was to fall short of aristocracy, and in spite of the deep dreads and disgusts that haunted his mind, he set about the business of its subjugation as if it were a spiritual amputation. But as he emerged from the egotism of adolescence he came to realise that this was too comprehensive an operation ; every one feels fear, and your true aristocrat is not one who has eliminated, but one who controls or ignores it. Brave men are men who do things when they are afraid to do them just as Nelson, even when he was seasick, and he was frequently seasick, was still master of the sea. Benham developed two leading ideas about fear ; one that it is worse at the first onset, and far worse than any real experience, and the other that fear is essentially a social instinct. He set himself upon these lines to study—what can we call it ?—the taming of fear, the nature, care, and management of fear. . . .

" Fear is very like pain in this, that it is a deterrent thing. It is superficial. Just as a man's skin is infinitely more sensitive than anything inside. . . . Once you have forced yourself or have been forced through the outward fear into vivid action or experience, you feel very little. The worst moment is before things happen. Rowe, the African sportsman, told me that he had seen cowardice often enough in the presence of lions, but he had never seen any one actually charged by a lion who did not behave well. I have heard the same thing of many sorts of dangers.

" I began to suspect this first in the case of falling or jumping down. Giddiness may be an almost intolerable torture, and falling nothing of the sort. I once saw the face of an old man who had flung himself out of a high window in Rome, and who had been killed instantly on the pavement ; it was not simply a serene face, it was glad, exalted. I suspect that when we have broken the shell of fear, falling may be delightful. Jumping down is, after all, only a steeper tobogganing, and tobogganing a milder jumping down. Always I used to funk at the top of the Cresta run. I suffered sometimes almost intolerably ; I found it almost impossible to get away. The first ten yards was like being slashed open with a sharp sword. But afterwards there was nothing but joyful thrills. All instinct, too, fought against me when I tried high diving. I managed it, and began to like it. I had to give it up because of my ears, but not until I had established the habit of stepping through that moment of disinclination.

" I was Challoner's passenger when he was killed at Sheerness. That was a queer unexpected experience, you may have supposed it an agony of terror, but indeed there was no fear in it at all. At any rate, I do not remember a moment of fear ; it has gone clean out of my memory if ever it was there. We were swimming high and fast, three thousand feet or so, in a clear, sweet air over the town of Sheerness. The river, with a string of battleships, was far away to the west of us, and the endless gray-blue flats of the Thames to the north. The sun was low behind a bank of cloud. I was watching a motor-car, which seemed to be crawling slowly enough, though, no doubt, it was making a respectable pace, between two hedges down below. It is extraordinary how slowly everything seems to be going when one sees it from such a height.

" Then the left wing of the monoplane came up like a door that slams, some wires whistled past my head, and one whipped off my helmet, and then, with the seat slipping away from me, down we went. I snatched unavailingly for the helmet, and then gripped the sides. It was like dropping in a boat suddenly into the trough of a wave—and going on dropping. We were both strapped, and I got my feet against the side and clung to the locked second wheel.

" The sensation was as though something like an intermittent electric current was pouring through me. It's a ridiculous image to use, I can't justify it, but it was as if I was having cold blue light squirted through every pore of my being. There was an astonishment, a feeling of confirmation. ' Of course these things do happen sometimes,' I told myself. I don't remember that Challoner looked round or said anything at all. I am not sure that I looked at him. . . .

" There seemed to be a long interval of intensely excited curiosity, and I remember thinking, ' Lord, but we shall come a smash in a minute ! ' Far ahead I saw the gray sheds of Eastchurch and people strolling about apparently unaware of our disaster. There was a sudden silence as Challoner stopped the engine. . . .

" But the point I want to insist upon is that I did not feel afraid. I was simply enormously, terribly *interested*. . . .

" There came a tremendous jolt and a lunge, and we were both tipped forward, so that we were hanging forehead down by our straps, and it looked as if the sheds were in the sky, then I saw nothing but sky, then came another vast swerve, and we were falling sideways, sideways. . . .

" I was altogether out of breath and *physically* astonished, and I remember noting quite intelligently as we hit the ground how the green grass had an effect of *pouring out* in every direction from below us. . . .

" Then I remember a jerk and a feeling that I was flying up again. I was astonished by a tremendous popping—fabric, wires, everything seemed going pop, pop, pop, like a machine-gun, and then came a flash of intense pain as my arm crumpled up. It was quite impersonal pain. As impersonal as seeing intense colour. *Splinters !* I remember the word came into my head instantly. I remember that very definitely.

" I thought, I suppose, my arm was in splinters. Or perhaps of the scraps and ends of rods and wires flying about us. It is curious that while I remember the word I cannot recall the idea. . . .

" When I became conscious again the chief thing present in my mind was that all those fellows round were young soldiers who wouldn't at all understand bad behaviour. My arm was—orchestral, but still far from being real suffering *in* me. Also I wanted to know what Challoner had got. They wouldn't understand my questions, and then I twisted round and saw from the negligent way his feet came out from under the engine that he must be dead. And dark red stains with bright red froth——

" Of course !

" There again the chief feeling was a sense of oddity. I wasn't sorry for him any more than I was for myself.

" It seemed to me that it was all right with us both, remarkable, vivid, but all right. . . ."

§ 8

" But though there is little or no fear in an aeroplane, even when it is smashing up, there is fear about aeroplanes. There is something that says very urgently, ' Don't ' to the man who looks up into the sky. It is very interesting to note how at a place like Eastchurch or Brooklands the necessary discretion trails the old visceral feeling with it, and how men will hang about, ready to go up, resolved to go up, but delaying. Men of indisputable courage will get into a state between dread and laziness, and waste whole hours of flying weather on any excuse or no excuse. Once they are up that inhibition vanishes. The man who was delaying and delaying half an hour ago will now be cutting the most venturesome capers in the air. Few men are in a hurry to get down again. I mean that quite apart from the hesitation of landing, they like being up there."

Then, abruptly, Benham comes back to his theory.

" Fear, you see, is the inevitable janitor, but it is not the ruler of experience. That is what I am driving at in all this. The bark of danger is worse than its bite. Inside the portals there may be events and destruction, but terror stays defeated at the door. It may be that when that old man was killed by a horse the child who watched suffered more than he did. . . .

" I am sure that was so. . . ."

§ 9

As White read Benham's notes and saw how his argument drove on, he was reminded again and again of those schoolboy

days and Benham's hardihood, and his own instinctive unreasonable reluctance to follow those gallant intellectual leads.
If fear is an ancient instinctive boundary that the modern life,
the aristocratic life, is bound to ignore and transcend, may
this not also be the case with pain ? We do a little adventure
into the "life beyond fear"; may we not also think of
adventuring into the life beyond pain ? Is pain any saner a
warning than fear ? May not pain just as much as fear keep us
from possible and splendid things ? But why ask a question
that is already answered in principle in every dentist's chair ?
Benham's idea, however, went much further than that ; he
was clearly suggesting that in pain itself, pain endured beyond
a certain pitch, there might come pleasure again, an intensity
of sensation that might have the colour of delight. He betrayed
a real anxiety to demonstrate this possibility, he had the
earnestness of a man who is sensible of dissentient elements
within. He hated the thought of pain even more than he hated
fear. His arguments did not in the least convince White, who
stopped to poke the fire and assure himself of his own comfort
in the midst of his reading.

Young people and unseasoned people, Benham argued, are
apt to imagine that if fear is increased and carried to an extreme
pitch it becomes unbearable, one will faint or die ; given a
weak heart, a weak artery or any such structural defect and
that may well happen, but it is just as possible that as the
stimulation increases one passes through a brief ecstasy of
terror to a new sane world, exalted but as sane as normal
existence. There is the calmness of despair. Benham had
made some notes to enforce this view, of the observed calm
behaviour of men already hopelessly lost, men on sinking ships,
men going to execution, men already maimed and awaiting
the final stroke, but for the most part these were merely
references to books and periodicals. In exactly the same way,
he argued, we exaggerate the range of pain as if it were limitless.
We think if we are unthinking that it passes into agony and
so beyond endurance to destruction. It probably does nothing
of the kind. Benham compared pain to the death range of the
electric current. At a certain voltage it thrills, at a greater it
torments and convulses, at a still greater it kills. But at
enormous voltages, as Tesla was the first to demonstrate, it
does no injury. And following on this came memoranda on
the recorded behaviour of martyrs, on the self-torture of
Hindoo ascetics, of the defiance of Red Indian prisoners.

" These things," Benham had written, " are much more
horrible when one considers them from the point of view of
an easy-chair " ; White gave an assenting nod—" *are they
really horrible at all ?* Is it possible that these charred and
slashed and splintered persons, those Indians hanging from
hooks, those walkers in the fiery furnace, have had glimpses
through great windows that were worth the price they paid

for them ? Haven't we allowed those checks and barriers that
are so important a restraint upon childish enterprise to creep
up into and distress and distort adult life ? . . .

"The modern world thinks too much as though painlessness
and freedom from danger were ultimate ends. It is fear-haunted,
it is troubled by the thoughts of pain and death, which it has
never met except as well-guarded children meet these things,
in exaggerated and untestable forms, in the menagerie or in
nightmares. And so it thinks the discovery of anæsthetics the
crowning triumph of civilisation, and cosiness and innocent
amusement, those ideals of the nursery, the whole purpose of
mankind. . . ."

"Mm," said White, and pressed his lips together and knotted
his brows and shook his head.

§ 10

But the bulk of Benham's discussion of fear was not concerned with this perverse and overstrained suggestion of
pleasure reached through torture, this exaggeration of the
man resolved not to shrink at anything ; it was an examination
of the present range and use of fear that led gradually to something like a theory of control and discipline. The second of his
two dominating ideas was that fear is an instinct arising only
in isolation, that in a crowd there may be a collective panic,
but that there is no real individual fear. Fear, Benham held,
drives the man back to the crowd, the dog to its master, the
wolf to the pack, and when it is felt that the danger is pooled,
then fear leaves us. He was quite prepared to meet the objection
that animals of a solitary habit do nevertheless exhibit fear.
Some of this apparent fear, he argued, was merely discretion,
and what is not discretion is the survival of an infantile characteristic. The fear felt by a tiger cub is certainly a social
emotion, that drives it back to the other cubs, to its mother
and the dark hiding of the lair. The fear of a fully grown tiger
sends it into the reeds and the shadows, to a refuge, that must
be " still reminiscent of the maternal lair." But fear has very
little hold upon the adult solitary animal, it changes with
extreme readiness to resentment and rage.

"Like most inexperienced people," ran his notes, " I was
astonished at the reported feats of men in war ; I believed
they were exaggerated, and that there was a kind of unpre-
meditated conspiracy of silence about their real behaviour.
But when on my way to visit India for the third time I turned
off to see what I could of the fighting before Adrianople, I
discovered at once that a thousand casually selected conscripts
will, every one of them, do things together that not one of
them could by any means be induced to do alone. I saw men
not merely obey orders that gave them the nearly certain prospect of death, but I saw them exceeding orders ; I saw men

leap out of cover for the mere sake of defiance, and fall shot through and smashed by a score of bullets. I saw a number of Bulgarians in the hands of the surgeon, several quite frightfully wounded, refuse chloroform merely to impress the English onlooker ; some of their injuries I could scarcely endure to see, and I watched a line of infantrymen go on up a hill and keep on quite manifestly cheerful with men dropping out and wriggling, and men dropping out and lying still until every other man was down. . . . Not one man would have gone up that hill alone, without onlookers. . . ."

Rowe, the lion hunter, told Benham that only on one occasion in his life had he given way to ungovernable fear, and that was when he was alone. Many times he had been in fearful situations in the face of charging lions and elephants, and once he had been bowled over and carried some distance by a lion, but on none of these occasions had fear demoralised him. There was no question of his general pluck. But on one occasion he was lost in rocky waterless country in Somaliland. He strayed out in the early morning while his camels were being loaded, followed some antelope too far, and lost his bearings. He looked up expecting to see the sun on his right hand and found it on his left. He became bewildered. He wandered some time, and then fired three signal shots and got no reply. Then losing his head he began shouting. He had only four or five more cartridges and no water-bottle. His men were accustomed to his going on alone, and might not begin to remark upon his absence until sundown. . . . It chanced, however, that one of the shikari noted the water-bottle he had left behind and organised a hunt for him.

Long before they found him he had passed to an extremity of terror. The world had become hideous and threatening, the sun was a pitiless glare, each rocky ridge he clambered became more dreadful than the last, each new valley into which he looked more hateful and desolate, the cramped thorn bushes threatened him gauntly, the rocks had a sinister lustre, and in every blue shadow about him the night and death lurked and waited. There was no hurry for them, presently they would spread out again and join and submerge him, presently in the confederated darkness he could be stalked and seized and slain. Yes, this he admitted was real fear. He had cracked his voice, yelling as a child yells. And then he had become afraid of his own voice. . . .

" Now this excess of fear in isolation, this comfort in a crowd, in support and in a refuge, even when support or refuge is quite illusory, is just exactly what one would expect of fear if one believed it to be an instinct which has become a misfit. In the case of the soldier fear is so much a misfit that instead of saving him for the most part it destroys him. Raw soldiers under fire bunch together and armies fight in masses, men are mowed down in swathes, because only so is the courage of the common men sustained, only so can they be brave ; albeit spread out, and handling their weapons as men of unqualified daring would handle them, they would be infinitely safer and more effective. . . .

" And all of us, it may be, are restrained by this misfit fear from a thousand bold successful gestures of mind and body ; we are held back from the attainment of mighty securities in pitiful temporary shelters that are perhaps in the end no better than traps. . . ."

From such considerations Benham went on to speculate how far the crowd can be replaced in a man's imagination, how far some substitute for that social backing can be made to serve the same purpose in neutralising fear. He wrote with the calm of a man who weighs the probabilities of a riddle, and with the zeal of a man lost to every material consideration. His writing, it seemed to White, had something of the enthusiastic whiteness of his face, the enthusiastic brightness of his eyes. We can no more banish fear from our being at present than we can carve out the fleshy pillars of the heart or the pineal gland in the brain. It is deep in our inheritance. As deep as hunger. And just as we have to satisfy hunger in order that it should leave us free, so we have to satisfy the unconquerable importunity of fear. We have to reassure our faltering instincts. There must be something to take the place of lair and familiars, something not ourselves but general, that we must carry with us into the lonely places. For it is true that man has now not only to learn to fight in open order instead of in a phalanx, but he has to think and plan and act in open order, to live in open order. . . .

Then with one of his abrupt transitions Benham had written, " This brings me to God."

" The devil it does ! " said White, roused to a keener attention.

" By no feat of intention can we achieve courage in loneliness so long as we feel indeed alone. An isolated man, an egoist, an Epicurean man, will always fail himself in the solitary place. There must be something more with us to sustain us against this vast universe than the spark of life that began yesterday and must be extinguished to-morrow. There can be no courage beyond social courage, the sustaining confidence of the herd, until there is in us the sense of God. But God is a word that covers a multitude of meanings. When I was a boy I was a passionate atheist, I defied God, and so far as God is the mere sanction of social traditions and pressures, a mere dressing up of the crowd's will in canonicals, I do still deny him and repudiate him. That God I heard of first from my nursemaid, and in very truth he is the proper God of all the nursemaids of mankind. But there is another God than that God of obedience, God the immortal adventurer in me, God who calls men from home and country, God scourged and crowned with thorns, who rose in a nail-pierced body out of death and came not to bring peace but a sword "

With something bordering upon intellectual consternation, White, who was a decent self-respecting sceptic, read these last clamberings of Benham's spirit. They were written in pencil ; they were unfinished when he died.

(Surely the man was not a Christian !)

" You may be heedless of death and suffering because you think you cannot suffer and die, or you may be heedless of death and pain because you have identified your life with the honour of mankind and the insatiable adventurousness of man's imagination, so that the possible death is negligible and the possible achievement altogether outweighs it. . . ."

White shook his head over these pencilled fragments.

He was a member of the Rationalist Press Association, and he had always taken it for granted that Benham was an orthodox unbeliever. But this was hopelessly unsound, heresy, perilous stuff ; almost, it seemed to him, a posthumous betrayal. . . .

§ 11

One night when he was in India the spirit of adventure came upon Benham. He had gone with Kepple, of the forestry department, into the jungle country in the hills above the Tapti. He had been very anxious to see something of that aspect of Indian life, and he had snatched at the chance Kepple had given him. But they had scarcely started before the expedition was brought to an end by an accident ; Kepple was thrown by a pony and his ankle broken. He and Benham bandaged it as well as they could, and a litter was sent for, and meanwhile they had to wait in the camp that was to have been the centre of their jungle raids. The second day of this waiting was worse for Kepple than the first, and he suffered much from the pressure of this amateurish bandaging. In the evening Benham got cool water from the well and rearranged things better ; the two men dined and smoked under their thatched roof beneath the big banyan, and then Kepple, tired out by his day of pain, was carried to his tent. Presently he fell asleep and Benham was left to himself.

Now that the heat was over he found himself quite indisposed to sleep. He felt full of life and anxious for happenings.

He went back and sat down upon the iron bedstead beneath the banyan that Kepple had lain upon through the day, and he watched the soft immensity of the Indian night swallow up the last lingering colours of the world. It left the outlines, it obliterated nothing, but it stripped off the superficial reality of things. The moon was full and high overhead, and the light had not so much gone as changed from definition and the blazing glitter and reflections of solidity to a translucent and unsubstantial clearness. The jungle that bordered the little encampment north, south, and west seemed to have crept a little nearer, enriched itself with blackness, taken to itself voices.

(Surely it had been silent during the day.)

A warm, faintly-scented breeze just stirred the dead grass and the leaves. In the day the air had been still.

Immediately after the sunset there had been a great crying of peacocks in the distance, but that was over now ; the crickets, however, were still noisy, and a persistent sound had become predominant, an industrious unmistakable sound, a sound that took his mind back to England, in midsummer. It was like a watchman's rattle—a nightjar !

So there were nightjars here in India, too ! One might have expected something less familiar. And then came another cry from far away over the heat-stripped tree-tops, a less familiar cry. It was repeated. Was that perhaps some craving leopard, a tiger cat, a panther ?——

" Hunt, Hunt ; " that might be a deer.

Then suddenly an angry chattering came from the dark trees quite close at hand. A monkey ? . . .

These great, scarce visible, sweeping movements through the air were bats. . . .

Of course, the day jungle is the jungle asleep. This was its waking hour. Now the deer were arising from their forms, the bears creeping out of their dens amidst the rocks and blundering down the gullies, the tigers and panthers and jungle cats stalking noiselessly from their lairs in the grass. Countless creatures that had hidden from the heat and pitiless exposure of the day stood now awake and alertly intent upon their purposes, grazed or sought water, flitting delicately through the moonlight and shadows. The jungle was awakening. Again Benham heard that sound like the belling of a stag. . . .

This was the real life of the jungle, this night life, into which man did not go. Here he was on the verge of a world that for all the stuffed trophies of the sportsman and the specimens of the naturalist is still almost as unknown as if it were upon another planet. What intruders men are, what foreigners in the life of this ancient system !

He looked over his shoulder, and there were the two little tents, one that sheltered Kepple and one that awaited him, and beyond, in an irregular line, glowed the ruddy smoky fires of the men. One or two turbaned figures still flitted about, and there was a voice—low, monotonous—it must have been telling a tale. Further, sighing and stirring ever and again, were tethered beasts, and then a great pale space of moonlight and the clumsy outlines of the village well. The clustering village itself slept in darkness beyond the mango trees, and still remoter the black encircling jungle closed in. One might have fancied this was the encampment of newly come invaders, were it not for the larger villages that are overgrown with thickets and altogether swallowed up again in the wilderness ; and for the deserted temples that are found rent asunder by the roots of trees and the ancient embankments that hold water only for the drinking of the sambur deer.

Benham turned his face to the dim jungle again. . . .

He had come far out of his way to visit this strange world of the ancient life, that now recedes and dwindles before our new civilisation, that seems fated to shrivel up and pass altogether before the dry advance of physical science and material organisation. He was full of unsatisfied curiosities about its fierce hungers and passions, its fears and cruelties, its instincts and its wellnigh incommunicable and yet most precious understandings. He had long ceased to believe that the wild beast is wholly evil, and safety and plenty the ultimate good for men. . . .

Perhaps he would never get nearer to this mysterious jungle life than he was now.

It was intolerably tantalising that it should be so close at hand and so inaccessible. . . .

As Benham sat brooding over his disappointment the moon, swimming on through the still circle of the hours, passed slowly over him. The lights and shadows about him changed by imperceptible gradations, and a long pale alley, where the native cart track drove into the forest, opened slowly out of the darkness, slowly broadened, slowly lengthened. It opened out to him with a quality of invitation. . . .

There was the jungle before him. Was it after all so inaccessible ?

" Come ! " the road said to him.

Benham rose and walked out a few paces into the moonlight and stood motionless.

Was he afraid ?

Even now some hungry watchful monster might lurk in yonder shadows, watching with infinite still patience. Kepple had told him how they would sit still for hours—staring unblinkingly as cats stare at a fire—and then crouch to advance. Beneath the shrill overtone of the nightjars, what noiseless gray shapes, what deep breathings and cracklings and creepings might there not be ? . . .

Was he afraid ?

That question determined him to go.

He hesitated whether he should take a gun. A stick ? A gun, he knew, was a dangerous thing to an inexperienced man. No ! He would go now, even as he was with empty hands. At least he would go as far as the end of that band of moonlight. If for no other reason than because he was afraid.

Now !

For a moment it seemed to him as though his feet were too heavy to lift, and then, hands in pockets, khaki-clad, an almost invisible figure, he strolled towards the cart-track.

Come to that, he halted for a moment to regard the distant fires of the men. No one would miss him. They would think he was in his tent. He faced the stirring quiet ahead. The cart-track was a rutted path of soft, warm sand, on which he went almost noiselessly. A bird squabbled for an instant in a thicket. A great white owl floated like a flake of moonlight across the track and vanished without a sound among the trees.

Along the moonlit path went Benham, and when he passed near trees his footsteps became noisy with the rustle and crash of dead leaves. The jungle was full of moonlight ; twigs, branches, creepers, grass-clumps came out acutely vivid. The trees and bushes stood in pools of darkness, and beyond were pale stretches of misty moonshine and big rocks shining with an unearthly lustre. Things seemed to be clear and yet uncertain. It was as if they dissolved or retired a little and then returned to solidity.

A sudden chattering broke out overhead, and black across the great stars soared a flying squirrel and caught a twig, and ran for shelter. A second hesitated in a tree-top and pursued. They chased each other and vanished abruptly. He forgot his sense of insecurity in the interest of these active little silhouettes. And he noted how much bigger and more wonderful the stars can look when one sees them through interlacing branches.

Ahead was darkness, but not so dark when he came to it that the track was invisible. He was at the limit of his intention, but now he saw that that had been a childish project. He would go on, he would walk right into the jungle. His first disinclination was conquered, and the soft intoxication of the subtropical moonshine was in his blood. . . . But he wished he could walk as a spirit walks, without this noise of leaves. . . .

Yes, this was very wonderful and beautiful, and there must always be jungles for men to walk in. Always there must be jungles. . . .

Some small beast snarled and bolted from under his feet. He stopped sharply. He had come into a darkness under great boughs, and now he stood still as the little creature scuttled away. Beyond the track emerged into a dazzling whiteness. . . .

In the stillness he could hear the deer belling again in the distance, and then came a fuss of monkeys in a group of trees near at hand. He remained still until this had died away into mutterings.

Then on the verge of movement he was startled by a ripe mango that slipped from its stalk and fell out of the tree and struck his hand. It took a little time to understand that, and then he laughed, and his muscles relaxed, and he went on again.

A thorn caught at him and he disentangled himself.

He crossed the open space, and the moon was like a great shield of light spread out above him. All the world seemed swimming in its radiance. The stars were like lamps in a mist of silvery blue.

The track led him on across white open spaces of shrivelled grass and sand, amidst trees where shadows made black patternings upon the silver, and then it plunged into obscurities. For a time it lifted, and then on one hand the bush fell away, and he saw across a vast moonlit valley wide undulations of open cultivation, belts of jungle, copses, and a great lake as black as ebony. For a time the path ran thus open, and then the jungle closed in again and there were more thickets, more levels of grass, and in one place far overhead among the branches he heard and stood for a time perplexed at a vast deep humming of bees. . . .

Presently a black monster with a hunched back went across his path heedless of him and making a great noise in the leaves. He stood quite still until it had gone. He could not tell whether it was a boar or hyæna ; most probably, he thought, a boar because of the heaviness of its rush.

The path dropped downhill for a time, crossed a ravine, ascended. He passed a great leafless tree on which there were white flowers. On the ground also, in the darkness under the tree, there were these flowers ; they were dropping noiselessly, and since they were visible in the shadows, it seemed to him that they must be phosphorescent. And they emitted a sweetish scent that lay heavily athwart the path. Presently he passed another such tree. Then he became aware of a tumult ahead of him, a smashing of leaves, a snorting and slobbering, grunting and sucking, a whole series of bestial sounds. He halted for a little while, and then drew nearer, picking his steps to avoid too great a noise. Here were more of those white-blossomed trees, and beneath, in the darkness, something very black and big was going to and fro, eating greedily. Then he found that there were two and then more of these black things, three or four of them.

Curiosity made Benham draw nearer, very softly.

Presently one showed in a patch of moonlight, startingly big, a huge, black hairy monster with a long white nose on a grotesque face, and he was stuffing armfuls of white blossom into his mouth with his curved fore claws. He took not the slightest notice of the still man, who stood perhaps twenty yards away from him. He was too blind and careless. He snorted and smacked his slobbering lips, and plunged into the shadows again. Benham heard him root among the leaves and grunt appreciatively. The air was heavy with the reek of the crushed flowers.

For some time Benham remained listening to and peering at these preoccupied gluttons. At last he shrugged his shoulders,

and left them and went on his way. For a long time he could
hear them ; then just as he was on the verge of forgetting them
altogether, some dispute arose among them, and there began
a vast uproar, squeals, protests, comments, one voice
ridiculously replete and authoritative, ridiculously suggestive of
a drunken judge with his mouth full, and a shrill voice of
grievance high above the others. . . .

The uproar of the bears died away at last, almost abruptly,
and left the jungle to the incessant nightjars. . . .

For what end was this life of the jungle ?

All Benham's senses were alert to the sounds and appearances about him, and at the same time his mind was busy with
the perplexities of that riddle. Was the jungle just an aimless
pool of life that man must drain and clear away ? Or is it to
have a use in the greater life of our race that now begins ?
Will man value the jungle as he values the precipice, for the
sake of his manhood ? Will he preserve it ?

Man must keep hard, man must also keep fierce. Will the
jungle keep him fierce ?

For life, thought Benham, there must be insecurity. . . .

He had missed the track. . . .

He was now in a second ravine. He was going downward,
walking on silvery sand amidst great boulders, and now there
was a new sound in the air—— It was the croaking of frogs.
Ahead was a solitary gleam. He was approaching a jungle
pool. . . .

Suddenly the stillness was alive, in a panic uproar. "*Honk !*"
cried a great voice, and "*Honk !*" There was a clatter of
hoofs, a wild rush—a rush as it seemed towards him. Was
he being charged ? He backed against a rock. A great pale
shape leaped by him, an antlered shape. It was a herd of big
deer bolting suddenly out of the stillness. He heard the swish
and smash of their retreat grow distant, disperse. He remained
standing with his back to the rock.

Slowly the strophe and antistrophe of frogs and goat-suckers
resumed possession of his consciousness. But now some
primitive instinct perhaps, or some subconscious intimation of
danger, made him meticulously noiseless.

He went on down a winding sound-deadening path of sand
towards the drinking-place. He came to a wide white place
that was almost level, and beyond it under clustering pale-
stemmed trees shone the mirror surface of some ancient tank,
and, sharp and black, a dog-like beast sat on its tail in the midst
of this space, started convulsively and went slinking into the
undergrowth. Benham paused for a moment and then walked
out softly into the light, and, behold ! as if it were to meet him
came a monster, a vast dark shape drawing itself lengthily out
of the blackness, and stopped with a start as if it had been
instantly changed to stone.

It had stopped with one paw advanced. Its **striped mask**

was light and dark gray in the moonlight, gray but faintly tinged with ruddiness, its mouth was a little open, its fangs and a pendant of viscous saliva shone vivid. Its great round-pupilled eyes regarded him steadfastly. At last the nightmare of Benham's childhood had come true, and he was face to face with a tiger, uncaged, uncontrolled.

For some moments neither moved, neither the beast nor the man. They stood face to face, each perhaps with an equal astonishment, motionless and soundless, in that mad Indian moonlight that makes all things like a dream.

Benham stood quite motionless, and body and mind had halted together. That confrontation had an interminableness that had nothing to do with the actual passage of time. Then some trickle of his previous thoughts stirred in the frozen quiet of his mind.

He spoke hoarsely. " I am Man," he said, and lifted a hand as he spoke. " The Thought of the world."

His heart leapt within him as the tiger moved. But the great beast went sideways, gardant, only that its head was low ; three noiseless instantaneous strides it made, and stood again watching him.

" Man," he said, in a voice that had no sound, and took a step forward.

" Wough ! " With two bounds the monster had become a great gray streak that crackled and rustled in the shadows of the trees. And then it had vanished, become invisible and inaudible with a kind of instantaneousness.

For some seconds or some minutes Benham stood rigid, fearlessly expectant, and then far away up the ravine he heard the deer repeat their cry of alarm, and understood with a new wisdom that the tiger had passed among them and was gone. . . .

He walked on towards the deserted tank, and now he was talking aloud.

" I understand the jungle. I understand. . . . If a few men die here, what matter ? There are worse deaths than being killed. . . .

" What is this fool's trap of security ?

" Every time in my life that I have fled from security I have fled from death. . . .

" Let men stew in their cities if they will. It is in the lonely places, in jungles and mountains, in snows and fires, in the still observatories and the silent laboratories, in those secret and dangerous places where life probes into life, it is there that the masters of the world, the lords of the beast, the rebel sons of Fate come to their own. . . .

" You sleeping away there in the cities ! Do you know what it means for you that I am here to-night ?

" Do you know what it means to you ?

" I am just one—just the precursor.

" Presently if you will not budge, those hot cities must be burnt about you. You must come out of them. . . ."

He wandered now uttering his thoughts as they came to him, and he saw no more living creatures because they fled and hid before the sound of his voice. He wandered until the moon, larger now and yellow tinged, was low between the black bars of the tree stems. And then it sank very suddenly behind a hilly spur and the light failed swiftly.

He stumbled and went with difficulty. He could go no farther among these rocks and ravines, and he sat down at the foot of a tree to wait for day.

He sat very still indeed.

A great stillness came over the world, a velvet silence that wrapped about him, as the velvet shadows wrapped about him. The corncrakes had ceased, all the sounds and stir of animal life had died away, the breeze had fallen. A drowsing comfort took possession of him. He grew more placid and more placid still. He was enormously content to find that fear had fled before him and was gone. He drifted into that state of mind when one thinks without ideas, when one's mind is like a starless sky, serene and empty.

§ 12

Some hours later Benham found that the trees and rocks were growing visible again, and he saw a very bright star he knew must be Lucifer rising amidst the black branches. He was sitting upon a rock at the foot of a slender-stemmed leafless tree. He had been asleep, and it was daybreak. Every thing was coldly clear and colourless.

He must have slept soundly.

He heard a cock crow, and another answer—jungle fowl these must be, because there could be no village within earshot —and then far away and bringing back memories of terraced houses and ripe walled gardens, was the scream of peacocks. And some invisible bird was making a hollow beating sound among the trees near at hand. *Tunk. . . . Tunk*, and out of the dry grass came a twittering.

There was a green light in the east that grew stronger, and the stars after their magnitudes were dissolving in the blue ; only a few remained faintly visible. The sound of birds increased. Through the trees he saw towering up a great mauve thing like the back of a monster—but that was nonsense, it was the crest of a steep hillside covered with woods of teak.

He stood up and stretched himself, and wondered whether he had dreamed of a tiger.

He tried to remember and retrace the course of his overnight wanderings.

A flight of emerald parakeets tore screaming through the trees, and then far away uphill he heard the creaking of a cart.

He followed the hint of a footmark, and went back up the glen slowly and thoughtfully.

Presently he came to a familiar place, a group of trees, a sheet of water, and the ruins of an old embankment. It was the ancient tank of his overnight encounter. The pool of his dream ?

With doubt still in his mind, he walked round its margin to the sandy level beyond, and cast about and sought intently, and at last found, and then found clearly, imposed upon the tracks of several sorts of deer and the footprints of many biggish birds, first the great spoor of the tiger and then his own. Here the beast had halted, and here it had leapt aside. Here his own footmarks stopped. Here his heels had come together.

It had been no dream.

There was a white mist upon the water of the old tank like the bloom upon a plum, and the trees about it seemed smaller and the sand-space wider and rougher than they had seemed in the moonshine. Then the ground had looked like a floor of frosted silver.

And thence he went on upward through the fresh morning, until just as the east grew red with sunrise, he reached the cart-track from which he had strayed overnight. It was, he found, a longer way back to the camp than he remembered it to be. Perhaps he had struck the path farther along. It curved about and went up and down and crossed three ravines. At last he came to that trampled place of littered white blossom under great trees where he had seen the bears.

The sunlight went before him in a sheaf of golden spears, and his shadow, that was at first limitless, crept towards his feet. The dew had gone from the dead grass and the sand was hot to his dry boots before he came back into the open space about the great banyan and the tents. And Kepple, refreshed by a night's rest and coffee, was wondering loudly where the devil he had gone.

THE STORY

CHAPTER ONE

THE BOY GROWS UP

§ I

BENHAM was the son of a schoolmaster. His father was assistant first at Cheltenham, and subsequently at Minchinghampton, and then he became head and later on sole proprietor of Martindale House, a high-class preparatory school at Seagate. He was extremely successful for some years, as success goes in the scholastic profession, and then disaster overtook him in the shape of a divorce. His wife, William Porphyry's mother, made the acquaintance of a rich young man named Nolan, who was recuperating at Seagate from the sequelæ of snake-bite, malaria, and a gun accident in Brazil. She ran away with him, and she was divorced. She was, however, unable to marry him because he died at Wiesbaden only three days after the Reverend Harold Benham obtained his decree absolute. Instead, therefore, being a woman of great spirit, enterprise and sweetness, she married Godfrey Marayne, afterwards Sir Godfrey Marayne, the great London surgeon.

Nolan was a dark, rather melancholy and sentimental young man, and he left about a third of his very large fortune entirely to Mrs. Benham and the rest to her in trust for her son, whom he deemed himself to have injured. With this and a husband already distinguished, she returned presently to London, and was on the whole fairly well received there.

It was upon the reverend gentleman at Seagate that the brunt of this divorce fell. There is perhaps a certain injustice in the fact that a schoolmaster who has lost his wife should also lose the more valuable proportion of his pupils, but the tone of thought in England is against any association of a schoolmaster with matrimonial irregularity. And also Mr. Benham remarried. It would certainly have been better for him if he could have produced a sister. His school declined and his efforts to resuscitate it only hastened its decay. Conceiving that he could now only appeal to the broader-minded, more progressive type of parent, he became an educational reformer, and wrote upon modernising the curriculum with increasing frequency to *The Times*. He expended a considerable fraction of his dwindling capital upon a science laboratory and a fives court ; he added a London Bachelor of Science with a Teaching Diploma to the school staff, and a library of about a thousand volumes, including the Hundred Best Books as selected by the late Lord Avebury, to the school equipment. None of these things did anything but enhance the suspicion of laxity his wife's escapade had created in the limited opulent and discreet class to which his establishment appealed. One boy who, under the influence of the Hundred Best Books, had quoted the *Zend-Avesta* to an irascible but influential grandfather, was withdrawn without notice or compensation in the middle of the term. It intensifies the tragedy of the Reverend Harold Benham's failure that in no essential respect did his school depart from the pattern of all other properly-conducted preparatory schools.

In appearance he was near the average of scholastic English gentlemen. He displayed a manifest handsomeness somewhat weakened by disregard and disuse, a large moustache and a narrow high forehead. His rather tired brown eyes were magnified by glasses. He was an active man in unimportant things, with a love for the phrase " ship-shape," and he played cricket better than any one else on the staff. He walked in wide strides, and would sometimes use the tail of his gown on the blackboard. Like so many clergymen and schoolmasters, he had early distrusted his natural impulse in conversation, and had adopted the defensive precaution of a rather formal and sonorous speech, which habit had made a part of him. His general effect was of one who is earnestly keeping up things that might otherwise give way, keeping them up by act and voice, keeping up an atmosphere of vigour and success in a school that was only too manifestly attenuated, keeping up a pretentious economy of administration in a school that must not be too manifestly impoverished, keeping up a claim to be in the scientific van and rather a flutterer of dovecots—with its method of manual training for example—keeping up *esprit de corps* and the manliness of himself and every one about him, keeping up his affection for his faithful second wife and his complete forgetfulness of and indifference to that spirit of distracting impulse and insubordination away there in London, who had once been his delight and insurmountable difficulty. " After my visits to her," wrote Benham, " he would show by a hundred little expressions and poses and acts how intensely he wasn't noting that anything of the sort had occurred."

But one thing that from the outset the father seemed to have failed to keep up thoroughly was his intention to mould and dominate his son.

The advent of his boy had been a tremendous event in the reverend gentleman's life. It is not improbable that his disposition to monopolise the pride of this event contributed to the ultimate disruption of his family. It left so few initiatives within the home to his wife. He had been an early victim to that wave of philoprogenitive and educational enthusiasm which distinguished the closing decade of the nineteenth century. He was full of plans in those days for the education of his boy, and the thought of the youngster played a large part in the series of complicated emotional crises with which he celebrated the departure of his wife, crises in which a number of old school and college friends very generously assisted—spending week-ends at Seagate for this purpose, and mingling tobacco, impassioned hand-clasps and suchlike consolation with much patient sympathetic listening to his carefully balanced analysis of his feelings. He declared that his son was now his one living purpose in life, and he sketched out a scheme of moral and intellectual training that he subsequently embodied in five very stimulating and intimate articles for the *School World*, but never put into more than partial operation.

" I have read my father's articles upon this subject," wrote Benham, " and I am still perplexed to measure just what I owe to him. Did he ever attempt this moral training he contemplated so freely ? I don't think he did. I know now, I knew then, that he had something in his mind. . . . There were one or two special walks we had together, he invited me to accompany him with a certain portentousness, and we would go out pregnantly making superficial remarks about the school cricket and return, discussing botany, with nothing said.

" His heart failed him.

" Once or twice, too, he seemed to be reaching out at me from the school pulpit.

" I think that my father did manage to convey to me his belief that there were these fine things, honour, high aims, nobilities. If I did not get this belief from him then I do not know how I got it. But it was as if he hinted at a treasure that had got very dusty in an attic, a treasure which he hadn't himself been able to spend. . . ."

The father who had intended to mould his son ended by watching him grow, not always with sympathy or under-standing. He was an overworked man assailed by many futile anxieties. One sees him striding about the establishment with his gown streaming out behind him, urging on the groundsman or the gardener, or, dignified, expounding the particular advantages of Seagate to inquiring parents ; one sees him unnaturally cheerful and facetious at the midday dinner-table ; one imagines him keeping up high aspirations in a rather too hastily scribbled sermon in the school pulpit, or keeping up an enthusiasm for beautiful language in a badly-prepared lesson on Virgil, or expressing unreal indignation and un-justifiably exalted sentiments to evil doers ; and one realises his disadvantage against the quiet youngster whose retentive memory was storing up all these impressions for an ultimate judgment ; and one understands, too, a certain relief that mingled with his undeniable emotion when at last the time came for young Benham, " the one living purpose " of his life, to be off to Minchinghampton and the next step in the mysterious ascent of the English educational system.

Three times at least, and with an increased interval, the

father wrote fine fatherly letters that would have stood the test of publication. Then his communications became comparatively hurried and matter of fact. His boy's return home for the holidays was always rather a stirring time for his private feelings, but he became more and more inexpressive. He would sometimes lay a hand on those growing shoulders and then withdraw it. They felt braced-up shoulders, stiffly inflexible or—they would wince. And when one has let the habit of indefinite feelings grow upon one, what is there left to say ? If one did say anything one might be asked questions...

One or two of the long vacations they spent abroad together. The last of these occasions followed Benham's convalescence at Montana and his struggle with the Bisse ; the two went to Zermatt and did several peaks and crossed the Theodule, and it was clear that their joint expeditions were a strain upon both of them. The father thought the son reckless, unskilful, and impatient ; the son found the father's insistence upon guides, ropes, precautions, the recognised way, the highest point and back again before you get a chill, and talk about it sagely but very, very modestly over pipes, tiresome. He wanted to wander in deserts of ice and see over the mountains, and discover what it is to be benighted on a precipice. And gradually he was becoming familiar with his father's repertory of Greek quotations. There was no breach between them, but each knew that holiday was the last they would ever spend together. . . .

The court had given the custody of young William Porphyry into his father's hands, but by a generous concession it was arranged that his mother should have him to see her for an hour or so five times a year. The Nolan legacy, however, coming upon the top of this, introduced a peculiar complication that provided much work for tactful intermediaries, and gave great and increasing scope for painful delicacies on the part of Mr. Benham as the boy grew up.

" I see," said the father over his study pipe and with his glasses fixed on remote distances above the head of the current sympathiser, " I see more and more clearly that the tale of my sacrifices is not yet at an end. . . . In many respects he is like her. . . . Quick. Too quick. . . . He must choose. But I know his choice. Yes, yes—I'm not blind. She's worked upon him. . . . I have done what I could to bring out the manhood in him. Perhaps it will bear the strain. . . . It will be a wrench, old man—God knows."

He did his very best to make it a wrench.

§ 2

Benham's mother, whom he saw quarterly and also on the first of May, because it was her birthday, touched and coloured his imagination far more than his father did. She was now Lady Marayne, and a prominent, successful, and happy little

lady. Her dereliction had been forgiven quite soon, and whatever whisper of it remained was very completely forgotten
during the brief period of moral kindliness which followed the
accession of King Edward the Seventh. It no doubt contributed
to her social reinstatement that her former husband was
entirely devoid of social importance, while, on the other hand,
Sir Godfrey Marayne's temporary monopoly of the cæcal
operation which became so fashionable in the last decade of
Queen Victoria's reign as to be practically epidemic, created a
strong feeling in her favour.

She was blue-eyed and very delicately complexioned,
quick-moving, witty, given to little storms of clean enthusiasm ;
she loved handsome things, brave things, successful things,
and the respect and affection of all the world. She did quite
what she liked upon impulse, and nobody ever thought ill of her.

Her family were the Mantons of Blent, quite good west-
country people. She had broken away from them before she
was twenty to marry Benham, whom she had idealised at a
tennis party. He had talked of his work and she had seen it
in a flash, the noblest work in the world, him at his daily divine
toil and herself a Madonna surrounded by a troupe of Blessed
Boys—all of good family, some of quite the best. For a time
she had kept it up even more than he had, and then Nolan
had distracted her with a realisation of the heroism that goes
to the ends of the earth. She became sick with desire for the
forests of Brazil, and the Pacific, and—a peak in Darien.
Immediately the school was frowsty beyond endurance, and
for the first time she let herself perceive how dreadfully a
gentleman and a scholar can smell of pipes and tobacco. Only
one course lay open to a woman of spirit. . . .

For a year she did indeed live like a woman of spirit ; and
it was at Nolan's bedside that Marayne was first moved to
admiration. She was plucky. All men love a plucky woman.

Sir Godfrey Marayne smelt a good deal of antiseptic soap,
but he talked in a way that amused her, and he trusted as well
as adored her. She did what she liked with his money, her own
money, and her son's trust money, and she did very well.
From the earliest Benham's visits were to a gracious presence
amidst wealthy surroundings. The transit from the moral
blamelessness of Seagate had an entirely misleading effect of
ascent.

Their earlier encounters became rather misty in his memory ;
they occurred at various hotels in Seagate. Afterwards he
would go, first taken by a governess, and later going alone,
to Charing Cross, where he would be met, in earlier times by a
maid and afterwards by a deferential manservant who called
him " Sir," and conveyed, sometimes in a hansom cab and
later in a smart brougham, by Trafalgar Square, Lower Regent
Street, Piccadilly, and streets of increasing wealth and sublimity to Sir Godfrey's house in Desborough Street. Very

naturally he fell into thinking of these discreet and well-governed West End streets as a part of his mother's atmosphere.

The house had a dignified portico, and always before he had got down to the pavement the door opened agreeably and a second respectful manservant stood ready. Then came the large hall, with its noiseless carpets and great Chinese jars, its lacquered cabinets and the wide staircase, and floating down the wide staircase, impatient to greet him, light and shining as a flower petal, sweet and welcoming, radiating a joyfulness as cool and clear as a dewy morning, came his mother. "*Well*, little man, my son," she would cry in her happy singing voice, "*Well?*"

So he thought she must always be, but indeed these meetings meant very much to her, she dressed for them and staged them, she perceived the bright advantages of her rarity and she was quite determined to have her son when the time came to possess him. She kissed him, but not oppressively, she caressed him cleverly ; it was only on these rare occasions that he was ever kissed or caressed, and she talked to his shy boyishness until it felt a more spirited variety of manhood. "What have you been doing," she asked, "since I saw you last ? "

She never said he had grown, but she told him he looked tall ; and though the tea was a marvellous display it was never an obtrusive tea, it wasn't poked at a fellow ; a various plenty flowed well within reach of one's arm, like an agreeable accompaniment to their conversation.

"What have you done ? All sorts of brave things ? Do you swim now ? I can swim. Oh ! I can swim half a mile. Some day we will swim races together. Why not ? And you ride ? . . .

"The horse bolted—and you stuck on ? Did you squeak ? I stick on, but I *have* to squeak. But you—of course, no ! you mustn't. I'm just a little woman. And I ride big horses. . . ."

And for the end she had invented a characteristic little ceremony.

She would stand up in front of him and put her hands on his shoulders and look into his face.

"Clean eyes ? " she would say. " ——still ? "

Then she would take his ears in her little firm hands and kiss very methodically his eyes and his forehead and his cheeks and at last his lips. Her own eyes would suddenly brim bright with tears.

"*Go*," she would say.

That was the end.

It seemed to Benham as though he was being let down out of a sunlit fairyland to this gray world again.

§ 3

The contrast between Lady Marayne's pretty amenities and the good woman at Seagate who urged herself almost hourly to forget that William Porphyry was not her own son, was entirely unfair. The second Mrs. Benham's conscientious spirit and a certain handsome ability about her fitted her far more than her predecessor for the onerous duties of a schoolmaster's wife, but whatever natural buoyancy she possessed was outweighed by an irrepressible conviction derived from an episcopal grandparent that the remarriage of divorced persons is sinful, and by a secret but well-founded doubt whether her husband loved her with a truly romantic passion. She might perhaps have borne either of these troubles singly, but the two crushed her spirit.

Her temperament was not one that goes out to meet happiness. She had reluctant affections and suspected rather than welcomed the facility of other people's. Her susceptibility to disagreeable impressions was however very ample, and life was fenced about with protections for her " feelings." It filled young Benham with inexpressible indignations that his sweet own mother, so gay, so brightly cheerful that even her tears were stars, was never to be mentioned in his stepmother's presence, and it was not until he had fully come to years of reflection that he began to realise with what honesty, kindness and patience this naturally not very happy lady had nursed, protected, mended for and generally mothered him.

§ 4

As Benham grew to look manly and bear himself with pride, his mother's affection for him blossomed into a passion. She made him come down to London from Cambridge as often as she could ; she went about with him ; she made him squire her to theatres and take her out to dinners and sup with her at the Carlton, and in the summer she had him with her at Chexington Manor, the Hertfordshire house Sir Godfrey had given her. And always when they parted she looked into his eyes to see if they were still clean—whatever she meant by that—and she kissed his forehead and cheeks and eyes and lips. She began to make schemes for his career, she contrived introductions she judged would be useful to him later.

Everybody found the relationship charming. Some of the more conscientious people, it is true, pretended to think that the Reverend Harold Benham was a first husband and long since dead, but that was all. As a matter of fact, in his increasingly futile way he wasn't, either at Seagate or in the Educational Supplement of the *Times*. But even the most conscientious of us are not obliged to go to Seagate or read the Educational Supplement of the *Times*.

Lady Marayne's plans for her son's future varied very pleasantly. She was an industrious reader of biographies, and more particularly of the large fair biographies of the recently contemporary ; they mentioned people she knew, they recalled scenes, each sowed its imaginative crop upon her mind, a crop that flourished and flowered until a newer growth came to oust it. She saw her son a diplomat, a prancing pro-consul, an empire builder, a trusted friend of the august, the bold leader of new movements, the saviour of ancient institutions, the youngest, brightest, modernest of prime ministers—or a tremendously popular poet. As a rule she saw him unmarried— with a wonderful little mother at his elbow. Sometimes in romantic flashes he was adored by German princesses or eloped with Russian grand-duchesses. But such fancies were *hors d'œuvre*. The modern biography deals with the career. Every project was bright, every project had *go*—tremendous go. And they all demanded a hero, debonair and balanced. And Benham, as she began to perceive, wasn't balanced. Something of his father had crept into him, a touch of moral stiffness. She knew the flavour of that moral stiffness so well. It was a stumbling, an elaboration, a spoil-sport and weakness. She tried not to admit to herself that even in the faintest degree it was there. But it was there.

" Tell me all that you are doing *now*," she said to him one afternoon when she had got him to herself during his first visit to Chexington Manor. " How do you like Cambridge ? Are you making friends ? Have you joined that thing— the Union is it ? — and delivered your maiden speech ? If you're for politics, Poff, that's your game. Have you begun it ? "

She lay among splashes of sunshine on the red cushions in the punt, a little curled-up figure of white, with her sweet pale animated face warmed by the reflection of her red sun- shade, and her eyes like little friendly heavens. And he, lean, and unconsciously graceful, sat at her feet and admired her beyond measure, and rejoiced that now at last they were going to be ever so much together, and doubted if it would be possible ever to love any other woman so much as he did her.

He tried to tell her of Cambridge and his friends and the undergraduate life he was leading, but he found it difficult. All sorts of things that seemed right and good at Trinity seemed out of drawing in the peculiar atmosphere she created about her. All sorts of clumsiness and youthfulness in him- self and his associates he felt she wouldn't accept, couldn't accept, that it would be wrong of her to accept. Before they could come before her they must wear a bravery. He couldn't, for instance, tell her how Billy Prothero, renouncing vanity and all social pretension, had worn a straw hat into November and the last stages of decay, and how it had been burnt by a special commission ceremonially in the great court. He couldn't convey to her the long sessions of beer and tobacco and high thinking that went on in Prothero's rooms into the small hours. A certain Gothic grayness and flatness and muddiness through which the Cambridge spirit struggles to its destiny, he concealed from her. What remained to tell was—attenuated. He could not romance. So she tried to fill in his jejune outlines. She tried to inspire a son who seemed most unaccountably up to nothing.

" You must make good friends," she said.   " Isn't young Lord Breeze at your college ? His mother the other day told me he was. And Sir Freddy Quenton's boy. And there are both the young Baptons at Cambridge."

He knew one of the Baptons.

" Poff," she said suddenly, " has it ever occurred to you what you are going to do afterwards ? Do you know you are going to be quite well off ? "

Benham looked up with a faint embarrassment. " My father said something. He was rather vague. It wasn't his affair— that kind of thing."

" You will be quite well off," she repeated, without any complicating particulars.   " You will be so well off that it will be possible for you to do anything almost that you like in the world. Nothing will tie you. Nothing. . . . "

" But—*how* well off ? "

" You will have several thousands a year."

" Thousands ? "

" Yes. Why not ? "

" But—— Mother, this is rather astounding. . . . Does this mean there are estates somewhere, responsibilities ? "

" It is just money. Investments."

" You know, I've imagined—— I've thought always I should have to *do* something."

" You *must* do something, Poff. But it needn't be for a living. The world is yours without that. And so you see you've got to make plans. You've got to know the sort of people who'll have things in their hands. You've got to keep out of—holes and corners. You've got to think of Parliament and abroad. There's the army, there's diplomacy. There's the Empire. You can be a Cecil Rhodes if you like. You can be a Winston. . . . "

§ 5

Perhaps it was only the innate eagerness of Lady Marayne which made her feel disappointed in her son's outlook upon life. He did not choose among his glittering possibilities, he did not say what he was going to be, pro-consul, ambassador, statesman, for days. And he talked *vaguely* of wanting to do something fine, but all in a fog. A boy of nearly nineteen ought to have at least the beginnings of *savoir faire*.

Was he in the right set ? Was he indeed in the right college ? Trinity, by his account, seemed a huge featureless place—and might he not conceivably be *lost* in it ? In those big crowds one had to insist upon oneself. Poff never insisted upon himself—except quite at the wrong moment. And there was this Billy Prothero. *Billy !* Like a goat or something. People called William don't get their Christian name insisted upon unless they are vulnerable somewhere. Any form of William stamps a weakness, Willie, Willy, Will, Billy, Bill ; it's a fearful handle for one's friends. At any rate Poff had escaped that. But this Prothero !

" But who *is* this Billy Prothero ? " she asked one evening in the walled garden.

" He was at Minchinghampton."

" But who *is* he ? Who is his father ? Where does he come from ? "

Benham sought in his mind for a space. " I don't know," he said at last. Billy had always been rather reticent about his people. She demanded descriptions. She demanded an account of Billy's furniture, Billy's clothes, Billy's form of exercise. It dawned upon Benham that for some inexplicable reason she was hostile to Billy. It was like the unmasking of an ambuscade. He had talked a lot about Prothero's ideas and the discussions of social reform and social service that went on in his rooms, for Billy read at unknown times, and was open at all hours to any argumentative caller. To Lady Marayne all ideas were obnoxious, a form of fogging ; all ideas, she held, were queer ideas. " And does he call himself a Socialist ? " she asked. " I *thought* he would."

" Poff," she cried suddenly, " you're not a *Socialist* ? "

" Such a vague term."

" But these friends of yours—they seem to be *all* Socialists. Red ties and everything complete."

" They have ideas," he evaded. He tried to express it better. " They give one something to take hold of."

She sat up stiffly on the garden-seat. She lifted her finger at him, very seriously. " I hope," she said with all her heart, " that you will have nothing to do with such ideas. Nothing. *Socialism !* "

" They make a case."

" Pooh ! Any one can make a case."

" But—— "

" There's no sense in them. What is the good of talking about upsetting everything ? Just disorder. How can one do anything then ? You mustn't. You mustn't. No. It's nonsense, little Poff. It's absurd. And you may spoil so much. . . . I *hate* the way you talk of it. . . . As if it wasn't all—absolutely—*rubbish*. . . . "

She was earnest almost to the intonation of tears.

Why couldn't her son go straight for his ends, clear tangible

ends, as she had always done ? This thinking about everything ! She had never thought about anything in all her life
for more than half an hour—and it had always turned out
remarkably well.

Benham felt baffled. There was a pause. How on earth
could he go on telling her his ideas if this was how they were
to be taken ?

" I wish sometimes," his mother said abruptly, with an
unusually sharp note in her voice, " that you wouldn't look
quite so like your father."

" But I'm *not* like my father ! " said Benham, puzzled.

" No," she insisted, and with an air of appealing to his
soberer reason, " so why should you go *looking* like him ?
That *concerned* expression. . . ."

She jumped to her feet. " Poff," she said, " I want to go
and see the evening primroses pop. You and I are talking
nonsense. *They* don't have ideas anyhow. They just pop—
as God meant them to do. What stupid things we human
beings are ! "

Her philosophical moments were perhaps the most baffling
of all.

§ 6

Billy Prothero became the symbol in the mind of Lady
Marayne for all that disappointed her in Benham. He had
to become the symbol, because she could not think of complicated or abstract things, she had to make things personal,
and he was the only personality available. She fretted over
his existence for some days therefore (once she awakened
and thought about him in the night), and then suddenly she
determined to grasp her nettle. She decided to seize and
obliterate this Prothero. He must come to Chexington and
be thoroughly and conclusively led on, examined, ransacked,
shown up, and disposed of for ever. At once. She was not
quite clear how she meant to do this, but she was quite resolved
that it had to be done. Anything is better than inaction.

There was a little difficulty about dates and engagements,
but he came, and through the season of expectation Benham,
who was now for the first time in contact with the feminine
nature, was delighted at the apparent change to cordiality.
So that he talked of Billy to his mother much more than he
had ever done before.

Billy had been his particular friend at Minchinghampton,
at least during the closing two years of his school life. Billy
had fallen into friendship with Benham, as some of us fall
in love, quite suddenly, when he saw Benham get down from
the fence and be sick after his encounter with the bull. Already
Billy was excited by admiration, but it was the incongruity
of the sickness conquered him. He went back to the school
with his hands more than usually in his pockets, and no eyes

for anything but this remarkable strung-up fellow creature. He felt he had never observed Benham before, and he was astonished that he had not done so.

Billy Prothero was a sturdy sort of boy, generously wanting in good looks. His hair was rough, and his complexion muddy, and he walked about with his hands in his pockets, long flexible lips protruded in a whistle, and a rather shapeless nose well up to show he didn't care. Providence had sought to console him by giving him a keen eye for the absurdity of other people. He had a suggestive tongue, and he professed and practised cowardice to the scandal of all his acquaintances. He was said never to wash behind his ears, but this report wronged him. There had been a time when he did not do so, but his mother had won him to a promise, and now that operation was often the sum of his simple hasty toilet. His desire to associate himself with Benham was so strong that it triumphed over a defensive reserve. It enabled him to detect accessible moments, do inobtrusive friendly services, and above all amuse his quarry. He not only amused Benham, he stimulated him. They came to do quite a number of things together. In the language of schoolboy stories they became " insepar- ables."

Prothero's first desire, so soon as they were on a footing that enabled him to formulate desires, was to know exactly what Benham thought he was up to in crossing a field with a bull in it instead of going round, and by the time he began to understand that, he had conceived an affection for him that was to last a lifetime.

" I wasn't going to be bullied by a beast," said Benham.

" Suppose it had been an elephant ? " Prothero cried. . . . " A mad elephant ? . . . A pack of wolves ? "

Benham was too honest not to see that he was entangled. " Well, suppose in *your* case it had been a wild cat ? . . . A fierce mastiff ? . . . A mastiff ? . . . A terrier ? . . . A lap dog ? "

" Yes, but my case is that there are limits."

Benham was impatient at the idea of limits. With a faintly malicious pleasure Prothero lugged him back to that idea.

" We both admit there are limits," Prothero concluded. " But between the absolutely impossible and the altogether possible there's the region of risk. You think a man ought to take that risk—— " He reflected. " I think—no—I think *not*."

" If he feels afraid," cried Benham, seeing his one point. " If he feels afraid. Then he ought to take it. . . . "

After a digestive interval, Prothero asked, " *Why* ? Why should he ? "

The discussion of that momentous question, that Why ? which Benham perhaps might never have dared ask himself, and which Prothero perhaps might never have attempted to answer if it had not been for the clash of their minds

was the chief topic of their conversation for many months.
From Why be brave ? it spread readily enough to Why be
honest ?   Why be clean ?—all the great whys of life. . . .
Because one believes. . . . But why believe it ?   Left to
himself Benham would have felt the mere asking of this
question was a thing ignoble, not to be tolerated.   It was,
as it were, treason to nobility.   But Prothero put it one
afternoon in a way that permitted no high dismissal of their
doubts.   " You can't build your honour on fudge, Benham.
Like committing sacrilege—in order to buy a cloth for the
altar."

By that Benham was slipped from the recognised code
and launched upon speculations which became the magnificent
research.

It was not only in complexion and stature and ways of
thinking that Billy and Benham contrasted.   Benham inclined a little to eloquence, he liked very clean hands, he
had a dread of ridiculous outlines.   Prothero lapsed readily
into ostentatious slovenliness, when his hands were dirty
he pitied them sooner than scrubbed them, he would have
worn an overcoat with one tail torn off rather than have
gone cold.   Moreover, Prothero had an earthy liking for
animals, he could stroke and tickle strange cats until they
wanted to leave father and mother and all earthly possessions
and follow after him, and he mortgaged a term's pocket
money and bought and kept a small terrier in the school
house against all law and tradition, under the baseless pretence
that it was a stray animal of unknown origin.   Benham, on
the other hand, was shy with small animals and faintly hostile
to big ones.   Beasts he thought were just beasts.   And Prothero
had a gift for caricature, while Benham's aptitude was for
music.

It was Prothero's eyes and pencil that first directed Benham
to the poor indolences and evasions and insincerities of the
masters.   It was Prothero's wicked pictures that made him
see the shrivelled absurdity of the vulgar theology.   But it
was Benham who stood between Prothero and that rather
coarsely conceived epicureanism that seemed his logical
destiny.   When quite early in their Cambridge days Prothero's
revolt against foppery reached a nadir of personal neglect,
and two philanthropists from the rooms below him, goaded
beyond the normal tolerance of Trinity, and assisted by two
sportsmen from Trinity Hall, burnt his misshapen straw
hat (after partly filling it with gunpowder and iron filings)
and sought to duck him in the fountain in the court, it was
Benham, in a state between distress and madness, and armed
with a hornhandled cane of exceptional size, who intervened,
turned the business into a blend of wrangle and scuffle, introduced the degrading topic of duelling into a simple wholesome rag of four against one, carried him off under the cloud

of horror created by this impropriety and so saved him, still only slightly wetted, not only from this indignity but from the experiment in rationalism that had provoked it.

Because Benham made it perfectly clear what he had thought and felt about this hat.

Such was the illuminating young man whom Lady Marayne decided to invite to Chexington, into the neighbourhood of herself, Sir Godfrey, and her circle of friends.

§ 7

He was quite anxious to satisfy the requirements of Benham's people and to do his friend credit. He was still in the phase of being a penitent pig, and he inquired carefully into the needs and duties of a summer guest in a country house. He knew it was quite a considerable country house, and that Sir Godfrey wasn't Benham's father, but like most people, he was persuaded that Lady Marayne had divorced the parental Benham. He arrived dressed very neatly in a brown suit that had only one fault, it had not the remotest suggestion of having been made for him. It fitted his body fairly well, it did annex his body with only a few slight incompatibilities, but it repudiated his hands and face. He had a conspicuously old Gladstone bag and a conspicuously new despatch case, and he had forgotten black ties and dress socks and a hair brush. He arrived in the late afternoon, was met by Benham, in tennis flannels, looking smartened up and a little unfamiliar, and taken off in a spirited dog-cart driven by a typical groom. He met his host and hostess at dinner.

Sir Godfrey was a rationalist and a residuum. Very much of him, too much perhaps, had gone into the acquirement and perfect performance of the cæcal operation ; the man one met in the social world was what was left over. It had the effect of being quiet, but in its unobtrusive way knobby. He had a knobby brow, with an air about it of having recently been intent, and his conversation was curiously spotted with little knobby arrested anecdotes. If any one of any distinction was named, he would reflect and say, " Of course—ah, yes, I know him, I know him. Yes, I did him a little service—in '96."

And something in his manner would suggest a satisfaction, or a dissatisfaction, with confidential mysteries.

He welcomed Billy Prothero in a colourless manner, and made conversation about Cambridge. He had known one or two of the higher dons. One he had done at Cambridge quite recently. " The inns are better than they are at Oxford, which is not saying very much, but the place struck me as being changed. The men seemed younger. . . ."

The burden of the conversation fell upon Lady Marayne. She looked extraordinarily like a flower to Billy ; a little diamond buckle on a black velvet band glittered between

the two masses of butter-coloured hair that flowed back
from her forehead, her head was poised on the prettiest neck
conceivable, and her shapely little shoulders and her shapely
little arms came decidedly but pleasantly out of a softness
and sparkle of white and silver and old rose. She talked
what sounded like innocent commonplaces a little spiced
by whim, though indeed each remark had an exploratory
quality, and her soft blue eyes rested ever and again upon
Billy's white tie. It seemed she did so by the merest inadvertency, but it made the young man wish he had after
all borrowed a black one from Benham. But the manservant
who had put his things out had put it out, and he hadn't
been quite sure. Also she noted all the little things he did
with fork and spoon and glass. She gave him an unusual
sense of being brightly, accurately, and completely visible.

Chexington, it seemed to Billy, was done with a large
and costly and easy completeness. The table with its silver
and flowers was much more beautifully done than any table
he had sat at before, and in the dimness beyond the brightness
there were two men to wait on the four of them. The old
gray butler was really wonderfully good. . . .

" You shoot, Mr. Prothero ? "

" You hunt, Mr. Prothero ? "

" You know Scotland well, Mr. Prothero ? "

These questions disturbed Prothero. He did not shoot,
he did not hunt, he did not go to Scotland for the grouse,
he did not belong, and Lady Marayne ought to have seen
that he did not belong, to the class that does these things.

" You ride much, Mr. Prothero ? "

Billy conceived a suspicion that these innocent inquiries
were designed to emphasise a contrast in his social quality.
But he could not be sure. One never could be sure with
Lady Marayne. It might be just that she did not understand the sort of man he was. And in that case ought he
to maintain the smooth social surface unbroken by pretending
as far as possible to be this kind of person, or ought he to
make a sudden gap in it by telling his realities ? He evaded
the shooting question anyhow. He left it open for Lady
Marayne and the venerable butler and Sir Godfrey and every
one to suppose he just happened to be the sort of gentleman
of leisure who doesn't shoot. He disavowed hunting, he
made it appear he travelled when he travelled in directions
other than Scotland. But the fourth question brought him
to bay. He regarded his questioner with his small rufous
eye.

" I have never been across a horse in my life, Lady Marayne."

" Tut, tut," said Sir Godfrey. " Why !—it's the best of
exercise. Every man ought to ride. Good for the health.
Keeps him fit. Prevents lodgments. Most trouble due to
lodgments."

"I've never had a chance of riding. And I think I'm afraid of horses."

"That's only an excuse," said Lady Marayne. "Everybody's afraid of horses and nobody's really afraid of horses."

"But I'm not used to horses. You see—I live on my mother. And she can't afford to keep a stable."

His hostess did not see his expression of discomfort. Her pretty eyes were intent upon the peas with which she was being served.

"Does your mother live in the country ? " she asked, and took her peas with fastidious exactness.

Prothero coloured brightly. "She lives in London."

"All the year ? "

"All the year."

"But isn't it dreadfully hot in town in the summer ? "

Prothero had an uncomfortable sense of being very red in the face. This kept him red. "We're suburban people," he said.

"But I thought—isn't there the seaside ? "

"My mother has a business," said Prothero, redder than ever.

"O-oh : " said Lady Marayne. "What fun that must be for her ? "

"It's a real business, and she has to live by it. Sometimes it's a worry."

"But a business of her own ! " She surveyed the confusion of his visage with a sweet intelligence. "Is it an amusing sort of business, Mr. Prothero ? "

Prothero looked mulish. "My mother is a dressmaker," he said. "In Brixton. She doesn't do particularly badly— or well. I live on my scholarship. I have lived on scholarships since I was thirteen. And you see, Lady Marayne, Brixton is a poor hunting country."

Lady Marayne felt she had unmasked Prothero almost indecently. Whatever happened there must be no pause. There must be no sign of a hitch.

"But it's good at tennis," she said. "You *do* play tennis, Mr. Prothero ? "

"I—I gesticulate," said Prothero.

Lady Marayne, still in flight from that pause, went off at a tangent.

"Poff, my dear," she said, "I've had a diving-board put at the deep end of the pond."

The remark hung answered for a moment. The transition had been too quick for Benham's state of mind.

"Do you swim, Mr. Prothero ? " the lady asked, though a moment before she had determined that she would never ask him a question again. But this time it was a lucky question.

"Prothero mopped up the lot of us at Minchinghampton

with his diving and swimming," Benham explained, and the tension was relaxed.

Lady Marayne spoke of her own swimming, and became daring and amusing at her difficulties with local feeling when first she swam in the pond. The high-road ran along the far side of the pond—" And it didn't wear a hedge or anything," said Lady Marayne. " That was what they didn't quite like. Swimming in an undraped pond. . . ."

Prothero had been examined enough. Now he must be entertained. She told stories about the village people in her brightest manner. The third story she regretted as soon as she was fairly launched upon it ; it was how she had interviewed the village dressmaker, when Sir Godfrey insisted upon her supporting local industries. It was very amusing but technical. The devil had put it into her head. She had to go through with it. She infused an extreme innocence into her eyes and fixed them on Prothero, although she felt a certain deepening pinkness in her cheeks was betraying her, and she did not look at Benham until her unhappy but otherwise quite amusing anecdote, was dead and gone and safely buried under another. . . .

But people ought not to go about having dressmakers for mothers. . . .

And coming into other people's houses and influencing their sons. . . .

§ 8

That night when everything was over Billy sat at the writing-table of his sumptuous bedroom—the bed was gilt wood, the curtains of the three great windows were tremendous, and there was a cheval glass that showed the full length of him and seemed to look over his head for more— and meditated upon this visit of his. It was more than he had been prepared for. It was going to be a great strain. The sleek young manservant in an alpaca jacket, who said " Sir " whenever you looked at him, and who had seized upon and unpacked Billy's most private Gladstone bag without even asking if he might do so, and put away and displayed Billy's things in a way that struck Billy as faintly ironical, was unexpected. And it was unexpected that the brown suit, with its pockets stuffed with Billy's personal and confidential sundries, had vanished. And apparently a bath in a bathroom far down the corridor was prescribed for him in the morning ; he hadn't thought of a dressing-gown. And after one had dressed, what did one do ? Did one go down and wander about the house looking for the breakfast-room or wait for a gong ? Would Sir Godfrey read Family Prayers? And afterwards did one go out or hang about to be entertained ? He knew now quite clearly that those wicked blue eyes would mark his every slip. She did not like him. She did not like him, he supposed, because he was common stuff. He didn't play up to her world and her. He was a discord in this rich, cleverly elaborate household. You could see it in the servants' attitudes. And he was committed to a week of this.

Billy puffed out his cheeks to blow a sigh, and then decided to be angry and say " Damn ! "

This way of living which made him uncomfortable was clearly an irrational and objectionable way of living. It was, in a cumbersome way, luxurious. But the waste of life of it, the servants, the observances, all concentrated on the mere detail of existence ! There came a rap at the door. Benham appeared, wearing an expensive-looking dressing-jacket which Lady Marayne had bought for him. He asked if he might talk for a bit and smoke. He sat down in a capacious chintz-covered easy-chair beside Prothero, lit a cigarette, and came to the point after only a trivial hesitation.

" Prothero," he said, " you know what my father is."

" I thought he ran a preparatory school."

There was the profoundest resentment in Prothero's voice.

" And, all the same, I'm going to be a rich man."

" I don't understand," said Prothero, without any shadow of congratulation.

Benham told Prothero as much as his mother had conveyed to him of the resources of his wealth. Her version had been adapted to his tender years and the delicacies of her position. The departed Nolan had become an eccentric godfather. Benham's manner was apologetic and he made it clear that only recently had these facts come to him. He had never suspected that he had had this eccentric godfather. It altered the outlook tremendously. It was one of the reasons that made Benham glad to have Prothero there ; one wanted a man of one's own age, who understood things a little to try over one's new ideas. Prothero listened with an unamiable expression.

" What would you do, Prothero, if you found yourself saddled with some thousands a year ? "

" Godfathers don't grow in Brixton," said Prothero concisely.

" Well, what am I to do, Prothero ? "

" Does all *this* belong to you ? "

" No, this is my mother's."

" Godfather too ? "

" I've not thought. . . . I suppose so. Or her own."

Prothero meditated.

" *This* life," he said at last, " this large expensiveness— . . ."

He left his criticism unfinished.

" I agree. It suits my mother somehow. I can't understand her living in any other way. But—for me. . . ."

" What can one do with several thousands a year ? "

Prothero's interest in this question presently swamped his petty personal resentments. " I suppose," he said, " one might have rather a lark with money like that. One would be free to go anywhere. To set all sorts of things going. . . . It's clear you can't sell all you have and give it to the poor. That is pauperisation nowadays. You might run a tremendously revolutionary paper. A real upsetting paper. How many thousands is it ? "

" I don't know. *Some.*"

Prothero's interest was growing as he faced the possibilities.

" I've dreamt of a paper," he said, " a paper that should tell the brute truth about things."

" I don't know that I'm particularly built to be a journalist," Benham objected.

" You're not," said Billy. . . . " You might go into Parliament as a perfectly independent member. . . . Only you wouldn't get in. . . ."

" I'm not a speaker," said Benham.

" Of course," said Billy, " if you don't decide on a game, you'll just go on like this. You'll fall into a groove, you'll —you'll hunt. You'll go to Scotland for the grouse."

For the moment Prothero had no further suggestions.

Benham waited for a second or so before he broached his own idea.

" Why, first of all, at any rate, Billy, shouldn't one use one's money to make the best of oneself ? To learn things that men without money and leisure find it difficult to learn ? By an accident, however unjust it is, one is in the position of a leader and a privileged person. Why not do one's best to give value as that ? "

" Benham, that's the thin end of aristocracy ! "

" Why not ? "

" I hate aristocracy. For you it means doing what you like. While you are energetic you will kick about and then you will come back to this."

" That's one's own look-out," said Benham, after reflection.

" No, it's bound to happen."

Benham retreated a little from the immediate question. " Well, we can't suddenly at a blow change the world. If it isn't to be plutocracy to-day it has to be aristocracy."

Prothero frowned over this, and then he made a sweeping proposition.

" *You cannot have aristocracy,*" he said, " *because, you see— all men are ridiculous.* Democracy has to fight its way out from under plutocracy. There is nothing else to be done."

" But a man in my position—— ? "

" It's a ridiculous position. You may try to escape being ridiculous. You won't succeed."

It seemed to Benham for a moment as though Prothero

had got to the bottom of the question, and then he perceived that he had only got to the bottom of himself. Benham was pacing the floor.

He turned at the open window, held out a long forefinger, and uttered his countervailing faith.

" Even if he is ridiculous, Prothero, a man may still be an aristocrat. A man may anyhow be as much of an aristocrat as he can be."

Prothero reflected. " No," he said, " it sounds all right, but it's wrong. I hate all these advantages and differences and distinctions. A man's a man. What you say sounds well, but it's the beginning of pretension, of pride——"

He stopped short.

" Better pride than dishonour," said Benham, " better the pretentious life than the sordid life. What else is there ? "

" A life isn't necessarily sordid because it isn't pretentious," said Prothero, his voice betraying a defensive disposition.

" But a life with a large income *must* be sordid unless it makes some sort of attempt to be fine. . . ."

§ 9

By transitions that were as natural as they were complicated and untraceable Prothero found his visit to Chexington developing into a tangle of discussions that all ultimately resolved themselves into an antagonism of the democratic and the aristocratic idea. And his part was, he found, to be the exponent of the democratic idea. The next day he came down early, his talk with Benham still running through his head, and after a turn or so in the garden he was attracted to the front door by a sound of voices, and found Lady Marayne had been up still earlier and was dismounting from a large effective black horse. This extorted an unwilling admiration from him. She greeted him very pleasantly and made a kind of introduction of her steed. There had been trouble at a gate, he was a young horse and fidgeted at gates ; the dispute was still bright in her. Benham she declared was still in bed. " Wait till I have a mount for him." She reappeared fitfully in the breakfast-room, and then he was left to Benham until just before lunch. They read and afterwards, as the summer day grew hot, they swam in the nude pond. She joined them in the water, splashing about in a costume of some elaboration and being very careful not to wet her hair. Then she came and sat with them on the seat under the big cedar and talked with them in a wrap that was pretty rather than prudish and entirely unmotherly. And she began a fresh attack upon him by asking him if he wasn't a Socialist and whether he didn't want to pull down Chexington and grow potatoes all over the park.

This struck Prothero as an inadequate statement of the

Socialist project, and he made an unsuccessful attempt to get
it amended.

The engagement thus opened was renewed with great
energy at lunch. Sir Godfrey had returned to London and
the inmost aspect of his fellow-creatures, but the party of
three was supplemented by a vague young lady from the
village and an alert agent from the neighbouring Tentington
estate who had intentions about a cottage. Lady Marayne
insisted upon regarding Socialism as a proposal to reinaugurate
the first French Revolution, as an inversion of society so
that it would be bottom upward, as an attack upon rule,
order, direction. " And what good are all these proposals ?
If you had the poor dear king beheaded, you'd only get a
Napoleon. If you divided all the property up between everybody, you'd have rich and poor again in a year."

Billy perceived no way of explaining away this version of
his Socialism that would not involve uncivil contradictions—
and nobody ever contradicted Lady Marayne.

" But, Lady Marayne, don't you think there is a lot of
disorder and injustice in the world ? " he protested.

" There would be ever so much more if your Socialists
had their way."

" But still don't you think——— . . ."

It is unnecessary even to recapitulate these universal controversies of our time. The lunch-table and the dinner-table
and the general talk of the house drifted more and more
definitely at its own level in the same direction as the private
talk of Prothero and Benham, towards the antagonism of
the privileged few and the many, of the trained and traditioned
against the natural and undisciplined, of aristocracy against
democracy. At the week-end Sir Godfrey returned to bring
fresh elements. He said that democracy was unscientific.
" To deny aristocracy is to deny the existence of the fittest.
It is on the existence of the fittest that progress depends."

" But do our social conditions exalt the fittest ? " asked
Prothero.

" That is another question," said Benham.

" Exactly," said Sir Godfrey. " That is another question.
But speaking with some special knowledge, I should say
that on the whole the people who are on the top of things
ought to be on the top of things. I agree with Aristotle that
there is such a thing as a natural inferior."

" So far as I can understand, Mr. Prothero," said Lady
Marayne, " he thinks that all the inferiors are the superiors
and all the superiors inferior. It's quite simple. . . ."

It made Prothero none the less indignant with this, that
there was indeed a grain of truth in it. He hated superiors,
he felt for inferiors.

§ 10

At last came the hour of tipping.   An embarrassed and miserable Prothero went slinking about the house distributing unexpected gold.

It was stupid, it was damnable ;   he had had to borrow the money from his mother. . . .

Lady Marayne felt he had escaped her.   The controversy that should have split these two young men apart had given them a new interest in each other.   When afterwards she sounded her son, very delicately, to see if indeed he was aware of the clumsiness, the social ignorance and uneasiness, the complete unsuitability of his friend, she could get no more from him than that exasperating phrase, " He has ideas ! "

What are ideas ?   England may yet be ruined by ideas.

He ought never to have gone to Trinity, that monster packet of everything.   He ought to have gone to some little *good* college, good all through.   She ought to have asked some one who *knew*.

§ 11

One glowing afternoon in October, as these two young men came over Magdalen Bridge after a long, disputatious and rather tiring walk to Drayton—they had been talking of Eugenics and the " family "—Benham was almost knocked down by an American trotter driven by Lord Breeze.   " Whup there ! " said Lord Breeze in a voice deliberately brutal, and Benham, roused from that abstraction which is partly fatigue, had to jump aside and stumbled against the parapet as the gaunt pacer went pounding by.

Lord Breeze grinned the sort of grin a man remembers. And passed.

" Damnation ! " said Benham with a face that had become suddenly very white.

Then presently.   " Any fool can do that who cares to go to the trouble."

" That," said Prothero, taking up their unquenchable issue, " that is the feeling of democracy."

" I walk because I choose to," said Benham.

The thing rankled.

" This equestrianism," he began, " is a matter of time and money—time even more than money.   I want to read. I want to deal with ideas. . . ."

" Any fool can drive. . . ."

" Exactly," said Prothero.

" As for riding, it means no more than the elaborate study and cultivation of your horse.   You have to know him.   All horses are individuals. A made horse perhaps goes its round like an omnibus, but for the rest. . . ."

Prothero made a noise of sympathetic assent.

" In a country where equestrianism is assertion I suppose one must be equestrian. . . ."

That night some malignant spirit kept Benham awake, and great American trotters with vast wide-striding feet and long yellow teeth, uncontrollable, hard-mouthed American trotters, pounded over his angry soul.

" Prothero," he said in hall next day, " we are going to drive to-morrow."

Next day, so soon as they had lunched, he led the way towards Maltby's, in Crosshampton Lane. Something in his bearing put a question into Prothero's mind. " Benham," he asked, " have you ever driven before ? "

" *Never*," said Benham.

" Well ? "

" I'm going to now."

Something between pleasure and alarm came into Prothero's eyes. He quickened his pace so as to get alongside his friend and scrutinise his pale determination. " Why are you doing this ? " he asked.

" I want to do it."

" Benham, is it—*equestrian* ? "

Benham made no audible reply. They proceeded resolutely in silence.

An air of expectation prevailed in Maltby's yard. In the shafts of a high, bleak-looking vehicle with vast side wheels, a throne-like vehicle that impressed Billy Prothero as being a gig, a very large angular black horse was being harnessed.

" This is mine," said Benham compactly.

" This is yours, sir," said an ostler.

" He looks—*quiet*."

" You'll find him fresh enough, sir."

Benham made a complicated ascent to the driver's seat and was handed the reins. " Come on," he said, and Prothero followed to a less exalted seat at Benham's side. They seemed to be at a very great height indeed. The horse was then led out into Crosshampton Lane, faced towards Trinity Street and discharged. " Check," said Benham, and touched the steed with his whip. They started quite well, and the ostlers went back into the yard, visibly unanxious. It struck Prothero that perhaps driving was less difficult than he had supposed.

They went along Crosshampton Lane, that high-walled gulley, with dignity, with only a slight suggestion of the inaccuracy that was presently to become apparent, until they met a little old bearded don on a bicycle. Then some misunderstanding arose between Benham and the horse, and the little bearded don was driven into the narrow pavement and had to get off hastily. He made no comment, but his face became like a gargoyle. " Sorry," said Benham, and gave his mind to the corner. There was some difficulty about whether they were to turn to the right or the left, but at last Benham, it seemed, carried his point, and they went along the narrow street, past the gray splendours of King's, and rather in the middle of the way.

Prothero considered the beast in front of him, and how proud and disrespectful a horse in a dog-cart can seem to those behind it ! Moreover, unaccustomed as he was to horses, he was struck by the strong resemblance a bird's-eye view of a horse bears to a fiddle, a fiddle with devil's ears.

" Of course," said Prothero, " this isn't a trotter."

" I couldn't get a trotter," said Benham.

" I thought I would try this sort of thing before I tried a trotter," he added.

And then suddenly came disaster.

There was a butcher's cart on the right, and Benham, mistrusting the intelligence of his steed, insisted upon an excessive amplitude of clearance. He did not reckon with the hand-barrow on his left, piled up with dirty plates from the lunch of Trinity Hall. It had been left there ; its custodian was away upon some mysterious errand. Heaven knows why Trinity Hall exhibited the treasures of its crockery thus stained and defiled in the Cambridge streets. But it did—for Benham's and Prothero's undoing. Prothero saw the great wheel over which he was poised entangle itself with the little wheel of the barrow. " God ! " he whispered, and craned, fascinated. The little wheel was manifestly intrigued beyond all self-control by the great wheel ; it clung to it, it went before it, heedless of the barrow, of which it was an inseparable part. The barrow came about with an appearance of unwillingness, it locked against the great wheel ; it reared itself towards Prothero and began, smash, smash, smash, to shed its higher plates. It was clear that Benham was grappling with a crisis upon a basis of inadequate experience. A number of people shouted haphazard things. Then, too late, the barrow had persuaded the little wheel to give up its fancy for the great wheel, and there was an enormous crash.

" Whoa ! " cried Benham. " Whoa ! " but also, unfortunately, he sawed hard at the horse's mouth.

The animal being in some perplexity, danced a little in the narrow street, and then it had come about and it was backing, backing, on the narrow pavement and towards the plate-glass window of a book and newspaper shop. Benham tugged at its mouth much harder than ever. Prothero saw the window bending under the pressure of the wheel. A sense of the profound seriousness of life and of the folly of this expedition came upon him. With extreme nimbleness he got down just as the window burst. It went with an explosion like a pistol shot, and then a clatter of falling glass. People sprang, it seemed, from nowhere, and jostled about Prothero, so that he became a peripheral figure in the discussion. He perceived that a man in a green apron was holding the horse, and that various people were engaged in simultaneous conversation with Benham, who with a pale serenity of face and an awful calm of manner, dealt with each of them in turn.

" I'm sorry," he was saying. " Somebody ought to have been in charge of the barrow. Here are my cards. I am ready to pay for any damage. . . .

" The barrow ought not to have been there. . . .

" Yes, I am going on. Of course I'm going on. Thank you."

He beckoned to the man who had held the horse and handed him half-a-crown. He glanced at Prothero as one might glance at a stranger. " Check ! " he said. The horse went on gravely. Benham lifted out his whip. He appeared to have clean forgotten Prothero. Perhaps presently he would miss him. He went on past Trinity, past the ruddy brick of St. John's. The curve of the street hid him from Prothero's eyes.

Prothero started in pursuit. He glimpsed the dogcart turning into Bridge Street. He had an impression that Benham used the whip at the corner, and that the dogcart went forward out of sight with a startled jerk. Prothero quickened his pace.

But when he got to the fork between the Huntingdon Road and the Cottenham Road, both roads were clear.

He spent some time in hesitation. Then he went along the Huntingdon Road until he came upon a road-mender, and learnt that Benham had passed that way. " Going pretty fast 'e was," said the road-mender, " and whipping 'is 'orse. Else you might 'a thought 'e was a boltin' with 'im." Prothero decided that if Benham came back at all he would return by way of Cottenham, and it was on the Cottenham Road that at last he encountered his friend again.

Benham was coming along at that good pace which all experienced horses when they are fairly turned back towards Cambridge display. And there was something odd about Benham, as though he had a large circular halo with a thick rim. This, it seemed, had replaced his hat. He was certainly hatless. The warm light of the sinking sun shone upon the horse and upon Benham's erect figure and upon his face, and gleams of fire kept flashing from his head to this rim, like the gleam of drawn swords seen from afar. As he drew nearer this halo detached itself from him and became a wheel sticking up behind him. A large, clumsy-looking bicycle was attached to the dog-cart behind. The expression of Benham's golden face was still a stony expression ; he regarded his friend with hard eyes.

"You all right, Benham ? " cried Prothero, advancing into the road.

His eye examined the horse. It looked all right, if anything it was a trifle subdued ; there was a little foam about its mouth, but not very much.

" Whoa ! " said Benham, and the horse stopped. " Are you coming up, Prothero ? "

Prothero clambered up beside him. " I was anxious," he said.

" There was no need to be."

" You've broken your whip."

" Yes. It broke. . . . *Get* up ! "

They proceeded on their way to Cambridge.

" Something has happened to the wheel," said Prothero, trying to be at his ease.

" Merely a splinter or so. And a spoke perhaps."

" And what is this behind ? "

Benham made a half-turn of the head. " It's a motor-bicycle."

Prothero took in details.

" Some of it is missing."

" No, the front wheel is under the seat."

" Oh ! "

" Did you find it ? " Prothero asked, after an interval.

" No."

" You mean ? "

" He ran into a motor-car—as I was passing. I was perhaps a little to blame. He asked me to bring his machine to Cambridge. He went on in the car. . . . It is all perfectly simple."

Prothero glanced at the splinters in the wheel with a renewed interest.

" Did your wheel get into it ? " he asked.

Benham affected not to hear. He was evidently in no mood for story-telling.

" Why did you get down, Prothero ? " he asked abruptly, with the note of suppressed anger thickening his voice.

Prothero became vividly red. " I don't know," he said, after an interval.

" I *do*," said Benham, and they went on in a rich and active silence to Cambridge, and the bicycle repair shop in Bridge Street, and Trinity College. At the gate of Trinity Benham stopped, and conveyed rather by acts than words that Prothero was to descend. He got down meekly enough, although he felt that the return to Maltby's yard might have many points of interest. But the spirit had gone out of him.

§ 12

For three days the two friends avoided each other, and then Prothero went to Benham's room. Benham was smoking cigarettes—Lady Marayne, in the first warmth of his filial

devotion, had prohibited his pipe—and reading Webb's
Industrial Democracy. " Hullo ! " he said coldly, scarcely
looking up, and continued to read that absorbing work.

" I keep on thinking how I jumped down from that damned
dog-cart," said Prothero, without any preface.

" It didn't matter in the least," said Benham distantly.

" Oh ! *Rot,*" said Prothero. " I behaved like a coward."

Benham shut the book.

" Benham," said Prothero, " you are right about aristocracy, and I am wrong. I've been thinking about it night
and day."

Benham betrayed no emotion. But his tone changed.
" Billy," he said, " there are cigarettes and whisky in the
corner. Don't make a fuss about a trifle."

" No whisky," said Billy, and lit a cigarette. " And it isn't
a trifle."

He came to Benham's hearthrug. " That business," he
said, " has changed all my views. No—don't say something
polite ! I see that if one hasn't the habit of pride one is bound
to get off a dog-cart when it seems likely to smash. You
have the habit of pride, and I haven't. So far as the habit
of pride goes, I come over to the theory of aristocracy."

Benham said nothing, but he put down Sidney and Beatrice
Webb, and reached out for and got and lit a cigarette.

" I give up ' Go as you please.' I give up the natural man.
I admit training. I perceive I am lax and flabby, unguarded,
I funk too much, I eat too much, and I drink too much.
And, yet, what I have always liked in you, Benham, is just
this—that you don't."

" I do," said Benham.

" Do what ? "

" Funk."

" Benham, I believe that naturally you funk as much as
I do. You're more a thing of nerves than I am, far more.
But you keep yourself up to the mark, and I have let myself
get flabby. You're so right. You're so utterly right. These
last nights I've confessed it—aloud. I had an inkling of it
—after that rag. But now it's as clear as daylight. I don't
know if you mean to go on with me, after what's happened,
but anyhow I want you to know, whether you end our
friendship or not——"

" Billy, don't be an old ass," said Benham.

Both young men paused for a moment. They made no
demonstrations. But the strain was at an end between them.

" I've thought it all out," Billy went on with a sudden
buoyancy. " We two are both of the same kind of men.
Only you see, Benham, you have a natural pride and I
haven't. You have pride. But we are both intellectuals.
We both belong to what the Russians call the Intelligentsia.
We have ideas, we have imagination, that is our strength.

And that is our weakness. That makes us moral light-weights. We are flimsy and uncertain people. All intellectuals are flimsy and uncertain people. It's not only that they are critical and fastidious ; they are weak-handed. They look about them ; their attention wanders. Unless they have got a habit of controlling themselves and forcing themselves and holding themselves together."

" The habit of pride."

" Yes. And then—then we are lords of the world."

" All this, Billy," said Benham, " I steadfastly believe."

" I've seen it all now," said Prothero. " Lord ! how clearly I see it ! The intellectual is either a prince or he is a Greek slave in a Roman household. He's got to hold his chin up or else he becomes—even as these dons we see about us— a thing that talks appointments, a toady, a port-wine bibber, a mass of detail, a conscious maker of neat sayings, a growing belly under a dwindling brain. Their gladness is drink or gratified vanity or gratified malice, their sorrow is indigestion or—old maid's melancholy. They are the lords of the world who will not take the sceptre. . . . And what I want to say to you, Benham, more than anything else is, *you* go on— *you* make yourself equestrian. You drive your horse against Breeze's, and go through the fire and swim in the ice-cold water and climb the precipice and drink little and sleep hard. And—I wish I could do so too."

" But why not ? "

" Because I can't. Now, I admit, I've got shame in my heart and pride in my head, and I'm strung up. I might do something—this afternoon. But it won't last. *You*— you have pride in your bones. My pride will vanish at a laugh. My honour will go at a laugh. I'm just exalted by a crisis. That's all. I'm an animal of intelligence. Soul and pride are weak in me. My mouth waters, my cheek brightens, at the sight of good things. And I've got a lickerish tail, Benham. You don't know. You don't begin to imagine. I'm secretive. But I quiver with hot and stirring desires. And I'm indolent—dirty indolent. Benham, there are days when I splash my bath about without getting into it. There are days when I turn back from a walk because there's a cow in the field. . . . But, I spare you the viler details. . . . And it's that makes me hate fine people and try so earnestly to persuade myself that any man is as good as any man, if not a trifle better. Because I know it isn't so. . . ."

" Billy," said Benham, " you've the boldest mind that ever I met."

Prothero's face lit with satisfaction. Then his countenance fell again. " I know I'm better there," he said, " and yet, see how I let in a whole system of lies to cover my secret humiliations. There, at least, I will cling to pride. I will at least *think* free and clean and high. But you can climb

higher than I can. You've got the grit to try to *live* high.
There you are, Benham."

Benham stuck one leg over the arm of his chair.

" Billy," he said, " come and be—equestrian, and stop this
nonsense."

" No."

" Damn it—you *dive* ! "

" You'd go in before me if a woman was drowning."

" Nonsense. I'm going to ride. Come and ride too. You've
a cleverer way with animals than I have. Why! that horse
I was driving the other day would have gone better alone.
I didn't drive it. I just fussed it. I interfered. If I ride for
ever, I shall never have decent hands, I shall always hang
on my horse's mouth at a gallop, I shall never be sure at a
jump. But at any rate I shall get hard. Come and get hard
too."

" You can," said Billy, " you can. But not I ! Heavens,
the *trouble* of it ! The riding-school ! The getting up early !
No !—for me the Trumpington Road on foot in the afternoon.
Four miles an hour and panting. And my fellowship and the
combination-room port. And, besides, Benham, there's the
expense. I can't afford the equestrian order."

" It's not so great."

" Not so great ! I don't mean the essential expense. But
—the incidentals. I don't know whether any one can realise
how a poor man is hampered by the dread of minor catastrophes. It isn't so much that he is afraid of breaking his
neck, Benham, as that he is afraid of breaking something
he will have to pay for. For instance—— Benham ! how much
did your little expedition the other day—— ? "

He stopped short and regarded his friend with round eyes
and raised eyebrows.

A reluctant grin overspread Benham's face. He was beginning to see the humour of the affair.

" The claim for the motor-bicycle isn't sent in yet. The
repair of the mudguards of the car is in dispute. Trinity
Hall's crockery, the plate-glass window, the whip-lash and
wheel and so forth, the hire of the horse and trap, sundry
gratuities. . . . I doubt if the total will come very much
under fifty pounds. And I seem to have lost a hat somewhere."

Billy regarded his toes and cleared his throat.

" Depending as I do on a widowed mother in Brixton
for all the expenditure that isn't covered by my pot-hunt-
ing——"

" Of course," said Benham, " it wasn't a fair sample afternoon."

" Still——"

" There's footer," said Benham, " we might both play footer."

" Or boxing."

" And, anyhow, you must come with me when I drive again. I'm going to start a trotter."

" If I miss another drive may I be—lost for ever," said Billy, with the utmost sincerity. " Never more will I get down, Benham, wherever you may take me. Short of muffing my fellowship I'm with you always. . . . Will it be an American trotter ? "

" It will be the rawest, gauntest, ungainliest brute that ever scared the motor-bicycles on the Northampton Road. It will have the legs and stride of an ostrich. It will throw its feet out like dealing cards. It will lift its head and look the sun in the eye like a vulture. It will have teeth like the English spinster in a French comic paper. . . . And we will fly. . . ."

" I shall enjoy it very much," said Prothero in a small voice after an interval for reflection. " I wonder where we shall fly ? It will do us both a lot of good. And I shall insure my life for a small amount in my mother's interest. . . . Benham, I think I will, after all, take a whisky. . . . Life is short. . . ."

He did so, and Benham strolled to the window and stood looking out upon the great court.

" We might do something this afternoon," said Benham.

" Splendid idea," reflected Billy over his whisky. " Living hard and thinking hard. A sort of Intelligentsia that is *blooded*. . . . I shall, of course, come as far as I can with you."

§ 13

In one of the bureau drawers that White in his capacity of literary executor was examining, there were two documents that carried back right to these early days. They were both products of this long wide undergraduate argumentation that had played so large a part in the making of Benham. One recorded the phase of maximum opposition, and one was the outcome of the concluding approach of the antagonists. They were debating club essays. One had been read to a club in Pembroke, a club called the *Enquirers*, of which White also had been a member, and as he turned it over he found the circumstances of its reading coming back to his memory. He had been present, and Carnac's share in the discussion with his shrill voice and stumpy gestures would alone have sufficed to have made it a memorable occasion. The later one had been read to the daughter club of the *Enquirers*, the *Social Enquirers*, in the year after White had gone down, and it was new to him.

Both these papers were folded flat and neatly docketed ; they were rather yellow and a little dog-eared, and with the outer sheet pencilled over with puzzling or illegible scribblings, Benham's memoranda for his reply. White took the earlier essay in his hand. At the head of the first page was written in large letters, " Go slowly, speak to the man at the back." It brought up memories of his own experiences, of rows of gaslit faces, and of a friendly helpful voice that said, " Speak up ! "

Of course this was what happened to every intelligent contemporary, this encounter with ideas, this restatement and ventilation of the old truths and the old heresies. Only in this way does a man make a view his own, only so does he incorporate it. These are our real turning points. The insignificant, the essential moments in the life of any one worth consideration are surely these moments when for the first time he faces towards certain broad ideas and certain broad facts. Life nowadays consists of adventures among generalisations. In class-rooms after the lecture, in studies in the small hours, among books or during solitary walks, the drama of the modern career begins. Suddenly a man sees his line, his intention. Yet though we are all of us writing long novels—White's world was the literary world, and that is how it looked to him—which profess to set out the lives of men, this part of the journey, this crucial passage among the Sphinxes, is still done—when it is done at all—slightly, evasively. Why ?

White fell back on his professionalism. " It does not make a book. It makes a novel into a treatise, it turns it into a dissertation."

But even as White said this to himself he knew it was wrong, and it slid out of his thoughts again. Was not this objection to the play of ideas merely the expression of that conservative instinct which fights for every old convention ? The traditional novel is a love story and takes ideas for granted, it professes a hero but presents a heroine. And to begin with at least, novels were written for the reading of heroines. Miss Lydia Languish sets no great store upon the contents of a man's head. That is just the stuffing of the doll. Eyes and heart are her game. And so there is never any more sphinx in the story than a lady may impersonate. And as inevitably the heroine meets a man. In his own first success, White reflected, the hero, before he had gone a dozen pages, met a very pleasant young woman very pleasantly in a sunlit thicket ; the second opened at once with a bicycle accident that brought two young people together so that they were never afterwards disentangled ; the third, failing to produce its heroine in thirty pages, had to be rearranged. The next——

White returned from an unprofitable digression to the matter before him.

§ 14

The first of Benham's early essays was written in an almost boyish hand, it was youthfully amateurish in its nervous disposition to definitions and distinctions, and in the elaborate linking of part to part. It was called *True Democracy*. Manifestly it was written before the incident of the Trinity Hall plates, and most of it had been done after Prothero's visit to Chexington. White could feel that now inaudible interlocutor. And there were even traces of Sir Godfrey Marayne's assertion that democracy was contrary to biology. From the outset it was clear that whatever else it meant, True Democracy, following the analogy of True Politeness, True Courage, True Honesty, and True Marriage, did not mean democracy at all. Benham was, in fact, taking Prothero's word, and trying to impose upon it his own solidifying and crystallising opinion of life.

They were not as yet very large or well-formed crystals. The proposition he struggled to develop was this, that True Democracy did not mean an equal share in the government, it meant an equal opportunity to share in the government. Men were by nature and in the most various ways unequal. True Democracy aimed only at the removal of artificial inequalities. . . .

It was on the truth of this statement, that men were by nature unequal, that the debate had turned. Prothero was passionately against the idea at that time. It was, he felt, separating himself from Benham more and more. He spoke with a personal bitterness. And he found his chief ally in a rigorous and voluble Frenchman named Carnac, an aggressive Roman Catholic, who opened his speech by saying that the first aristocrat was the devil, and shocked Prothero by claiming him as probably the only other sound Christian in the room. Several biologists were present, and one tall, fair youth with a wearisome forefinger tried to pin Carnac with questions.

" But you must admit some men are taller than others ? "

" Then the others are broader."

" Some men are smaller altogether."

" Nimbler—it's notorious."

" Some of the smaller are less nimble than the others."

" Then they have better nightmares. How can you tell ? "

The biologist was temporarily incapacitated, and the talk went on over his prostrate attempts to rally and protest.

A second biologist seemed to Benham to come nearer the gist of the dispute when he said that they were not discussing the importance of men, but their relative inequalities. Nobody was denying the equal importance of everybody. But there was a virtue of this man and a virtue of that. Nobody could dispute the equal importance of every wheel in a machine, of every atom in the universe. Prothero and Carnac were angry because they thought the denial of absolute equality was a denial of equal importance. That was not so. Every man mattered in his place. But politically, or economically, or intellectually that might be a lowly place. . . .

At this point Carnac interrupted with a whooping and great violence, and a volley of obscure French colloquialisms.

He was understood to convey that the speaker was a Jew, and did not in the least mean what he was saying. . . .

§ 15

The second paper was an altogether maturer and more characteristic production. It was no longer necessary to answer Prothero. Prothero had been incorporated. And Benham had fairly got away with his great idea. It was evident to White that this paper had been worked over on several occasions since its first composition, and that Benham had intended to make it a part of his book. There were corrections in pencil and corrections in a different shade of ink, and there was an unfinished new peroration that was clearly the latest addition of all. Yet its substance had been there always. It gave the youth just grown to manhood, but anyhow fully grown. It presented the far-dreaming intellectualist shaped.

Benham had called it *Aristocracy*. But he was far away by now from political aristocracy.

This time he had not begun with definitions and generalisations, but with a curiously subjective appeal. He had not pretended to be theorising at large any longer, he was manifestly thinking of his own life and as manifestly he was thinking of life as a matter of difficulty and unexpected thwartings.

" We see life," he wrote, " not only life in the world outside us, but life in our own selves, as an immense choice of possibilities ; indeed, for us in particular who have come up here, who are not under any urgent necessity to take this line or that, life is apparently pure choice. It is quite easy to think we are all going to choose the pattern of life we like best and work it out in our own way. . . . And, meanwhile, there is no great hurry. . . .

" I want to begin by saying that choice isn't so easy and so necessary as it seems. We think we are going to choose presently, and in the end we may never choose at all. Choice needs perhaps more energy than we think. The great multitude of older people we can observe in the world outside there, haven't chosen either in the matter of the world outside, where they shall go, what they shall do, what part they shall play, or in the matter of the world within, what they will be and what they are determined they will never be. They are still in much the same state of suspended choice as we seem to be in, but in the meanwhile *things happen to them*. And things are happening to us, things will happen to us, while we still suppose ourselves in the wings waiting to be consulted about the casting of the piece. . . .

" Nevertheless this immense appearance of choice which we get in the undergraduate community here, is not altogether illusion ; it is more reality than illusion even if it has not the stable and complete reality it appears to have. And it is more a reality for us than it was for our fathers, and much more a reality now than it was a few centuries ago. The world is more confused and multitudinous than ever it was, the practicable world far wider, and ourselves far less under the pressure of inflexible moulding forces and inevitable necessities than any preceding generations. I want to put very clearly how I see the new world, the present world, the world of novel choice to which our youth and inexperience faces, and I want to define to you a certain selection of choices which I am going to call aristocratic, and to which it is our manifest duty and destiny as the elect and favoured sons of our race to direct ourselves.

" It isn't any choice of Hercules I mean, any mere alternative whether we will be—how shall I put it ?—the bridegrooms of pleasure or the bridegrooms of duty. It is infinitely vaster and more subtly moral than that. There are a thousand good lives possible, of which we may have one, lives which are soundly good, or a thousand bad lives, if you like, lives which are thoroughly bad—that's the old and perpetual choice, that has always been—but what is more evident to me and more remarkable and disconcerting is that there are nowadays ten thousand muddled lives lacking even so much moral definition, even so much consistency as is necessary for us to call them either good or bad ; there are planless indeterminate lives, more and more of them, opening out as the possible lives before us, a perfect wilderness between salvation and damnation, a wilderness so vast and crowded that at last it seems as though the way to either hell or heaven would be lost in its interminable futility. Such planless indeterminate lives, plebeian lives, mere lives, fill the world ; and the spectacle of whole nations, our whole civilisation, seems to me to re-echo this planlessness, this indeterminate confusion of purpose. Plain issues are harder and harder to find ; it is as if they had disappeared. Simple living is the countryman come to town. We are deafened and jostled and perplexed. There are so many things afoot that we get nothing. . . .

" That is what is in my mind when I tell you that we have to gather ourselves together much more than we think. We have to clench ourselves upon a chosen end. We have to gather ourselves together out of the swill of this brimming world.

" Or—we are lost. . . . "

("Swill of this brimming world," said White. "Some of this sounds uncommonly like Prothero." He mused for a moment and then resumed his reading.)

"That is what I was getting at when, three years ago, I made an attack upon Democracy to the mother society of this society, an attack that I expressed ill and failed to drive home. That is what I have come down now to do my best to make plainer. This age of confusion is Democracy; it is all that Democracy can ever give us. Democracy, if it means anything, means the rule of the planless man, the rule of the unkempt mind. It means as a necessary consequence this vast boiling up of collectively meaningless things.

"What is the quality of the common man, I mean of the man that is common to all of us, the man who is the Standard for such men as Carnac, the man who seems to be the ideal of the Catholic Democrat ? He is the creature of a few fundamental impulses. He begins in blind imitation of the life about him. He lusts and takes a wife, he hungers and tills a field or toils in some other way to earn a living, a mere aimless living, he fears and so he does not wander, he is jealous and stays by his wife and his job, is fiercely yet often stupidly and injuriously defensive of his children and his possessions, and so until he wearies. Then he dies and needs a cemetery. He needs a cemetery because he is so afraid of dissolution that even when he has ceased to be, he still wants a place and a grave to hold him together and prevent his returning to the All that made him. Our chief impression of long ages of mankind comes from its cemeteries. And this is the life of man, as the common man conceives and lives it. Beyond that he does not go, he never comprehends himself collectively at all; the state happens about him; his passion for security, his gregarious self-defensiveness, makes him accumulate upon himself until he congests in cities that have no sense of citizenship and states that have no structure; the clumsy, inconsecutive lying and chatter of his newspapers, his hoardings and music-halls give the measure of his congested intelligences; the confusion of ugly, half empty churches and chapels and meeting-halls gauges the intensity of his congested souls; the tricks and slow blundering dishonesties of Diet and Congress and Parliament are his statecraft and his wisdom. . . .

"I do not care if this instant I am stricken dead for pride. I say here now to you and to High Heaven that *this life is not good enough for me*. I know there is a better life than this muddle about us, a better life possible now. I know it. A better individual life and a better public life. If I had no other assurances, if I were blind to the glorious intimations of art, to the perpetually widening promise of science, to the mysterious beckonings of beauty in form and colour and the inaccessible mockery of the stars, I should still know this from the insurgent spirit within me. . . .

"Now this better life is what I mean when I talk of Aristocracy. This idea of a life breaking away from the common life to something better, is the consuming idea in my mind.

"Constantly, recurringly, struggling out of the life of the farm and the shop, the inn and the market, the street and the crowd, is something that is not of the common life. Its way of thinking is Science, its dreaming is Art, its will is the purpose of mankind. It is not the common thing. But also it is not an unnatural thing. It is not as common as a rat, but it is no less natural than a panther.

"For it is as natural to be an explorer as it is to be a potato grower, it is rarer but it is as natural; it is as natural to seek explanations and arrange facts as it is to make love, or adorn a hut, or show kindness to a child. It is a folly I will not even dispute about, that man's only natural implement is the spade. Imagination, pride, exalted desire are just as much Man, as are hunger and thirst and sexual curiosities and the panic dread of unknown things. . . .

"Now you see better what I mean about choice. Now you see what I am driving at. We have to choose each one for himself and also each one for the race, whether we will accept the muddle of the common life, whether we ourselves will be muddled, wealky nothings, children of luck, steering our artful courses for mean success and tawdry honours, or whether we will be aristocrats, for that is what it amounts to, each one in the measure of his personal quality an aristocrat, refusing to be restrained by fear, refusing to be restrained by pain, resolved to know and understand up to the hilt of his understanding, resolved to sacrifice all the common stuff of his life to the perfection of his peculiar gift, a purged man, a trained, selected, artificial man not simply free, but lordly free, filled and sustained by pride. Whether you or I make that choice and whether you or I succeed in realising ourselves, though a great matter to ourselves, is, I admit, a small matter to the world. But the great matter is this, that *the choice is being made*, that it will continue to be made, and that all around us, so that it can never be arrested and darkened again, is the dawn of human possibility. . . ."

(White could also see his dead friend's face with its enthusiastic paleness, its disordered hair and the glowing darknesses in the eyes. On such occasions Benham always had an expression of *escape*. Temporary escape. And thus would his hand have clutched the reading-desk; thus would his long fingers have rustled these dry papers.)

"Man has reached a point when a new life opens before him. . . .

"The old habitual life of man is breaking up all about us, and for the new life our minds, our imaginations, our habits and customs are all unprepared. . . .

"It is only now, after some years of study and living that

I begin to realise what this tremendous beginning we call Science means to mankind. Every condition that once justified the rules and imperatives, the manners and customs, the sentiments, the morality, the laws and limitations which make up the common life, has been or is being destroyed. . . . Two or three hundred years more and all that life will be as much a thing past and done with as the life that was lived in the age of unpolished stone. . . .

"Man is leaving his ancestral shelters and going out upon the greatest adventure that ever was in space or time, he is doing it now, he is doing it in us as I stand here and read to you."

CHAPTER TWO

THE YOUNG MAN ABOUT TOWN

§ 1

THE oldest novel in the world at any rate, White reflected, was a story with a hero and no love interest worth talking about. It was the story of Tobias and how he came out from the shelters of his youth into this magic and intricate world. Its heroine was incidental, part of the spoil, a seven times relict. . . .

White had not read the book of Tobit for many years, and what he was really thinking of was not that ancient story at all, but Botticelli's picture, that picture of the sunlit morning of life. When you say "Tobias" that is what most intelligent people will recall. Perhaps you will remember how gaily and confidently the young man strides along with the armoured angel by his side. Absurdly enough, Benham and his dream of high aristocracy reminded White of that. . . .

"We have all been Tobias in our time," said White.

If White had been writing this chapter he would have in all probability called it *The Tobias Stage*, forgetful that there was no Tobit behind Benham and an entirely different Sara in front of him.

§ 2

From Cambridge Benham came to London. For the first time he was to live in London. Never before had he been in London for more than a few days at a time. But now, guided by his mother's advice, he was to have a flat in Finacue Street, just round the corner from Desborough Street, a flat very completely and delightfully furnished under her supervision. It had an admirable study, in which she had arranged not only his books, but a number of others in beautiful old leather bindings that it had amused her extremely to buy ; it had a splendid bureau and business-like letter-filing cabinets, a

neat little drawing-room and a dining-room, well placed
abundant electric lights, and a man called Merkle whom she
had selected very carefully and who she felt would not only
see to Benham's comfort but keep him, if necessary, up to the
mark.

This man Merkle seemed quite unaware that humanity
" here and now "—even as he was engaged in meticulously
putting out Benham's clothes—was " leaving its ancestral
shelters and going out upon the greatest adventure that ever
was in space or time." If we had been told as much by Benham
he would probably have said, " Indeed, sir," and proceeded
accurately with his duties. And if Benham's voice had seemed
to call for any additional remark, he would probably have
added, " It's 'igh time, sir, something of the sort was done.
Will you have the white wesket as before, sir, or a fresh one
this evening ? . . . Unless it's a very special occasion, sir. . . .
Exactly, sir. *Thank* you, sir."

And when her son was properly installed in his apartments
Lady Marayne came round one morning with a large experi-
enced-looking portfolio and rendered an account of her stewardship of his estate that was already some months overdue. It
was all very confused and confusing, and there were inexplicable
incidents, a heavy overdraft at the bank for example, but this
was Sir Godfrey's fault, she explained. " He never would help
me with any of this business," she said. " I've had to add
sometimes for *hours*. But, of course, you are a man, and when
you've looked through it all, I know you'll understand."

He did look through it enough to see that it was undesirable
that he should understand too explicitly, and, anyhow, he
was manifestly very well off indeed, and the circumstances
of the case, even as he understood them, would have made any
business-like book-keeping ungracious. The bankers submitted
the corroborating account of securities, and he found himself
possessed of his unconditional six thousand a year, with, as
she put it, " the world at his feet." On the whole it seemed
more wonderful to him now than when he had first heard of
it. He kissed her and thanked her, and left the portfolio open
for Merkle's entirely honest and respectful but very exact
inspection, and walked back with her to Desborough Street,
and all the while he was craving to ask the one tremendous
question he knew he would never ask, which was just how
exactly this beneficent Nolan came in. . . .

Once or twice in the small hours, and on a number of other
occasions, this unspeakable riddle assumed a portentous pre-
dominance in his mind. He was forced back upon his inner
consciousness for its consideration. He could discuss it with
nobody else, because that would have been discussing his mother.

Probably most young men who find themselves with riches
at large in the world have some such perplexity as this mixed
in with the gift. Such men as the Cecils perhaps not, because

they are in the order of things, the rich young Jews perhaps not, because acquisition is their principle, but for most other intelligent inheritors there must be this twinge of conscientious doubt. "Why particularly am *I* picked out for so tremendous an advantage?" If the riddle is not Nolan, then it is rent, or it is the social mischief of the business, or the particular speculative *coup* that established their fortune.

"*Pecunia non olet*," Benham wrote, "and it is just as well. Or the west-ends of the world would reek with deodorisers. Restitution is inconceivable; how and to whom? And in the meanwhile here we are lifted up by our advantage to a fantastic appearance of opportunity. Whether the world looks to us or not to do tremendous things, it ought to look to us. And above all we ought to look to ourselves. *Richesse oblige.*"

§ 3

It is not to be supposed that Benham came to town only with a general theory of aristocracy. He had made plans for a career. Indeed, he had plans for several careers. None of them when brought into contrast with the great spectacle of London retained all the attractiveness that had saturated them at their inception.

They were all more or less political careers. Whatever a democratic man may be, Prothero and he had decided that an aristocratic man is a public man. He is made and protected in what he is by laws and the state and his honour goes out to the state. The aristocrat has no right to be a voluptuary or a mere artist or a respectable nonentity or any such purely personal things. Responsibility for the aim and ordering of the world is demanded from him as imperatively as courage.

Benham's deliberate assumption of the equestrian rôle brought him into contact with a new set of acquaintances, conscious of political destinies. They were amiable, hard young men, almost affectedly unaffected; they breakfasted before dawn to get in a day's hunting, and they saw to it that Benham's manifest determination not to discredit himself did not lead to his breaking his neck. Their bodies were beautifully tempered, and their minds were as flabby as Prothero's body. Among them were such men as Lord Breeze and Peter Westerton, and that current set of Corinthians who supposed themselves to be resuscitating the Young England movement and Tory Democracy. Poor movements which indeed have never so much lived as suffered chronic resuscitation. These were days when Tariff Reform was only an inglorious possibility for the Tory Party, and Young England had yet to demonstrate its mental quality in an anti-socialist campaign. Seen from the perspectives of Cambridge and Chexington, the Tory party was still a credible basis for the adventure of a young man with an aristocratic theory in his mind.

These were the days when the strain and extremity of a dangerous colonial war were fresh in people's minds, when the quality of the public consciousness was braced up by its recent response to unanticipated demands. The conflict of stupidities that had caused the war was overlaid and forgotten by a hundred thousand devotions, by countless heroic deaths and sufferings, by a pacification largely conceived and broadly handled. The nation had displayed a belated regard for its honour and a sustained passion for great unities. It was still possible for Benham to regard the empire as a splendid opportunity, and London as the conceivable heart of the world. He could think of Parliament as a career and of a mingling of aristocratic socialism based on universal service with a civilising imperialism as a purpose. . . .

But his thoughts had gone wider and deeper than that. . . .

Already when Benham came to London he had begun to dream of possibilities that went beyond the accidental states and empires of to-day. Prothero's mind, replete with historical detail, could find nothing but absurdity in the alliances and dynasties and loyalties of our time. " Patched-up things, Benham, temporary, pretentious. All very well for the undignified man, the democratic man, to take shelter under, all very well for the humorist to grin and bear, all very well for the crowd and the quack, but not for the aristocrat—No !— his mind cuts like steel and burns like fire. Lousy sheds they are, plastered hoardings . . . and such a damned nuisance too ! For any one who wants to do honourable things ! With their wars and their diplomacies, their tariffs and their encroachments ; all their humbugging struggles, their bloody and monstrous struggles, that finally work out to no end at all. . . . If you are going for the handsome thing in life then the world has to be a united world, Benham, as a matter of course. That was settled when the railways and the telegraph came. Telephones, wireless telegraphy, aeroplanes insist on it. We've got to mediatise all this stuff, all these little crowns and boundaries and creeds, and so on, that stand in the way. Just as Italy had to be united in spite of all the rotten little dukes and princes and republics, just as Germany had to be united in spite of its scores of kingdoms and duchies and liberties, so now the world. Things as they are may be fun for lawyers and politicians and court people and—douaniers, they may suit the loan-mongers and the armaments shareholders, they may even be more comfortable for the middle-aged, but what, except as an inconvenience, does that matter to you or me ? "

Prothero always pleased Benham when he swept away empires. There was always a point when the rhetoric broke into gesture.

" We've got to sweep them away, Benham," he said, with a wide gesture of his arm. " We've got to sweep them all away."

Prothero helped himself to some more whisky, and spoke hastily, because he was afraid some one else might begin. He was never safe from interruption in his own room. The other young men present sucked at their pipes and regarded him doubtfully. They were never quite certain whether Prothero was a prophet or a fool. They could not understand a mixed type, and he was so manifestly both.

" The only sane political work for an intelligent man is to get the world-state ready. For that we have to prepare an aristocracy—— "

" Your world-state will be aristocratic ? " some one interpolated.

" Of course it will be aristocratic. How can uninformed men think all round the globe ? Democracy dies five miles from the parish pump. It will be an aristocratic republic of all the capable men in the world. . . . "

" Of course," he added, pipe in mouth, as he poured out his whisky, " it's a big undertaking. It's an affair of centuries. . . . "

And then, as a further afterthought : " All the more reason for getting to work at it. . . . "

In his moods of inspiration Prothero would discourse through the tobacco smoke until that great world-state seemed imminent—and Part Two in the Tripos a thing relatively remote. He would talk until the dimly-lit room about him became impalpable, and the young men squatting about it in elaborately careless attitudes caught glimpses of cities that are still to be, bridges in wild places, deserts tamed and oceans conquered, mankind no longer wasted by bickerings, going forward to the conquest of the stars. . . .

An aristocratic world state ; this political dream had already taken hold of Benham's imagination when he came to town. But it was a dream, something that had never existed, something that indeed may never materialise, and such dreams, though they are vivid enough in a study at night, fade and vanish at the rustle of a daily newspaper or the sound of a passing band. To come back again. . . . So it was with Benham. Sometimes he was set clearly towards this world-state that Prothero had talked into possibility. Sometimes he was simply abreast of the patriotic and socially constructive British Imperialism of Breeze and Westerton. And there were the moods when the two things were confused in his mind, and the glamour of world dominion rested wonderfully on the slack and straggling British Empire of Edward the Seventh—and Mr. Rudyard Kipling and Mr. Chamberlain. He did go on for a time honestly entertaining both these projects in his mind, each at its different level, the greater impalpable one and the lesser concrete one within it. In some unimaginable way he could suppose that the one by some miracle of ennoblement—and neglecting the Frenchman, the Russian, the German, the American, the Indian, the Chinaman, and, indeed, the greater part of mankind from the problem—might become the other. . . .

All of which is recorded here, without excess of comment, as it happened, and as, in a mood of astonished reminiscences, he came finally to perceive it, and set it down for White's meditative perusal.

§ 4

But to the enthusiasm of the young, dreams have something of the substance of reality, and realities something of the magic of dreams. The London to which Benham came from Cambridge and the disquisitions of Prothero was not the London of a mature and disillusioned vision. It was London seen magnified and distorted through the young man's crystalline intentions. It had for him a quality of multitudinous, unquenchable activity. Himself filled with an immense appetite for life, he was unable to conceive of London as fatigued. He could not suspect these statesmen he now began to meet and watch, of jaded wills and petty spites; he imagined that all the important and influential persons in this large world of affairs were as frank in their private lives and as unembarrassed in their financial relationships as his untainted self. And he had still to reckon with stupidity. He believed in the statecraft of leader-writers and the sincerity of political programmes. And so regarded, what an avenue to Empire was Whitehall! How momentous was the sunrise in St. James's Park, and how significant the clustering knot of listeners and speakers beneath the tall column that lifts our Nelson to the windy sky!

For a time Benham was in love with the idea of London. He got maps of London and books about London. He made plans to explore its various regions. He tried to grasp it all, from the conscious picturesqueness of its garden suburbs to the factories of Croydon, from the clerk-villadoms of Ealing to the inky streams of Bow. In those days there were passenger steamboats that would take one from the meadows of Hampton Court past the whole spectacle of London out to the shipping at Greenwich and the towed liners, the incessant tugs, the heaving portals of the sea. . . . His time was far too occupied for him to carry out a tithe of these expeditions he had planned, but he had many walks that bristled with impressions. Northward and southward, eastward and westward a dreaming young man could wander into a wilderness of population, polite or sombre, poor, rich, or middle-class, but all ceaselessly active, all urgently pressing, as it seemed, to their part in the drama of the coming years. He loved the late afternoon, when every artery is injected and gorged with the multitudinous home-going of the daily workers, he loved the time of lighting up, and the clustering excitements of the late hours. And he went out southward and eastward into gaunt regions of reeking toil. As yet he knew nothing of the realities of industrialism. He saw only the beauty of the great chimneys that rose against the sullen smoke-barred sunsets, and he felt only the romance of the lurid shuddering flares that burst out from squat stacks of brickwork and lit the emptiness of strange and slovenly streets. . . .

And this London was only the foreground of the great scene upon which he, as a prosperous, well-befriended young Englishman, was free to play whatever part he could. This narrow turbid tidal river by which he walked ran out under the bridges eastward beneath the gray-blue clouds towards Germany, towards Russia, and towards Asia, which still seemed in those days so largely the Englishman's Asia. And when you turned about at Blackfriars Bridge this sense of the round world was so upon you that you faced not merely Westminster, but the icy Atlantic and America, which one could yet fancy was a land of Englishmen—Englishmen a little estranged. At any rate they assimilated, they kept the tongue. The shipping in the lower reaches below the Tower there carried the flags of every country under the sky. . . . As he went along the riverside he met a group of dusky students, Chinese or Japanese. Cambridge had abounded in Indians, and beneath that tall clock tower at Westminster it seemed as though the world might centre. The background of the Englishman's world reached indeed to either pole, it went about the earth, his background it was—for all that he was capable of doing. All this had awaited him. . . .

Is it any wonder if a young man with an excitable imagination came at times to the pitch of audible threats ? If the extreme indulgence of his opportunity and his sense of ability and vigour lifted his vanity at moments to the kingly pitch ? If he ejaculated and made a gesture or so as he went along the Embankment ?

§ 5

In the disquisition upon choice that opened Benham's paper on *Aristocracy*, he showed himself momentarily wiser than his day-dreams. For in these day-dreams he did seem to himself to be choosing among unlimited possibilities. Yet while he dreamt other influences were directing his movements. There were, for instance, his mother, Lady Marayne, who saw a very different London from what he did, and his mother Dame Nature, who cannot see London at all. She was busy in his blood as she is busy in the blood of most healthy young men ; common experience must fill the gaps for us ; and patiently and thoroughly she was preparing for the entrance of that heroine whom not the most self-centred of heroes can altogether avoid. . . .

And then there was the power of every day. Benham

imagined himself at large on his liberating steed of property while indeed he was mounted on the made horse of Civilisation; while he was speculating whither he should go, he was already starting out upon the round. One hesitates upon the magnificent plan and devotion of one's lifetime and meanwhile there is usage, there are engagements. Every morning came Merkle, the embodiment of the established routine, the herald of all that the world expected and required Benham to be and do. Usually he awakened Benham with the opening of his door and the soft tinkle of the curtain rings as he let in the morning light. He moved softly about the room, gathering up and removing the crumpled hulls of yesterday; that done he reappeared at the bedside with a cup of admirable tea and one thin slice of bread-and-butter, reported on the day's weather, stood deferential for instructions. "You will be going out for lunch, sir. Very good, sir. White slips of course, sir. You will go down into the country in the afternoon. Will that be the serge suit, sir, or the brown?"

These matters settled, the new aristocrat could yawn and stretch like any aristocrat under the old dispensation, and then, as the sound of running water from the bathroom ceased, stick his toes out of bed.

The day was tremendously indicated. World-states and aristocracies of steel and fire, things that were as real as coal-scuttles in Billy's rooms away there at Cambridge, were now remoter than Sirius.

He was expected to shave, expected to bath, expected to go in to the bright warmth and white linen and silver and china of his breakfast-table. And there he found letters and invitations, loaded with expectation. And beyond the coffee-pot, neatly folded, lay the *Times*, and the *Daily News* and the *Telegraph* all with an air of requiring his attention. There had been more fighting in Thibet and Mr. Ritchie had made a Free Trade speech at Croydon. The Japanese had torpedoed another Russian ironclad and a British cruiser was ashore in the East Indies. A man had been found murdered in an empty house in Hoxton and the King had had a conversation with General Booth. Tadpole was in for North Winchelsea, beating Taper by nine votes, and there had been a new cut in the Atlantic passenger rates. He was expected to be interested and excited by these things.

Presently the telephone bell would ring and he would hear the clear little voice of his mother full of imperative expectations. He would be round for lunch? Yes, he would be round to lunch. And the afternoon, had he arranged to do anything with his afternoon? No!—put off Chexington until to-morrow. There was this new pianist, it was really an *experience*, and one might not get tickets again. And then tea at Panton's. It was rather fun at Panton's. . . . Oh!—

Weston Massinghay was coming to lunch. He was a useful man to know. So *clever.* . . . So long, my dear little Son, till I see you. . . .

So life puts out its Merkle threads, as the poacher puts his hair noose about the pheasant's neck, and while we theorise takes hold of us. . . .

It came presently home to Benham that he had been down from Cambridge for ten months, and that he was still not a step forward with the realisation of the new aristocracy. His political career waited. He had done a quantity of things, but their net effect was incoherent. He had not been merely passive, but his efforts to break away into creative realities had added to rather than diminished his accumulating sense of futility.

The natural development of his position under the influence of Lady Marayne had enormously enlarged the circle of his acquaintances. He had taken part in all sorts of social occasions, and sat and listened to a representative selection of political and literary and social personages, he had been several times to the opera and to a great number and variety of plays, he had been attentively inconspicuous in several really good week-end parties. He had spent a golden October in North Italy with his mother, and escaped from the glowing lassitude of Venice for some days of climbing in the Eastern Alps. In January in an outbreak of inquiry, he had gone with Lionel Maxim to Petrograd and had eaten zakuska, brightened his eyes with vodka, talked with a number of charming people of the war that was then imminent, listened to gipsy singers until dawn, careered in sledges about the most silent and stately of capitals, and returned with Lionel, discoursing upon autocracy and assassination, Japan, the Russian destiny, and the government of Peter the Great. That excursion was the most after his heart of all the dispersed employments of his first year. Through the rest of the winter he kept himself very fit, and still further qualified that nervous dislike for the horse that he had acquired from Prothero by hunting once a week in Essex. He was incurably a bad horseman ; he rode without sympathy, he was unready and convulsive at hedges and ditches, and he judged distances badly. His white face and rigid seat and a certain joylessness of bearing in the saddle earned him the singular nickname, which never reached his ears, of the " Galvanised Corpse." He got through, however, at the cost of four quite trifling spills and without damaging either of the horses he rode. And his physical self-respect increased.

On his writing-desk appeared a few sheets of manuscript that increased only very slowly. He was trying to express his Cambridge view of aristocracy in terms of Finacue Street, West.

The artistic and intellectual movements of London had made their various demands upon his time and energies. Art came to him with a noble assumption of his interest and an intention that presently became unpleasantly obvious to sell him pictures that he did not want to buy and explain away pictures that he did. He bought one or two modern achievements, and began to doubt if art and aristocracy had any necessary connection. At first he had accepted the assumption that they had. After all, he reflected, one lives rather for life and things than for pictures of life and things or pictures arising out of life and things. This Art had an air of saying something, but when one came to grips with it what had it to say? Unless it was Yah! The drama, and more particularly the intellectual drama, challenged his attention. In the hands of Shaw, Barker, Masefield, Galsworthy, and Hankin, it, too, had an air of saying something, but he found it extremely difficult to join on to his own demands upon life anything whatever that the intellectual drama had the air of having said. He would sit forward in the front row of the dress-circle with his cheek on his hand and his brow slightly knit. His intentness amused observant people. The drama that did not profess to be intellectual he went to with Lady Marayne, and usually on first nights. Lady Marayne loved a big first night at St. James's Theatre or His Majesty's. Afterwards, perhaps, Sir Godfrey would join them at a supper party, and all sorts of clever and amusing people would be there saying keen intimate things about each other. He met Yeats, who told amusing stories about George Moore, and afterwards he met George Moore, who told amusing stories about Yeats, and it was all, he felt, great fun for the people who were in it. But he was not in it, and he had no very keen desire to be in it. It wasn't his stuff. He had, though they were nowadays rather at the back of his mind, quite other intentions. In the meanwhile all these things took up his time and distracted his attention.

There was, as yet, no practicable aviation to beguile a young man of spirit, but there were times when Benham found himself wondering whether there might not be something rather creditable in the possession and control of a motor-car of exceptional power. Only one might smash people up. Should an aristocrat be deterred by the fear of smashing people up? If it is a selfish fear of smashing people up, if it is nerves rather than pity? At any rate it did not come to the car.

§ 6

Among other things that delayed Benham very greatly in the development of his aristocratic experiments was the advice that was coming to him from every quarter. It came in extraordinary variety and volume, but always it had one unvarying feature. It ignored and tacitly contradicted his private intentions.

We are all of us disposed to be propagandists of our way of living, and the spectacle of a wealthy young man quite at large is enough to excite the most temperate of us without distinction of age or sex. " If I were you," came to be a familiar phrase in his ear. This was particularly the case with political people ; and they did it not only from the natural infirmity of humanity, but because, when they seemed reluctant or satisfied with him as he was, Lady Marayne egged them on.

There was a general assumption that he was to go into Parliament, and most of his counsellors assumed further that on the whole his natural sympathies would take him into the Conservative party. But it was pointed out to him that just at present the Liberal party was the party of a young man's opportunity ; sooner or later the swing of the pendulum which would weed the Conservatives and proliferate Liberals was bound to come, there was always more demand and opportunity for candidates on the Liberal side, the Tariff Reformers were straining their ministerial majority to the splitting point, and most of the old Liberal leaders had died off during the years of exile. The party was no longer dominated ; it would tolerate ideas. A young man who took a distinctive line—provided it was not from the party point of view a vexatious or impossible line—might go very rapidly far and high. On the other hand, it was urged upon him that the Tariff Reform adventure called also for youth and energy. But there, perhaps, there was less scope for the distinctive line—and already they had Garvin. Quite a number of Benham's friends pointed out to him the value of working out some special aspect of our national political interests. A very useful speciality was the Balkans. Mr. Pope, the well-known publicist, whose very sound and considerable reputation was based on the East Purblow Labour Experiment, met Benham at lunch and proposed to go with him in a spirit of instructive association to the Balkans, rub up their Greek together, and settle the problem of Albania. He wanted, he said, a foreign speciality to balance his East Purblow interest. But Lady Beach Mandarin warned Benham against the Balkans ; the Balkans were getting to be too handy for Easter and summer holidays, and now that there were several good hotels in Serbia and Montenegro and Sofia, they were being overdone. Everybody went to the Balkans and came back with a pet nationality. She loathed pet nationalities. She believed most people loathed them nowadays. It was stale ; it was *Gladstonian*. She was all for specialisation in social reform. She thought Benham ought to join the Fabian Society and consult the Webbs. Quite a number of able young men had been placed with the assistance of the Webbs. They were, she said, " a perfect fount. . . . " Two other people, independently of each other, pointed out to Benham the helpfulness of a few articles in the half-crown monthlies. . . .

" What are the assumptions underlying all this ? " Benham asked himself in a phase of lucidity.

And after reflection ; " Good God ! The assumptions ! What do they think will satisfy me ? . . . "

Everybody, however, did not point to Parliament. Several people seemed to think Travel, with a large T, was indicated. One distant cousin of Sir Godfrey's, the kind of man of the world who has long moustaches, was for big game shooting. " Get right out of all this while you are young," he said. " There's nothing to compare with stopping a charging lion at twenty yards. I've done it, my boy. You can come back for all this pow-wow afterwards." He gave the diplomatic service as a second choice. " There you are," he said, " first-rate social position, nothing to do, theatres, operas, pretty women, colour, life. The best of good times. Barring Washington, that is. But Washington, they say, isn't as bad as it used to be—since Teddy has Europeanised 'em. . . . "

Even the Reverend Harold Benham took a subdued but thoughtful share in his son's admonition. He came up to the flat—due precautions were taken to prevent a painful encounter—he lunched at his son's new club, and he was visibly oppressed by the contrasts between the young man's youthful fortunes and his own. As visibly he bore up bravely. " There are few men, Poff, who would not envy you your opportunities," he said. " You have the Feast of Life spread out at your feet. . . . I hope you have had yourself put up for the Athenæum. They say it takes years. When I was a young man—and ambitious—I thought that some day I might belong to the Athenæum. . . . One has to learn. . . . "

§ 7

And with an effect of detachment, just as though it didn't belong to the rest of him at all, there was beginning a sort of backstairs and underside to Benham's life. There is no need to discuss how inevitable that may or may not be in the case of a young man of spirit and large means, nor to embark upon the discussion of the temptations and opportunities of large cities. Several ladies, of various positions and qualities, had reflected upon his manifest need of education. There was in particular Mrs. Skelmersdale, a very pretty little widow with hazel eyes, black hair, a mobile mouth, and a pathetic history, who talked of old music to him and took him to a Dolmetsch concert in Clifford's Inn, and expanded that common interest to a general participation in his indefinite outlook. She advised him about his probable politics—everybody did that — but when he broke through his usual reserve and suggested views of his own, she was extraordinarily sympathetic. She was so sympathetic, and in such a caressing way, that she created a temporary belief in her understanding, and it was quite imperceptibly that he was drawn into the discussion of modern ethical problems. She herself was a rather stimulating instance of modern ethical problems. She told him something of her own story, and then their common topics narrowed down very abruptly. He found he could help her in several ways. There is, unhappily, a disposition on the part of many people, who ought to know better, to regard a rôle played by Joseph during his earlier days in Egypt as a ridiculous one. This point of view became very inopportunely dominant in Benham's mind when he was lunching *tête à tête* with Mrs. Skelmersdale at her flat. . . .

The ensuing intimacy was of an entirely concealed and respectable nature, but a certain increased preoccupation in his manner set Lady Marayne thinking. He had as a matter of fact been taken by surprise.

Still he perceived that it is no excuse for a man that he has been taken by surprise. Surprises in one's own conduct ought not to happen. When they do happen then an aristocrat ought to stick to what he has done. He was now in a subtle and complicated relationship to Mrs. Skelmersdale, a relationship in which her pride had become suddenly a matter of tremendous importance. Once he had launched himself upon this affair, it was clear to him that he owed it to her never to humiliate her. And to go back upon himself now would be a tremendous humiliation for her. You see, he had helped her a little financially. And she looked to him, she wanted him. . . .

She wasn't, he knew, altogether respectable. Indeed, poor dear, her ethical problems, already a little worn, made her seem at times anything but respectable. He had met her first one evening at Jimmy Gluckstein's when he was forming his opinion of Art. Her manifest want of interest in pictures had attracted him. And that had led to music. And to the mention of a Clementi piano, that short, gentle, sad, old, little sort of piano people will insist upon calling a spinet, in her flat.

And so to this. . . .

It was very wonderful and delicious, this first indulgence of sense.

It was shabby and underhand.

The great god Pan is a glorious god. (And so was Swinburne.) And what can compare with the warmth of blood and the sheen of sunlit limbs ?

But Priapus. . . .

She was the most subtle, delightful and tender of created beings.

She had amazing streaks of vulgarity.

And some astonishing friends.

Once she had seemed to lead the talk deliberately to money matters.

She loved him and desired him. There was no doubt of it.

There was a curious effect about her as though when she went round the corner she would become somebody else. And a curious recurrent feeling that round the corner there was somebody else.

He had an extraordinary feeling that his mother knew about this business. This feeling came from nothing in her words or acts, but some indefinable change in her eyes and bearing towards him. But how could she know ?

It was unlikely that she and Mrs. Skelmersdale would ever meet, and it seemed to him that it would be a particularly offensive incident for them to meet.

There were times now when life took on a gray and boring quality such as it had never had before he met Mrs. Skelmersdale, and the only remedy was to go to her. She could restore his nervous tranquillity—his feeling of solidity and reality, his pride in himself. For a time that is.

Nevertheless his mind was as a whole pervaded by the feeling that he ought not to have been taken by surprise.

And he had the clearest conviction in his mind that if now he could be put back again to the day before that lunch. . . .

No ! he should not have gone there to lunch.

He had gone there to see her Clementi piano.

Had he or had he not thought beforehand of any other possibility ?

On a point so vital his memory was curiously unsure.

§ 8

The worry and disorganisation of Benham's life and thoughts increased as the spring advanced. His need in some way to pull things together became overpowering. He began to think of Billy Prothero, more and more did it seem desirable to have a big talk with Billy and place everything that had got disturbed. Benham thought of going to Cambridge for a week of exhaustive evenings. Small engagements delayed that expedition. . . .

Then came a day in April when all the world seemed wrong to Benham. He was irritable ; his will was unstable ; whatever presented itself to be done presented itself as undesirable ; he could settle to nothing. He had been keeping away from Mrs. Skelmersdale, and in the morning there came a little note from her designed to correct this abstention. She understood the art of the attractive note. But he would not decide to go to her. He left the note unanswered.

Then came his mother at the telephone and it became instantly certain to Benham that he could not play the dutiful son that evening. He answered her that he could not come to dinner. He had engaged himself. " Where ? "

" With some men."

There was a pause and then his mother's voice came, flat

tened by disappointment. " Very well then, little Poff. Perhaps I shall see you to-morrow."

He replaced the receiver and fretted back into his study where the notes on aristocracy lay upon his desk, the notes he had been pretending to work over all the morning.

" Damned liar ! " he said, and then, " Dirty liar ! "

He decided to lunch at the club, and in the afternoon he was moved to telephone an appointment with his siren. And having done that he was bound to keep it.

About one o'clock in the morning he found himself walking back to Finacue Street. He was no longer a fretful conflict of nerves, but if anything he was less happy than he had been before. It seemed to him that London was a desolate and inglorious growth.

London ten years ago was much less nocturnal than it is now. And not so brightly lit. Down the long streets came no traffic but an occasional hansom. Here and there a cat halted or bolted in the road. Near Piccadilly a policeman hovered artfully in a doorway, and then came a few belated prostitutes waylaying the passers-by, and a few youths and men, wearily lust driven.

As he turned up New Bond Street he saw a figure that struck him as familiar. Surely !—it was Billy Prothero ! Or at any rate it was astonishingly like Billy Prothero. He glanced again and the likeness was more doubtful. The man had his back to Benham ; he was halting and looking back at a woman.

By some queer flash of intuition it came to Benham that even if this was not Prothero, still Prothero did these things. It might very well be Prothero even though, as he now saw, it wasn't. Everybody did these things. . . .

It came into Benham's head for the first time that life could be tiresome.

This Bond Street was a tiresome place ; with its shops all shut and muffled, its shops where in the crowded daytime one bought costly furniture, costly clothes, costly scent, sweets, bibelots, pictures, jewellery, presents of all sorts, clothes for Mrs. Skelmersdale, sweets for Mrs. Skelmersdale, presents for Mrs. Skelmersdale, all the elaborate fittings and equipage of—*that !*

" Good-night, dear," a woman drifted by him.

" I've *said* good-night," he cried, " I've *said* good night," and so went on to his flat. The unquenchable demand, the wearisome insatiability of sex ! When everything else has gone, then it shows itself bare in the bleak small hours. And at first it had seemed so light a matter ! He went to bed, feeling dog-tired—he went to bed at an hour and with a finished completeness that Merkle would have regarded as entirely becoming in a young gentleman of his position.

And a little past three o'clock in the morning he awoke

to a mood of indescribable desolation. He awoke with a start
to an agony of remorse and self-reproach.

§ 9

For a time he lay quite still staring at the darkness, then
he groaned and turned over. Then, suddenly, like one
who fancies he hears a strange noise, he sat up in bed and
listened.

" Oh, God ! " he said at last.

And then : " Oh ! The *dirtiness* of life ! The dirty muddle
of life !

" What are we doing with life ? What are we all doing
with life ?

" It isn't only this poor Milly business. This only brings
it to a head. Of course she wants money. . . . "

His thoughts came on again.

" But the ugliness !

" Why did I begin it ? "

He put his hands upon his knees and pressed his eyes against
the backs of his hands and so remained very still, a blankness beneath his own question.

After a long interval his mind moved again.

And now it was as if he looked upon his whole existence ;
he seemed to see in a large, clear, cold comprehensiveness
all the wasted days, the fruitless activities, the futilities, the
perpetual postponements that had followed his coming to
London. He saw it all as a joyless indulgence, as a confusion
of playthings and undisciplined desires, as a succession of
days that began amiably and weakly, that became steadily
more crowded with ignoble and trivial occupations, that had
sunken now to indignity and uncleanness. He was overwhelmed by that persuasion, which only freshly soiled youth
can feel in its extreme intensity, that life was slipping away
from him, that the sands were running out, that in a little
while his existence would be irretrievably lost.

By some trick of the imagination he saw life as an interminable Bond Street, lit up by night lamps, desolate, full of
rubbish, full of the very best rubbish, trappings, temptations,
and down it all he drove, as the damned drive, wearily,
inexplicably.

What are we up to with life ? What are we making of life ?

But hadn't he intended to make something tremendous of
life ? Hadn't he come to London trailing a glory ? . . .

He began to remember it as a project. It was the project
of a great World-State sustained by an aristocracy of noble
men. He was to have been one of those men, too fine and far-
reaching for the dull manœuvres of such politics as rule the
world to-day. The project seemed still large, still whitely
noble, but now it was unlit and dead, and in the foreground
he sat in the flat of Mrs. Skelmersdale, feeling dissipated and

fumbling with his white tie. And she was looking tired. " God ! " he said. " How did I get there ? "

And then suddenly he reached out his arms in the darkness and prayed aloud to the silences.

" Oh, God ! Give me back my visions ! Give me back my visions ! "

He could have imagined he heard a voice calling upon him to come out into life, to escape from the body of this death. But it was his own voice that called to him. . . .

§ 10

The need for action became so urgent in him, that he got right out of his bed and sat on the edge of it. Something had to be done at once. He did not know what it was, but he felt that there could be no more sleep, no more rest, no dressing nor eating nor going forth before he came to decisions. Christian before his pilgrimage began was not more certain of this need of flight from the life of routine and vanities.

What was to be done ?

In the first place he must get away and think about it all, think himself clear of all these—these immediacies, these associations and relations and holds and habits. He must get back his vision, get back to the God in his vision. And to do that he must go alone.

He was clear he must go alone. It was useless to go to Prothero, one weak man going to a weaker. Prothero he was convinced could help him not at all, and the strange thing is that this conviction had come to him and had established itself incontestably because of that figure at the street corner, which had for just one moment resembled Prothero. By some fantastic intuition Benham knew that Prothero would not only participate but excuse. And he knew that he himself could endure no excuses. He must cut clear of any possibility of qualification. This thing had to be stopped. He must get away, he must get free, he must get clean. In the extravagance of his reaction Benham felt that he could endure nothing but solitary places and to sleep under the open sky.

He wanted to get right away from London and everybody and lie in the quiet darkness and stare up at the stars.

His plans grew so definite that presently he was in his dressing-gown and turning out the maps in the lower drawer of his study bureau. He would go down into Surrey with a knapsack, wander along the North Downs until the Guildford gap was reached, strike across the Weald country to the South Downs and then beat eastward. The very thought of it brought a coolness to his mind. He knew that over those southern hills one could be as lonely as in the wilderness and as free to talk to God. And there he would settle something. He would make a plan for his life and end this torment.

When Merkle came in to him in the morning he was fast asleep.

The familiar curtain rings awakened Benham. He turned his head over, stared for a moment and then remembered.

" Merkle," he said, " I am going for a walking tour. I am going off this morning. Haven't I a rücksack ? "

" You 'ave a sort of canvas bag, sir, with pockets to it," said Merkle. " Will you be needing the *very* 'eavy boots with 'obnails—Swiss, I fancy, sir—or your ordinary shooting boots ? "

" And when may I expect you back, sir ? " asked Merkle, as the moment for departure drew near.

" God knows," said Benham, " I don't."

" Then will there be any address for forwarding letters, sir ? "

Benham hadn't thought of that. For a moment he regarded Merkle's scrupulous respect with a transient perplexity.

" I'll let you know, Merkle," he said. " I'll let you know."

For some days at least, notes, telephone messages, engagements, all this fuss and clamour about nothing, should clamour for him in vain. . . .

§ 11

" But how closely," cried White, in a mood of cultivated enthusiasm ; " how closely must all the poor little stories that we tell to-day follow in the footsteps of the Great Exemplars ! A little while ago and the springtime freshness of Tobias irradiated the page. Now, see ! it is Christian—— "

Indeed it looked extremely like Christian as Benham went up across the springy turf from Epsom Downs station towards the crest of the hill. Was he not also fleeing in the morning sunlight from the City of Destruction ? Was he not also seeking that better city whose name is Peace ? And there was a bundle on his back. It was the bundle, I think, that seized most firmly upon the too literary imagination of White.

But the analogy of the bundle was a superficial one. Benham had not the slightest desire to lose it from his shoulders. It would have inconvenienced him very greatly if he had done so. It did not contain his sins. Our sins nowadays are not so easily separated. It contained a light, warm cape-coat he had bought in Switzerland and which he intended to wrap about him when he slept under the stars, and in addition Merkle had packed it with his silk pyjamas, an extra pair of stockings, tooth-brush, brush and comb, a safety razor. . . . And there were several sheets of the Ordnance map.

§ 12

The urgency of getting away from something dominated Benham to the exclusion of any thought of what he might be getting to. That muddle of his London life had to be left behind. First, escape. . . .

Over the downs great numbers of larks were singing. It was warm April that year, and early. All the cloud stuff in the sky was gathered into great towering, slow-sailing masses, and the rest was blue of the intensest. The air was so clean that Benham felt it clean in the substance of his body. The chestnuts down the hill to the right were flowering, the beeches were luminously green, and the oaks in the valley foaming gold. And sometimes it was one lark filled his ears, and sometimes he seemed to be hearing all the larks for miles about him. Presently over the crest he would be out of sight of the grand stand and the men exercising horses, and that brace of red-jacketed golfers. . . .

What was he to do ?

For a time he could think of nothing to do except to keep up and out of the valley. His whole being seemed to have come to his surfaces to look out at the budding of the year and hear the noise of the birds. And then he got into a long road from which he had to escape, and trespassing southward through plantations he reached the steep edge of the hills and sat down over above a great chalk pit somewhere near Dorking and surveyed all the tumbled wooded spaces of the Weald. . . .
It is after all not so great a country this Sussex, nor so hilly, from deepest valley to highest crest is not six hundred feet, yet what a greatness of effect it can achieve ! There is something in those downland views which, like sea views, lifts a mind out to the skies. All England it seemed was there to Benham's vision, and the purpose of the English, and his own purpose in the world. For a long time he surveyed the large delicacy of the detail before him, the crests, the tree-protected houses, the fields and the farmsteads, the distant gleams of water. And then he became interested in the men who were working in the chalk pit down below.

They at any rate were not troubled with the problem of what to do with their lives.

§ 13

Benham found his mind was now running clear, and so abundantly that he could scarcely, he felt, keep pace with it. As he thought his flow of ideas was tinged with a fear that he might forget what he was thinking. In an instant, for the first time in his mental existence, he could have imagined he had discovered Labour and seen it plain. A little while ago and he had seemed a lonely man among the hills, but indeed he was not lonely, these men had been with him all the time, and he was free to wander, to sit here, to think and choose simply because those men down there were not free. *He was spending their leisure*. . . . Not once but many times with Prothero had he used the phrase *Richesse oblige*. Now he remembered it. He began to remember a mass of ideas that had been overlaid and stifling within him. This was what Merkle and the club servants and the entertainments and engagements and his mother and the artistic touts and the theatrical touts and the hunting and the elaboration of games and—Mrs. Skelmersdale and all that had clustered thickly round him in London had been hiding from him. Those men below there had not been trusted to choose their work; they had been given it. And he had been trusted. . . .

And now to grapple with it! Now to get it clear! What work was he going to do? That settled, he would deal with his distractions rapidly enough. Until that was settled he was lax and exposed to every passing breeze of invitation.

" What work am I going to do? What work am I going to do? " He repeated it.

It is the only question for the aristocrat. What amusement? That for a footman on holiday. That for a silly child, for any creature that is kept or led or driven. That perhaps for a tired invalid, for a toiler worked to a rag. But able-bodied amusement! The arms of Mrs. Skelmersdale were no worse than the solemn aimlessness of hunting, and an evening of dalliance not an atom more reprehensible than an evening of chatter. It was the waste of him that made the sin. His life in London had been of a piece together. It was well that his intrigue had set a light on it, put a point to it, given him this saving crisis of the nerves. That, indeed, is the chief superiority of idle love-making over other more prevalent forms of idleness and self-indulgence; it does at least bear its proper label. It is reprehensible. It brings your careless honour to the challenge of concealment and shabby evasions and lies. . . .

But in this pellucid air things took their proper proportions again.

And now what was he to do?

" Politics," he said aloud to the turf and the sky.

Is there any other work for an aristocratic man? . . . Science? One could admit science in that larger sense that sweeps in History, or Philosophy. Beyond that whatever work there is is work for which men are paid. Art? Art is nothing aristocratic except when it is a means of scientific or philosophical expression. Art that does not argue nor demonstrate nor discover is merely the craftsman's impudence.

He pulled up at this and reflected for a time with some distinguished instances in his mind. They were so distinguished, so dignified, they took their various arts with so admirable a gravity that the soul of this young man recoiled from the verdicts to which his reasoning drove him. " It's not for me to judge them," he decided, " except in relation to myself. For them there may be tremendous significances in Art. But if these do not appear to me, then so far as I am concerned they do not exist for me. They are not in my world. So far as they attempt to invade me and control my attitudes or my outlook, or to judge me in any way, there is no question of their impudence. Impudence is the word for it. My world is real. I want to be really aristocratic, really brave, really paying for the privilege of not being a driven worker. The things the artist makes are like the things my private dream-artist makes, relaxing, distracting. What can Art at its greatest be, pure Art that is, but a more splendid, more permanent, transmissible reverie ? The very essence of what I am after is *not* to be an artist. . . ."

After a large and serious movement through his mind he came back to Science, Philosophy or Politics as the sole three justifications for the usurpation of leisure.

So far as devotion to science went, he knew he had no specific aptitude for any departmentalised subject, and equally he felt no natural call to philosophy. He was left with politics. . . .

" Or else, why shouldn't I go down there and pick up a shovel and set to work ? To make leisure for my betters. . . ."

And now it was that he could take up the real trouble that more than anything else had been keeping him ineffective and the prey of every chance demand and temptation during the last ten months. He had not been able to get himself into politics, and the reason why he had not been able to do so was that he could not induce himself to fit in. Statecraft was a remote and faded thing in the political life of the time ; politics was a choice of two sides in a game, and either side he found equally unattractive. Since he had come down from Cambridge the Tariff Reform people had gone far to capture the Conservative party. There was little chance of a candidature for him without an adhesion to that. And he could find nothing he could imagine himself working for in the declarations of the Tariff Reform people. He distrusted them, he disliked them. They took all the light and pride out of imperialism, they reduced it to a shabby conspiracy of the British and their colonies against foreign industrialism. They were violent for armaments and hostile to education. They could give him no assurance of any scheme of growth and unification, and no guarantees against the manifest dangers of economic disturbance and political corruption a tariff involves. Imperialism without noble imaginations, it seemed to him, was simply nationalism with megalomania. It was swaggering, it was greed, it was German ; its enthusiasm was forced, its nobility a vulgar lie. No. And when he turned to the opposite party he found little that was more attractive. They were prepared, it seemed, if they came into office, to pull the legislature of the British Isles to pieces in obedience to the Irish demand for Home Rule, and they were totally unprepared with any scheme for doing this that had even a chance of success. In the twenty years that had elapsed since

Gladstone's hasty and disastrous essay in political surgery they had studied nothing, learnt nothing, produced no ideas whatever in the matter. They had not had the time. They had just negotiated, like the mere politicians they were, for the Nationalist vote. They seemed to hope that by a marvel God would pacify Ulster. Lord Dunraven, Plunkett, were voices crying in the wilderness. The sides in the party game would as soon have heeded a poet. . . . But unless Benham was prepared to subscribe either to Home Rule or Tariff Reform there was no way whatever open to him into public life. He had had some decisive conversations. He had no illusions left upon that score. . . .

Here was the real barrier that had kept him inactive for ten months. Here was the problem he had to solve. This was how he had been left out of active things, a prey to distractions, excitements, idle temptations—and Mrs. Skelmersdale.

Running away to shoot big game or explore wildernesses was no remedy. That was just running away. Aristocrats do not run away. What of his debt to those men down there in the quarry ? What of his debt to the unseen men in the mines away in the north ? What of his debt to the stokers on the liners, and to the clerks in the city ? He reiterated the cardinal article of his creed. The aristocrat is a privileged man in order that he may be a public and political man.

But how is one to be a political man when one is not in politics ?

Benham frowned at the Weald. His ideas were running thin.

He might hammer at politics from the outside. And then again how ? He would make a list of all the things that he might do. For example, he might write. He rested one hand on his knee and lifted one finger and regarded it. *Could* he write ? There were one or two men who ran papers and seemed to have a sort of independent influence. Strachey, for example, with his *Spectator* ; Maxse, with his *National Review*. But they were grown up, they had formed their ideas. He had to learn first.

He lifted a second finger. How to learn ? For it was learning that he had to do.

When one comes down from Oxford or Cambridge one falls into the mistake of thinking that learning is over and action must begin. But until one perceives clearly just where one stands action is impossible.

How is one with no experience of affairs to get an experience of affairs when the door of affairs is closed to one by one's own convictions ? Outside of affairs how can one escape being flimsy ? How can one escape becoming merely an intellectual like those wordy Fabians, those writers, poseurs, and sham publicists whose wrangles he had attended ? And, moreover, there is danger in the leisure of your intellectual. One cannot

be always reading and thinking and discussing and inquiring.
. . . *Would it not be better after all to make a concession, swallow
Home Rule or Tariff Reform, and so at least get his hands on
things ?*

And then in a little while the party conflict would swallow
him up !

Still it would engage him, it would hold him. If, perhaps,
he did not let it swallow him up. If he worked with an eye
open for opportunities of self-assertion. . . .

The party game had not altogether swallowed " Mr
Arthur " . . .

But every one is not a Balfour. . . .

He reflected profoundly. On his left knee his left hand
rested with two fingers held up. By some rapid mental alchemy
these fingers had now become Home Rule and Tariff Reform.
His right hand, which had hitherto taken no part in the controversy, had raised its index finger by imperceptible degrees.
It had been raised almost subconsciously. And by still obscurer
processes this finger had become Mrs. Skelmersdale. He recognised her sudden reappearance above the threshold of
consciousness with mild surprise. He had almost forgotten her
share in these problems. He had supposed her dismissed to an
entirely subordinate position. . . .

Then he perceived that the workmen in the chalk pit far
below had knocked off and were engaged upon their midday
meal. He understood why his mind was no longer moving
forward with any alacrity.

Food ?

The question where he should eat arose abruptly and dismissed all other problems from his mind. He unfolded a
map.

Here must be the chalk pit, here was Dorking. That village
was Brockham Green. Should he go down to Dorking, or this
way over Box Hill to the little inn at Burford Bridge ? He
would try the latter.

§ 14

The April sunset found our young man talking to himself
for greater emphasis, and wandering along a turfy cart-track
through a wilderness mysteriously planted with great bushes
of rhododendra on the Downs above Shere. He had eaten a
belated lunch at Burford Bridge, he had got some tea at a
little inn near a church with a splendid yew tree, and for the
rest of the time he had wandered and thought. He had travelled
perhaps a dozen or fifteen miles, and a good way from his first
meditations above the Dorking chalk pit.

He had recovered long ago from that remarkable conception
of an active if dishonest political career as a means of escaping
Mrs. Skelmersdale and all that Mrs. Skelmersdale symbolised.
That would be just louting from one bad thing to another.

He had to settle Mrs. Skelmersdale clean and right, and he had to do as exquisitely right in politics as he could devise. If the public life of the country had got itself into a stupid antagonism of two undesirable things, the only course for a sane man of honour was to stand out from the parties and try to get them back to sound issues again. There must be endless people of a mind with himself in this matter. And even if there were not, if he was the only man in the world, he still had to follow his lights and do the right. And his business was to find out the right. . . .

He came back from these imaginative excursions into contemporary politics with one idea confirmed in his mind, an idea that had been indeed already in his mind during his Cambridge days. This was the idea of working out for himself, thoroughly and completely, a political scheme, a theory of his work and duty in the world, a plan of the world's future that should give a rule for his life. The Research Magnificent was emerging. It was an alarmingly vast proposal, but he could see no alternative but submission, a plebeian's submission to the currents of life about him.

Little pictures began to flit before his imagination of the way in which he might build up this tremendous inquiry. He would begin by hunting up people ; everybody who seemed to have ideas and promise ideas he would get at. He would travel far—and exhaustively. He would, so soon as the ideas seemed to indicate it, hunt out facts. He would learn how the world was governed. He would learn how it did its thinking. He would live sparingly. (" Not *too* sparingly," something interpolated.) He would work ten or twelve hours a day. Such a course of investigation must pass almost of its own accord into action and realisation. He need not trouble now how it would bring him into politics. Inevitably somewhere it would bring him into politics. And he would travel. Almost at once he would travel. It is the manifest duty of every young aristocrat to travel. Here he was, ruling India. At any rate, passively, through the mere fact of being English, he was ruling India. And he knew nothing of India. He knew nothing indeed of Asia. So soon as he returned to London his preparations for this travel must begin, he must plot out the men to whom he would go, and so contrive that also he would go round the world. Perhaps he would get Lionel Maxim to go with him. Or if Maxim could not come, then possibly Prothero. Some one surely could be found, some one thinking and talking of state-craft and the larger idea of life. All the world is not swallowed up in every day. . . .

§ 15

His mind shifted very suddenly from these large proposals to an entirely different theme. These mental landslips are not unusual when men are thinking hard and wandering. He found himself holding a trial upon himself for Presumptuousness, for setting himself up against the wisdom of the ages, and the decisions of all the established men in the world, for being in short a Presumptuous Sort of Ass. He was judge and jury and prosecutor, but rather inexplicably the defence was conducted in an irregular and undignified way by some inferior stratum of his being.

At first the defence contented itself with arguments that did at least aim to rebut the indictment. The decisions of all the established men in the world were notoriously in conflict. However great was the gross wisdom of the ages the nett wisdom was remarkably small. Was it after all so very immodest to believe that the Liberals were right in what they said about Tariff Reform, and the Tories right in their criticism of Home Rule ?

And then suddenly the defence threw aside its mask and insisted that Benham had to take this presumptuous line because there was no other tolerable line possible for him.

" Better die with the Excelsior chap up the mountains," the defence interjected.

Than what ?

Consider the quality Benham had already betrayed. He was manifestly incapable of a decent modest mediocre existence. Already he had ceased to be—if one may use so fine a word for genteel abstinence—virtuous. He didn't ride well, he hadn't good hands, and he hadn't good hands for life. He must go hard and harsh, high or low. He was a man who needed *bite* in his life. He was exceptionally capable of boredom. He had been bored by London. Social occasions irritated him, several times he had come near to gross incivilities ; art annoyed him ; sport was an effort, wholesome perhaps, but unattractive ; music he loved, but it excited him. The defendant broke the sunset calm by uttering amazing and improper phrases.

" I can't smug about in a state of falsified righteousness like these Crampton chaps.

" I shall roll in women. I shall rollick in women. If, that is, I stay in London with nothing more to do than I have had this year past.

" I've been sliding fast to it. . . .

" *No ! I'm damned if I do ! . . .* "

§ 16

For some time he had been bothered by a sense of something, something else, awaiting his attention. Now it came swimming up into his consciousness. He had forgotten. He was, of course, going to sleep out under the stars.

He had settled that overnight, that was why he had this cloak in his rücksack, but he had settled none of the details.

Now he must find some place where he could lie down. *Here*, *perhaps*, in this strange forgotten wilderness of rhododendra.

He turned off from the track and wandered among the bushes. One might lie down anywhere here. But not yet; it was as yet barely twilight. He consulted his watch. *Half-past seven.*

Nearly dinner-time. . . .

No doubt Christian during the earlier stages of his pilgrimage noticed the recurrence of the old familiar hours of his life of emptiness and vanity. Or rather of vanity—simply. Why drag in the thought of emptiness just at this point ? . . .

It was very early to go to bed.

He might perhaps sit and think for a time. Here for example was a mossy bank, a seat, and presently a bed. So far there were only three stars visible, but more would come. He dropped into a reclining attitude. *Damp !*

When one thinks of sleeping out under the stars one is apt to forget the dew.

He spread his Swiss cloak out on the soft thick carpeting of herbs and moss, and arranged his knapsack as a pillow. Here he would lie and recapitulate the thoughts of the day. (That squealing might be a young fox.) At the club at present men would be sitting about holding themselves back from dinner. Excellent the clear soup always was at the club ! Then perhaps a Chateaubriand. That—what was that ? Soft and large and quite near and noiseless. An owl !

The damp feeling was coming through his cloak. And this April night air had a knife-edge. Early ice coming down the Atlantic perhaps. It was wonderful to be here on the top of the round world and feel the icebergs away there. Or did this wind come from Russia ? He wasn't quite clear just how he was oriented, he had turned about so much. Which was east ? Anyhow it was an extremely cold wind.

What had he been thinking ? Suppose after all that ending with Mrs. Skelmersdale was simply a beginning. So far he had never looked sex in the face. . . .

He sat up and sneezed violently.

It would be ridiculous to start out seeking the clue to one's life and be driven home by rheumatic fever. One should not therefore incur the risk of rheumatic fever.

Something squealed in the bushes.

It was impossible to collect one's thoughts in this place. He stood up. The night was going to be bitterly cold, savagely, cruelly cold. . . .

No. There was no thinking to be done here, no thinking at all. He would go on along the track and presently he would strike a road and so come to an inn. One can solve no problems when one is engaged in a struggle with the elements. The thing to do now was to find that track again. . . .

It took Benham two hours of stumbling and walking, with

a little fence climbing and some barbed wire thrown in, before he got down into Shere to the shelter of a friendly little inn. And then he negotiated a satisfying meal, with beef-steak as its central fact, and stipulated for a fire in his bedroom.

The landlord was a pleasant-faced man ; he attended to Benham himself and displayed a fine sense of comfort. He could produce wine, a half-bottle of Australian hock, Big Tree brand No. 8, a virile wine ; he thought of sardines to precede the meal, he provided a substantial Welsh rarebit by way of a savoury, he did not mind in the least that it was nearly ten o'clock. He ended by suggesting coffee. " And a liqueur ? "

Benham had some Benedictine !

One could not slight such sympathetic helpfulness. The Benedictine was genuine. And then came the coffee.

The cup of coffee was generously conceived and honestly made. A night of clear melancholy ensued. . . .

§ 17

Hitherto Benham had not faced in any detail the problem of how to break with Mrs. Skelmersdale. Now he faced it pessimistically. She would, he knew, be difficult to break with. (He ought never to have gone there to lunch.) There would be something ridiculous in breaking off. In all sorts of ways she might resist. And face to face with her he might find himself a man divided against himself. That opened preposterous possibilities. On the other hand it was out of the question to do the business by letter. A letter hits too hard ; it lies too heavy on the wound it has made. And in money matters he could be generous. He must be generous. At least financial worries need not complicate her distresses of desertion. But to suggest such generosities on paper, in cold ink, would be outrageous. And, in brief—he ought not to have gone there to lunch. After that he began composing letters at a great rate. Delicate—explanatory. Was it on the whole best to be explanatory ? . . .

It was going to be a tremendous job, this breaking with her. And it had begun so easily. . . .

There was, he remembered with amazing vividness, a little hollow he had found under her ear, and how when he kissed her there it always made her forget her worries and ethical problems for a time and turn to him. . . .

" No," he said grimly, " it must end," and rolled over and stared at the black. . . .

Like an insidious pedlar that old rascal whom young literary gentlemen call the Great God Pan, began to spread his wares in the young man's memory. . . .

After long and feverish wanderings of the mind, and some talking to himself and walking about the room, he did at last get a little away from Mrs. Skelmersdale.

He perceived that when he came to tell his mother about this journey round the world there would be great difficulties. She would object very strongly, and if that did not do then she would become extremely abusive, compare him to his father, cry bitterly, and banish him suddenly and heart-brokenly from her presence for ever. She had done that twice already—once about going to the opera instead of listening to a lecture on Indian ethnology, and once about a week-end in Kent. . . . He hated hurting his mother, and he was beginning to know now how easily she was hurt. It is an abominable thing to hurt one's mother—whether one has a justification or whether one hasn't.

Recoiling from this, he was at once resumed by Mrs. Skelmersdale ; who had in fact an effect of really never having been out of the room. But now he became penitent about her. His penitence expanded until it was on a nightmare scale. At last it blotted out the heavens. He felt like one of those unfortunate victims of religious mania who are convinced they have committed the Sin against the Holy Ghost. (Why had he gone there to lunch ? That was the key to it. *Why* had he gone there to lunch ?) . . . He began to have remorse for everything, for everything he had ever done, for everything he had ever not done, for everything in the world. In a moment of lucidity he even had remorse for drinking that stout honest cup of black coffee. . . .

And so on and so on and so on.

When daylight came it found Benham still wide awake. Things crept mournfully out of the darkness into a reproachful clearness. The sound of birds that had been so delightful on the yesterday was no longer agreeable. The thrushes, he thought, repeated themselves a great deal.

He fell asleep as it seemed only a few minutes before the landlord, accompanied by a great smell of frying bacon, came to call him.

§ 18

The second day opened rather dully for Benham. There was not an idea left in his head about anything in the world. It was—*solid*. He walked through Bramley and Godalming and Witley and so came out upon the purple waste of Hindhead. He strayed away from the road and found a sunny place of turf amidst the heather and lay down and slept for an hour or so. He arose refreshed. He got some food at the Huts Inn on the Hindhead crest and went on across sunlit heathery wildernesses variegated by patches of spruce and fir and silver birch. And then suddenly his mental inanition was at an end and his thoughts were wide and brave again. He was astonished that for a moment he could have forgotten that he was vowed to the splendid life.

" Continence by preoccupation " ; he tried the phrase. . .

" A man must not give in to fear ; neither must he give in to sex. It's the same thing really. The misleading of instinct."

This set the key of his thought throughout the afternoon—until Amanda happened to him.

CHAPTER THREE

AMANDA

§ 1

AMANDA happened to Benham very suddenly.

From Haslemere he had gone on to further heaths and gorse beyond Liphook, and thence he had wandered into a pretty district beset with Hartings. He had found himself upon a sandy ridge looking very beautifully into a sudden steep valley that he learnt was Harting Coombe ; he had been through a West Harting and a South Harting and read finger-posts pointing to others of the clan ; and in the evening, at the foot of a steep hill where two roads met, he sat down to consider whether he should go back and spend the night in one of the two kindly-looking inns of the latter place or push on over the South Downs towards the unknown luck of Singleton or Chichester. As he sat down two big retrievers, black and brown, came headlong down the road. The black carried a stick, the brown disputed and pursued. As they came abreast of him the foremost a little relaxed his hold, the pursuer grabbed at it, and in an instant the rivalry had flared to rage and a first-class dog-fight was in progress.

Benham detested dog-fights. He stood up, pale and distressed. " Lie down ! " he cried. " Shut up, you brutes ! " and was at a loss for further action.

Then it was Amanda leapt into his world, a light, tall figure of a girl, fluttering a short petticoat. Hatless she was, brown, flushed, and her dark hair tossing loose, and in a moment she had the snarling furious dogs apart, each gripped firmly by its collar. Then with a wriggle black was loose and had closed again. Inspired by the best traditions of chivalry Benham came to her assistance. He was not expert with dogs. He grasped the black dog under its ear. He was bitten in the wrist, rather in excitement than malice, and with a certain excess of zeal he was strangling the brute before you could count ten.

Amanda seized the fallen stick and whacked the dog she held, reasonably but effectively until its yelps satisfied her. " There ! " she said pitching her victim from her, and stood erect again. She surveyed the proceedings of her helper for the first time.

" You needn't," she said, " choke Sultan any more."

" Ugh ! " she said, as though that was enough for Sultan.
And peace was restored.

" I'm obliged to you. But—— , . . I say ! He didn't bite
you, did he ? Oh, *Sultan ! "*

Sultan tried to express his disgust at the affair. Rotten
business. When a fellow is fighting one can't be meticulous.
And if people come interfering. Still—*sorry !* So Sultan by
his code of eye and tail.

" May I see ? . . . Something ought to be done to this. . . . "

She took his wrist in her hand, and her cheek and eye-
lashes came within a foot of his face.

Some observant element in his composition guessed, and
guessed quite accurately, that she was nineteen. . . .

§ 2

She had an eyebrow like a quick stroke of a camel's-hair
brush, she had a glowing face, half childish imp, half-woman,
she had honest hazel eyes, a voice all music, a manifest decision
of character. And he must have this bite seen to at once.
She lived not five minutes away. He must come with her.

She had an aunt who behaved like a mother and a mother
who behaved like a genteel visitor, and they both agreed
with Amanda that although Mr. Walter Long and his dreadful
muzzles and everything did seem to have stamped out rabies,
yet you couldn't be too careful with a dog bite. A dog bite
might be injurious in all sorts of ways—particularly Sultan's
bite. He was, they had to confess, a dog without refinement,
a coarse-minded omnivorous dog. Both the elder ladies insisted upon regarding Benham's wound as clear evidence of
some gallant rescue of Amanda from imminent danger—
" she's always so *reckless* with those dogs," as though Amanda
was not manifestly capable of taking care of herself ; and
when he had been Listerined and bandaged, they would have
it that he should join them at their supper-dinner, which
was already prepared and waiting. They treated him as if
he were still an undergraduate, they took his arrangements
in hand as though he was a favourite nephew. He must stay
in Harting that night. Both the Ship and the Coach and
Horses were excellent inns, and over the Downs there would
be nothing for miles and miles. . . .

The house was a little long house with a veranda and a
garden in front of it with flint-edged paths ; the room in
which they sat and ate was long and low and equipped with
pieces of misfitting good furniture, an accidental-looking gilt
tarnished mirror, and a sprinkling of old and middle-aged
books. Some one had lit a fire, which cracked and spurted
about cheerfully in a motherly fireplace, and a lamp and
some candles got lit. Mrs. Wilder, Amanda's aunt, a comfortable dark broad-browed woman, directed things, and sat
at the end of the table and placed Benham on her right hand

between herself and Amanda. Amanda's mother remained un-developed, a watchful little woman with at least an eyebrow like her daughter's. Her name, it seemed, was Morris. No servant appeared, but two cousins of a vague dark picturesqueness and with a stamp of thirty upon them, the first young women Benham had ever seen dressed in djibbahs, sat at the table or moved about and attended to the simple needs of the service. The reconciled dogs were in the room and shifted inquiring noses from one human being to another.

Amanda's people were so easy and intelligent and friendly, and Benham after his thirty hours of silence so freshly ready for human association, that in a very little while he could have imagined he had known and trusted this household for years. He had never met such people before, and yet there was something about them that seemed familiar—and then it occurred to him that something of their easy-going freedom was to be found in Russian novels. A photographic enlargement of somebody with a vegetarian expression of face and a special kind of slouch hat gave the atmosphere a flavour of Socialism, and a press and tools and stamps and pigments on an oak table in the corner, suggested some such socialistic art as bookbinding. They were clearly " advanced " people. And Amanda was tremendously important to them, she was their light, their pride, their most living thing. They focused on her. When he talked to them all in general he talked to her in particular. He felt that some introduction of himself was due to these welcoming people. He tried to give it mixed with an itinerary and a sketch of his experiences. He praised the heather country and Harting Coombe and the Hartings. He told them that London had suddenly become intolerable—" In the spring sunshine."

" You live in London ? " said Mrs. Wilder.

Yes. And he had wanted to think things out. In London one could do no thinking——

" Here we could do nothing else," said Amanda.

" Except dog-fights," said the elder cousin.

" I thought I would just wander and think and sleep in the open air. Have you ever tried to sleep in the open air ? "

" In the summer we all do," said the younger cousin. " Amanda makes us. We go out on to the little lawn at the back."

" You see Amanda has some friends at Limpsfield. And there they all go out and camp and sleep in the woods."

" Of course," reflected Mrs. Wilder, " in April it must be different."

" It *is* different," said Benham with feeling ; " the night comes five hours too soon. And it comes wet." He described his experiences and his flight to Shere and the kindly landlord and the cup of coffee. " And after that I thought with a vengeance."

" Do you write things ? " asked Amanda abruptly, and it seemed to him with a note of hope.

" No. No, it was just a private puzzle. It was something I couldn't get straight."

" And you have got it straight ? " asked Amanda.

" I think so."

" You were making up your mind about something ? "

" Amanda *dear* ! " cried her mother.

" Oh ! I don't mind telling you," said Benham.

They seemed such unusual people that he was moved to unusual confidences. They had that effect one gets at times with strangers freshly met as though they were not really in the world. And there was something about Amanda that made him want to explain himself to her completely.

" What I wanted to think about was what I should do with my life."

" Haven't you any *work*—— ? " asked the elder cousin.

" None that I'm obliged to do."

" That's where a man has the advantage," said Amanda with the tone of profound reflection. " You can choose. And what are you going to do with your life ? "

" Amanda," her mother protested, " really you mustn't ! "

" I'm going round the world to think about it," Benham told her.

" I'd give my soul to travel," said Amanda.

She addressed her remark to the salad in front of her.

" But have you no ties ? " asked Mrs. Wilder.

" None that hold me," said Benham. " I'm one of those unfortunates who needn't do anything at all. I'm independent. You see my riddles. East and west and north and south, it's all my way for the taking. There's not an indication."

" If I were you," said Amanda, and reflected. Then she half turned herself to him. " I should go first to India," she said, " and I should shoot, one, two, three, yes, three tigers. And then I would see Farukhabad Sikri—I was reading in a book about it yesterday—where the jungle grows in the palaces ; and then I would go right up the Himalayas ; and then, then I would have a walking tour in Japan ; and then I would sail in a sailing ship down to Borneo and Java and set myself up as a Ranee—— . . . And then I would think what I would do next."

" All alone, Amanda ? " asked Mrs. Wilder.

" Only when I shoot tigers. You and mother should certainly come to Japan."

" But Mr. Benham perhaps doesn't intend to shoot tigers, Amanda," said Amanda's mother.

"Not at once. My way will be a little different. I think I shall go first through Germany. And then down to Constantinople. And then I've some idea of getting across Asia Minor and Persia to India. That would take some time. One must ride."

"Asia Minor ought to be fun," said Amanda. "But I should prefer India because of the tigers. It would be so jolly to begin with the tigers right away."

"It is the towns and governments and peoples I want to see rather than tigers," said Benham. "Tigers if they are in the programme. But I want to find out about—other things."

"Don't you think there's something to be found out at home?" said the elder cousin, blushing very brightly and speaking with the effort of one who speaks for conscience' sake.

"Betty's a Socialist," Amanda said to Benham with a suspicion of apology.

"Well, we're all rather that," Mrs. Wilder protested.

"If you are free, if you are independent, then don't you owe something to the workers?" Betty went on, getting graver and redder with each word.

"It's just because of that," said Benham, "that I am going round the world."

§ 3

He was as free with these odd people as if he had been talking to Prothero. They were—alert. And he had been alone and silent and full of thinking for two clear days. He tried to explain why he found Socialism at once obvious and inadequate. . . .

Presently the supper things got themselves put away and the talk moved into a smaller room with several arm-chairs and a fire. Mrs. Wilder and the cousins and Amanda each smoked a cigarette as if it were symbolical ; and they were joined by a grave gray-bearded man with a hyphenated name and slightly Socratic manner, dressed in a very blue linen shirt and collar, a very woolly mustard-coloured suit and loose tie, and manifestly devoted to one of those branches of exemplary domestic decoration that grow upon Socialist soil in England. He joined Betty in the opinion that the duty of a free and wealthy young man was to remain in England and give himself to democratic Socialism and the abolition of "profiteering." "Consider that chair," he said. But Benham had little feeling for the craftsmanship of chairs.

Under cross-examination Mr. Rathbone - Sanders became entangled and prophetic. It was evident he had never thought out his "democratic," he had rested in some vague tangle of idealism from which Benham now set himself with the zeal of a specialist to rout him. Such an argument sprang up as one meets with rarely beyond the happy undergraduate's range. Everybody lived in the discussion, even Amanda's mother listened visibly. Betty said she herself was certainly democratic and Mrs. Wilder had always thought herself to be so, and outside the circle round the fire Amanda hovered impatiently, not quite sure of her side as yet, but eager to come down with emphasis at the first flash of intimation.

She came down vehemently on Benham's.

And being a very clear-cutting personality with an instinct for the material rendering of things, she also came and sat beside him on the little square cornered sofa.

" Of course, Mr. Rathbone-Sanders," she said, " of course the world must belong to the people who dare. Of course people aren't all alike, and dull people, as Mr. Benham says, and spiteful people, and narrow people have no right to any voice at all in things. . . . "

§ 4

In saying this she did but echo Benham's very words, and all she said and did that evening was in quick response to Benham's earnest expression of his views. She found Benham a delightful novelty. She liked to argue because there was no other talk so lively, and she had perhaps a lurking intellectual grudge against Mr. Rathbone-Sanders that made her welcome an ally. Everything from her that night that even verges upon the notable has been told, and yet it sufficed, together with something in the clear, long line of her limbs, in her voice, in her general physical quality, to convince Benham that she was the freest, finest, bravest spirit that he had ever encountered.

In the papers he left behind him was to be found his perplexed endeavours to explain this mental leap, that after all his efforts still remained unexplained. He had been vividly impressed by the decision and courage of her treatment of the dogs ; it was just the sort of thing he could not do. And there was a certain contagiousness in the petting admiration with which her family treated her. But she was young and healthy and so was he, and in a second mystery lies the key of the first. He had fallen in love with her, and that being so whatever he needed that instantly she was. He needed a companion, clean and brave and understanding. . . .

In his bed in the Ship that night he thought of nothing but her before he went to sleep, and when next morning he walked on his way over the South Downs to Chichester his mind was full of her image and of a hundred pleasant things about her. In his confessions he wrote, " I felt there was a sword in her spirit. I felt she was as clean as the wind."

Love is the most chastening of powers, and he did not even remember now that two days before he had told the wind and the twilight that he would certainly " roll and rollick in women " unless there was work for him to do. She had a peculiarly swift and easy stride that went with him in his thoughts along the turf by the wayside halfway and

more to Chichester. He thought always of the two of them as
being side by side. His imagination became childishly romantic. The open down about him with its scrub of thorn
and yew became the wilderness of the world, and through
it they went—in armour, weightless armour—and they wore
long swords. There was a breeze blowing and larks were
singing, and something, something dark and tortuous, dashed
suddenly in headlong flight from before their feet. It was an
ethical problem such as those Mrs. Skelmersdale nursed in
her bosom. But at the sight of Amanda it had straightened
out—and fled. . . .

And interweaving with such imaginings, he was some day
to record, there were others. She had brought back to his
memory the fancies that had been aroused in his first reading
of Plato's *Republic* ; she made him think of those women
Guardians, who were the friends and mates of men. He wanted
now to re-read that book and the *Laws*. He could not remember
if the Guardians were done in the *Laws* as well as in the *Republic*. He wished he had both these books in his rücksack,
but as he had not, he decided he would hunt for them in
Chichester. When would he see Amanda again ? He would
ask his mother to make the acquaintance of these very interesting people, but as they did not come to London very much
it might be some time before he had a chance of seeing her
again. And besides, he was going to America and India. The
prospect of an exploration of the world was still noble and
attractive ; but he realised it would stand very much in the
way of his seeing more of Amanda. Would it be a startling
and unforgivable thing if presently he began to write to her ?
Girls of that age and spirit living in out-of-the-way villages
have been known to marry. . . .

Marriage didn't at this stage strike Benham as an agreeable aspect of Amanda's possibilities ; it was an inconvenience ; his mind was running in the direction of pedestrian
tours in armour of no particular weight, amidst scenery of a
romantic wildness. . . .

When he had gone to the house and taken his leave that
morning it had seemed quite in the vein of the establishment
that he should be received by Amanda alone and taken up
the long garden before anybody else appeared, to see the
daffodils and the early apple-trees in blossom and the pear-
trees white and delicious.

Then he had taken his leave of them all and made his
social tentatives. Did they ever come to London ? When
they did they must let his people know. He would so like
them to know his mother, Lady Marayne. And so on with
much gratitude.

Amanda had said that she and the dogs would come with
him up the hill, she had said it exactly as a boy might have
said it ; she had brought him up to the corner of Up Park

and had sat down there on a heap of stones and watched him until he was out of sight, waving to him when he looked back. "Come back again," she had cried.

In Chichester he found a little green-bound *Republic* in a second-hand bookshop near the Cathedral, but there was no copy of the *Laws* to be found in the place. Then he was taken with the brilliant idea of sleeping the night in Chichester and going back next day via Harting to Petersfield station and London. He carried out this scheme and got to South Harting neatly about four o'clock in the afternoon. He found Mrs. Wilder and Mrs. Morris and Amanda and the dogs entertaining Mr. Rathbone-Sanders at tea, and they all seemed a little surprised, and, except Mr. Rathbone-Sanders, they all seemed pleased to see him again so soon. His explanation of why he hadn't gone back to London from Chichester struck him as a little unconvincing in the cold light of Mr. Rathbone-Sanders's eye. But Amanda was manifestly excited by his return, and he told them his impressions of Chichester and described the entertainment of the evening guest at a country inn and suddenly produced his copy of the *Republic*. "I found this in a bookshop," he said, "and I brought it for you, because it describes one of the best dreams of aristocracy there has ever been dreamt."

At first she praised it as a pretty book in the dearest little binding, and then realised that there were deeper implications, and became grave and said she would read it through and through, she loved such speculative reading.

She came to the door with the others and stayed at the door after they had gone in again. When he looked back at the corner of the road to Petersfield she was still at the door and waved farewell to him.

He only saw a light slender figure, but when she came back into the sitting-room Mr. Rathbone-Sanders noted the faint flush in her cheek and an unwonted abstraction in her eye.

And in the evening she tucked her feet up in the arm-chair by the lamp and read the *Republic* very intently and very thoughtfully, occasionally turning over a page.

§ 5

When Benham got back to London he experienced an unwonted desire to perform his social obligations to the utmost.

So soon as he had had some dinner at his club he wrote his South Harting friends a most agreeable letter of thanks for their kindness to him. In a little while he hoped he should see them again. His mother, too, was most desirous to meet them. . . . That done, he went on to his flat and to various aspects of life for which he was quite unprepared.

But here we may note that Amanda answered him. Her reply came some four days later. It was written in a square

schoolgirl hand, it covered three sheets of notepaper, and it
was a very intelligent essay upon the *Republic* of Plato. " Of
course," she wrote, " the Guardians are inhuman, but it was a
glorious sort of inhumanity. They had a spirit—like sharp
knives cutting through life."

It was her best bit of phrasing and it pleased Benham very
much. But, indeed, it was not her own phrasing ; she had
culled it from a disquisition into which she had led Mr. Rathbone-Sanders, and she had sent it to Benham as she might
have sent him a flower.

§ 6

Benham re-entered the flat from which he had fled so pre-
cipitately with three very definite plans in his mind. The first
was to set out upon his grand tour of the world with as little
delay as possible, to shut up this Finacue Street establishment
for a long time, and get rid of the soul-destroying perfections
of Merkle. The second was to end his ill-advised intimacy
with little Mrs. Skelmersdale as generously and cheerfully as
possible. The third was to bring Lady Marayne into social
relations with the Wilder and Morris *ménage* at South Harting.
It did not strike him that there was any incompatibility
among these projects or any insurmountable difficulty in any
of them until he was back in his flat.

The accumulation of letters, packages, and telephone
memoranda upon his desk included a number of notes and
slips to remind him that both Mrs. Skelmersdale and his mother
were ladies of some determination. Even as he stood turning
over the pile of documents the mechanical vehemence of the
telephone filled him with a restored sense of the adverse will
in things. " Yes, mam," he heard Merkle's voice, " yes, mam.
I will tell him, mam. Will you keep possession, mam." And
then in the doorway of the study, " Mrs. Skelmersdale, sir.
Upon the telephone, sir."

Benham reflected with various notes in his hand. Then
went to the telephone.

" You Wicked Boy, where have you been hiding ? "

" I've been away. I may have to go away again."

" Not before you have seen me. Come round and tell me
all about it."

Benham lied about an engagement.

" Then to-morrow in the morning." . . . Impossible.

" In the afternoon. You don't *want* to see me." Benham
did want to see her.

" Come round and have a jolly little evening to-morrow
night. I've got some more of that harpsichord music. And
I'm dying to see you. Don't you understand ? "

Further lies. " Look here," said Benham, " can you come
and have a talk in Kensington Gardens ? You know the place,
near that Chinese garden. Paddington Gate. . . . "

The lady's voice fell to flatness. She agreed. "But why not come to see me *here* ? " she asked.

Benham hung up the receiver abruptly.

He walked slowly back to his study. " Phew ! " he whispered to himself. It was like hitting her in the face. He didn't want to be a brute, but short of being a brute there was no way out for him from this entanglement. Why, oh ! why the devil had he gone there to lunch ? . . .

He resumed his examination of the waiting letters with a ruffled mind. The most urgent thing about them was the clear evidence of gathering anger on the part of his mother. He had missed a lunch party at Sir Godfrey's on Tuesday and a dinner engagement at Philip Magnet's, quite an important dinner in its way, with various promising young Liberals, on Wednesday evening. And she was furious at "this stupid mystery. Of course you're bound to be found out, and of course there will be a scandal." . . . He perceived that this last note was written on his own paper. "Merkle ! " he cried sharply.

" Yessir ! "

Merkle had been just outside, on call.

" Did my mother write any of these notes here ? " he asked.

" Two, sir. Her ladyship was round here three times, sir."

" Did she see all these letters ? "

" Not the telephone calls, sir. I 'ad put them on one side. But . . . It's a little thing, sir."

He paused and came a step nearer. " You see, sir," he explained with the faintest flavour of the confidential softening his mechanical respect, " yesterday, when 'er ladyship was 'ere, sir, some one rang up on the telephone——"

" But you, Merkle——"

" Exactly, sir. But 'er ladyship said, ' *I'll* go to that, Merkle,' and just for a moment I couldn't exactly think 'ow I could manage it, sir, and there 'er ladyship was, at the telephone. What passed, sir, I couldn't 'ear. I 'eard her say, ' Any message ? ' And I *fancy*, sir, I 'eard 'er say, " I'm the 'ousemaid,' but that, sir, I think must have been a mistake, sir."

" Must have been," said Benham. " Certainly—must have been. And the call you think came from—— ? "

" There again, sir, I'm quite in the dark. But of course, sir, it's usually Mrs. Skelmersdale, sir. Just about her time in the afternoon. On an average, sir. . . ."

§ 7

" I went out of London to think about my life."

It was manifest that Lady Marayne did not believe him.

" Alone ? " she asked.

" Of course alone."

" *Stuff!* " said Lady Marayne.

She had taken him into her own little sitting-room, she had thrown aside gloves and fan and theatre wrap, curled herself comfortably into the abundantly cushioned corner by the fire, and proceeded to a mixture of cross-examination and tirade that he found it difficult to make head against. She was vibrating between distressed solicitude and resentful anger. She was infuriated at his going away and deeply concerned at what could have taken him away. " I was worried," he said. " London is too crowded to think in. I wanted to get myself alone."

" And there I was while you were getting yourself alone, as you call it, wearing my poor little brains out to think of some story to tell people. I had to stuff them up you had a sprained knee at Chexington, and for all I knew any of them might have been seeing you that morning. Besides, what has a boy like you to worry about ? It's all nonsense, Poff."

She awaited his explanations. Benham looked for a moment like his father.

" I'm not getting on, mother," he said. " I'm scattering myself. I'm getting no grip. I want to get a better hold upon life, or else I do not see what is to keep me from going to pieces—and wasting existence. It's rather difficult sometimes to tell what one thinks and feels——"

She had not really listened to him.

" Who is that woman," she interrupted suddenly, " Mrs. Fly-by-Night or some such name, who rings you up on the telephone ? "

Benham hesitated, blushed, and regretted it.

" Mrs. Skelmersdale," he said after a little pause.

" It's all the same. Who is she ? "

" She's a woman I met at a studio somewhere, and I went with her to one of those Dolmetsch concerts."

He stopped.

Lady Marayne considered him in silence for a little while. " All men," she said at last, " are alike. Husbands, sons, and brothers, they are all alike. Sons ! One expects them to be different. They aren't different. Why should they be ? I suppose I ought to be shocked, Poff. But I'm not. She seems to be very fond of you."

" She's—she's very good—in her way. She's had a difficult life. . . . "

" You can't leave a man about for a moment," Lady Marayne reflected. " Poff, I wish you'd fetch me a glass of water."

When he returned she was looking very fixedly into the fire. " Put it down," she said, " anywhere. Poff ! is this Mrs. Helter-Skelter a discreet sort of woman ? Do you like her ? " She asked a few additional particulars and Benham made his grudging admission of facts. " What I still don't understand, Poff, is why you have been away."

" I went away," said Benham, " because I want to clear things up."

" But why ? Is there some one else ?"

" No."

" You went alone ? All the time ? "

" I've told you I went alone. Do you think I tell you lies, mother ? "

" Everybody tells lies somehow," said Lady Marayne. " Easy lies or stiff ones. Don't *flourish*, Poff. Don't start saying things like a moral windmill in a whirlwind. It's all a muddle. I suppose every one in London is getting in or out of these entanglements—or something of the sort. And this seems a comparatively slight one. I wish it hadn't happened. They do happen."

An expression of perplexity came into her face. She looked at him. " Why do you want to throw her over ? "

" I *want* to throw her over," said Benham.

He stood up and went to the hearthrug, and his mother reflected that this was exactly what all men did at just this phase of a discussion. Then things ceased to be sensible.

From overhead he said to her : " I want to get away from this complication, this servitude. I want to do some—some work. I want to get my mind clear and my hands clear. I want to study government and the big business of the world."

" And she's in the way ? "

He assented.

" You men ! " said Lady Marayne after a little pause. " What queer beasts you are ! Here is a woman who is kind to you. She's fond of you. I could tell she's fond of you directly I heard her. And you amuse yourself with her. And then its Gobble, Gobble, Gobble, Great Work, Hands Clear, Big Business of the World. Why couldn't you think of that before, Poff ? Why did you begin with her ? "

" It was unexpected. . . ."

" *Stuff !* " said Lady Marayne for a second time.

" Well," she said, " well. Your Mrs. Fly-by-Night—oh, it doesn't matter !—whatever she calls herself, must look after herself. I can't do anything for her. I'm not supposed even to know about her. I dare say she'll find her consolations. I suppose you want to go out of London and get away from it all. I can help you there perhaps. I'm tired of London, too. It's been a tiresome season. Oh ! tiresome and disappointing ! I want to go over to Ireland and travel about a little. The Pothercareys want us to come. They've asked us twice. . . ."

Benham braced himself to face fresh difficulties. It was amazing how different the world could look from his mother's little parlour and from the crest of the North Downs.

" But I want to start round the world," he cried with a note of acute distress. " I want to go to Egypt and India and see what is happening in the East, all this wonderful waking

p of the East : I know nothing of the way the world is
oing—— . . ."

"India !" cried Lady Marayne. " The East. Poff, what
s the *matter* with you ? Has something happened—something
lse ? Have you been having a love affair ?—a *real* love
ffair ? "

" Oh, *damn* love affairs ! " cried Benham. " Mother !—
'm sorry, mother ! But don't you see there's other things in
he world for a man than having a good time and making
ove. I'm for something else than that. You've given me the
splendidest time—— . . ."

" I see," cried Lady Marayne, " I see. I've bored you.
I might have known I should have bored you."

" You've *not* bored me ! " cried Benham.

He threw himself on the rug at her feet. " Oh, mother ! "
he said, " little, dear, gallant mother, don't make life too
hard for me. I've got to do my job, I've got to find my job."

" I've bored you," she wept.

Suddenly she was weeping with all the unconcealed distressing
grief of a disappointed child. She put her pretty be-ringed
little hands in front of her face and recited the accumulation
of her woes.

" I've done all I can for you, planned for you, given all my
time for you and I've *bored* you."

" Mother ! "

" Don't come near me, Poff ! Don't *touch* me ! All my
plans. All my ambitions. Friends—every one. You don't
know all I've given up for you. . . ."

He had never seen his mother weep before. Her self-abandonment amazed him. Her words were distorted by her
tears. It was the most terrible and distressing of crises. . . .

" Go away from me ! How can you help me ? All I've done
has been a failure ! Failure ! Failure ! "

§ 8

That night the silences of Finacue Street heard Benham's
voice again. " I must do my job," he was repeating, " I must
do my job. Anyhow. . . ."

And then after a long pause, like a watchword and just a
little unsurely ; " Aristocracy. . . ."

The next day his resolution had to bear the brunt of a
second ordeal. Mrs. Skelmersdale behaved beautifully and this
made everything tormentingly touching and difficult. She
convinced him she was really in love with him, and indeed if
he could have seen his freshness and simplicity through her
experienced eyes he would have known there was sound
reason why she should have found him exceptional. And
when his clumsy hints of compensation could no longer be
ignored she treated him with a soft indignation, a tender
resentment, that left him soft and tender. She looked at him

with pained eyes and a quiver of the lips. What did he think
she was ? And then a little less credibly, did he think she
would have given herself to him if she hadn't been in love
with him ? Perhaps that was not altogether true, but at any
rate it was altogether true to her when she said it, and it was
manifest that she did not for a moment intend him to have
the cheap consolation of giving her money. But, and that
seemed odd to Benham, she would not believe, just as Lady
Marayne would not believe, that there was not some other
woman in the case. He assured her and she seemed reassured,
and then presently she was back at exactly the same question.
Would no woman ever understand the call of Asia, the pride
of duty, the desire for the world ?

One sort of woman perhaps. . . .

It was odd that for the first time now, in the sunshine of
Kensington Gardens, he saw the little gossamer lines that tell
that thirty years and more have passed over a face, a little
wrinkling of the eyelids, a little hardening of the mouth. How
slight it is, how invisible it has been, how suddenly it appears !
And the sunshine of the warm April afternoon, heightened it
may be by her determined unmercenary pose, betrayed too
the faintest hint of shabbiness in her dress. He had never
noticed these shadows upon her or her setting before, and their
effect was to fill him with a strange regretful tenderness. . . .

Perhaps men only begin to love when they cease to be
dazzled and admire. He had thought she might reproach him,
he had felt and feared she might set herself to stir his senses,
and both these expectations had been unjust to her he saw
now that he saw her beside him, a brave, rather ill-advised and
unlucky little struggler, stung and shamed. He forgot the
particulars of that first lunch of theirs together and he remembered his mother's second contemptuous " *Stuff !* "

Indeed he knew now it had not been unexpected.

Why hadn't he left this little sensitive soul and this little
sensitive body alone ? And since he hadn't done so, what
right had he now to back out of their common adventure ?
He felt a sudden wild impulse to marry Mrs. Skelmersdale, in
a mood between remorse and love and self-immolation, and
then a sunlit young woman with a leaping stride in her paces,
passed across his heavens, pointing to Asia and Utopia and
forbidding even another thought of the banns. . . .

" You will kiss me good-bye, dear, won't you ? " said Mrs.
Skelmersdale, brimming over. " You will do that."

He couldn't keep his arm from her little shoulders. And
as their lips touched he suddenly found himself weeping
also. . . .

His spirit went limping from that interview. She chose
to stay behind in her chair and think, she said, and each time
he turned back she was sitting in the same attitude looking
at him as he receded, and she had one hand on the chair back

nd her arm drawn up to it. The third time he waved his hat
:lumsily, and she started and then answered with her hand.
Then the trees hid her. . . .

This sex business was a damnable business. If only because
t made one hurt women. . . .

He had trampled on Mrs. Skelmersdale, he had hurt and
disappointed his mother. Was he a brute ? Was he a cold-
blooded prig ? What was this aristocracy ? Was his belief
anything more than a theory ? Was he only dreaming of a
debt to the men in the quarry, to the miners, to the men in
the stokeholes, to the drudges on the fields ? And while he
dreamt he wounded and distressed real living creatures in
the sleep-walk of his dreaming. . . .

So long as he stuck to his dream he must at any rate set
his face absolutely against the establishment of any further
relations with women.

Unless they were women of an entirely different type,
women hardened and tempered, who would understand.

§ 9

So Benham was able to convert the unfortunate Mrs. Skelmersdale into a tender but for a long time an entirely painful
memory. But mothers are not so easily disposed of, and more
particularly a mother whose conduct is coloured deeply by
an extraordinary persuasion of having paid for her offspring
twice over. Nolan was inexplicable ; he was, Benham understood quite clearly, never to be mentioned again ; but somehow from the past his shadow and his legacy cast a peculiar
and perplexing shadow of undefined obligation upon Benham's
outlook. His resolution to go round the world carried on his
preparations rapidly and steadily, but at the same time his
mother's thwarted and angry bearing produced a torture of
remorse in him. It was constantly in his mind, like the suit of
the importunate widow, that he ought to devote his life to
the little lady's happiness and pride, and his reason told him
that even if he wanted to make this sacrifice he couldn't ;
the mere act of making it would produce so entirely catastrophic a revulsion. He could as soon have become a croquet
champion or the curate of Chexington church, lines of endeavour which for him would have led straightly and simply to
sacrilegious scandal or manslaughter with a mallet.

There is so little measure in the wild atonements of the
young that it was perhaps as well for the Research Magnificent
that the remorses of this period of Benham's life were too
complicated and scattered for a cumulative effect. In the
background of his mind and less subdued than its importance
could seem to warrant was his promise to bring the Wilder-
Morris people into relations with Lady Marayne. They had
been so delightful to him that he felt quite acutely the slight
he was putting upon them by this delay. Lady Marayne's

moods, however, had been so uncertain that he had found no occasion to broach this trifling matter, and when at last the occasion came he perceived in the same instant the fullest reasons for regretting it.

"Ah !" she said, hanging only for a moment, and then "you told me you were alone ! "

Her mind leapt at once to the personification of these people as all that had puzzled and baffled her in her son since his flight from London. They were the enemy, they had got hold of him.

"When I asked you if you were alone you pretended to be angry," she remembered with a flash. " You said, ' Do I tell lies ? ' "

"I *was* alone. Until—— It was an accident. On my walk I was alone."

But he flinched before her accusing, her almost triumphant forefinger.

From the instant she heard of them she hated these South Harting people unrestrainedly. She made no attempt to conceal it. Her valiant bantam spirit caught at this quarrel as a refuge from the rare and uncongenial ache of his secession. "And who are they ? What are they ? What sort of people can they be to drag in a passing young man ? I suppose this girl of theirs goes out every evening—Was she painted, Poff ? "

She whipped him with her questions as though she was slashing his face. He became dead-white and grimly civil, answering every question as though it was the sanest, most justifiable inquiry.

"Of course I don't know who they are. How should I know ? What need is there to know ? "

"There are ways of finding out," she insisted. " If I am to go down and make myself pleasant to these people because of you."

" But I implore you not to."

"And five minutes ago you were imploring me to ! Of course I shall."

" Oh, well !—well ! "

" One has to know *something* of the people to whom one commits oneself, surely."

" They are decent people ; they are well-behaved people."

" Oh !—I'll behave well. Don't think I'll disgrace your casual acquaintances. But who they are, what they are, I *will* know. . . ."

On that point Lady Marayne was to score beyond her utmost expectations.

" Come round," she said over the telephone, two mornings later. " I've something to tell you."

She was so triumphant that she was sorry for him. When it came to telling him, she failed from her fierceness.

" Poff, my little son," she said, " I'm so sorry I hardly

know how to tell you. Poff, I'm sorry. I have to tell you
—and it's utterly beastly."

"But what?" he asked.

"These people are dreadful people."

"But how?"

"You've heard of the great Kent and Eastern Bank smash
and the Marlborough Building Society frauds eight or nine
years ago?"

"Vaguely. But what has that to do with them?"

"That man Morris."

She stopped short, and Benham nodded for her to go on.

"Her father," said Lady Marayne.

"But who was Morris? Really, mother, I don't remember."

"He was sentenced to seven years—ten years—I forget.
He had done all sorts of dreadful things. He was a swindler.
And when he went out of the dock into the waiting-room—
He had a signet-ring with prussic acid in it—— . . ."

"I remember now," he said.

A silence fell between them.

Benham stood quite motionless on the hearthrug and stared
very hard at the little volume of Henley's poetry that lay
upon the table.

He cleared his throat presently.

"You can't go and see them then," he said. "After all
——since I am going abroad so soon—— . . . It doesn't
so very much matter."

§ 10

To Benham it did not seem to be of the slightest importance
that Amanda's father was a convicted swindler who had
committed suicide. Never was a resolved and conscious
aristocrat so free from the hereditary delusion. Good parents,
he was convinced, are only an advantage in so far as they
have made you good stuff, and bad parents are no discredit
to a son or daughter of good quality. Conceivably he had a
bias against too close an examination of origins, and he held
that the honour of the children should atone for the sins
of the fathers and the questionable achievements of any intervening testator. Not half a dozen rich and established
families in all England could stand even the most conventional
inquiry into the foundations of their pride, and only a universal
amnesty could prevent ridiculous distinctions. But he brought
no accusation of inconsistency against his mother. She looked
at things with a lighter logic and a kind of genius for the
acceptance of superficial values. She was condoned and
forgiven, a rescued lamb, re-established, notoriously bright
and nice, and the Morrises were damned. That was their
status, exclusion, damnation, as fixed as colour in Georgia
or caste in Bengal. But if his mother's mind worked in that
way there was no reason why his should. So far as he was

concerned, he told himself, it did not matter whether Amanda
was the daughter of a swindler or the daughter of a god.
He had no doubt that she herself had the spirit and quality
of divinity. He had seen it.

So there was nothing for it in the failure of his mother's
civilities but to increase his own. He would go down to Harting
and take his leave of these amiable outcasts himself. With
a certain effusion. He would do this soon because he was
now within sight of the beginning of his world tour. He had
made his plans and prepared most of his equipment. Little
remained to do but the release of Merkle, the wrappering
and locking up of Finacue Street, which could await him
indefinitely, and the buying of tickets. He decided to take
the opportunity afforded by a visit of Sir Godfrey and Lady
Marayne to the Blights, big iron people in the North of England
of so austere a morality that even Benham was ignored by it.
He announced his invasion in a little note to Mrs. Wilder.
He parted from his mother on Friday afternoon ; she was
already, he perceived, a little reconciled to his project of
going abroad ; and contrived his arrival at South Harting
for that sunset hour which was for his imagination the natural
halo of Amanda.

" I'm going round the world," he told them simply. " I
may be away for two years, and I thought I would like to
see you all again before I started."

That was quite the way they did things.

The supper-party included Mr. Rathbone-Sanders, who displayed a curious tendency to drift in between Benham and
Amanda ; a literary youth with a Byronic visage, dark very
curly hair, and a number of extraordinary mature chins ;
a girl-friend of Betty's who had cycled down from London,
and who it appeared maintained herself at large in London
by drawing for advertisements ; and a silent colourless friend
of Mr. Rathbone-Sanders. The talk lit by Amanda's enthusiasm
circled actively round Benham's expedition. It was clear that
the idea of giving some years to thinking out one's possible
work in the world was for some reason that remained obscure
highly irritating to both Mr. Rathbone-Sanders and the Byronic
youth. Betty too regarded it as levity when there was " so
much to be done," and the topic whacked about and rose to
something like a wrangle, and sat down and rested and got
up again reinvigorated, with a continuity of interest that
Benham had never yet encountered in any London gathering.
He made a good case for his modern version of the Grand
Tour, and he gave them something of his intellectual enthusiasm
for the distances and views, the cities and seas, the multitudinous wide spectacle of the world he was to experience.
He had been reading about Benares and North China. As
he talked Amanda, who had been animated at first, fell
thoughtful and silent. And then it was discovered that the

night was wonderfully warm and the moon shining. They drifted out into the garden, but Mr. Rathbone-Sanders was suddenly entangled and drawn back by Mrs. Wilder and the young woman from London upon some technical point, and taken to the work-table in the corner of the dining-room to explain. He was never able to get to the garden.

Benham found himself with Amanda upon a side path, a little isolated by some swaggering artichokes and a couple of apple trees and so forth from the general conversation. They cut themselves off from the continuation of that by a little silence, and then she spoke abruptly and with the quickness of a speaker who has thought out something to say and fears interruption : " Why did you come down here ? "

" I wanted to see you before I went."

" You disturb me. You fill me with envy."

" I didn't think of that. I wanted to see you again."

" And then you will go off round the world, you will see the Tropics, you will see India, you will go into Chinese cities all hung with vermilion, you will climb mountains Oh ! men can do all the splendid things. Why do you come here to remind me of it ? I have never been anywhere, anywhere at all. I never shall go anywhere. Never in my life have I seen a mountain. Those Downs there—look at them !—are my highest. And while you are travelling I shall think of you—and think of you. . . ."

" Would *you* like to travel ? " he asked as though that was an extraordinary idea.

" Do you think *every* girl wants to sit at home and rock a cradle ? "

" I never thought *you* did."

" Then what did you think I wanted ? "

" What *do* you want ? "

She held her arms out widely, and the moonlight shone in her eyes as she turned her face to him.

" Just what you want," she said ; " —*the whole World !* "

" Life is like a feast," she went on ; " it is spread before everybody and nobody must touch it. What am I ? Just a prisoner. In a cottage garden. Looking for ever over a hedge. I should be happier if I couldn't look. I remember once, only a little time ago, there was a cheap excursion to London. Our only servant went. She had to get up at an unearthly hour, and I—I got up too. I helped her to get off. And when she was gone I went up to my bedroom again and cried. I cried with envy for any one, any one who could go away. I've been nowhere—except to school at Chichester and three or four times to Emsworth and Bognor—for eight years. When you go "—the tears glittered in the moonlight —" I shall cry. It will be worse than the excursion to London. . . . Ever since you were here before I've been thinking of it."

It seemed to Benham that here indeed was the very sister of his spirit. His words sprang into his mind as one thinks of a repartee. " But why shouldn't you come too ? " he said.

She stared at him in silence. The two white-lit faces examined each other. Both she and Benham were trembling.

" *Come too ?* " she repeated.

" Yes, with me."

" But—*how ?* "

Then suddenly she was weeping like a child that is teased ; her troubled eyes looked out from under puckered brows. " You don't mean it," she said. " You don't mean it."

And then indeed he meant it.

" Marry me," he said very quickly, glancing towards the dark group at the end of the garden. " And we will go together."

He seized her arm and drew her to him. " I love you," he said. " I love your spirit. You are not like any one else."

There was a moment's hesitation.

Both he and she looked to see how far they were still alone.

Then they turned their dusky faces to each other. He drew her still closer.

" Oh ! " she said, and yielded herself to be kissed !

Their lips touched, and for a moment he held her lithe body against his own.

" I want you," he whispered close to her. " You are my mate. From the first sight of you I knew that. . . ."

They embraced—alertly furtive.

Then they stood a little apart. Some one was coming towards them. Amanda's bearing changed swiftly. She put up her little face to his, confidently and intimately.

" Don't *tell* any one," she whispered eagerly, shaking his arm to emphasise her words. " Don't tell any one—not yet. Not for a few days. . . ."

She pushed him from her quickly as the shadowy form of Betty appeared in a little path between the artichokes and raspberry canes.

" Listening to the nightingales ? " cried Betty.

" Yes, aren't they ? " said Amanda inconsecutively.

" That's our very own nightingale ! " cried Betty, advancing. " Do you hear it, Mr. Benham ? No, not that one. That is a quite inferior bird that performs in the vicarage trees. . . ."

§ 11

When a man has found and won his mate then the best traditions demand a lyrical interlude. It should be possible to tell, in that ecstatic manner which melts words into moonshine, makes prose almost uncomfortably rhythmic, and brings all the freshness of every spring that ever was across the page, of the joyous exaltation of the happy lover. This at any rate was what White had always done in his novels

hitherto, and what he would certainly have done at this
point had he had the telling of Benham's story uncontrolledly
in his hands. But, indeed, indeed, in real life, in very truth,
the heart has not this simplicity. Only the heroes of romance,
and a few strong simple clean-shaven Americans have that
much emotional integrity. (And even the Americans do at
times seem to an observant eye to be putting in work at
the job and keeping up their gladness.) Benham was excited
that night, but not in the proper bright-eyed, red-cheeked
way ; he did not dance down the village street of Harting
to his harbour at the Ship, and the expression in his eyes
as he sat on the edge of his bed was not the deep elemental
wonder one could have wished there, but amazement. Do
not suppose that he did not love Amanda, that a rich majority
of his being was not triumphantly glad to have won her,
that the image of the two armour-clad lovers was not still
striding and flourishing through the lit wilderness of his
imagination. For three weeks things had pointed him to this.
They would do everything together now, he and his mate,
they would scale mountains together and ride side by side
towards ruined cities across the deserts of the World. He
could have wished no better thing. But at the same time,
even as he felt and admitted this and rejoiced at it, the sky
of his mind was black with consternation. . . .

It is remarkable, White reflected, as he turned over the
abundant, but confused notes upon this perplexing phase of
Benham's development that lay in the third drawer devoted
to the Second Limitation, how dependent human beings
are upon statement. Man is the animal that states a case.
He lives not in things but in expressed ideas, and what was
troubling Benham inordinately that night, a night that should
have been devoted to purely blissful and exalted expectations,
was the sheer impossibility of stating what had happened
in any terms that would be tolerable either to Mrs. Skelmersdale or Lady Marayne. The thing had happened with the
suddenness of a revelation. Whatever had been going on in
the less illuminated parts of his mind, his manifest resolution
had been merely to bid South Harting good-bye—— And
in short they would never understand. They would accuse
him of the meanest treachery. He could see his mother's
face, he could hear her voice saying, " And so because of
this sudden infatuation for a swindler's daughter, a girl who
runs about the roads with a couple of retrievers hunting for
a man, you must spoil all my plans, ruin my year, tell me a
lot of pretentious stuffy lies. . . ." And Mrs. Skelmersdale
too would say, " Of course he just talked of the world and
duty and all that rubbish to save my face. . . ."

It wasn't so at all.

But it looked so frightfully like it !

Couldn't they realise that he had fled out of London before

ever he had seen Amanda ? They might be able to do it perhaps, but they never would. It just happened that in the very moment when the edifice of his noble resolutions had been ready, she had stepped into it—out of nothingness and nowhere. She wasn't an accident ; that was just the point upon which they were bound to misjudge her ; she was an embodiment. If only he could show her to them as she had first shown herself to him, swift, light, a little flushed from running but not in the least out of breath, quick as a leopard upon the dogs. . . . But even if the improbable opportunity arose, he perceived it might still be impossible to produce the Amanda he loved, the Amanda of the fluttering short skirt and the clear enthusiastic voice. Because, already he knew she was not the only Amanda. There was another, there might be others, there was this perplexing person who had flashed into being at the very moment of their mutual confession, who had produced the entirely disconcerting demand that nobody must be told. Then Betty had intervened. But that sub-Amanda and her carneying note had to be dealt with on the first occasion, because when aristocrats love they don't care a rap who is told and who is not told. They just step out into the light side by side. . . .

" Don't tell any one," she had said, " not for a few days. . . . "

This sub-Amanda was perceptible next morning again, flitting about in the background of a glad and loving adventuress, a pre-occupied Amanda who had put her head down while the real Amanda flung her chin up and contemplated things on the Asiatic scale, and who was apparently engaged in disentangling something obscure connected with Mr. Rathbone-Sanders that ought never to have been entangled. . . .

" A human being," White read, " the simplest human being, is a clustering mass of aspects. No man will judge another justly who judges everything about him. And of love in particular is this true. We love not persons but revelations. The woman one loves is like a goddess hidden in a shrine ; for her sake we live on hope and suffer the kindred priestesses that make up herself. The art of love is patience till the gleam returns. . . ."

Sunday and Monday did much to develop this idea of the intricate complexity of humanity in Benham's mind. On Monday morning he went up from the Ship again to get Amanda alone and deliver his ultimatum against a further secrecy, so that he could own her openly and have no more of the interventions and separations that had barred him from any intimate talk with her throughout the whole of Sunday. The front door stood open, the passage hall was empty, but as he hesitated whether he should proclaim himself with the knocker or walk through, the door of the little drawing-room flew open and a black-clad cylindrical clerical person entirely unknown to Benham stumbled over the threshold,

blundered blindly against him, made a sound like " *Moo* "
and a pitiful gesture with his arm, and fled forth. . . .

It was a curate and he was weeping bitterly. . . .

Benham stood in the doorway and watched a clumsy
broken-hearted flight down the village street.

He had been partly told and partly left to infer, and anyhow he was beginning to understand about Mr. Rathbone-
Sanders. That he could dismiss. But—why was the curate in
tears ?

§ 12

He found Amanda standing alone in the room from which
this young man had fled. She had a handful of daffodils in
her hand, and others were scattered over the table. She had
been arranging the big bowl of flowers in the centre. He left
the door open behind him and stopped short with the table
between them. She looked up at him—intelligently and calmly.
Her pose had a divine dignity.

" I want to tell them now," said Benham without a word
of greeting.

" Yes," she said, " tell them now."

They heard steps in the passage outside. " Betty ! " cried
Amanda.

Her mother's voice answered, " Do you want Betty ? "

" We want you all," answered Amanda. " We have something to tell you. . . . "

" Carrie ! " they heard Mrs. Morris call her sister after an
interval, and her voice sounded faint and flat and unusual.
There was the soft hissing of some whispered words outside
and a muffled exclamation. Then Mrs. Wilder and Mrs. Morris
and Betty came into the room. Mrs. Wilder came first, and
Mrs. Morris with an alarmed face as if sheltering behind her.
" We want to tell you something," said Amanda.

" Amanda and I are going to marry each other," said
Benham, standing in front of her.

For an instant the others made no answer ; they looked at
each other.

" *But does he know ?* " Mrs. Morris said in a low voice.

Amanda turned her eyes to her lover. She was about to
speak, she seemed to gather herself for an effort, and then he
knew that he did not want to hear her explanation. He checked
her by a gesture.

" *I know*," he said, and then, " I do not see that it matters
to us in the least."

He went to her holding out both his hands to her.

She took them and stood shyly for a moment, and then
the watchful gravity of her face broke into soft emotion.
" Oh ! " she cried and seized his face between her hands in a
passion of triumphant love and kissed him.

And then he found himself being kissed by Mrs. Morris.

She kissed him thrice, with solemnity, with thankfulness, with relief, as if in the act of kissing she transferred to him precious and entirely incalculable treasures.

CHAPTER FOUR

THE SPIRITED HONEYMOON

§ 1

IT was a little after sunrise one bright morning in September that Benham came up on to the deck of the sturdy Austrian steamboat that was churning its way with a sedulous deliberation from Spalato to Cattaro, and lit himself a cigarette and seated himself upon a deck chair. Save for a yawning Greek sailor busy with a mop the first-class deck was empty.

Benham surveyed the haggard beauty of the Illyrian coast. The mountains rose gaunt and enormous and barren to a jagged fantastic silhouette against the sun; their almost vertical slopes, still plunged in blue shadow, broke only into a little cold green and white edge of olive terraces and vegetation and houses before they touched the clear blue water. An occasional church or a house perched high upon some seemingly inaccessible ledge did but accentuate the vast barrenness of the land. It was a land desolated and destroyed. At Ragusa, at Salona, at Spalato and Zara and Pola, Benham had seen only variations upon one persistent theme, a dwindled and uncreative human life living amidst the giant ruins of preceding times, as worms live in the sockets of a skull. Forward an unsavoury group of passengers still slumbered amidst fruit-peel and expectorations, a few soldiers, some squalid brigands armed with preposterous red umbrellas, a group of curled-up human lumps brooded over by an aquiline individual caparisoned with brass like a horse, his head wrapped picturesquely in a shawl. Benham surveyed these last products of the " life force " and resumed his pensive survey of the coast. The sea was deserted save for a couple of little lateen craft with suns painted on their gaudy sails, sea butterflies that hung motionless as if unawakened close inshore. . . .

The travel of the last few weeks had impressed Benham's imagination profoundly. For the first time in his life he had come face to face with civilisation in defeat. From Venice hitherward he had marked with cumulative effect the clustering evidences of effort spent and power crumbled to nothingness. He had landed upon the marble quay of Pola and visited its deserted amphitheatre; he had seen a weak provincial life going about ignoble ends under the walls of the great Venetian fortress and the still more magnificent cathedral of Zara; he had visited Spalato, clustered in sweltering grime within the ample compass of the walls of Diocletian's villa, and a few troublesome sellers of coins and iridescent glass and fragments of tessellated pavement and such-like loot was all the population he had found amidst the fallen walls and broken friezes and columns of Salona. Down this coast there ebbed and flowed a mean residual life, a life of violence and dishonesty, peddling trades, vendettas and war. For a while the unstable Austrian ruled this land and made a sort of order that the incalculable chances of international politics might at any time shatter. Benham was drawing near now to the utmost limit of that extended peace. Ahead beyond the mountain capes was Montenegro and, further, Albania and Macedonia, lands of lawlessness and confusion. Amanda and he had been warned of the impossibility of decent travel beyond Cattaro and Cettinjé, but this had but whetted her adventurousness and challenged his spirit. They were going to see Albania for themselves.

The three months of honeymoon they had been spending together had developed many remarkable divergences of their minds that had not been in the least apparent to Benham before their marriage. Then their common resolve to be as spirited as possible had obliterated all minor considerations. But that was the limit of their unanimity. Amanda loved wild and picturesque things, and Benham strong and clear things ; the vines and brushwood amidst the ruins of Salona that had delighted her had filled him with a sense of tragic retrogression. Salona had revived again in the acutest form a dispute that had been smouldering between them throughout a fitful and lengthy exploration of north and central Italy. She could not understand his disgust with the mediæval colour and confusion that had swamped the pride and state of the Roman Empire, and he could not make her feel the ambition of the ruler, the essential discipline and responsibilities of his aristocratic idea. While his adventurousness was conquest, hers, it was only too manifest, was brigandage. His thoughts ran now into the form of an imaginary discourse, that he would never deliver to her, on the decay of states, on the triumphs of barbarians over rulers who will not rule, on the relaxation of patrician orders and the return of the robber and assassin as lordship decays. This coast was no theatrical scenery for him ; it was a shattered empire. And it was shattered because no men had been found, united enough, magnificent and steadfast enough, to hold the cities and maintain the roads, keep the peace and subdue the brutish hates and suspicions and cruelties that devastated the world.

And as these thoughts came back into his mind, Amanda flickered up from below, light and noiseless as a sunbeam, and stood behind his chair.

Freedom and the sight of the world had if possible brightened and invigorated her. Her costume and bearing were subtly touched by the romance of the Adriatic. There was a flavour of the pirate in the cloak about her shoulders and the light knitted cap of scarlet she had stuck upon her head. She surveyed his preoccupation for a moment, glanced forward, and then covered his eyes with her hands. In almost the same movement she had bent down and nipped the tip of his ear between her teeth.

" Confound you, Amanda ! "

" You'd forgotten my existence, you star-gazing Cheetah. And then, you see, these thing happen to you ! "

" I was thinking."

" Well—*don't* . . . I distrust your thinking. . . . This coast is wilder and grimmer than yesterday. It's glorious."

She sat down on the chair he unfolded for her.

" Is there nothing to eat ? " she asked abruptly.

" It is too early."

§ 2

" This coast is magnificent," she said presently.

" It's hideous," he answered. " It's as ugly as a heap of slag."

" It's nature at its wildest."

" That's Amanda at her wildest."

" Well, isn't it ? "

" No ! This land isn't nature. It's waste. Not wilderness. It's the other end. Those hills were covered with forests ; this was a busy civilised coast just a little thousand years ago. The Venetians wasted it. They cut down the forests ; they filled the cities with a mixed mud of population, *that* stuff. Look at it ! "—he indicated the sleepers forward by a movement of his head.

" I suppose they *were* rather feeble people," said Amanda.

" Who ? "

" The Venetians."

" They were traders—and nothing more. Just as we are. And when they were rich they got splendid clothes and feasted and rested. Much as we do."

Amanda surveyed him. " We don't rest."

" We idle."

" We are seeing things."

" Don't be a humbug, Amanda. We are making love. Just as they did. And it has been—ripping. In Salona they made love tremendously. They did nothing else until the barbarians came over the mountains. . . ."

" Well," said Amanda virtuously, " we will do something else."

He made no answer, and her expression became profoundly thoughtful. Of course this wandering must end. He had been growing impatient for some time. But it was difficult, she perceived, to decide just what to do with him. . . .

Benham picked up the thread of his musing.

He was seeing more and more clearly that all civilisation was an effort, and so far always an inadequate and very partially successful effort. Always it had been aristocratic, aristocratic in the sense that it was the work of minorities, who took power, who had a common resolution against the inertia, the indifference, the insubordination and instinctive hostility of the mass of mankind. And always the set-backs, the disasters of civilisation, had been failures of the aristocratic spirit. Why had the Roman purpose faltered and shrivelled ? Every order, every brotherhood, every organisation carried with it the seeds of its own destruction. Must the idea of statecraft and rule perpetually reappear, reclothe itself in new forms, age, die, even as life does—making each time its almost infinitesimal addition to human achievement ? Now the world is crying aloud for a renascence of the spirit that orders and controls. Human affairs sway at a dizzy height of opportunity. Will they keep their footing there, or stagger ? We have got back at last to a time as big with opportunity as the early empire. Given only the will in men and it would be possible now to turn the dazzling accidents of science, the chancy attainments of the nineteenth century, into a sane and permanent possession, a new starting-point. . . What a magnificence might be made of life !

He was aroused by Amanda's voice.

" When we go back to London, old Cheetah," she said, " we must take a house."

For some moments he stared at her, trying to get back to their point of divergence.

" Why ? " he asked at length.

" We must have a house," she said.

He looked at her face. Her expression was profoundly thoughtful, her eyes were fixed on the slumbering ships poised upon the transparent water under the mountain shadows.

" You see," she thought it out, " you've got to *tell* in London. You can't just sneak back there. You've got to strike a note of your own. With all these things of yours."

" But how ? "

" There's a sort of little house, I used to see them when I was a girl and my father lived in London, about Brook Street and that part. Not too far north. . . You see, going back to London for us is just another adventure. We've got to capture London. We've got to scale it. We've got advantages of all sorts. But at present we're outside. We've got to march in."

Her clear hazel eyes contemplated conflicts and triumphs.

She was roused by Benham's voice.

" What the deuce are you thinking of, Amanda ? "

She turned her level eyes to his. " London," she said. " For you."

" I don't want London," he said.

" I thought you did. You ought to. I do."

" But to take a house ! Make an invasion of London ! "

" You dear old Cheetah, you can't be always frisking about in the wilderness, staring at the stars."

" But I'm not going back to live in London in the old way, theatres, dinner-parties, chatter——"

" Oh no ! We aren't going to do that sort of thing. We aren't going to join the ruck. We'll go about in holiday times all over the world. I want to see Fusiyama. I mean to swim in the South Seas. With you. We'll dodge the sharks. But all the same we shall have to have a house in London. We have to be *felt* there."

She met his consternation fairly. She lifted her fine eye-brows. Her little face conveyed a protesting reasonableness.

" Well, *mustn't* we ? "

She added, " If we want to alter the world we ought to live in the world."

Since last they had disputed the question she had thought out these new phrases.

" Amanda," he said. " I think sometimes you haven't the remotest idea of what I am after. I don't believe you begin to suspect what I am up to."

She put her elbows on her knees, dropped her chin between her hands and regarded him impudently. She had a char-acteristic trick of looking up with her face downcast that never failed to soften his regard.

" Look here, Cheetah, don't you give way to your early morning habit of calling your own true love a fool," she said.

" Simply I tell you I will not go back to London."

" You will go back with me, Cheetah."

" I will go back as far as my work calls me there."

" It calls you through the voice of your mate and slave and doormat to just exactly the sort of house you ought to have. . . . It is the privilege and duty of the female to choose the lair."

For a space Benham made no reply. This controversy had been gathering for some time, and he wanted to state his view as vividly as possible. The Benham style of connubial conver-sation had long since decided for emphasis rather than delicacy.

" I think," he said slowly, " that this wanting to take London by storm is a beastly *vulgar* thing to want to do."

Amanda compressed her lips.

" I want to work out things in my mind," he went on. " I do not want to be distracted by social things, and I do not want to be distracted by picturesque things. This life— it's all very well on the surface, but it isn't real. I'm not getting hold of reality. Things slip away from me. God ! but how they slip away from me ! "

He got up and walked to the side of the boat.

She surveyed his back for some moments. Then she went and leant over the rail beside him.

" I want to go to London," she said.

" I don't."

" Where do you want to go ? "

" Where I can see into the things that hold the world together."

" I have loved this wandering—I could wander always. But . . . Cheetah ! I tell you I *want* to go to London."

He looked over his shoulder into her warm face. " *No*," he said.

" But, I ask you."

He shook his head.

She put her face closer and whispered. " Cheetah ! big beast of my heart. Do you hear your mate asking for something ? "

He turned his eyes back to the mountains. " I must go my own way."

" Haven't I, so far, invented things, made life amusing, Cheetah ? Can't you trust the leopard's wisdom ? "

He stared at the coast inexorably.

" I wonder," she whispered.

" What ? "

" You *are* that Cheetah, that lank, long, *eager* beast——"

Suddenly with a nimble hand she had unbottoned and rolled up the sleeve of her blouse. She stuck her pretty blue-veined arm before his eyes. " Look here, sir, it was you, wasn't it ? It was your powerful jaw inflicted this bite upon the arm of a defenceless young leopardess——"

" Amanda ! "

" Well." She wrinkled her brows.

He turned about and stood over her, he shook a finger in her face, and there was a restrained intensity in his voice as he spoke.

" Look here, Amanda ! " he said, " if you think that you are going to make me agree to any sort of project about London, to any sort of complication of our lives with houses in smart streets and a campaign of social assertion—by *that*, then may I be damned for an uxorious fool ! "

Her eyes met his and there was mockery in her eyes.

" This, Cheetah, is the morning mood," she remarked.

" This is the essential mood. Listen, Amanda——"

He stopped short. He looked towards the gangway, they both looked. The magic word " Breakfast " came simultaneously from them.

" Eggs," she said ravenously, and led the way.

A smell of coffee as insistent as a herald's trumpet had called a truce between them.

§ 3

Their marriage had been a comparatively inconspicuous one, but since that time they had been engaged upon a honeymoon of great extent and variety. Their wedding had taken place at South Harting church in the marked absence of Lady Marayne, and it had been marred by only one untoward event. The Reverend Amos Pugh, who in spite of the earnest advice of several friends had insisted upon sharing in the ceremony, had suddenly covered his face with the sleeves of his surplice and fled with a swift rustle to the vestry, whence an uproar of inadequately smothered sorrow came as an obligato accompaniment to the more crucial passages of the service. Amanda appeared unaware of the incident at the time, but afterwards she explained things to Benham. " Curates," she said, " are such pent-up men. One ought, I suppose, to remember that. But he never had anything to go upon at all—not anything—except his own imaginations."

" I suppose when you met him you were nice to him."

" I was nice to him, of course. . . . "

They drove away from Harting, as it were, over the weeping remains of this infatuated divine. His sorrow made them thoughtful for a time, and then Amanda nestled closer to her lover and they forgot about him, and their honeymoon became so active and entertaining that only very rarely and transitorily did they ever think of him again.

The original conception of their honeymoon had been identical with the plans Benham had made for the survey and study of the world, and it was through a series of modifications, replacements, and additions that it became at last a prolonged and very picturesque tour in Switzerland, the Austrian Tyrol, North Italy, and down the Adriatic coast. Amanda had never seen mountains, and longed, she said, to climb. This took them first to Switzerland. Then, in spite of their exalted aims, the devotion of their lives to noble purposes, it was evident that Amanda had no intention of scamping the detail of love, and for that what background is so richly beautiful as Italy ? An important aspect of the grand tour round the world as Benham had planned it, had been interviews, inquiries and conversations with every sort of representative and understanding person he could reach. An unembarrassed young man who wants to know and does not promise to bore may reach almost any one in that way, he is as impersonal as pure reason and as mobile as a letter, but the presence of a lady in his train leaves him no longer unembarrassed. His approach has become a social event. The wife of a great or significant personage must take notice or decide not to take notice. Of course, Amanda was prepared to go anywhere, just as Benham's shadow ; it was the world that was unprepared. And a second leading aspect of his original scheme had been the examination of the ways of government in cities and the shifting and mixture of nations and races. It would have led to back streets, and involved and complicated details, and there was something in the fine flame of girlhood beside him that he felt was incompatible with those shadows and that dust. And also they were lovers, and very deeply in love. It was amazing how swiftly that draggled shameful London sparrow-gamin, Eros, took heart from Amanda, and became wonderful, beautiful, glowing, life-giving, confident, clear-eyed ; how he changed from flesh to sweet fire, and grew until he filled the sky. So that you see they went to Switzerland and Italy at last very like two ordinary young people who were not aristocrats at all, had no theory about the world or their destiny, but were simply just ardently delighted with the discovery of one another.

Nevertheless Benham was for some time under a vague impression that in a sort of way still he was going round the world and working out his destinies.

It was part of the fascination of Amanda that she was never what he had supposed her to be, and that nothing that he set out to do with her ever turned out as they had planned it. Her appreciations marched before her achievement, and when it came to climbing it seemed foolish to toil to summits over which her spirit had flitted days before. Their Swiss expeditions which she had foreseen as glorious wanderings amidst the blue ice of crevasses and nights of exalted hardihood became a walking tour of fitful vigour and abundant fun and delight. They spent a long day on the ice of the Aletsch glacier, but they reached the inn on its eastward side with magnificent appetites a little late for dinner.

Amanda had revealed an unexpected gift for nicknames and pretty fancies. She named herself the Leopard, the spotless Leopard ; in some obscure way she intimated that the colour was black, but that was never to be admitted openly, there was supposed to be some lurking traces of a rusty brown, but the word was spotless and the implication white, a dazzling white ; she would play a thousand variations on the theme ; in moments of despondency she was only a black cat, a common lean black cat, and sacks and half-bricks almost too good for her. But Benham was always a Cheetah. That had come to her as a revelation from heaven. But so clearly he was a Cheetah. He was a Hunting Leopard ; the only beast that has an up-cast face and dreams and looks at you with absent-minded eyes like a man. She laced their journeys with a fantastic monologue telling in the third person what the Leopard and the Cheetah were thinking and seeing and doing. And so they walked up mountains and over passes and swam in the warm clear water of romantic lakes and loved each other mightily always, in chestnut woods and olive orchards and flower-starred alps and pine forests and awning-covered boats, and by sunset and moonlight and starshine; and out of these agreeable solitudes they came brown and dusty, striding side by side into sunlit entertaining fruit-piled market-places and envious hotels. For days and weeks together it did not seem to Benham that there was anything that mattered in life but Amanda and the elemental joys of living. And then the Research Magnificent began to stir in him again. He perceived that Italy was not India, that the clue to the questions he must answer lay in the crowded new towns that they avoided, in the packed bookshops and the talk of men, and not in the picturesque and flowery solitudes to which their love-making carried them.

Moods began in which he seemed to forget Amanda altogether.

This happened first in the Certosa di Pavia, whither they had gone one afternoon from Milan. That was quite soon after they were married. They had a bumping journey thither in a motor-car, a little doubtful if the excursion was worth while, and they found a great amazement in the lavish beauty and decorative wealth of that vast church and its associated cloisters, set far away from any population as it seemed in a flat wilderness of reedy ditches and patchy cultivation. The distilleries and outbuildings were deserted—their white walls were covered by one monstrously great and old wisteria in flower—the soaring marvellous church was in possession of a knot of unattractive guides. One of these conducted them through the painted treasures of the gold and marble chapels; he was an elderly but animated person who evidently found Amanda more wonderful than any church. He poured out great accumulations of information and compliments before her. Benham dropped behind, went astray and was presently recovered dreaming in the great cloister. The guide showed them over two cells that opened thereupon, each a delightful house for a solitary, bookish and clean, and each with a little secret walled garden of its own. He was covertly tipped, against all regulations, and departed regretfully with a beaming dismissal from Amanda. She found Benham wondering why the Carthusians had failed to produce anything better in the world than a liqueur. "One might have imagined that men would have done something in this beautiful quiet; that there would have come thought from here or will from there."

"In these dear little nests they ought to have put lovers," said Amanda.

"Oh, of course, *you* would have made the place Thelema."

But as they went shaking and bumping back along the evil road to Milan, he fell into a deep musing. Suddenly, he said, "Work has to be done. Because this order or that has failed, there is no reason why we should fail. And look at those ragged children in the road ahead of us, and those dirty women sitting in the doorways, and the foul ugliness of these

gaunt nameless towns through which we go ! They are what
they are, because we are what we are—idlers, excursionists.
In a world we ought to rule. . . .

"Amanda, we've got to get to work. . . . "

That was his first display of this new mood, which presently
became a common one. He was less and less content to let
the happy hours slip by, more and more sensitive to the reminders in giant ruin and deserted cell, in a chance encounter
with a string of guns and soldiers on their way to manœuvres
or in the sight of a stale newspaper, of a great world process
going on in which he was now playing no part at all. And a
curious irritability manifested itself more and more plainly,
whenever human pettiness obtruded upon his attention,
whenever some trivial dishonesty, some manifest slovenliness,
some spiritless failure, a cheating waiter or a wayside beggar
brought before him the shiftless, selfish, aimless elements in
that war against the great dream of life made glorious.
"Accursed things," he would say, as he flung some importunate cripple at a church door a ten-centime piece ; "why
were they born ? Why do they consent to live ? They
are no better than some chance fungus that is because it
must."

"It takes all sorts to make a world," said Amanda.

"Nonsense," said Benham. "Where is the megatherium ?
That sort of creature has to go. Our sort of creature has to
end it."

"Then why did you give it money ? "

"Because—— I don't want the thing to be more wretched
than it is. But if I could prevent more of them—. . . . What
am I doing to prevent them ? "

"These beggars annoy you," said Amanda after a pause.
"They do me. Let us go back into the mountains."

But he fretted in the mountains.

They made a ten days' tour from Macugnaga over the
Monte Moro to Sass, and thence to Zermatt and back by the
Theodule to Macugnaga. The sudden apparition of douaniers
upon the Monteo Moro annoyed Benham, and he was also
irritated by the solemn English mountain climbers at Saas
Fee. They were as bad as golfers, he said, and reflected momentarily upon his father. Amanda fell in love with Monte
Rosa, she wanted to kiss its snowy forehead, she danced like
a young goat down the path to Mattmark, and rolled on the
turf when she came to gentians and purple primulas. Benham
was tremendously in love with her most of the time, but one
day when they were sitting over the Findelen glacier his per-
ceptions blundered for the first time upon the fundamental
antagonism of their quality. She was sketching out jolly
things that they were to do together, expeditions, entertainments, amusements, and adventures, with a voluble swiftness,
and suddenly in a flash his eyes were opened, and he saw

that she would never for a moment feel the quality that made
life worth while for him.   He saw it in a flash, and in that
flash he made his urgent resolve not to see it.   From that
moment forth his bearing was poisoned by his secret determination not to think of this, not to admit it to his mind.
And, forbidden to come into his presence in its proper form,
this conflict of intellectual temperaments took on strange
disguises, and the gathering tension of his mind sought to
relieve itself along grotesque irrelevant channels.

There was, for example, the remarkable affair of the drive
from Macugnaga to Piedimulera.

They had decided to walk down in a leisurely fashion,
but with the fatigues of the precipitous clamber down from
Switzerland still upon them they found the white road between rock above and gorge below wearisome, and the valley
hot in the late morning sunshine, and already before they
reached the inn they had marked for lunch Amanda had
suggested driving the rest of the way.   The inn had a number
of brigand-like customers consuming such sustenance as garlic
and salami and wine ; it received them with an indifference
that bordered on disrespect, until the landlord, who seemed
to be something of a beauty himself, discovered the merits of
Amanda.   Then he became markedly attentive.   He was a
large, fat, curly-headed person with beautiful eyes, a cherished
moustache, and an air of great gentility, and when he had
welcomed his guests and driven off the slatternly waiting-
maid, and given them his best table, and consented, at Amanda's request, to open a window, he went away and put on a
tie and collar.   It was an attention so conspicuous that even
the group of men in the far corner noticed and commented on
it, and then they commented on Amanda and Benham, assuming an ignorance of Italian in the visitors that was only partly
justifiable.   " Bellissima," " bravissima," " signorina," " Ing-
lesa," one need not be born in Italy to understand such words
as these.   Also they addressed sly comments and encourage-
ments to the landlord as he went to and fro.

Benham was rather still and stiff during the meal, but it
ill becomes an English aristocrat to discuss the manners of an
alien population, and Amanda was amused by the effusion
of the landlord and a little disposed to experiment upon him.
She sat radiating light amidst the shadows.

The question of the vehicle was broached.   The landlord
was doubtful ; then an idea, it was manifestly a questionable
idea, occurred to him.   He went to consult an obscure brown-
faced individual in the corner, disappeared, and the world
without became eloquent.   Presently he returned and announced that a carozza was practicable.   It had been difficult,
but he had contrived it.   And he remained hovering over the
conclusion of their meal, asking questions about Amanda's
mountaineering and expressing incredulous admiration.

His bill, which he presented with an uneasy flourish, was large and included the carozza.

He ushered them out to the carriage with civilities and compliments. It had manifestly been difficult and contrived. It was dusty and blistered, there had been a hasty effort to conceal its recent use as a hen-roost, the harness was mended with string. The horse was gaunt and scandalous, a dirty white, and it carried its head apprehensively. The driver had but one eye, through which there gleamed a concentrated hatred of God and man.

" No wonder he charged for it before we saw it," said Benham.

" It's better than walking," said Amanda.

The company in the inn gathered behind the landlord and scrutinised Amanda and Benham intelligently. The young couple got in. " Avanti," said Benham, and Amanda bestowed one last ineradicable memory on the bowing landlord.

Benham did not speak until just after they turned the first corner, and then something portentous happened, considering the precipitous position of the road they were upon. A small boy appeared sitting in the grass by the wayside, and at the sight of him the white horse shied extravagantly. The driver rose in his seat ready to jump. But the crisis passed without a smash. " Cheetah ! " cried Amanda suddenly. " This isn't safe." " Ah ! " said Benham, and began to act with the vigour of one who has long accumulated force. He rose in his place and gripped the one-eyed driver by the collar. " Aspetto," he said, but he meant " Stop ! " The driver understood that he meant " Stop," and obeyed.

Benham wasted no time in parleying with the driver. He indicated to him and to Amanda by a comprehensive gesture that he had business with the landlord, and with a gleaming appetite upon his face went running back towards the inn.

The landlord was sitting down to a little game of dominoes with his friends when Benham reappeared in the sunlight of the doorway. There was no misunderstanding Benham's expression.

For a moment the landlord was disposed to be defiant. Then he changed his mind. Benham's earnest face was within a yard of his own, and a threatening forefinger was almost touching his nose.

" Albergo cattivissimo," said Benham. " Cattivissimo ! Pranzo cattivissimo 'orrido. Cavallo cattivissimo, dangerousissimo. Gioco abominablissimo, damnissimo. Capisce. Eh ? "[1]

The landlord made deprecatory gestures.

" *You* understand all right," said Benham. " Da me il argento per il carozza. Subito ? "[2]

---

[1] This is vile Italian. It may—with a certain charity to Benham—be rendered: "The beastliest inn! The beastliest! The beastliest, most awful lunch! The vilest horse! Most dangerous! Abominable trick! Understand ?"

[2] " Give me back the money for the carriage. *Quickly !* "

The landlord was understood to ask whether the signor no longer wished for the carriage.

" *Subito !* " cried Benham, and giving way to a long-restrained impulse seized the padrone by the collar of his coat and shook him vigorously.

There were dissuasive noises from the company, but no attempt at rescue. Benham released his hold.

" Adesso!"[1] said Benham.

The landlord decided to disgorge. It was at any rate a comfort that the beautiful lady was not seeing anything of this. And he could explain afterwards to his friends that the Englishman was clearly a lunatic, deserving pity rather than punishment. He made some sound of protest, but attempted no delay in refunding the money Benham had prepaid.

Outside sounded the wheels of the returning carriage. They stopped. Amanda appeared in the doorway and discovered Benham dominant.

He was a little short of breath, and as she came in he was addressing the landlord with much earnestness in the following compact sentences.

" Attendez ! Ecco ! Adesso noi andiamo con questa cattivissimo cavallo a Piedimulera. Si noi arrivero in safety, securo, that is, pagaremo. Non altro. Si noi abbiamo accidento Dio—Dio have mercy on your sinful soul. See ! Capisce ? That's all."[2]

He turned to Amanda. " Get back into the thing," he said. " We won't have these stinking beasts think we are afraid of the job. I've just made sure he won't have a profit by it if we smash up. That's all. I might have known what he was up to when he wanted the money beforehand." He came to the doorway and with a magnificent gesture commanded the perplexed driver to turn the carriage.

While that was being done he discoursed upon his adjacent fellow-creatures. " A man who pays beforehand for anything in this filthy sort of life is a fool. You see the standards of the beasts. They think of nothing but their dirty little tricks to get profit, their garlic, their sour wine, their games of dominoes, their moments of lust. They crawl in this place like cockroaches in a warm corner of the fireplace until they die. Look at the scabby frontage of the house. Look at the men's faces. . . Yes. So ! Adequato. Aspettate. . . . Get back into the carriage, Amanda."

" You know it's dangerous, Cheetah. The horse is a shier. That man is blind in one eye."

" Get back into the carriage," said Benham, whitely angry. " *I am going to drive !* "

[1] "*Now !*"
[2] " Now we will go with this beastly horse to Piedimulera. If we get there safely I will pay. If we have an accident then——"

" But—— ! "

Just for a moment Amanda looked scared. Then with a
queer little laugh she jumped in again.

Amanda was never a coward when there was excitement
afoot. " We'll smash ! " she cried, by no means woefully.

"Get up beside me," said Benham speaking in English to
the driver, but with a gesture that translated him. Power
over men radiated from Benham in this angry mood. He
took the driver's seat. The little driver ascended, and then
with a grim calmness that brooked no resistance Benham
reached over, took and fastened the apron over their knees
to prevent any repetition of the jumping-out tactics.

The recovering landlord became voluble in the doorway.

" In Piedimulera pagaro," said Benham over his shoulder
and brought the whip across the white outstanding ribs.
" Get up ! " said Benham.

Amanda gripped the sides of the seat as the carriage started
into motion.

He laid the whip on again with such vigour that the horse
forgot altogether to shy at the urchin that had scared it before.

" Amanda," said Benham, leaning back. " If we do happen
to go over on *that* side, jump out. It's all clear and wide for
you. This side won't matter so—— "

" *Mind !* " screamed Amanda and recalled him to his
duties. He was off the road and he had narrowly missed an
outstanding chestnut tree.

" No you don't," said Benham presently, and again their
career became erratic for a time as after a slight struggle he
replaced the apron over the knees of the deposed driver.
It had been furtively released. After that Benham kept
an eye on it that might have been better devoted to the
road.

The road went down in a series of curves and corners. Now
and then there were pacific interludes when it might have
been almost any road. Then, again, it became specifically an
Italian mountain road. Now and then only a row of all too
infrequent granite stumps separated them from a sheer precipice. Some of the corners were miraculous, and once they
had a wheel in a ditch for a time, they shaved the parapet of
a bridge over a gorge and they drove a cyclist into a patch of
maize, they narrowly missed a goat and jumped three gullies,
thrice the horse stumbled and was jerked up in time, there
were sickening moments, and withal they got down to Piedimulera unbroken and unsplit. It helped perhaps that the brake,
with its handle like a barrel organ, had been screwed up before
Benham took control. And when they were fairly on the level
outside the town Benham suddenly pulled up, relinquished the
driving into the proper hands and came into the carriage
with Amanda.

" Safe now," he said compactly.

The driver appeared to be murmuring prayers very softly as he examined the brake.

Amanda was struggling with profound problems. " Why didn't you drive down in the first place," she asked, " without going back ? "

" The landlord annoyed me," he said. " I had to go back. . . . I wish I had kicked him. Hairy beast ! If anything had happened, you see, he would have had his mean money. I couldn't bear to leave him."

" And why didn't you let *him* drive ? " She indicated the driver by a motion of the head.

" I was angry," said Benham. " I was angry at the whole thing."

" Still—— "

" You see, I think I did that because he might have jumped off if I hadn't been up there to prevent him—I mean if we had had a smash. I didn't want him to get out of it."

" But you too—— "

" You see I was angry. . . . "

" It's been as good as a switchback," said Amanda after reflection. " But weren't you a little careless about me, Cheetah ? "

" I never thought of you," said Benham, and then as if he felt that inadequate : " You see—I was so annoyed. It's odd at times how annoyed one gets. Suddenly when that horse shied I realised what a beastly business life was—as those brutes up there live it. I want to clear out the whole hot, dirty, little aimless nest of them. . . .

" No, I'm sure," he repeated after a pause as though he had been digesting something, " I wasn't thinking about you at all."

§ 4

The suppression of his discovery that his honeymoon was not in the least the great journey of world exploration he had intended, but merely an impulsive pleasure hunt, was by no means the only obscured and repudiated conflict that disturbed the mind and broke out upon the behaviour of Benham. Beneath that issue he was keeping down a far more intimate conflict. It was in those lower, still less recognised depths that the volcanic fire arose and the earthquakes gathered strength. The Amanda he had loved, the Amanda of the gallant stride and fluttering skirt, was with him still ; she marched rejoicing over the passes, and a dearer Amanda, a soft whispering creature with dusky hair, who took possession of him when she chose, a soft creature who was nevertheless a fierce creature, was also interwoven with his life. But—— But there was now also a multitude of other Amandas who had this in common—that they roused him to opposition, that they crossed his moods and jarred upon his spirit. And particularly there was the Conquering Amanda, not so much proud of her beauty as eager to test it, so that she was not unmindful of the stir she made in hotel lounges, nor of the magic that may shine memorably through the most common-place incidental conversation.   This Amanda was only too manifestly pleased to think that she made peasant lovers discontented and hotel porters unmercenary ; she let her light shine before men. We lovers, who had deemed our own subjugation a profound privilege, love not this further ex-pansiveness of our lady's empire. But Benham knew that no aristocrat can be jealous ; jealousy he held to be the vice of the hovel and farmstead and suburban villa, and at an enor-mous expenditure of will he ignored Amanda's waving flags and roving glances. So, too, he denied that Amanda who was sharp and shrewd about money matters, that flash of an Amanda who was greedy for presents and possessions, that restless Amanda who fretted at any cessation of excitement, and that darkly thoughtful Amanda whom chance observa-tions and questions showed to be still considering an account she had to settle with Lady Marayne. He resisted these im-pressions, he shut them out of his mind, but still they worked into his thoughts, and presently he could find himself asking, even as he and she went in step striding side by side through the red-scarred pinewoods in the most perfect outward har-mony, whether after all he was so happily mated as he declared himself to be a score of times a day, whether he wasn't catching glimpses of reality through a veil of delusion that grew thinner and thinner and might leave him disillusioned in the face of a relationship——

Sometimes a man may be struck by a thought as though he had been struck in the face, and when the name of Mrs. Skelmersdale came into his head, he glanced at his wife by his side as if it were something that she might well have heard. Was this indeed the same thing as that ? Wonderful, fresh as the day of Creation, clean as flame, yet the same ! Was Amanda indeed the sister of Mrs. Skelmersdale—wrought of clean fire, but her sister ? . . .

But also beside the inimical aspects which could set such doubts afoot there were in her infinite variety yet other Amandas neither very dear nor very annoying, but for the most part delightful, who entertained him as strangers might, Amandas with an odd twist which made them amusing to watch, jolly Amandas who were simply irrelevant.   There was, for example, Amanda the Dog Mistress, with an astonish-ing tact and understanding of dogs, who could explain dogs and the cock of their ears and the droop of their tails and their vanity and their fidelity, and why they looked up and why they suddenly went off round the corner, and their pride in the sound of their voices and their dastardly thoughts and sniffing satisfactions, so that for the first time dogs had souls for Benham to see ; and there was an Amanda with a striking passion for the sleekness and soft noses of horses. And there was an Amanda extremely garrulous who was a biographical dictionary and critical handbook to all the girls in the school she had attended at Chichester—they seemed a very girlish lot of girls—and an Amanda who was very knowing—knowing was the only word for it—about pictures and architecture. And these and all the other Amandas agreed together to develop and share this one quality in common—that altogether they pointed to no end, they converged on nothing. She was, it grew more and more apparent, a miscellany bound in a body. She was an animated discursiveness. That passion to get all things together into one aristocratic aim, that restraint of purpose, that imperative to focus, which was the structural essential of Benham's spirit, was altogether foreign to her composition.

There were so many Amandas, they were as innumerable as the Venuses—Cytherea, Cypria, Paphia, Popularia, Euploea, Area, Verticordia, Etaira, Basilea, Myrtea, Libertina, Freya, Astarte, Philommedis, Telessigamma, Anadyomene, and a thousand others to whom men have bowed and built temples, a thousand and the same, and yet it seemed to Benham there was still one wanting.

The Amanda he had loved most wonderfully was that Amanda in armour who had walked with him through the wilderness of the world along the road to Chichester—and that Amanda came back to him no more.

§ 5

Amanda too was making her observations and discoveries.

These moods of his perplexed her ; she was astonished to find he was becoming irritable ; she felt that he needed a firm but gentle discipline in his deportment as a lover. At first he had been perfect. . . .

But Amanda was more prepared for human inconsecutiveness than Benham, because she herself was inconsecutive and her dissatisfaction with his irritations and preoccupation broadened to no general discontent. He had seemed perfect and he wasn't. So nothing was perfect. And he had to be managed, just as one must manage a dog or a cousin or a mother or a horse. Anyhow she had got him, she had no doubt that she held him by a thousand ties ; the spotless leopard had him between her teeth, he was a prisoner in the dusk of her hair, and the world was all one vast promise of entertainment.

§ 6

But the raid into the Balkans was not the tremendous success she had expected it to be. They had adventures, but they were not the richly coloured, mediæval affairs she had anticipated. For the most part until Benham broke loose beyond Ochrida they were adventures in discomfort. In those remote parts of Europe inns die away and cease, and it had never occurred to Amanda that inns could die away anywhere. She had thought that they just became very simple and natural and quaint. And she had thought that when benighted people knocked at a door it would presently open hospitably. She had not expected shots at random from the window. And it is not usual in Albania generally for women, whether they are Christian or Moslem, to go about unveiled ; when they do so it leads to singular manifestations. The moral sense of the men is shocked and staggered, and they show it in many homely ways. Small boys at that age when feminine beauty does not yet prevail with them, pelt. Also in Maho-metan districts they pelt men who do not wear fezzes, while occasionally Christians of the shawl-headed or skull-cap persuasions will pelt a fez. Sketching is always a peltable or mobable offence, as being contrary to the Koran, and sitting down tempts the pelter. Generally they pelt. The dogs of Albania are numerous, big, dirty, white dogs, large and hostile, and they attack with little hesitation. The women of Albania are secluded and remote, and indisposed to be of service to an alien sister. Roads are infrequent and most bridges have broken down. No bridge has been repaired since the later seventeenth century, and no new bridge has been made since the decline and fall of the Roman Empire.

There are no shops at all. The scenery is magnificent but precipitous, and many of the high-roads are difficult to trace. And there is rain. In Albania there is sometimes very heavy rain.

Yet in spite of these drawbacks they spent some splendid hours in their exploration of that wild lost country beyond the Adriatic headlands. There was the approach to Cattaro, for example, through an arm of the sea, amazingly beautiful on either shore, that wound its way into the wild mountains and ended in a deep blue bay under the tremendous declivity of Montenegro. The quay, with its trees and lateen craft, ran along under the towers and portcullised gate of the old Vene-tian wall ; within clustered the town ; and then the fortifi-cations zigzagged up steeply to a monstrous fantastic fortress perched upon a great mountain headland that overhung the town. Behind it the rocks, slashed to and fro with the road to Cettinjé, continued to ascend into blue haze, upward and upward until they became a purple curtain that filled half the heavens. The paved still town was squalid by day, but in the evening it became theatrically incredible, with an outdoor café amidst flowers and creepers, a Hungarian military band, a rabble of promenaders like a stage chorus in gorgeous cos-tumes, and a great gibbous yellow moon.

And there was Kroia, which Benham and Amanda saw first

through the branches of the great trees that bordered the broad green track they were following. The town and its castle were poised at a tremendous height, sunlit and brilliant against a sombre mass of storm cloud, over vast cliffs and ravines. Kroia continued to be beautiful through a steep laborious approach up to the very place itself, a clustering group of houses and bazaars crowned with a tower and a minaret, and from a painted corridor upon this crest they had a wonderful view of the great seaward levels, and even far away the blue sea itself stretching between Scutari and Durazzo. The eye fell in succession down the stages of a vast and various descent, on the bazaars and tall minarets of the town, on jagged rocks and precipices, on slopes of oak forest and slopes of olive woods, on blue hills dropping away beyond blue hills to the coast. And behind them when they turned they saw great mountains, sullenly magnificent, cleft into vast irregular masses, dense with woods below and grim and desolate above.

These were unforgettable scenes, and so too was the wild lonely valley through which they rode to Ochrida amidst walnut and chestnut trees and scattered rocks, and the first vision of that place itself, with its fertile levels dotted with sheep and cattle, its castle and clustering mosques, its spacious blue lake and the great mountains rising up towards Olympus under the sun. And there was the first view of the blue Lake of Presba seen between silvery beech stems, and that too had Olympus in the far background, plain now and clear and un-expectedly snowy. And there were midday moments when they sat and ate under vines and heard voices singing very pleasantly, and there were forest glades and forest tracks in a great variety of beauty with mountains appearing through their parted branches, there were ilex woods, chestnut woods, beech woods, and there were strings of heavily-laden mules staggering up torrent-worn tracks, and strings of blue-swathed mysterious-eyed women with burdens on their heads passing silently, and white remote houses and ruins and deep gorges and precipices and ancient half-ruinous bridges over unruly streams. And if there was rain there was also the ending of rain, rainbows, and the piercing of clouds by the sun's incandescence and sunsets and the moon, first full, then new, and then growing full again as the holiday wore on.

They found tolerable accommodation at Cattaro and at Cettinjé and at a place half-way between them. It was only when they had secured a guide and horses, and pushed on into the south-east of Montenegro that they began to realise the real difficulties of their journey. They aimed for a place called Podgoritza, which had a partially justifiable reputation for an inn, they missed the road and spent the night in the open beside a fire, rolled in the blankets they had very for-tunately bought in Cettinjé. They supped on biscuits and Benham's brandy flask. It chanced to be a fine night, and,

drawn like moths by the fire, four heavily-armed moun-
taineers came out of nowhere, sat down beside Benham and
Amanda, rolled cigarettes, achieved conversation in bad
Italian through the muleteer, and awaited refreshment.
They approved of the brandy highly, they finished it, and
towards dawn warmed to song. They did not sing badly,
singing in chorus, but it appeared to Amanda that the hour
might have been better chosen. In the morning they were
agreeably surprised to find one of the Englishmen was an
Englishwoman, and followed every accessible detail of her
toilet with great interest. They were quite helpful about
breakfast when the trouble was put to them ; two vanished
over a crest and reappeared with some sour milk, a slabby
kind of bread, goat's cheese young but hardened, and coffee
and the means of making coffee, and they joined spiritedly
in the ensuing meal. It ought to have been extraordinarily
good fun, this camp under the vast heavens and these wild
visitors, but it was not such fun as it ought to have been
because both Amanda and Benham were extremely cold,
stiff, sleepy, grubby and cross, and when at last they were
back in the way to Podgoritza and had parted, after some
present-giving, from their chance friends, they halted in a
sunlit grassy place, rolled themselves up in their blankets
and recovered their arrears of sleep.

Podgoritza was their first experience of a khan, those
Oriental substitutes for hotels, and it was a deceptively good
khan, indeed it was not a khan at all, it was an inn ; it provided meals, it had a kind of bar, or at any rate a row of bottles
and glasses, it possessed an upper floor with rooms, separate
rooms, opening on to a gallery. The room had no beds, but
it had a shelf about it on which Amanda and Benham rolled
up in their blankets and slept. " We can do this sort of thing
all right," said Amanda and Benham. " But we mustn't
lose the way again."

" In Scutari," said Benham, " we will get an extra horse
and a tent."

The way presently became a lake and they reached Scutari
by boat towards the dawn of the next day. . . .

The extra horse involved the addition of its owner, a small
suspicious Latin Christian, to the company, and of another
horse for him and an ugly almost hairless boy attendant.
Moreover, the British consul prevailed with Benham to accept
the services of a picturesque Arnaut cavasse, complete with
a rifle, knives, and other implements and the name of Giorgio.
And as they got up into the highlands beyond Scutari they
began to realise the deceitfulness of Podgoritza and the real
truth about khans. Their next one they reached after a rainy
evening, and it was a cavernous room with a floor of indurated
mud and full of eye-stinging wood-smoke and wind and the
smell of beasts, unpartitioned, with a weakly hostile custodian

from whom no food could be got but a little goat's flesh and
bread. The meat Giorgio stuck upon a skewer in gobbets
like cat's-meat and cooked before the fire. For drink there
was coffee and raw spirits. Against the wall in one corner
was a slab of wood rather like the draining board in a scullery,
and on this the guests were expected to sleep. The horses
and the rest of the party camped loosely about the adjacent
corner after a bitter dispute upon some unknown point between the horse owner and the custodian.

Amanda and Benham were already rolled up on their
slanting board like a couple of chrysalids when other company
began to arrive through the open door out of the moonlight,
drawn thither by the report of a travelling Englishwoman.

They were sturdy men in light-coloured garments adorned
ostentatiously with weapons ; they moved mysteriously
about in the firelit darknesses and conversed in undertones
with Giorgio. Giorgio seemed to have considerable powers
of exposition and a gift for social organisation. Presently
he came to Benham and explained that raki was available
and that hospitality would do no harm ; Benham and Amanda
sat up and various romantic figures with splendid moustaches
came forward and shook hands with him, modestly ignoring
Amanda. There was drinking, in which Benham shared,
incomprehensible compliments, much ineffective saying of
" *Buona notte*," and at last Amanda and Benham counter-
feited sleep. This seemed to remove a check on the conversation and a heated discussion in tense undertones went on,
it seemed interminably. . . . Probably very few aspects of
Benham and Amanda were ignored. . . . Towards morning
the twanging of a string proclaimed the arrival of a querulous-
faced minstrel with a sort of embryonic one-stringed horse-
headed fiddle, and after a brief parley singing began, a long
high-pitched solo. The fiddle squealed pitifully under the
persuasion of a semicircular bow. Two heads were lifted
inquiringly.

The singer had taken up his position at their feet and faced
them. It was a compliment.

" *Oh !* " said Amanda, rolling over.

The soloist obliged with three songs and then, just as day
was breaking, stopped abruptly and sprawled suddenly on
the floor as if he had been struck asleep. He was vocal even
in his sleep. A cock in the far corner began crowing and was
answered by another outside. . . .

But this does not give a full account of the animation of
the khan. " *Oh !* " said Amanda, rolling over again with the
suddenness of accumulated anger.

" They're worse than in Scutari," said Benham, understanding her trouble instantly.

" It isn't days and nights we are having," said Benham
a few days later, " it's days and nightmares."

But both he and Amanda had one quality in common. The deeper their discomfort the less possible it was to speak of turning back from the itinerary they had planned. . . .

They met no robbers, though an excited little English Levantine in Scutari had assured them they would do so and told a vivid story of a ride to Ipek, a delay on the road due to a sudden inexplicable lameness of his horse after a halt for refreshment, a political discussion that delayed him, his hurry through the still twilight to make up for lost time, the coming on of night and the sudden silent apparition out of the darkness of the woods about the road of a dozen armed men each protruding a gun-barrel. " Sometimes they will wait for you at a ford or a broken bridge," he said. " In the mountains they rob for arms. They assassinate the Turkish soldiers even. It is better to go unarmed unless you mean to fight for it. . . . Have you got arms ? "

" Just a revolver," said Benham.

But it was after that that he closed with Giorgio.

If they found no robbers in Albania they met soon enough with bloodshed. They came to a village where a friend of a friend of Giorgio's was discovered, and they slept at his house in preference to the unclean and crowded khan. Here for the first time Amanda made the acquaintance of Albanian women and was carried off to the women's region at the top of the house, permitted to wash, closely examined, shown a baby, and confided in as generously as gesture and some fragments of Italian would permit. Benham slept on a rug on the first floor in a corner of honour beside the wood fire. There had been much confused conversation and some singing, he was dog-tired and slept heavily, and when presently he was awakened by piercing screams he sat up in a darkness that seemed to belong neither to time nor place. . . .

Near his feet was an ashen glow that gave no light.

His first perplexity gave way to dismay at finding no Amanda by his side. " Amanda ! " he cried. . . .

Her voice floated down through a chink in the floor above. " What can it be, Cheetah ? "

Then : " It's coming nearer."

The screaming continued, heart-rending, eviscerating shrieks. Benham, still confused, lit a match. All the men about him were stirring or sitting up and listening, their faces showing distorted and ugly in the flicker of his light. " *Che e ?* " he tried. No one answered. Then one by one they stood up and went softly to the ladder that led to the stable-room below. Benham struck a second match and a third.

" Giorgio ! " he called.

The cavasse made an arresting gesture and followed discreetly and noiselessly after the others, leaving Benham alone in the dark.

Benham heard their shuffling patter, one after the other,

down the ladder, the sounds of a door being unbarred softly, and then no other sound but that incessant shrieking in the darkness.

Had they gone out ? Were they standing at the door looking out into the night and listening ?

Amanda had found the chink and her voice sounded nearer. " It's a woman," she said.

The shrieking came nearer and nearer, long, repeated, throat-tearing shrieks. Far off there was a great clamour of dogs. And there was another sound, a whisper— ?

" *Rain !* "

The shrieks seemed to turn into a side street and receded. The tension of listening relaxed. Men's voices sounded below in question and answer. Dogs close at hand barked shortly and then stopped inquiringly.

Benham seemed to himself to be sitting alone for an interminable time. He lit another match and consulted his watch. It was four o'clock and nearly dawn. . . .

Then slowly and stumbling up the ladder the men began to return to Benham's room.

" Ask them what it is," urged Amanda.

But for a time not even Giorgio would understand Benham's questions. There seemed to be a doubt whether he ought to know. The shrieking approached again and then receded. Giorgio came and stood, a vague thoughtful figure, by the embers of the fire. Explanation dropped from him reluctantly. It was nothing. Some one had been killed : that was all. It was a vendetta. A man had been missing overnight, and this morning his brother who had been prowling and searching with some dogs had found him, or rather his head. It was on this side of the ravine, thrown over from the other bank on which the body sprawled stiffly, wet through, and now growing visible in the gathering daylight. Yes—the voice was the man's wife. It was raining hard. . . . There would be shrieking for nine days. Yes, nine days. Confirmation with the fingers when Benham still fought against the facts. Her friends and relatives would come and shriek too. Two of the dead man's aunts were among the best keeners in the whole land. They could keen marvellously. It was raining too hard to go on. . . . The road would be impossible in rain. . . . Yes, it was very melancholy. Her house was close at hand. Perhaps twenty or thirty women would join her. It was impossible to go on until it had stopped raining. It would be tiresome, but what could one do ? . . .

§ 7

As they sat upon the parapet of a broken bridge on the road between Elbassan and Ochrida Benham was moved to a dissertation upon the condition of Albania and the politics of the Balkan peninsula.

" Here we are," he said, " not a week from London, and you see the sort of life that men live when the forces of civilisation fail. We have been close to two murders——"

" Two ? "

" That little crowd in the square at Scutari—— That was a murder. I didn't tell you at the time."

" But I knew it was," said Amanda.

" And you see the filth of it all, the toiling discomfort of it all. There is scarcely a house here in all the land that is not filthier and viler than the worst slum in London. No man ventures far from his village without arms, everywhere there is fear. The hills are impassable because of the shepherds' dogs. Over those hills a little while ago a stranger was torn to pieces by dogs—and partially eaten. Amanda, those dogs madden me ! I shall let fly at the beasts. The infernal indignity of it ! But that is by the way. You see how all this magnificent country lies waste with nothing but this crawling, ugly mockery of human life."

" They sing," said Amanda.

" Yes," said Benham and reflected, " they do sing. I suppose singing is the last thing left to men. When there is nothing else you can still sit about and sing. Miners who have been buried in mines will sing, people going down in ships."

" The Sussex labourers don't sing," said Amanda. " These people sing well."

" They would probably sing as well if they were civilised. Even if they didn't I shouldn't care. All the rest of their lives is muddle and cruelty and misery. Look at the women. There was that party of bent creatures we met yesterday, carrying great bundles, carrying even the men's cloaks and pipes, while their rascal husbands and brothers swaggered behind. Look at the cripples we have seen and the mutilated men. If we have met one man without a nose we have met a dozen. And stunted people. All these people are like evil schoolboys ; they do nothing but malicious mischief ; there is nothing adult about them but their voices ; they are like the heroic dreams of young ruffians in a penitentiary. You saw that man at Scutari in the corner of the bazaar, the gorgeous brute, you admired him——"

" The man with the gold inlaid pistols and the diamonds on his yataghan. He wanted to show them to us."

" Yes. You let him see you admired him."

" I liked the things on his stall."

" Well, he has killed nearly thirty people."

" In duels ? "

" Good Lord ! *No !* Assassinations. His shoemaker annoyed him by sending in a bill. He went to the man's stall, found him standing with his child in his arms and blew out his brains. He blundered against a passer-by in the road and shot

him. Those are his feats. Sometimes his pistols go off in
the bazaar just by accident."

" Does nobody kill him ? "

" I wanted to," said Benham and became thoughtful for
a time. " I think I ought to have made some sort of quarrel.
But then as I am an Englishman he might have hesitated.
He would have funked a strange beast like me. And I couldn't
have shot him if he had hesitated. And if he hadn't——"

" But doesn't a blood feud come down on him ? "

" It only comes down on his family. The shoemaker's
son thought the matter over and squared accounts by putting
the muzzle of a gun into the small of the back of our bully's
uncle. It was easier that way. . . . You see you're dealing
with men of thirteen years old or thereabouts, the boy who
doesn't grow up."

" But doesn't the law—— ? "

" There's no law. Only custom and the Turkish tax collector.

" You see this is what men are where there is no power,
no discipline, no ruler, no responsibility. This is a master-
less world. This is pure democracy. This is the natural state
of men. This is the world of the bully and the brigand and
assassin, the world of the mud-pelter and brawler, the world
of the bent woman, the world of the flea and the fly, the open
drain and the baying dog. This is what the British senti-
mentalist thinks a noble state for men."

" They fight for freedom."

" They fight among each other. There are their private
feuds and their village feuds and above all that great feud
religion. In Albania there is only one religion and that is
hate. But there are three churches for the better cultivation
of hate and cruelty, the Latin, the Greek and the Mahometan."

" But no one has ever conquered these people."

" Any one could, the Serbians, the Bulgarians, the Greeks,
the Italians, the Austrians. Why, they can't even shoot !
It's just the balance of power and all that foolery keeps this
country a roadless wilderness. Good God, how I tire of it !
These men who swagger and stink, their brawling dogs, their
greasy priests and dervishes, the down-at-heel soldiers, the
bribery and robbery, the cheating over the money. . . ."

He slipped off the parapet, too impatient to sit any longer,
and began to pace up and down in the road.

" One marvels that no one comes to clear up this country,
one itches to be at the job, and then one realises that before
one can begin here, one must get to work back there, where the
fools and pedants of *Welt Politik* scheme mischief one against
another. This country frets me. I can't see any fun in it,
can't see the humour of it. And the people away there know
no better than to play off tribe against tribe, sect against
sect, one peasant prejudice against another. Over this pass
the foolery grows grimmer and viler. We shall come to where

the Serbian plots against the Bulgarian and the Greek against
both, and the Turk, with spasmodic massacres and indulgences,
broods over the brew. Every division is subdivided. There
are two sorts of Greek church, Exarchic, Patriarchic, both
teaching by threat and massacre. And there is no one, no
one, with the sense to over-ride all these squalid hostilities.
All those fools away there in London and Vienna and St.
Petersburg and Rome take sides as though these beastly
tribes and leagues and superstitions meant anything but
blank, black, damnable ignorance. One fool stands up for
the Catholic Albanians, another finds heroes in the Serbians,
another talks of Brave Little Montenegro, or the Sturdy
Bulgarian, or the Heroic Turk. There isn't a religion in the
whole Balkan peninsula, there isn't a tribal or national sentiment that deserves a moment's respect from a sane man.
They're things like niggers' nose-rings and Chinese secret
societies ; childish things, idiot things that have to go. Yet
there is no one who will preach the only possible peace, which
is the peace of the world-state, the open conspiracy of all
the sane men in the world against the things that break us
up into wars and futilities. And here am I—who have the
light—*wandering !* Just wandering ! "

He shrugged his shoulders and came to stare at the torrent
under the bridge.

" You're getting ripe for London, Cheetah," said Amanda
softly.

" I want somehow to get to work, to get my hands on
definite things."

" How can we get back ? "

She had to repeat her question presently.

" We can go on. Over the hills is Ochrida and then over
another pass is Presba, and from there we go down into Monastir
and reach a railway and get back to the world of our own times
again."

§ 8

But before they reached the world of their own times
Macedonia was to show them something grimmer than Albania.

They were riding through a sunlit walnut wood beyond
Ochrida when they came upon the thing.

The first they saw of it looked like a man lying asleep on
a grassy bank. But he lay very still indeed, he did not look
up, he did not stir as they passed, the pose of his hand was
stiff, and when Benham glanced back at him, he stifled a
little cry of horror. For this man had no face and the flies had
been busy upon him. . . .

Benham caught Amanda's bridle so that she had to give
her attention to her steed.

" Ahead ! " he said, " ahead ! Look, a village ! "

(Why the devil didn't they bury the man ? Why ?

And that fool Giorgio and the others were pulling up and beginning to chatter. After all she might look back.)

Through the trees now they could see houses. He quickened his pace and jerked Amanda's horse forward. . . .

But the village was a still one. Not a dog barked.

Here was an incredible village without even a dog !

And then, then they saw some more people lying about. A woman lay in a doorway. Near her was something muddy that might have been a child, beyond were six men all spread out very neatly in a row with their faces to the sky.

" Cheetah ! " cried Amanda, with her voice going up. " They've been killed. Some one has killed them."

Benham halted beside her and stared stupidly.

" It's a band," he said. " It's—propaganda. Greeks or Turks or Bulgarians."

" But their feet and hands are fastened ! And—— . . . *What have they been doing to them?* . . ."

" I want to kill," cried Benham. " Oh ! I want to kill people. Come on, Amanda ! It blisters one's eyes. Come away. Come away ! Come ! "

Her face was white and her eyes terror-stricken. She obeyed him mechanically. She gave one last look at those bodies. . . .

Down the deep-rutted soil of the village street they clattered. They came to houses that had been set on fire. . . .

" What is that hanging from a tree ? " cried Amanda. " Oh, Oh ! "

" Come on. . . ."

Behind them rode the others scared and hurrying.

The sunlight had become the light of hell. There was no air but horror. Across Benham's skies these fly-blown trophies of devilry dangled mockingly in the place of God. He had no thought but to get away.

Presently they encountered a detachment of Turkish soldiers, very greasy and ragged, with worn-out boots and yellow faces, toiling up the stony road belatedly to the village. Amanda and Benham riding one behind the other in a stricken silence passed this labouring column without a gesture, but presently they heard the commander stopping and questioning Giorgio. . .

Then Giorgio and the others came clattering to overtake them.

Giorgio was too full to wait for questions. He talked eagerly to Benham's silence.

It must have happened yesterday, he explained. They were Bulgarians—traitors. They had been converted to the Patriarchists by the Greeks—by a Greek band, that is to say. They had betrayed one of their own people. Now a Bulgarian band had descended upon them. Bulgarian bands it see ned were always particularly rough on Bulgarian speaking Patriarchists. . . .

§ 9

That night they slept in a dirty little room in a peasant's house in Resnia, and in the middle of the night Amanda woke up with a start and heard Benham talking. He seemed to be sitting up as he talked. But he was not talking to her and his voice sounded strange.

" Flies," he said, " in the sunlight ! "

He was silent for a time, and then he repeated the same words.

Then suddenly he began to declaim. " Oh ! Brutes together. Apes. Apes with knives. Have they no lord, no master, to save them from such things ? This is the life of men when no man rules. . . . When no man rules. . . . Not even himself. . . . It is because we are idle, because we keep our wits slack and our wills weak that these poor devils live in hell. These things happen here and everywhere when the hand that rules grows weak. Away in China now they are happening. Persia. Africa. . . . Russia staggers. And I who should serve the law, I who should keep order, wander and make love. . . . My God ! May I never forget ! May I never forget ! Flies in the sunlight ! That man's face. And those six men !

" Grip the savage by the throat.

" The weak savage in the Foreign Office, the weak savage at the party headquarters, feud and indolence and folly. It is all one world. This and that are all one thing. The spites of London and the mutilations of Macedonia. The maggots that eat men's faces and the maggots that rot their minds. Rot their minds. Rot their minds. Rot their minds. . . ."

To Amanda it sounded like delirium.

" *Cheetah !* " she said suddenly between remonstrance and a cry of terror.

The darkness suddenly became quite still. He did not move. She was afraid. " Cheetah ! " she said again.

" What is it, Amanda ? "

" I thought—— Are you all right ? "

" Quite."

" But do you feel well ? "

" I've got this cold I caught in Ochrida. I suppose I'm feverish. But—yes, I'm well."

" You were talking."

Silence for a time.

" I was thinking," he said.

" You talked."

" I'm sorry," he said after another long pause.

§ 10

The next morning Benham had a pink spot on either cheek, his eyes were feverishly bright, he would touch no food and instead of coffee he wanted water. " In Monastir there will be a doctor," he said. " Monastir is a big place. In Monastir I will see a doctor. I want a doctor."

They rode out of the village in the freshness before sunrise and up long hills, and sometimes they went in the shade of woods and sometimes in a flooding sunshine. Benham now rode in front, preoccupied, intent, regardless of Amanda, a stranger, and she rode close behind him wondering.

" When you get to Monastir, young man," she told him, inaudibly, " you will go straight to bed and we'll see what has to be done with you."

" *Ammalato*," said Giorgio, confidentially coming abreast of her.

" *Medico in Monastir*," said Amanda.

" *Si—molti medici, Monastir*," Giorgio agreed.

Then came the inevitable dogs, big white brutes, three in full cry charging hard at Benham and a younger less enterprising beast running along the high bank above yapping and making feints to descend.

The goatherd reclining under the shadow of a rock, awaited Benham's embarrassment with an indolent malice.

" You *uncivilised* Beasts ! " cried Benham, and before Amanda could realise what he was up to, she heard the crack of his revolver and saw a puff of blue smoke drift away above his right shoulder. The foremost beast rolled over and the goatherd had sprung to his feet. He shouted with something between anger and dismay as Benham, regardless of the fact that the other dogs had turned and were running back, let fly a second time. Then the goatherd had clutched at the gun that lay on the grass near at hand. Giorgio was bawling in noisy remonstrance and also getting ready to shoot, and the horse-owner and his boy were clattering back to a position of neutrality up the stony road. " *Bang !* " came a flight of lead within a yard of Benham and then the goatherd was in retreat behind a rock and Giorgio was shouting, " *Avanti, Avanti !* " to Amanda.

She grasped his intention and in another moment she had Benham's horse by the bridle and was leading the retreat. Giorgio followed close, driving the two baggage mules before him.

" I am tired of dogs," Benham said. " Tired to death of dogs. All savage dogs must be shot. All through the world. I am tired——"

Their road carried them down through the rocky pass and then up a long slope in the open. Far away on the left they saw the goatherd running and shouting and other armed goatherds appearing among the rocks. Behind them the horse-owner and his boy came riding headlong across the zone of danger.

" Dogs must be shot," said Benham, exalted. " Dogs must be shot."

" Unless they are *good* dogs," said Amanda, keeping beside him with an eye on his revolver.

" Unless they are good dogs to every one," said Benham.

They rushed along the road in a turbulent dusty huddle of horses and mules and riders. The horse-owner, voluble in Albanian, was trying to get past them. His boy pressed behind him. Giorgio in the rear had unslung his rifle and got it across the front of his saddle. Far away they heard the sound of a shot and a kind of shudder in the air overhead witnessed to the flight of the bullet. They crested a rise and suddenly between the tree boughs Monastir was in view, a wide stretch of white town, with many cypress and plane trees, a winding river with many wooden bridges, clustering minarets of pink and white, a hilly cemetery, and scattered patches of soldiers' tents like some queer white crop to supplement its extensive barracks.

As they hurried down towards this city of refuge a long string of mules burdened with great bales of green stuff appeared upon a convergent track to the left. Besides the customary muleteers there were, by way of an escort, a couple of tattered Turkish soldiers. All these men watched the headlong approach of Benham's party with apprehensive inquiry. Giorgio shouted some sort of information that made the soldiers brighten up and stare up the hill, and set the muleteers whacking and shouting at their convoy. It struck Amanda that Giorgio must be telling lies about a Bulgarian band. In another moment Benham and Amanda found themselves swimming in a torrent of mules. Presently they overtook a small flock of fortunately nimble sheep, and picked up several dogs, dogs that happily disregarded Benham in the general confusion. They also comprehended a small springless cart, two old women with bundles and an elderly Greek priest, before their dusty, barking, shouting cavalcade reached the outskirts of Monastir. The two soldiers had halted behind to cover the retreat.

Benham's ghastly face was now bedewed with sweat and he swayed in his saddle as he rode. " This is *not* civilisation, Amanda," he said, " this is *not* civilisation."

And then suddenly with extraordinary pathos : "Oh! I want to go to *bed*! I want to go to *bed*! A bed with sheets. . . ."

To ride into Monastir is to ride into a maze. The streets go nowhere in particular. At least that was the effect on Amanda and Benham. It was as if Monastir too had a temperature and was slightly delirious. But at last they found an hotel—quite a civilised hotel. . . .

The doctor in Monastir was an Armenian with an ambition that outran his capacity to speak English. He had evidently studied the language chiefly from books. He thought *these* was pronounced " theser " and *those* was pronounced " thoser," and that every English sentence should be taken at a rush. He diagnosed Benham's complaint in various languages and failed to make his meaning clear to Amanda. One combination of words he clung to obstinately, having clearly the utmost faith in its expressiveness. To Amanda it sounded like, " May Ah ! Slays," and it seemed to her that he sought to intimate a probable fatal termination of Benham's fever. But it was clear that the doctor was not satisfied that she understood. He came again with a queer little worn book, a parallel vocabulary of half-a-dozen European languages.

He turned over the pages and pointed to a word. " May ! Ah ! Slays ! " he repeated, reproachfully, almost bitterly.

" Oh, *measles !* " cried Amanda. . . .

So the spirited honeymoon passed its zenith.

§ 11

The Benhams went as soon as possible down to Smyrna and thence by way of Uskub tortuously back to Italy. They recuperated at the best hotel of Locarno in golden November weather, and just before Christmas they turned their faces back to England.

Benham's plans were comprehensive but entirely vague ; Amanda had not so much plans as intentions. . . .

CHAPTER FIVE

THE ASSIZE OF JEALOUSY

§ 1

IT was very manifest from the disorder of papers amidst which White spent so many evenings of interested perplexity before his novel began to be written that Benham had never made any systematic attempt at editing or revising his accumulation at all. There were not only overlapping documents, in which he had returned again to old ideas and re-stated them in the light of fresh facts and an apparent unconsciousness of his earlier effort, but there were mutually destructive papers ; new views quite ousting the old had been tossed in upon the old, and the very definition of the second limitation, as it had first presented itself to the writer, had been abandoned. To begin with, this second division had been labelled " Sex," in places the heading remained ; no effective substitute had been chosen for some time, but there was a closely-written memorandum, very much erased and written over and amended, which showed Benham's early dissatisfaction with that crude rendering of what he had in mind. This memorandum was tacked to an interrupted fragment of autobiography, a manuscript soliloquy in which Benham had been discussing his married life.

" It was not until I had been married for the better part of a year, and had spent more than six months in London, that I faced the plain issue between the aims I had set before myself and the claims and immediate necessities of my personal life. For all that time I struggled not so much to reconcile them as to serve them simultaneously. . . ."

At that the autobiography stopped short, and the intercalary note began.

This intercalary note runs as follows :—

" I suppose a mind of my sort cannot help but tend towards simplification, towards making all life turn upon some one dominant idea, complex perhaps in its reality but reducible at last to one consistent simple statement, a dominant idea which is essential as nothing else is essential, which makes and sustains and justifies. This is perhaps the innate disposition of the human mind, at least of the European mind—for I have some doubts about the Chinese. Theology drives obstinately towards an ultimate unity in God, science towards an ultimate unity in law, towards a fundamental element and a universal material truth from which all material truths evolve, and in matters of conduct there is the same tendency to refer to a universal moral law. Now this may be a simplification due to the need of the human mind to comprehend, and its inability to do so until the load is lightened by neglecting factors. William James has suggested that on account of this, theology may be obstinately working away from the truth, that the truth may be that there are several or many incompatible and incommensurable gods ; science, in the same search for unity, may follow divergent methods of inquiry into ultimately uninterchangeable generalisations ; and there may be not only not one universal moral law, but no effective reconciliation of the various rights and duties of a single individual. At any rate I find myself doubtful to this day about my own personal systems of right and wrong. I can never get all my life into one focus. It is exactly like examining a rather thick section with a microscope of small penetration ; sometimes one level is clear and the rest foggy and monstrous, and sometimes another.

" Now the ruling *me*, I do not doubt, is the man who has set his face to this research after aristocracy, and from the standpoint of this research it is my duty to subordinate all other considerations to this work of clearing up the conception of rule and nobility in human affairs. This is my aristocratic self. What I did not grasp for a long time, and which now grows clearer and clearer to me, is firstly that this aristocratic self is not the whole of me, it has absolutely nothing to do with a pain in my ear or in my heart, with a scar on my hand or my memory ; and secondly that it is not altogether mine. Whatever knowledge I have of the quality of science, whatever will I have towards right, is of it ; but if from without, from the reasoning or demonstration or reproof of some one else, there comes to me clear knowledge, clarified will, that also is as it were a part of my aristocratic self coming home to me from the outside. How often have I not found my own mind in Prothero after I have failed to find it in myself ? It is, to be paradoxical, my impersonal personality, this Being that I have in common with all scientific-spirited and aristocratic-spirited men. This it is that I am trying to get clear from the great limitations of humanity. When I assert a truth for the sake of truth to my own discomfort or injury, there again is this incompatibility of the aristocratic self and the accepted, confused, conglomerate self of the unanalysed man. The two have a separate system of obligations. One's affections, compounded as they are in the strangest way of physical reactions and emotional associations, one's implicit pledges to particular people, one's involuntary reactions, one's pride and jealousy, all that one might call the dramatic side of one's life, may be in conflict with the definitely seen rightnesses of one's higher use. . . ."

The writing changed at this point.

" All this seems to me at once as old as the hills and too new to be true. This is like the conflict of the Superior Man of Confucius to control himself, it is like the Christian battle of the spirit with the flesh, it savours of that eternal wrangle between the general and the particular which is metaphysics ; it was for this aristocratic self, for righteousness' sake, that men have hungered and thirsted, and on this point men have left father and mother and child and wife and followed after salvation. This world-wide, ever-returning antagonism has filled the world in every age with hermits and lamas, recluses and teachers, devoted and segregated lives. It is a perpetual effort to get above the simplicity of barbarism. Whenever men have emerged from the primitive barbarism of the farm and the tribe, then straightway there has emerged this conception of a specialised life a little lifted off the earth ; often, for the sake of freedom, celibate, usually disciplined, sometimes directed, having a generalised aim beyond personal successes and bodily desires. So it is that the philosopher, the scientifically concentrated man, has appeared, often, I admit, quite ridiculously at first, setting out upon the long journey that will end only when the philosopher is king. . . .

" At first I called my Second Limitation, Sex. But from the outset I meant more than mere sexual desire, lust and lustful imaginings, more than personal reactions to beauty and spirited living, more even than what is called love. On the one hand I had in mind many appetites that are not sexual yet turn to bodily pleasure, and on the other there are elements of pride arising out of sex and passing into other regions, all the elements of rivalry, for example, that have strained my first definition to the utmost. And I see now that this Second Limitation as I first imagined it spreads out without any definite boundary, to include one's rivalries with old schoolfellows, for example, one's generosities to beggars and dependents, one's desire to

avenge an injured friend, one's point of honour, one's regard
for the good opinion of an aunt, and one's concern for the health
of a pet cat. All these things may enrich, but they may also
impede and limit the aristocratic scheme. I thought for a time
I would call this ill-defined and miscellaneous wilderness of
limitation the Personal Life. But at last I have decided to
divide this vast territory of difficulties into two sub-divisions
and make one of these Indulgence, meaning thereby pleasurable
indulgence of sense or feeling, and the other a great mass of
self-regarding motives that will go with a little stretching under
the heading of Jealousy. I admit motives are continually
playing across the boundary of these two divisions, I should
find it difficult to argue a case for my classification, but in
practice these two groupings have a quite definite meaning
for me. There is pride in the latter group of impulses and not
in the former ; the former are always a little apologetic. Fear,
Indulgence, Jealousy, these are the First Three Limitations
of the soul of man. And the greatest of these is Jealousy because
it can use pride. Over them the Life Aristocratic, as I conceive
it, marches to its end. It saves itself for the truth rather than
sacrifices itself romantically for a friend. It justifies vivisection
if thereby knowledge is won for ever. It upholds that Brutus
who killed his sons. It forbids devotion to women, courts of
love, and all such decay of the chivalrous idea. And it resigns—
so many things that no common Man of Spirit will resign. Its
intention transcends these things. Over all the world it would
maintain justice, order, a noble peace, and it would do this
without indignation, without resentment, without mawkish
tenderness or individualised enthusiasm or any queen of
beauty. It is of a cold austere quality, commanding sometimes
admiration but having small hold upon the affections of men.
So that it is among its foremost distinctions that its heart is
steeled. . . ."

There this odd fragment ended and White was left to resume
the interrupted autobiography.

§ 2

What moods, what passions, what nights of despair and
gathering storms of anger, what sudden cruelties and amazing
tendernesses are buried and hidden and implied in every love
story ! What a waste is there of exquisite things ! So each
spring sees a million glorious beginnings, a sunlit heaven in
every opening leaf, warm perfection in every stirring egg, hope
and fear and beauty beyond computation in every forest tree ;
and in the autumn before the snows come they have all gone—
of all that incalculable abundance of life, of all that hope and
adventure, excitement and deliciousness there is scarcely more
to be found than a soiled twig, a dirty seed, a dead leaf, black
mould or a rotting feather. . . .

White held the ten or twelve pencilled pages that told how

Benham and Amanda drifted into antagonism and estrangement, and as he held it he thought of the laughter and delight
they must have had together, the exquisite excitement of her
eye, the racing colour of her cheek, the gleams of light upon her
skin, the flashes of wit between them, the sense of discovery, the
high rare paths they had followed, the pools in which they had
swum together. And now it was all gone into nothingness,
there was nothing left of it, nothing at all, but just those sheets
of statement, and it may be, stored away in one single mind,
like things forgotten in an attic, a few neglected faded
memories. . . .

And even those few sheets of statement were more than most
love leaves behind it. For a time White would not read them.
They lay neglected on his knee as he sat back in Benham's most
comfortable chair and enjoyed an entirely beautiful melancholy.

White too had seen and mourned the spring.

Indeed, poor dear! he had seen and mourned several
springs. . . .

With a sigh he took up the manuscript and read Benham's
desiccated story of intellectual estrangement, and how in the
end he had decided to leave his wife and go out alone upon that
journey of inquiry he had been planning when first he met her.

§ 3

Amanda had come back to England in a state of extravagantly vigorous womanhood. Benham's illness, though it
lasted only two or three weeks, gave her a sense of power and
leadership for which she had been struggling instinctively ever
since they came together. For a time at Locarno he was lax-
minded and indolent, and in that time she formed her bright
and limited plans for London. Benham had no plans as yet,
but only a sense of divergence, as though he was being pulled
in opposite directions by two irresistible forces. To her it was
plain that he needed occupation, some distinguished occupation,
and she could imagine nothing better for him than a political
career. She perceived he had personality, that he stood out
among men so that his very silences were effective. She loved
him immensely, and she had tremendous ambitions for him
and through him.

And also London, the very thought of London filled her
with appetite. Her soul thirsted for London. It was like some
enormous juicy fruit waiting for her pretty white teeth, a
place almost large enough to give her avidity the sense of
enough. She felt it waiting for her, household servants, a
carriage, shops and the jolly delight of buying and possessing
things, the opera, first-nights, picture exhibitions, great dinner-
parties, brilliant lunch parties, crowds seen from a point of
vantage, the carriage in a long string of fine carriages with the
lamp-lit multitude peering, Amanda in a thousand bright
settings, in a thousand various dresses. She had had love ;

it had been glorious, it was still glorious, but her love-making became now at times almost perfunctory in the contemplation of these approaching delights and splendours and excitements.

She knew, indeed, that ideas were at work in Benham's head ; but she was a realist. She did not see why ideas should stand in the way of a career. Ideas are a brightness, the good looks of the mind. One talks ideas, but *the thing that is, is the thing that is.* And though she believed that Benham had a certain strength of character of his own, she had that sort of confidence in his love for her and in the power of her endearments that has in it the assurance of a faint contempt. She had mingled pride and sense in the glorious realisation of the power over him that her wit and beauty gave her. She had held him faint with her divinity, intoxicated with the pride of her complete possession, and she did not dream that the moment when he should see clearly that she would deliberately use these ultimate delights to rule and influence him, would be the end of their splendour and her power. Her nature, which was just a nest of vigorous appetites, was incapable of suspecting his gathering disillusionment until it burst upon her.

Now with her attention set upon London ahead he could observe her. In the beginning he had never seemed to be observing her at all, they dazzled one another ; it seemed extraordinary now to him to note how much he had been able to disregard. There were countless times still when he would have dropped his observation and resumed that mutual exaltation very gladly, but always now other things possessed her mind. . . .

There was still an immense pleasure for him in her vigour ; there was something delightful in her pounce, even when she was pouncing on things superficial, vulgar or destructive. She made him understand and share the excitement of a big night at the opera, the glitter and prettiness of a smart restaurant, the clustering little acute adventures of a great reception of gay people, just as she had already made him understand and sympathise with dogs. She picked up the art world where he had laid it down, and she forced him to feel dense and slow before he rebelled against her multitudinous enthusiasms and admirations. South Harting had had its little group of artistic people ; it is not one of your sleepy villages, and she slipped back at once into the movement. Those were the great days of John, the days before the Post-Impressionist outbreak. John, Orpen, Tonks, she bought them with vigour. Artistic circles began to revolve about her. Very rapidly she was in possession. . . . And among other desirable things she had, it seemed, pounced upon and captured Lady Marayne.

At any rate, it was clear that that awful hostile silence and aloofness were to end. Benham never quite mastered how it was done. But Amanda had gone in one morning to Desborough Street, very sweetly and chastely dressed, had abased herself and announced a possible (though sub-sequently disproved) grandchild. And she had appreciated the little lady so highly and openly, she had so instantly caught and reproduced her tone, that her success, though only temporary in its completeness, was immediate. In the afternoon Benham was amazed by the apparition of his mother amidst the scattered unsettled furnishings of the new home Amanda had chosen in Lancaster Gate. He was in the hall, the door stood open awaiting packing-cases from a van without. In the open doorway she shone, looking the smallest of dainty things. There was no effect of her coming but only of her having arrived there, as a little blue butterfly will suddenly alight on a flower.

" Well, Poff ! " said Lady Marayne, ignoring abysses, " what are you up to now, Poff ? Come and embrace me. . . .

" No, not so," she said, " stiffest of sons. . . ."

She laid hold of his ears in the old fashion and kissed one eye.

" Congratulations, dear little Poff. Oh ! congratulations ! In heaps. I'm so *glad*."

Now what was tl t for ?

And then Amanda came out upon the landing upstairs, saw the encounter with an involuntary cry of joy, and came downstairs with arms wide open. It was the first intimation he had of their previous meeting. He was for some minutes a stunned, entirely inadequate Benham. . . .

§ 4

At first Amanda knew nobody in London, except a few people in the Hampstead Garden suburb that she had not the slightest wish to know, and then very quickly she seemed to know quite a lot of people. The artistic circle brought in people, Lady Marayne brought in people ; they spread. It was manifest the Benhams were a very bright young couple ; he would certainly do something considerable presently, and she was bright and daring, jolly to look at and excellent fun, and, when you came to talk to her, astonishingly well informed. They passed from one hostess's hand to another : they reciprocated. The Clynes people and the Rushtones took her up ; Mr. Evesham was amused by her, Lady Beach Mandarin proclaimed her charm like a trumpet, the Young Liberal people made jealous advances, Lord Moggeridge found she listened well, she lit one of the brightest week-end parties Lady Marayne had ever gathered at Chexington. And her descriptions of recent danger and adventure in Albania not only entertained her hearers, but gave her just that flavour of personal courage which completes the fas-cination of a young woman. People in the gaps of a halting dinner-table conversation would ask : " Have you met Mrs. Benham ? "

Meanwhile Benham appeared to be talking. A smiling and successful young woman, who a year ago had been nothing more than a leggy girl with a good lot of miscellaneous reading in her head, and vaguely engaged, or at least friendly to the pitch of engagement, to Mr. Rathbone-Sanders, may be forgiven if in the full tide of her success she does not altogether grasp the intention of her husband's discourse. It seemed to her that he was obsessed by a responsibility for civilisation and the idea that he was aristocratic. (Secretly she was inclined to doubt whether he was justified in calling himself aristocratic; at the best his mother was county-stuff; but still if he did there was no great harm in it nowadays.) Clearly his line was Tory-Democracy, social reform through the House of Lords and friendly intimacy with the more spirited young peers. And it was only very slowly and reluctantly that she was forced to abandon this satisfactory solution of his problem. She reproduced all the equipment and comforts of his Finacue Street study in their new home, she declared constantly that she would rather forgo any old social thing than interfere with his work, she never made him go anywhere with her without first asking if his work permitted it. To relieve him of the burden of such social attentions she even made a fag or so. The making of fags out of manifestly stricken men, the keeping of tamed and hopeless admirers, seemed to her to be the most natural and reasonable of feminine privileges. They did their useful little services until it pleased the Lord Cheetah to come to his own. That was how she put it. . . .

But at last he was talking to her in tones that could no longer be ignored. He was manifestly losing his temper with her. There was a novel austerity in his voice and a peculiar whiteness about his face on certain occasions that lingered in her memory.

He was indeed making elaborate explanations. He said that what he wanted to do was to understand " the collective life of the world," and that this was not to be done in a West-end study. He had an extraordinary contempt, it seemed, for both sides in the drama of British politics. He had extravagant ideas of beginning in some much more fundamental way. He wanted to understand this " collective life of the world," because ultimately he wanted to help control it. (Was there ever such nonsense?) The practical side of this was serious enough, however; he was back at his old idea of going round the earth. Later on that might be rather a jolly thing to do, but not until they had struck root a little more surely in London.

And then with amazement, with incredulity, with indignation, she began to realise that he was proposing to go off by himself upon this vague extravagant research, that all this work she had been doing to make a social place for him in London was as nothing to him, that he was thinking of himself as separable from her. . . .

"But Cheetah! How can you leave your spotless leopard? You would howl in the lonely jungle!"

"Possibly I shall. But I am going."

"Then I shall come."

"No." He considered her reasons. "You see you are not interested.

"But I am."

"Not as I am. You would turn it all into a jolly holiday. You don't want to see things as I want to do. You want romance. All the world is a show for you. As a show I can't endure it. I want to lay hands on it."

"But, Cheetah!" she said, "this is separation."

"You will have your life here. And I shall come back."

"But, Cheetah! How can we be separated?"

"We are separated," he said.

Her eyes became round with astonishment. Then her face puckered.

"Cheetah!" she cried in a voice of soft distress, "I love you. What do you mean?"

And she staggered forward, tear-blinded, and felt for his neck and shoulders so that she might weep in his arms. . . .

§ 5

"Don't say we are separated," she whispered, putting her still wet face close to his.

"No. We're mates," he answered softly, with his arm about her.

"How could we ever keep away from each uvver?" she whispered.

He was silent.

"How *could* we?"

He answered aloud. "Amanda," he said, "I mean to go round the world."

She disentangled herself from his arm and sat up beside him.

"What is to become of me," she asked suddenly in a voice of despair, "while you go round the world? If you desert me in London," she said, "if you shame me by deserting me in London—— If you leave me, I will never forgive you, Cheetah! Never." Then in an almost breathless voice, and as if she spoke to herself, "Never in all my days."

§ 6

It was after that that Amanda began to talk about children. There was nothing involuntary about Amanda. "Soon," she said, "we must begin to think of children. Not just now, but a little later. It's good to travel and have our fun, but life is unreal until there are children in the background. No woman is really content until she is a mother. . . ."

And for nearly a fortnight nothing more was said about that solitary journey round the world.

But children were not the only new topic in Amanda's talk. She set herself with an ingenious subtlety to remind her husband that there were other men in the world. The convenient fags, sometimes a little embarrassed, found their inobtrusive services being brought into the light before Benham's eyes. Most of them were much older men than himself, elderly philanderers of whom it seemed to him no sane man need be jealous, men often of forty or more, but one was a contemporary, Sir Philip Easton, a man with a touch of Spanish blood and a suggestion of Spanish fire, who quite manifestly was very much in love with Amanda, and of whom she spoke with a slight perceptible difference of manner that made Benham faintly uneasy. He was ashamed of the feeling. Easton it seemed was a man of a peculiarly fine honour, so that Amanda could trust herself with him to an extent that would have been inadvisable with men of a commoner substance, and he had a gift of understanding and sympathy that was almost feminine ; he could cheer one up when one was lonely and despondent. For Amanda was so methodical in the arrangement of her time that even in the full rush of a London season she could find an hour now and then for being lonely and despondent. And he was a liberal and understanding purchaser of the ascendant painters ; he understood that side of Amanda's interests, a side upon which Benham was notably deficient. . . .

" Amanda seems to like that dark boy, Poff ; what is his name ?—Sir Philip Easton ? " said Lady Marayne.

Benham looked at her with a slightly hostile intelligence, and said nothing.

" When a man takes a wife, he has to keep her," said Lady Marayne.

" No," said Benham after consideration. " I don't intend to be a wife-herd."

" What ? "

" Wife-herd—same as goat-herd."

" Coarse, you are sometimes, Poff—nowadays."

" It's exactly what I mean. I can understand the kind of curator's interest an Oriental finds in shepherding a large establishment, but to spend my days looking after one person who ought to be able to look after herself——"

" She's very young."

" She's quite grown up. Anyhow I'm not a moral nurse-maid."

" If you leave her about and go abroad——"

" Has she been talking to you, mother ? "

" The thing shows."

" But about my going abroad ? "

" She said something, my little Poff."

Lady Marayne suddenly perceived that beneath Benham's indifference was something strung very tight, as though he had been thinking inordinately. He weighed his words before he spoke again. " If Amanda chooses to threaten me with a sort of conditional infidelity, I don't see that it ought to change the plans I have made for my life. . . ."

§ 7

" No aristocrat has any right to be jealous," Benham wrote. " If he chances to be mated with a woman who does not see his vision or naturally go his way, he has no right to expect her, much less to compel her, to go his way. What is the use of dragging an unwilling companion through morasses of uncongenial thought to unsought ends ? What is the use of dragging even a willing pretender, who has no inherent will to seek and live the aristocratic life ?

" But that does not excuse him from obedience to his own call. . . ."

He wrote that very early in his examination of the Third Limitation. Already he had thought out and judged Amanda. The very charm of her, the sweetness, the nearness and magic of her, was making him more grimly resolute to break away. All the elaborate process of thinking her over had gone on behind the mask of his silences while she had been preoccupied with her housing and establishment in London ; it was with a sense of extraordinary injustice, of having had a march stolen upon her, of being unfairly trapped, that Amanda found herself faced by foregone conclusions. He was ready now even with the details of his project. She should go on with her life in London exactly as she had planned it. He would take fifteen hundred a year for himself, and all the rest she might spend without check or stint as it pleased her. He was going round the world for one or two years. It was even possible he would not go alone. There was a man at Cambridge he might persuade to come with him, a don called Prothero who was peculiarly useful in helping him to hammer out his ideas. . . .

To her it became commandingly necessary that none of these things should happen.

She tried to play upon his jealousy, but her quick instinct speedily told her that this only hardened his heart. She perceived that she must make a softer appeal. Now of a set intention she began to revive and imitate the spontaneous passion of the honeymoon ; she perceived for the first time clearly how wise and righteous a thing it is for a woman to bear a child. " He cannot go if I am going to have a child," she told herself. But that would mean illness, and for illness in herself or others Amanda had the intense disgust natural to her youth. Yet even illness would be better than this

intolerable publication of her husband's ability to leave her
side. . . .

She had a wonderful facility of enthusiasm, and she set
herself forthwith to cultivate a philoprogenitive ambition,
to communicate it to him. Her dread of illness disappeared ;
her desire for offspring grew.

" Yes," he said, " I want to have children, but I must go
round the world none the less."

She argued with all the concentrated subtlety of her fine
keen mind. She argued with persistence and repetition. And
then suddenly, so that she was astonished at herself, there
came a moment when she ceased to argue.

She stood in the dusk in a window that looked out upon
the park, and she was now so intent upon her purpose as
to be still and self-forgetful ; she was dressed in a dinner-
dress of white and pale green, that set off her slim erect body
and the strong clear lines of her neck and shoulders very
beautifully ; some greenish stones caught a light from without
and flashed soft whispering gleams from amidst the misty
darkness of her hair. She was going to Lady Marayne and
the opera, and he was bound for a dinner at the House with
some young Liberals at which he was to meet two representative Indians with a grievance from Bengal. Husband and
wife had but a few moments together. She asked about his
company, and he told her.

" They will tell you about India."

" Yes."

She stood for a moment looking out across the lights and
the dark green trees, and then she turned to him.

" Why cannot I come with you ? " she asked with sudden
passion. " Why cannot I see the things you want to see ? "

" I tell you you are not interested. You would only be
interested through me. That would not help me. I should
just be dealing out my premature ideas to you. If you cared
as I care, if you wanted to know as I want to know, it would
be different. But you don't. It isn't your fault that you
don't. It happens so. And there is no good in forced interest,
in prescribed discovery."

" Cheetah," she asked, " what is it that you want to know
—that I don't care for ? "

" I want to know about the world. I want to rule the
world."

" So do I."

" No, you want to have the world."

" Isn't it the same ? "

" No. You're a greedier thing than I am, you Black Leopard
you—standing there in the dusk. You're a stronger thing.
Don't you know you're stronger ? When I am with you,
you carry your point, because you are more concentrated,
more definite, less scrupulous. When you run beside me you

push me out of my path. . . . You've made me afraid of you.
. . . And so I won't go with you, Leopard. I go alone. It
isn't because I don't love you. I love you too well. It isn't
because you aren't beautiful and wonderful. . ."

" But, Cheetah! nevertheless you care more for this that
you want than you care for me."

Benham thought of it. " I suppose I do," he said.

" What is it that you want? Still I don't understand."

Her voice had the break of one who would keep reasonable
in spite of pain.

" I ought to tell you."

" Yes, you ought to tell me."

" I wonder if I can tell you," he said very thoughtfully,
and rested his hands on his hips. " I shall seem ridiculous
to you."

" You ought to tell me."

" I think what I want is to be king of the world."

She stood quite still staring at him.

" I do not know how I can tell you of it. Amanda, do you
remember those bodies—you saw those bodies—those mutilated
men ? "

" I saw them," said Amanda.

" Well. Is it nothing to you that those things happen ? "

" They must happen."

" No. They happen because there are no kings but pitiful
kings. They happen because the kings love their Amandas
and do not care."

" But what can *you* do, Cheetah ? "

" Very little. But I can give my life and all my strength.
I can give all I can give."

" But how ? How can you help it—help things like that
massacre ? "

" I can do my utmost to find out what is wrong with my
world and rule it and set it right."

" *You!* Alone."

" Other men do as much. Every one who does so, helps
others to do so. You see—— . . . In this world one may
wake in the night and one may resolve to be a king, and
directly one has resolved one is a king. Does that sound
foolishness to you ? Anyhow, it's fair that I should tell you
though you count me a fool. This—this kingship—this dream
of the night—is my life. It is the very core of me. Much
more than you are. More than anything else can be. I mean
to be a king in this earth. *King.* I'm not mad. . . . I see
the world staggering from misery to misery and there is little
wisdom, less rule, folly, prejudice, limitation, the good things
come by chance and the evil things recover and slay them,
and it is my world and I am responsible. Every man to
whom this light has come is responsible. As soon as this
light comes to you, as soon as your kingship is plain to you,

there is no more rest, no peace, no delight, except in work, in service, in utmost effort. As far as I can do it I will rule my world. I cannot abide in this smug city, I cannot endure its self-complacency, its routine, its gloss of success, its rottenness. . . . I shall do little, perhaps I shall do nothing, but what I can understand and what I can do I will do. Think of that wild beautiful country we saw, and the mean misery, the filth and the warring cruelty of the life that lives there, tragedy, tragedy without dignity ; and think, too, of the limitless ugliness here, and of Russia slipping from disorder to massacre, and China, that sea of human beings, sliding steadily to disaster. Do you think these are only things in the newspapers ? To me at any rate they are not things in newspapers ; they are pain and failure, they are torment, they are blood and dust and misery. They haunt me day and night. Even if it is utterly absurd I will still do my utmost. It *is* absurd. I'm a madman, and you and my mother are sensible people. . . . And I will go my way. . . . I don't care for the absurdity. I don't care a rap."

He stopped abruptly.

" There you have it, Amanda. It's rant, perhaps. Sometimes I feel it's rant. And yet it's the breath of life to me. . . . There you are. . . . At last I've been able to break silence and tell you. . . ."

He stopped with something like a sob and stood regarding the dusky mystery of her face. She stood quite still, she was just a beautiful outline in the twilight, her face was an indistinctness under the black shadow of her hair, with eyes that were two patches of darkness.

He looked at his watch, lifting it close to his face to see the time. His voice changed. " Well—if you provoke a man enough, you see he makes speeches. Let it be a lesson to you, Amanda. Here we are talking instead of going to our dinners. The car has been waiting ten minutes."

Amanda, so still, was the most disconcerting of all Amandas. . . .

A strange exaltation seized upon her very suddenly. In an instant she had ceased to plot against him. A vast wave of emotion swept her forward to a resolution that astonished her.

" Cheetah ! " she said, and the very quality of her voice had changed, " give me one thing. Stay until June with me."

" Why ? " he asked.

Her answer came in a voice so low that it was almost a whisper.

" Because—now—no, I don't want to keep you any more —I am not trying to hold you any more. . . . I want . . ."

She came forward to him and looked up closely at his face.

" Cheetah," she whispered almost inaudibly, " Cheetah— I didn't understand. But now—— I want to bear your child."

He was astonished. " Old Leopard ! " he said.

" No," she answered, putting her hands upon his shoulders and drawing very close to him, " Queen—if I can be—to your King."

" You want to bear me a child ! " he whispered, profoundly moved.

§ 8

The Hindu agitators at the cavernous dinner under the House of Commons came to the conclusion that Benham was a dreamer. And over against Amanda at her dinner-party sat Sir Sidney Umber, one of those men who know that their judgments are quoted.

" Who is the beautiful young woman who is seeing visions ? " he asked of his neighbour in confidential undertones. . . .

He tittered. " I think, you know, she ought to seem just *slightly* aware that the man to her left is talking to her. . . ."

§ 9

A few days later Benham went down to Cambridge, where Prothero was now a Fellow of Trinity and Brissenden Trust Lecturer. . . .

All through Benham's writing there was manifest a persuasion that in some way Prothero was necessary to his mind. It was as if he looked to Prothero to keep him real. He suspected, even while he obeyed, that upward flourish which was his own essential characteristic. He had a peculiar feeling that somehow that upward bias would betray him ; that from exaltation he might presently float off, into the higher, the better, and so to complete unreality. He fled from priggishness and the terror of such sublimity alike to Prothero. Moreover, in relation to so many things Prothero in a peculiar distinctive manner *saw*. He had less self-control than Benham, less integrity of purpose, less concentration, and things that were before his eyes were by the very virtue of these defects invariably visible to him. Things were able to insist upon themselves with him. Benham on the other hand, when facts contradicted his purpose too stoutly, had a way of becoming blind to them. He repudiated inconvenient facts. He mastered and made his world ; Prothero accepted and recorded his. Benham was a will towards the universe where Prothero was a perception and Amanda a confusing responsive activity. And it was because of his realisation of this profound difference between them that he was possessed by the idea of taking Prothero with him about the world, as a detachable kind of vision—rather like that eye the Graiae used to hand one another. . . .

After the busy sunlit streets of Maytime Cambridge Prothero's rooms in Trinity, their windows full of Gothic perspectives and light-soaked blue sky, seemed cool and quiet.

A flavour of scholarship pervaded them—a little blended
with the flavour of innumerable breakfasts nearly but not
completely forgotten. Prothero's door had been locked against
the world, and he had appeared after a slight delay looking
a little puffy and only apprehending who his visitor was after
a resentful stare for the better part of a second. He might
have been asleep, he might have been doing anything but
the examination papers he appeared to be doing. The two
men exchanged personal details ; they had not met since
some months before Benham's marriage, and the visitor's
eye went meanwhile from his host to the room and back to
his host's face as though they were all aspects of the thing
he was after, the Prothero humour, the earthly touch, the
distinctive Prothero flavour. Then his eye was caught by a
large red, incongruous, meretricious looking volume upon
the couch that had an air of having been flung aside, *Venus
in Gem and Marble*, its cover proclaimed. . . .

His host followed that glance and blushed. " They send
me all sorts of inappropriate stuff to review," he remarked.

And then he was denouncing celibacy.

The transition wasn't very clear to Benham. His mind
had been pre-occupied by the problem of how to open his
own large project. Meanwhile Prothero got, as it were, the
conversational bit between his teeth and bolted. He began
to say the most shocking things right away, so that Benham's
attention was caught in spite of himself.

" Inflammatory classics."

" What's that ? "

" Celibacy, my dear Benham, is maddening me," said
Prothero. " I can't stand it any longer."

It seemed to Benham that somewhere, very far away, in
another world, such a statement might have been credible.
Even in his own life—it was now indeed a remote, forgotten
stage—there had been something distantly akin. . . .

" You're going to marry ? "

" I must."

" Who's the lady, Billy ? "

" I don't know. Venus."

His little red-brown eyes met his friend's defiantly.

" So far as I know, it is Venus Anadyomene." A flash of
laughter passed across his face and left it still angrier, still
more indecorously defiant. " I like her best, anyhow. I do
indeed. But, Lord ! I feel that almost any of them——"

" Tut, tut ! " said Benham.

Prothero flushed deeply but stuck to his discourse.

" Wasn't it always your principle, Benham, to look facts
in the face ? I am not pronouncing an immoral principle.
Your manner suggests I am. I am telling you exactly how
I feel. That is how I feel. I want—Venus. I don't want
her to talk to or anything of that sort. . . . I have been

studying that book, yes, that large, vulgar, red book, all the morning, instead of doing any work. Would you like to see it ? . . . *No !* . . .

" This spring, Benham, I tell you, is driving me mad. It is a peculiarly erotic spring. I cannot sleep, I cannot fix my mind, I cannot attend to ordinary conversation. These feelings, I understand, are by no means peculiar to myself. . . . No, don't interrupt me, Benham ; let me talk now that the spirit of speech is upon me. When you came in you said, ' How are you ? ' I am telling you how I am. You brought it on yourself. Well—I am—inflamed. I have no strong moral or religious convictions to assist me either to endure or deny this—this urgency. And so why should I deny it ? It's one of our chief problems here. The majority of my fellow dons who look at me with secretive faces in hall and court and combination-room are in just the same case as myself. The fever in oneself detects the fever in others. I know their hidden thoughts. Their fishy eyes defy me to challenge their hidden thoughts. Each covers his miserable secret under the cloak of a wholesome manly indifference. A tattered cloak. . . . Each tries to hide his abandonment to this horrible vice of continence——"

" Billy, what's the matter with you ? "

Prothero grimaced impatience. " Shall I *never* teach you not to be a humbug, Benham ? " he screamed, and in screaming became calmer. " Nature taunts me, maddens me. My life is becoming a hell of shame. ' Get out from all these books,' says Nature, ' and serve the Flesh.' The Flesh, Benham. Yes—I insist—the Flesh. Do I look like a pure spirit ? Is any man a pure spirit ? And here am I at Cambridge like a lark in a cage, with too much port and no Aspasia. Not that I should have liked Aspasia."

" Mutual, perhaps, Billy."

" Oh ! you can sneer ! "

" Well, clearly—Saint Paul is my authority—it's marriage, Billy."

Prothero had walked to the window. He turned round.

" I *can't* marry," he said. " The trouble has gone too far. I've lost my nerve in the presence of women. I don't like them any more. They come at one—done up in a lot of ridiculous clothes, and chattering about all sorts of things that don't matter. . . ."

He surveyed his friend's thoughtful attitude.

" I'm getting to hate women, Benham. I'm beginning now to understand the bitterness of spinsters against men. I'm beginning to grasp the unkindliness of priests. The perpetual denial. To you, happily married, a woman is just a human being. You can talk to her, like her, you can even admire her calmly ; you've got, you see, no grudge against her. . . ."

He sat down abruptly.

Benham, upon the hearthrug before the empty fireplace, considered him.

"Billy! this is delusion," he said. "What's come over you?"

"I'm telling you," said Prothero.

"No," said Benham.

Prothero awaited some further utterance.

"I'm looking for the cause of it. It's feeding, Billy. It's port and stimulants where there is no scope for action. It's idleness. I begin to see now how much fatter you are, how much coarser."

"Idleness! Look at this pile of examination answers. Look at that filing system like an arsenal of wisdom. Useless wisdom, I admit, but anyhow not idleness."

"There's still bodily idleness. No. That's your trouble. You're stuffy. You've enlarged your liver. You sit in this room of a warm morning after an extravagant breakfast—— And peep and covet."

"Just eggs and bacon!"

"Think of it! Coffee and toast, it ought to be. Come out of it, Billy, and get aired."

"How can one?"

"Easily. Come out of it now. Come for a walk, you Pig!"

"It's an infernally warm morning."

"Walk with me to Grantchester."

"We might go by boat. You could row."

"*Walk.*"

"I ought to do these papers."

"You weren't doing them."

"No. . . ."

"Walk with me to Grantchester. All this affliction of yours is—horrid—and just nothing at all. Come out of it! I want you to come with me to Russia and about the world. I'm going to leave my wife——"

"Leave your wife!"

"Why not? And I came here hoping to find you clear-headed, and instead you are in this disgusting state. I've never met anything in my life so hot and red and shiny and shameless. Come out of it, man! How can one talk to you?"

§ 10

"You pull things down to your own level," said Benham as they went through the heat of Grantchester.

"I pull them down to truth," panted Prothero.

"Truth! As though being full of gross appetites was truth, and discipline and training some sort of falsity!"

"Artificiality. And begetting pride, Benham, begetting a prig's pride."

For a time there was more than the heat of the day between them. . . .

The things that Benham had come down to discuss were thrust into the background by the impassioned materialism of Prothero.

" I'm not talking of Love," he said, remaining persistently outrageous. " I'm talking of physical needs. That first. What is the good of arranging systems of morality and sentiment before you know what is physically possible ? . . ."

" But how can one disentangle physical and moral necessities ? "

" Then why don't we up and find out ? " said Billy.

He had no patience with the secrecy, the ignorance, the emotion that surrounded these questions. We didn't worship our ancestors when it came to building bridges or working metals or curing disease or studying our indigestion, and why should we become breathless or wordless with awe and terror when it came to this fundamental affair. Why here in particular should we give way to Holy Fear and stifled submission to traditional suppressions and the wisdom of the ages ? " What is the wisdom of the ages ? " said Prothero. " Think of the corners where that wisdom was born. . . . Flea-bitten sages in stone-age hovels. . . . Wandering wise man with a rolling eye, a fakir under a tree, a Jewish sheik, an Arab epileptic. . . ."

" Would you sweep away the experience of mankind ? " protested Benham.

The experience of mankind in these matters had always been bitter experience. Most of it was better forgotten. It didn't convince. It had never worked things out. In this matter just as in every other matter that really signified things had still to be worked out. Nothing had been worked out hitherto. The wisdom of the ages was a Cant. People had been too busy quarrelling, fighting, and running away. There wasn't any digested experience of the ages at all. Only the mis-remembered hankey-pankey of the Dead Old Man.

" Is this love-making a physical necessity for most men and women or isn't it ? " Prothero demanded. " There's a simple question enough, and is there anything whatever in your confounded wisdom of the ages to tell me yes or no ? Can an ordinary celibate be as healthy and vigorous as a mated man ? Is a spinster of thirty-eight a healthy human being ? Can she be ? I don't believe so. Then why in thunder do we let her be ? Here am I at a centre of learning and wisdom and I don't believe so ; and there is nothing in all our colleges, libraries, and rooms full of wiseacres here, to settle that plain question for me, plainly and finally. My life is a grubby torment of cravings because it isn't settled. If sexual activity *is* a part of the balance of life, if it *is* a necessity, well let's set about making it accessible and harmless and have done with it. Swedish exercises. That sort of thing. If it isn't, if it can be reduced and done without, then let us set about teaching people *how* to control themselves and reduce and get rid of this vehement passion. But all this muffled mystery, this pompous sneak's way we take with it!"

"But, Billy! How can one settle these things? It's a matter of idiosyncrasy. What is true for one man isn't true for another. There's infinite difference of temperaments."

"Then why haven't we a classification of temperaments and a moral code for each sort? Why am I ruled by the way of life that is convenient for Rigdon the vegetarian and fits Bowler the saint like a glove? It isn't convenient for me. It fits me like a hair-shirt. Of course there are temperaments, but why can't we formulate them and exercise the elementary charity of recognising that one man's health in these matters is another man's death? Some want love and gratification and some don't. There are people who want children and people who don't want to be bothered by children but who are full of vivid desires. There are people whose only happiness is chastity, and women who would rather be courtesans than mothers. Some of us would concentrate upon a single passion or a single idea; others overflow with a miscellaneous—tenderness. Yes—and you smile! Why spit upon and insult a miscellaneous tenderness, Benham? Why grin at it? Why try every one by the standards that suit oneself? We're savages, Benham, shamefaced savages, still. Shamefaced and persecuting.

"I was angry about sex by seventeen," he went on. "Every year I live I grow angrier."

His voice rose to a squeal of indignation as he talked.

"Think," he said, "of the amount of thinking and feeling about sex that is going on in Cambridge this morning. The hundreds out of these thousands full of it. A vast tank of cerebration. And we put none of it together; we work nothing out from that but poor little couplings and casual stories, patchings up of situations, misbehaviours, blunders, disease, trouble, escapes; and the next generation will start, and the next generation after that will start with nothing but your wisdom of the ages, which isn't wisdom at all, which is just awe and funk, taboos and mystery and the secretive cunning of the savage. . . .

"What I really want to do is my work," said Prothero, going off quite unexpectedly again. "That is why all this business, this incessant craving and the shame of it and all makes me so infernally angry. . . ."

§ 11

"There I'm with you," cried Benham, struggling out of the thick torrent of Prothero's prepossessions. "What we want to do is our work."

He clung to his idea. He raised his voice to prevent Prothero getting the word again.

"It's this, that you call Work, that I call—what do I call it?—living the aristocratic life, which takes all the coarse

simplicity out of this business. **If it was only submission.** . . .
You think it is only submission—giving way. . . . It isn't
only submission. We'd manage sex all right, we'd be the happy
swine our senses would make us, if we didn't know all the
time that there was something else to live for, something far
more important. And different. Absolutely different and
contradictory. So different that it cuts right across all these
considerations. It won't fit in. . . . I don't know what this
other thing is ; it's what I want to talk about with you. But
I know that it *is*, in all my bones. . . . *You* know. . . . It
demands control, it demands continence, it insists upon
disregard."

But the ideas of continence and disregard were unpleasant
ideas to Prothero that day.

" Mankind," said Benham, " is overcharged with this sex.
It suffocates us. It gives life only to consume it. We struggle
out of the urgent necessities of a mere animal existence. We
are not so much living as being married and given in marriage.
All life is swamped in the love story. . . ."

" Man is only overcharged because he is unsatisfied," said
Prothero, sticking stoutly to his own view.

§ 12

It was only as they sat at a little table in the orchard at
Grantchester after their lunch that Benham could make head
against Prothero and recover that largeness of outlook which
had so easily touched the imagination of Amanda. And then
he did not so much dispose of Prothero's troubles as soar over
them. It is the last triumph of the human understanding
to sympathise with desires we do not share, and to Benham
who now believed himself to be loved beyond the chances of
life, who was satisfied and tranquil and austerely content, it
was impossible that Prothero's demands should seem anything
more than the grotesque and squalid squealings of the beast
that has to be overridden and rejected altogether. It is a
freakish fact of our composition that these most intense feelings
in life are just those that are most rapidly and completely
forgotten ; hate one may recall for years, but the magic of
love and the flame of desire serve their purpose in our lives
and vanish, leaving no trace, like the snows of Venice. Benham
was still not a year and a half from the meretricious delights of
Mrs. Skelmersdale, and he looked at Prothero as a marble
angel might look at a swine in its sty. . . .

What he had now in mind was an expedition to Russia.
When at last he could sufficiently release Prothero's attention,
he unfolded the project that had been developing steadily in
him since his honeymoon experience.

He had discovered a new reason for travelling. The last
country we can see clearly, he had discovered, is our own
country. It is as hard to see one's own country as it is to see

the back of one's head. It is too much behind us, too much ourselves. But Russia is like England with everything larger, more vivid, cruder ; one felt that directly one walked about St. Petersburg. St. Petersburg upon its Neva was like a savage untamed London on a larger Thames ; they were seagull-haunted tidal cities, like no other capitals in Europe. The shipping and buildings mingled in their effects. Like London it looked over the heads of its own people to a limitless polyglot empire. And Russia was an aristocratic land, with a middle-class that had no pride in itself as a class ; it had a British toughness and incompetence, a British disregard of logic and meticulous care. Russia, like England, was outside Catholic Christendom ; it had a state church and the opposition to that church was not secularism but dissent. One could draw a score of such contrasted parallels. And now it was in a state of intolerable stress, that laid bare the elemental facts of a great social organisation. It was having its South Africa war, its war at the other end of the earth, with a certain defeat instead of a dubious victory. . . .

"There is far more freedom for the personal life in Russia than in England," said Prothero, a little irrelevantly.

Benham went on with his discourse about Russia. . . .

"At the college of Troitzka," said Prothero, " which I understand is a kind of monster Trinity unencumbered by a University, Binns tells me that although there is a profession of celibacy within the walls, the arrangements of the town and more particularly of the various hotels are conceived in a spirit of extreme liberality."

Benham hardly attended at all to these interruptions.

He went on to point out the elemental quality of the Russian situation. He led up to the assertion that to go to Russia, to see Russia, to try to grasp the broad outline of the Russian process, was the manifest duty of every responsible intelligence that was free to do as much. And so he was going, and if Prothero cared to come too——

" Yes," said Prothero, " I should like to go to Russia."

§ 13

But throughout all their travel together that summer Benham was never able to lift Prothero away from his obsession. It was the substance of their talk as the Holland boat stood out past waiting destroyers and winking beacons and the lights of Harwich, into the smoothly undulating darkness of the North Sea ; it rose upon them again as they sat over the cakes and cheese of a Dutch breakfast in the express for Berlin. Prothero filled the Sièges Alleés with his complaints against nature and society, and distracted Benham in his contemplation of Polish agriculture from the windows of the train with turgid sexual liberalism. So that Benham during this period, until Prothero left him and until the tragic enormous spectacle of

Russia in revolution took complete possession of him, was as it were thinking upon two floors. Upon the one he was thinking of the vast problems of a society of a hundred million people staggering on the verge of anarchy, and upon the other he was perplexed by the feverish inattention of Prothero to the tremendous things that were going on all about them. It was only presently when the serenity of his own private life began to be ruffled by disillusionment, that he began to realise the intimate connexion of these two systems of thought. Yet Prothero put it to him plainly enough.

" Inattentive," said Prothero, " of course I am inattentive. What is really the matter with all this—this social mess people are in here, is that nearly everybody is inattentive. These Big Things of yours, nobody is thinking of them really. Everybody is thinking about the Near Things that concern himself."

" The bombs they threw yesterday ? The Cossacks and the whips ? "

" Nudges. Gestures of inattention. If everybody was thinking of the Res Publica would there be any need for bombs ? "

He pursued his advantage. " It's all nonsense to suppose people think of politics because they are in 'em. As well suppose that the passengers on a liner understand the engines, or soldiers a war. Before men can think of to-morrow, they must think of to-day. Before they can think of others, they must be sure about themselves. First of all, food ; the private, the personal economic worry. Am I safe for food ? Then sex, and until one is tranquil and not ashamed, not irritated and dissatisfied, how can one care for other people, or for next year or the Order of the World ? How can one, Benham ? "

He seized the illustration at hand. " Here we are, in Warsaw —not a month after bomb-throwing and Cossack charging. Windows have still to be mended, smashed doors restored. There's bloodstains still on some of the houses. There are hundreds of people in the Citadel and in the Ochrana prison. This morning there were executions. Is it anything more than an eddy in the real life of the place ? Watch the customers in the shops, the crowd in the streets, the men in the cafés who stare at the passing women. They are all swallowed up again in their own business. They just looked up as the Cossacks galloped past ; they just shifted a bit when the bullets spat. . . ."

And when the streets of Moscow were agog with the grotesque amazing adventure of the Potemkin mutineers, Prothero was in the full tide of the private romance that severed him from Benham and sent him back to Cambridge—changed.

Before they reached Moscow, Benham was already becoming accustomed to disregard Prothero. He was looking over him at the vast heaving trouble of Russia, which now was like a sea that tumbles under the hurrying darknesses of an approaching storm. In those days it looked as though it must be an overwhelming storm. He was drinking in the wide and massive Russian effects, the drifting crowds in the entangling streets, the houses with their strange lettering in black and gold, the innumerable barbaric churches, the wildly driven droshkys, the sombre red fortress of the Kremlin, with its bulbous churches clustering up into the sky, the crosses, the innumerable gold crosses, the mad church of St. Basil, carrying the Russian note beyond the pitch of permissible caricature, and in this setting the obscure drama of clustering, staring, sash-wearing peasants, long-haired students, sane-eyed women, a thousand varieties of uniform, a running and galloping to and fro of messengers, a flutter of little papers, whispers, shouts, shots, a drama elusive and portentous, a gathering of forces, an accumulation of tension going on to a perpetual clash and clamour of bells. Benham had brought letters of introduction to a variety of people ; some had vanished, it seemed. They were " away," the porters said, and they continued to be " away,"—it was the formula, he learnt, for arrest—others were evasive, a few showed themselves extraordinarily anxious to inform him about things, to explain themselves and things about them exhaustively. One young student took him to various meetings and showed him in great detail the scene of the recent murder of the Grand Duke Sergius. The buildings opposite the old French cannons were still under repair. " The assassin stood just there. The bomb fell there, look ! right down there towards the gate ; that was where they found his arm. He was torn to fragments. He was scraped up. He was mixed with the horses. . . ."

Every one who talked spoke of the outbreak of revolution as a matter of days or at the utmost weeks. And whatever question Benham chose to ask these talkers were prepared to answer. Except one. " And after the revolution," he asked, " what then ? . . ." Then they waved their hands, and failed to convey meanings by reassuring gestures.

He was absorbed in his effort to understand this universal ominous drift towards a conflict. He was trying to piece together a process, if it was one and the same process, which involved riots in Lodz, fighting at Libau, wild disorder at Odessa, remote colossal battlings in Manchuria, the movements of a disastrous fleet lost somewhere now in the Indian seas, steaming clumsily to its fate, he was trying to rationalise it all in his mind, to comprehend its direction. He was struggling strenuously with the obscurities of the language in which these things were being discussed about him, a most difficult language demanding new sets of visual images because of its strange alphabet. Is it any wonder that for a time he failed to observe that Prothero was involved in some entirely disconnected affair ?

They were staying at the big Cosmopolis Bazaar in the Theatre Square. Thither, through the doors that are opened by distraught-looking men with peacocks' feathers round their caps, came Benham's friends and guides to take him out and show him this and that. At first Prothero always accompanied Benham on these expeditions ; then he began to make excuses. He would stay behind in the hotel. Then when Benham returned Prothero would have disappeared. When the porter was questioned about Prothero his nescience was profound.

One night no Prothero was discoverable at any hour, and Benham, who wanted to discuss a project for going on to Kieff and Odessa, was alarmed.

"Moscow is a late place," said Benham's student friend. "You need not be anxious until after four or five in the morning. It will be quite time—*quite* time to be anxious to-morrow. He may be—close at hand."

When Benham hunted up Prothero in his room next morning he found him sleepy and irritable.

"I don't trouble if *you* are late," said Prothero, sitting up in his bed with a red resentful face and crumpled hair. "I wasn't born yesterday."

"I wanted to talk about leaving Moscow."

"I don't want to leave Moscow."

"But Odessa—Odessa is the centre of interest just now."

"I want to stay in Moscow."

Benham looked baffled.

Prothero stuck up his knees and rested his night-shirted arms upon them. "I don't want to leave Moscow," he said, "and I'm not going to do so."

"But haven't we done——"

Prothero interrupted. "You may. But I haven't. We're not after the same things. Things that interest you, Benham, don't interest me. I've found—different things."

His expression was extraordinarily defiant.

"I want," he went on, "to put our affairs on a different footing. Now you've opened the matter we may as well go into it. You were good enough to bring me here. . . . There was a sort of understanding we were working together. . . . We aren't. . . . The long and short of it is, Benham, I want to pay you for my journey here and go on my own—independently."

His eye and voice achieved a fierceness that Benham found nearly incredible in him.

Something that had got itself overlooked in the press of other matters jerked back into Benham's memory. It popped back so suddenly that for an instant he wanted to laugh. He turned towards the window, picked his way among Prothero's carelessly dropped garments, and stood for a moment staring into the square, with its drifting, assembling and dispersing fleet of trams and its long line of blue-coated *izvoshtchiks*. Then he turned.

"Billy," he said, "didn't I see you the other evening driving towards the Hermitage ? "

" Yes," said Prothero, and added, " that's it."

" You were with a lady."

" And she *is* a lady," said Prothero, so deeply moved that his face twitched as though he was going to weep.

" She's a Russian ? "

" She had an English mother. Oh, you needn't stand there and look so damned ironical ! She's—she's a woman. She's a thing of kindness. . . ."

He was too full to go on.

" Billy, old boy," said Benham distressed, " I don't want to be ironical——"

Prothero had got his voice again.

" You'd better know," he said, " you'd better know. She's one of those women who live in this hotel."

" Live in this hotel ! "

" On the fourth floor. Didn't you know ? It's the way in most of these big Russian hotels. They come down and sit about after lunch and dinner. A woman with a yellow ticket. Oh ! I don't care. I don't care a rap. She's been kind to me ; she's—she's dear to me. How are you to understand ? I shall stop in Moscow. I shall take her to England. I can't live without her, Benham. And then—— And then you come worrying me to come to your damned Odessa ! "

And suddenly this extraordinary young man put his hands to his face as though he feared to lose it and would hold it on, and after an apoplectic moment burst noisily into tears. They ran between his fingers. " Get out of my room," he shouted suffocatingly. " What business have you to come prying on me ? "

Benham sat down on a chair in the middle of the room and stared round-eyed at his friend. His hands were in his pockets. For a time he said nothing.

" Billy," he began at last, and stopped again. " Billy, in this country somehow one wants to talk like a Russian. Billy, my dear—I'm not your father, I'm not your judge. I'm—unreasonably fond of you. It's not my business to settle what is right or wrong for you. If you want to stay in Moscow, stay in Moscow. Stay here, and stay as my guest. . . ."

He stopped and remained staring at his friend for a little space.

" I didn't know," said Prothero brokenly ; " I didn't know it was possible to get so fond of a person. . . ."

Benham stood up. He had never found Prothero so attractive and so abominable in his life before.

" I shall go to Odessa alone, Billy. I'll make things all right here before I go. . . ."

He closed the door behind him and went in a state of profound thought to his own room. . . .

Presently Prothero came to him with a vague inopportune desire to explain what so evidently did not need explaining.

He walked about the room trying ways of putting it, while Benham packed.

In an unaccountable way Prothero's bristling little mind seemed to have shrunken to something sleek and small.

" I wish," he said, " you could stay for a later train and have lunch and meet her. She's not the ordinary thing. She's —different."

Benham plumbed depths of wisdom. " Billy," he said, " no woman *is* the ordinary thing. They are all—different. . . ."

§ 14

For a time this affair of Prothero's seemed to be a matter as disconnected from the Research Magnificent as one could imagine any matter to be. While Benham went from Moscow and returned, and travelled hither and thither, and involved himself more and more in the endless tangled threads of the revolutionary movement in Russia, Prothero was lost to all those large issues in the development of his personal situation. He contributed nothing to Benham's thought except attempts at discouragement. He reiterated his declaration that all the vast stress and change of Russian national life was going on because it was universally disregarded. " I tell you, as I told you before, that nobody is attending. You think because all Moscow, all Russia, is in the picture, that everybody is concerned. Nobody is concerned. Nobody cares what is happening. Even the men who write in newspapers and talk at meetings about it don't care. They are thinking of their dinners, of their clothes, of their money, of their wives. They hurry home. . . ."

That was his excuse.

Manifestly it was an excuse.

His situation developed into remarkable complications of jealousy and divided counsels that Benham found altogether incomprehensible. To Benham in those days everything was very simple in this business of love. The aristocrat had to love ideally ; that was all. He had to love Amanda. He and Amanda were now very deeply in love again, more in love, he felt, than they had ever been before. They were now writing love-letters to each other and enjoying a separation that was almost voluptuous. She found in the epistolary treatment of her surrender to him and to the natural fate of women, a delightful exercise for her very considerable powers of expression. Life pointed now wonderfully to the great time ahead when there would be a Cheetah cub in the world, and meanwhile the Cheetah loped about the wild world upon a mighty quest. In such terms she put it. Such foolishness written in her invincibly square and youthful hand went daily from London to Russia and stacked up against his return in the porter's office at the Cosmopolis Bazaar or pursued him down through the jarring disorders of south-

west Russia, or waited for him at ill-chosen post-offices that
deflected his journeyings wastefully, or in several instances
went altogether astray. Perhaps they supplied self-educating
young strikers in the postal service with useful exercises in
the deciphering of manuscript English. He wrote back five-
hundred different ways of saying that he loved her extravagantly. . . .

It seemed to Benham in those days that he had found
the remedy and solution of all those sexual perplexities that
distressed the world ; Heroic Love to its highest note—and
then you go about your business. It seemed impossible not
to be happy and lift one's chin high and diffuse a bracing
kindliness among the unfortunate multitudes who stewed
in affliction and hate because they had failed as yet to find
this simple, culminating elucidation. And Prothero—Prothero,
too, was now achieving the same grand elementariness ; out
of his lusts and protests and general physical squalor he had
flowered into love. For a time it is true it made rather an
ineffective companion of him, but this was the mere goose-
stepping for the triumphal march ; this way ultimately lay
exaltation. Benham had had as yet but a passing glimpse
of this Anglo-Russian, who was a lady and altogether unlike
her fellows ; he had seen her for a doubtful second or so as
she and Prothero drove past him, and his impression was
of a rather little creature, white-faced with dusky hair under
a red cap, paler and smaller but with something in her, a
quiet alertness, that gave her a touch of kinship with Amanda.
And if she liked old Prothero—— And, indeed, she must
like old Prothero or could she possibly have made him so
deeply in love with her ?

They must stick to each other, and then, presently, Prothero's
soul would wake up and face the world again. What did
it matter what she had been ?

Through stray shots and red conflict, long tediums of
strained anxiety, and the physical dangers of a barbaric
country staggering towards revolution, Benham went with
his own love like a lamp within him and this affair of Prothero's reflecting its light, and he was quite prepared for the
most sympathetic and liberal behaviour when he came back
to Moscow to make the lady's acquaintance. He intended
to help Prothero to marry and take her back to Cambridge,
and to assist by every possible means in destroying and forgetting the official yellow ticket that defined her status in
Moscow. But he reckoned without either Prothero or the
young lady in this expectation.

It only got to him slowly through his political preoccupations that there were obscure obstacles to this manifest course.
Prothero hesitated ; the lady expressed doubts.

On closer acquaintance her resemblance to Amanda diminished. It was chiefly a similarity of complexion. She had a

more delicate face than Amanda, and its youthful brightness
was deadened ; she had none of Amanda's glow, and she
spoke her mother's language with a pretty halting limp that
was very different from Amanda's clear decisions.

She put her case compactly.

" I would not *do* in Cambridge," she said, with an infinitesimal glance at Prothero.

" Mr. Benham," she said, and her manner had the gravity
of a woman of affairs, " now do you see me in Cambridge ?
Now do you see me ?   Kept outside the walls ?   In a little
datcha ? With no occupation ? Just to amuse him."

And on another occasion when Prothero was not with
her she achieved still completer lucidity.

" I would come if I thought he wanted me to come," she
said. " But you see if I came he would not want me to come.
Because then he would have me and so he wouldn't want me.
He would just have the trouble. And I am not sure if I should
be happy in Cambridge. I am not sure I should be happy
enough to make him happy. It is a very learned and intelligent and charming society, of course ; but here, *things
happen*. At Cambridge nothing happens—there is only education. There is no revolution in Cambridge ; there are not
even sinful people to be sorry for. . . . And he says himself
that Cambridge people are particular. He says they are
liberal but very, very particular, and perhaps I could not
always act my part well. Sometimes I am not always well
behaved. When there is music I behave badly sometimes,
or when I am bored. He says the Cambridge people are so
liberal that they do not mind what you are, but he says they
are so particular that they mind dreadfully how you are
what you are.   So that it comes to exactly the same
thing. . . ."

" Anna Alexievna," said Benham suddenly, " are you in
love with Prothero ? "

Her manner became conscientiously scientific.

" He is very kind and very generous—too generous. He
keeps sending for more money—hundreds of roubles. I try
to prevent him."

" Were you *ever* in love ? "

" Of course. But it's all gone long ago. It was like being
hungry. Only very fine hungry. Exquisite hungry. . . .
And then being disgusted. . . ."

" He is in love with you."

" What is love ? " said Anna. " He is grateful. He is by
nature grateful." She smiled a smile, like the smile of a pale
Madonna who looks down on her bambino.

" And you love nothing ? "

" I love Russia—and being alone, being completely alone.
When I am dead perhaps I shall be alone. Not even my own
body will touch me then."

Then she added, " But I shall be sorry when he goes."

Afterwards Benham talked to Prothero alone. " Your Anna," he said, " is rather wonderful. At first, I tell you now frankly I did not like her very much, I thought she looked ' used ' ; she drank vodka at lunch, she was gay, uneasily ; she seemed a sham thing—all that was prejudice. She thinks ; she's generous, she's fine."

" She's tragic," said Prothero, as though it was the same thing.

He spoke as though he noted an objection. His next remark confirmed this impression. " That's why I can't take her back to Cambridge," he said.

" You see, Benham," he went on, " she's human. She's not really feminine. I mean, she's—unsexed. She isn't fitted to be a wife or a mother any more. We've talked about the possible life in England, very plainly. I've explained what a household in Cambridge would mean. . . . It doesn't attract her. . . In a way she's been let out from womanhood, forced out of womanhood, and I see now that when women are let out from womanhood there's no putting them back. I could give a lecture on Anna. I see now that if women are going to be wives and mothers and homekeepers and ladies, they must be got ready for it from the beginning, sheltered, never really let out into the wild chances of life. She has been. Bitterly. She's *really* emancipated. And it's let her out into a sort of nothingness. She's no longer a woman, and she isn't a man. She ought to be able to go on her own —like a man. But I can't take her back to Cambridge. Even for her sake."

His perplexed eyes regarded Benham.

" You won't be happy in Cambridge—alone," said Benham.

" Oh, damnably not ! But what can I do ? I had at first some idea of coming to Moscow for good—teaching."

He paused. " Impossible. I'm worth nothing here. I couldn't have kept her."

" Then what are you going to do, Billy ? "

" I don't *know* what I'm going to do, I tell you. I live for the moment. To-morrow we are going out into the country."

" I don't understand," said Benham with a gesture of resignation. " It seems to me that if a man and woman love each other—well, they insist upon each other. What is to happen to her if you leave her in Moscow ? "

" Damnation ! Is there any need to ask that ? "

" Take her to Cambridge, man. And if Cambridge objects, teach Cambridge better manners."

Prothero's face was suddenly transfigured with rage.

" I tell you she won't come ! " he said.

" Billy ! " said Benham, " you should make her ! "

" I can't."

" If a man loves a woman he can make her do anything——"

" But I don't love her like that," said Prothero, shrill with anger. " I tell you I don't love her like that."

Then he lunged into further deeps. " It's the other men," he said, " it's the things that have been. Don't you understand ? Can't you understand ? The memories—she must have memories—they come between us. It's something deeper than reason. It's in one's spine and under one's nails. One could do anything, I perceive, for one's very own woman. . . ."

" *Make* her your very own woman," said the exponent of heroic love.

" I shirk deeds, Benham, but you shirk facts. How could any man make her his very own woman now ? You—you don't seem to understand—*anything*. She's nobody's woman —for ever. That—that might-have-been has gone for ever. . . . It's nerves—a passion of the nerves. There's a cruelty in life and—— She's *kind* to me. She's so kind to me. . . ."

And then again Prothero was weeping like a vexed child.

§ 15

The end of Prothero's first love affair came to Benham in broken fragments in letters. When he looked for Anna Alexievna in December—he never learnt her surname— he found she had left the Cosmopolis Bazaar soon after Prothero's departure and he could not find whither she had gone. He never found her again. Moscow and Russia had swallowed her up.

Of course she and Prothero parted ; that was a foregone conclusion. But Prothero's manner of parting succeeded in being at every phase a shock to Benham's ideas. It was clear he went off almost callously ; it would seem there was very little crying. Towards the end it was evident that the two had quarrelled. The tears only came at the very end of all. It was almost as if he had got through the passion and was glad to go. Then came regret, a regret that increased in geometrical proportion with every mile of distance.

In Warsaw it was that grief really came to Prothero. He had some hours there and he prowled the crowded streets, seeing girls and women happy with their lovers, abroad upon bright expeditions and full of delicious secrets, girls and women who ever and again flashed out some instant resemblance to Anna. . . .

In Berlin he stopped a night and almost decided that he would go back. " But now I had the damned frontier," he wrote, " between us."

It was so entirely in the spirit of Prothero, Benham thought, to let the " damned frontier " tip the balance against him.

Then came a scrawl of passionate confession, so passionate that it seemed as if Prothero had been transfigured. " I can't stand this business," he wrote. " It has things in it, possibilities of emotional disturbance—you can have no idea ! In the train—luckily I was alone in the compartment—I sat and thought, and suddenly, I could not help it, I was weeping —noisy weeping, an uproar ! A beastly German came and stood in the corridor to stare. I had to get out of the train. It is disgraceful, it is monstrous we should be made like this. . . .

" Here I am stranded in Hanover with nothing to do but to write to you about my dismal feelings. . . ."

After that surely there was nothing before a broken-hearted Prothero but to go on with his trailing wing to Trinity and a life of unappeasable regrets ; but again Benham reckoned without the invincible earthliness of his friend. Prothero stayed three nights in Paris.

" There is an extraordinary excitement about Paris," he wrote. " A levity. I suspect the gypsum in the subsoil— some as yet undescribed radiations. Suddenly the world looks brightly cynical. . . . None of those tear-compelling German emanations. . . .

" And, Benham, I have found a friend.

" A woman. Of course you will laugh, you will sneer. You do not understand these things. . . . Yet they are so simple. It was the strangest accident brought us together. There was something that drew us together. A sort of instinct. Near the Boulevard Poissonière. . . ."

" Good heavens ! " said Benham. " A sort of instinct ! "

" I told her all about Anna ! "

" Good Lord ! " cried Benham.

" She understood. Perfectly. None of your so-called ' respectable ' women could have understood. . . . At first I intended merely to talk to her. . . ."

Benham crumpled the letter in his hand.

" Little Anna Alexievna ! " he said, " you were too clean for him."

§ 16

Benham had a vision of Prothero returning from all this foreign travel meekly, pensively, a little sadly, and yet not without a kind of relief to the gray mildness of Trinity. He saw him, capped and gowned, and restored to academic dignity again, nodding greetings, resuming friendships.

The little man merged again into his rare company of discreet Benedicts and restrained celibates at the high tables. They ate on in their mature wisdom long after the undergraduates had fled. Presently they would withdraw processionally to the combination-room. . . .

There would be much to talk about over the wine.

Benham speculated what account Prothero would give of Moscow. . . .

He laughed abruptly.

And with that laugh Prothero dropped out of Benham's world for a space of years. There may have been other letters, but if so they were lost in the heaving troubles of a revolution-strained post-office. Perhaps to this day they linger sere and yellow in some forgotten pigeon-hole in Kishinev or Ekaterinoslav. . . .

§ 17

In November, after an adventure in the trader's quarter of Kieff which had brought him within an inch of death, and because an emotional wave had swept across him and across his correspondence with Amanda, Benham went back suddenly to England and her. He wanted very greatly to see her, and also he wanted to make certain arrangements about his property. He returned by way of Hungary, and sent telegrams like shouts of excitement whenever the train stopped for a sufficient time. " Old Leopard, I am coming, I am coming," he telegraphed, announcing his coming for the fourth time. It was to be the briefest of visits, very passionate, the mutual refreshment of two noble lovers, and then he was returning to Russia again.

Amanda was at Chexington, and there he found her installed in the utmost dignity of expectant maternity. Like many other people he had been a little disposed to regard the bearing of children as a common human experience ; at Chexington he came to think of it as a rare and sacramental function. Amanda had become very beautiful in quiet, gray, dove-like tones ; her sun-touched boy's complexion had given way to a soft glow of the utmost loveliness, her brisk little neck that had always reminded him of the stalk of a flower was now softened and rounded ; her eyes were tender, and she moved about the place in the manner of one who is vowed to a great sacrifice. She dominated the scene, and Lady Marayne, with a certain astonishment in her eyes and a smouldering disposition to irony, was the half-sympathetic, half-resentful priestess of her daughter-in-law's unparalleled immolation. The *motif* of motherhood was everywhere, and at his bedside he found—it had been put there for him by Amanda—among much other exaltation of woman's mission, that most wonderful of all philoprogenitive stories, Hudson's *Crystal Age.*

Everybody at Chexington had an air of being grouped about the impending fact. An epidemic of internal troubles, it is true, kept Sir Godfrey in the depths of London society, but to make up for his absence Mrs. Morris had taken a little cottage down by the river and the Wilder girls were with her, both afire with fine and subtle feelings, and both, it seemed, and more particularly Betty, prepared to be keenly critical of Benham's attitude.

He did a little miss his cue in these exaltations, because he had returned in a rather different vein of exaltation.

In missing it he was assisted by Amanda herself, who had at moments an effect upon him of a priestess confidentially disrobed. It was as if she put aside for him something official, something sincerely maintained, necessary, but at times a little irksome. It was as if she was glad to take him into her confidence and unbend. Within the pre-natal Amanda an impish Amanda still lingered.

There were aspects of Amanda that it was manifest dear Betty must never know. . . .

But the real Amanda of that November visit even in her most unpontifical moods did not quite come up to the imagined Amanda who had drawn him home across Europe. At times she was extraordinarily jolly. They had two or three happy walks about the Chexington woods ; that year the golden weather of October had flowed over into November, and except for a carpet of green and gold under the horse-chestnuts most of the leaves were still on the trees. Gleams of her old wanton humour shone on him. And then would come something else, something like a shadow across the world, something he had quite forgotten since his idea of the heroic love had flooded him, something that reminded him of those long explanations with Mr. Rathbone-Sanders that had never been explained, and of the curate in the doorway of the cottage and his unaccountable tears.

On the afternoon of his arrival at Chexington he was a little surprised to find Sir Philip Easton coming through the house into the garden, with an accustomed familiarity. Sir Philip perceived him with a start that was instantly controlled, and greeted him with unnatural ease.

Sir Philip, it seemed, was fishing and reading and playing cricket in the neighbourhood, which struck Benham as a poor way of spending the summer, the sort of soft holiday a man learns to take from scholars and literary men. A man like Sir Philip, he thought, ought to have been aviating or travelling.

Moreover, when Sir Philip greeted Amanda it seemed to Benham that there was a flavour of established association in their manner. But then Sir Philip was also very assiduous with Lady Marayne. She called him " Pip," and afterwards Amanda called across the tennis-court to him, " Pip ! " And then he called her " Amanda." When the Wilder girls came up to join the tennis he was just as brotherly. . . .

The next day he came to lunch.

During that meal Benham became more aware than he had ever been before of the peculiar deep expressiveness of this young man's eyes. They watched him and they watched Amanda with a solicitude that seemed at once pained and tender. And there was something about Amanda, a kind of hard brightness, an impartiality and an air of something undefinably suspended, that gave Benham an intuitive certitude that that afternoon Sir Philip would be spoken to privately, and that then he would pack up and go away in a state of illumination from Chexington. But before he could be spoken to he contrived to speak to Benham.

They were left to smoke after lunch, and then it was he took advantage of a pause to commit his little indiscretion.

" Mrs. Benham," he said, " looks amazingly well—extraordinarily well, don't you think ? "

" Yes," said Benham, startled. " Yes. She certainly keeps very well."

" She misses you terribly," said Sir Philip ; " it is a time when a woman misses her husband. But, of course, she does not want to hamper your work. . . ."

Benham felt it was very kind of him to take so intimate an interest in these matters, but on the spur of the moment he could find no better expression for this than a grunt.

" You don't mind," said the young man with a slight catch in the breath that might have been apprehensive, " that I sometimes bring her books and flowers and things ? Do what little I can to keep life interesting down here ? It's not very congenial. . . . She's so wonderful. I think she is the most wonderful woman in the world."

Benham perceived that so far from being a modern aristocrat he was really a primitive barbarian in these matters.

" I've no doubt," he said, " that my wife has every reason to be grateful for your attentions."

In the little pause that followed Benham had a feeling that Sir Philip was engendering something still more personal. If so, he might be constrained to invert very gently but very firmly the bowl of chrysanthemums over Sir Philip's head, or kick him in an improving manner. He had a ridiculous belief that Sir Philip would probably take anything of the sort very touchingly. He scrambled in his mind for some remark that would avert this possibility.

" Have you ever been in Russia ? " he asked hastily. " It is the most wonderful country in Europe. I had an odd adventure near Kiev. During a pogrom."

And he drowned the developing situation in a flood of description. . . .

But it was not so easy to drown the little things that were presently thrown out by Lady Marayne. They were so much more in the air. . . .

§ 18

Sir Philip suddenly got out of the picture even as Benham had foreseen.

" Easton has gone away," he remarked three days later to Amanda.

" I told him to go. He is a bore with you about. . . . But otherwise he is rather a comfort, Cheetah." She meditated upon Sir Philip. " And he's an *honourable* man," she said. " He's safe. . . ."

§ 19

After that visit it was that the notes upon love and sex began in earnest. The scattered memoranda upon the perfectness of heroic love for the modern aristocrat ended abruptly. Instead there came the first draft for a study of jealousy. The note was written in pencil on Chexington notepaper and manifestly that had been supported on the ribbed cover of a book. There was a little computation in the corner, converting forty-five degrees Réaumur into degrees Fahrenheit, which made White guess it had been written in the Red Sea. But, indeed, it had been written in a rather amateurishly stoked corridor-train on Benham's journey to the gathering revolt in Moscow. . . .

" I think I have been disposed to underrate the force of sexual jealousy. . . . I thought it was something essentially contemptible, something that one dismissed and put behind oneself in the mere effort to be aristocratic, but I begin to realise that it is not quite so easily settled with. . . .

" One likes to know. . . . Possibly one wants to know too much. . . . In phases of fatigue, and particularly in phases of sleeplessness, when one is leaving all that one cares for behind, it becomes an irrational torment. . . .

" And it is not only in oneself that I am astonished by the power of this base motive. I see, too, in the queer business of Prothero how strongly jealousy, how strongly the sense of proprietorship, weighs with a man. . . .

" There is no clear reason why one should insist upon another human being being one's ownest own—utterly one's own. . . .

" There is, of course, no clear reason for most human motives. . . .

" One does. . . .

" There is something dishonouring in distrust—to both the distrusted and the one who distrusts. . . ."

After that, apparently, it had been too hot and stuffy to continue.

§ 20

Benham did not see Amanda again until after the birth of their child. He spent his Christmas in Moscow, watching the outbreak, the fitful fighting and the subsequent breakup of the revolution, and taking care of a lost and helpless English family whose father had gone astray temporarily on the way home from Baku. Then he went southward to Rostov and thence to Astrakhan. Here he really began his travels. He determined to get to India by way of Herat, and for the first time in his life rode out into an altogether lawless wilderness. He went on obstinately because he found himself disposed to funk the journey, and because discouragements were put in his way. He was soon quite cut off from all the ways of living he had known. He learnt what it is to be flea-bitten—saddle sore, hungry and, above all, thirsty. He was haunted by a dread of fever, and so contrived strange torments for himself with over-doses of quinine. He ceased to be traceable from Chexington in March, and he reappeared in the form of a telegram from Karachi demanding news in May. He learnt he was the father of a man-child and that all was well with Amanda.

He had not expected to be so long away from any communication with the outer world, and something in the nature of a stricken conscience took him back to England. He found a second William Porphyry in the world, dominating Chexington, and Amanda tenderly triumphant and passionate, the Madonna enthroned. For William Porphyry he could feel no emotion. William Porphyry was very red and ugly and protesting, feeble and aggressive, a matter for a skilled nurse. To see him was to ignore him and dispel a dream. It was to Amanda Benham turned again.

For some days he was content to adore his Madonna and listen to the familiar flatteries of her love. He was a leaner, riper man, Amanda said, and wiser, so that she was afraid of him. . . .

And then he became aware that she was requiring him to stay at her side. " We have both had out adventures," she said, which struck him as an odd phrase.

It forced itself upon his obstinate incredulity that all those conceptions of heroic love and faithfulness he had supposed to be so clearly understood between them had vanished from her mind. She had absolutely forgotten that twilight moment at the window which had seemed to him the crowning instant, the real marriage of their lives. It had gone, it had left no recoverable trace in her. And upon his interpretations of that he had loved her passionately for a year. She was back at exactly the ideas and intentions that ruled her during their first settlement in London. She wanted a joint life in the social world of London—she demanded his presence, his attention, the daily practical evidences of love. It was all very well for him to be away when the child was coming, but now everything was different. Now he must stay by her.

This time he argued no case. These issues he had settled for ever. Even an indignant dissertation from Lady Marayne, a dissertation that began with appeals and ended in taunts, did not move him. Behind these things now was India. The huge problems of India had laid an unshakeable hold upon his imagination. He had seen Russia, and he wanted to balance that picture by a vision of the East. . . .

He saw Easton only once during a week-end at Chexington. The young man displayed no further disposition to be confidentially sentimental. But he seemed to have something on his mind. And Amanda said not a word about him. He was a young man above suspicion, Benham felt. . . .

And from his departure the quality of the correspondence of these two larger carnivores began to change. Except for the repetition of accustomed endearments, they ceased to be love-letters in any sense of the word. They dealt chiefly with the "Cub," and even there Benham felt presently that the enthusiasm diminished. A new amazing quality for Amanda appeared—triteness. The very writing of her letters changed as though it had suddenly lost backbone. Her habitual liveliness of phrasing lost its point. Had she lost her animation? Was she ill unknowingly? Where had the light gone? It was as if her attention was distracted. . . . As if every day when she wrote her mind was busy about something else.

Abruptly at last he understood. A fact that had never been stated, never formulated, never in any way admitted, was suddenly pointed to convergently by a thousand indicating fingers, and beyond question perceived to be *there*. . . .

He left a record of that moment of realisation.

" Suddenly one night I woke up and lay still, and it was as if I had never seen Amanda before. Now I saw her plainly, I saw her with that same dreadful clearness that sometimes comes at dawn, a pitiless, a scientific distinctness that has neither light nor shadow. . . .

" Of course," I said, and then presently I got up very softly. . . .

" I wanted to get out of my intolerable, close, personal cabin. I wanted to feel the largeness of the sky. I went out upon the deck. We were off the coast of Madras, and when I think of that moment, there comes back to me also the faint flavour of spice in the air, the low line of the coast, the cool flooding abundance of the Indian moonlight, the swish of the black water against the side of the ship. And a perception of infinite loss, as if the limitless heavens above this earth and below to the very uttermost star were just one boundless cavity from which delight had fled. . . .

" Of course I had lost her. I knew it with absolute certainty. I knew it from her insecure temperament, her adventurousness, her needs. I knew it from every line she had written me in the last three months. I knew it intuitively. She had been unfaithful. She must have been unfaithful.

" What had I been dreaming about to think that it would not be so ? "

§ 21

" Now let me write down plainly what I think of these matters. Let me be at least honest with myself, whatever self-contradictions I may have been led into by force of my passions. Always I have despised jealousy. . . .

" Only by the conquest of four natural limitations is the aristocratic life to be achieved. They come in a certain order, and in that order the spirit of man is armed against them less and less efficiently. Of fear and my struggle against fear I have told already. I am fearful. I am a physical coward until I can bring shame and anger to my assistance, but in overcoming fear I have been helped by the whole body of human tradition. Every one, the basest creatures, every Hottentot, every stunted creature that ever breathed poison in a slum, knows that the instinctive constitution of man is at fault here and that fear is shameful and must be subdued. The race is on one's side. And so there is a vast traditional support for a man against the Second Limitation, the limitation of physical indulgence. It is not so universal as the first ; there is a grinning bawling humour on the side of grossness, but common pride is against it. And in this matter my temperament has been my help ; I am fastidious, I eat little, drink little, and feel a shivering recoil from excess. It is no great virtue ; it happens so ; it is something in the nerves of my skin. I cannot endure myself unshaven or in any way unclean ; I am tormented by dirty hands or dirty blood or dirty memories, and after I had once loved Amanda I could not— unless some irrational impulse to get equal with her had caught me—have broken my faith to her, whatever breach there was in her faith to me. . .

" I see that in these matters I am cleaner than most men and more easily clean ; and it may be that it is in the vein of just that distinctive virtue that I fell so readily into a passion of resentment and anger.

" I despised a jealous man. There is a traditional discredit of jealousy, not so strong as that against cowardice, but still very strong. But the general contempt of jealousy is curiously wrapped up with the supposition that there is no cause for jealousy, that it is unreasonable suspicion. Given a cause then tradition speaks with an uncertain voice. . . .

" I see now that I despised jealousy because I assumed that it was impossible for Amanda to love any one but me ; it was intolerable to imagine anything else, I insisted upon believing that she was as fastidious as myself and as faithful as myself, made indeed after my image, and I went on disregarding the most obvious intimations that she was not, until that still moment in the Indian Ocean, when silently, gently as a drowned body might rise out of the depths of a pool, that knowledge of love dead and honour gone for ever floated up into my consciousness.

" And then I felt that Amanda had cheated me ! Outrageously. Abominably.

" Now, so far as my intelligence goes, there is not a cloud

upon this question. My demand upon Amanda was outrageous and I had no right whatever to her love or loyalty. I must have that very clear. . . .

" This aristocratic life, as I conceive it, must be, except accidentally here and there, incompatible with the domestic life. It means going hither and thither in the universe of thought as much as in the universe of matter, it means adventure, it means movement and adventure that must needs be hopelessly encumbered by an inseparable associate, it means self-imposed responsibilities that will not fit into the welfare of a family. In all ages, directly society had risen above the level of a barbaric tribal village, this need of a release from the family for certain necessary types of people has been recognised. It was met sometimes informally, sometimes formally, by the growth and establishment of special classes and orders, of priests, monks, nuns, of pledged knights, of a great variety of non-family people, whose concern was the larger collective life that opens out beyond the simple necessities and duties and loyalties of the steading and of the craftsman's house. Sometimes, but not always, that release took the form of celibacy ; but besides that there have been a hundred institutional variations of the common life to meet the need of the special man, the man who must go deep and the man who must go far. A vowed celibacy ceased to be a tolerable rule for an aristocracy directly the eugenic idea entered the mind of man, because a celibate aristocracy means the abandonment of the racial future to a proletariat of base unleaderly men. That was plain to Plato. It was plain to Campanella. It was plain to the Protestant reformers. But the world has never yet gone on to the next step beyond that recognition, to the recognition of feminine aristocrats, rulers and the mates of rulers, as untrammelled by domestic servitudes and family relationships as the men of their kind. That I see has always been my idea since in my undergraduate days I came under the spell of Plato. It was a matter of course that my first gift to Amanda should be his *Republic*. I loved Amanda transfigured in that dream. . . .

" There are no such women. . . .

" It is no excuse for me that I thought she was like-minded with myself. I had no sound reason for supposing that. I did suppose that, I did not perceive that not only was she younger than myself, but that while I had been going through a mill of steely education, kept close, severely exercised, polished by discussion, she had but the weak training of a not very good school, some scrappy reading, the vague discussions of village artists, and the draped and decorated novelties of the " advanced." It all went to nothing on the impact of the world. . . . She showed herself the woman the world has always known, no miracle, and the alternative was for me to give myself to her in the ancient way, to serve

her happiness, to control her and delight and companion her,
or to let her go. . . .

"The normal woman centres upon herself ; her mission
is her own charm and her own beauty and her own setting ;
her place is her home. She demands the concentration of
a man. Not to be able to command that is her failure.
Not to give her that is to shame her. As I had shamed
Amanda. . . ."

§ 22

"There are no such women." He had written this in and
struck it out, and then at some later time written it in again.
There it stayed now as his last persuasion, but it set White
thinking and doubting. And, indeed, there was another sheet
of pencilled broken stuff that seemed to glance at quite another
type of womanhood.

§ 23

"It is clear that the woman aristocrats who must come
to the remaking of the world will do so in spite of limitations
at least as great as those from which the aristocratic spirit
of man escapes. These women must become aristocratic
through their own innate impulse, they must be self-called
to their lives, exactly as men must be ; there is no making
an aristocrat without a predisposition for rule and nobility.
And they have to discover and struggle against just exactly
the limitations that we have to struggle against. They have
to conquer not only fear but indulgence, indulgence of a softer,
more insidious quality, and jealousy—proprietorship. . . .

"It is as natural to want a mate as to want bread, and a
thousand times in my work and in my wanderings I have
thought of a mate and desired a mate. A mate—not a possession. It is a need almost naïvely simple. If only one could
have a woman who thought of one and with one ! Though
she were on the other side of the world and busied about a
thousand things. . . .

"'*With* one', I see it must be rather than '*of* one.'
That ' of one ' is just the unexpurgated egotistical demand
coming back again. . . .

"Man is a mating creature. It is not good to be alone.
But mating means a mate. . . .

"We should be lovers, of course ; that goes without
saying. . . .

"And yet not specialised lovers, not devoted, *attending*
lovers. ' Dancing attendance '—as they used to say. We
should meet upon our ways as the great carnivores do. . . .

"That at any rate was a sound idea. Though we only played
with it.

"But that mate desire is just a longing that can have no
possible satisfaction now for me. What is the good of dream-

ing ? Life and chance have played a trick upon my body and soul. I am mated, though I am mated to a phantom. I loved and I love Amanda, not Easton's Amanda, but Amanda in Armour, the Amanda of my dreams. Sense, and particularly the sense of beauty, lies deeper than reason in us. There can be no mate for me now unless she comes with Amanda's voice and Amanda's face and Amanda's quick movements and her clever hands. . . ."

§ 24

" Why am I so ungrateful to her still for all the happiness she gave me ?

" There were things between us two as lovers—love, things more beautiful than anything else in the world, things that set the mind hunting among ineffectual images in a search for impossible expression, images of sunlight shining through blood-red petals, images of moonlight in a scented garden, of marble gleaming in the shade, of far-off wonderful music heard at dusk in a great stillness, of fairies dancing softly, of floating happiness and stirring delights, of joys as keen and sudden as the knife of an assassin, assassin's knives made out of tears, tears that are happiness ; wordless things ; and surprises, expectations, gratitudes, sudden moments of contemplation, the sight of a soft eyelid closed in sleep, shadowy tones in the sound of a voice heard unexpectedly ; sweet, dear magical things that I can find no words for. . . .

" If she was a goddess to me, should it be any affair of mine that she was not a goddess to herself ; that she could hold all this that has been between us more cheaply than I did ? It does not change one jot of it for me. At the time she did not hold it cheaply. She forgets where I do not forget. . . ."

§ 25

Such were the things that Benham could think and set down.

Yet for whole days he was possessed by the thought of killing Amanda and himself.

He did not at once turn homeward. It was in Ceylon that he dropped his work and came home. At Colombo he found a heap of letters awaiting him, and there were two of these that had started at the same time. They had been posted in London on one eventful afternoon. Lady Marayne and Amanda had quarrelled violently. Two earnest, flushed, quick-breathing women, full of neat but belated repartee, separated to write their simultaneous letters. Each letter trailed the atmosphere of that truncated encounter. Lady Marayne told her story ruthlessly. Amanda, on the other hand, generalised, and explained. Sir Philip's adoration of her was a love-friendship, it was beautiful, it was pure. Was there no trust nor courage in the world ? She would defy all jealous scandal. She would not even banish him from her side. Surely the Cheetah could trust her. But the pitiless facts of Lady Marayne went beyond Amanda's explaining. The little lady's dignity had been stricken. " I have been used as a cloak," she wrote.

Her phrases were vivid. She quoted the very words of Amanda, words she had overheard at Chexington in the twilight. They were no invention. They were the very essence of Amanda, the lover. It was as sure as if Benham had heard the sound of her voice, as if he had peeped and seen, as if she had crept by him, stooping and rustling softly. It brought back the living sense of her, excited, flushed, reckless ; his wild-haired Amanda of infinite delight. . . .

All day those words of hers pursued him. All night they flared across the black universe. He buried his face in the pillows and they whispered softly in his ear.

He walked his room in the darkness longing to smash and tear.

He went out from the house and shook his ineffectual fists at the stirring quiet of the stars.

He sent no notice of his coming back. Nor did he come back with a definite plan. But he wanted to get at Amanda.

§ 26

It was with Amanda he had to reckon. Towards Easton he felt scarcely any anger at all. Easton he felt only existed for him because Amanda willed to have it so.

Such anger as Easton did arouse in him was a contemptuous anger. His devotion filled Benham with scorn. His determination to serve Amanda at any price, to bear the grossest humiliations and slights for her, his humility, his service and tenderness, his care for her moods and happiness, seemed to Benham a treachery to human nobility. That rage against Easton was like the rage of a trade-unionist against a blackleg. Are all the women to fall to the men who will be their master-slaves and keepers ? But it was not simply that Benham felt men must be freed from this incessant attendance ; women too must free themselves from their almost instinctive demand for an attendant. . . .

His innate disposition was to treat women as responsible beings. Never in his life had he thought of a woman as a pretty thing to be fooled and won and competed for and fought over. So that it was Amanda he wanted to reach and reckon with now, Amanda who had mated and ruled his senses only to fling him into this intolerable pit of shame and jealous fury. But the forces that were driving him home now were the forces below the level of reason and ideas, organic forces compounded of hate and desire, profound aboriginal urgencies. He thought, indeed, very little as he lay in his berth or sulked on deck ; his mind lay waste under a pitiless invasion of exasperating images that ever and again would so wring him that his muscles would tighten and his hands clench or he would find himself restraining a snarl, the threat of the beast, in his throat.

Amanda grew upon his imagination until she overshadowed the whole world. She filled the skies. She bent over him and mocked him. She became a mystery of passion and dark beauty. She was the sin of the world. One breathed her in the winds of the sea. She had taken to herself the greatness of elemental things. . . .

So that when at last he saw her he was amazed to see her, and see that she was just a creature of common size and quality, a rather tired and very frightened-looking white-faced young woman, in an evening-dress of unfamiliar fashion, with little common trinkets of gold and colour about her wrists and neck.

In that instant's confrontation he forgot all that had brought him homeward. He stared at her as one stares at a stranger whom one has greeted in mistake for an intimate friend.

For he saw that she was no more the Amanda he hated and desired to kill than she had ever been the Amanda he had loved.

§ 27

He took them by surprise. It had been his intention to take them by surprise. Such is the inelegance of the jealous state.

He reached London in the afternoon and put up at a hotel near Charing Cross. In the evening about ten he appeared at the house in Lancaster Gate. The butler was deferentially amazed. Mrs. Benham was, he said, at a theatre with Sir Philip Easton, and he thought some other people also. He did not know when she would be back. She might go on to supper. It was not the custom for the servants to wait up for her.

Benham went into the study that reduplicated his former rooms in Finacue Street and sat down before the fire the butler lit for him. He sent the man to bed, and fell into profound meditation.

It was nearly two o'clock when he heard the sound of her latchkey and went out at once upon the landing.

The half-door stood open and Easton's car was outside. She stood in the middle of the hall and relieved Easton of the gloves and fan he was carrying.

" Good-night," she said, " I am so tired."

" My wonderful goddess," he said.

She yielded herself to his accustomed embrace, then started, stared, and wrenched herself out of his arms.

Benham stood at the top of the stairs looking down upon them, white-faced and inexpressive. Easton dropped back a pace. For a moment no one moved nor spoke, and then very quietly Easton shut the half-door and shut out the noises of the road.

For some seconds Benham regarded them, and as he did so his spirit changed. . . .

Everything he had thought of saying and doing vanished out of his mind.

He stuck his hands into his pockets and descended the staircase. When he was five or six steps above them, he spoke, " Just sit down here," he said, with a gesture of one hand, and sat down himself upon the stairs. " *Do* sit down," he said with a sudden testiness as they continued standing. " I know all about this affair. Do please sit down and let us talk. . . . Everybody's gone to bed long ago."

" Cheetah ! " she said. " Why have you come back like this ? "

Then at his mute gesture she sat down at his feet.

" I wish you would sit down, Easton," he said in a voice of subdued savagery.

" Why have you come back ? " Sir Philip Easton found his voice to ask.

" *Sit* down," Benham spat, and Easton obeyed unwillingly.

" I came back," Benham went on, " to see to all this. Why else ? I don't—now I see you—feel very fierce about it. But it has distressed me. You look changed, Amanda, and fagged. And your hair is untidy. It's as if something had happened to you and made you a stranger. . . . You two people are lovers. Very natural and simple, but I want to get out of it. Yes, I want to get out of it. That wasn't quite my idea, but now I see it is. It's queer, but on the whole I feel sorry for you. All of us, poor humans—— There's reason to be sorry for all of us. We're full of lusts and uneasiness and resentments that we haven't the will to control. What do you two people want me to do to you ? Would you like a divorce, Amanda ? It's the clean, straight thing, isn't it ? Or would the scandal hurt you ? "

Amanda sat crouched together, with her eyes on Benham.

" Give us a divorce," said Easton, looking to her to confirm him.

Amanda shook her head.

" I don't want a divorce," she said.

" Then what do you want ? " asked Benham with sudden asperity.

" I don't want a divorce," she repeated, " Why do you, after a long silence, come home like this, abruptly, with no notice ? "

" It was the way it took me," said Benham, after a little interval.

" You have left me for long months."

" Yes. I was angry. And it was ridiculous to be angry.

I thought I wanted to kill you, and now I see you I see that all I want to do is to help you out of this miserable mess—and then get away from you. You two would like to marry. You ought to be married."

" I would die to make Amanda happy," said Easton.

" Your business, it seems to me, is to live to make her happy. That you may find more of a strain. Less tragic and more tiresome. I, on the other hand, want neither to die nor live for her." Amanda moved sharply. " It's extraordinary what amazing vapours a lonely man may get into his head. If you don't want a divorce then I suppose things might go on as they are now."

" I hate things as they are now," said Easton. " I hate this falsehood and deception."

" You would hate the scandal just as much," said Amanda.

" I would not care what the scandal was unless it hurt you."

" It would be only a temporary inconvenience," said Benham. " Every one would sympathise with you. . . . The whole thing is so natural . . . People would be glad to forget very soon. They did with my mother."

" No," said Amanda, " it isn't so easy as that."

She seemed to come to a decision.

" Pip," she said, " I want to talk to—*him*—alone."

Easton's brown eyes were filled with distress and perplexity. " But why ? " he asked.

" I do," she said.

" But this is a thing for *us*."

" Pip, I want to talk to him alone. There is something—something I can't say before you. . . . "

Sir Philip rose slowly to his feet.

" Shall I wait outside ? "

" No, Pip. Go home. Yes—there are some things you must leave to me."

She stood up too and turned so that she and Benham both faced the younger man. The strangest uneasiness mingled with his resolve to be at any cost splendid. He felt—and it was a most unexpected and disconcerting feeling—that he was no longer confederated with Amanda ; that prior, more fundamental and greater associations prevailed over his little new grip upon her mind and senses. He stared at husband and wife aghast in this realisation. Then his resolute romanticism came to his help. " I would trust you—— " he began. " If you tell me to go—— "

Amanda seemed to measure her hold upon him.

She laid her hand upon his arm. " Go, my dear Pip," she said. " Go."

He had a moment of hesitation, of anguish, and it seemed to Benham as though he eked himself out with unreality, as though somewhen, somewhere, he had seen something of the sort in a play and filled in a gap that otherwise he could not have supplied.

Then the door had closed upon him, and Amanda, pale and darkly dishevelled, faced her husband, silently and intensely.

" *Well ?* " said Benham.

She held out her arms to him.

" Why did you leave me, Cheetah ?   Why did you leave me ? "

§ 28

Benham affected to ignore those proffered arms. But they recalled in a swift rush the animal anger that had brought him back to England. To remind him of desire now was to revive an anger stronger than any desire. He spoke seeking to hurt her.

" I am wondering now," he said, " why the devil I came back."

" You had to come back to me."

" I could have written just as well about these things."

" *Cheetah,*" she said softly, and came towards him slowly, stooping forward and looking into his eyes, " you had to come back to see your old Leopard. Your wretched Leopard. Who has rolled in the dirt. And is still yours."

" Do you want a divorce ?   How are we to fix things, Amanda ? "

" Cheetah, I will tell you how we will fix things."

She dropped upon the step below him. She laid her hands with a deliberate softness upon him, she gave a toss so that her disordered hair was a little more disordered, and brought her soft chin down to touch his knees. Her eyes implored him.

" Cheetah," she said.   " You are going to forgive."

He sat rigid, meeting her eyes.

" Amanda," he said at last, " you would be astonished if I kicked you away from me and trampled over you to the door. That is what I want to do."

" Do it," she said, and the grip of her hands tightened. " Cheetah dear !   I would love you to kill me."

" I don't want to kill you."

Her eyes dilated.   " Beat me."

" And I haven't the remotest intention of making love to you," he said, and pushed her soft face and hands away from him as if he would stand up.

She caught hold of him again.   " Stay with me," she said.

He made no effort to shake off her grip. He looked at the dark cloud of her hair that had ruled him so magically, and the memory of old delights made him grip a great handful almost inadvertently as he spoke.   " Dear Leopard," he said, " we humans are the most streaky of conceivable things.   I thought I hated you. I do. I hate you like poison. And also I do not hate you at all."

Then abruptly he was standing over her.

She rose to her knees.

" Stay here, old Cheetah ! " she said. " This is your house. I am your wife."

He went towards the unfastened front door.

" Cheetah ! " she cried with a note of despair.

He halted at the door.

" Amanda, I will come to-morrow. I will come in the morning, in the sober London daylight, and then we will settle things."

He stared at her, and to her amazement he smiled. He spoke as one who remarks upon a quite unexpected fact. . . .

" Never in my life, Amanda, have I seen a human being that I wanted so little to kill."

§ 29

White found a fragment that might have been written within a week of those last encounters of Benham and Amanda.

" The thing that astonished me most in Amanda was the change in her mental quality.

" With me in the old days she had always been a sincere person ; she had deceived me about facts, but she had never deceived me about herself. Her personal, stark frankness had been her essential strength. And it was gone. I came back to find Amanda an accomplished actress, a thing of poses and calculated effects. She was a surface, a sham, a Lorelei. Beneath that surface I could not discover anything individual at all. Fear and a grasping quality, such as God gave us all when He gave us hands ; but the individual I knew, the humorous wilful Spotless Leopard was gone. Whither, I cannot imagine. An amazing disappearance. Clean out of space and time like a soul lost for ever.

" When I went to see her in the morning, she was made up for a scene, she acted an intricate part, never for a moment was she there in reality. . . .

" I have got a remarkable persuasion that she lost herself in this way, by cheapening love, by making base love to a lover she despised. . . . There can be no inequality in love. Give and take must balance. One must be one's natural self or the whole business is an indecent trick, a vile use of life ! To use inferiors in love one must needs talk down to them, interpret oneself in their insufficient phrases, pretend, sentimentalise. And it is clear that unless oneself is to be lost, one must be content to leave alone all those people that one can reach only by sentimentalising. But Amanda—and yet somehow I love her for it still—could not leave any one alone. So she was always feverishly weaving nets of false relationship. Until her very self was forgotten. So she will go on until the end. With Easton it had been necessary for her to key herself to a simple exalted romanticism that was entirely insincere. She had so accustomed herself to these poses that her innate gestures were forgotten. She could not recover them ; she could not even reinvent them. Between us there were momentary gleams as though presently we should be our frank former selves again. They were never more than momentary. . . ."

And that was all that this astonishing man had seen fit to tell of his last parting from his wife.

Perhaps he did Amanda injustice. Perhaps there was a stronger thread of reality in her desire to recover him than he supposed. Clearly he believed that under the circumstances Amanda would have tried to recover anybody.

She had dressed for that morning's encounter in a very becoming and intimate wrap of soft mauve and white silk, and she had washed and dried her dark hair so that it was a vapour about her face. She set herself with a single mind to persuade herself and Benham that they were inseparable lovers, and she would not be deflected by his grim determination to discuss the conditions of their separation. When he asked her whether she wanted a divorce, she offered to throw over Sir Philip and banish him for ever as lightly as a great lady might sacrifice an objectionable poodle to her connubial peace.

Benham passed through perplexing phrases, so that she herself began to feel that her practice with Easton had spoilt her hands. His initial grimness she could understand and partially its breakdown into irritability. But she was puzzled by his laughter. For he laughed abruptly.

" You know, Amanda, I came home in a mood of tremendous tragedy. And really—you are a Lark."

And then overriding her altogether, he told her what he meant to do about their future and the future of their little son.

" You don't want a divorce and a fuss. Then I'll leave things. I perceive I've no intention of marrying any more. But you'd better do the straight thing. People forget and forgive. Especially when there is no one about making a fuss against you.

" Perhaps, after all, there is something to be said for shirking it. We'll both be able to get at the boy then. You'll not hurt him, and I shall want to see him. It's better for the boy anyhow not to have a divorce.

" I'll not stand in your way. I'll get a little flat and I shan't come too much to London, and when I do, you can get out of town. You must be discreet about Easton, and if people say anything about him, send them to me. After all, this is our private affair.

" We'll go on about money matters as we have been going. I trust to you not to run me into overwhelming debts. And, of course, if at any time you do want to marry—on account of children or anything—if nobody knows of this conversation we can be divorced then. . . . ''

Benham threw out these decisions in little dry sentences while Amanda gathered her forces for her last appeal.

It was an unsuccessful appeal, and at the end she flung herself down before him and clung to his knees. He struggled ridiculously to get himself clear, and when at last he succeeded she dropped prostrate on the floor with her dishevelled hair about her.

She heard the door close behind him, and still she lay there, a dark Guinevere, until with a start she heard a step upon the thick carpet without. He had come back. The door reopened. There was a slight pause, and then she raised her face and met the blank stare of the second housemaid. There are moments, suspended fragments of time rather than links in its succession, when the human eye is more intelligible than any words.

The housemaid made a rapid apologetic noise and vanished with a click of the door.

" *Damn !* " said Amanda.

Then slowly she rose to her knees.

She meditated through vast moments.

" It's a cursed thing to be a woman," said Amanda.

She stood up. She put her hand on the telephone in the corner and then she forgot about it. After another long interval of thought she spoke.

" Cheetah ! " she said, " old Cheetah ! . . .

" I didn't *think* it of you. . . . ''

Then presently with the even joyless movements of one who does a reasonable business, with something indeed of the manner of one who packs a trunk, she rang up Sir Philip Easton.

§ 30

The head chambermaid on the first floor of the Westwood Hotel in Danebury Street had a curious and perplexing glimpse of Benham's private processes the morning after this affair.

Benham had taken Room 27 on the afternoon of his return to London. She had seen him twice or three times, and he had struck her as a coldly decorous person, tall, white-faced, slow speaking ; the last man to behave violently or surprise a head chambermaid in any way. On the morning of his departure she was told by the first-floor waiter that the occupant of Room 26 had complained of an uproar in the night, and almost immediately she was summoned to see Benham.

He was standing facing the door and in a position which did a little obscure the condition of the room behind him. He was carefully dressed, and his manner was more cold and decorous than ever. But one of his hands was tied up in a white bandage.

" I am going this morning," he said ; " I am going down now to breakfast. I have had a few little accidents with some of the things in the room and I have cut my hand. I want you to tell the manager and see that they are properly charged for on the bill. . . . Thank you."

The head chambermaid was left to consider the accidents.

Benham's things were all packed up and the room had an air of having been straightened up neatly and methodically after a destructive cataclysm. One or two items that the chambermaid might possibly have overlooked in the normal course of things were carefully exhibited. For example, the sheet had been torn into half a dozen strips and they were lying side by side on the bed. The clock on the mantelpiece had been knocked into the fireplace and then pounded to pieces. All the looking-glasses in the room were smashed, apparently the electric lamp that stood on the night table by the bedside had been wrenched off and flung or hammered about amidst the other breakables. And there was a considerable amount of blood splashed about the room. The head chambermaid felt unequal to the perplexities of the spectacle and summoned her most convenient friend, the head chambermaid on the third floor, to her aid. The first-floor waiter joined their deliberations and several housemaids displayed a respectful interest in the matter. Finally they invoked the manager. He was still contemplating the scene of the disorder when the precipitate retreat of his subordinates warned him of Benham's return.

Benham was smoking a cigarette and his bearing was reassuringly tranquil.

" I had a kind of nightmare," he said. " I am fearfully sorry to have disarranged your room. You must charge me for the inconvenience as well as for the damage."

§ 31

" An aristocrat cannot be a lover.

" One cannot serve at once the intricacies of the wider issues of life and the intricacies of another human being. I do not mean that one may not love. One loves the more because one does not concentrate one's love. One loves nations, the people passing in the street, beasts hurt by the wayside, troubled scoundrels and university dons in tears. . . .

" But if one does not give one's whole love and life into a woman's hands I do not think one can expect to be loved.

" An aristocrat must do without close personal love. . . ."

This much was written at the top of a sheet of paper. The writing ended halfway down the page. Manifestly it was an abandoned beginning. And it was, it seemed to White, the last page of all this confusion of matter that dealt with the Second and Third Limitations. Its incompleteness made its expression perfect. . . .

There Benham's love experience ended. He turned to the great business of the world. Desire and Jealousy should deflect his life no more ; like Fear they were to be dismissed as far as possible and subdued when they could not be altogether dismissed. Whatever stirrings of blood or imagination there were in him after that parting, whatever failures from this resolution, they left no trace on the rest of his research, which was concerned with the hates of peoples and classes and war and peace and the possibilities science unveils and starry speculations of what mankind may do.

§ 32

But Benham did not leave England again until he had had an encounter with Lady Marayne.

The little lady came to her son in a state of extraordinary anger and distress. Never had she seemed quite so resolute nor quite so hopelessly dispersed and mixed. And when for a moment it seemed to him that she was not as a matter of fact dispersed and mixed at all, then with an instant eagerness he dismissed that one elucidatory gleam. " What are you doing in England, Poff ? " she demanded. " And what are you going to do ?

" Nothing ! And you are going to leave her in your house, with your property and a lover. If that's it, Poff, why did you ever come back ? And why did you ever marry her ? You might have known ; her father was a swindler. She's begotten of deceit. She'll tell her own story while you are away, and a pretty story she'll make of it."

" Do you want me to divorce her and make a scandal ? "

" I never wanted you to go away from her. If you'd stayed and watched her as a man should, as I begged you and implored you to do—— Didn't I tell you, Poff ? Didn't I warn you ? "

" But now what am I to do ? "

" There you are ! That's just a man's way. You get yourself into this trouble, you follow your passion and your fancies and fads and then you turn to me ! How can I help you now, Poff ? If you'd listened to me before ! "

Her blue eyes were demonstratively round.

" Yes, but——"

" I warned you," she interrupted. " I warned you. I've done all I could for you. It isn't that I haven't seen through her. When she came to me at first with that made-up story of a baby ! And all about loving me like her own mother. But I did what I could. I thought we might still make the best of a bad job. And then—— I might have known she couldn't leave Pip alone. . . . But for weeks I didn't dream. I wouldn't dream. Right under my nose. The impudence of it !"

Her voice broke. " Such a horrid mess ! Such a hopeless horrid mess ! "

She wiped away a bright little tear. . . .

" It's all alike. It's your way with us. All of you. There isn't a man in the world deserves to have a woman in the world. We do all we can for you. We do all we can to amuse you, we dress for you and we talk for you. All the sweet, warm little women there are ! And then you go away from us ! There never was a woman yet who pleased and satisfied a man, who did not lose him. Give you everything and off you must go ! Lovers, mothers. . . ."

It dawned upon Benham dimly that his mother's troubles did not deal exclusively with himself.

" But Amanda," he began.

" If you'd looked after her properly, it would have been right enough. Pip was as good as gold until she undermined him. . . . A woman can't wait about like an umbrella in a stand. . . . He was just a boy. . . . Only of course there she was—a novelty. It is perfectly easy to understand. She flattered him. . . . Men are such fools."

" Still—it's no good saying that now."

" But she'll spend all your money, Poff ! She'll break your back with debts. What's to prevent her ? With him living on her ! For that's what it comes to practically."

" Well, what am I to do ? "

" You aren't going back without tying her up, Poff ? You ought to stop every farthing of her money—every farthing. It's your duty."

" I can't do things like that."

" But have you no Shame ? To let that sort of thing go on ! "

" If I don't feel the Shame of it—— And I don't."

" And that money—— I got you that money, Poff ! It was my money."

Benham stared at her perplexed. " What am I to do ? " he asked.

" Cut her off, you silly boy ! Tie her up ! Pay her through a solicitor. Say that if she sees him *once* again—— ! "

He reflected. " No," he said at last.

" Poff ! " she cried, " every time I see you, you are more and more like your father. You're going off —just as he did. That baffled, *mulish* look—priggish—solemn ! Oh ! it's strange the stuff a poor woman has to bring into the world. But you'll do nothing. I know you'll do nothing. You'll stand everything. You—you Cuckold ! And she'll drive by me, she'll pass me in theatres with the money that ought to have been mine ! Oh ! Oh ! "

She dabbed her handkerchief from one swimming eye to the other. But she went on talking. Faster and faster, less and less coherently ; more and more wildly abusive. Presently in a brief pause of the storm Benham sighed profoundly. . . .

It brought the scene to a painful end. . . .

For weeks her distress pursued and perplexed him.

He had an extraordinary persuasion that in some obscure way he was in default, that he was to blame for her distress, that he owed her—he could never define what he owed her.

And yet, what on earth was one to do ?

And something his mother had said gave him the odd idea that he had misjudged his father, that he had missed depths of perplexed and kindred goodwill. He went down to see him before he returned to India. But if there was a hidden well of feeling in Mr. Benham, senior, it had been very carefully boarded over. The parental mind and attention were entirely engaged in a dispute in the *School World* about the heuristic method. Somebody had been disrespectful to Martindale House, and the thing was rankling almost unendurably. It seemed to be a relief to him to show his son very fully the essentially illogical position of his assailant. He was entirely inattentive to Benham's carefully made conversational opportunities. He would be silent at times while Benham talked, and then he would break out suddenly with : " What seems to me so unreasonable, so ridiculous, in the whole of that fellow's second argument—if one can call it an argument——
. . . A man who reasons as he does is bound to get laughed at. If people will only see it. . . . "

CHAPTER SIX

THE NEW HAROUN AL RASCHID

§ 1

BENHAM corresponded with Amanda until the summer of 1913. Sometimes the two wrote coldly to one another, sometimes with warm affection, sometimes with great bitterness. When he met White in Johannesburg during the strike period of 1913, he was on his way to see her in London and to settle their relationship upon a new and more definite footing. It was her suggestion that they should meet.

About her he felt an enormous, inexorable dissatisfaction. He could not persuade himself that his treatment of her and that his relations to her squared with any of his preconceptions of nobility, and yet at no precise point could he detect where he had definitely taken an ignoble step. Through Amanda he was coming to the full experience of life. Like all of us he had been prepared, he had prepared himself, to take life in a certain way, and life had taken him, as it takes all of us, in an entirely different and unexpected way. . . . He had been ready for noble deeds and villainies, for achievements and failures, and here as the dominant fact of his personal life was a perplexing riddle. He could not hate and condemn her for ten minutes at a time without a flow of exoneration ; he could not think of her tolerantly or lovingly without immediate shame and resentment, and with the utmost will in the world he could not banish her from his mind.

During the intervening years he had never ceased to have her in his mind ; he would not think of her, it is true, if he could help it, but often he could not help it ; and as a negative presence, as a thing denied, she was almost more potent than she had been as a thing accepted. Meanwhile he worked. His nervous irritability increased, but it did not hinder the steady development of his Research.

Long before his final parting from Amanda he had worked out his idea and method for all the more personal problems in life ; the problems he put together under his headings of the first three " Limitations." He had resolved to emancipate himself from fear, indulgence, and that instinctive preoccupation with the interests and dignity of self which he chose to term Jealousy, and with the one tremendous exception of Amanda he had to a large extent succeeded. Amanda. Amanda. Amanda. He stuck the more grimly to his Research to drown that beating in his brain.

Emancipation from all these personal things he held now to be a mere prelude to the real work of a man's life, which was to serve this dream of a larger human purpose. The bulk of his work was to discover and define that purpose, that purpose which must be the directing and comprehending form of all the activities of the noble life. One cannot be noble, he had come to perceive, at large ; one must be noble to an end. To make human life, collectively and in detail, a thing more comprehensive, more beautiful, more generous and coherent than it is to-day seemed to him the fundamental intention of all nobility. He believed more and more firmly that the impulses to make and help and subserve great purposes are abundantly present in the world, that they are inhibited by hasty thinking, limited thinking and bad thinking, and that the real ennoblement of human life was not so much a creation as a release. He lumped the preventive and destructive forces that keep men dispersed, unhappy and ignoble under the heading of Prejudice ; and he made this Prejudice his fourth and greatest and most difficult limitation. In one place he had written it, " Prejudice or Divisions." That being subdued in oneself and in the world, then in the measure of its subjugation, the new life of our race, the great age, the noble age, would begin.

So he set himself to examine his own mind and the mind of the world about him for prejudice, for hampering follies, disguised disloyalties and mischievous distrusts ; and the great bulk of the papers that White struggled with at Westhaven Street were devoted to various aspects of this search for " Prejudice." It seemed to White to be at once the most magnificent and the most preposterous of enterprises. It was indeed no less than an inquiry into all the preventible sources of human failure and disorder. . . . And it was all too manifest to White also that the last place in which Benham was capable of detecting a prejudice was at the back of his own head. . . .

Under this Fourth Limitation he put the most remarkable array of influences, race-hatred, national suspicion, the evil side of patriotism, religious and social intolerance, every social consequence of muddle-headedness, every dividing force indeed except the purely personal dissensions between man and man. And he developed a metaphysical interpretation of these troubles. " No doubt," he wrote in one place, " much of the evil between different kinds of men is due to uncultivated feeling, to natural bad feeling, but far more is it due to bad thinking. At times he seemed on the verge of the persuasion that most human trouble is really due to bad metaphysics. It was, one must remark, an extraordinary journey he had made ; he had started from chivalry and arrived at metaphysics ; every knight he held must be a logician, and ultimate bravery is courage of the mind. One thinks of his coming to this conclusion with knit brows and balancing intentness above whole gulfs of bathos—very much as he had once walked the Leysin Bisse. . . .

" Men do not know how to think," he insisted—getting along the planks ; " and they will not realise that they do not know how to think. Nine-tenths of the wars in the world have arisen out of misconceptions. . . . Misconception is the sin and dishonour of the mind, and muddle thinking as ignoble as dirty conduct. . . . Infinitely more disastrous."

And again he wrote : " Man, I see, is an over-practical creature, too eager to get into action. There is our deepest trouble. He takes conclusions ready-made, or he makes them in a hurry. Life is so short that he thinks it better to err than wait. He has no patience, no faith in anything but himself. He thinks he is a being when in reality he is only a link in a being, and so he is more anxious to be complete than right. The last devotion of which he is capable is that devotion of the mind which suffers partial performance, and before he is dead it is already being abandoned and begun all over again by some one else in the same egotistical haste. . . "

It is, I suppose, a part of the general humour of life that these words should have been written by a man who walked the plank to fresh ideas with the dizziest difficulty unless he had Prothero to drag him forward, and who acted time after time with an altogether disastrous hastiness.

§ 2

Yet there was a kind of necessity in this journey of Benham's from the cocked hat and wooden sword of Seagate and his early shame at cowardice and baseness to the spiritual megalomania of his complete Research Magnificent. You can no more resolve to live a life of honour nowadays and abstain from social and political scheming on a world-wide scale, than you can profess religion and refuse to think about God. In the past it was possible to take all sorts of things for granted and be loyal to unexamined things. One could be loyal to unexamined things because they were unchallenged things. But now everything is challenged. By the time of his second visit to Russia, Benham's ideas of conscious and deliberate aristocracy reaching out to an idea of universal responsibility had already grown into the extraordinary fantasy that he was, as it were, an uncrowned king in the world. To be noble is to be aristocratic, that is to say a ruler. Thence it follows that aristocracy is multiple kingship, and to be an aristocrat is to partake both of the nature of philosopher and king. . . .

Yet it is manifest that the powerful people of this world are by no means necessarily noble, and that most modern kings, poor in quality, petty in spirit, conventional in outlook, controlled and limited, fall far short of kingship. Nevertheless, there *is* nobility, there *is* kingship, or this earth is a dustbin and mankind but a kind of skin-disease upon a planet. From that it is an easy step to this idea, the idea whose first expression had already so touched the imagination of Amanda, of a sort of diffused and voluntary kingship scattered throughout mankind. The aristocrats are not at the high table, the kings are not enthroned, those who are enthroned are but pretenders and *simulacra*, kings of the vulgar ; the real king and ruler is every man who sets aside the naïve passions and self-interest of the common life for the rule and service of the world.

This is an idea that is now to be found in much contemporary writing. It is one of those ideas that seem to appear simultaneously at many points in the world, and it is impossible to say now how far Benham was an originator of this idea, and how far he simply resonated to its expression by others. It was far more likely that Prothero, getting it heaven knows where, had spluttered it out and forgotten it, leaving it to germinate in the mind of his friend. . . .

This lordly, this kingly dream became more and more essential to Benham as his life went on. When Benham walked the Bisse he was just a youngster resolved to be individually brave ; when he prowled in the jungle by night he was there for all mankind. With every year he became more and more definitely to himself a consecrated man as kings are consecrated. Only that he was self-consecrated, and anointed

only in his heart. At last he was, so to speak Haroun al Raschid
again, going unsuspected about the world, because the palace
of his security would not tell him the secrets of men's disorders.
He was no longer a creature of circumstances ; he was kingly,
unknown, Alfred in the camp of the Danes. In the great later
accumulations of his Research the personal matter, the introspection, the intimate discussion of motive, becomes less and
less. He forgets himself in the exaltation of kingliness. He
worries less and less over the particular rightness of his definite
acts. In these later papers White found Benham abstracted,
self-forgetful, trying to find out with an ever increased self-
detachment, with an ever deepening regal solicitude, why
there are massacres, wars, tyrannies and persecutions, why
we let famine, disease and beasts assail us and want to dwarf
and cripple vast multitudes in the midst of possible plenty.
And when he found out, and as far as he found out, he meant
quite simply and earnestly to apply his knowledge. . . .

§ 3

The intellectualism of Benham intensified to the end. His
definition of Prejudice impressed White as being the most
bloodless and philosophical formula that ever dominated the
mind of a man.

" Prejudice," Benham had written, " is that common
incapacity of the human mind to understand that a difference
in any respect is not a difference in all respects, reinforced
and rendered malignant by an instinctive hostility to what
is unlike ourselves. We exaggerate classification and then
charge it with mischievous emotion by referring it to ourselves." And under this comprehensive formula he proceeded to study and attack Family Prejudice, National Prejudice, Race Prejudice, War, Class Prejudice, Professional
Prejudice, Sex Prejudice, in the most industrious and elaborate
manner. Whether one regards oneself or others he held that
these prejudices are evil things. " From the point of view
of human welfare they break men up into wars and conflicts,
make them an easy prey to those who trade upon suspicion
and hostility, prevent sane collective co-operations, cripple
and embitter life. From the point of view of personal aristocracy they make men vulgar, violent, unjust and futile. All
the conscious life of the aristocrat must be a constant
struggle against false generalisations ; it is as much his duty
to free himself from that as from fear, indulgence, and
jealousy ; it is a larger and more elaborate task, but it is
none the less cardinal and essential. Indeed it is more
cardinal and essential. The true knight has to be not only
no coward, no self-pamperer, no egotist. He has to be a
philosopher. He has to be no hasty or foolish thinker. His
judgment no more than his courage is to be taken by
surprise.

"To subdue fear, desire and jealousy is the aristocrat's personal affair, it is his ritual and discipline, like a knight watching his arms ; but the destruction of division and prejudice and all their forms and establishments is his real task, that is the common work of knighthood. It is a task to be done in a thousand ways ; one man working by persuasion, another by example, this one overthrowing some crippling restraint upon the freedom of speech and the spread of knowledge, and that preparing himself for a war that will shatter a tyrannous presumption. Most imaginative literature, all scientific investigation, all sound criticism, all good building, all good manufacture, all sound politics, every honesty and every reasoned kindliness, contribute to this release of men from the heat and confusions of our present world."

It was clear to White that as Benham progressed with this major part of his research, he was more and more possessed by the idea that he was not making his own personal research alone, but, side by side with a vast, masked, hidden and once unsuspected multitude of others ; that this great idea of his was under kindred forms the great idea of thousands, that it was breaking as the dawn breaks, simultaneously to great numbers of people, and that the time was not far off when the new aristocracy, the disguised rulers of the world, would begin to realise their common bent and effort. Into these latter papers there creeps more and more frequently a new phraseology, such expressions as the "Invisible King" and the "Spirit of Kingship," so that as Benham became personally more and more solitary, his thoughts became more and more public and social.

Benham was not content to define and denounce the prejudices of mankind. He set himself to study just exactly how these prejudices worked, to get at the nature and habits and strengths of each kind of prejudice, and to devise means for its treatment, destruction or neutralisation. He had no great faith in the power of pure reasonableness ; his psychological ideas were modern, and he had grasped the fact that the power of most of the great prejudices that strain humanity lies deeper than the intellectual level. Consequently he sought to bring himself into the closest contact with prejudices in action and prejudices in conflict in order to discover their sub-rational springs.

A large proportion of that larger moiety of the material at Westhaven Street which White from his extensive experience of the public patience decided could not possibly "make a book," consisted of notes and discussions upon the first-hand observations Benham had made in this or that part of the world. He began in Russia during the revolutionary trouble of 1906, he went thence to Odessa, and from place to place in Bessarabia and Kieff, where during a pogrom he had his first really illuminating encounter with race and culture prejudice. His examination of the social and political condition of Russia seems to have left him much more hopeful than was the common feeling of liberal-minded people during the years of depression that followed the revolution of 1906, and it was upon the race question that his attention concentrated.

The Swadeshi outbreak drew him from Russia to India. Here in an entirely different environment was another discord of race and culture, and he found in his study of it much that illuminated and corrected his impressions of the Russian issue. A whole drawer was devoted to a comparatively finished and very thorough inquiry into human dissensions in lower Bengal. Here there were not only race but culture conflicts, and he could work particularly upon the differences between men of the same race who were Hindus, Christians, and Mahometans respectively. He could compare the Bengali Mahometan not only with the Bengali Brahminist, but also with the Mahometan from the north-west. " If one could scrape off all the creed and training, would one find much the same thing at the bottom or something fundamentally so different that no close homogeneous social life and not even perhaps a life of just compromise is possible between the different races of mankind ? "

His answer to that was a confident one. " There are no such natural and unalterable differences in character and quality between any two sorts of men whatever, as would make their peaceful and kindly co-operation in the world impossible," he wrote.

But he was not satisfied with his observations in India. He found the prevalence of caste ideas anti-pathetic and complicating. He went on after his last parting from Amanda into China, it was the first of several visits to China, and thence he crossed to America. White found a number of American press-cuttings of a vehemently anti-Japanese quality still awaiting digestion in a drawer, and it was clear to him that Benham had given a considerable amount of attention to the development of the " white " and " yellow " race hostility on the Pacific slope ; but his chief interest at that time had been the negro. He went to Washington and thence south ; he visited Tuskeegee and Atlanta, and then went off at a tangent to Hayti. He was drawn to Hayti by Hesketh Pritchard's vivid book, *Where Black Rules White,* and like Hesketh Pritchard he was able to visit that wonderful monument to kingship, the hidden fastness of La Ferrière, the citadel built a century ago by the " Black Napoleon," the Emperor Christophe. He went with a young American demonstrator from Harvard.

§ 4

It was a memorable excursion. They rode from Cap Haytien for a day's journey along dusty uneven tracks through a steaming plain of luxurious vegetation, that presented the strangest mixture of unbridled jungle with populous country. They passed countless villages of thatched huts alive with curiosity and swarming with naked black children, and yet all the time they seemed to be in a wilderness. They forded rivers, they had at times to force themselves through thickets, once or twice they lost their way, and always ahead of them, purple and sullen, the great mountain peak with La Ferrière upon its crest rose slowly out of the background until it dominated the landscape.   Long after dark they blundered upon rather than came to the village at its foot where they were to pass the night.   They were interrogated under a flaring torch by peering ragged black soldiers, and passed through a firelit crowd into the presence of the local commandant to dispute volubly about their right to go further.   They might have been in some remote corner of Nigeria.   Their papers, laboriously got in order, were vitiated by the fact which only became apparent by degrees, that the commandant could not read. They carried their point with difficulty.

But they carried their point, and, watched and guarded by a hungry nalf-naked negro in a kepi and the remains of a sky-blue pair of trousers, they explored one of the most exemplary memorials of imperialism that humanity has ever made. The roads and parks and prospects constructed by this vanished Emperor of Hayti had long since disappeared, and the three men clambered for hours up ravines and precipitous jungle tracks, occasionally crossing the winding traces of a choked and ruined road that had once been the lordly approach to his fastness.   Below they passed an abandoned palace of vast extent, a palace with great terraces and the still traceable outline of gardens, though there were green things pushing between the terrace steps, and trees thrust out of the empty windows.   Here from a belvedere of which the skull-like vestige still remained, the negro Emperor Christophe, after fourteen years of absolute rule, had watched for a time the smoke of the burning of his cane-fields in the plain below, and then, learning that his bodyguard had deserted him, had gone in and blown out his brains.

He had christened the place, after the best of examples, " Sans Souci."

But the citadel above, which was to have been his last defence, he never used.   The defection of his guards made him abandon that.   To build it, they say, cost Hayti thirty thousand lives.   He had the true Imperial lavishness.   So high it was, so lost in a wilderness of trees and bush, looking out over a land relapsed now altogether to a barbarism of patch and hovel, so solitary and chill under the tropical sky —for even the guards who still watched over its suspected treasures feared to live in its ghostly galleries and had made hovels outside its walls—and at the same time so huge and grandiose—there were walls thirty feet thick, galleries with scores of rust-eaten cannon, circular dining-halls, king's apartments, and queen's apartments, towering battlements and great arched doorways—that it seemed to Benham to embody the power and passing of that miracle of human history, tyranny, the helpless bowing of multitudes before one man and the transitoriness of such glories, more completely than anything he had ever seen or imagined in the world before. Beneath the battlements—they were choked above with jungle grass and tamarinds and many flowery weeds—the precipice fell away a sheer two thousand feet, and below spread a vast rich green plain populous and diversified, bounded at last by the blue sea, like an amethystine wall. Over this precipice Christophe was wont to fling his victims, and below this terrace were bottle-shaped dungeons where men, broken and torn, thrust in at the neck-like hole above, starved and died ; it was his headquarters here, here he had his torture chambers and the means for nameless cruelties. . . .

" Not a hundred years ago," said Benham's companion, and told the story of the disgraced favourite, the youth who had offended.

" Leap," said his master, and the poor hypnotised wretch after one questioning glance at the conceivable alternatives made his last gesture of servility, and then stood out against the sky, swayed, and with a convulsion of resolve, leapt and shot headlong down through the shimmering air.

Came presently the little faint sound of his fall.

The Emperor, satisfied, turned away, unmindful of the fact that this projectile he had launched had caught among the bushes below, and presently struggled and found itself still a living man. It could scramble down to the road and, what is more wonderful, hope for mercy. An hour and it stood before Christophe again, with an arm broken and bloody and a face torn, a battered thing now but with a faint flavour of pride in its bearing. " Your bidding has been done, Sire," it said.

" So," said the Emperor unappeased. " And you live ? Well—— Leap again. . . ."

And then came other stories. The young man told them as he had heard them, stories of ferocious wholesale butcheries, of men standing along the walls of the banqueting chamber to be shot one by one as the feast went on, of exquisite and terrifying cruelties, and his one note of wonder, his refrain was, " *Here !* Not a hundred years ago. . . . It makes one almost believe that somewhere things of this sort are being done now."

They ate their lunch together amidst the weedy flowery ruins. The lizards which had fled their coming crept out again to bask in the sunshine. The soldier-guide and guard scrabbled about with his black fingers in the ruinous and rifled tomb of Christophe in a search for some saleable memento. . . .

Benham sat musing in silence. The thought of deliberate cruelty was always an actual physical distress to him. He sat bathed in the dreamy afternoon sunlight and struggled against the pictures that crowded into his mind, pictures of men aghast at death, and of fear-driven men toiling in agony, and of the shame of extorted obedience and of cringing and crawling black figures, and the defiance of righteous hate beaten down under blow and anguish. He saw eyes alight with terror and lips rolled back in agony, he saw weary hopeless flight before striding proud destruction, he saw the poor trampled mangled dead, and he shivered in his soul. . . .

He hated Christophe and all that made Christophe ; he hated pride, and then the idea came to him that it is not pride that makes Christophes but humility.

There is in the medley of man's composition, deeper far than his superficial working delusion that he is a separated self-seeking individual, an instinct for co-operation and obedience. Every natural sane man wants, though he may want it unwittingly, kingly guidance, a definite direction for his own partial life. At the bottom of his heart he feels, even if he does not know it definitely, that his life is partial. He is driven to join himself on. He obeys decision and the appearance of strength as a horse obeys its rider's voice. One thinks of the pride, the uncontrolled frantic will of this black ape of all Emperors, and one forgets the universal docility that made him possible. Usurpation is a crime to which men are tempted by human dirigibility. It is the orderly peoples who create tyrants, and it is not so much restraint above as stiff insubordination below that has to be taught to men. There are kings and tyrannies and imperialisms, simply because of the unkingliness of men.

And as he sat upon the battlements of La Ferrière, Benham cast off from his mind his last tolerance for earthly kings and existing States, and expounded to another human being for the first time this long-cherished doctrine of his of the Invisible King who is the lord of human destiny, the spirit of nobility, who will one day take the sceptre and rule the earth. . . . To the young American's naïve American response to any simply felt emotion, he seemed with his white earnestness and his glowing eyes a veritable prophet. . . .

" This is the root idea of aristocracy," said Benham.

" I have never heard the underlying spirit of democracy, the real true Thing in democracy, so thoroughly expressed," said the young American.

§ 5

Benham's notes on race and racial cultures gave White tantalising glimpses of a number of picturesque experiences. The adventure in Kieff had first roused Benham to the reality of racial quality. He was caught in the wheels of a pogrom.

" Before that time I had been disposed to minimise and deny race. I still think it need not prevent men from the completest social co-operation, but I see now better than I did how difficult it is for any man to purge from his mind the idea that he is not primarily a Jew, a Teuton, or a Kelt, but a man. You can persuade any one in five minutes that he or she belongs to some special and blessed and privileged sort of human being ; it takes a lifetime to destroy that persuasion. There are these confounded differences of colour, of eye and brow, of nose or hair, small differences in themselves except that they give a foothold and foundation for tremendous fortifications of prejudice and tradition, in which hostilities and hatreds may gather. When I think of a Jew's nose, a Chinaman's eyes, or a negro's colour I am reminded of that fatal little pit which nature has left in the vermiform appendix, a thing no use in itself and of no significance, but a gathering-place for mischief. The extremest case of race-feeling is the Jewish case ; and even here, I am convinced, it is the Bible and the Talmud and the exertions of those inevitable professional champions who live upon racial feeling, far more than their common distinction of blood, which holds this people together banded against mankind."

Between the lines of such general propositions as this White read little scraps of intimation that linked with the things Benham let fall in Johannesburg to reconstruct the Kieff adventure.

Benham had been visiting a friend in the country on the further side of the Dnieper. As they drove back along dusty stretches of road amidst fields of corn and sunflower, and through bright little villages, they saw against the evening blue under the full moon a smoky red glare rising from amidst the white houses and dark trees of the town. " The pogrom's begun," said Benham's friend, and was surprised when Benham wanted to end a pleasant day by going to see what happens after the beginning of a pogrom.

He was to have several surprises before at last he left Benham in disgust and went home by himself.

For Benham, with that hastiness that so flouted his exalted theories, passed rapidly from an attitude of impartial inquiry to active intervention. The two men left their carriage and plunged into the network of unlovely dark streets in which the Jews and traders harboured. . . . Benham's first intervention was on behalf of a crouching and yelping bundle of humanity that was being dragged about and kicked at a street corner.

The bundle resolved itself into a filthy little old man, and made off with extraordinary rapidity, while Benham remonstrated with the kickers. Benham's tallness, his very Gentile face, his good clothes, and an air of tense authority about him had its effect, and the kickers shuffled off with remarks that were partly apologies. But Benham's friend revolted. This was no business of theirs.

Benham went on unaccompanied towards the glare of the burning houses.

For a time he watched. Black figures moved between him and the glare, and he tried to find out the exact nature of the conflict by inquiries in clumsy Russian. He was told that the Jews had insulted a religious procession, that a Jew had spat at an ikon, that the shop of a cheating Jew trader had been set on fire, and that the blaze had spread to the adjacent group of houses. He gathered that the Jews were running out of the burning block on the other side "like rats." The crowd was mostly composed of town roughs with a sprinkling of peasants. They were mischievous but undecided. Among them were a number of soldiers, and he was surprised to see a policeman, brightly lit from head to foot, watching the looting of a shop that was still untouched by the flames.

He held back some men who had discovered a couple of women's figures slinking along in the shadow beneath a wall. Behind his remonstrances the Jewesses escaped. His anger against disorder was growing upon him. . . .

Late that night Benham found himself the leading figure amidst a party of Jews who had made a counter attack upon a gang of roughs in a court that had become the refuge of a crowd of fugitives. Some of the young Jewish men had already been making a fight, rather a poor and hopeless fight, from the windows of the house near the entrance of the court, but it is doubtful if they would have made an effective resistance if it had not been for this tall excited stranger who was suddenly shouting directions to them in sympathetically murdered Russian. It was not that he brought powerful blows or subtle strategy to their assistance, but that he put heart into them and perplexity into his adversaries because he was so manifestly non-partisan. Nobody could ever have mistaken Benham for a Jew. When at last towards dawn a not too zealous governor called out the troops and began to clear the streets of rioters, Benham and a band of Jews were still keeping the gateway of that court behind a hasty but adequate barricade of furniture and hand-barrows.

The ghetto could not understand him, nobody could understand him, but it was clear a rare and precious visitor had come to their rescue, and he was implored by a number of elderly, dirty, but very intelligent-looking old men to stay with them and preserve them until their safety was assured.

They could not understand him, but they did their utmost

to entertain him and assure him of their gratitude. They seemed to consider him as a representative of the British Government, and foreign intervention on their behalf is one of those unfortunate fixed ideas that no persecuted Jews seem able to abandon.

Benham found himself, refreshed and tended, sitting beside a wood fire in an inner chamber richly flavoured by humanity and listening to a discourse in evil but understandable German. It was a discourse upon the wrongs and the greatness of the Jewish people—and it was delivered by a compact middle-aged man with a big black beard and long-lashed but animated eyes. Beside him a very old man dozed and nodded approval. A number of other men crowded the apartment, including several who had helped to hold off the rioters from the court. Some could follow the talk and ever and again endorsed the speaker in Yiddish or Russian ; others listened with tantalised expressions, their brows knit, their lips moving.

It was a discourse Benham had provoked. For now he was at the very heart of the Jewish question, and he could get some light upon the mystery of this great hatred at first hand. He did not want to hear tales of outrages, of such things he knew, but he wanted to understand what was the irritation that caused these things.

So he listened. The Jews dilated at first on the harmlessness and usefulness of the Jews.

" But do you never take a certain advantage ? " Benham threw out.

" The Jews are cleverer than the Russians. Must we suffer for that ? "

The spokesman went on to the more positive virtues of his race. Benham suddenly had that uncomfortable feeling of the Gentile who finds a bill being made against him. Did the world owe Israel nothing for Philo, Aron ben Asher, Solomon Gabriol, Halévy, Mendelssohn, Heine, Meyerbeer, Rubinstein, Joachim, Zangwill ? Does Britain owe nothing to Lord Beaconsfield, Montefiore, or the Rothschilds ? Can France repudiate her debt to Fould, Gaudahaux, Oppert, or Germany to Fürst, Steinschneider, Herxheimer, Lasker, Auerbach, Traube and Lazarus and Benfey ? . . .

Benham admitted under the pressure of urgent tones and gestures that these names did undoubtedly include the cream of humanity, but was it not true that the Jews did press a little financially upon the inferior peoples whose lands they honoured in their exile ?

The man with the black beard took up the challenge bravely.

" They are merciful creditors," he said. " And it is their genius to possess and control. What better stewards could you find for the wealth of nations than the Jews. And for the honours ? That always had been the rôle of the Jews—stewardship. Since the days of Joseph in Egypt. . . . "

Then in a lower voice he went on to speak of the deficiencies of the Gentile population. He wished to be just and generous, but the truth was the truth. The Christian Russians loved drink and laziness ; they had no sense of property ; were it not for unjust laws even now the Jews would possess all the land of South Russia. . . .

Benham listened with a kind of fascination. "But," he said.

It was so. And with a confidence that aroused a protest or so from the onlookers, the Jewish apologist suddenly rose up, opened a safe close beside the fire and produced an armful of documents.

"Look ! " he said, " all over South Russia there are these ! "

Benham was a little slow to understand, until half a dozen of these papers had been thrust into his hand. Eager fingers pointed, and several voices spoke. These things were illegalities that might some day be legal ; there were the records of loans and hidden transactions that might at any time put all the surrounding soil into the hands of the Jew. All South Russia was mortgaged. . . .

" But is it so ? " asked Benham, and for a time ceased to listen and stared into the fire.

Then he held up the papers in his hand to secure silence and, feeling his way in unaccustomed German, began to speak and continued to speak in spite of a constant insurgent undertone of interruption from the Jewish spokesman.

All men, Benham said, were brothers. Did they not remember Nathan the Wise ?

" I did not claim him." said the spokesman, misunderstanding. " He is a character in fiction."

But all men are brothers, Benham maintained. They had to be merciful to one another and give their gifts freely to one another. Also they had to consider each other's weaknesses. The Jews were probably justified in securing and administering the property of every community into which they came, they were no doubt right in claiming to be best fitted for that task ; but also they had to consider, perhaps more than they did, the feelings and vanities of the host population into which they brought these beneficent activities. What was said of the ignorance, incapacity and vice of the Roumanians and Russians was very generally believed and accepted, but it did not alter the fact that the peasant, for all his incapacity, did like to imagine he owned his own patch and hovel and did have a curious irrational hatred of debt. . . .

The faces about Benham looked perplexed.

" *This*," said Benham, tapping the papers in his hand. " They will not understand the ultimate benefit of it. It will be a source of anger and fresh hostility. It does not follow because your race has supreme financial genius that you must always follow its dictates to the exclusion of other considerations. . . ."

The perplexity increased.

Benham felt he must be more general. He went on to emphasise the brotherhood of man, the right to equal opportunity, equal privilege, freedom to develop their idiosyncrasies as far as possible, unhindered by the idiosyncrasies of others. He could feel the sympathy and understanding of his hearers returning. " You see," said Benham, " you must have generosity. You must forget ancient scores. Do you not see the world must make a fresh beginning ? "

He was entirely convinced he had them with him. The heads nodded assent, the bright eyes and lips followed the slow disentanglement of his bad German.

" Free yourselves and the world," he said.

Applause.

" And so," he said, breaking unconsciously into English, " let us begin by burning these *beastly* mortgages ! "

And with a noble and dramatic gesture Benham cast his handful on the fire. The assenting faces became masks of horror. A score of hands clutched at those precious papers, and a yell of dismay and anger filled the room. Some one caught at his throat from behind. " Don't kill him ! " cried some one. " He fought for us ! " . . .

§ 6

An hour later Benham returned in an extraordinarily dishevelled and battered condition to his hotel. He found his friend in anxious consultation with the hotel proprietor.

" We were afraid that something had happened to you," said his friend.

" I got a little involved," said Benham.

" Hasn't some one clawed your cheek ? "

" Very probably," said Benham.

" And torn your coat ? And hit you rather heavily upon the neck ? "

" It was a complicated misunderstanding," said Benham. " Oh ! pardon ! I'm rather badly bruised upon that arm you're holding."

§ 7

Benham told the story to White as a jest against himself.

" I see now of course that they could not possibly understand my point of view," he said. . . .

" I'm not sure if they quite followed my German. . . .

" It's odd, too, that I remember saying, ' Let's burn these mortgages,' and at the time I'm almost sure I didn't know the German for mortgage. . . . "

It was not the only occasion on which other people had failed to grasp the full intention behind Benham's proceedings. His aristocratic impulses were apt to run away with his conceptions of brotherhood, and time after time it was only too manifest to White that Benham's pallid flash of anger had astonished the subjects of his disinterested observations extremely. His explorations in Hayti had been terminated abruptly by an affair with a native policeman that had necessitated the intervention of the British Consul. It was begun with that suddenness that was too often characteristic of Benham, by his hitting the policeman. It was in the main street of Cap Haytien, and the policeman had just clubbed an unfortunate youth over the head with the heavily loaded wooden club which is the normal instrument of Haytien discipline. His blow was a repartee, part of a triangular altercation in which a large, voluble, mahogany-coloured lady whose head was tied up in a blue handkerchief played a conspicuous part, but it seemed to Benham an entirely unjustifiable blow.

He allowed an indignation with negro policemen in general that had been gathering from the very moment of his arrival at Port-au-Prince to carry him away. He advanced with the kind of shout one would hurl at a dog, and smote the policeman to the earth with the stout stick that the peculiar social atmosphere of Hayti had disposed him to carry. By the local standard his blow was probably a trivial one, but the moral effect of his indignant pallor and a sort of rearing tallness about him on these occasions was always very considerable. Unhappily these characteristics could have no effect on a second negro policeman who was approaching the affray from behind, and he felled Benham by a blow on the shoulder that was meant for the head, and with the assistance of his colleague overpowered him, while the youth and the woman vanished.

The two officials dragged Benham in a state of vehement protest to the lock-up, and only there, in the light of a superior officer's superior knowledge, did they begin to realise the grave fact of his British citizenship.

The memory of the destruction of the Haytien fleet by a German gunboat was still vivid in Port-au-Prince, and to that Benham owed it that in spite of his blank refusal to compensate the man he had knocked over, he was after two days of anger, two days of extreme insanitary experience, and much meditation upon his unphilosophical hastiness, released.

Quite a number of trivial incidents of a kindred sort diversified his inquiries into Indian conditions. They too turned for the most part on his facile exasperation at any defiance of his deep-felt desire for human brotherhood. At last indeed came an affair that refused ultimately to remain trivial, and tangled him up in a coil that invoked newspaper articles and heated controversies.

The effect of India upon Benham's mind was a peculiar mixture of attraction and irritation. He was attracted by the Hindu spirit of intellectualism and the Hindu repudiation of brutality, and he was infuriated by the spirit of caste that cuts the great world of India into a thousand futile little worlds,

all aloof and hostile one to the other. " I came to see India,"
he wrote, " and there is no India. There is a great number of
Indias, and each goes about with its chin in the air, quietly
scorning everybody else."

His Indian adventures and his great public controversy
on caste began with a tremendous row with an Indian civil
servant who had turned an Indian gentleman out of his first-class
compartment, and culminated in a disgraceful fracas with a
squatting brown holiness at Benares, who had thrown aside
his little brass bowlful of dinner because Benham's shadow
had fallen upon it.

" You unendurable snob ! " said Benham, and then lapsing
into the forceful and inadvisable, " By Heaven, you *shall*
eat it ! . . ."

§ 8

Benham's detestation of human divisions and hostilities was
so deep in his character as to seem almost instinctive. But
he had too a very clear reason for his hostility to all these
amazing breaks in human continuity in his sense of the gathering dangers they now involve. They had always, he was convinced, meant conflict, hatred, misery, and the destruction of
human dignity, but the new conditions of life that have been
brought about by modern science were making them far more
dangerous than they had ever been before. He believed that
the evil and horror of war was becoming more and more tremendous with every decade, and that the free play of national
prejudice and that stupid filching ambitiousness that seems to
be inseparable from monarchy, were bound to precipitate
catastrophe, unless a real international aristocracy could be
brought into being to prevent it.

In the drawer full of papers labelled " Politics," White found
a paper called " The Metal Beast." It showed that for a time
Benham had been greatly obsessed by the thought of the
armaments that were in those days piling up in every country
in Europe. He had gone to Essen, and at Essen he had met a
German who had boasted of Zeppelins and the great guns that
were presently to smash the effete British fleet and open the
Imperial way to London.

" I could not sleep," he wrote, " on account of this man
and his talk and the streak of hatred in his talk. He
distressed me not because he seemed exceptional, but because
he seemed ordinary. I realised that he was more human than
I was, and that only killing and killing could come out of such
humanity. I thought of the great ugly guns I had seen, and
of the still greater guns he had talked about, and how gloat-
ingly he thought of the destruction they could do. I felt as
I used to feel about that infernal stallion that had killed a man
with its teeth and feet, a despairing fear, a sense of monstrosity
in life. And this creature who had so disturbed me was only

a beastly snuffy little man in an ill-fitting frock-coat, who laid his knife and fork by their tips on the edge of his plate, and picked his teeth with gusto and breathed into my face as he talked to me. The commonest of representative men. I went about that Westphalian country after that, with the conviction that headless, soulless, blood-drinking metal monsters were breeding all about me. I felt that science was producing a poisonous swarm, a nest of black dragons. They were crouching here and away there in France and England, they were crouching like beasts that bide their time, mewed up in forts, kennelled in arsenals, hooded in tarpaulins as hawks are hooded. . . . And I had never thought very much about them before, and there they were, waiting until some human fool like that frock-coated thing of spite, and fools like him multiplied by a million, saw fit to call them out to action. Just out of hatred and nationalism and faction. . . . ''

Then came a queer fancy.

" Great guns, mines, battleships, all that cruelty-apparatus ; I see it more and more as the gathering revenge of dead joyless matter for the happiness of life. It is a conspiracy of the lifeless, an enormous plot of the rebel metals against sensation. That is why in particular half-living people seem to love these things. La Ferrière was a fastness of the kind of tyranny that passes out of human experience, the tyranny of the strong man over men. Essen comes, the new thing, the tyranny of the strong machine. . . .

" Science is either slave or master. These people—I mean the German people and militarist people generally—have no real mastery over the scientific and economic forces on which they seem to ride. The monster of steel and iron carries Kaiser and Germany and all Europe captive. It has persuaded them to mount upon its back, and now they must follow the logic of its path. Whither ? . . . Only kingship will ever master that beast of steel which has got loose into the world. Nothing but the sense of unconquerable kingship in us all will ever dare withstand it. . . . Men must be kingly aristocrats—it isn't *may* be now, it is *must* be—for these confederated metals, these things of chemistry and metallurgy, these explosives and mechanisms, will trample the blood and life out of our race into mere red-streaked froth and filth. . . . ''

Then he turned to the question of this metallic beast's release. Would it ever be given blood ?

" Men of my generation have been brought up in this threat of a great war that never comes ; for forty years we have had it, so that it is with a note of incredulity that one tells oneself, ' After all this war may happen. But can it happen ? ' ''

He proceeded to speculate upon the probability whether a great war would ever devastate western Europe again, and it was very evident to White that he wanted very much to persuade himself against that idea. It was too disagreeable for him to think it probable. The paper was dated 1910. It was in October, 1914, that White, who was still working upon the laborious uncertain account of Benham's life and thought he has recently published, read what Benham had written. Benham concluded that the common sense of the world would hold up this danger until reason could get " to the head of things."

" There are already mighty forces in Germany," Benham wrote, " that will struggle very powerfully to avoid a war. And these forces increase. Behind the coarseness and the threatenings, the melodrama and the display of the vulgarer sort there arises a great and noble people. . . . I have talked with Germans of the better kind. . . . You cannot have a whole nation of Christophes. . . . There also the true knighthood discovers itself. . . I do not believe this war will overtake us."

" Well ! " said White.

" I must go back to Germany and understand Germany better," the notes went on.

But other things were to hold Benham back from that resolve. Other things were to hold many men back from similar resolves until it was too late for them. . . .

" It is preposterous that these monstrous dangers should lower over Europe, because a certain threatening vanity has crept into the blood of a people, because a few crude ideas go inadequately controlled. . . . Does no one see what that metallic beast will do if they once let it loose ? It will trample cities ; it will devour nations. . . ."

White read this on the 9th of October, 1914. One crumpled evening paper at his feet proclaimed in startled headlines : " Rain of Incendiary Shells. Antwerp Ablaze." Another declared untruthfully but impressively : " Six Zeppelins drop Bombs over the Doomed City."

He had bought all the evening papers, and had read and re-read them and turned up maps and worried over strategic problems for which he had no data at all—as everyone did at that time—before he was able to go on with Benham's manuscripts.

These pacific reassurances seemed to White's war-troubled mind like finding a flattened and faded flower, a girl's love-token, between the pages of some torn and scorched and blood-stained book picked out from a heap of loot after rapine and murder had had their fill. . . .

" How can we ever begin over again ? " said White, and sat for a long time staring gloomily into the fire, forgetting, forgetting, forgetting too that men who are tired and weary die, and that new men are born to succeed them. . . .

" We have to begin over again," said White at last, and took up Benham's papers where he had laid them down. . . .

§ 9

One considerable section of Benham's treatment of the Fourth Limitation was devoted to what he called the Prejudices of Social Position. This section alone was manifestly expanding into a large treatise upon the psychology of economic organisation. . . .

It was only very slowly that he had come to realise the important part played by economic and class hostilities in the disordering of human affairs. This was a very natural result of his peculiar social circumstances. Most people born to wealth and ease take the established industrial system as the natural method in human affairs ; it is only very reluctantly and by real feats of sympathy and disinterestedness that they can be brought to realise that it is natural only in the sense that it has grown up and come about, and necessary only because nobody is strong and clever enough to rearrange it. Their experience of it is a satisfactory experience. On the other hand, the better off one is, the wider is one's outlook and the more alert one is to see the risks and dangers of international dissensions. Travel and talk to foreigners open one's eyes to aggressive possibilities ; history and its warnings become conceivable. It is in the nature of things that socialists and labour parties should minimise international obligations and necessities, and equally so that autocracies and aristocracies and plutocracies should be negligent of and impatient about social reform.

But Benham did come to realise this broader conflict between worker and director, between poor man and possessor, between resentful humanity and enterprise, between unwilling toil and unearned opportunity. It is a far profounder and subtler conflict than any other in human affairs. " I can forsee a time," he wrote, " when the greater national and racial hatreds may all be so weakened as to be no longer a considerable source of human limitation and misery, when the suspicions of complexion and language and social habit are allayed, and when the element of hatred and aggression may be clean washed out of most religious cults ; but I do not begin to imagine a time, because I cannot imagine a method when there will not be great friction between those who employ, those who direct collective action, and those whose part it is to be the rank and file in industrialism. This, I know, is a limitation upon my confidence due very largely to the restricted nature of my knowledge of this sort of organisation. Very probably resentment and suspicion in the mass and self-seeking and dishonesty in the fortunate few are not so deeply seated, so necessary, as they seem to be, and if men can be cheerfully obedient and modestly directive in war time, there is no reason why ultimately they should not be so in the business of peace.

But I do not understand the elements of the methods by which this state of affairs can be brought about.

" If I were to confess this much to an intelligent working man I know that at once he would answer ' Socialism,' but Socialism is no more a solution of this problem than eating is a solution when one is lost in the wilderness and hungry. Of course everybody with any intelligence wants Socialism ; everybody, that is to say, wants to see all human efforts directed to the common good and a common end, but brought face to face with practical problems Socialism betrays a vast insufficiency of practical suggestions. I do not say that Socialism would not work, but I do say that so far Socialists have failed to convince me that they could work it. The substitution of a stupid official for a greedy proprietor may mean a vanished dividend, a limited output, and no other human advantage whatever. Socialism is in itself a mere eloquent gesture, inspiring, encouraging, perhaps, but beyond that not very helpful, towards the vast problem of moral and material adjustment before the race. That problem is incurably miscellaneous and intricate, and only by great multitudes of generous workers, one working at this point and one at that, secretly devoted knights of humanity, hidden and dispersed kings, unaware of one another, doubting each his right to count himself among those who do these kingly services, is this elaborate rightening of work and guidance to be done."

So from these most fundamental social difficulties he came back to his panacea. All paths and all inquiries led him back to his conception of aristocracy, conscious, self-disciplined, devoted, self-examining yet secret, making no personal nor class pretences, as the supreme need not only of the individual but the world.

§ 10

It was the Labour trouble in the Transvaal which had brought the two schoolfellows together again. White had been on his way to Zimbabwe. An emotional disturbance of unusual intensity had driven him to seek consolations in strange scenery and mysterious desolations. It was as if Zimbabwe called to him. Benham had come to South Africa to see into the question of Indian immigration, and he was now on his way to meet Amanda in London. Neither man had given much heed to the gathering social conflict on the Rand until the storm burst about them. There had been a few paragraphs in the papers about a dispute upon a point of labour etiquette, a question of the recognition of Trade Union officials, a thing that impressed them both as technical, and then suddenly a long incubated quarrel flared out in rioting and violence, the burning of houses and furniture, attacks on mines, attempts to dynamite trains. White stayed in Johannesburg because he did not want to be stranded up country by the railway strike that was among the possibilities of the situation. Benham stayed because he was going to London very reluctantly, and he was glad of this justification for a few days' delay. The two men found themselves occupying adjacent tables in the Sherborough Hotel, and White was the first to recognise the other. They came together with a warmth and readiness of intimacy that neither would have displayed in London.

White had not seen Benham since the social days of Amanda at Lancaster Gate, and he was astonished at the change a few years had made in him. The peculiar contrast of his pallor and his dark hair had become more marked, his skin was deader, his features seemed more prominent and his expression intenser. His eyes were very bright and more sunken under his brows. He had suffered from yellow fever in the West Indies, and these it seemed were the marks left by that illness. And he was much more detached from the people about him; less attentive to the small incidents of life, more occupied with inner things. He greeted White with a confidence that White was one day to remember as pathetic.

" It is good to meet an old friend," Benham said. " I have lost friends. And I do not make fresh ones. I go about too much by myself, and I do not follow the same tracks that other people are following." . . .

What track was he following? It was now that White first heard of the Research Magnificent. He wanted to know what Benham was doing, and Benham after some partial and unsatisfactory explanation of his interest in insurgent Hindoos, embarked upon larger expositions. " It is, of course, a part of something else," he amplified. He was writing a book, " an enormous sort of book." He laughed with a touch of shyness. It was about " everything," about how to live and how not to live. And " aristocracy, and all sorts of things." White was always curious about other people's books. Benham became more earnest and more explicit under encouragement, and to talk about his book was soon to talk about himself. In various ways, intentionally and inadvertently, he told White much. These chance encounters, these intimacies of the train and hotel, will lead men at times to a stark frankness of statement they would never permit themselves with habitual friends.

About the Johannesburg labour trouble they talked very little, considering how insistent it was becoming. But the wide propositions of the Research Magnificent with its large indifference to immediate occurrences, its vast patience, its tremendous expectations, contrasted very sharply in White's memory with the bitterness, narrowness and resentment of the events about them. For him the thought of that first discussion of this vast inchoate book into which Benham's life was flowering, and which he was ultimately to summarise, trailed with it a fringe of vivid little pictures; pictures of crowds of men hurrying on bicycles and afoot under a lowering twilight sky towards murmuring centres of disorder, of startling flares seen suddenly afar off, of the muffled galloping of troops through the broad dusty street in the night, of groups of men standing and watching down straight broad roads, roads that ended in groups of chimneys and squat buildings of corrugated iron. And once there was a marching body of white men in the foreground and a complicated wire fence, and a clustering mass of Kaffirs watching them over this fence and talking eagerly amongst themselves.

" All this affair here is little more than a hitch in the machinery," said Benham, and went back to his large pre-occupation. . . .

But White, who had not seen so much human disorder as Benham, felt that it was more than that. Always he kept the tail of his eye upon that eventful background while Benham talked to him.

When the firearms went off he may for the moment have even given the background the greater share of his attention. . . .

§ 11

It was only as White burrowed through his legacy of documents that the full values came to very many things that Benham said during these last conversations. The papers fitted in with his memories of their long talks like text with commentary; so much of Benham's talk had repeated the private writings in which he had first digested his ideas that it was presently almost impossible to disentangle what had been said and understood at Johannesburg from the fuller statement of those patched and corrected manuscripts. The two things merged in White's mind as he read. The written text took upon itself a resonance of Benham's voice ; it eked out the hints and broken sentences of his remembered conversation.

But some things that Benham did not talk about at all, left by their mere marked absence an impression on White's mind. And occasionally after Benham had been talking for a long time there would be an occasional aphasia, such as is often apparent in the speech of men who restrain themselves from betraying a pre-occupation. He would say nothing about Amanda or about women in general, he was reluctant to speak of Prothero, and another peculiarity was that he referred perhaps half a dozen times or more to the idea that he was a " prig ." He seemed to be defending himself against some inner accusation, some unconquerable doubt of the entire adventure of his life. These half hints and hints by omission exercised the quick intuitions of White's mind very keenly, and he drew far closer to an understanding of Benham's reserves than Benham ever suspected. . . .

At first after his parting from Amanda in London Benham had felt completely justified in his treatment of her. She had betrayed him and he had behaved, he felt, with dignity and self-control. He had no doubt that he had punished her very effectively, and it was only after he had been travelling in China with Prothero for some time and in the light of one or two chance phrases in her letters that he began to have doubts whether he ought to have punished her at all. And one night at Shanghai he had a dream in which she stood before him, dishevelled and tearful, his Amanda, very intensely his Amanda, and said that she was dirty and shameful and spoilt for ever, because he had gone away from her. Afterwards the dream became absurd, she showed him the black leopard's fur as though it was a rug, and it was now moth-eaten and mangy, the leopard skin that had been so bright and wonderful such a little time ago, and he awoke before he could answer her, and for a long time he was full of unspoken answers explaining that in view of her deliberate unfaithfulness the position she took up was absurd. She had spoilt her own fur. But what was more penetrating and distressing in this dream was not so much the case Amanda stated as the atmosphere of unconquerable intimacy between them, as though they still belonged to each other, soul to soul, as though nothing that had happened afterwards could have destroyed their common responsibility and the common interest of their first unstinted union. She was hurt, and of course he was hurt. He began to see that his marriage to Amanda was still infinitely more than a technical bond.

And having perceived that much he presently began to doubt whether she realized anything of the sort. Her letters fluctuated very much in tone, but at times they were as detached and guarded as a schoolgirl writing to a cousin. Then it seemed to Benham an extraordinary fraud on her part that she should presume to come into his dream with an entirely deceptive closeness and confidence. She began to sound him in these latter letters upon the possibility of divorce. This, which he had been quite disposed to concede in London, now struck him as an outrageous suggestion. He wrote to ask her why, and she responded exasperatingly that she thought it was "better." But, again, why better? It is remarkable that although his mind had habituated itself to the idea that Easton was her lover in London, her thought of being divorced, no doubt to marry again, filled him with jealous rage. She asked him to take the blame in the divorce proceedings. There, again, he found himself ungenerous. He did not want to do that. Why should he do that ? As a matter of fact he was by no means reconciled to the price he had paid for his Research Magnificent ; he regretted his Amanda acutely. He was regretting her with a regret that grew when by all the rules of life it ought to be diminishing.

It was in consequence of that regret and his controversies with Prothero while they travelled together in China that his concern about what he called priggishness arose. It is a concern that one may suppose has a little afflicted every reasonably self-conscious man who has turned from the natural passionate personal life to religion or to public service or any abstract devotion. These things that are at least more extensive than the interests of flesh and blood have a trick of becoming unsubstantial, they shine gloriously and inspiringly upon the imagination, they capture one and isolate one and then they vanish out of sight. It is far easier to be entirely faithful to friend or lover than it is to be faithful to a cause or to one's country or to a religion. In the glow of one's first service that larger idea may be as closely spontaneous as a hand-clasp, but in the darkness that comes as the glow dies away there is a fearful sense of unreality. It was in such dark moments that Benham was most persecuted by his memories of Amanda and most distressed by this suspicion that the Research Magnificent was a priggishness, a pretentious logomachy. Prothero could indeed hint as much so skilfully that at times the dream of nobility seemed an insult to the sunshine, to the careless laughter of children, to the good light in wine, and all the warm happiness of existence. And then Amanda would peep out of the dusk and whisper, " Of course if you could leave me—— ! Was I not *life* ? Even now if you cared to come back to me—— ! For I loved you best and loved you still, old Cheetah, long after you had left me to follow your dreams. . . . Even now I am drifting further into lies and the last shreds of dignity drop from me ; a dirty, lost, and shameful leopard I am now, who was once clean and bright. . . . You could come back, Cheetah, and you could save me yet. If you would love me. . . ."

In certain moods she could wring his heart by such imagined speeches, the very quality of her voice was in them, a softness that his ear had loved, and not only could she distress him, but when Benham was in this heartache mood, when once she had set him going, then his little mother also would rise against him, touchingly indignant, with her blue eyes bright with tears ; and his frowsty father would back towards him and sit down complaining that he was neglected, and even little Mrs. Skelmersdale would reappear, bravely tearful on her chair looking after him as he slunk away from her through Kensington Gardens ; indeed every personal link he had ever had with life could in certain moods pull him back through the door of self-reproach Amanda opened, and set him aching and accusing himself of harshness and self-concentration. The very kittens of his childhood revived forgotten moments of long-repented hardness. For a year before Prothero was killed there were these heartaches. That tragedy gave them their crowning justification. All these people said in this form or that, " You owed a debt to us, you evaded it, you betrayed us, you owed us life out of yourself, love and services, and you have gone off from us all with this life that was ours, to live by yourself in dreams about the rule of the world, and with empty phantoms of power and destiny. All this was intellectualisation. You sacrificed us to the thin things of the mind. There is no rule of the world at all, or none that a man like you may lay hold upon. The rule of the world is a fortuitous result of incalculably multitudinous forces. But all of us you could have made happier. You could have spared us distresses. Prothero died because of you. Presently it will be the turn of your father, your mother —Amanda perhaps. . . ."

He made no written note of his heartaches, but he made several memoranda about priggishness that White read and came near to understanding. In spite of the tugging at his heart-strings, Benham was making up his mind to be a prig. He weighed the cold uningratiating virtues of priggishness against his smouldering passion for Amanda, and against his obstinate sympathy with Prothero's grossness and his mother's personal pride, and he made his choice. But it was a reluctant choice.

One fragment began in the air. " Of course I had made myself responsible for her life. But it was, you see, such a confoundedly energetic life, as vigorous and as slippery as an eel. . . . Only by giving all my strength to her could I have held Amanda. . . . So what was the good of trying to hold Amanda ? . . .

" All one's people have this sort of claim upon one. Claims made by their pride and their self-respect, and their weaknesses and dependences. You've no right to hurt them, to kick about and demand freedom when it means snapping and tearing the silly suffering tendrils they have wrapped about you. The true aristocrat, I think, will have enough grasp, enough steadiness, to be kind and right to every human being and still do the work that ought to be his essential life. I see that now. It's one of the things this last year or so of loneliness has made me realise ; that in so far as I have set out to live the aristocratic life I have failed. Instead I've discovered it—and found myself out. I'm an over-strung man. I go harshly and continuously for one idea. I live as I ride. I blunder through my fences, I take off too soon. I've no natural ease of mind or conduct of body. I am straining to keep hold of a thing too big for me and do a thing beyond my ability. Only after Prothero's death was it possible for me to realise the prig I have always been, first as regards him and then as regards Amanda and my mother and every one. A necessary unavoidable priggishness. . . .

" I do not see how certain things can be done without prigs—people, that is to say, so concentrated and specialised in interest as to be a trifle inhuman, so resolved as to be rather rhetorical and forced. . . . All things must begin with clumsiness, there is no assurance about pioneers. . . .

"Some one has to talk about aristocracy, some one has to explain aristocracy. . . . But the very essence of aristocracy as I conceive it, is that it does not explain nor talk about itself. . . .

"After all it doesn't matter what I am. . . . It's just a private vexation that I haven't got where I meant to get. That does not affect the truth I have to tell. . . .

"If one has to speak the truth with the voice of a prig, still one must speak the truth. I have worked out some very considerable things in my research, and the time has come when I must set them out clearly and plainly. That is my job anyhow. My journey to London to release Amanda will be just the end of my adolescence and the beginning of my real life. It will release me from my last entanglement with the fellow creatures I have always failed to make happy. . . . It's a detail in the work. . . . And I shall go on.

"But I shall feel very like a man who goes back for a surgical operation.

"It's very like that. A surgical operation, and when it is over perhaps I shall think no more about it.

"And beyond these things there are great masses of work to be done. So far I have but cleared up for myself a project and outline of living. I must begin upon these masses now, I must do what I can upon the details, and, presently, I shall see more clearly where other men are working to the same ends. . . ."

§ 12

Benham's expedition to China with Prothero was essentially a wrestle between his high resolve to work out his conception of the noble life to the utmost limit and his curiously invincible affection and sympathy for the earthliness of that inglorious little don. Although Benham insisted upon the dominance of life by noble imaginations and relentless reasonableness, he would never altogether abandon the materialism of life. Prothero had once said to him, " You are the advocate of the brain and I of the belly. Only, only we respect each other." And at another time, " You fear emotions and distrust sensations. I invite them. You do not drink gin because you think it would make you weep. But if I could not weep in any other way I would drink gin." And it was under the influence of Prothero that Benham turned from the haughty intellectualism, the systematised superiorities and refinements, the caste marks and defensive dignities of India to China, that great teeming stinking tank of humorous yellow humanity.

Benham had gone to Prothero again after a bout of elevated

idealism. It was only very slowly that he reconciled his mind to the idea of an entirely solitary pursuit of his aristocratic dream. For some time as he went about the world he was trying to bring himself into relationship with the advanced thinkers, the liberal-minded people who seemed to promise at least a mental and moral co-operation. Yet it is difficult to see what co-operation was possible unless it was some sort of agreement that presently they should all shout together. And it was after a certain pursuit of Rabindranath Tagore, whom he met in Hampstead, that a horror of perfect manners and perfect finish came upon him, and he fled from that starry calm to the rich uncleanness of the most undignified fellow of Trinity. And as an advocate and exponent of the richness of the lower levels of life, as the declared antagonist of caste and of the uttermost refinements of pride, Prothero went with Benham by way of Siberia to the Chinese scene.

Their controversy was perceptible at every dinner-table in their choice of food and drink. Benham was always wary and Prothero always appreciative. It peeped out in the distribution of their time, in the direction of their glances. Whenever women walked about, Prothero gave way to a sort of ethnological excitement. " That girl—a wonderful racial type." But in Moscow he was sentimental. He insisted on going again to the Cosmopolis Bazaar, and when he had ascertained that Anna Alexievna had vanished and left no trace he prowled the streets until the small hours.

In the eastward train he talked intermittently of her. " I should have defied Cambridge," he said.

But at every stopping station he got out upon the platform ethnologically alert. . . .

Theoretically Benham was disgusted with Prothero. Really he was not disgusted at all. There was something about Prothero like a sparrow, like a starling, like a Scotch terrier. . . . These, too, are morally objectionable creatures that do not disgust. . . .

Prothero discoursed much upon the essential goodness of Russians. He said they were a people of genius, that they showed it in their faults and failures just as much as in their virtues and achievements. He extolled the " germinating disorder " of Moscow far above the " implacable discipline " of Berlin. Only a people of inferior imagination, a base materialist people, could so maintain its attention upon precision and cleanliness. Benham was roused to defence against this paradox. " But all exaltation neglects," said Prothero. " No religion has ever boasted that its saints were spick and span." This controversy raged between them in the streets of Irkutsk. It was still burning while they picked their way through the indescribable filth of Pekin.

" You say that all this is a fine disdain for material things," said Benham. " But look out there ! "

Apt to their argument a couple of sturdy young women came shuffling along, cleaving the crowd in the narrow street by virtue of a single word and two brace of pails of human ordure.

" That is not a fine disdain for material things," said Benham. " That is merely individualism and unsystematic living."

" A mere phase of frankness. Only frankness is left to them now. The Manchus crippled them, spoilt their roads and broke their waterways. European intervention paralyses every attempt they make to establish order on their own lines. In the Ming days China did not reek. . . . And, anyhow, Benham, it's better than the silly waste of London. . . ."

And in a little while Prothero discovered that China had tried Benham and found him wanting, centuries and dynasties ago.

What was this new-fangled aristocratic man, he asked, but the ideal of Confucius, the superior person, " the son of the King ? " There you had the very essence of Benham, the idea of self-examination, self-preparation under a vague Theocracy. (" Vaguer," said Benham, " for the Confucian Heaven could punish and reward.") Even the elaborate sham modesty of the two dreams was the same. Benham interrupted and protested with heat. And this Confucian idea of the son of the King, Prothero insisted, had been the cause of China's paralysis. " My idea of nobility is not traditional but expectant," said Benham. " After all, Confucianism has held together a great pacific state far longer than any other polity has ever lasted. I accept your Confucianism. I've not the slightest objection to finding China nearer salvation than any other land. Do but turn it round so that it looks to the future and not to the past, and it will be the best social and political culture in the world. That, indeed, is what is happening. Mix Chinese culture with American enterprise and you will have made a new lead for mankind."

From that Benham drove on to discoveries. " When a man thinks of the past he concentrates on self ; when he thinks of the future he radiates from self. Call me a neo-Confucian ; with the cone opening forward away from me, instead of focusing on me. . . ."

" You make me think of an extinguisher," said Prothero.

" You know I am thinking of a focus," said Benham. " But all your thought now has become caricature. . . . You have stopped thinking. You are fighting after making up your mind. . . ."

Prothero was a little disconcerted by Benham's prompt endorsement of his Chinese identification. He had hoped it would be exasperating. He tried to barb his offence. He amplified the indictment. All cultures must be judged by their reaction and fatigue products, and Confucianism had produced formalism, priggishness, humbug. . . . No doubt its ideals had had their successes ; they had unified China, stamped the idea of universal peace and good manners upon the greatest mass of population in the world, paved the way for much beautiful art and literature and living. " But in the end, all your stern orderliness, Benham," said Prothero, " only leads to me. The human spirit rebels against this everlasting armour on the soul. After Han came T'ang. Have you never read Ling Po? There's scraps of him in English in that little book you have—what is it ?—the *Lute of Jade* ? He was the inevitable Epicurean ; the Omar Khayyam after the Prophet. Life must relax at last. . . ."

" No ! " cried Benham. " If it is traditional, I admit, yes ; but if it is creative, no. . . ."

Under the stimulation of their undying controversy Benham was driven to closer inquiries into Chinese thought. He tried particularly to get to mental grips with English-speaking Chinese. " We still know nothing of China," said Prothero. " Most of the stuff we have been told about this country is mere middle-class tourist's twaddle. We send merchants from Brixton and missionaries from Glasgow and what doesn't remind them of these delectable standards seems either funny to them or wicked. I admit the thing is slightly pot-bound, so to speak, in the ancient characters and the ancient traditions, but for all that, they *know*, they *have*, what all the rest of the world has still to find and get. When they begin to speak and write in a modern way and handle modern things and break into the soil they have scarcely touched, the rest of the world will find just how much it is behind. . . . Oh ! not soldiering ; the Chinese are not such fools as that, but *life*. . . ."

Benham was won to a half belief in these assertions.

He came to realise more and more clearly that while India dreams or wrestles weakly in its sleep, while Europe is still hopelessly and foolishly given over to militant monarchies, racial vanities, delirious religious feuds, and an altogether imbecile fumbling with loaded guns, China, even more than America, develops steadily into a massive possibility of ordered and aristocratic liberalism. . . .

The two men followed their associated and disconnected paths. Through Benham's chance speeches and notes, White caught glimpses, as one might catch glimpses through a moving trellis, of that bilateral adventure. He saw Benham in conversation with liberal-minded mandarins, grave-faced, bald-browed persons with disciplined movements, who sat with their hands thrust into their sleeves, talking excellent English ; while Prothero pursued inquiries of an intenser, more recondite sort with gentlemen of a more confidential type. And, presently, Prothero began to discover and discuss the merits of opium.

For if one is to disavow all pride and priggishness, if one

is to find the solution of life's problem in the rational enjoyment of one's sensations, why should one not use opium ? It
is art materialised. It gives tremendous experiences with a
minimum of exertion, and if presently its gifts diminish one
need but increase the quantity. Moreover, it quickens the
garrulous mind, and steadies the happiness of love. Across
the varied adventures of Benham's journey in China fell the
shadow first of a suspicion and then of a certainty. . . .

The perfected and ancient vices of China wrapped about
Prothero like some tainted but scented robe, and all too late
Benham sought to drag him away. And then in a passion of
disgust turned from him.

" To this," cried Benham, " one comes ! Save for pride and
fierceness ! "

" Better this than cruelty," said Prothero, talking quickly
and clearly because of the evil thing in his veins. " You think
that you are the only explorer of life, Benham, but while
you toil up the mountains I board the house-boat and float
down the stream. For you the stars, for me the music and
the lanterns. You are the son of a mountaineering don, and
I am a Chinese philosopher of the riper school. You force
yourself beyond fear of pain, and I force myself beyond fear
of consequences. What are we either of us but children groping
under the black cloak of our Maker ?—who will not blind us
with his light. Did he not give us also these lusts, the keen
knife and the sweetness, these sensations that are like pine-
apple smeared with saltpetre, like salted olives from heaven,
like being flayed with delight. . . . And did he not give us
dreams fantastic beyond any lust whatever ? What is the
good of talking ? Speak to your own kind. I have gone, Benham. I am lost already. There is no resisting any more, since
I have drugged away resistance. Why then should I come
back ? I know now the symphonies of the exalted nerves ;
I can judge ; and I say better lie and hear them to the end
than come back again to my old life, to my little tin-whistle
solo, my—effort ! My *effort* ! . . . I ruin my body. I know.
But what of that ? . . . I shall soon be thin and filthy. What of
the grape-skin when one has had the pulp ? "

" But," said Benham, " the cleanness of life ! "

" While I perish," said Prothero still more wickedly, " I
say good things. . . . "

§ 13

White had a vision of a great city with narrow crowded
streets, hung with lank banners and gay with vertical vermilion labels, and of a pleasant large low house that stood
in a garden on a hillside, a garden set with artificial stones
and with beasts and men and lanterns of white porcelain, a
garden which overlooked this city. Here it was that Benham
stayed and talked with his host, a man robed in marvellous

silks and subtle of speech even in the European languages he used ; and meanwhile Prothero, it seemed, had gone down into the wickedness of the town below. It was a very great town indeed, spreading for miles along the banks of a huge river, a river that divided itself indolently into three shining branches so as to make islands of the central portion of the place. And on this river swarmed for ever a vast flotilla of ships and boats, boats in which people lived, boats in which they sought pleasure, moored places of assembly, high-pooped junks, steam-boats, passenger sampans, cargo craft, such a water town in streets and lanes, endless miles of it, as no other part of the world save China can display. In the daylight it was gay with countless sunlit colours embroidered upon a fabric of yellow and brown ; at night it glittered with a hundred thousand lights that swayed and quivered and were reflected quiveringly upon the black flowing waters.

And while Benham sat and talked in the garden above came a messenger who was for some reason very vividly realised by White's imagination. He was a tall man with lack-lustre eyes and sunken cheeks that made his cheek bones very prominent, and gave his thin-lipped mouth something of the geniality of a skull, and the arm he thrust out of his yellow robe to hand Prothero's message to Benham was lean as a pole. So he stood out in White's imagination, against the warm afternoon sky and the brown roofs and blue haze of the great town below, and was with one exception the distinctest thing in the story. The message he bore was scribbled by Prothero himself in a nerveless scrawl ; " Send a hundred dollars by this man. I am in a frightful fix."

Now Benham's host had been twitting him with the European patronage of opium, and something in this message stirred his facile indignation. Twice before he had had similar demands. And on the whole they had seemed to him to be unreasonable demands. He was astonished that while he was sitting and talking of the great world-republic of the future and the secret self-directed aristocracy that would make it possible, his own friend, his chosen companion should thus, by this inglorious request and this ungainly messenger, disavow him. He felt a wave of intense irritation.

" No," he said, " I will not."

And he was too angry to express himself in any language understandable by his messenger.

His host intervened and explained after a few questions that the occasion was serious. Prothero, it seemed, had been gambling.

" No," said Benham. " He is shameless. Let him do what he can."

The messenger was still reluctant to go.

And scarcely had he gone before misgivings seized Benham.

" Where *is* your friend ? " asked the mandarin.

" I don't know," said Benham.

" But they will keep him ! They may do all sorts of things when they find he is lying to them."

" Lying to them ? "

" About your help."

" Stop that man," cried Benham, suddenly realising his mistake. But when the servants went to stop the messenger their intentions were misunderstood, and the man dashed through the open gate of the garden and made off down the winding road.

" Stop him ! " cried Benham, and started in pursuit, suddenly afraid for Prothero.

The Chinese are a people of great curiosity, and a small pebble sometimes starts an avalanche. . . .

White pieced together his conception of the circles of disturbance that spread out from Benham's pursuit of Prothero's flying messenger.

For weeks and months the great town had been uneasy in all its ways because of the insurgent spirits from the south and the disorder from the north, because of endless rumours and incessant intrigue. The stupid manœuvres of one European " power " against another, the tactlessness of missionaries, the growing Chinese disposition to meet violence and force with violence and force, had fermented and brewed the possibility of an outbreak. The sudden resolve of Benham to get at once to Prothero was like the firing of a mine. This tall, pale-faced, incomprehensible stranger charging through the narrow streets that led to the pleasure-boats in the south river seemed to many a blue-clad citizen like the White Peril embodied. Behind him came the attendants of the rich man up the hill ; but they surely were traitors to help this stranger.

Before Benham could at all realise what was happening he found his way to the river-boat on which he supposed Prothero to be detained, barred by a vigorous street fight. Explanations were impossible ; he joined in the fight.

For three days that fight developed round the mystery of Prothero's disappearance.

It was a complicated struggle into which the local foreign traders on the river-front and a detachment of modern drilled troops from the up-river barracks were presently drawn. It was a struggle that was never clearly explained, and at the end of it they found Prothero's body flung out upon a waste place near a little temple on the river bank, stabbed while he was asleep. . . .

And from the broken fragments of description that Benham let fall, White had an impression of him hunting for all those three days through the strange places of a Chinese city, along narrow passages, over queer Venetian-like bridges, through the vast spaces of empty warehouses, in the incense-scented darkness of temple yards, along planks that passed to the dark hulls of secret barges, in quick-flying boats that slipped noiselessly among the larger craft ; and sometimes he hunted alone, sometimes in company, sometimes black figures struggled in the darkness against dim-lit backgrounds and sometimes a swarm of shining yellow faces screamed and shouted through the torn paper windows. . . . And then at the end of this confused effect of struggle, this Chinese kinematograph film, one last picture jerked into place and stopped and stood still, a white wall in the sunshine come upon suddenly round a corner, a dirty flagged passage, and a stiff crumpled body that had for the first time an inexpressive face. . . .

§ 14

Benham sat at a table in the smoking-room of the Sherborough Hotel at Johannesburg and told of these things. White watched him from an arm-chair. And as he listened he noted again the intensification of Benham's face, the darkness under his brows, the pallor of his skin, the touch of red in his eyes. For there was still that red gleam in Benham's eyes ; it shone when he looked out of a darkness into a light. And he sat forward with his arms folded under him, or moved his long lean hand about over the things on the table.

" You see," he said, " this is a sort of horror in my mind. Things like this stick in my mind. I am always seeing Prothero now, and it will take years to get this scar off my memory again. Once before—about a horse, I had the same kind of distress. And it makes me tender, sore-minded about everything. It will go, of course, in the long run, and it's just like any other ache that lays hold of one. One can't cure it. One has to get along with it. . . .

" I know, White, I ought to have sent that money, but how was I to know then that it was so imperative to send that money ? . . .

" At that time it seemed just pandering to his vices. . . .

" I was angry. I shall never subdue that kind of hastiness altogether. It takes me by surprise. Before the messenger was out of sight I had repented. . . .

" I failed him. I have gone about in the world dreaming of tremendous things and failing most people. My wife too. . . ."

He stopped talking for a little time and folded his arms tight and stared hard in front of himself, his lips compressed.

" You see, White," he said, with a kind of setting of the teeth, " this is the sort of thing one has to stand. Life is imperfect. Nothing can be done perfectly. And on the whole—— " He spoke still more slowly, " I would go through again with the very same things that have hurt my people. If I had to live over again, I would try to do the things without hurting the people, but I would do the things anyhow. Because I'm raw with remorse, it does not follow that on the whole I am not doing right. Right doing isn't balm. If I could have contrived not to hurt these people as I have done, it would have been better, just as it would be better to win a battle without any killed or wounded. I was clumsy with them and they suffered, I suffer for their suffering, but still I have to stick to the way I have taken. One's blunders are accidents. If one thing is clearer than another it is that the world isn't accident-proof. . . .

" But I wish I had sent those dollars to Prothero. . . . God ! White, but I lie awake at night thinking of that messenger as he turned away. . . . Trying to stop him. . . .

" I didn't send those dollars. So fifty or sixty people were killed and many wounded. . . . There for all practical purposes the thing ends. Perhaps it will serve to give me a little charity for some other fool's haste and blundering. . . .

" I couldn't help it, White. I couldn't help it. . . .

" The main thing, the impersonal thing, goes on. One thinks, one learns, one adds one's contribution of experience and understanding. The spirit of the race goes on to light and comprehension. In spite of accidents. In spite of individual blundering.

" It would be absurd anyhow to suppose that nobility is so easy as to come slick and true on every occasion. . . .

" If one gives oneself to any long aim one must reckon with minor disasters. This Research I undertook grows and grows. I believe in it more and more. The more it asks from me the more I give to it. When I was a youngster I thought the thing I wanted was just round the corner. I fancied I would find out the noble life in a year or two, just what it was, just where it took one, and for the rest of my life I would live it. Finely. But I am just one of a multitude of men, each one going a little wrong, each one achieving a little right. And the noble life is a long, long way ahead. . . . We are working out a new way of living for mankind, a new rule, a new conscience. It's no small job for all of us. There must be lifetimes of building up and lifetimes of pulling down and trying again. Hope and disappointments and much need for philosophy. . . . I see myself now for the little workman I am upon this tremendous undertaking. And all my life hereafter goes to serve it. . . ."

He turned his sombre eyes upon his friend. He spoke with a grim enthusiasm. " I'm a prig. I'm a fanatic, White. But I have something clear, something better worth going on with than any adventure of personal relationship could possibly be. . . ."

And suddenly he began to tell White as plainly as he could of the faith that had grown up in his mind. He spoke with a touch of defiance, with the tense force of a man who shrinks but overcomes his shame. " I will tell you what I believe."

He told of his early dread of fear and baseness, and of the slow development, expansion and complication of his idea of self-respect until he saw that there is no honour nor pride for a man until he refers his life to ends and purposes beyond himself. An aristocrat must be loyal. So it has ever been, but a modern aristocrat must also be lucid ; there it is that one has at once the demand for kingship and the repudiation of all existing states and kings. In this manner he had come to his idea of a great world republic that must replace the little warring kingdoms of the present, to the conception of an unseen kingship ruling the whole globe, to his King Invisible, who is the Lord of Truth and all sane loyalty. " There," he said, " is the link of our order, the new knighthood, the new aristocracy, that must at last rule the earth. There is our Prince. He is in me, he is in you ; he is latent in all mankind. I have worked this out and tried it and lived it and I know that outwardly and inwardly this is the way a man must live, or else be a poor thing and a base one. On great occasions and small occasions I have failed myself a thousand times, but no failure lasts if your faith lasts. What I have learnt, what I have thought out and made sure, I want now to tell the world. Somehow I will tell it, as a book I suppose, though I do not know if I shall ever be able to make a book. But I have away there in London or with me here all the masses of notes I have made in my search for the life that is worth while living. . . . We who are self-appointed aristocrats, who are not ashamed of kingship, must speak to one another. . . .

" We can have no organisation, because organisations corrupt. . . .

" No recognition. . .

" But we can speak plainly. . . ."

(As he talked his voice was for a space drowned by the jingle and voices of mounted police riding past the hotel.)

" But on one side your aristocracy means revolution," said White. " It becomes a political conspiracy."

" Manifestly. An open conspiracy. It denies the king upon stamps and the flag upon the wall. It is the continual pro- clamation of the Republic of Mankind."

§ 15

The earlier phases of violence in the Rand outbreak in 1913 were manifest rather in the outskirts of Johannesburg than at the centre. " Pulling out " was going on first at this mine and then that, there were riots in Benoni, attacks on strike breakers, and the smashing up of a number of houses. It was not until July the 4th that, with the suppression of a public meeting in the market-place, Johannesburg itself became the storm centre.

Benham and White were present at this market-place affair, a confused crowded occasion, in which a little leaven of active men stirred through a large uncertain multitude of decently dressed onlookers. The whole big square was astir, a swaying crowd of men. A ramshackle platform improvised upon a trolley struggled through the swarming straw hats to a street corner, and there was some speaking. At first it seemed as though military men were using this platform, and then it was manifestly in possession of an excited knot of labour leaders with red rosettes. The military men had said their say and got down. They came close by Benham, pushing their way across the square. "We've warned them," said one. A red flag, like some misunderstood remark at a tea-party, was fitfully visible and incomprehensible behind the platform. Somebody was either pitched or fell off the platform. One could hear nothing from the speakers except a minute bleating. . . .

Then there were shouts that the police were charging. A number of mounted men trotted into the square. The crowd began a series of short rushes that opened lanes for the passage of the mounted police as they rode to and fro. These men trotted through the crowd, scattering knots of people. They carried pick-handles, but they did not seem to be hitting with them. It became clear that they aimed at the capture of the trolley. There was only a feeble struggle for the trolley ; it was captured and hauled through the scattered spectators in the square to the protection of a small impassive body of regular cavalry at the opposite corner. Then quite a number of people seemed to be getting excited and fighting. They appeared to be vaguely fighting the foot-police, and the police seemed to be vaguely pushing through them and dispersing them. The roof of a little one-story shop became prominent as a centre of vigorous stone-throwing.

It was no sort of battle. Merely the normal inconsecutiveness of human affairs had become exaggerated and pugnacious. A meeting was being prevented, and the police engaged in the operation were being pelted or obstructed. Mostly people were just looking on.

"It amounts to nothing," said Benham. "Even if they held a meeting, what could happen ? Why does the Government try to stop it ? "

The drifting and charging and a little booing went on for some time. Every now and then some one clambered to a point of vantage, began a speech and was pulled down by policemen. And at last across the confusion came an idea, like a wind across a pond.

The strikers were to go to the Power Station.

That had the effect of a distinct move in the game. The Power Station was the centre of Johannesburg's light and energy. There if anywhere it would be possible to express one's disapproval of the administration, one's desire to embarrass and confute it. One could stop all sorts of things from the Power Station. At any rate it was a repartee to the suppression of the meeting. Everybody seemed gladdened by a definite project.

Benham and White went with the crowd.

At the intersection of two streets they were held up for a time ; the scattered drift of people became congested. Gliding slowly across the mass came an electric tram, an entirely unbattered tram with even its glass undamaged, and then another and another. Strikers, with the happy expression of men who have found something expressive to do, were escorting the trams off the street. They were being meticulously careful with them. Never was there less mob violence in a riot. They walked by the captured cars almost deferentially, like rough men honoured by a real lady's company. And when White and Benham reached the Power House the marvel grew. The rioters were already in possession and going freely over the whole place, and they had injured nothing. They had stopped the engines, but they had not even disabled them. Here too, manifestly, a majority of the people were, like White and Benham, merely lookers-on.

" But this is the most civilised rioting," said Benham. " It isn't rioting ; it's drifting. Just as things drifted in Moscow. Because nobody has the rudder. . . .

" What maddens me," he said, " is the democracy of the whole thing. White ! I *hate* this modern democracy. Democracy and inequality ! Was there ever an absurder combination? What is the good of a social order in which the men at the top are commoner, meaner stuff than the men underneath, the same stuff, just spoilt, spoilt by prosperity and opportunity and the conceit that comes with advantage ? This trouble wants so little, just a touch of aristocracy, just a little cultivated magnanimity, just an inkling of responsibility, and the place might rise instantly out of all this squalor and evil temper. . . . What does all this struggle here amount to ? On one side unintelligent greed, unintelligent resentment on the other ; suspicion everywhere. . . .

" And you know, White, at bottom *they all want to be decent !*

" If only they had light enough in their brains to show them how.

" It's such a plain job they have here, too—a new city, the simplest industries, freedom from war, everything to make a good life for men, prosperity, glorious sunshine, a kind of happiness in the air. And mismanagement, fear, indulgence, jealousy, prejudice, stupidity, poison it all. A squabble about working on a Saturday afternoon, a squabble embittered by this universal shadow of miner's phthisis that the masters were too incapable and too mean to prevent.

" Oh, God ! " cried Benham, " when will men be princes and take hold of life ? When will the kingship in us wake up and come to its own ? . . . Look at this place ! Look at this place ! . . . The easy, accessible happiness ! The manifest prosperity. The newness and the sunshine. And the silly bitterness, the rage, the mischief and miseries ! . . ."

And then : " It's not our quarrel. . . .

" It's amazing how every human quarrel draws one in to take sides. Life is one long struggle against the incidental. I can feel my anger gathering against the Government here in spite of my reason. I want to go and expostulate. I have a ridiculous idea that I ought to go off to Lord Gladstone or Botha and expostulate. . . . What good would it do ? They move in the magic circles of their own limitations, an official, a politician—how would they put it ?—' with many things to consider. . . .'

" It's my weakness to be drawn into quarrels. It's a thing I have to guard against. . . .

" What does it all amount to ? It is like a fight between navvies in a tunnel to settle the position of the Pole star. It doesn't concern us. . . . Oh ! it doesn't indeed concern us. It's a scuffle in the darkness, and our business, the business of all brains, the only permanent good work, is to light up the world. . . . There will be mischief and hatred here and sup- pression and then forgetfulness, and then things will go on again, a little better or a little worse. . . .

" I'm tired of this place, White, and of all such places. I'm tired of the shouting and running, the beating and shooting. I'm sick of all the confusions of life's experience, which tells only of one need amidst an endless multitude of distresses. I've seen my fill of wars and disputes and struggles. I see now how a man may grow weary at last of life and its disorders, its unreal exacting disorders, its blunders and its remorse. No ! I want to begin upon the realities I have made for my- self. For they are the realities. I want to go now to some quiet corner where I can polish what I have learnt, sort out my accumulations, be undisturbed by these transitory symp- tomatic things. . . .

" What was that boy saying ? They are burning the *Star* office. . . . Well, let them. . . . "

And as if to emphasise his detachment, his aversion, from the things that hurried through the night about them, from the red flare in the sky and the distant shouts and revolver shots and scuffling flights down side streets, he began to talk again of aristocracy and the making of greatness and a new great spirit in men. All the rest of his life, he said, must be given to that. He would say his thing plainly and honestly and afterwards other men would say it clearly and beautifully ; here it would touch a man and there it would touch a man ; the Invisible King in us all would find him- self and know himself a little in this and a little in that, and at last a day would come when fair things and fine things would rule the world and such squalor as this about them would be as impossible any more for men as a Stone Age Corroboree. . . .

Late or soon ?

Benham sought for some loose large measure of time.

"Before those constellations above us have changed their shapes. . . .

"Does it matter if we work at something that will take a hundred years or ten thousand years ? It will never come in our lives, White. Not soon enough for that. But after that everything will be soon—when one comes to death then everything is at one's finger-tips—I can feel that greater world I shall never see as one feels the dawn coming through the last darkness. . . ."

§ 16

The attack on the Rand Club began while Benham and White were at lunch in the dining-room at the Sherborough on the day following the burning of the *Star* office. The Sherborough dining-room was on the first floor, and the Venetian window beside their table opened on to a veranda above a piazza. As they talked they became aware of an excitement in the street below, shouting and running and then a sound of wheels and the tramp of a body of soldiers marching quickly. White stood up and looked. "They're seizing the stuff in the gunshops," he said, sitting down again. "It's amazing they haven't done it before."

They went on eating and discussing the work of a medical mission at Mukden that had won Benham's admiration. . . .

A revolver cracked in the street and there was a sound of glass smashing. Then more revolver shots. "That's at the big club at the corner, I think," said Benham and went out upon the veranda.

Up and down the street mischief was afoot. Outside the Rand Club in the cross street a considerable mass of people had accumulated, and was being hustled by a handful of khaki-clad soldiers. Down the street people were looking in the direction of the market-place, and then suddenly a rush of figures flooded round the corner, first a froth of scattered individuals and then a mass, a column, marching with an appearance of order and waving a flag. It was a poorly disciplined body, it fringed out into a swarm of sympathisers and spectators upon the side walk, and at the head of it two men disputed. They seemed to be differing about the direction of the whole crowd. Suddenly one smote the other with his fist, a blow that hurled him sideways, and then turned with a triumphant gesture to the following ranks, waving his arms in the air. He was a tall lean man, hatless and collarless, gray-haired and wild-eyed. On he came, gesticulating gauntly, past the hotel.

And then up the street something happened. Benham's attention was turned round to it by a checking, by a kind of catch in the breath, on the part of the advancing procession under the veranda.

The roadway beyond the club had suddenly become clear.

Across it a dozen soldiers had appeared and dismounted methodically and lined out, with their carbines in readiness. The mounted men at the club corner had vanished, and the people there had swayed about towards this new threat. Quite abruptly the miscellaneous noises of the crowd ceased. Understanding seized upon everyone.

These soldiers were going to fire. . . .

The brown uniformed figures moved like automata ; the rifle shots rang out almost in one report. . . .

There was a rush in the crowd towards doorways and side streets, an inquiring pause, the darting back of a number of individuals into the roadway, and then a derisive shouting. Nobody had been hit. The soldiers had fired in the air.

" But this is a stupid game," said Benham. " Why did they fire at all ? "

The tall man who had led the mob had run out into the middle of the road. His commando was a little disposed to assume a marginal position, and it had to be reassured. He was near enough for Benham to see his face. For a time it looked anxious and thoughtful. Then he seemed to jump to his decision. He unbuttoned and opened his coat wide as if defying the soldiers. " Shoot," he bawled, " Shoot, if you dare ! "

A little uniform movement of the soldiers answered him. The small figure of the officer away there was inaudible. The coat of the man below flapped like the wings of a crowing cock before a breast of dirty shirt, the hoarse voice cracked with excitement, " Shoot, if you dare. Shoot, if you dare ! See ! "

Came the metallic bang of the carbines again, and in the instant the leader collapsed in the road, a sprawl of clothes, hit by half a dozen bullets. It was an extraordinary effect. As though the figure had been deflated. It was incredible that a moment before this thing had been a man, an individual, a hesitating complicated purpose.

" Good God ! " cried Benham, " but—this is horrible ! "

The heap of garments lay still. The red hand that stretched out towards the soldiers never twitched.

The spectacular silence broke into a confusion of sounds, women shrieked, men cursed, some fled, some sought a corner from which they might still see, others pressed forward. " Go for the swine ! " bawled a voice, a third volley rattled over the heads of the people, and in the road below a man with a rifle halted, took aim, and answered the soldier's fire. " Look out ! " cried White, who was watching the soldiers, and ducked. " This isn't in the air ! "

Came a straggling volley again, like a man running a metal hammer very rapidly along iron corrugations, and this time people were dropping all over the road. One white-faced man not a score of yards away fell with a curse and a sob, struggled up, staggered for some yards with blood running abundantly from his neck, and fell and never stirred again. Another went down upon his back clumsily in the roadway and lay wringing his hands faster and faster until suddenly with a movement like a sigh they dropped inert by his side. A straw-hatted youth in a flannel suit ran and stopped and ran again. He seemed to be holding something red and strange to his face with both hands ; above them his eyes were round and anxious. Blood came out between his fingers. He went right past the hotel and stumbled and suddenly sprawled headlong at the opposite corner. The majority of the crowd had already vanished into doorways and side streets. But there was still shouting and there was still a remnant of amazed and angry men in the roadway—and one or two angry women. They were not fighting. Indeed they were unarmed, but if they had had weapons now they would certainly have used them.

" But this is preposterous ! " cried Benham, " Preposterous. Those soldiers are never going to shoot again ! This must stop."

He stood hesitating for a moment and then turned about and dashed for the staircase. " Good Heaven ! " cried White. " What are you going to do ? "

Benham was going to stop that conflict very much as a man might go to stop a clock that is striking unwarrantably and amazingly. He was going to stop it because it annoyed his sense of human dignity.

White hesitated for a moment and then followed, crying, " Benham ! "

But there was no arresting this last outbreak of Benham's all too impatient kingship. He pushed aside a ducking German waiter who was peeping through the glass doors, and rushed out of the hotel. With a gesture of authority he ran forward into the middle of the street, holding up his hand, in which he still held his dinner napkin clenched like a bomb. White believes firmly that Benham thought he would be able to dominate everything. He shouted out something about " Foolery ! "

Haroun al Raschid was flinging aside all his sublime in-difference to current things. . . .

But the carbines spoke again.

Benham seemed to run unexpectedly against something invisible. He spun right round and fell down into a sitting position. He sat looking surprised.

After one moment of blank funk White drew out his pocket handkerchief, held it arm high by way of a white flag, and ran out from the piazza of the hotel.

§ 17

" Are you hit ? " cried White, dropping to his knees and making himself as compact as possible. " Benham ! "

Benham, after a moment of perplexed thought answered in a strange voice, a whisper into which a whistling note had been mixed.

" It was stupid of me to come out here. Not my quarrel. Faults on both sides. And now I can't get up. I will sit here a moment and pull myself together. Perhaps I'm—I must be shot. But it seemed to come—inside me. . . . If I should be hurt. Am I hurt ? . . . Will you see to that book of mine, White ? It's odd. A kind of faintness. . . . What ? "

" I will see after your book," said White and glanced at his hand because it felt wet, and was astonished to discover it bright red. He forgot about himself then, and the fresh flight of bullets down the street.

The immediate effect of this blood was that he said something more about the book, a promise, a definite promise. He could never recall his exact words, but their intention was binding. He conveyed his absolute acquiescence with Benham's wishes whatever they were. His life for that moment was unreservedly at his friend's disposal. . . .

White never knew if his promise was heard. Benham had stopped speaking quite abruptly with that " What ? "

He stared in front of him with a doubtful expression, like a man who is going to be sick, and then, in an instant, every muscle seemed to give way, he shuddered, his head flopped, and White held a dead man in his arms.

Printed by H. Henderson at the Villafield Press, Bishopbriggs